Thomas Hartley, Emanuel Swedenborg, Samuel Noble,   Making of America Project

Heaven and its Wonders the World of Spirits and Hell

from things heard and seen

Thomas Hartley, Emanuel Swedenborg, Samuel Noble,   Making of America Project

Heaven and its Wonders the World of Spirits and Hell
from things heard and seen

ISBN/EAN: 9783337388355

Printed in Europe, USA, Canada, Australia, Japan

Cover: Foto ©Andreas Hilbeck / pixelio.de

More available books at **www.hansebooks.com**

HEAVEN

AND ITS WONDERS,

THE WORLD OF SPIRITS,

AND HELL:

FROM THINGS HEARD AND SEEN

Translated from the Latin of
EMANUEL SWEDENBORG,
Servant of the Lord Jesus Christ.

ORIGINALLY PUBLISHED AT LONDON IN LATIN, MDCCLVIII

TRANSLATED BY THE .
REV SAMUEL NOBLE, OF LONDON.

NEW YORK:
AMERICAN SWEDENBORG PRINTING AND PUBLISHING SOCIETY

Published by THE AMERICAN SWEDENBORG PRINTING AND PUBLISHING SOCIETY, *organized for the purpose of Stereotyping, Printing, and Publishing Uniform Editions of the Theological Writings of* EMANUEL SWEDENBORG, *and incorporated in the State of New York,* A. D. 1850.

ADVERTISEMENT.

THE following translation is a copy of the one recently published in London, from the pen of the Rev. Samuel Noble, entitled "Heaven and its Wonders, the World of Spirits (or the intermediate region, which is the first receptacle of man after death), and Hell; described by one who had heard and seen what he relates. From the Latin of Emanuel Swedenborg, servant of the Lord Jesus Christ. Translated by the Rev. Samuel Noble. Second edition, carefully revised, with a new preface by the Translator, including explanatory notes and observations. Together with the original English preface by the Rev. Thomas Hartley, A.M. London, James S. Hodson, 22 Portugal Street, Lincoln's Inn, 1851."

Most of the notes are retained; and Hartley's preface (published by private subscription) is bound in some of the copies; but the excellent critical preface by the Rev. Mr. Noble is omitted, not being appropriate to this edition.

NEW-YORK, *November,* 1851.

CONTENTS.

OF THE WORLD OF SPIRITS, AND OF THE STATE OF MAN AFTER DEATH.

OF HELL.

PREFACE

BY

The Rev. THOMAS HARTLEY, A.M.,

Late Rector of Winwick, in Northamptonshire.

BESIDES the more general provisions made by the Father of lights for the instruction of His church and people in divine things, under the public dispensations of the law and the gospel, He has also been graciously pleased at sundry times and in divers manners, as occasions and the needs of the church might require it, to make extraordinary discoveries and revelations to particular persons, either for more private or public use, to answer various ends of His wisdom and goodness: and, indeed, were it true that all things proceeded according to one invariable rule of government in His administrations, in grace, in providence, and also in the natural world, without His interposing any particular acts of His divine authority and power, God's government of the world would be less attended to and believed in, His cognizance of human affairs be questioned by many, and such a settled sameness in the course of things be construed into a blind fatality. Nor is it easily to be conceived by us, how one unchangeable mode of proceedings could be adapted to the present condition of mankind, as free agents, under their continual fluctuations and deviations from the rule of obedience, their backslidings, rebellions, and apostacy ; and accordingly we read how the Lord varied His particular dealings with the Israelites, according to their states and circumstances respectively, for direction, for warning, for correction, &c., by visions, by voices, by signs and wonders, and by the mission of angels, to reclaim and convert them ! and this is so far from arguing any variableness in God, that it evidences His unchangeableness in mercy and goodness, by accommodating His dealings and dispensations to the needs and requirements of His poor frail creatures : agreeably to that declaration, "I am the Lord, I change not, therefore ye sons of Jacob are not consumed."*

How things went with the Antediluvians in regard to divine manifestations, the sacred records give us but little intelligence ; but thus much we may collect from them, that in the line of Seth, as contradistinguished from that of Cain, there was a church of devout worshippers then on earth, in which Enoch was highly favored of God, and a man of renown, whose prophetic writings continued in the church down to the times of the apostles, as appears from the Epistle of Jude.† In

---

* Mal. iii. 6.

† Mr. Hartley here speaks according to the ideas commonly entertained from the literal sense of the Word ; but according to Emanuel Swedenborg, by Enoch is not to be understood any individual so named, but a branch or society of the most ancient church, by whom the knowledges which were seen perceptively by the most ancient

this line of Seth (from what is mentioned of Enoch and Noah) we may conclude, that the church of God, before the general apostacy brought on the flood, was instructed and conducted by particular revelation from heaven; and that an intercourse between angels and the holy men of those early days (called the sons of God), was no unfrequent thing.

On the call of Abraham, heaven was again opened to man in the way of divine communications externally, and he was taught of God the things that be of God, by the ministry of angels'; so that what we now call extraordinary dispensations, were then the *ordinary* way of conveying divine knowledge :* and from these more immediate discoveries of Himself to the patriarchs, we apprehend it was, that God styled Himself the God of Abraham, the God of Isaac, and the God of Jacob.

Nor was the delivery of the law, as a stated directory to the Israelites for duty and worship, intended to supersede particular revelations from heaven, or communications with angels; nay, the promise of an angel to "go before them in the way," was immediately annexed to it :† and the prophetic dispensation under the law, appears as a supplement of superior excellency to the law itself, by expounding and illustrating the typical parts of it in reference to that ministration of righteousness by Jesus Christ, which should far exceed it in glory. Thus the law and the prophets made together, as it were, but one dispensation, and all serious Jews looked upon divine manifestations, by prophecy and vision, as such standing tokens of God's favor towards them, that any occasional cessation of them was considered as a mark of the divine displeasure. Thus the Psalmist: "We see not our tokens, there is not one prophet more,"‡ and hence it was that the Seers, or true Visionaries, were held in such honor by the godly of that church. Thus, "The word of the Lord was precious in those days; there was no open vision."§ "Her prophets find no vision from the Lord."‖ And it is observable, that from the time of Malachi to a little before the advent of Christ, during which period prophecy and vision ceased in the Jewish church (at least in persons of a public character), was the most horrid degeneracy of that people from all things sacred and moral; intestine divisions, bribery, and libertinism, diffused their poison through church and state; the very temple was often polluted with the blood of hostile factions: and the high priesthood was bought and sold, nay, the nomination to it submitted to heathen princes, who conferred the same on the highest bidder: thus fulfilling the truth of Solomon's words,¶ "Where there is no vision the people perish;" meaning thereby, that where there is a cessation of all

people, were reduced into a doctrinal form: and by its being said that "he was not for God took him," is signified that the doctrinals thus arranged, not being agreeable to the genius of the most ancient church, the members of which, being able to see divine things by intuitive perception, had no need of being instructed by the posterior way of doctrine, were withdrawn for the present, and reserved by Divine Providence for the use of posterity (See *Arc. Cœl.* n. 521). The book ascribed to Enoch, and containing the passage quoted from it by Jude, has, since the above Preface was written, been brought to light, and an English translation of it, by Abp. Lawrence, has been printed. It is a supposititious production, of an age far posterior the age of those called Enoch.—*N.*

* See *Bromley on Extraordinary Dispensations,* at the end of his *Way to the Sabbath of Rest.* A book which I much recommend to the reader.—*H.*
† Exod. iii. 20. ‡ Psalm lxxiv. 10. § 1 Sam. iii. 4.
‖ Isaiah iii. 1. ¶ Prov. xxix. 18.

divine communications, the sense of religion decays, and all things tend to ruin.

When the time was fully come, as foretold by the prophets, for the Sun of Righteousness to arise with healing in His wings: for God to manifest Himself in the flesh to destroy the works of the devil, and to supply what was lacking in all preceding dispensations: then the heavens were again opened, and celestial communications renewed with men; an angel foretold the birth of Him who should be the harbinger to this Prince of Peace: the same heavenly messenger was sent to the highly favored virgin, with a salutation, on her miraculous conception of Him; and a host of angels proclaimed the joyful news of His gracious advent; angels ministered unto Him during His abode on earth, and announced His resurrection from the dead. But when all was finished relating to our adorable Redeemer's ministry, sufferings, and life in the flesh, and the dispensation of the Holy Ghost took place according to His promise, were all extraordinary dispensations then to cease? By no means; for this very public solemnity on the day of Pentecost, was attended with a gracious promise of their continuance in the church to future generations; as declared to all present by Peter, who, on quoting the prophecy of Joel,* concerning the same vouchsafements, applies them to the times of the gospel dispensations: "For the promise is to you and to your children, and to them that are afar off."† And they certainly continued with the apostles, as more particularly appears from the visions of angels to Peter, Paul, Philip, and John the divine; plainly evincing, that they were not superseded by the giving of the Holy Ghost.

Such as are no friends to the belief of extraordinary gifts and communications, have labored all they could to confine them to the times of the apostles; but in so contradicting the current testimony of the church-history, they show much prejudice and little modesty. The apostolical fathers, Barnabas, Clement, and Hermas (whose writings were reverenced as of canonical authority for four hundred years, and were read, together with the canonical Scriptures, in many of the churches), confirm the truth of prophecy, divine visions, and miraculous gifts, continuing in the church after the apostolical age, both by their testimony and experience: and to pass over many other venerable names (among whom Tertullian and Origen are witnesses to the same truth afterwards), Eusebius, Cyprian, and Lactantius, still lower down, declare that extraordinary divine manifestations were not uncommon in their days. Cyprian is very express on this subject, praising God on that behalf, with respect to himself, to divers of the clergy, and many of the people, using these words: "The discipline of God over us never ceases by night and by day to correct and reprove; for not only by visions of the night, but also by day, even the innocent age of children among us is filled with the Holy Spirit, and they see, and hear, and speak in ecstasy, such things as the Lord vouchsafes to admonish and instruct us by:"‡ and it was the settled belief of the early fathers of the church, that these divine communications, for direction, edification, and comfort, would never wholly cease therein.

That extraordinary gifts became more rare in the church about the

* Joel iii. 28, 29.   † Acts ii. 39.   ‡ Epist. 16.

middle of the third century, is allowed by Cyprian himself, and such other writers, both contemporary and subsequent, as at the same time testified to the reality of them ; and they account for it from the encouragement given to the pernicious doctrines of Epicurus, and other materialists, at that time, which disposed many to turn every thing supernatural and spiritual into mockery and contempt. In the next century, when the profession of Christianity became established by Constantine as the religion of the empire, and millions adopted it from its being the religion of the court, the fashion of the times, or the road to temporal emoluments, then Christianity appeared indeed more gorgeous in her apparel, but became less glorious within ; was more splendid in form, but less vigorous in power ; and so what the church gained in surface she lost in depth. She suffered her faith to be corrupted by the impure mixtures of the heathenish philosophy ; whilst the honors, riches, and pleasures of the world, insinuated themselves into her affections, stole away her graces, and so robbed her of her best treasure ; insomuch, that many have made it a doubt whether, in the times here spoken of, Paganism was more christianized, or Christianity more paganized.

This being the condition of things, it is no wonder that we hear so little of divine visions and extraordinary spiritual gifts in those days : for however external men are apt to glory in the pompous appearance of a visible church, yet the true spiritual church may be considered at that time, and indeed ever since, as in her wilderness state, withdrawn from the multitude to keep herself unspotted from the world, and to preserve a holy intercourse with her beloved, in a life and conversation becoming the gospel of Christ : nor were her heavenly vouchsafements less than before, but only less proper to be divulged, as less likely to be received, or to be received only with derision, as were the dreams of Joseph by his brethren. We always mean to except, under this distinction, many excellent persons, mixed with carnal professors in common life, yet walking in all good conscience, fearing God, and working righteousness. Nor is any thing here said with a design to suggest, as though the establishment of Christianity in the Roman empire were without its great beneficial effects; for it was a means appointed by Providence for spreading the knowledge of the truth over a great part of the known world, whereby great numbers, under very defective and corrupt administrations of it, were converted from the error of their ways, and, by passing through the *outward forms* and *ordinances* to the *inward power*, became burning and shining lights in the church. Besides, divine truth is of a diffusive nature, like the precious ointment upon the head of Aaron, that fell down to the skirts of his garments. Thus the Christian religion, in the weakest administrations of it, was not without good influence on the nations that received it, by civilizing their manners, improving their systems of morality, repressing their enormous vices, and regulating their polity by more wholesome laws and institutes.

To trace the Christian religion in the various revolutions of its progress, from its first civil establishment down to the present times, would be the province of the historian ; we shall therefore pass over all the intervening periods of it, to consider the subject before us, in the way both of scriptural and rational inquiries in relation to ourselves. And here it must be owned, that the belief of all extraordinary or supernatural dispensations, is at a very low ebb with us, and that from several assignable causes, two or three of which shall here be noticed.

And first, from an undue exaltation of man's natural rational faculties and powers, as the sufficient test of revealed truths; and this gross error has prevailed more among men of human learning for this century past, than perhaps ever before; to which it is owing, that almost every thing in religion has been run into question and controversy, and that a general disbelief of all things supernatural has, in a great measure, banished faith, and introduced Sadducism amongst us, to the denying of all spiritual visions and apparitions of angels as things incredible.

Secondly, This doubting and unbelief in things of a spiritual nature, has spread to a greater extent among all classes, from an excessive attachment to worldly interest, and the love of money in the trading nations of Christendom, through the vast increase of commerce and navigation in the two last centuries; whereby the affections and pursuits of such great numbers have been so engaged on the side of filthy lucre, as to turn an employment, in itself innocent and useful, into the occasion of sin. Hence a sordid avarice, and *making haste to be rich*, by frauds, extortion, and injustice, which lay an invincible obstacle in the way of faith; since we are told, that every one that would name the name of Christ, as his Saviour, must first depart from iniquity.

Another great hindrance to the belief of all communications with the world of spirits, is, a life of pleasure, which the apostle calls a state of death,* as it chains down the mind to the objects of the senses, and things of outward observation, and totally indisposes it for the consideration of things inward and spiritual: and this is not only the case of the voluptuous and libertine part of mankind, but of those also, who, from an indulged levity and dissipation of mind, abandon themselves to vain pastimes and amusements, are carried away with every wind of fashion and folly, or, like the Athenians, spend their time in nothing else, but either to tell or to hear some new thing. Should an apostle reveal any thing concerning heaven or hell to persons thus indisposed to receive his report, is it not to be expected that they would reply in derision, like the philosophers or Athenians before mentioned, at the preaching of Paul, "What will this babbler say?" Nor can it be expected that the contents of the following volume should meet with a more favorable reception from such. All things relating to the other world, and the condition of departed souls, are of a most interesting nature, and call for great seriousness and awful attention; and they that bring not with them minds so prepared for the consideration of these subjects, however they may boast of their reason, are not as yet qualified for judges in these matters. And this leads to an observation or two on the subject of reason.

There is nothing more talked of and pretended to, than reason, and yet nothing which people of every rank and age are less agreed in; that which generally passes for reason, being of a vague, uncertain nature, varying according to the tempers, inclinations, and circumstances of men.

* 1 Tim. v. 6.

Thus it happens, that the reason of one at thirty years of age is seldom the reason of the same person at fifty ; the reason of the majority is not the reason of the minority ; nay, in every profession, art, and science, men reason differently, and often oppositely, except where reason has least place, as in mathematics, geometry, and arithmetic. And yet there is a right reason in all things, where men are qualified to find it out ; but these are few, and we see by far the greater part perpetually wrangling, disputing, and contradicting one another in relation to right and wrong in most things ; and the main cause of it is the want of simplicity, and a right disposition of the will and affections, which are absolutely necessary, in order to a right judgment : but whilst men dignify their passions, humors, and false interests, with the venerable name of reason, it remains in them no other than the operation of their present state of mind on the errors, prejudices, and wrong principles they have before imbibed, and which they are resolved to maintain with the most words, and such arguments as they are masters of ; and hence it is that we have so many critics, politicians, and divines, who are utter strangers to the truth of the matters they take in hand.

But reason has also its specific differences and measures, according to the nature of the subject to be investigated : thus ethics, physics, and metaphysics, have each their respective principles, and consequently a distinct kind of reason ; and he that is a good proficient in the knowledge of one, may be very deficient in another. Thus every part of knowledge has its standard, adequate and proper to itself : so natural things are known by natural reason, and spiritual things are discerned by a spiritual light : and this distinction is founded on the authority of Scripture, in which we are told, that " the natural man receiveth not the things of the Spirit of God, for they are foolishness unto him ; neither can he know them, because they are spiritually discerned ;"* that is, the animal or sensual man, with all his natural faculties and endowments, cannot of himself attain to the knowledge of spiritual things, they being too far above his reach ; and therefore it must be given him from above, or he cannot have it : nay, so contrary are they to the propensities and apprehensions of his sensual fallen nature, that whilst he presumes on a fancied sufficiency in himself to comprehend these things, the deeper he plunges himself into the darkness of human ignorance concerning them, and the more accounts them foolishness : and thus God is said to make foolish the wisdom of this world, by leaving such to their wilful blindness, who choose darkness rather than light.

Nothing is here said to depreciate external rational knowledge, even in its lowest sphere, when joined with the fear of God in men of humble minds : for this also is the gift of God, and is not only helpful to us in all the purposes of this life, but, in due place and subordination, subservient to the divine life : it is the abuse of this knowledge only that falls under our censure ; as when natural knowledge and human learning are employed to unsettle men's minds with respect to the things of the other world, and to rob them of the precious hopes of a glorious immortality through the redemption that is in Christ Jesus. All such kind of sophistry, mistaken for reason, is no better than vain deceit, and science falsely so called ; and all that exercise themselves therein are disturbers of the

* 1 Cor. ii. 14.

peace of mankind, as well as enemies to the church of God. Nor can we here forbear to pass a reproof on all those, who, whilst they profess a reverence for the Gospel revelation, patronize, at the same time, the infidelity of the Sadducees, as touching angels and spirits, and all extraordinary dispensations : for to deny all communications with the spiritual world, whether by visions, or any other means, naturally leads to Atheism ; and their pernicious reasonings in this way have had dreadful effects upon the present times, by weakening the sense of religion and conscience in the lower classes of the people. The belief of an intercourse with the other world, according to the truth of it, keeps alive and cherishes faith in the immortality of the soul, in all ranks of people, and familiarizes the mind to its existence separate from the body : and it is not to be doubted, that such gracious vouchsafements were granted to the Jews under the law, and have been continued since to the church under the Gospel, in aid and assistance to men's faith in the written traditions of both dispensations ; such being the goodness of the Lord in compassion to the weakness of our nature, and the dulness of our minds, which stand so much in need of fresh awakening incitements to call off our attention from earthly to heavenly things. And therefore we cannot but lament, that any men of name in the church (though little deserving of it on this account), have gone so far beyond this line, as to assert, that all extraordinary gifts and supernatural dispensations have totally ceased since the third century : but we have no authority for this but their own, and therefore do upon much better grounds assert, that extraordinary gifts and vouchsafements never did nor will cease in the church, till that which is perfect shall come ; that is, till such extraordinary become ordinary dispensations, and angels shall converse with men as familiarly as they did with Adam before the fall ; and, in the mean time, we confidently rely upon the divine promise, that the same Lord, who " gave some apostles, and some prophets, and some evangelists, and some pastors and teachers, for the perfecting of the saints, for the work of the ministry, for the edifying of the body of Christ," will fulfil the same promise, " till we all come in the unity of the faith, and the knowledge of the Son of God, unto a perfect man, unto the measure of the stature of the fulness of Christ."*

But it may be said here, that seers of visions are not mentioned along with prophets, &c., in the foregoing quotation from the apostle : and therefore as the first are principally referred to in this preface, it will be here apposite to observe, that the name of prophet in Scripture, is not confined to the gift of prediction or foretelling things to come, but signifies one to whom any divine manifestation was made for the use of others; and as this was generally by vision, so we read that prophets in ancient times were usually called seers, that is, see-ers of visions. Thus, in 1 Sam. ix. 9, " Before time in Israel, when a man went to inquire of God, thus he spake, Come, and let us go to the seer ; for he that is now called a prophet was before time called a seer ;" and afterwards, in the same chapter, Samuel calls himself a seer : and in 2 Sam. xxiv. 11, we read, " that the word of the Lord came unto the prophet Gad, David's seer ;" of such honorable repute was the name of seer in those times. When therefore the apostle gives it in charge to the church, not to despise

* Eph. iv. 11.

prophesyings, we have no warrant to exclude visions from the general charge, especially as we are well informed from ecclesiastical history, that the custom of communicating to the church the visions of holy persons, particularly such as were of authority in the ministry, continued down at least to the days of Cyprian, the good bishop of Carthage, who speaks of manifestations by visions throughout his epistles, and also of his own; for he had many visions, and, among others, one concerning his own martyrdom, and the particular manner of it, which happened accordingly.

St. Paul,* speaking of the superior excellence and blessedness of the New Covenant, says, "But ye are come to mount Sion, and unto the city of the living God, the heavenly Jerusalem, and to an innumerable company of angels," &c. By which words we cannot suppose him to mean less, than that by Christ, the mediator of this better covenant, a more free intercourse with heaven, and a more intimate fellowship with saints and angels, is now opened for us, if we debar not ourselves of this blessed privilege. What then hinders our conversing with angels now, as the patriarchs and prophets did of old? What but our own fault and unfitness for such glorious company? Why do we not now see them descending and ascending between heaven and earth, as Jacob did on the typical ladder? Why, but for our own unbelief, our dulness, our earthly-mindedness; from which deep sleep, as to the things of God, if we are truly awakened, we should see cause to own, in the words of the same patriarch, when he awaked from the vision of the night, "surely the Lord is in this place, and I knew it not."† Heaven is as near to the heavenly soul, as the soul is to the body; for we are not separated from it by distance of place, but only by *condition of state;* thus when Elisha was surrounded in Dothan by Syrians, his servant saw not the chariots and horsemen [the angelical host] that surrounded his master for defence, as Elisha did, till the Lord opened his eyes. Just so it is with us unbelief and sin keep us from seeing the things that are about us and near to us, and also from giving credit to the reports of those who are in the experience of them.

The same apostle who cautions against despising prophesyings, does also give us to understand, that angels were not to discontinue their visits to men in future times of the church; as, when exhorting us not to "be forgetful to entertain strangers," he adds, "for thereby some have entertained angels unawares."‡ Now there would be no encouragement nor argument in the latter part of the verse, unless the same might happen to be the case with us also. But wherefore should we doubt that those blessed friendly beings should take delight in exercising their good-will to men by many kind offices, both visible and invisible, according to the good pleasure of our common Lord: as by preserving us in many dangers, protecting us against the assaults of evil men and evil spirits, and by counselling, warning, and helping us, by various ways and means we know not of? We ought not so to doubt of this, as we are apt to do, nor wonder at it: "For are they not all ministering spirits, sent forth to minister to them who shall be heirs of salvation."§ But whether manifested to us or not, sure it is, that we are more indebted to them for their kind assistance and ministrations than is generally believed;

* Heb. xii. 22.   † Gen. xxvii. 16.   ‡ Heb. xiii. 2.   § Heb. i. 14.

as evidently appears to have been the sense of the Church of England, heretofore at least, as thus expressed in her collect for St. Michael and all angels: "O everlasting God, who hast ordained and constituted the service of angels and men in a wonderful order, mercifully grant, that as thy holy angels always do thee service in heaven, so by thy appointment they may succor and defend us on earth."

As to the argument offered by those, who maintain the total cessation of these and other extraordinary dispensations, on the establishment of the Christian religion, or its protection by the civil powers; viz., that the ordinary gifts of the Spirit, together with its settled ecclesiastical economy, are sufficient for salvation, and the welfare of the church, and therefore what is more is needless, and not to be expected:—be it answered, first, that the opposers of extraordinary dispensations do here take for granted the very point in question, viz. that they are ceased, which it is impossible for them to prove; nay, we appeal for the reality of them to the authority of universal ecclesiastical history, as also to the records of every particular church and nation in Christendom, not to insist on the testimony given thereto in numberless books, tracts, and narratives, some or other of which have fallen in the way of every person of any reading and conversation. What credit is to be given to or withheld from them respectively, is another matter of inquiry; but that all should be invention and forgery, requires a higher degree of credulity than is sufficient for believing the greater part of them; and as to the reproachful epithets of monkish and legendary, so liberally bestowed on well-attested narratives of this kind, by such as resolve to believe nothing but what they can see with their eyes or touch with their hands, they are not to be regarded, where the grounds of credulity and evidence are the points in question. Many of the Roman Catholic writers stand confessedly chargeable with an over credulity; and it is to be wished, that many of the Protestant writers were less censurable than they are for incredulity; and the medium between both these extremes will be found the proper ground from whence to take the clearest view of these matters. Sure it is, that we are at this time very dangerously infected with doubting and unbelief, as to the things supernatural; and that the general idea of Reformation, amongst us, means rather a departure from certain Popish errors and superstitions, than any advances in true faith and godliness.

Secondly, As to what is alleged for the sufficiency of the ordinary means of grace, under a legal establishment of religion, for faith and salvation; may we not ask such bold pronouncers, by what commission they take upon them to determine concerning sufficiency in this matter, and who gave authority to teach, that the Lord is become more sparing of His benefits and gifts to His church than in former times, nay, than He has promised to be towards it; or do they suppose, that what is called an establishment of religion by the civil powers, is equivalent to the extraordinary gifts bestowed on the primitive Christians? Wherefore should they go about to limit the loving-kindness of the Lord by their own scanty measure of sufficiency, since it is His usual way to give not only for mere necessity, but also for delectation; His gracious attribute is, not only to be good, but abundant in goodness in all His works, both of nature and grace, where men render not themselves unqualified for the same; and He that giveth one talent, is as ready to bestow ten talents on a due improvement of the former; for so He giveth grace for grace.

Thirdly, The inference they draw against the usefulness of miraculous gifts, and other extraordinary dispensations, from those words of Abraham, in the parable of Dives and Lazarus, "If they hear not Moses and the prophets, neither will they be persuaded if one should rise from the dead," is not at all conclusive in this case; as that saying appears to respect such only as have hardened themselves in unbelief, by departing from faith in the written Word, under the ordinary means of salvation; and not such as are weak in the faith, but not obdurate, as was the case with the disciples, who, though under our Lord's own teachings, yet, through the dulness of their apprehension, seemed to need some mighty work to make an impression on their feeble minds: and accordingly, when Jesus was on the way with them to raise Lazarus from the dead, he speaks of the ensuing miracle as useful for them among others, and takes satisfaction on their account, that he was not present with Lazarus in his sickness to heal him: "I am glad for your sakes that I was not there, to the intent that ye may believe;"* that is, by seeing him raised from the dead. So then we are to make a wide distinction between an evil heart of unbelief, as where men, through an incorrigible attachment to sinful courses, or by taking pains to confirm themselves in infidelity, are proof against evidence sufficient for their conviction; and where they are in unbelief through present inattention, distraction of mind from worldly hindrances, dulness of apprehension, and the like causes, but without any wilful opposition to the truth. In these last cases extraordinary means have often salutary effects, by calling off the mind from its wandering, by alarming and converting the sinner from the error of his ways.

From what has been observed on the foregoing subject, we shall conclude, that the same Lord, who in times past sent His prophets, wise men, and seers, and gave extraordinary tokens and warnings to awaken a careless world to a sense of its danger, has not wholly ceased in these last ages to manifest His power and goodness for the same end, in various instances, to co-operate as assisting means with the more general and stated provisions of His revealed will, for our incitement and benefit: and though some, through their unbelief and obduracy in sin, refuse to profit by any methods of His goodness, whether ordinary or extraordinary, yet many others may not be so far departed from the faith and fear of God, as to continue unreclaimable by His more particular and alarming visitations. Thus we read, that many were converted on seeing the miracles which Jesus did; whilst the scribes, Pharisees, and rulers endeavored to stifle their report, and remained wilful unbelievers to the end; and we well know what like opposition we have to expect from men of the same leaven, to every thing that may here be advanced in favor of extraordinary manifestations; but were their names and number greater than they are, it would have no weight with us, being no strangers to their little length and breadth, and their want of depth, and ready to meet them in the field of argument, as well as prepared to answer every objection they have to offer, wishing them at the same

* John xi. 16.

time more modesty, for their own sakes, than to dictate to the church what is sufficient, without scriptural authority.   In the general division I am speaking of, there is a class of modest, well-meaning men, who are no further concerned in the matter before us, than to justify the ways of God to man upon a supposition that all things are left to one settled scheme of things and means, as not seeing any thing beyond it, who are established in the faith under the use of ordinary means, and have no invincible prejudice against the extraordinary, but only think them not granted in these ages of the church : and with such I have no controversy ; but address myself only to those, who declare open war against all supernatural manifestations, whether they are in the profession of Christianity or not.

And here I must ask all such, To what purpose is your opposition to the belief of any fresh discoveries of the other world ?   Is it not a subject of the highest importance to us to know, what and where we shall be to all eternity, after a short passage over this bridge of time ?   Are there not different degrees of evidence in these matters ; and supposing that your convictions were at all times so full in relation thereto, as to exclude all shadow of doubting, yet are there not infinite particulars and circumstances relating to the world of spirits, which may serve as an inexhaustible fund of fresh discoveries, many of which may have been revealed to others, though not to us, and for us to receive from them ? How comes it then, that you are so void of all reasonable curiosity, as to prefer ignorance to information in these things, nay, to study objections to the belief of them ?   Were any prejudice allowable in this case, it should rather be for than against them, especially where they have a tendency to promote faith, virtue, and godliness.   If any knowledge is to be coveted, surely it is that of the laws, ways, and accommodations of that good country, which we hope to go to and live in forever. Besides, such extraordinary manifestations are greatly conducive to the good of this world, by laying before us fresh motives and encouragements in our way through it, to strive lawfully for the high prize that is set before us in a better, and by rousing every power and faculty of the mind by fresh news from heaven.   If we believe the Scriptures, we must allow of such an intercourse between heaven and earth in former times ; and if it be less frequent now, it is owing to the infidelity and apostacy of the times : for God's goodness endureth the same forever, and good spirits are equally desirous of holding communication with men now, as formerly ; but then there must be a suitableness for it on the part of the latter, something of that innocence and simplicity of life, which in ancient times served for the basis of such fellowship.

Cautionary reserves, however, may be justifiable, nay prudent, where the manifestation appears to respect only the party to whom it is made, or for private use to some few others, according as discretion may direct ; yet, where it is evidently given for public benefit and use, as in the case of this author ; more especially if by express command ; here the person is to be considered as standing in the prophetic character, and therefore is not to consult with flesh and blood in this matter, nor to regulate his measures by human prudence ; but to deliver his message boldly, and leave the event to God, lest he suffer for his disobedience, as Jonah did, and be obliged to deliver it at last.

But it may be asked here, if it be not reasonable to expect that every such message from heaven should have the attestation of a miracle to evince the truth of it; to which it might suffice to answer, in the words of Job,* that "The Lord giveth not an account of His matters." This, however, is certain, that wherever He sends a message, He also gives power sufficient with it to convince, or to condemn the rejection of it. Our Lord, in the days of His flesh, wrought miracles, sometimes to convince the understanding, sometimes to take away all excuse from the hardened and impenitent; and sometimes He refrained from doing them, to prevent the greater condemnation of unbelievers; thus he is said not to have done many mighty works in Galilee, because of their unbelief.

But the foregoing query may be further urged into an objection of such apparent strength, as may be thought deserving of a more particular answer. Thus it may be asked, if any particular revelation for public use and benefit, either in the way of instruction, direction, or warning, rests only on the credit and authority of the revealer, are we not liable to much deception in the matter; and though the messenger may be a true one, yet might not our receiving him as such give encouragement to pretenders and impostors, to assume the like character in order to deceive, and to come with "Thus saith the Lord," in their mouths, when the Lord hath not spoken it? In this case, what rule have we to go by, and how shall we tread firm on such slippery ground? To this it is replied, that as in old times there were false as well as true prophets and seers, so nothing hinders but there may be like counterfeits now o'days; for in this mixed world of good and evil, where men stand in their liberty of speaking and acting, no infallible provision against hypocrisy and imposture can take effect, but the enemy will sow his tares in the same field where the good husbandman has sowed his wheat, and Satan will at all times transform himself into an angel of light. Every thing has its contrary here, where good and evil are set one against the other; but then the help and means are provided for our direction and safety: if offences are many, so also are our defences; if errors are manifold, there are diversities of gifts to detect and refute them; and if the father of lies and his emissaries are busy to deceive us, the good Spirit of God is ever ready to lead us into all truth: so that we have not only light in the Scriptures, but, through supplication and prayer, may also have light within us, from above, for the discerning of spirits, and for our security against all the powers of darkness. We are not therefore to reject truth and error indiscriminately in whatever forms they may appear, because the latter may wear a like garb with the former, but to try the spirits, and hold fast to that which is good; herein imitating the fishers mentioned in the gospel, who, "when they had filled their net with fish of every kind, gathered the good into vessels, and cast the bad away."† Nay, the most illiterate Christian, walking humbly in the fear of God, and working righteousness according to his best knowledge, never was nor will be suffered to fall into any fatal delusion: simplicity and uprightness of heart place him under the protection of the Almighty; and he is in the essence of truth, though without the formal ideas of it; for "all the paths of the Lord are mercy and truth, to such as keep His covenant and His testimonies."‡ Mistake

* Ch. xxxii. 18.   † Matt. xiii. 48.   ‡ Psalm xxv 10.

he may, but cannot dangerously err; for his very errors are innocent, and love sanctifies all he thinks, says, and does. Thus the pure in heart see God in all things, and from all things reap benefit without hazard of loss; whilst the perverse and ungodly "change even the truth of God into a lie,"* by turning that which was designed for their good into the occasion of their sin.

But to resume the subject: If it were allowed to be a justifiable cause for the rejection of every extraordinary dispensation that comes supported by credible evidence, because some may falsely pretend to the same, the objection would be of equal force, on the side of numbers, against listening to their established pastors and teachers, because some among them are ignorant, some unsound in doctrine, and some handle the Word of God deceitfully; and though this must be allowed to be a pitiable case where it happens, yet the salvation of the conscientious worshipper does by no means lie upon any such hazard; for ordinary and extraordinary means are all one with the Lord, and rather than any sincerely pious and seeking soul should perish for lack of knowledge, He would send, if need were, an angel from heaven to be its teacher. But all such have an unerring guide, even the good Spirit of God; and "them that are meek shall He guide in judgment, and such as are gentle, them shall He teach his way."†

Lastly, it is to be observed under this article, that all who professedly oppose every kind of communication with the world of spirits, do not only deny the authority of the Sacred Records, but also set aside that evidence which is given to the truth of this matter, by the concurrent testimony of every age and nation: so that matter of fact is against them, and proves all their pretensions to reason and philosophy to be vain, whilst they go about to invalidate all authority, except that of their own senses; and, I may add, even to render that doubtful likewise; nay, I have heard one of this skeptical class declare, that he would not believe the testimony of his own senses in such a case. It is well known, that the heathens believed themselves to be under the care of their gods through the ministry of genii or tutelary spirits, and held the existence both of good demons, and of evil or caco-demons; for dark as their dispensation was, they had shadows of truth among them sufficient to keep alive their belief of the soul's immortality, and they have transmitted down to us in their histories many instances of supernatural visions and apparitions, and of warnings by dreams: so that many of our modern unbelievers have less of faith in things of the other world than the very Gentiles, several of whom have declared themselves indebted to good and visible agents for the wisdom of their laws, for many valuable discoveries in physic, for warnings, predictions, and extraordinary deliverances.‡ To give only one saying of Cicero, among many, to the same purpose: "I know not," says he, "any one nation, polite or barbarous, which does not hold, that some persons have the gift of foretelling future events."§

But I chiefly confine myself here to celestial visions, answerable to the following work, and which are by no means to be considered on the level with apparitions, whether of ghosts departed, or of spirits of any other order, these last being of a far inferior kind to the first; and

---

* Rom. i. 25.   † Psalm xxv. 9.   ‡ Cicero de Divinatione.   § Ibid. Lib. I.

yet it will not be going far out of my way to speak a few words of the latter.

There is a climax in God's works of nature, or a scale ascending from the lowest to the highest of them, till they terminate in the great adorable Original, who is the Alpha and Omega of the universe. From these gradations, discovered or discoverable in the natural world, we may from analogy (which is our best rule here to go by) conclude, that the like progression takes place in the spiritual worlds, and that there is not that wide chasm between one and the other that is generally supposed, but that the most refined part of the material meets the grossest part of the immaterial system of beings, visible thus ending where invisible begins ; and consequently, that there are spirits very near us, though not discernible by us, except when, according to certain unknown laws of their existence, or the particular will of the Lord, they become manifested to us, either visibly or audibly ; and highly credible it is, that all nature is peopled with them in its several regions of the air and earth, and its subterraneous dwellings, according to their different classes, subordinations, and allotments.* Milton finely expresses himself on this subject, as follows :

> " Think not, though men were none,
> That heaven would want spectators, God want praise :
> Millions of spiritual creatures walk the earth
> Unseen, both when we wake, and when we sleep," &c.

Now to argue against their existence from their being inconspicuous, is an absurd conclusion for men who pretend to philosophy ; especially when all know what a new world of animalcula, invisible before, has been discovered to us by the improved microscope ; and who will say, that the natural† eye of man is incapable of such further assistance, as may enable us to discern the subtile vehicles of certain spirits, whether consisting of air or ether ; certain it is, that either by condensation, or some other way, they can make themselves visible, and converse with us, as man with man ; and so innumerable are the instances hereof, as also of their discoveries, warnings, predictions, &c., that I may venture to affirm, with an appeal to the public for the truth of it, that there are few ancient families in any county of Great Britain, that are not possessed of

---

* The pious Author of this Preface here seems, agreeably to the popular belief, to recognize the existence of spirits not originally derived from the human race. But though the opinion is supported by the authority of the poet, Milton, it is clearly shown, in the following work, that all spirits whatever came first into existence as men on this or some other earth. But this fact does not militate against the position, that there are spirits of very different orders and classes, besides angels, or the inhabitants of heaven, and devils, or the inhabitants of hell ; and that they operate with most power, respectively, in different localities, corresponding, respectively, to their states. All that the Author of the Preface advances respecting spirits, not immediate inhabitants either of heaven or hell, is perfectly true, when understood of the various classes of spirits whose abode is in what is called, in the following work, the world of spirits, where all are prepared for their final home, either in the heavenly or infernal regions. These, as is shown in the following work, are the immediate spiritual associates of men in the world.—N.

† The learned Writer of this Preface here, again, speaks according to the ordinary views of philosophers and divines. It is, however, clearly shown, in the following work, that it is impossible for spirits to be seen by the *natural* eye ; and that when they are made visible to man, it is not by clothing themselves with vehicles of air or ether, and condensing these into a visible natural substance, but by the opening of the sight of man's spirit, before which spirits are seen as plainly, in their own spiritual substance, and proper form, as are natural objects before man's natural sight.—N.

records or traditions of the same in their own houses, however the prevailing Sadducism of these times may have sunk the credit of them, as well as in a great measure cut off communications of this kind.

These spirits are of both sorts, like men on earth, good and bad ; as to the latter, they are the agents of Satan, to promote the .interests of his kingdom, and, like their chief, " go to and fro in the earth, walking up and down in it,"* seeking whom they may deceive and destroy. These are enemies to good men, and the willing associates of men of evil dispositions, over whom they have great power through the consent of their will, but none otherwise, practising upon their minds and understanding " with all deceivableness of unrighteousness in them that perish, because they received not the love of the truth, that they might be saved."† This power of enticing, prompting, and instigating such as become their willing captives, to all kinds of evil ; and the heinous sin of the latter, in freely surrendering themselves into their hands to be practised upon ; stand confessed even in the form of proceeding in our courts of judicature in the case of atrocious delinquents, it being part in the charge of indictment, that they did such and such things at the instigation of the devil, inferring it as the aggravation of their crime, that they could choose the service of so bad a master.

To continue insensible of our danger from evil spirits, whether from ignorance, inattention, or the disbelief of them, is one of the sorest evils that can befall us, and is in the church at this day a misery to be lamented with tears of blood, as it leads to a fatal carelessness, exposes us to their subtle devices, and gives them an advantage over us every way. Nor are they an enemy lightly to be accounted of, being watchful, diligent, and full of stratagems for our ruin ; and they have moreover a hold on the corrupt part of our nature, and well know how to use it, being furnished with traps of all sorts to catch the unwary, and with baits adapted to every vicious appetite and inclination ; having a great part of the honors and riches of this world at their disposal, through the power and influence of those that are subject to them ; and therefore it behoves us to be well furnished for this part of our spiritual welfare, and to put on the whole armor of God, seeing those we have to do with are not to be subdued with carnal weapons ; for here, as the apostle tells us, " we wrestle against principalities, against powers, against the rulers of the darkness of this world, against spiritual wickedness in high places."‡ But we come now to speak of better spirits, and more to satisfaction.

If there be legions of spirits about and near us to deceive, tempt, and annoy us, can we doubt of there being as many appointed to serve, help, and defend us, according to their several classes and offices, in this our world ? The conclusion is natural from parity of reason, and the law of opposites, according to which the Great Governor of the world has contrasted evil with a counterbalance of good ; consequently, such beneficent beings there doubtless always have been, and are, in readiness to succor the fallen human race by their friendly ministrations, and to fill up the distance in the scale of created beings between men and angels. The darkness of the heathen world most certainly did not separate them from the care of that good God, who is loving to every man, and whose mercy is over all his works : and though their condition might not admit

* Job i. 7.   † 2 Thess. ii. 10.   ‡ Eph. vi. 12.

of communion with angels, but in rare instances, yet the good offices of
these kindly affectioned ministers in their respective provinces, might, in
a sort, be angelical to them answerably to their dispensation, and serve
as the lowest step in Jacob's ladder for their communication with the
heavenly world: and by what is handed down to us by authors of credit
concerning communications of this kind to eminent persons in the heathen
ancient world, as Socrates and others, whether by checks and warnings,
impulses, dreams, voices, or visions, we are not at liberty to doubt of an
intercourse between good spirits and the well-disposed heathens of all
ranks, as a dispensation not so unfrequent as many suppose ; seeing that
the instances of this kind amongst ourselves, that come to public knowledge, bear no proportion in number to those that are concealed from
us.   This, however, we are assured of upon the best authority, that
many shall come from the east and from the west [in the Gentile world].
and sit down with Abraham, Isaac, and Jacob, in the kingdom of heaven;
and that many of the children of the kingdom [professors of the truth]
shall be cast out.*

Though we now stand in a far higher dispensation than the heathens,
and are called to an innumerable company of angels, and to the fellowship of the Holy Ghost, yet we are not therefore to suppose, that all
intercourse with good spirits of an inferior order is now ceased among
us ; as many, who have not yet attained to the glorious privileges of the
gospel, and the immediate guardianship of angels, may nevertheless
stand indebted, under God, to the ministry of such good spirits for many
important services, both in their spiritual and temporal affairs; nay, they
may be, to all of us in the natural world, what the good angels are in
that which is purely spiritual, and by their great knowledge in the laws
and powers of this mundane system, and by various impressions on our
animal spirits and faculties, may contribute much to our relief, comfort,
and preservation, in many difficulties, distresses, and dangers; and perhaps few that take a serious review of the most remarkable occurrences
of their past lives, will not be led to ascribe much of assistance to the
instrumentality of such invisible friends ; nay, who can say that they are
not constituted subordinate agents on various occasions in conducting the
scheme both of general and particular providences ?   There is nothing in
this supposition that offers violence to reason or religion; and sure it is,
that we have abundant credible testimonies to wonderful discoveries
made by them, of a very interesting nature, both to individuals, and also
to society ; as of concealed writings and treasures, of murders, conspira-
cies, and other matters leading to the administration of justice, both dis-
tributive and punitive ;† as is well known of all conversant with men
and books ; so that to give the lie to all such relations as credited by
the learned, the wise, the good of all classes, must appear nothing less
than impudence joined with infidelity.

It has been made a common objection to the credibility of many
apparitions, that they have been either silent, or not delivered any thing
worthy of such extraordinary visits ; and, consequently, that such
visions were no other than the effect of imagination and fancy, as not
answering to any use or purpose.   To which be it answered, That the
use of such visits may be very important, though nothing should pass in

* Matt. viii. 11, 12.   † See, in particular, Miscellanies, by J. Aubrey, Esq., F.R.S.

the way of conversation between the parties during the interview; as, First, by convincing the spectator of the reality of such beings as spirits, and so removing doubts concerning a future state, as well as by preparing him for the return of such visits to further purpose. Secondly, by affecting the conscience with a tender sense of duty, or with remorse for past offences, and impressing the mind with awful thoughts of its own existence in a separate state. Thirdly, by giving us to know, that we are the objects of regard to beings in the other world, and visible to them when we think not of it; which may serve as a means to restrain us from indecent and offensive liberties in our most retired hours, when the more weighty consideration of the Divine Omnipresence may not be attended to, and so lose its proper effect upon us.

But here we are called off from answering more objections on this subject, to observe, that this labored opposition to the belief of all intercourse betwixt us and the other world, too often proceeds both from a practical and speculative kind of atheism, and, consequently, the disbelief of a future state. Hence proceeds that countenance given to some late writers in favor of infidelity; as also, that dreadful apostacy amongst so many in these last days, of exalting I know not what natural religion, in order to lessen the authority of Divine Revelation: whereas it may truly be affirmed, that all such resistance to, or departure from, the faith, under the light of the Gospel, however it may be covered or colored with the name of natural religion, is nothing better than atheism. O wretched men, here spoken of, what are you doing? What but the greatest possible injury to your own souls? What but robbing yourselves of every comfort that reason and religion can supply to make this life a blessing? And all in the miserable, mad hope, that when you die, you shall be of no more account than a dead dog. If there be any folly, it is yours; if any insanity in the world, you are possessed of it: for if there be a God, you make Him your enemy through your unbelief; if a heaven, what lot have you to hope for in such inheritance? If a hell, how will you escape it? And here also let it be asked, what is your character and estimation in society; if true members of society you can be called, who have no pledge to give of your obedience and fidelity to government, as acknowledging no sanctity in an oath, which is inseparably connected with the belief of a future state? Thus void of faith, void of conscience, void of honor (for what is honor without conscience?) what have you left for a support to the slenderest virtue? What have you to engage the smallest confidence from man? Can any firm bond of compact or friendship find place in that heart, which has no interest in *hereafter* to care for, and wherein every motive and measure must take its rise and direction from the love of self and the love of this world? In this case, it is more for our comfort to go by our hopes than our fears, and therefore one would be willing to believe, from tenderness to human nature, and also from charity, that the number of those who are in this horrible degree of infidelity is but small. But however that may be, it will be proper to observe here, that to the many general causes of infidelity, some of which have been briefly touched on before—as the undue exaltation of natural reason, a life of pleasure, and confirmed habits of vice—we may add the spirit of controversy and dispute, long ago introduced into the church by the artificial logic of Aristotle, and

3

encouraged and kept up in the schools as a necessary part of education in theology; to the engendering of perplexity and doubting on every subject, and keeping the mind from fixing in any settled principles of religion. The several churches of Christendom have confessedly been infected with this poison of fierce contention and debate, to the banishing of sweet peace and brotherly love; whilst a pretended zeal for truth has served for a cloak to that "wrath of man, which worketh not the righteousness of God." But such carnal weapons ill befit the Christian warfare; all such kind of striving for victory among ourselves gives advantage to the enemies of our holy faith, and causes the Philistines to rejoice. The best way of healing differences is, by composedness and gentleness of mind; and the truth of the gospel of peace is most suitably offered, and most readily received, by humble men, and such as are of a meek and quiet spirit. It is obvious to remark in this place, that Deism, Sadducism, and Atheism, did never more abound amongst us, than since the itch of controversy and wrangling, on all occasions, has filled the world so full of false reasoning and perverse disputings. Nay, the contagion has descended to private life, and turned much of our conversation into contradiction and a strife of words, and introduced a bold behavior and an assuming talkativeness, offensive to all modest persons; insomuch that we are now in general fallen under that reprehension of the apostle applied to the contentious, who "come together, not for the better, but for the worse."*

After what has been replied to objections against the credibility of extraordinary manifestations, and also offered concerning some causes of unbelief in this case, we are here led to declare, not only our belief, but full assurance, that extraordinary communications, however now less frequent than formerly, are still continued to several particular members of the different churches, though not publicly revealed by them; and that they are not to be considered only as a particular privilege, but as making part of the state of certain persons (not all) of eminent purity and piety: and the way to be inwardly convinced of this ourselves is, to make some approach to their state; for however we may come short of them as to like vouchsafements, yet, both in the ordinary and extraordinary gifts and graces of the spirit, we are led, not only to rejoice with them, but by mutual fellowship do participate with them in the blessing; for as in the natural body, so also in the mystical body of Christ, the inferior as well as the superior members jointly contribute to the nourishment and welfare of the whole, by a circulation of that which every one supplieth, so that the highest cannot say to the lowest, I have no need of thee. Thus the meekness, the patience, and the humble condescension, in some, may countervail the high illuminations and splendid ministrations of others; whilst a common sense of their mutual dependence and relation joins them all in the unity of the Spirit, to the edifying of the church in love; and therefore where any, whether in the stated office of the ministry, or others, go about to vilify or obstruct the success of any extraordinary way that has a manifest tendency to promote more true godliness, they would do well to consider and stand in awe, lest they be found to oppose themselves to a work of God; for neither can they be sure that we are not now come to the near approach of that

* 1 Cor xi 7.

glorious state of the church spoken of in so many places by the prophets; when the Lord shall do great things for her in the latter days by a revival of His work in righteousness and peace, shall pour out His Spirit upon all flesh, restore the old paths of heavenly communications, and make His Sion a praise in the earth.   However unpromising the times are, yet, praised be God! we can draw comfort from the promises of better days, even under the "present falling away, and the revelation of the man of sin," foretold* to precede the day of the Lord's coming in the power of His Spirit, to sanctify and cleanse His church, and to purify unto Himself a peculiar people zealous of good works; trusting in hope that this time is near at hand, i. e., that He that shall come, will come, and will not tarry. And though there has been for a season a withholding, in a measure, from Sion, of the ordinary consolations of the Spirit, in the way of a judgment-work (under grace) for self-condemnation, humiliation, and subsequent glorification: yet we are assured that such judgment is sent forth unto victory over the remainder of indwelling sin: for there is a judgment unto righteousness, as well as a judgment unto condemnation; and accordingly in the former sense it is said, that "Zion shall be redeemed with judgment, and her converts with righteousness;"† so that her tribulation is for purification, and exaltation; as it is said in another place, "For a small moment have I forsaken thee, but with great mercies will I gather thee, saith the Lord, thy Redeemer."‡ And as to the restitution of·her gifts, graces, and extraordinary dispensations, signified by precious stones, under her figurative denomination of the Lord's House or Temple, the prophet proceeds thus: "O thou afflicted, tossed with tempest, and not comforted, behold I will lay thy stones with fair colors, and thy foundations with sapphires, and all thy borders with pleasant stones; and all thy children shall be taught of the Lord, and great shall be the peace of thy children: in righteousness shalt thou be established."§

The above is but a small part of the glorious things that are spoken, by the evangelical Prophet, of the city of God, the spiritual church under the Gospel-dispensation in the latter days, when she shall have filled up the measure of her persecutions and sufferings, both from her open enemies, and also in the house of her friends.   And we trust that the time draws very nigh for this glorious dispensation of the New Jerusalem to take place: and particularly, among other important considerations, from instances of extraordinary communications from above, by visions and other ways, particularly in the case of our illuminated Author.   Nor did ever any extraordinary revolution come to pass in the church of God, without previous notices of it first given to some chosen vessels for a testimony to the times, to strengthen the weak in faith, to comfort the afflicted, to alarm the careless and impenitent, or to answer other good purposes of the Divine Providence and Goodness.

Other instances of the kind above-mentioned are ready at hand to offer, and which were received in their day, according to the dignity of their character, by such as were qualified to profit by their message and ministry; but, as is usual in these cases, they were rejected by the greater part; and their names are here passed over, as it is one design of this preface to guard, as far as possible, against giving occasion for

* 2 Thess. ii. 3.   † Isa. i. 27.   ‡ Isa. liv. 7.   § Isa. liv. 11, 18.

critical cavilling and dispute ; it being sufficient for the main intent of it,
to recommend and enforce, to the best of our power, the credibility and
authority of the following Treatise by the honorable and learned Author,
Emanuel Swedenborg, a native of Sweden, of eminence and distinction
in his own country, having had an honorable employment under the
crown, and being of the first Senatorial Order* of the kingdom ; of
respected estimation in the royal family during the late reigns ; of extensive learning, as his voluminous writings demonstrate ; and, as to private
life and character, irreproachable. Something more particular, as to his
personal character, has been spoken in the Preface to the *Treatise on
the Intercourse between the Soul and the Body:* and Mr. Swedenborg's
Letter to a Friend, giving a particular account of himself and family,
annexed to that work, is subjoined to this Preface, the original of which
is in my hands.

It must be owned, that the following Treatise contains so many
wonderful particulars relating to the world of spirits, warranted for truth
by the ocular testimony of the writer, according to his solemn affirma-
tion, as would appear impossible for man in this mortal body to come at
the knowledge of, but for the like instances delivered down to us on the
authority of the Sacred Records, and the promise therein made to the
church of the continuance of such manifestations in it ; and the visions of
our Author must appear to us the more extraordinary, when we consider
that they were of the most exalted nature, as not being exhibited
objectively to the bodily organs or external senses, nor yet merely
intellectual, by representations in the mind, but purely spiritual, whereby
spiritual beings and things were actually seen and perceived by his
spiritual senses, as one spirit beholds another, and answering to those
expressions in Scripture, of " being in the spirit," and of being " caught
up by the spirit ;" as likewise to that rapt, trance, or ecstasy of the apostle,
during which he says " whether he was in the body, or out of the body,
he could not tell."†

The same question that will be asked here, has been briefly noticed
already, viz., If a testimony to so extraordinary a dispensation does not
require the extraordinary seal of miracles to render it credible ? To
which be it further answered, that many of the prophets worked no
miracles, and yet were believed upon their own private testimony ; and
that we believe many things of the highest consequence in religion upon
human authority, where the persons transmitting and delivering them

---

* By the phrase " first Senatorial Order," here used by Mr. Hartley, is not to be
understood that select body called *the Senate*, which, prior to the revolution in 1772,
exercised an authority even greater than that of the king ; but he means the first order
of the States or Diet of the kingdom. For the States of Sweden do not, like our
parliament, consist of two houses only, but of four, viz., the House of Nobles, the House
of the Clergy, the House of Burghers, and the House of Peasants ; in the first of which,
the head or representative of every noble family in the kingdom, whether enjoying the
title of Count or Baron, or only ranking as a simple gentleman, has a seat. Of this
House, Swedenborg was a member ; and it is owing to this circumstance, joined to the
difficulty which we find in this country of forming an idea of a nobleman without a
title, that it has become necessary to give him the title of Baron, which he did not
really enjoy. He speaks of himself, in the letter given at the conclusion of this Preface, as taking his seat in the Diet with the Nobles of the *Equestrian Order;*
evidently denoting a rank below that of Count and Baron, the only *titles* of Nobility in
Sweden.—*N.*

† 2 Cor. xii. 2.

appear properly qualified and circumstanced to give credibility to what they relate. But this argument has been considered in the Preface to the *Treatise on the Intercourse between the Soul and the Body*, before mentioned,* and from the reasons adduced, and such as are ready to be further produced, if called for, we look upon our author's testimony as worthy of our acceptation in this matter, and venture to rely on his own integrity and piety, and his disinterested and indefatigable labors to instruct the world in the most important truths relating to salvation, at the expense of his fortune, and the sacrifice of all worldly enjoyments during the last thirty years of his life. And if we further reflect, that the whole scope and tendency of his writings is to promote the love of God and of our neighbor ; to inculcate the highest reverence to the Holy Scriptures ; to urge the necessity of practical holiness ; and to confirm our faith in the divinity of our Lord and Saviour Jesus Christ : these considerations, I think, may be allowed to be sufficient credentials (as far as human testimony can go) of his extraordinary mission and character, and as convincing marks of his sincerity and truth ; especially as we have to add, upon the credit of two worthy persons (one of them a learned physician,† who attended him in his last sickness), that he confirmed the truth of all that he had published relating to his communications with the world of spirits, by his solemn testimony, a very short time before he departed this life, in London, Anno Dom. 1772.

Reader, might it not seem a wonder, if a person of so extraordinary and so apostolical a character, should better escape the imputation of madness than the prophets of old ? And accordingly some have given out, that he was beside himself, and, in particular, that it was occasioned by a fever which he had about twenty years before his death. Now it is well known by all his acquaintance, that our author recovered of that fever after the manner of other men : that his extraordinary communications commenced many years before that time, and that his writings, both prior and subsequently to it, entirely harmonize, and proceed upon the same principles with an exact correspondence ; and that in the whole of his conversation, transactions, and conduct of life, he continued to the end of it the same uniform excellent man. Now, if to write many large volumes on the most important of all subjects with unvaried consistency, to reason accurately, and to give proofs of an astonishing memory all the way ; and if hereto be joined propriety and dignity of character in all the relative duties of the Christian life ; if all this can be reconciled with the true definition of madness, why then there is an end of all distinction between sane and insane, between wisdom and folly. Fie upon those uncharitable prejudices, which have led so many in all ages to credit and propagate slanderous reports of the best of men, even whilst they have been employed in the heavenly work of turning many from darkness to light. and from the power of Satan unto God !

Were an angel from heaven to come and dwell incarnate amongst us, may we not suppose that his conversation, discoveries, and conduct of life, would in many things be so contrary to the errors and prejudices,

---

* And in several works since published ; as in *Hindmarsh's Letters to Priestley*, and *Vindication*, &c., in answer to Pike ; *Clowes's Letters to a Member of Parliament*, &c., in answer to Barruel ; and *Noble's Appeal.—N.*
† The late Dr. Messiter.—*N.*

the ways and fashions of this world, that many would say with one consent, He is beside himself? And where any one of our brethren, through the divine favor, attains to any high degree of angelical illumination and communications, may he not expect the like treatment? I forget the name of the philosopher, whose precepts and lectures were so repugnant to the dissolute manners of the Athenians, that they sent to Hippocrates to come and cure him of his madness; to which message that great physician returned this answer, That it was not the philosopher, but the Athenians that were mad.* In like manner, the wise in every city and country are the smaller part, and therefore must be content to suffer the reproachful name that in truth belongs to the majority. This has been the case of all extraordinary messengers for good to mankind; and the world is not altered in this respect. But it may be said, that though it be thus with the ignorant and profane, yet men of education and learning will form a more righteous judgment of the matter, and be determined impartially according to the nature of the evidence: and it would be well if this were so; but in general it is far otherwise. Human learning, considered merely in itself, neither makes a man a believer nor an unbeliever, but confirms him in truth or error, according to his prejudices, inclinations, or interest: at least it is commonly so; and therefore we find, that in all ages such among the learned as devoted themselves to support the credit and interest of their particular professions, were always the most violent persecutors of the truth; for though truth has its conveyance through the intellectual part in man, yet it never gains its effect, or operates as a principle, till it be received into the affection and will; and so man is said in Scripture to be of an understanding heart. So that knowledge is productive of the greatest good, or the greatest evil, according to the ground or disposition in which it resides: when joined with piety and humility, it adds both lustre and force to truth; when joined with the corrupt passions of our nature, it is the most violent persecutor of it. This was the case with the scribes and Pharisees, and doctors of the law; no greater enemies to Christ than they; the pride of reputation for learning, and the authority of public teachers, unfitted them for becoming learners at the feet of the lowly Jesus; and therefore to them were directed those words of our Lord: "How can ye believe, who receive honor one of another, and seek not the honor that cometh of God only?"† giving us hereby to understand that the dominion of any wrong passion over the mind, will prove a certain hindrance in our way to divine truth.

Great as our loss is by the fall, yet something of that correspondent relation, which originally subsisted between the human soul and divine truth, is still remaining with us (through grace): otherwise we should no more be capable of receiving it when offered, than the brute beasts, which have no understanding: but then, that all may not be lost by wilful sin, and we rendered thereby incapable of conversion, we must be careful not to set up idols in our hearts, nor suffer any false interest to mislead us; as thereby the mind is tinctured with prejudice against the truth, and the understanding receives a wrong bias, and so we become

---

* The story of Democritus and the citizens of *Abdera* seems to be that here alluded to.—*N.*.   † John v. 44.

like the false wise ones spoken of in Job,* who "meet with darkness in the day time, and grope in the noon day as in the night." This difference in the state of the heart and the affections, occasions the difference we see both in the unlearned and learned of equal natural and acquired abilities ; that whilst some readily receive the truth in the light and love of it, others are always disputing, and always seeking, without ever coming to the knowledge of it.

As there is a correspondence, or mutual relation, between rightly disposed minds and truth in general, so likewise there is a particular correspondence or congruity between certain minds and certain truths in particular, producing an aptitude in the former to receive the latter as soon as offered, and that by a kind of intuition without reasoning : and hence it comes to pass, that such as have a remarkable fitness for this or that particular class of truths (which we usually term genius) are less qualified for any considerable proficiency in certain others. Thus the mathematician seldom excels in metaphysical knowledge ; and he that may be very expert in systematical divinity, is often a stranger to mystical theology ; one member thus supplying what another lacketh ; whilst all may learn thereby to esteem and love one another, and praise the Lord for His diversity of gifts for the common benefit of his church. Let not then such as walk in the simplicity of a naked faith, without needing any other evidence : let not such, I say, censure in the following book what they do not understand, or cannot receive ; as it may be of use to others, who are led more in the way of knowledge than themselves. We judge not them, nay, love them ; wherefore then should they come short of us in charity ? Are we not brethren, and travelling to the same good land ? Why then should we fall out by the way ? Even the scribes could say, as touching Paul, " If a spirit or an angel hath spoken to him, let us not fight against God :"† and who can say, that what this our Author delivers to us, as from vision and revelation in the other world, is not the very truth ?

Let it be observed here, in regard to the ensuing work, that though the narrative part of it should appear to the reader strange on account of its novelty, yet both that and the doctrinal part, which is confirmed by plain Scripture, certainly merits his serious attention ; nay, many things therein, touching which the Scriptures are silent, carry weight and internal evidence along with them in the judgment of impartial minds, and will often be found useful to illustrate the most important religious topics ; as also to enrich the mind, to familiarize heavenly things to the thoughts, and to wean the affections from the toys and vanities of a miserable world lying in wickedness. It is allowed that our author does not, in all places throughout his writings, follow the commonly received interpretation of the Scriptures ; but so neither do all churches, nor all expositors in the same church. Though as to life and godliness, and consequently what pertains to salvation, the Scriptures are sufficiently plain, yet, with respect to many difficult and mysterious parts of them, they continue wrapped up in a venerable obscurity, to be opened according to the needs and states of the church throughout all ages ; and we doubt not to affirm, that the highly illuminated Swedenborg has been instrumental in bringing hidden things to light, and in revealing the

* Chap. v. 14.   † Acts xxiii. 9.

spiritual sense of the Sacred Records, above any other person, since the church became possessed of that divine treasure. In the present dark night of general apostasy has this new star appeared in our northern hemisphere, to guide and comfort the bewildered traveller on his way to Bethlehem.

It is further to be remarked on our Author's writings, that the representation he therein gives us of the heavenly kingdom, sets before us that world of desires so objectively to the human intellect and reason, nay, even to our sensible apprehension, as to accommodate the description of it to the clear ideas of our minds, whether they be called innate, acquired, or (as he pronounces them) influxive from the spiritual world. He gives us to know, from ocular experience, that heaven is not so dull a place as some foolishly suppose it, who having no ideas of it, so neither desire to have any; and this through a superstitious fear, in some, of profaning the subject by any association of natural ideas; whereas nature, in the state of man's innocence, was constituted a fair representation of the first or lowest heaven; and though it be now sadly corrupted and deformed through the entrance and dominion of sin, yet as far as we can separate the evil from the good, so far it adumbrates to us celestial things; nay, even the art and ingenuity of man, as displayed in works of nature, is a ray of the divine skill manifested in the human mind. Thus Bezaleel and Aholiab are said to have wrought curious work for the service of the sanctuary, by wisdom and understanding given them from the Lord.* If, then, we receive innocent satisfaction here from viewing beautiful houses and gardens, why should we be so averse from thinking that there are celestial mansions and paradises in the kingdom of our Father? Does music delight us? Why may we not hope to be entertained with more ravishing harmony from the vocal and instrumental melody of the angels in heaven? How cheering both to the mind and senses, and also helpful to pious meditations in good men, are the sweetly variegated scenes of nature in the prime of the year! And can we be unwilling to believe that corresponding heavenly scenes are provided for the delectation of departed happy souls in the land of bliss? especially when we understand (as understand we may) that all that is truly pleasing, beautiful, and harmonious in nature, is by influx from the spiritual into the natural world; in which latter, archetypal glories are faintly represented to us by earthly images. It was a profane saying of a well-known jester and epicure, who was also a celebrated performer on the stage, that, "as to heaven, he had no great longing for the place, as he could not see what great pleasure there could be in sitting forever on a cloud, singing psalms." But had that person reflected, that heaven or hell must be the everlasting portion of every one in the other world; and, had he been acquainted with our Author's writings; he would not have treated the glories of the place with such ludicrous profaneness,† but have thought, and spoken, and lived, better than he did; nay, he might have wished his lot to be there, even from a principle of epicurism, in a certain sense. For all spiritual beings must have spiritual senses;

---

* Exod. xxxvi. 1.
† For he would then have known that the employments and joys of heaven do not consist in an eternal round of prayer and psalmody; as is abundantly shown in the following work.—N.

and if in heaven, those senses must be gratified with delights adapted thereto: but where any one is so grossly sensual, as to place the supreme felicity of a spirit in such gratifications as suit only with the corporeal part of our present degraded nature, may it not be said of such a one, that he has degraded it still lower, even to the level of an ass in his understanding, and to that of a swine by his affections? The work before us will help the reader to very exalted conceptions of the heavenly kingdom, even as to those particular beatitudes which are most nearly accommodated to the ideas of sense; and he may also therein learn, that all the relative duties, all the social virtues, and all the tender affections, that give consistence and harmony to society and do honor to humanity, find place and exercise, in the utmost purity, in those delectable abodes, where every thing that can delight the eye or rejoice the heart, entertain the imagination or exalt the understanding, conspires with innocence, love, joy, and peace, to bless the spirits of just men made perfect, and to make glad the city of our God.

Such, dear reader, and so excellent, are the things here offered for thine entertainment and instruction by this wonderful traveller. But if, after all, thou canst not read him as the enlightened seer, and the extraordinary messenger of important news from the other world, read him as the Christian divine, and sage interpreter of the Scriptures; read him as the judicious moralist, and acute metaphysician; or read him as the profound philosopher: or if he cannot please thee in either of these characters, read him, at least, as the ingenious author of a divine romance. But if neither as such he can give thee content, I have only to add: Go thy way, and leave the book to such, as know how to make a better use of it. And such, I trust, are not a few among the serious; being willing to hope, for the honor of our country, that if such a ludicrous representation of hell as passes under the title of *the Visions of Don Quevedo,* could make its way amongst us through no less than ten editions, there will not be wanting in the land a sufficient number of persons of sober reflection and contemplative minds, to give all due encouragement to a work so well calculated, as this is, to promote true wisdom and godliness, by credible testimony to the realities of the world of spirits, and to the respective states and conditions of departed souls.

As to the persons concerned in translating and conducting the publication of the following extraordinary work, I may venture to say, that they deserve well of the public, as far as the most disinterested pains and benevolent intentions can justify the expression: and though we are far from obtruding the contents of this book on any, as demanding an implicit faith therein, yet we cannot but zealously recommend them to the most serious attention of those who are qualified to receive them, as subjects of the greatest importance, high as heaven and deep as hell, and comprehending all that is within us, and without us; as a key that unlocks all worlds, and opens to us wonderful mysteries both in nature and grace; as displaying many hidden secrets of time and eternity, and acquainting us with the laws of the spiritual worlds; as leading us from heaven to heaven, and bringing us, as it were, into the company of angels, nay, into the presence chamber of the King of saints, and Lord of glory. In a word, whatever is most desirable to know, whatever is most deserving our affections, and whatever is most interesting in things pertaining to salvation; all this is the subject of the following volume.

We are not unprepared for the opposition that may be expected to any fresh discoveries of truth; especially, as has been observed before, where the credit or interest of any considerable profession or body of men is concerned. Established doctrines and opinions are considered as sacred, and the sanction of custom gives them, with many, the firmness of a rock; as is known to have been the case in physic, astronomy, and natural philosophy, in which truth, though supported by the evidence of demonstration, has scarcely been able to make its way in a century. Besides, the pride of learning is strong on the side of established institutes; and for men to part with what they have been building up with much study and pains for a great part of their lives, is a mortifying consideration; they are startled at the thoughts of becoming thus poor, and some would be as willing to part with their lives as with their acquisitions of this kind; and hence it is, that we read of so many martyrs to error and folly in all ages. These things considered, we are not to wonder that our author's publications have met with no better encouragement hitherto in his own country (as is usually the case with prophets), we being informed some time ago by a worthy merchant residing at Gottenburg, that but few of the clergy (as far as had come to his knowledge) had there received them; and that the Reverend Dr. Beyer, a learned man, and professor in divinity in that university, had suffered much persecution for adopting and propagating the truths contained in his writings, and was not suffered to print his explication and defence of them in Sweden.* But, to the honor of our constitution, we can as yet call the liberty of the press (and a liberty within the bounds of decency may it always be) the privilege of Englishmen, and therefore may reasonably hope for better success to our author's writings in this land of freedom; not that we expect any encouragement on their behalf from our Pharisees and bigots of any denomination, for they are the same everywhere; but our hopes are from men of unprejudiced minds, dead to self and the world, of a simplified understanding, and such as are friends to wisdom wherever they find her; in a word, whose spirit harmonizes with truth, and whose hearts are in unison with heavenly things.

I cannot think of concluding this preface without speaking somewhat particularly to a point of doctrine, the knowledge of which is the more necessary to the reader for the right understanding of the author's writings, as, in the vast variety of subjects and new discoveries that he presents to us, it has a principal connection with most of them; nay, is the true key in his hand that opens the secrets of the visible and invisible worlds, explains man to himself, and also reveals the spiritual sense of the Sacred Writings. The doctrine I am here speaking of is that of correspondence.

Correspondence, in a philosophical sense, is a kind of analogy that one thing bears to another, or the manner in which one thing represents, images, or answers to another; and this doctrine, as it refers to things in heaven and in earth, according to their natural relations, is given us in the following adage of the renowned Hermes Trismegistus:—*Omnia*

---

* It is to be recollected that this was written in the year 1778; since which period the number of friends to the truth in Sweden has very greatly increased.—*N.*

quæ in cœlis, sunt in terris terrestri modo ; omnia quæ in terris, sunt in cœlis cœlesti modo.*

This natural or material world, in which we live as to the body, proceeds derivatively from the spiritual world, and subsists by continual influx from it: it is a spiritual thing formed into a palpable and material thing, as an essence clothing itself with a form, or as a soul making to itself a body. Therefore this world, and all things in it, as far as they stand in the divine order, correspond to heaven and heavenly things ; but now (through the fall of man) standing in evil as well as good, the dark, evil, or hellish world has gained a form in outward nature. Hence it is, that so many evil men, evil beasts, and poisonous things, together with all the disorders in the natural world, bear its impressions and properties, and make this world a kind of torment-house to us. Man, considered in himself, is a little image of heaven or hell, and also of this outward world, which no other being is ; and therefore he is the most wonderful of all God's creatures. At death, he puts off his part in this material kingdom, and passes into one of the other two, being its servant to which he obeys or unites himself here by his will and affections ; and therefore he is commanded to set his "affections on things above,"† as they constitute the band of union betwixt heaven or hell and the soul of man. These three worlds may be called principles ; as, first, the light or heavenly world ; secondly, the dark or hellish world ; and thirdly, this natural or material world ; and man's reasoning faculty stands in the centre of the three, and receives impressions from each, as it turns to one or other of them, then speculates on the materials it derives thence, and contends for or against right and truth, even as the affections are set, for these bias, lead, or bribe it ; and therefore, if reason be not enlightened from above, under the conduct of good affections, it is a mere mercenary, ready to enlist on any side.

The human nature was so almost universally corrupted at the time of our Saviour's advent in the flesh, that unless Jesus Christ had come into the world when He did, to restore the heavenly principle of light and grace, or truth and goodness, through the medium of His Humanity (all immediate communication between God and the soul being well nigh ceased), the human race must have perished, by falling irrecoverably into the evil principle, to the utter extinction of truth, and the loss of all free-will to good ; but by the entrance of this Divine Friend into the human nature, He opened the closed gate of communication between heaven and earth, God and the soul, and so became our great Mediator and gracious Redeemer. But still we are at liberty to receive or reject Him as our sanctification and complete redemption ; for man can only be saved consistently with choice and free-will.

Men had lost the true original language of nature (which expressed things according to their qualities and properties) before the flood, even so much of it as remained among the posterity of Seth and Enoch for a considerable time ; and this ignorance they fell into on their losing the knowledge of nature in its correspondence to divine and heavenly things ; for nature in its proper order, as observed before, is the book of God,

---

* *All things which are in the heavens exist also in the earth in an earthly manner, and all things which are in the earth exist also in the heavens in a heavenly manner.*

† Col. iii. 2.

and exhibits spiritual things in material forms. In the room, therefore, of this, was substituted a language by letters and reading in books, to help him this way for attaining to divine knowledge, as rudiments leading thereto in our present state of ignorance, in which literature is mistaken by most for wisdom itself: however, the door was and still is open for immediate heavenly communications; but through unbelief, earthly-mindedness, and other sad impediments, few at this time are qualified for so high a privilege.

The early ancients after the flood had a knowledge of correspondence derived down to them by tradition, though without any perception of it in themselves: and it remained longest among the Egyptians, of which their hieroglyphics or sacred sculptures were a principal part; but by degrees they became so far corrupted and blind, as to lose sight of the things represented, and to worship their representatives or images. Hence the original of their foolish idolatry of beasts, birds, fishes, and vegetables. Our enlightened author, had he lived longer, designed, as he told me, to give us the key to the ancient hieroglyphical learning, saying at the same time, that none but himself could do it; but this he did not live to publish.

The knowledge of correspondence is now almost entirely lost, especially in Europe, where even the name is little understood; and this is one main cause of the obscurity of the Scriptures of the Old Testament, which were wholly written by the rules of this science; nay, man also, as an image of the spiritual and natural worlds, contains in himself the correspondences of both, of the former in his interior, and of the latter in his exterior or bodily part, and so is called the microcosm, or little world. Thus for example; all the organs of his senses, his features, bowels, and vessels, even to the minutest vein and nerve, correspond to something in the soul or spiritual part. On the other hand, the affections and passions of the mind represent themselves naturally in the face and features, so that the countenance would be the natural index to the mind, were men in a state of simplicity, without guile and dissimulation; and yet, as matters stand at present, so much still appears of the mind, in the corre-spondent features of the face, as to serve for a type, signature, or impres-sion thereof. Thus love, hatred, hope, fear, joy, sorrow, assent, contempt, surprise, &c., do naturally, and often involuntarily, manifest themselves in the visage; in like manner the will, by the actions and motions of the body; the understanding expresses itself in the speech, and the affections in the tone of voice; and all these by influx from within, and corre-spondence from without; and as the features correspond to the affec-tions, so does the eye to the intellect, the nose to the faculty of discerning, and the ears to attention and obedience; accordingly we use the word *quick-sighted*, to signify a ready apprehension; and penetration or dis-cernment is sometimes expressed by *smelling a thing out*; and to *hearken*, in Scripture, means to *obey*. Be it likewise observed, that the heart corresponds to sincerity of love; the loins, &c., to conjugal affection; the hands and fingers to operation, &c.; and so much of the language of nature still remains, as to express by these outward representatives the corresponding powers, passions, and affections of the soul, which influ-ences and actuates these several members and parts; as every one experiences. And as the body in its several parts and offices corresponds to the soul and its operations, so does the soul in its several faculties and powers to the heavenly world in all things good, and to the hellish world in all things evil. Thus wisdom, love, purity, innocence, &c., have reference to the celestial kingdom, as being communications by influx from thence; and therefore it is that heaven bears a near analogy to man (as standing in his right order), and is called by our author *The Grand Man:* for the human form is the most perfect of all, and, accordingly, God assumed it in condescension to man,* represents Himself to us by it, and manifests Himself in it, at times, to the holy angels: so likewise the angelical societies, according to their distinguishing qualities and excellence, bear a particular relation to this or that part of the human form. Thus, as our author informs us, one society corresponds to, or is in, the province of the head, and they are such as excel in wisdom; another to the heart, being such as excel in love; and some to the arms, as being of superior strength; and so on. Thus, as the body corresponds to the soul, so the soul, in its true state and order, corresponds to heaven, and heaven to God, who is the only original fountain of goodness and truth, of all blessedness and perfection; from whom they descend, in their different kinds and degrees, through the heavenly and spiritual worlds, down to this last and lowest form of creation, the earth in which we now dwell.

The earth likewise, in its different kingdoms, animal, vegetable, and mineral, corresponds to things in the spiritual world. Thus not only the beasts of the field, and the birds of the air, according to their different properties, have a representative meaning in Scripture, but also trees and plants of various kinds; so, in particular, those of the aromatic kind, as also the olive, the vine, and the cedar, do figure divine gifts and graces, and other rare endowments in the human heart and mind; and in like manner, gold, silver, precious stones, and other particulars of rich furniture in the tabernacle and temple, are mentioned in Scripture with a corresponding reference to goodness, truth, purity of affection, holiness, &c.: and so the wisest interpreters have expounded them, and this not by arbitrary significations, but as *outward proper signs of things inward and spiritual.* Thus all nature is a theatre of divine wonders, representative of the invisible world to such as are of a right understanding and discernment; as our author has exemplified in a thousand instances. It is hoped, that what has been here offered on the subject of correspondence, will be found useful to such as are in a disposition to give the following work an attentive perusal.

From the great variety of important subjects and discoveries to be met with in our Author's writings, I cannot refrain from observing on one more, as deserving our particular regard, as also to prepare the reader for what he is to meet with in this volume, viz., the doctrine of the intermediate state of departed souls, called here *the World of Spirits,* as being that in which they all meet after death (except a very few, who pass directly to heaven or hell), in order to their last preparation for final

---

* We are not to understand by this expression that the Lord was not in a human form prior to the incarnation; what He then assumed in condescension to man, or for our redemption, was the human nature in last or lowest principles, as He had always been a Man in first principles; man being a man, and in a human form, from Him, being created after His image and likeness.—*N.*

bliss or misery.   This doctrine has long been received in the church, and revealed to many by their departed friends; but having been much disfigured and misrepresented, like some other truths, by erroneous additions and lucrative figments in the church of Rome, it was not admitted by our first Reformers, who, instead of reforming the doctrine, totally rejected it, under the opprobrious name of a Popish purgatory; however, it has been retained by most of the spiritual, otherwise called mystic writers, in all churches, and I have seen a judicious defence of it by the Hon. Archibald Campbell in our own; but the book, I believe, is scarce. Sure it is, that as far as our Author's credit and authority extend, the truth of the doctrine will not be questioned, as he relates that he had frequent translations of spirit to that intermediate world, and had there seen and conversed with most, if not all, his departed friends and acquaintance, besides a great number of others, to the amount of very many thousands.   In this intermediate world, the good spirits are gradually purified from all the stains and defilements of sin which they had contracted in this world; whilst the good principle predominating in them takes full possession of all their faculties and powers, confirms them in good habits, and renders them meet to be partakers of heavenly joys; on which they are translated to heaven: on the other hand, the bad spirits are gradually divested of those superficial and apparent virtues, and all that adventitious, external good, which before had served as covers to the evil principle within, which now predominates without reserve or control, confirming them in their evil habits, and their repugnancy to all good; which being effected, they precipitate themselves into the infernal pit, to join company with such as are like themselves.   Thus what is a state of purification to the good, is to bad spirits a state of separation of all extraneous good from that radical evil which constitutes the essence of their nature.

Now this doctrine appears consonant, first, to reason, as it accords with the tenor of the divine administration in the government of this world, in which all things proceed to their limit or completion in a regular and gradual process.   Secondly, it is consonant to religion, as it vindicates the divine attributes from all imputation of undue severity, by laying man's destruction at the proper door, and as the inevitable consequence of his own free choice.   Thirdly, this doctrine yields consolation to the humble pious Christian, as the time of his departure draws nigh.   Few such, upon a strict examination of themselves, are so well satisfied with their state, as to find nothing lacking, but that they are already fitly qualified for the society of the holy angels; whereas the belief that an intermediate state is appointed, wherein every thing that now hindereth shall be removed out of the way, and their souls purified from every pollution and spot contracted by their union with this fleshly nature, through the prevailing power and energy of the divine principle within them, and so bringing them into the state of just men made perfect, is a consideration well calculated to afford them comfort, and enable them to meet their change with a holy confidence.

If this be so, and that the same intermediate state which purifies the good spirits leaves the bad under the total dominion of evil by their own free choice, that so both may be possessed by their own proper principle respectively, and go to their own proper place; how say some, that the devils will be eventually transformed into angels of light, at a certain time appointed by the Father? We desire here to oppose, with the greatest tenderness, a doctrine which we have heretofore judged favorably of, and modestly to offer the reasons of our present dissent, wishing rather that we could agree with some excellent men on the other side of the question: but human wishes are no rule of the divine proceedings, and even charity must be directed by the principle of truth, and the established laws and nature of things. We find ourselves called upon to offer a few observations on this subject, at a time when there is much reason to believe, that many have revived this doctrine more to quiet their fears, and to lull them into a false peace, than from any conviction of their understanding; whereas they may be supplied with a much surer remedy against those fears in the comfortable promises to the truly penitent delivered in the gospel of our most compassionate Saviour, whose last declaration to His disciples before His ascension was, " That repentance and remission of sins should be preached in His name among all nations."*

It is evident that the plainest Scriptures (and such we are to go by) are against the doctrine before mentioned; and that the same force of words that is therein used to express the eternal happiness of those that are saved, is also made use of to express the eternity of their state who are lost. But the advocates for that side of the question rest their plea, and the stress of their argument, on the foot of Divine Mercy; and God forbid that we should go about to straiten that mercy towards others (though even devils), to which the very best of us stand indebted both for all we have, and all we have to hope for; and did the matter of the question turn merely upon mercy, in like manner as a gaol-delivery depends on the arbitrary clemency of an earthly prince, I doubt not, that either one single soul would not go to hell, or if any, that a host of angels would be sent thither with a message of mercy; nay, if necessary to their salvation, that even Jesus Christ Himself would condescend so far, as to visit those unhappy prisoners with a free offer of peace and reconciliation for their redemption. But here it must be observed, that mercy misunderstood and misapplied, is no other than man's own *false idea* of mercy. God's mercy in regard to man, respects him as a creature that He has endowed with freedom of will, and whose happiness or misery depends on the right or wrong direction of his choice and affections, by which he becomes capable or incapable of the Divine Mercy. Now to *compel* such a creature, is to undo him, to *unmake him* what he is; and therefore mercy, with regard to him, is to provide for him such means and motives as may influence his understanding, will, and affections, to what is good, as his free choice. Now, through the mercy of God, every thing is done in this life (which is man's only state of probation) in order to this end, though man knoweth it not; how then are we to expect, that any means of this kind should be more effectual in the other world, wherein all things are represented to us as unchangeable, where the tree lieth as it falls, for heaven or hell? Praised be the name of the Lord, for his mercy endureth forever! And as it is infinite, so it extends to all possible cases: but to make us good, that we may be qualified for happiness *against our will*, is no possible case, seeing that to be good, is

* Luke xxiv. 47.

to *will* good with desire and affection, which the self-hardened and impenitent are averse to, and therefore render themselves unreceptive of mercy. Now the very idea of diabolism carries in it repugnance and hatred to God and goodness, and consequently the greatest contrariety to the possibility of conversion. Were it otherwise, and that the most malignant spirit in hell could sincerely say, "Lord, I am weary and ashamed of this evil nature, and sorry for the sins that have brought me into it; O help and deliver me, through Thy mercy, from it, that I may be converted, and become Thy servant!" in this case, he would instantly cease to be a devil, and become an object of the Divine Mercy; but repentance, prayer, and the desire of good, is all from the grace of God, and can in no wise dwell in those who are the willing servants of sin, and therefore only free *from*, not *to*, righteousness.*

It is supposed by some, that length of suffering will at last subdue the reluctance of the will, melt the heart into tenderness, and turn the worst of evil spirits to repentance and supplication for pardoning mercy, and qualify them for it; but this, as just now observed, is the sole effect of that grace which they are *not admissive of*, and is not the effect of suffering, which has no such power belonging to it; but has its different effects relative to the different states of those who are the subjects of its operation. Thus we see, that as the same fire which melts the wax, hardens the clay, so the sharpest sufferings have contrary effects on different persons. They who have any remnant of grace in their inmost soul (however unrighteous they have been outwardly), any spark of the divine life still remaining in their interior, are softened and ameliorated by them, and become obedient to the heavenly voice that cries within them, "Why will ye die? Turn unto the Lord, that iniquity may not be your ruin:" whilst the obdurate and impenitent say in their hearts with Pharaoh, "Who is the Lord, that we should obey him?" and turn that punishment which should be for their amendment into the occasion of their blasphemy and despair. I desire not to strain any argument beyond its proper strength against an hypothesis, which I find myself more ready to receive, upon any satisfactory grounds, than to reject: but *let truth be ever held sacred* and inviolable, whether it be according or contrary to our natural inclinations and wishes: nor let that be called a want of charity, where charity is not concerned, or would suffer perversion and abuse.

We are encouraged to hope, that many things which have been offered in the course of this Preface will be found properly introductory to the following volume; and shall now conclude it with two or three short remarks to the serious reader, as no other is capable of reaping any benefit from our author's writings; nor to others have we any thing to say, unless it be to caution them against treating with derision or scurrility such matter as they may be more nearly concerned in than they at present suppose. Even the very dreams of good men, in relation to the things of the other world, have at times something divine in them, and are not lightly to be regarded: but where such communicate to us important instructions and discoveries as by commission, and from their own experience, and that with deliberation, consistency, and clearness, they demand our attention and reverence. And here it is to be observed,

*Rom. iv. 20.

that what this Author has published to the world concerning the states
of departed souls respectively, the laws of the invisible worlds, and a
thousand particular circumstances belonging thereto, appear such as
could never enter into heart of man to conceive, unless they had been
given to him from above, and also carry something of an internal evidence
along with them, as soon as they are received by a serious mind; for,
after all, it is more the right temper and disposition of the mind, than its
sagacity, that gives us to see these things in their proper light. It is
every wise man's care to guard against a stubborn incredulity on the one
hand, as well as against any delusion that an overhasty belief might
expose him to on the other; and in this age of doubting and disputing
all things of a spiritual nature, our greater danger is confessedly from
the former side, and therefore it behoves us to give the more heed, that
we lean not to the error of the times. Besides, the weight and importance of the subjects here treated of adds to the credibility of the
message, as coinciding with our confidence in the promises of the Lord,
that He will reveal His secrets to His servants, and not forsake His
church in the time of her extremity, but send His extraordinary messengers and ministers, endued with light and power from on high to alarm
the careless, to call back the wanderers, to confirm the wavering, and to
comfort the spirit of the humble and contrite ones with glad tidings from
the heavenly Canaan, the lot of their inheritance; and this in order to
make ready a people prepared for the Lord against His second advent in
spirit, to build up the walls of the New Jerusalem: and when should
such messengers be more expected, or when entitled to a better welcome,
than in this our time of desolations, when faith and charity have so far
failed amongst us, and when darkness is on the face of the deep,—darkness in the church, and darkness in the state,—darkness in the minds of
good men, and darkness on all the dispensations of Providence; so as to
give emphatical application of those words of the Psalmist to our present
condition: "It is time, O Lord, that Thou have mercy upon Sion, yea,
the time is come."* But who are they that most reject the testimony
of those special messengers, and those faithful witnesses to the truth,
which the Father of Lights has sent from time to time for the edification
of His church, and the confirmation of the faith of many in it? Who but
such as are ever calling out for more evidence for believing, and pleading
the want of it in justification of their unbelief; whilst at the same time
they labor all they can to invalidate the evidence of all human testimony,
which is the ordinary medium through which divine truth is conveyed
to us?

And now, dear reader, I bid you farewell, sincerely wishing that you
may be of the number of those who take the Holy Scriptures for their
guide, as their authentic outward rule of faith and life, and in an honest
and good heart receive the Word of God, and keep it; and may the
Spirit of Wisdom give us a right judgment in all things pertaining to
salvation, that so we may be preserved from error through an over-hasty
credulity on the one hand, and an obstinate incredulity on the other;
neither rejecting the testimony of men fearing God, and of good report,
as to what great things the Lord hath done for them, and to be communicated by them for the benefit of their brethren; not suffering

* Psalm cii. 13.
4

ourselves to be imposed on by the cunning craftiness of such as lie in wait to deceive: and as it is more profitable for us to have the heart established in grace, and to glorify God in our lives, than to be gifted with visions and particular revelations (through danger of being exalted above measure thereby), so let us not be high-minded, but fear nor, because others have been so favored, expect or desire the same ourselves, but walk humbly and contentedly in the way of God's ordinary dispensations, lest presumption or a vain curiosity should expose us to the danger of delusion from our spiritual enemy. As to those that cannot receive many of the things delivered in the following work; and also as to those that do receive them; let them not judge one another, but follow the rule of moderation laid down by the Apostle,* every one abiding by that of which he is persuaded in his own mind, in a candid forbearance towards others. In men of a Christian spirit, charity easily beareth all such things, believeth all things for good, and hopeth all things for the best; and as we are all brethren on a journey to the same heavenly country, so let us hold on our way together in peace, and that love which is more than knowledge: and may the God of peace and love be with us.

* Rom. xiv.

AN ANSWER TO A LETTER FROM A FRIEND,

BY THE AUTHOR.

I TAKE pleasure in the friendship you express for me in your letter, and return you thanks for the same; but as to the praises which you bestow upon me, I only receive them as tokens of your love of the truths contained in my writings, and so refer them to the Lord our Saviour, from whom is the all of truth, because HE IS THE TRUTH (John xiv. 6). It is the concluding part of your letter that chiefly engages my attention, where you say as follows: "As after your departure from England disputes may arise on the subject of your writings, and so give occasion to defend their author against such false reports and aspersions, as they who are no friends to truth may invent to the prejudice of his character, may it not be of use, in order to refute any calumnies of that kind, that you leave in my hands some short account of yourself; as concerning, for example, your degrees in the university, the offices you have borne, your family and connections, the honors which I am told have been conferred upon you, and such other particulars as may serve to the vindication of your character, if attacked; that so any ill-grounded prejudices may be obviated or removed? For where the honor and interest of truth are concerned, it certainly behoves us to employ all lawful means in its defence and support." After reflecting on the foregoing passage, I was induced to comply with your friendly advice, by briefly communicating the following circumstances of my life.

I was born at Stockholm, in the year of our Lord 1689,[*] Jan. 29th. My Father's name was Jesper Swedberg, who was Bishop of Westrogothia, and a man of celebrity in his day. He was also elected a member of the English Society for the Propagation of the Gospel; and he was appointed as Bishop over the Swedish churches in Pensylvania and London by King Charles XII. In the year 1710, I began my travels, first into England, and afterwards into Holland, France, and Germany, and returned home in 1714. In the year 1716, and afterwards, I frequently conversed with Charles XII., King of Sweden, who was pleased to bestow on me a large share of his favor, and in that year appointed me to the office of Assessor in the Metallic College; in which office I continued from that time till the year 1747, when I quitted the office, but still retain the salary annexed to it as an appointment for life. The sole reason of my withdrawing from the business of that employment was, that I might be more at liberty to apply myself to that new function to which the Lord had called me. A higher degree of rank was then offered me, which I declined to accept, lest pride on account of it should enter my mind. In 1719 I was ennobled by Queen Ulrica Eleonora, and named *Swedenborg*; from which time I have taken my seat with the Nobles of the Equestrian Order, in the Triennial Assemblies of the States. I am a Fellow, by invitation, of the Royal Academy of Sciences at Stockholm; but have never sought admission into any other literary society,[†] as I belong to an angelical society, in which things relating to heaven and the

---

[*] It has been ascertained that this should be 1688.—*N*.
[†] It appears, however, from Sandel, that he was also a member of the Academy of Sciences of St. Petersburg, from which a diploma of fellowship was sent him on the

soul are the only subjects of discourse and entertainment; whereas in our literary societies the attention is wholly taken up with things relating to the world and the body. In the year 1734, I published the *Regnum Minerale*, at Leipsic, in three volumes, folio; and in 1738 I took a journey into Italy, and staid a year at Venice and Rome.

With respect to my family connections: I had four sisters; one of them was married to Erich Benzelius, afterwards promoted to the Archbishopric of Upsal; and thus I became related to the two succeeding Archbishops of that see, both named Benzelius, and younger brothers of the former. My second sister was married to Lars Benzelstierna, who was promoted to a provincial government. But these are both dead: however, two bishops who are related to me are still living. One of them is named Filenius, Bishop of Ostrogothia, who now officiates as President of the Ecclesiastical Order in the Diet at Stockholm, in the room of the Archbishop, who is infirm; he married the daughter of my sister. The other, who is named Benzelstierna, Bishop of Westermannia and Dalecarlia, is the son of my second sister. Not to mention others of my family who enjoy stations of dignity. I converse freely, and am in friendship, with all the bishops of my country, who are ten in number; and also with the sixteen Senators, and the rest of the Peers, who love and honor me, as knowing that I am in fellowship with angels. The King and Queen themselves, as also the three Princes their sons, show me all kind countenance; and I was once invited to dine with the King and Queen at their table (an honor granted only to the Peers of the realm); and likewise, since, with the Hereditary Prince. All in my own country wish for my return home; so far am I from having the least fear of being persecuted there, as you seem to apprehend, and are also kindly solicitous to provide against; and should any thing of that kind befall me elsewhere, it will give me no concern.

Whatever of worldly honor and advantage may appear to be in the things before mentioned, I hold them as matters of respectively little moment, because, what is far better, I have been called to a holy office by the Lord Himself, who most graciously manifested Himself in person to me His servant, in the year 1743,* and then opened my sight into the spiritual world, and endowed me with the gift of conversing with spirits and angels, which has been continued to me to this day. From that time I began to print and publish various *arcana*, that have been either seen by me or revealed to me; as concerning heaven and hell; the state of man after death; the true worship of God; the spiritual sense of the Word; and many other highly important matters tending to salvation and true wisdom: and the only motive which has induced me at different times to leave my home and visit foreign countries, was the desire of being useful, and of communicating the arcana intrusted to me. As to this world's wealth, I have sufficient, and more I neither seek nor wish for.

Your letter has drawn the mention of these things from me, with a view, as you suggest, that any ill-grounded prejudices may be removed. Farewell; and from my heart I wish you all felicity both in this world and in the next; which I make no doubt of your obtaining, if you look and pray to our Lord.

London, 1769.   EMAN. SWEDENBORG.

* It appears from a passage in his *Spiritual Diary*, n. 397, lately published, that the last figure must be an error, the actual year being 1745.

HEAVEN AND HELL.

INTRODUCTION.

1. In the Lord's discourse with his disciples respecting the consummation of the age,* which means the last time of the church,(¹) at the close of his predictions concerning the successive states through which it would pass in regard to love and faith,(²) are these words : *"Immediately after the tribulation of those days, shall the sun be darkened, and the moon shall not give her light, and the stars shall fall from heaven, and the powers of the heavens shall be shaken. And then shall appear the sign of the Son of man in heaven: and then shall all the tribes of the earth mourn ; and they shall see the Son of man coming in the clouds of heaven with power and great glory. And he shall send his angels with a great sound of a trumpet, and they shall gather together his elect from the four winds, from one end of heaven to the other."*—Matt. xxiv. 29, 30, 31. They who understand these words according to the literal sense, have no other idea, than that, at the last time, which is called the last judgment, all these circumstances will happen according to their literal description : thus they not only imagine that the sun and moon will be darkened, that the stars will fall from heaven, that the sign of the Lord will appear in heaven, and that they shall see him in the clouds attended by angels with trumpets, but they also suppose, from predictions in other places, that the whole visible world will perish, and that a new heaven and a new earth will afterwards be established. This is the opinion of many within the church at this day. But they who entertain these notions are unacquainted with the arcana which are contained in every part of the Word. In every part of the Word there is an internal sense, in which natural and worldly

---

* *The consummation of the age*, is the true rendering from the original Greek, and not *the end of the world*, as in the common translation ; the word Αιων never properly signifying the *world*, but an age or period of time, or a dispensation of things.—*H.*
(¹) That the consummation of the age is the last time of the church, nn. 4535, 10,622.
(²) The particulars which the Lord predicted in Matthew, Chs. xxiv. and xxv., respecting the consummation of the age and his advent, thus respecting the successive devastation of the church and the last judgment, are explained in the introductory articles to several of the chapters of Genesis, viz., from Ch. xxvi. to Ch. xl.; nn. 3353, 3354, 3355, 3486—3488, 3650—3655, 3751—3757, 3897—3901, 4056—4060, 4229—4231, 4332—4335, 4422—4424, 4635—4638, 4661—4664, 4807—4810, 4954—4959, 5063—5071.

1

things, such as are mentioned in the literal sense, are not treated of, but spiritual and celestial things. This is the case not only with respect to the sense of several words taken together, but even with respect to every single expression; ([3]) for the Word is written by pure correspondences,([4]) in order that an internal sense may be contained in every part of it. The nature of that sense may be manifest from the particulars which are stated and shown concerning it in the ARCANA CŒLESTIA; which may also be seen collected together in the little work on the WHITE HORSE mentioned in the Revelation. The words which the Lord spoke, in the place quoted above, concerning his advent in the clouds of heaven, are to be understood, according to that sense, thus : By the sun there mentioned, which would be darkened, is signified the Lord with respect to love ;([5]) by the moon, the Lord with respect to faith ; ([6]) by the stars, the knowledges of good and truth, or of love and faith ; ([7]) by the sign of the Son of man in heaven, the manifestation of Divine Truth ; by the tribes of the earth, which would mourn, all things relating to truth and good, or to faith and love ; ([8]) by the coming of the Lord in the clouds of heaven with power and glory, his presence in the Word, and revelation of its true import ; ([9]) by clouds is signified the literal sense of the Word,([10]) and by glory, its internal sense ; ([11]) by the angels with a great sound of a trumpet, is signified heaven, whence it is that the revelation of divine truth is made. ([12]) Hence it may appear, that by these words of the Lord is meant, that at the end of the church, when there no longer remains any love, and thence not any faith, the Lord will open the Word as to its internal sense, and will reveal arcana of heaven.

([3]) That there is an internal or spiritual sense in all the particulars of the Word, even to the most minute, nn. 1143, 1984, 2135, 2333, 2395, 2495, 4442, 9048, 9063, 9086.
([4]) That the Word is written by pure correspondences, and that thence all the particulars contained in it, even to the most minute, signify spiritual things, un. 1404, 1408, 1409, 1540, 1619, 1659, 1709, 1783, 2900, 9086.
([5]) That the sun, when mentioned in the Word, signifies the Lord with respect to love, and thence love to the Lord, nn. 1529, 1837, 2441, 2495, 4060, 4696, (4966,)* 7083, 10,809.
([6]) That the moon, when mentioned in the Word, signifies the Lord with respect to faith, and thence faith in the Lord, nn. 1529, 1530, 2495, 4060, 4696, 7083.
([7]) That the stars, when mentioned in the Word, signify the knowledges of good and truth, nn. 2495, 2849, 4697.
([8]) That the tribes signify all truths and goods in the complex, thus all things of faith and love, nn. 3858, 3926, 4060, 6335.
([9]) That the advent of the Lord is His presence in the Word, and revelation, nn. 3900, 4060.
([10]) That clouds, when mentioned in the Word, signify the Word in the letter, or its literal sense, nn. 4060, 4391, 5922, 6343, 6752. 8106, 8781, 9430, 10,551, 10,574.
([11]) That glory, when mentioned in the Word, signifies the Divine Truth such as it is in heaven, and such as it is in the internal sense of the Word, nn. 4809, (5292,) 5922, 8267, 8427, 9429, 10,574.
([12]) That a trumpet or horn, when mentioned in the Word, signifies Divine Truth in heaven, and revealed from heaven, nn. 8815, 8823, 8915. And a voice likewise, nn. 6971, 9926.

* Respecting the above erroneous number, being the first that occurs (in note ([5])) it may be observed, that it most probably has originated from the preceding correct number, 4696, and ought to be omitted altogether. The case is similar in other instances.—N.

2

The arcana which are revealed in the following pages are such as relate to heaver and hell, and to the life of man after death. The members of the church at this day know scarcely any thing concerning heaven and hell, nor yet concerning their own life after death, although these things are all described in the Word; nay, many, though born within the church, even deny their existence, saying in their heart, Who has come from thence and declared the fact? Lest, therefore, such a negative state, which chiefly prevails among those who possess much worldly wisdom, should also infect and corrupt the simple in heart and faith, it has been granted me to be admitted into the society of angels, and to converse with them as one man converses with another; and also to see the things that exist in heaven and those that exist in hell. I have enjoyed this privilege for the space of thirteen years: and I am now permitted to describe the heavens and the hells from the testimony of my own sight and hearing; in the hope that ignorance may thus be enlightened, and incredulity dissipated. The reason that such an immediate revelation is made at this day, is, because this is what is meant by the coming of the Lord.

8

OF HEAVEN.

---

2. THE first thing necessary to be known is, who is the God of heaven; for every thing else depends on this. In the universal heaven, no other is acknowledged for its God, but the Lord Alone: they say there, as He Himself taught, *that He is One with the Father; that the Father is in Him, and He in the Father; that whosoever seeth Him, seeth the Father; and that every thing holy proceeds from Him.*—John x. 30, 38; xiv. 10, 11; xvi. 13, 14, 15. I have often conversed with the angels on this subject, and they constantly declared, that they are unable to divide the Divine Being into three, because they know and perceive that the Divine Being is One, and that he is One in the Lord. They said, also, that persons belonging to the church who arrive there from the world, having an idea of three Divine Beings, cannot be admitted into heaven, because their thought wanders from one to another, and it is not allowed there to have three in the thoughts and profess one with the lips. (¹) Every one in heaven speaks from his thought, speech there being the utterance of thought, or thought speaking: wherefore they who in the world had divided the Divine Being into three, and have acquired a separate idea concerning each, and have not concentrated and made it one in the Lord, cannot be admitted. In heaven there is a communication of the thoughts of all, wherefore if any one should come there who has three in his thoughts while he professes one with his lips, he would be immediately discovered and rejected. But it is to be observed, that all those who have not separated truth from good, or faith from love, on being instructed in the other life, receive the heavenly idea concerning the Lord, namely, that He is the God of the universe: but it is otherwise with those who have separated faith from life, that is, who have not lived according to the precepts of a true faith.

3. Those within the church who have denied the Lord, and

(¹) That certain Christians were explored in the other life, as to what idea they had of the One God, when it was found that they had an idea of three Gods, nn. 2329, 5256, 10,736, 10,738, 10,821. That the Divine Trinity in the Lord is acknowledged in heaven, nn. 14, 15, 1729, 2005, 5256, 9303.

4

have acknowledged the Father alone, and have confirmed themselves in such a faith, are out of heaven ; and as no influx from heaven, where the Lord Alone is worshipped, can be received by them, they are deprived by degrees of the faculty of thinking truth on any subject whatever, and at length they either become like dumb persons, or they talk foolishly, and wander in and out as they walk, with their arms dangling as if void of strength in the joints. They who have denied the divinity of the Lord, and have only acknowledged his humanity, like the Socinians, are likewise out of heaven, and are borne forwards a little towards the right,* where they are let down into a deep place, and thus are entirely separated from the rest of those that come from the Christian world. But it was found that those who profess to believe in an invisible Divinity, which they call the *Ens Universi,*† from which all things existed, and who reject all faith concerning the Lord, believe in no God ; because this invisible Divinity is, according to them, like nature in its first principles, which cannot be an object of faith and love, since no idea can be formed of it :([2]) such persons have their lot among those who are called Naturalists. It is different with those who are born without the church, and are called gentiles, who will be treated of in the following pages.

4. All infants, of whom a third part of heaven consists, are initiated into the acknowledgment and faith, that the Lord is their Father : and afterwards, that He is the Lord of all, and consequent the God of heaven and earth. That infants grow up in the heavens, and are perfected by means of knowledges even to angelic intelligence and wisdom, will be seen in the following pages.

5. That the Lord is the God of heaven, cannot be doubted by those who belong to the church : for he himself taught *that all things of the Father are His* (Matt. xi. 27 ; John xvi. 15 ; xvii. 2), *and that He hath all power in heaven and in earth* (Matt. xxviii. 16). He says, "in heaven and in earth," because He that governs heaven governs the earth also, for the one depends on the other.([3]) To govern heaven and earth, signifies,

---

* The place of the spirits in the other world, as also their ascent into heaven, or descent into hell, is constantly described by the author in reference to the body of the spectator : and the meaning of this passage is, that the spirits here mentioned appear to sink down in front, a little towards the right, into the particular place appointed for them. This will be better comprehended when the reader understands what is said in the following pages, respecting *the Quarters in Heaven*, nn. 141, &c.—*H.*

† Literally, the *Being of the Universe ;* but this not being in use among English writers, the original term, employed in Latin philosophical writings, is retained.—*N.*

([2]) That a Divine Being that cannot be comprehended by any idea, cannot be an object of faith, nn. 4733, 5110, (5633,) 6982, 6996. 7004, 7211. (9267,) 9359, 9972, 10,067.

([3]) That the universal heaven is the Lord's. nn. 2751, 7086. That all power in the heavens and on earth belongs to Him, nn. 1607, 10,089, 10,827. That as the Lord governs heaven, He also governs all things which depend thereon, thus all things in the world, nn. 2026, 2037, 4523, 4524. That the Lord alone has the power of removing the hells from man, of withholding him from evils, of keeping him in good, thus of saving him, n. 10,019.

5

to receive from Him all the good which is the object of love, and all the truth which is the object of faith, thus all intelligence and wisdom, and thereby all happiness; in short, eternal life. This the Lord also taught when he said, "*He that believeth on the Son, hath everlasting life; and he that believeth not the Son, shall not see life*" (John iii. 36). Again: "*I am the resurrection and the life: he that believeth in me, though he were dead, yet shall he live; and whosoever liveth and believeth in me, shall never die*" (John xi. 25, 26). And again: "*I am the way, the truth, and the life*" (John xiv. 6).

6. There were certain spirits, who, when they lived in the world, professed to believe in the Father, but had no other idea of the Lord than as of a mere man, whence they did not believe him to be the God of heaven : wherefore it was permitted them to ramble about, and inquire wherever they pleased, whether there were any other heaven than that which belongs to the Lord. They continued their search for some days, but found none. They belonged to that class of persons who make the happiness of heaven to consist in pomp and dominion; and because they could not obtain their desire, and were informed that heaven does not consist in such things, they were angry, and would have a heaven in which they might domineer over others, and excel others in magnificence, after the fashion of this world.

THAT THE DIVINE SPHERE OF THE LORD CONSTITUTES HEAVEN.

7. The angels, taken collectively, are called heaven, because they compose it: but still it is the Divine Sphere proceeding from the Lord, which enters the angels by influx, and is by them received, which essentially constitutes it, both in general and in particular. The Divine Sphere proceeding from the Lord, is the good of love, and the truth of faith : in proportion, therefore, as the angels receive good and truth from the Lord, so far they are angels, and so far they are heaven.

8. Every one in the heavens knows and believes, yea, feels by interior perception, that he can neither will nor do any thing of good, nor think and believe any thing of truth, from himself, but only from the Divine Being, thus from the Lord; and that the good and truth which are from himself, are not really such, because there is no life within them from a Divine Source. The angels of the inmost heaven, also, have a clear perception and sensation of the influx; and so far as they receive it, so far they seem to themselves to be in heaven, because they are so far in love and in faith, and so far in the light of intelligence and wisdom, and thence in heavenly joy. As all these things proceed from the Divine Sphere which emanates from the Lord

and it is in these that heaven, as enjoyed by the angels, consists, it is evident that the Divine Sphere of the Lord constitutes heaven, and that it is not constituted by the angels by virtue of any thing proper to themselves.([1]) It is on this account that heaven is called, in the Word, the Lord's habitation, or dwelling-place, and his throne ; and that its inhabitants are said to be in the Lord.([2]) But in what manner the Divine Sphere proceeds from the Lord, and fills heaven, will be shown in the following pages.

9. The angels, by virtue of their wisdom, go still further They not only say that all good and truth are from the Lord, but also, that the all of life is from the Lord. This they confirm by the consideration, that nothing can exist from itself, but only from something prior to itself ; consequently, that all things *exist* from a First Cause, which they call the Very Esse* of the life of all things ; and that they *subsist* in a similar manner, because subsistence is perpetual existence ; wherefore, whatever is not kept in connection with the First Cause by intermediate links, instantly falls away, and is utterly dissipated. They say, also, that there is only One Fountain of life, and that the life of man is a stream flowing from it, which, if it were not continually supplied from its fountain, would instantly flow away. They say, moreover, that nothing proceeds from that One Fountain of life, which is the Lord, but divine good and divine truth, and that these affect every one according to his reception of them ; that those who receive them in faith and life, have in them heaven ; but that those who reject or suffocate them, turn them into hell, because they turn good into evil, and truth into falsity ; thus life into death. That the all of life is from the \ Lord, they also confirm by this consideration : That all things in the universe have relation to good and truth, the life of man's will, which is the life of his love, having relation to good, and the life of man's understanding, which is the life of his faith, having relation to truth ; wherefore, since all good and truth come from above, it follows that the all of life comes from above too. As this is the belief of the angels, they reject all return of thanks on account of the good which they do, and are displeased,

---

(1) That the angels of heaven acknowledge all good to be from the Lord, and nothing of it from themselves; and that the Lord dwells with them in what is His Own, and not in any thing proper to themselves, nn. 9338, 10,125, 10,151, 10,157. That therefore by angels, when mentioned in the Word, is understood something of the Lord, nn. 1925, 2821, 3039, 4085, 1202, 10,528. And that therefore the angels are called gods from their reception of the Divine Sphere proceeding from the Lord, nn. 4295, 4402, 7268, 7873, 8301, 8192 That all good which is good, and all truth which is truth, consequently all peace, love, charity, and faith, are also from the Lord, nn 1614, 2016, 2751, 2882, 2883, 2891, 2892, 2904. And likewise all wisdom and intelligence, nn. 109, 112, 121, 124.

(2) That those who are in heaven are said to be in the Lord, nn. 3637, 3638.

* *Esse* is a Latin word that literally signifies *to be*, whence it is used by philosophers to express the very ground of the existence of the thing of which they are treating.—N.

7

and withdraw themselves, if any one attributes good to them, as the authors of it. They wonder how any one can believe that he possesses wisdom, or does good, from himself. Good done for the sake of self, they do not call good at all, because it is done from self ; but good done for its own sake, they call good from the Divine Source, and affirm that this good is what constitutes heaven, because such good is the Lord.(³)

10. Spirits, who, when they lived in the world had confirmed themselves in the belief, that the good which they do, and the truth which they believe, are from themselves, or are appropriated to them as their own, (which belief is entertained by all who place merit in their good deeds and arrogate righteousness to themselves,) are not received into heaven. The angels avoid them, regarding them as fools or as thieves ; as fools, because they continually look to themselves and not to the Divine Being ; and as thieves, because they rob the Lord of what is His. Such persons are opposed to the faith of heaven, namely, that the Divine Sphere of the Lord, received by the angels, constitutes heaven.

11. That the inhabitants of heaven, and the members of the church, are in the Lord, and the Lord in them, he also teaches, saying, "*Abide in me, and I in you. As the branch cannot bear fruit of itself, except it abide in the vine ; no more can ye, except ye abide in me. I am the vine, ye are the branches ; he that abideth in me, and I in him, the same bringeth forth much fruit. For without me, ye can do nothing*" (John xv. 4, 5).

12. From these considerations it may now be evident, that the Lord dwells with the angels of heaven in what is His Own, and thus that the Lord is the All in all of heaven. The reason of this is, because good from the Lord is the Lord with those who receive it ; for whatever is from him, is himself. Consequently, good from the Lord is heaven to the angels, and not any thing proper to themselves.

THAT THE DIVINE SPHERE OF THE LORD IN HEAVEN IS LOVE TO HIM AND CHARITY TOWARDS THE NEIGHBOR.

13. The Divine Sphere proceeding from the Lord is called in heaven Divine Truth, f r a reason that will appear in what follows. This Divine Truth flows into heaven from the Lord out of His Divine Love. Divine Love, and Divine Truth thence derived, are, comparatively, like the fire of the sun, and the light thence proceeding in the world ; love being like the fire of the sun, and truth thence derived like light from the sun.

(³) That good from the Lord has the Lord inwardly in it, but not good from proprium, 'nn. 1802, 3951, 8480.

Fire also signifies love, from correspondence; and light signifies the truth thence proceeding.([1]) Hence may appear what is the quality of the Divine Truth proceeding from the Lord's Divine Love; namely, that, in its essence, it is Divine Good in conjunction with Divine Truth; and by virtue of this conjunction it imparts life to all things of heaven, as the heat of the sun in the world, in conjunction with its light, renders fruitful all the productions of the earth; as is experienced in the season of spring and summer. It is otherwise when heat is not conjoined with the light, thus when the light is cold; for then all things become torpid and lie dead. This Divine Good, which is compared to heat, is, when received by the angels, the good of love; and the Divine Truth, which is compared to light, is that, by and from which the good of love is communicated to them.

14. The reason that the Divine Sphere in heaven, which constitutes it heaven, is love, is, because love is spiritual conjunction. It conjoins the angels with the Lord, and it conjoins them mutually with each other; and this it effects in such a manner, that they all, in the sight of the Lord, form a one. Moreover, love is the very *esse* of every one's life; wherefore both angels and men derive their life from it. That the inmost vital principle of man is derived from love, every one may know who considers the subject; for at its presence he grows warm, at its absence he grows cold, and on the privation of it he dies.([2]) But it is to be observed, that the quality of the life of every one is the same as that of his love.

15. There are in heaven two distinct kinds of love—love to the Lord, and love towards the neighbor. The love that prevails in the inmost or third heaven, is love to the Lord; and that which reigns in the second or middle heaven, is love towards the neighbor. Each proceeds from the Lord, and each constitutes heaven. How these two kinds of love are distinguished from each other, and how they are conjoined together, appears, in heaven, in the clearest light; but can only be seen obscurely in the world. In heaven, by loving the Lord, is not understood to love him as to his person, but to love the good which proceeds from him; and to love good, is to will and do good from love. So, by loving their neighbor, they do not understand the love of their companions as to their person, but to love the truth which is from the Word; and to love truth is to will and do truth. It hence is evident, that these two kinds

([1]) That fire, when mentioned in the Word, signifies love both in a good and a bad sense, nn. 934, 4906, 5215. That sacred and heavenly fire signifies divine love, and every affection which belongs to that love, nn. 934, 6314, 6832. That the light thence proceeding signifies truth proceeding from the good of love; and that light, in heaven, is divine truth, nn. (3395,) 3485, 3636, 3643, 3993, 4302, 4413, 4415, 9548, 9684.

([2]) That love is the fire of life, and that life is actually derived from it, nn. 4906, 5071, 6032, 6314.

9

of love are distinguished from each other as good and truth are, and that they are conjoined together as good is conjoined with truth.(³) But he who does not know what love is, what good is, and what the neighbor is, can with difficulty form an idea on these subjects.(⁴)

16. I have sometimes conversed on this subject with the angels, who expressed their wonder that men belonging to the church should not be aware, that to love the Lord and to love the neighbor, is to love good and truth, and to do them from inclination; when yet they might know that every one testifies his love for another, by willing and doing what is agreeable to the will of the other; in consequence of which he is loved by the other in return, and conjunction with him is effected; which does not ensue on loving the other without doing what is agreeable to his will, since this, regarded in itself, is not loving him: and when they also might know, that the good proceeding from the Lord is his likeness, because He is in it, and that those become likenesses of Him, and attain conjunction with Him, who make good and truth the principles of their life, by willing and doing them. To will, also, is, to love to do. This the Lord likewise teaches, saying, "*He that hath my commandments, and keepeth them, he it is that loveth me ;—and I will love him, and will manifest myself unto him*" (John xiv. 21). And in another place: "*If ye keep my commandments, ye shall abide in my love*" (John xv. 10).

17. That the Divine Sphere proceeding from the Lord, which affects the angels and constitutes heaven, is love, all experience in heaven testifies: for all there are forms of love and charity They appear of ineffable beauty; and love beams forth from their face, from their speech, and from every particular of their life.(⁵) Moreover, from every angel and spirit proceed spiritual spheres of life, which are circumfused around them, and by means of which their quality, as to the affections which belong to their love, is sometimes perceived at a considerable distance. For those spheres flow from the life of the affection, and thence of the thought, of every one; or from the life of his love and thence of his faith: and the spheres proceeding from the angels are so full of love, that they affect the inmost grounds of the life of those in their company: they have sometimes been per-

(³) That to love the Lord and our neighbor is to live according to the Lord's precepts, nn. 10,143, 10,153, 10,310, 10,578, 10,648

(⁴) That to love the neighbor is not to love his person, but to love that in him by which he is constituted a neighbor, thus truth and good, nn. 5028, 10,336. That those who love the person, and not that in him by which he is constituted a neighbor, love evil as well as good, n. 3820. That charity consists in willing truths, and being affected by truths, for their own sake, nn. 3876, 3877. That charity towards our neighbor consists in doing what is good, just, and right, in every work and in every office, nn. 8120, 8121, 8122.

(⁵) That the angels are forms of love and charity, nn. 3804, 4735, 4797, 4985, 5199, 5530, 9879, 10,177.

ceived by me, when they affected me in this manner.(6) That love is the principle from which the life of the angels is derived, is also evident from hence, that every one in the other life turns himself in a direction agreeing with his love; those who are principled in love to the Lord, and in love towards their neighbor, turn themselves constantly to the Lord; but those who are principled in the love of self constantly turn themselves away from the Lord. This continues to be the case in every motion of their bodies: for spaces, in the other life, depend on the state of the interiors of those who dwell there, as do the quarters likewise, which are not fixed there, as they are in the world. but are determined according to the aspect of the faces of the inhabitants. It is not, however, the angels who turn themselves to the Lord, but it is the Lord who turns all those to himself who love to do those things that are from him.(7) More will be said on these subjects in the following pages, when the Quarters in the other life are treated of.

18. The reason that the Divine Sphere of the Lord in heaven is love, is, because love is the receptacle of all the constituents of heaven, which are peace, intelligence, wisdom, and happiness. For love receives all things whatever that are congenial to itself; it desires them, it seeks for them, and it imbibes them as it were spontaneously; for it is continually desirous of being enriched and perfected by them.(8) This is also known to man: for in him, love inspects as it were the stores of his memory, and calls forth thence such of its contents as agree with itself: these it collects together and arranges in and under itself,—in itself that they may be its own, and under itself that they may be ready for its service: but whatever does not agree with itself, it rejects and exterminates. That every faculty for receiving the truths congenial to it, and the desire of conjoining them to itself, are inherent in love, clearly appears, also, from those who are raised to heaven; all of whom, though they may have been simple persons when they lived in the world, nevertheless, on coming among the angels, enter fully into their angelic wisdom, and the felicities of heaven: the reason is, because they had loved good and truth for their own sake, and had implanted them in their life, and thereby acquired the faculty of receiving heaven, with all its ineffable perfections. But those who are immersed in the love of self and of the world possess no faculty

(6) That a spiritual sphere, which is the sphere of his life, flows and exudes from every man, spirit, and angel, and spreads around him, nn. 4464, 5179, 7454, 8630. That it flows from the life of his affection and thence of his thought, nn. 2489, 4464 6206.

(7) That spirits and angels turn themselves constantly to their loves, and that those in heaven turn themselves constantly to the Lord, nn. 10,130, 10,189, 1(,420, 10,702. That the quarters in the other life depend with every one on the aspect of his face, and are thence determined, differently from what takes place in the world, nn. 10,130, 10,189, 10,420, 10,702.

(8) That innumerable things are inherent in love, and that love receives to itself all things that agree with it, nn. 2500, 2572, 3079, 3189, 6323, 7490, 7750.

11

of receiving such gifts : they feel aversion for them, they reject them, they flee away at their first touch and influx, and associate themselves with those in hell who are immersed in the same kinds of love as themselves. There were certain spirits who doubted whether such faculties were inherent in heavenly love, and desired to know the truth; wherefore, the obstacles in themselves being for a time removed, they were let into a state of heavenly love, and borne forward to some distance where there was an angelic heaven; whence they conversed with me, saying, that they had a perception of interior happiness which they were unable to express by words, and grieving exceedingly that they must return into their former state. Some others, also, were taken up into heaven, and in proportion as their elevation became more interior and exalted, they entered into such intelligence and wisdom, as to be capable of seeing things with clear perception which before they were unable to comprehend at all. Hence it is manifest, that love proceeding from the Lord is the receptacle of heaven and of all its perfections.

19. That love to the Lord and love towards the neighbor comprehend in themselves all divine truths, may appear from what the Lord declared concerning them, when he said, " *Thou shalt love the Lord thy God with all thy heart, and with all thy soul, and with all thy mind. This is the first and great commandment. And the second is like unto it : Thou shalt love thy neighbor as thyself. On these two commandments hang all the law and the prophets*" (Matt. xxii. 37—40). The law and the prophets are the whole Word, thus all Divine Truth.

. THAT HEAVEN IS DIVIDED INTO TWO KINGDOMS.

20. As in heaven there are infinite varieties, and no society is exactly like another, nor indeed any angel,(¹) therefore heaven is divided in a general, in a specific, and in a particular manner. It is divided, in general, into two kingdoms, specifically, into three heavens, and in particular, into innumerable societies. Each division shall be treated of distinctly.

The general divisions are styled *kingdoms*, because heaven is called *the kingdom of God*.

21. There are angels who receive the Divine Sphere proceeding from the Lord more and less interiorly. They who receive

(¹) That variety is infinite, and that one thing is never the same as another, nn. 7236, 9002. That in the heavens, also, there is infinite variety, nn. 684, 690, 3744, 5598, 7236. That varieties in the heavens are varieties of good, nn. 3744, 4005. 7236, 7833, 7836, 9002. That thereby all the societies of heaven, and all the angels in each society, are distinguished from each other nn. 690, 3241, 3519, 3804, 3986, 4067, 4149, 4263, 7236, 7833, 7836. But that they all, nevertheless, make a one, by means of love from the Lord, nn. 457, 3986.

12

it more interiorly are called celestial angels; but they who receive it less interiorly are called spiritual angels. Hence heaven is divided into two kingdoms; one of which is called the CELESTIAL KINGDOM, and the other, the SPIRITUAL KINGDOM.([2])

22. The angels who constitute the celestial kingdom, because they receive the Divine Sphere proceeding from the Lord more interiorly, are called interior, and also, superior angels; and thence, also, the heavens which they constitute are called interior and superior heavens.([3]) They are styled *superior* and *inferior*, because things *interior* and *exterior*, respectively, are so called.([4])

23. The love in which those who dwell in the celestial kingdom are principled, is called celestial love; and the love in which those who dwell in the spiritual kingdom are principled, is called spiritual love. Celestial love is love to the Lord, and spiritual love is charity towards the neighbor. And as all good has relation to love, since whatever any one loves he deems good, therefore, also, the good of one kingdom is called celestial good, and that of the other, spiritual good. Hence it is evident in what respect those two kingdoms are distinguished from each other, namely, that the distinction between them is like that between the good of love to the Lord and the good of charity towards the neighbor:([5]) and as the former good is interior good, and that love is interior love, therefore the celestial angels are interior angels, and are called superior.

24. The celestial kingdom is also called the Sacerdotal Kingdom of the Lord, and, in the Word, His dwelling-place or habitation; and the spiritual kingdom is called His Regal Kingdom, and, in the Word, His Throne. It is, also, from His Divine Celestial Principle, that the Lord, in the world, was called JESUS; and it is by virtue of His Divine Spiritual Principle, that He was called CHRIST.

25. The angels in the Lord's celestial kingdom far excel the angels of His spiritual kingdom in wisdom and glory, by reason that they more interiorly receive the Lord's Divine Sphere: for they are grounded in love to Him, and thence they are nearer to Him, and in closer conjunction with Him.() The reason

([2]) That the whole heaven is distinguished into two kingdoms, the celestial kingdom, and the spiritual kingdom, nn. 3887, 4138. That the angels of the celestial kingdom receive the Divine Sphere proceeding from the Lord in the will part, thus more interiorly than the spiritual angels, who receive it in the intellectual part, nn. 5113, 6367, 8521, 9936, 9995, 10,124.

([3]) That the heavens which constitute the celestial kingdom are styled superior heavens, but those which constitute the spiritual kingdom, inferior heavens, n. 10,068.

([4]) That what is interior is expressed by what is superior, and that what is superior signifies what is interior, nn. 2148, 3084, 4599, 5146, 8325.

([5]) That the good of the celestial kingdom is the good of love to the Lord, and that the good of the spiritual kingdom is the good of charity towards the neighbor, nn. 8691, 6435, 9468, 9680, 9683, 9780.

([6]) That the celestial angels immensely excel the spiritual angels in wisdom, nn. 2718, 9995. What is the difference between the celestial and the spiritual angels, nn. 2088, 2849, 2705, 2715, 3235, 3241, 4788, 7053, 8521, 9277, 10,295.

13

that these angels are of such a quality, is, because they had received, when in the world, and continue to receive still, divine truths immediately in the life, and do not, like the spiritual, first deposit them in the memory and the thought. From this cause, they have them inscribed on their hearts: they have a perception of their reality, and, as it were, see them in themselves : nor do they ever reason about them, to ascertain whether the truth be so or not.(⁷) They are such as are described in Jeremiah : "*I will put my law in their inward parts, and write it in their hearts.—They shall teach no more every man his neighbor, and every man his brother, saying, Know ye Jehovah ; for they shall all know me, from the least of them unto the greatest of them, saith Jehovah*" (ch. xxxi. 33, 34). And they are called in Isaiah, The "*taught of Jehovah*" (ch. liv. 13). That the taught of Jehovah are they who are taught of the Lord, the Lord himself teaches in John (vi. 45).

26. It was observed, that the celestial angels excel the others in wisdom and glory, because they had received, when in the world, and continue to receive still, divine truths immediately in the life : for as soon as they hear them, they will and do them, and do not first deposit them in the memory, and afterwards think whether they be true or not. They who are of such a quality, know immediately, by an influx from the Lord, whether what they hear be true or not : for the Lord enters by influx into man's faculty of willing immediately, and mediately, through that, into his faculty of thinking ; or, what is the same, the Lord enters by influx into good immediately, and mediately, through good, into truth :(⁸) for that is called good which has its abode in the will, and thence proceeds into act ; and that is called truth which has its seat in the memory, and is thence made an object of the thought. All truth, also, is turned into good, and is implanted in the love, as soon as it enters the will ; but so long as it is in the memory, and thence in the thought, it does not become good, nor has it life, nor is it appropriated to the man ; for man is man by virtue of his will, and of his understanding as thence exercised, and not by virtue of his understanding in separation from his will.(⁹)

(⁷) That the celestial angels do not reason concerning the truths of faith, because they have a perception of them in themselves, but that the spiritual angels reason concerning them, to ascertain whether a thing be so or not, nn. 202, 337, 597, 607, 784, 1121, 1384, (1398,) 1919, 8246, 4448, 7680, 7877, 8780, 9277, 10,786.

(⁸) That there is an influx of the Lord into good, and through good into truth, and not *vice versa ;* thus into the will, and through that into the understanding, and not *vice versa,* nn. 5482, 5649, 6027, 8685, 8701, 10,153.

(⁹) That the will of man is the very *esse* of his life, and is the receptacle of the good of love ; and that his understanding is his *existere* of life thence derived, and is the receptacle of the truth and good of faith, nn. 3619, 5002, 9282. Thus that the life of his will is the principal life of man, and that the life of his understanding proceeds from it, nn. 585, 590, 3619, 7342, 8885, 9282, 10,076, 10,109, 10,110. That those things which are received in the will, become principles of the life, and are appropriated to man, nn. 3161, 9386, 9393. That man is man by virtue of his will, and thence by vir-

14

27. As there is such a difference between the angels of the celestial kingdom and those of the spiritual kingdom, they do not dwell together, nor have they any mutual intercourse. There is only a communication between them by means of intermediate angelic societies, called celestial-spiritual; through which the celestial kingdom enters by influx into the spiritual.([10]) It is owing to this influx, that although heaven is divided into two kingdoms, still it forms a one. The Lord always provides such intermediate angels, by means of whom communication and conjunction are effected.

28. As the angels of both these kingdoms are much treated of in the following pages, it is unnecessary to state any further particulars here.

THAT THERE ARE THREE HEAVENS.

29. There are three heavens, which are perfectly distinct from each other; namely, the Inmost or Third Heaven, the Middle or Second Heaven, and the Ultimate or First. They follow each other in order, and are mutually related, like the highest part of man, which is called the head, his middle part, which is called the body, and his lowest part, which is the feet; and like the highest, the middle, and the lowest stories of a house. The Divine Sphere which proceeds and descends from the Lord, is also in the same order; and hence, from its necessary conformity to order, heaven is disposed according to a threefold arrangement.

30. The interiors of man, belonging to his internal and external minds,* are also in similar order: he has an inmost, a middle, and an ultimate. For when man was created, all the principles of Divine Order were collated into him, so that he was made Divine Order in form, and thence a heaven in minia-

---

tue of his understanding, nn. 8911, 9069, 9071, 10,076, 10,109, 10,110. That also, every man whose will and understanding are good, is loved and esteemed by others; while he whose will and understanding are not good, is rejected and despised, nn. (8911,) (10,076.) That man also continues after death such as his will is and his understanding thence, and that those things which are entertained by his understanding and not at the same time by his will, then vanish, because they are not in the man, nn. 9069, 9071, 9232, 9386, 10,153.

([10]) That there is communication and conjunction between the two heavens, by means of angelic societies which are called celestial-spiritual, nn. 4047, 6435, 8787, 8802. Of the influx of the Lord through the celestial kingdom into the spiritual, nn. 3969, 6366.

* Our Author frequently uses two Latin words together (*mens* and *animus*) to denote the mind, meaning by the former the intellectual or rational mind, which is respectively internal, and by the latter the natural or animal mind, which is respectively external. The distinction is common with the philosophers, and is indicated in the Apostolic writings by the distinct terms *pneuma* and *psyche*. This explanation should be remembered wherever the words "internal and external minds" occur in the following pages.—*N.*

ture.(¹) Thus also man, with respect to his interiors, has communication with the heavens, and also rises to the angelic abodes after death; entering into the society of the angels of the inmost, second, or ultimate heaven, according to his reception of divine good and truth from the Lord during his life in the world.

31. The Divine Sphere which enters by influx from the Lord, and is received in the third or inmost heaven, is called the *Divine Celestial Sphere;* whence the angels there are called *celestial angels;* and the Divine Sphere which enters by influx from the Lord, and is received, in the second or middle heaven, is called the *Divine Spiritual Sphere,* whence the angels there are called *spiritual angels:* but the *Divine Sphere* which enters by influx from the Lord, and is received, in the ultimate or first heaven, is called the *Divine Natural Sphere.* As, however, the natural sphere of that heaven is not like the natural sphere in which this world exists, but has the spiritual and celestial spheres within it, that heaven is called *spiritual-and-celestial-natural;* whence the angels there are called *spiritual-and-celestial-natural angels:*(²) those are styled *spiritual-natural* who receive their influx out of the middle or second heaven, which is the spiritual heaven; and those are styled *celestial-natural* who receive their influx out of the third or inmost heaven, which is the celestial heaven. The spiritual-and-celestial-natural angels dwell apart from each other, but still they constitute but one heaven, because they are in the same degree.

32. In every heaven there is an Internal and an External; and those who are in the internal are called there internal angels, but those who are in the external are called external angels. The internal and the external in the heavens, and in every heaven, are like the will-faculty, and its intellectual faculty, appertaining to man, the internal being like the will-faculty, and the external like its intellectual faculty. Every species of will-faculty has its own intellectual faculty, the one not existing without the other; the will-faculty being comparatively like a flame, and its intellectual faculty like the light proceeding from it.

33. It is carefully to be noted, that the interiors of the angels

(¹) That all the principles of Divine Order are collated into man, and that man, from creation, is Divine Order in a form, nn. 4219, 4222, 4223, 4523, 4524, 5114, (5368,) 6013, 6057, 6605, 6626, 9706, 10,156, 10,472. That, with man, his internal man is formed after the image of heaven, and his external after the image of the world, and that, therefore, man was called by the ancients a microcosm, or little world, nn. 4523, 5368, 6013, 6057, 9279, 9706, 10,156, 10,472. That thus man is, from creation, with respect to his interiors, a heaven in miniature, formed after the image of heaven at large; and that the man who is born anew, or regenerated by the Lord, is such also, nn. 911, 1900, 1928, 3624—3631, 3634, 3884, 4041, 4279, 4523, 4524, 4625, 6013, 9279, 9632.
(²) That there are three heavens, the inmost, the middle, and the ultimate; or the third, the second, and the first, nn. 684, 9594, 10,270. That goods, there, also follow each other in a triple order, nn. 4938, 4939, 9992, 10,005, 10,017. That the good of the inmost or third heaven is called celestial good, that of the middle or second, spiritual good, and that of the ultimate or first, natural good, nn. 4279, 4286, 4938, 9992, 10,005, 10,017, 10,068.

are what determine their situation in one or other of these heavens; for they inhabit a more interior heaven in proportion as their interiors are more open to the Lord. There exist with every one, whether angel, spirit, or man, three degrees of the interiors: those with whom the third degree is open, are in the inmost heaven; and those with whom the second degree, or only the first, is open, are either in the middle or ultimate heaven. The interiors are opened by the reception of divine good and divine truth. Those who are affected with divine truths, and admit them immediately into the life, thus into the will and thence into act, are in the inmost or third heaven, their situation there being according to their reception of good from the affection of truth; those who do not admit divine truths immediately into the life, but into the memory and from that into the understanding, and thence will and do them, are in the middle or second heaven; but those who lead a moral life, and believe in the Divine Being, without caring much to be instructed, are in the ultimate or first heaven.([*]) Hence it may appear, that the states of the interiors are what constitute heaven, and that heaven is within every one, and not without him; as the Lord also teaches, saying, "*The kingdom of God cometh not with observation, neither shall they say, Lo here! or Lo there! for behold, the kingdom of God is within you*" (Luke xvii. 20, 21).

34. All perfection, also, increases as it advances towards the interiors, and decreases as it descends towards the exteriors; because interior things are nearer to the Divine Nature, and in themselves more pure; but exterior things are further removed from the Divine Nature, and in themselves more gross.([†]) Angelic perfection consists in intelligence, wisdom, love, and every good, and thence in happiness, but not in happiness without the former; for, without those graces, happiness is external and not internal. As, in the angels of the inmost heaven, the interiors are open in the third degree, their perfection immensely surpasses that of the angels in the middle heaven, whose interiors are open in the second degree: and the perfection of the angels of the middle heaven exceeds that of the angels of the ultimate heaven in a similar manner.

35. The difference between them being so great, an angel of one heaven cannot intrude among the angels of another heaven;

([*]) That there are as many degrees of life in man as there are heavens, and that they are opened after death according to his life, nn. 3747, 9594. That heaven is in man, n. 3884. Hence, that whoever receives heaven in himself in the world, comes into heaven after death, n. 10,717.

([†]) That interior things are more perfect, because nearer to the Divine Being, nn. 3405, 5146, 5147. That there are thousands and thousands of things in the internal, which in the external appear as one general thing, n. 5707. That so far as any one is elevated from external things towards interior things, so far he comes into light, and thus into intelligence; and that such elevation is like passing out of a mist into a clear atmosphere, nn. 4598, 6183, 6313.

that is, no one can ascend from an inferior heaven, nor descend from a superior one. Whoever ascends from an inferior to a superior heaven, is seized with an anxiety amounting to anguish; nor can he see those who dwell there, still less can he converse with them; and whoever descends from a superior to an inferior heaven is deprived of his wisdom, stammers in his speech, and is filled with despair. There were certain angels of the ultimate heaven who had not yet learned that heaven has its seat in the interiors of the angels, believing that they should come into superior heavenly happiness, could they but enter a heaven inhabited by angels by whom such happiness is enjoyed. They were also permitted: but when they came there, though they looked about for the angels, and there was a great multitude present, they could see no one: for the interiors of the strangers were not opened in the same degree as the interiors of the angels who dwelt there, consequently, neither was their sight. Soon afterwards they were seized with anguish of heart, to such a degree, that they scarcely knew whether they were alive or not: wherefore they speedily betook themselves away to the heaven from which they came, rejoicing on their arrival amongst their own companions, and promising that they would never more covet any higher enjoyments than such as were in agreement with their life. I have also seen some angels let down out of a superior into an inferior heaven; who were deprived of their wisdom to such a degree, that they did not know of what quality their own heaven was. But this does not happen, when the Lord, as is frequently the case, elevates any angels from an inferior to a superior heaven that they may see its glory; for they then are previously prepared, and are surrounded by intermediate angels, by means of whom communication is effected. It is evident from these facts, that the three heavens are perfectly distinct from each other.

36. All, however, who reside in the same heaven can hold intercourse with each other; only the enjoyments of their intercourse depend upon the affinity between the kinds of good in which they are principled. But this will be treated of in the following sections.

37. But though the three heavens are so distinct that the angels of one heaven cannot have intercourse with those of another, yet the Lord conjoins them all into one by immediate and mediate influx; by immediate influx from himself into all the heavens, and by mediate influx from one heaven into another.([5]) The result of this is, that the three heavens form a

([5]) That the influx proceeding from the Lord is both immediate from Himself, and mediate through one heaven into another; and that the influx from the Lord with man takes place into his interiors in a similar manner, nn. 6063, 6307, 6472, 9682, 9683. Of the immediate influx of the Divine Sphere proceeding from the Lord, nn. 6058, 6474—6478, 8717, 8728. Of the mediate influx through the spiritual world into the natural world, nn. 6982, 6985, 6996.

united whole, and are all kept in connection, from the First Cause to ultimate effects, so that nothing which is not in such connection can be found: for whatever is not connected with the First Cause by intermediate links, cannot subsist, but is dissipated and falls to nothing.([6])

38. He who does not know the regulations of divine order with respect to degrees cannot comprehend in what manner the heavens are distinct from each other, nor even what is meant by the internal and external man. Most persons in the world have no other idea of things interior and exterior, or superior and inferior, than as of something continuous, or cohering by continuity, from a purer state to a grosser; whereas things interior and exterior are not continuous with respect to each other, but discrete.* Degrees are of two kinds, there being continuous degrees and degrees not continuous. Continuous degrees are like the degrees of light, decreasing as it recedes from flame, which is its source, till it is lost in obscurity; or like the degrees of visual clearness, decreasing as the sight passes from the objects in the light to those in the shade; or like the degrees of the purity of the atmosphere from its base to its summit: these degrees being determined by the respective distances. But degrees that are not continuous, but discrete, differ from each other like what is prior and what is posterior, like cause and effect, and like that which produces and that which is produced. Whoever investigates this subject will find, that in all the objects of creation, both general and particular, there are such degrees of production and composition, and that from one thing proceeds another, and from that a third, and so on. He that has not acquired a clear apprehension of these degrees, cannot be acquainted with the difference between the various heavens, and between the interior and exterior faculties of man; nor can he be acquainted with the difference between the spiritual world and the natural, nor between the spirit of man and his body; nor, consequently, can he understand what correspondences and representations are, and their origin; nor what is the nature of Influx. Sensual men cannot comprehend these distinctions, for they suppose increase and decrease, even with respect to these degrees, to be continuous; on which account they can form no other conception of what is spiritual, than as something more purely natural. Thus they stand, as it were, without the gate, far remote from all that constitutes intelligence.([7])

---

* *Discrete* is a philosophical term signifying *separate*, and is applied to two or more things that do not run into one another, but, though contiguous, have each their distinct boundary.—*N.*

([6]) That all things exist from things prior to themselves, thus from a First Cause; and that they subsist in like manner, because subsistence is perpetual existence; and that therefore nothing unconnected is to be found, nn. 3626, 3627, 3628, 3648, 4523, 4524, 6040, 6056.

([7]) That things interior and exterior are not continuous, but distinct and discrete according to degrees; and that every degree is terminated, nn. 3691, 5145, 5114, 8603.

39. In the last place, a certain arcanum may be mentioned respecting the angels of the three heavens, which never before entered the mind of any one, because no man has hitherto understood the doctrine of degrees. There is in every angel, and also in every man, an inmost and supreme degree, or a certain inmost and supreme region of the soul, and faculty of reception, into which the Divine Sphere of the Lord first or proximately flows, and from which it regulates the other interior receptive faculties, which follow in succession according to the degrees of order. This inmost or supreme region of the soul may be called the Lord's entrance to angels and men, and his most immediate dwelling-place in them. It is owing to his having this inmost or supreme abode for the Lord that a man is a man, and is distinguished from the brute animals, which do not possess it. It is by virtue of this, that man, differently from animals, with respect to all the interiors, or the faculties belonging to his internal and external minds, is capable of being elevated by the Lord to himself, of believing in him, of being affected with love to him, and thus of seeing him; and is capable of. receiving intelligence and wisdom, and of conversing in a rational manner: and it is also by virtue of this, that man lives to eternity. But the arrangements and provisions that are made by the Lord in this inmost region, do not come manifestly to the perception of any angel, because they are above his sphere of thought, and transcend his wisdom.

40. These particulars are such as are common to all the three heavens; but, in what follows, each heaven will be treated of specifically.

THAT THE HEAVENS CONSIST OF INNUMERABLE SOCIETIES.

41. The angels of each heaven do not dwell all together in one place, but are divided into larger and smaller societies, according to the differences of the good of love and faith in which they are grounded; those who are grounded in similar good forming one society. There is an infinite variety of kinds of good in the heavens; and every angel is such in quality as is the good belonging to him.[1]

10,099. That one thing is formed from another, and that the things thus formed are not purer and grosser by continuity, nn. 6326, 6465. That whoever does not perceive the distinction between things interior and exterior, according to degrees, can form no conception of the internal and external man, nor of the interior and exterior heavens, nn. 5146, 6465, 10,099, 10,181.

[1] That variety is infinite, and that no one thing is ever the same as another, nn. 7236, 9002. That there is also an infinite variety in the heavens, nn. 684, 690, 3744, 5598, 7236. That the varieties in the heavens, which are infinite, are varieties of good, nn. 3744, 4005, 7236, 7833, 7836, 9002. That these varieties exist by means of the multiplicity of truths, from which every one acquires good, nn. 3470, 3804, 4149, 6917.

42. The angelic societies in the heavens are also at a distance from each other, in proportion to the general and specific differences of their species of good. For there is no other origin of distances, in the spiritual world, than the difference of the state of the interiors, thus, in the heavens, the difference of the states of love. Those who differ much in this respect, are at a great distance from each other, and those who differ little, are at a little distance; but those whose states of love are similar dwell together.(²)

43. All the angels in one society are distinctly arranged among themselves in a similar manner. Those who are more perfect, that is, who excel in good, and consequently in love, wisdom, and intelligence, are stationed in the middle; and those who excel less are located round about them, being more distant by degrees in proportion as they diminish in perfection. In this respect they may be compared to light, which decreases as it recedes from its centre to the circumference: those who are in the middle are, also, in the greatest light, but those towards the circumference are in less and less.

44. The angels who are of a similar quality come into each other's society as it were spontaneously; for when they are in company with such as are like themselves, they feel as if they were amongst their own relations, and in their own home; but when they are in company with others, they feel as among strangers, and abroad. When they are amongst those that are like themselves, they also feel at liberty, and thence in the full enjoyment of their life.

45. Hence it is evident, that good is what connects all the angels in the heavens together in society, and that they are distinctly located according to its quality. Yet it is not the angels who thus connect themselves together in society, but the Lord, from whom all good proceeds: He leads them, conjoins them, distinctly arranges them, and preserves them in a state of liberty, in proportion as they are grounded in good; thus He preserves every one in the life of his own love, his own faith, his own intelligence and wisdom, and consequently in happiness.(³)

46. All the angels who are grounded in similar good, also

7236. That hence all the societies in heaven, and all the angels in every society, are distinct from each other, nn. 690, 3241, 3519, 3804, 3986, 4067, 4149, 4263, 7236, 7833, 7836. B·.e that, nevertheless, they all act in unity by means of love from the Lord, nn. 457, 3986.

(²) That all the societies of heaven have a fixed situation, according to the difference of their state of life, thus according to their differences of love and faith, nn. 1274, 3633. 3639. Some wonderful particulars in the other life, or in the spiritual world, respecting distance, situation, place, space, and time, nn. 1273—1277.

(³) That all liberty is of love or affection, because what a man loves, that he does freely, nn. 2870, 3158, 8987, 9990, 9585, 9591. That as liberty is what is of the love, it consequently is the life of every one, and his delight, n. 2873. That nothing appears to a man as his own, but what is of his liberty, n. 2880. That the very essence of liberty is to be led by the Lord, because this is to be led by the love of good and truth, nn. 892, 905, 2872, 2886, 2890, 2891, 2892 9586—9491.

21

know each other, though they never met before, as well as men
in the world know their kindred, relations, and friends: the
reason of which is, because in the other life there are no other
relationships, affinities, and friendships, than such as are spiritual, thus such as are the result of love and faith.(⁴) This it
has been frequently granted me to see, when I have been in the
spirit, and thus withdrawn from the body, and in company with
angels. At such times, I have seen some who appeared to have
been known to me from infancy; whilst others seemed not
known to me at all: those whom I appeared to know, were
such as were in a state similar to that of my spirit; but those
whom I did not know, were such whose state was dissimilar.

47. All the angels who form one society, have a common
likeness of countenance, but with a difference in particular.
An idea may, in some measure, be formed respecting such
general likenesses with particular variations, from similar cases
existing in the world. Thus it is well known that every race
of people has some common likeness in the face and eyes, by
which it is recognized, and is distinguished from other races;
which is yet more the case in particular families : but this takes
place in much greater perfection in the heavens, because there,
all the interior affections appear and shine forth from the face,
which is there the external and representative form of those
affections; for to have any other face than such as is proper to
the affections of its possessor, is not possible in heaven. It has
also been shown me, in what manner the general resemblance
is particularly varied in the individuals composing one society.
There appeared to me a face like that of an angel, which was
varied according to the affections of good and truth, as they
exist with the angels who dwell in one society. These variations continued a long time; and I observed that the same general countenance continued as the plane or groundwork of the
rest, and that these were only derivations and propagations proceeding from it. In the same manner, by means of this face,
the affections of a whole society, according to which the faces
of all its inmates are varied, were shown me: for, as observed
above, the faces of angels are the forms of their interiors, thus
of the affections which belong to their love and faith.

48. It is from this cause that an angel who excels in wisdom
can immediately see what is the quality of another by his face;
for no one there can disguise his interiors by his countenance,
and put on an appearance which does not belong to him; and
it is quite impossible to utter falsehood, and to deceive by craft
and hypocrisy. It, indeed, sometimes happens that hypocrites
insinuate themselves into angelic societies, having learned how

---

(⁴) That all proximities, relationships, affinities and as it were, consanguinities, in
heaven, are derived from good, and are according to its agreements and differences.
n .. 685, 917, 1394, 2739, 3612, 3815, 4121.

to conceal their interiors, and so to fashion their exteriors as to appear in the form of the good in which the members of the society are grounded, and thus to feign themselves angels of light: but they cannot long abide there; for they soon begin to feel interior anguish, are tormented, turn black in the face, and are deprived, as it were, of life; experiencing these alterations, from the opposite nature of the life which there enters by influx, and operates upon them: wherefore they quickly cast themselves down into the hell inhabited by spirits like themselves, and have no wish to ascend any more. These are such as are signified by the man who was found amongst the guests, at the marriage-supper, not clothed with a wedding garment, and who was cast into outer darkness (Matt. xxii. 11, &c.).

49. All the societies of heaven communicate with each other, though not by open intercourse; for few go out of their own society into another, because to go out of their society is like going out of themselves, or out of their own life, and passing into another which does not so well agree with them; but they all communicate by an extension of the sphere which proceeds from the life of each. The sphere of the life is a sphere of the affections which belong to their love and faith. This sphere diffuses itself far and wide into the surrounding societies, and the more so, in proportion as the affections are more interior and perfect.[5] The angels enjoy intelligence and wisdom in proportion to the extent of this diffusion: and those who dwell in the inmost heaven, and in the central parts of it, have a diffusion of sphere that pervades the whole of heaven. Thus is produced a communication of all the societies of heaven with every individual angel, and of every individual angel with the whole.[6] But this diffusion will be more fully treated of, in the Section concerning the heavenly form, according to which the angelic societies are arranged; and likewise in the Section that treats of the wisdom and intelligence of the angels; for all the diffusions of the affections and thoughts proceed according to that form.

50. It was observed above, that there are larger and smaller societies in the heavens; the larger consist of myriads of angels, the smaller of several thousands, and the smallest of some hundreds. There are also some angels who dwell alone, as by houses and families; but though these live thus dispersed, yet they are arranged in a similar manner with those who dwell in

---

[5] That a spiritual sphere, which is the sphere of their life, flows out of every man, spirit, and angel, and surrounds them, nn. 4464, 5179, 7454, 8630. That it flows from the life of their affection and thought, nn. 2489, 4464, 6206. That those spheres extend themselves far into the angelic societies, in proportion to the quality and quantity of their good, nn. 6603, 8063, 8794, 8797.

[6] That a communication of the goods of all prevails in heaven, because heavenly love communicates every thing that is its own to others, nn. 549, 550, 1390, 1391, 1392, 10,130, 10,723.

23

societies; that is, the wiser among them are in the middle, and the more simple in the boundaries. These are more immediately under the divine auspices of the Lord, and are the best of the angels.

THAT EVERY SOCIETY IS A HEAVEN ON A SMALLER SCALE, AND EVERY ANGEL IS A HEAVEN IN MINIATURE.

51. The reason that every society is a heaven on a smaller scale, and every angel is a heaven in miniature, is, because the good of love and faith is what constitutes heaven; and that good exists in every society of heaven, and in every angel of such society. It matters not that this good is everywhere different and various; still it is the good of heaven; the only difference is, that heaven is of one quality in one place, and of another in another. It is therefore said, when a person is elevated into any heavenly society, that he is gone to heaven; and of its inhabitants, that they are in heaven, and every one in his own heaven. This is known to all in the other life; wherefore those who stand without or below heaven, and view the abodes of the angelic assemblies from a distant situation, say that heaven is there, or there. This may be compared to the lords, officers, and attendants, in a royal palace or court; who, although they dwell by themselves in separate apartments or chambers, one above and another below, are still all in one palace or court, ready to serve the king in their several capacities. This shows what is meant by the Lord's words, "*In my Father's house are many mansions*" (John xiv. 2); and what is meant by *the habitations of heaven*, and *the heaven of heavens*, in the prophets.

52. That every society is a heaven on a smaller scale, may also appear from this circumstance, that the heavenly form is the same in each society as it is in the whole heaven; for in the whole heaven, those angels who excel the rest dwell in the middle, and around them even to the boundaries, decreasing in order, are those who excel less, as is stated in the preceding Section, n. 43. It may also appear from this circumstance, that the Lord guides all in the whole heaven as if they were one angel; and likewise those in each society; on which account an entire angelic society sometimes appears as one object, in the form of an angel; which sight has been granted me by the Lord to behold. When, also, the Lord appears in the midst of the angels, he does not appear surrounded by a multitude, but as One Being in an angelic form; which is the reason that the Lord, in the Word, is called an angel; as is also an entire society; for Michael, Gabriel, and Raphael, are nothing but an-

24

gelic societies, which are so named from t'ıe functions they discharge.([1])

53. As an entire society is a heaven on a smaller scale, so also is an angel a heaven in miniature; because heaven is not without an angel, but within him. For his interiors, which belong to his mind, are arranged into the form of heaven, and thus are adapted to the reception of all the elements of heaven that exist without him; and he also does receive them according to the quality of the good which is in him from the Lord. Hence an angel, also, is a heaven.

54. It can by no means be said that heaven is without any one, but that it is within him; for every angel receives the heaven that is without him according to the heaven that is within him. This shows how they are deceived, who imagine, that to go to heaven is only to be taken up amongst the angels, let the quality of the individual with respect to his interior life be what it may; and thus that an abode in heaven may be conferred on any one by an immediate act of grace;([2]) when, nevertheless, unless heaven be within a person, nothing of the heaven that is without him can enter into him, and be received. Many spirits entertain the above opinion, and, on account of such being their belief, some have been taken up into heaven; but when they came there, their interior life being contrary to that in which the angels were grounded, they began to grow blind as to their intellectual faculties till they became like idiots, and to feel torture as to their will-faculties till they behaved like madmen. In short, those who get into heaven after having lived ill, gasp for breath, and writhe about like fishes taken out of the water into the air, or like animals in the ether of an exhausted receiver, after the air has been extracted. Hence it may be evident, that heaven is within a person, and not without him.([3])

55. As all receive the heaven which is without them, according to the nature of the heaven which is within them, they of course receive the Lord in the same manner, because the Divine Sphere of the Lord is what constitutes heaven. Hence when the Lord manifests Himself as present in any society, He appears there according to the quality of the good in which the society is grounded, thus not the same in one society as in another; not that there is any variableness in Him, but the dis-

---

([1]) That the Lord is called an angel in the Word, nn. 6280, 6831, 8192, 9303. That an entire angelic society is called an angel, and that Michael and Raphael are angelic societies so named from their functions, n. 8192. That the societies of heaven, and the angels, have not any name, but that they are known from the quality of their good, and from an idea respecting it, nn. 1705, 1754.

([2]) That heaven is not granted from immediate mercy, but according to the life, and that every principle of life by means of which man is led to heaven by the Lord, is from mercy, and is what is meant by it, nn. 5057, 10,659. That if heaven were granted from immediate mercy, it would be granted to all, n. 2401. Of certain evil spirits that were cast down from heaven, who imagined that heaven was granted to every one from immediate mercy, n 4226.

([3]) That heaven is in man, n. 3884.

similitude is in the angels, who view Him from their own good, and according to it. The angels are also affected at the sight of the Lord, according to the quality of their love: those who love Him most interiorly, are most interiorly affected, and those who love Him less are less affected; but the evil spirits, who are out of heaven, are tormented at His presence. When the Lord appears in any society, He appears there as an angel: but He is distinguished from the others by the Divinity which shines through Him.

56. Heaven also exists wherever the Lord is acknowledged, believed in, and loved: and the various modes of worshipping Him, proceeding from that variety of good in different societies, are not injurious, but advantageous; for the perfection of heaven is the result of that variety. That the perfection of heaven is the result of that variety, can hardly be intelligibly explained, without the assistance of the forms of expression in use in the learned world, and unless it be thereby shown how one whole, to be perfect, is formed of various parts. Every whole is composed of various parts; for a whole which is not composed of various parts, is not any thing, having no form, and consequently no quality; but when a whole is composed of various parts, and these are arranged in a perfect form, in which each part adjoins itself to the others in harmonious accordance and regular series, the quality that results is that of perfection. Now heaven is one whole, composed of various parts arranged in the most perfect form; for the heavenly form is the most perfect of all forms. That all perfection results from such harmonious variety, is evident from all the beauty, pleasantness, and agreeableness, which affect both the senses and the mind: for these qualities exist and proceed from no other source, than the concert and harmony of various concordant and consentient parts, arranged either in coexistent or in successive order, and do not result from any single thing without more. Hence the proverb, that variety is charming; and it is known that its charms depend upon its quality. From these considerations it may be seen, how perfection results from variety, even in heaven; for the objects of the spiritual world may be seen, as in a mirror, from those of the natural.[4]

57. The same assertion may be made respecting the church as respecting heaven; for the church is the Lord's heaven on earth. This has many branches; and yet each is called the church, and also is the church, so far as the good of love and faith reigns in it: and here, also, the Lord makes one whole out of various parts, thus one church out of many.[5] The same

[4] That every whole results from the harmony and agreement of various parts, and that otherwise it has no quality, n. 457. That hence the universal heaven is one, n. 457. Because all therein regard one end, which is the Lord, n. 9828.

[5] That if good were the characteristic and essential of the church, and not truth without good, the church would be one, nn. 1285, 1316, 2982, 3267, 3445, 3451, 3452

may also be said of each member of the church in particular, as
of the church in general, namely, that the church is within the
man, and not without him, and that every man, in whom the
Lord is present in the good of love and faith, is a church.(6)
The same, too, may be said respecting a man in whom the
church is, as respecting an angel in whom heaven is, namely,
that he is a church in miniature, as the angel is a heaven in
miniature: and further, that a man in whom the church is, is a
heaven, equally with an angel: for man was created to go to
heaven and become an angel; wherefore he who receives good
from the Lord is a man-angel.(7) It may be expedient to
mention what is common both to men and angels, and what,
compared with angels, is peculiar to man. *It is common both
to man and angels*, to have their interiors formed after the image
of heaven; and also, to become images of heaven in proportion
as they are grounded in the good of love and faith: and *it is
peculiar to man compared with the angels*, to have his exteriors
formed after the image of the world, and, so far as he is grounded in good, to have his worldly part rendered subordinate to
his heavenly part, so as to serve it;(8) and then to-have the
Lord present with him in both, as in his heaven; for the Lord
is in His own divine order everywhere, God being order itself.(9)

58. It may lastly be stated, that whoever has heaven in himself, not only enjoys it in his greatest or most general parts and
faculties, but also in his least or individual ones; for the least
things in him present an image of the greatest. The reason of
this is, because every one is his own love, and is of such a quality as his reigning love is: for whatever reigns, flows into and
arranges the most minute particulars, and induces everywhere
the likeness of itself.(10) The reigning love in the heavens is love

That all the churches, also, make one church in the sight of the Lord from good, nn.
7396, 9276.
(6) That the church is in man and not without him, and that the church at large
consists of men in whom the church is, n. 3884.
(7) That the man in whom the church is, is a heaven in miniature after the image
of heaven-at large, because the interiors which are of his mind are arranged into the
form of heaven, and thus are adapted to the reception of all things of heaven, nn. 911,
1900, 1928, 3624—3631, 3634, 3884, 4041, 4279, 4523, 4524, 4625, 6013, 6057, 9279, 9632.
(8) That man has an internal and an external, and that his internal is formed from
creation after the image of heaven, and his external after the image of the world, and
that therefore man was called by the ancients a microcosm, nn. 4523, 4524, 5368, 6013,
6057, 9279, 9706, 10,156, 10,472. That therefore man was so created, that the world
with him might serve heaven; as it also does with the good; but that with the evil
the case is inverted, and heaven serves the world; nn. 9283, 9278.
(9) That the Lord is Order, because Divine Good and Truth, which proceed from
the Lord, constitute Order, nn. 1728, 1919, (2201,) 2258, (5110,) 5703, 8988, 10,330,
10,619. That divine truths are the laws of order, nn. 2247, 7995. That so far as a
man lives according to order, thus so far as he lives in good according to divine truths,
so far he is a man, and heaven and the church are in him, nn 4839, 6605, (8067.)
(10) That the governing or ruling love with every one resides in all and each of the
things belonging to his life, thus in all and each of the things belonging to his thought
and will, nn. 6159, 7648, 8067, 8853. That man is of such a quality is the governing
principle of his life is, nn. (918,) 1040, 1568, 1571, 3570, 6571, 6934, 6938, 9853, 8857,
10,076, 10,109, 10,110, 10,284. That love and faith, when they govern, are in the minutest particulars of a man's life, though he does not know it, nn. 8854, 8864, 9865.

to the Lord, because the Lord is there loved above all things:
hence the Lord is there the All in all.   He enters by influx into
all the angels, both collectively and individually, arranges them,
and induces on them the likeness of Himself, constituting heaven
by His presence.   From this cause it is, that an angel is a
heaven in miniature, a society is a heaven on a larger scale, and
all the societies together are heaven on the largest; that the
Divine Sphere of the Lord constitutes heaven, and is the All in
all, may be seen above, n. 7—12.

THAT THE WHOLE HEAVEN, VIEWED COLLECTIVELY, IS IN FORM AS ONE MAN.

59. That heaven, viewed collectively, is in form as one man,
is an arcanum which is not yet known in the world: but it is
well known in the heavens; for the knowledge of this arcanum,
with the particular and most particular circumstances relating
to it, is the chief article of the intelligence of the angels; since
many other things depend upon it, which, without a knowledge
of this as their common centre, could not possibly enter distinctly
and clearly into their ideas. As they know that all the heavens,
together with their societies, are in form as one man, they also
call heaven the GRAND AND DIVINE MAN.([1]) They call it divine,
because the Divine Sphere of the Lord constitutes heaven, as
shown above, n. 7—12.

60. They who have not a just idea respecting such subjects,
cannot conceive that things spiritual and celestial can be arranged and conjoined into that form and image.   They imagine
that the earthly and material elements which compose the ultimate of man, are what make him such, and that he would not be
a man without them: But be it known to such, that a man is
not a man by virtue of having those elementary particles attached to him, but by virtue of his being endowed with a capacity to understand what is true and will what is good.   These are
spiritual and celestial things; and these are what constitute him
a man.   It is also generally known, that the quality of every
one, as a man, is such as is that of his understanding and will;
and it might be known, further, that his earthly body is formed
for the service, in the world, of those faculties, and to perform
uses in conformity with their behests in the ultimate sphere of
nature.   On this account, also, the body has no activity of itself, but is made to act in passive compliance with the pleasure
of the understanding and will; and this so absolutely, that what-

([1]) That heaven, in the whole complex, appears in form like a man, and that it is
thence called the Grand or Greatest Man, nn. 2996, 2998, 3624—3649, 3741—3745,
4625.

ever the man thinks, he utters with the tongue and lips, and whatever he pleases to do, he executes by the body and members, so that the understanding and will are the agent, and the body, of itself, not at all so. Hence it is evident, that the powers belonging to his understanding and will are what make the man; and that their form is like that of the body, because they act upon the most minute and individual parts and fibres of the body, as what is internal on what is external. Man, therefore, by virtue of those faculties, is called an internal and spiritual man. Such a man, in his greatest and most perfect form, is heaven.

61. Such is the idea which the angels entertain concerning man; wherefore they pay no attention whatever to the things which man does with the body, but to the will from which the body acts. This they call the man himself; and the understanding also, so far as it acts in unity with the will.[2]

62. The angels do not, indeed, see all heaven, collectively, in such a form, for the whole of heaven is too vast to be grasped by the sight of any angel; but they occasionally see distant societies, consisting of many thousands of angels, as one object in such a form; and from a society, as a part, they form their conclusion respecting the whole, which is heaven. For in a most perfect form, wholes are as their parts, and parts as their wholes; the only difference being like that between similar things of greater and less magnitude. Hence the angels say, that the whole heaven is such in the sight of the Lord, as a single society is when seen by them; because the Divine Being, from his inmost and supreme residence, sees all together.

63. Such being the form of heaven, it also is governed by the Lord as one man, and thus as one whole. For it is well known, although man consists of an innumerable variety of things, both in the whole and in part; consisting, *in the whole*, of members, organs, and viscera, and *in part*, of series of fibres, nerves, and blood-vessels; thus of members within members, and of parts within parts; that nevertheless, when he acts, he acts as one man. Such also is heaven, under the government and guidance of the Lord.

64. The reason that so many various things in man are as one, is, because there is nothing in him which does not contribute its share to the common good, and perform its proper use. The whole performs use to its parts, and the parts perform use to the whole: for the whole consists of the parts, and the parts constitute the whole: wherefore they provide for each other's necessities, have respect to each other's state, and are

[2] That the will of man is the very *esse* of his life, and that the understanding is the *existere* of his life thence derived, nn. 3619, 5002, 9282. That the life of the will is the principal life of man, and that the life of the understanding proceeds from it, nn. 585, 590, 3619, 7342, 8885, 9282, 10,076, 10,109, 10,110. That man is man by virtue of his will, and thence by virtue of his understanding, nn. 8911, 9069, 9071, 10,076, 10,109, 10,110.

combined in such a form, that they all, both generally and individually, act with reference to the whole and its good. Thus it is that they act as a one. It is in this manner that societies are connected together in the heavens. The inhabitants are there combined into such a form according to their capacity of performing uses; and they who contribute nothing to the good of the community, are cast out, as being foreign to the nature of heaven. To perform uses consists in cherishing good-will to others for the sake of the common good; but not to perform uses consists in cherishing good-will to others, not for the sake of the common good, but for that of self. These are the characters who love themselves above all things; but the former are those who love the Lord above all things. It is thus that the inhabitants of heaven are as a one, and that they are so, not from themselves, but from the Lord: for they regard Him as the One Only Being from whom all good proceeds, and his kingdom as the community whose good is to be sought. This is meant by the Lord's words, "*Seek ye first the kingdom of God, and his righteousness, and all these things shall be added unto you.*"— (Matt. vi. 33.) To seek his righteousness means, his good.[*] They who, in the world, love the good of their country more than their own, and that of their neighbor as their own, are those who, in the other life, love and seek the kingdom of God; for there the kingdom of God is in the place of their country; and they who love to do good to others, not for their own sake, but out of regard to good itself, are those who love their neighbor; for there, good is their neighbor.[+] All who are of such a character have a place in the Grand Man, that is, in heaven.

65. Since heaven, as a whole, resembles one man, and is, also, a Divine-spiritual man in the greatest form, even with respect to shape, it necessarily has the same distinctions, as to members and parts, as man has, bearing similar names. The angels, also, know in what member this or the other society is situated; which they express by saying, that this society is in the member, or in some province, of the head—that, in the member, or in some province, of the breast—that other, in the member, or in some province, of the loins; and so with respect to others. In general, the supreme or third heaven composes the head, as far as the neck; the middle or second heaven composes the breast or body, to the loins and knees; and the ultimate or first heaven composes the legs and feet down to the soles; as also, the arms down to the fingers; for the arms and hands are parts of the ul

(*) That justice, in the Word, is predicated of good, and judgment of truth; and hence to do justice and judgment is to do what is good and true, nn. 2235, 9857.
(+) That, in the supreme sense, the Lord is our neighbor; and hence that to love the Lord is to love that which is from Him, because in all which is from Him He is, thus it is to love what is good and true, nn. 2425, 3419, 6706, 6711, 6819, 6823, 8123. Hence, that all good which is from the Lord is the neighbor, and that to will and to do that good is to love our neighbor, nn. 5028, 10,336.

timates of man, though placed at the sides. Hence, again, it is evident why there are three heavens.

66. The spirits who are beneath heaven are exceedingly astonished, when they hear and see, that heaven is below as well as above : because they entertain the same belief and opinion as men do in the world, supposing heaven to be nowhere but over head. For they are not aware that the situation of the heavens is like that of the members, organs, and viscera, in man, some of which are above and others beneath ; and like the situation of the parts in every member, organ, and viscus, some of which are within and some without. Thus their ideas, on the subject of heaven, are all confusion.

67. These particulars are stated respecting heaven, as the Grand Man, because, without a knowledge of these facts, what further remains to be stated respecting heaven cannot possibly be comprehended. Neither can any distinct idea be conceived of the Form of Heaven, of the Conjunction of the Lord with Heaven, of the Conjunction of Heaven with Man, nor of the Influx of the Spiritual World into the Natural ; and none whatever respecting Correspondence ; of which subjects, in their order, we are to proceed to treat. To throw light upon them, therefore, the above is premised.

THAT EVERY SOCIETY IN THE HEAVENS IS IN FORM AS ONE MAN.

68. That every society of heaven is likewise as one man, and also has the form of a man, it has been occasionally granted me to see. There was a certain society, into which many spirits had insinuated themselves, who knew how to feign themselves to be angels of light, being hypocrites. When these were being separated from the angels, I saw that the whole society at first appeared as one indistinct mass; afterwards, by degrees, but still indistinctly, in the human form ; and at last, distinctly, as a man. They who were in that man, and composed him, were those that were grounded in the good proper to that society ; but the others, who were not in that man, and did not compose him, were hypocrites. These were rejected, and the others retained. Thus a separation was effected. Hypocrites are such as talk well, and also act well, but who, in whatever they say or do, have respect to themselves. They talk like angels about the Lord, about heaven, about love, and about the heavenly life: and they also act well, so as to appear to be such as their discourse would imply : but their thoughts are different : they believe nothing of what they say, and do not cherish good-will to any but themselves. When they do good, it is only for the sake

of themselves; and if they also do good for the sake of others, it is that they may have the reputation of it; and thus, st.ll, for the sake of themselves.

69. That a whole angelic society, when the Lord exhibits himself as present, appears as one object in a human f.rm, it has also been granted me to see. There appeared on high, towards the east, something like a cloud, inclining from white to red, and encompassed with little stars. It was descending; and as it descended, it became, by degrees, more clear, and at length was seen in a form perfectly human. The little stars surrounding the cloud were angels, who had that appearance in consequence of the light proceeding from the Lord.

70. It is to be observed, that although all who reside in one heavenly society, when seen together, appear as one object, having the likeness of a man, still one society does not compose exactly such a man as another does. They differ from each other like the faces of different persons of the same family. The cause of this is that mentioned above (n. 47); namely, that they vary as to form according to the varieties of good in which they are grounded, and by which their forms are determined. The societies which appear in the most perfect and beautiful human form, are those that compose the inmost or highest heaven, and which occupy its central region.

71. It is worthy of mention, that in proportion as the members of any heavenly society are more numerous, all acting as a one, the more perfect is the human form of that society; for variety, arranged in a heavenly form, produces perfection (as shown above, n. 56): and it is numbers that produce variety. Every society of heaven, also, increases in number daily; and as it does so, it also increases in perfection: the consequence of which is, that not only is that society rendered more perfect, but, also, heaven at large; for heaven at large is composed of its various societies. Since heaven advances in perfection as its inhabitants increase in multitude, it is evident how much they are mistaken who imagine, that heaven will be shut when full; whereas the contrary is the truth, namely, that it will never be shut, and that the greater its fulness the greater its perfection. There is nothing, therefore, which the angels more earnestly desire, than to receive additional angels, as new guests, among them.

72. The reason that every society, on being viewed together, appears as one object in the shape of a man, is, because heaven at large has that shape (as shown in the preceding section); and in a form that is most perfect, such as that of heaven, the parts bear the likeness of the whole, and the smaller objects that of the greatest. The smaller objects and parts of heaven, are the societies of which it consists; which, also, are heavens on a smaller scale (as shown above, nn. 51—58). The reason that such

32

a likeness constantly prevails, is, because, in the heavens, the
kinds of good in which all are grounded are derived from one
love, thus from one source; and the single love from which is
the source of all the kinds of good which prevail there, is love
to the Lord derived from Himself. Hence, heaven, as a whole,
is His likeness in general; every society, less generally; and
every angel, in particular. (See, also, what was said on this
subject above, n. 58.)

THAT HENCE EVERY ANGEL IS IN A PERFECT HUMAN FORM.

73. It has been shown in the two preceding Sections, that
heaven, taken collectively, is in form as one man; and every society in heaven likewise: and it follows in order, from the causes
there stated, that the same is true respecting every angel. As
heaven is a man in the greatest form, and every society in a less,
so is every angel in the least; for in a most perfect form, such
as that of heaven, the whole has its likeness in every part, and
every part in the whole. The reason of this is, because heaven
is a communion; for it communicates all that belongs to it, to
every inhabitant, and every inhabitant receives all that belongs
to him from that communion. An angel is a receptacle of what
is thus communicated; whence, also, he is a heaven in miniature (as shown, in a specific Section, above). So also man, so
far as he receives heaven in himself, is such a receptacle, is a
heaven, and is an angel (see above, n. 57). This is described in
the Revelation in these words: "*And he measured the wall
thereof, a hundred and forty and four cubits; according to the
measure of a man, that is, of an angel*" (ch. xxi. 17). Jerusalem,
there spoken of, is the Lord's church, and, in a more exalted
sense, heaven :([1]) its wall is truth, as protecting it from the attacks
of falsities and evils :([2]) the number a hundred and forty-four
denotes all truths and goods collectively :([3]) the measure means
its quality :([4]) a man is the subject in whom they all have their
residence, in general and in particular, thus, in whom heaven
abides: and because an angel is also a man by virtue of his receiving those endowments. therefore it is said, "the measure of a

---

([1]) That Jerusalem is the church, nn. 402, 3654, 9166.
([2]) That a wall denotes truth that protects from the assault of falsities and of evils,
n. 6419.
([3]) That twelve denotes all truths and goods in the complex, nn. 577, 2089, 2129,
2130, 3272, 3858, 3913. In like manner seventy-two, and a hundred and forty-four,
since a hundred and forty-four arises from twelve multiplied into itself, n. 7973.
That all numbers, in the Word, signify things, nn. 482, 487, 647, 648, 755, 813, 1963,
1988, 2075, 2252, 3252, 4264, 4495, 5265. That numbers multiplied signify the same
with the simple ones from which they arise by multiplication, nn. 5291, 5335, 5708,
7973.
([4]) That measure, in the Word, signifies the quality of a thing as to truth and good,
nn. 3104, 9603.

man, that is, of an angel."(⁵)* This is the spiritual sense of those words; and without that sense who could understand what is meant by the wall of the holy Jerusalem being "the measure of a man, that is, of an angel?"

74. But to certify this from experience. That angels are human forms, or men, I have seen a thousand times : for I have conversed with them as one man does with another, sometimes with one alone, and sometimes with many in company : nor did I ever see in them any thing differing, as to their form, from man. I have sometimes wondered at finding them such ; and lest it should be objected that I was deceived by some fallacy or visionary fancy, it has been granted me to see them when I was wide awake, or when all my bodily senses were in activity, and I was in a state to perceive every thing clearly. I have also frequently told them, that men in the Christian world are in such gross ignorance respecting angels and spirits, as to suppose them to be minds without a form, or mere thoughts, of which they have no other idea than as something ethereal possessing a vital principle ; and as they thus attribute to them nothing belonging to man except a faculty of thinking, they imagine that they cannot see, being without eyes, nor hear, being without ears, nor speak, having neither mouth nor tongue. The angels said in reply, that they are aware that such a belief exists with many in the world, and that it particularly prevails among the learned, and also, at which they marvelled, among the clergy. They also explained the reason of this ; namely, that the learned, who had been guides of others, and who first broached such notions about angels and spirits, thought respecting them from the sensual apprehensions of the external man ; and they who think from their sensual apprehensions, and not from interior light, and from the general idea inherent in every one, cannot but form such inventions, since the sensual faculties of the external man can comprehend nothing but what is within the sphere of nature, and not any thing above that sphere, consequently, nothing whatever that relates to the spiritual world.(⁶) From these authorities, as leaders, that erroneous mode of thinking respecting angels was derived to others, who did not think for themselves, but took their opinions from them ; and those who first take their opinions from others, and make them

---

(*) Respecting the spiritual or internal sense of the Word, see the little tract on *the White Horse mentioned in the Revelation,* and the Appendix to the chapter on the Word in the *New Jerusalem and its Heavenly Doctrine.*

(⁶) That man, unless he be elevated above the sensual principles of the external man, makes little progress in wisdom, n. 5089. That a wise man thinks above those sensual principles, nn. 5089, 5094. That when man is elevated above those sensual principles, he comes into a clearer light, and at length into heavenly light, nn. 6183, 6313, 6315, 9407, 9730, 9922. That elevation and abstraction from those sensual principles was known to the ancients, n. 6313.

* "*An* angel" is the correct translation; not "*the* angel," as in the common version.--*N.*

points of faith with themselves, and afterwards view them as such from their own understanding, can with difficulty give them up; wherefore they usually rest satisfied with confirming them as true. The angels said, further, that the simple in faith and heart do not form such conceptions respecting angels, but have an idea of them as heavenly men, by reason that they have not extinguished, by erudition, their inherent perception, derived from heaven, and can conceive of nothing as being without form. Hence it is, that angels are never represented in churches, either in sculpture or in painting, otherwise than as men. Of that inherent faculty of perception derived from heaven, they said, that it is the Divine Sphere entering by influx with those who are grounded in good as to faith and life.

75. From all my experience, and which I have now enjoyed for many years, I can declare and affirm, that angels, as to form, are in every respect men; that they have faces, eyes, ears, a body, arms, hands, feet, and that they see, hear, and converse with each other; in short, that they are deficient in nothing that belongs to a man, except that they are not super-invested with a material body. I have seen them in their own light, which exceeds in brightness, by many degrees, the noonday light of the word; and in that light I have beheld all the features of their faces more distinctly and clearly than it is possible to see the features of men on earth. It also has been granted me to see an angel of the inmost heaven. His face was more bright and resplendent than those of the angels of the lower heavens. I examined him; and I can declare, that he had the human form in its utmost perfection.

76. But it is to be observed, that angels cannot be seen by man with the eyes of his body, but only with the eyes of the spirit which is within man,([7]) because this is in the spiritual world, whereas all the parts of the body are in the natural world. Like sees like, because from a like ground. Besides, the organ of sight belonging to the body, which is the eye, is so obtuse, that, as is known to every one, it cannot even discern, except by the aid of optical glasses, the smaller objects of nature;— much less can it discern objects which are above the sphere of nature, as are all those of the spiritual world. These, however, may be seen by man, when he is withdrawn from the sight of his body, and that of his spirit is opened. This, also, is done in an instant, when it is the pleasure of the Lord that the things of the spiritual world should be seen by man; nor is he at all aware, at the time, that he does not behold him with the eyes of his body. It was thus that angels were seen by Abraham, Lot, Manoah, and the prophets: it was thus that the Lord was

([7]) That man, as to his interiors, is a spirit, n. 1594. And that the spirit is the man himself, and that the body lives from it, nn. 447, 4622, 6054.

seen by the disciples after his resurrection: and it was thus, also, that angels have been seen by me. As the prophets enj)yed this mode of vision, they were therefore called *seers, and men whose eyes were open* (1 Sam. ix. 9; Num. xxiii. 3); and to cause them to see in this way was called *opening their eyes;* as was done to Elisha's servant, of whom we read, "And Elisha prayed, and said, Jehovah, *I pray thee, open his eyes, that he may see. And Jehovah opened the eyes of the young man; and he saw:* and, behold, the mountain was full of horses and chariots of fire round about Elisha."—(2 Kings vi. 17.)

77. Good spirits, with whom, also, I have conversed on this subject, were deeply grieved that such ignorance respecting the state of heaven, and respecting spirits and angels, should prevail in the church; and they desired me, with indignation, to say from them, that they are not formless minds, nor ethereal puffs of breath, but they are men as to shape, and that they see, hear, and possess every sense, equally with men in the world.[*]

THAT IT IS BY DERIVATION FROM THE LORD'S DIVINE HUMANITY, THAT HEAVEN, BOTH IN THE WHOLE AND IN ITS PARTS, IS IN FORM AS A MAN.

78. That it is by derivation from the Lord's Divine Humanity, that heaven, both in the whole and in its parts, is in form as a man, follows as a conclusion from all that has been advanced and shown in the preceding Sections. It has there been shown, I. *That the Lord is the God of heaven:* II. *That the Divine Sphere of the Lord constitutes heaven:* III. *That heaven consists of innumerable societies; and that each society is a heaven on a smaller scale, and every angel is a heaven in miniature:* IV. *That the whole heaven, viewed collectively, is in form as one man:* V. *That every society in the heavens is also in form as one man:* VI. *That thence every angel is in a perfect human form.* All these truths point to this conclusion: That the Divine Being, whose Proceeding Sphere is what constitutes heaven, is Human in form. That this is the Lord's Divine Humanity, will be still more clearly seen, because in a compendious form, from the extracts which, by way of corollary, are adduced below from the *Arcana Cœlestia.* That the Lord's Humanity is Divine, and that it is not true, as generally believed in the church, that His Humanity is not Divine, may also be seen

---

[*] That every angel, inasmuch as he is a recipient of Divine Order from the Lord, is in a human form, perfect and beautiful according to such reception, nn. 322, 1880, 1881, 3633, 3804, 4622, 4735, 4797, 4985, 5199, 5530, 6054, 9879, 10,177, 10,594. That the Divine Truth is the principle by which order is effected, and the Divine Good is the essential of order, nn. 2451, 3166, 4390, 4409, 5232, 7256, 10,122, 10,555.

from those Extracts; and likewise, from the *Doctrine of the New Jerusalem*, near the end, in the Section respecting the Lord.

79. That such is the fact, has been evinced to me by much experience, part of which shall now be related. No angel in all the heavens ever has a perception of the Divine Being under any other form than the Human; and, what is wonderful, those who inhabit the superior heavens cannot think of the Divine Being in any other manner. They derive the necessity of so thinking from the Divine Sphere itself which enters them by influx; and also, from the form of heaven, according to which their thoughts diffuse themselves around. For every thought conceived by the angels diffuses itself into heaven round about them, and they enjoy intelligence and wisdom according to the extent of that diffusion. Hence it is that all in heaven acknowledge the Lord, because there is no Divine Humanity except in Him. These truths have not only been related to me by the angels, but it has also been granted me to have a perception of them myself, when I have been elevated into the interior sphere of heaven. Hence it is evident, that the wiser the angels are, the more clearly do they perceive this truth. Hence also it is, that the Lord appears to them: for the Lord appears in a Divine Angelic Form, which is the Human, to those who acknowledge and believe in a visible Divine Being, but not to the worshippers of an invisible Divinity: for the former can see their God; but the latter cannot.

80. As the angels have no perception of an invisible Divine Being, which they call a God without form, but of a Divine Being visible in Human Form, it is common with them to say, that the Lord Alone is a Man, and that they are men by derivation from Him; also, that every one is a man in proportion as he receives Him. By receiving the Lord, they mean, to receive good and truth, which are from Him; since the Lord is in His own good and His own truth. This, also, they call wisdom and intelligence: they say, that every one may know that intelligence and wisdom are what constitute a man, and not a human face without them. That such is the fact, is also apparent from the angels of the interior heavens. Being grounded in good and truth, and thence in wisdom and intelligence, from the Lord, they appear in the most beautiful and most perfect human form. The angels of the lower heavens also appear in a human form, though not so perfect and beautiful. But in hell, the case is reversed. Its inhabitants, when seen in the light of heaven, scarcely appear as men at all, but as monsters: for they are grounded in evil and falsity, not in goodness and truth, and thence in the opposites to wisdom and intelligence: wherefore, also, their life is not called life, but spiritual death.

81. Since heaven, both in the whole and in its parts, presents the form of a man, by derivation from the Lord's Divine Hu-

manity, it is customary for the angels to say, that they are in the Lord; and some, that they are in his body, by which they mean, in the good of his love: as, also, the Lord himself teaches, saying, "*Abide in Me, and I in you. As the branch cannot bear fruit of itself, except it abide in the vine; no more can ye, except ye abide in Me.——For without Me, ye can do nothing. ——Continue ye in My love. If ye keep My commandments, ye shall abide in My love.*"—(John xv. 4—10.)

82. Since such is the perception respecting the Divine Being that exists in heaven, it is inherent in every man, who receives any influx from heaven, to think of God under a Human Shape. Thus did the ancients: thus also do the moderns, those without the church as well as those within it: simple persons view him in thought as an Old Man surrounded with brightness. But this inherent perception has been extinguished by all those who exclude the influx from heaven, either by self-derived intelligence, or by a life of evil: those who have extinguished it by self-derived intelligence, will have none but an invisible God; and they who have done so by a life of evil, no God at all. Neither class is aware that any such inherent perception exists, since it does not exist with them; and yet this is that very Divine celestial principle which primarily enters man by influx from heaven, because man is born for heaven, and none can go there without an idea of the Divine Being.

83. Hence it results, that he who is destitute of a right idea of heaven, that is, of an idea of the Divine Being from whom heaven exists, cannot be elevated to the lowest threshold of the heavenly kingdom. As soon as he approaches it, he is sensible of a resistance, and a strong repelling effort: the reason is, because, in him, the interiors, which should be open for the reception of heaven, are closed, because they are not in the form of heaven; indeed, the nearer he comes to heaven, they are closed the more tightly. Such is the lot of those within the church who deny the Lord, and of those who, like the Socinians, deny his Divinity. But what is the lot of those who are born without the church, to whom the Lord is not known because they are not in possession of the Word, will be seen in the following pages.

84. That the ancients had an idea of Humanity connected with their idea of the Divine Being, is evident from his appearances to Abraham, Lot, Joshua, Gideon, Manoah, his wife, and others; all of whom, though they saw God as a Man, nevertheless worshipped him as the God of the universe, calling him the God of heaven and earth, and Jehovah. That it was the Lord who was seen by Abraham, He teaches himself in John (Ch. viii. 56): and that it was He, also, who appeared to the others, is evident from His words, when He said, "*Ye have neither heard His [the Father's] voice at any time, nor seen His shape*" (Ch. v. 37; i. 18).

38

85. But that God is a Man, can with difficulty be conceived by those who judge of every thing from the sensual apprehensions of the external man. For a sensual man can only think of the Divine Being from the world and its objects; thus he can only think of a Divine and Spiritual Man as of a corporeal and natural man. Hence he concludes, that if God were a man, he must be as big as the universe; and that if, as a Man, he governs heaven and earth, he must do it by a multitude of lieutenants, as kings govern their distant provinces in the world. If he were told, that in heaven there is not extension of space, such as exists in the world, he would not comprehend it: for he who thinks solely from nature and its light, can form no idea of any other sort of extension than such as is before his eyes. They are, however, exceedingly mistaken when they apply such ideas to heaven. The extension which there exists is not such as that in the world; for extension, in the world, is determinate, and thence capable of being measured; but extension, in heaven, is not determinate, and thence not capable of mensuration: but respecting extension in heaven see a subsequent Section, treating of space and time in the Spiritual World. Besides, every one knows how amazingly far the sight of the eye can reach, even to the sun and the stars, of which the distances from us are so enormous; every one, also, who thinks deeply, is aware, that the internal sight, which is that of the thought, can reach still further; and, consequently, that a sight still more interior must have a wider range still: what then can be beyond the reach of the Divine Sight, which is the inmost and highest of all? Since the thoughts have such an extension, all things belonging to heaven are communicated to every inhabitant; consequently, all things belonging to the Divine Sphere which constitutes heaven, and fills it, are thus communicated—as shown in the preceding Sections.

86. The inhabitants of heaven are astonished, that men should imagine themselves intelligent, while they think of God as an invisible Being, that is, as incomprehensible under any form; and that they should call those who think differently, not intelligent, and mere simpletons; whereas the contrary is the truth. The angels say, " If such self-esteemed intelligent ones were to examine themselves, would they not find that they regard nature as God? some of them, nature as existing before the sight, and some of them, nature in her invisible recesses? And are they not blinded to such a degree, as not to know what God is, what an angel is, what a spirit, what their own soul which is to live after death, what the life of heaven in man; with other subjects belonging to intelligence? When, nevertheless, those whom they call simpletons understand all these points in their own way. Of their God, they have an idea, that He is a Divine Being in a Human Form; of an angel, that he is a heavenly

man; of their own soul which is to live after death, that it is such a being as an angel; and of the life of heaven in man. that it consists in living according to the divine commandments." These, therefore, the angels call intelligent, and fitted for heaven; but the others, on the contrary, not intelligent.[1]

[1] *Extracts from the* ARCANA CŒLESTIA, *respecting the Lord and respecting His Divine Humanity.*

That the Lord had a Divine Essence from conception itself, nn. 4641, 4963, 5041, 5157, 6716, 10,125. That the Lord alone had Divine seed, n. 1438. That His soul was Jehovah, nn. 1999, 2004, 2005, 2018, 2025. That thus the inmost of the Lord was the Essential Divinity, and that the clothing was from the mother, n. 5041. That the Essential Divinity was the *Esse* of the Lord's life, from which the Humanity afterwards went forth, and was made the *Existere* from that *Esse*, nn. 3194, 3210, 10,370, 10,372.

That within the church, where the Word is, and where, by it, the Lord is known, the Divine Essence of the Lord ought not to be denied, nor the Holy Emanation proceeding from him, n. 2359. That those within the church who do not acknowledge the Lord, have no conjunction with the Divine Being: it is otherwise with those who are out of the church, n. 10,205. That it is an essential of the church to acknowledge the Lord's Divinity, and His union with the Father, nn. 10,083, 10,112, 10,370, 10,738, 10,730, 10,816, 10,817, 10,818, 10,820.

That the subject treated of in the Word, in many passages, is the glorification of the Lord, n. 10,828. And that this subject is everywhere treated of in the internal sense of the Word, nn. 2249, 2523, 3245. That the Lord glorified His Humanity, and not His Divinity, because the latter was glorified in itself, n. 10,057. That the Lord came into the world that He might glorify His Humanity, nn. 3637, 4180, 9315. That the Lord glorified His Humanity by the Divine Love which was in Himself from conception, n. 4727. That the love of the Lord towards the universal human race was the life of the Lord in the world, n. 2253. That the Lord's love transcends all human understanding, n. 2077. That the Lord saved the human race by glorifying His Humanity, nn. 4180, 10,019, 10,152, 10,655, 10,659, 10,828. That otherwise the whole human race would have perished in eternal death, n. 1676. Of the Lord's states of glorification and humiliation, nn. 1785, 1999, 2159, 6866. That glorification, where it is predicated of the Lord, denotes the uniting of His Humanity with His Divinity, and that to glorify is to make Divine, nn. 1603, 10,053, 10,828. That the Lord, when He glorified His Humanity, put off all the humanity derived from the mother, until at length He was not her son, nn. 2159, 2574, 2649, 3036, 10,830.

That the Son of God from eternity was the Divine Truth in heaven, nn. (2628,) (2798,) 2803, 3195, 3704. That the Lord also made His Humanity Divine Truth from the Divine Good which was in Him, when He was in the world, nn. 2803, 3194, 3195, 3210, 6716, 6864, 7014, 7499, 8127, 8724, 9199. That the Lord at that time arranged all things appertaining to Himself into a celestial form, which is according to Divine Truth, nn. 1928, 3633. That on this account the Lord was called the Word, which is the Divine Truth, nn. 2533, 2813, 2859, 2894, 3393, 3712. That the Lord alone had perception and thought from Himself, and above all angelic perception and thought, nn. 1904, 1914, 1919.

That the Lord united the Divine Truth, which was Himself. with the Divine Good, which was in himself, nn. 10,047, 10,062, 10,076. That the union was reciprocal, nn. 2004, 10,067. That the Lord, when He departed from the world. made His Humanity also Divine Good, nn. 3194, 3210, 6864, 7499, 8724, 9199, 10,076. That this is meant by His coming forth from the Father, and returning to the Father, nn. 3736, 3210. That that was made One with the Father, nn. 2751, 3704, 4766. That since the union, the Divine Truth proceeds from the Lord, nn. 3704, 3712, 3969, 4577, 5704, 7499, 8127, 8241, 9199, 9398. In what manner the Divine Truth proceeds, illustrated, nn. 7270, 9407. That the Lord, from His own proper power, united the Humanity with the Divinity, nn. 1616, 1749, 1752, 1813, 1921, 2025, 2026, 2523, 3141, 5005, 5045, 6716. That hence it may be manifest, that the Humanity of the Lord was not as the humanity of another man, because he was conceived from the Divine Being Himself, nn. 10,125, 10,826. That His union with the Father, from whom He had His soul, was not like that between two persons, but like that between the soul and the body, nn. 3737, 10,824.

That the most ancient people could not adore the Divine *Esse*, but the Divine *Existere*, which is the Divine Humanity, and that the Lord therefore came into the world, that He might be made the Divine *Existere* from the Divine *Esse*, nn. 4687, 5321. That the ancients acknowledged the Divine Being, because He appeared to them in a human form, and that this was the Divine Humanity, nn. 5110, 5663, 6846, 10,737.

40

THAT THERE IS A CORRESPONDENCE BETWEEN ALL THINGS BE-
LONGING TO HEAVEN, AND ALL THINGS BELONGING TO MAN.

87. It is unknown at this day what correspondence is. This
ignorance is owing to various causes; the chief of which is, that

That the Infinite *Esse* could not flow into heaven with the angels, nor with men,
except by or through the Divine Humanity, nn. (1646,) 1990, 2016, 2034. That in
heaven, no other Divine Being is perceived but the Divine Humanity, nn. 6475, 9303,
(9367,) 10,067. That the Divine Humanity from eternity was the Divine Truth in
heaven, and the Divine Emanation passing through heaven, thus the Divine *Existere*,
which afterwards in the Lord was made the Divine *Esse* by Itself, from which is the
Divine *Existere* in heaven, nn. 3061, 6280, 8880, 10,579. What was the quality of the
state of heaven before the coming of the Lord, nn. 6371, 6372, 6373. That the Divine
Emanation was not perceptible, except when it had passed through heaven, nn. 6982,
6996, 7004.
That the inhabitants of all the earths adore the Divine Being under a human form,
thus the Lord, nn. 6700, 8541—8547, 10,736, 10,737, 10,738. That they rejoice when
they hear that God was actually made a Man, n. 9361. That the Lord receives all who
are in good, and who adore the Divine Being under a human form, n. 9359. That
God cannot be thought of except in a human form, and that what is incomprehensible
falls into no idea, thus is no object of faith, nn. 9359, 9972. That man is capable of
worshipping what he has some idea of, but not what he has no idea of, nn. 4733, 5110,
5633, 7211, 9356, 10,067. That, therefore, by the generality in the universal terrestrial globe, the Divine Being is worshipped under a human form, and that this is the
effect of an influx from heaven, n. 10,159. That all who are principled in good as to
life, when they think of the Lord, think of a Divine Humanity, and not of the Humanity separate from the Divinity; it is otherwise with those who are not principled
in good as to life, nn. 2326, 4724, 4731, 4766, 8878, 9193, 9198. That in the church at
this day, those who are in evil as to life, also who are in faith separate from charity,
think of the Humanity of the Lord without the Divinity, and likewise do not comprehend what a Divine Humanity is; and the reasons thereof, nn. 3212, 3241, 4689,
4692, 4724, 4731, 5321, (6372,) 8878, 9193, 9198. That the Humanity of the Lord is
Divine, because from the *Esse* of the Father, which was His soul, illustrated by the
likeness of the father in the children, nn. 10,269, (10,372,) 10,823: and because it was
from the Divine Love, which was the very *Esse* of His life from conception, n. 6872.
That every man is such as his love is, and that he is his own love, nn. 6872, 10,177,
10,284. That the Lord made all the Humanity, both internal and external, Divine, nn.
1603, 1815, 1902, 1926, 2093, 2083. That, therefore, He rose again as to the whole
body, differently from any man, nn. 1729, 2083, 5078, 10,825.
That the Humanity of the Lord is Divine, is acknowledged from His omnipresence
in the holy supper, nn. 2343, (2359,) and from His transfiguration before His three disciples, n. 3212: and also from the Word of the Old Testament, in which His Humanity
is called God, n. 10,254; and is called Jehovah, nn. (1603,) 1736, 1815, 1902, 2921,
3035, 5110, 6281, 6303, 8864, 9194, 9315. That a distinction is made in the sense of
the letter between the Father and the Son, or between Jehovah and the Lord, but not
in the internal sense of the Word, in which the angels of heaven are, n. 3035. That
in the Christian world, the Humanity of the Lord has been acknowledged to be not
Divine, and this was effected in a council for the sake of the Pope, that he might be
acknowledged as his vicar, n. 4738.
That Christians in the other life were explored as to the idea they held concerning
one God, and that it was found that they had an idea of three Gods, nn. 2329, 5256,
10,736, 10,737, 10,738, 10,821. That a Trinity or Divine Trine, may be conceived of
in one person, and thus one God, but not in three persons, nn. 10,738, 1815, 10,821, 10,824.
That the Divine Trine in the Lord is acknowledged in heaven, nn. 14, 15, 1729, 2005,
5256, 9303. That the Trine in the Lord is the Essential Divinity, which is called the
Father, the Divine Humanity, which is called the Son, and the Divine Proceeding,
which is called the Holy Spirit; and that this Divine Trine is One, nn. 2149, 2156,
2288, 2321, 2329, 2447, 3704, 6993, 7182, 10,733, 10,822, 10,823. That the Lord Himself teaches that the Father and He are One, nn. 1729, 2004, 2005, 2018, 2025, 2751,
3704, 3736, 4766; and that the Holy Divine Emanation proceeds from Him, and is His,
nn. 3569, 4673, 6788, 6993, 7499, 8127, 8302, 9199, (9228,) 9229, 9270, 9407, 9818, 9829,
10,330.
That the Divine Humanity flows into heaven, and constitutes heaven, n. 3088.
That the Lord is the all in heaven, and that He is the life of heaven, nn. 7211, (9128.)

man has removed himself from heaven, through cherishing the love of self and of the world. For he that supremely loves himself and the world, cares only for worldly things, because they soothe the external senses and are agreeable to his natural disposition ; but has no concern about spiritual things, because these only soothe the internal senses, and are agreeable to the internal or rational mind. These, therefore, they cast aside, saying, that they are too high for man's comprehension. Not so did the ancients. With them, the science of correspondences was the chief of all sciences ; by means of its discoveries, also, they imbibed intelligence and wisdom ; and such of them as belonged to the church had by it communication with heaven ; for the science of correspondences is the science of angels. The most ancient people, who were celestial men, absolutely thought from correspondence, as do the angels ; whence, also, they conversed with angels ; and whence, likewise, the Lord often appeared to them, communicating instruction. But, at the present day, that science is so utterly lost, that it is even unknown what correspondence is.([1])

88. Without an apprehension of what correspondence is, not any thing can be clearly known respecting the spiritual world ; nor respecting its influx into the natural world ; nor, indeed, respecting what that which is spiritual is, compared with that which is natural ; since, also, nothing can be clearly known respecting the spirit of man, which is called the soul, and its operation upon the body ; nor yet concerning the state of man

That the Lord dwells in the angels in what is His own, nn. 9338, 10,125, 10,151, 10,157. That hence those who are in heaven are in the Lord, nn. 3637, 3638. That the conjunction of the Lord with the angels is according to the reception of the good of love and of charity from Him, nn. 904, 4198, 4205, 4211, 4220, (6280,) 6832, 7042, 8819, 9680, 9682, 9683, (10,106,) (10,811.) That the universal heaven has reference to the Lord, nn. 551, 552. That the Lord is the common centre of heaven, nn. 3633. That all in heaven turn themselves to the Lord, who is above the heavens, nn. 9828, 10,130, 10,189. That nevertheless the angels do not turn themselves to the Lord, but the Lord turns them to Himself, n. 10,189. That there is not a presence of the angels with the Lord, but a presence of the Lord with the angels, n. 9415. That in heaven there is no conjunction with the Essential Divinity, but with the Divine Humanity, nn. 4211, 4724, (5633.)

That heaven corresponds with the Divine Humanity of the Lord ; and that thence heaven at large is as one man; and that on this account heaven is called the Grand Man, nn. 2996, 2998, 3624—3649, 3741—3745, 4625. That the Lord is the Only Man, and those only are men who receive what is Divine from Him, n. 1894. That so far as they receive, so far they are men, and not images of Him, n. 8547. That therefore the angels are forms of love and charity in a human form, and that this is from the Lord, nn. 3804, 4735, 4797, 4985, 5199, 5530, 9879, 10,177.

That the universal heaven is the Lord's, nn. 2751, 7086. That He has all power in the heavens and on earth, nn. 1607, 10,089, 10,827. That the Lord rules the universal heaven, and that he also rules all things which thence depend, thus all things in the world, nn. 2026, 2027, 4523, 4524. That the Lord alone has the power of removing the hells, of withholding from evils, and of holding in good, thus of saving, n. 10,919.

([1]) How far the science of correspondences excels other sciences, n. 4280. That the chief science amongst the ancients was the science of correspondences, but at this day it is obliterated, nn. 3024, 3419, 4280, 4749, 4844, 4964, 4966, 6004, 7729, 10,252. That with the orientals, and in Egypt, the science of correspondences flourished, nn. 5702, 6692, 7097, 7779, 9391, 10,407.

after death : therefore it is necessary to show what correspondence is, and what its nature : which, also, will prepare the way
for what is to follow.

89. It shall first be stated what correspondence is. The whole
natural world corresponds to the spiritual world ; and not only
the natural world collectively, but also in its individual parts :
wherefore every object in the natural world existing from some
thing in the spiritual world, is called its correspondent. It is to
be observed, that the natural world exists and subsists from the
spiritual world, just as the effect exists from its efficient cause.
All *that* is called the natural world, which lies below the sun,
and thence receives its heat and light; and all the objects
which thence subsist belong to that world : but the spiritual
world is heaven ; and the objects of that world are all that are
in the heavens.

90. Since man is both a heaven and a world in miniature,
formed after the image of heaven and the world at large (see
above, n. 57), he, also, has belonging to him both a spiritual
world and a natural world. The interiors, which belong to his
mind, and have relation to his understanding and will, constitute his spiritual world ; but his exteriors, which belong to his
body, and have reference to its senses and actions, constitute his
natural world. Whatever, therefore, exists in his natural world,
that is, in his body, with its senses and actions, by derivation
from his spiritual world, that is, from his mind, with its understanding and will, is called its correspondent.

91. The nature of correspondence may be seen from the face
in man. In a countenance which has not been taught to dis-
semble, all the affections of the mind display themselves visibly,
in a natural form, as in their type ; whence the face is called
the index of the mind. Thus man's spiritual world shows itself
in his natural world. In the same manner, the ideas of his
understanding reveal themselves in his speech, and the determinations of his will in the gestures of his body. All things,
therefore, which take effect in the body, whether in the countenance, the speech, or the gestures, are called correspondences.

92. From these observations may also be seen what the internal man is, and what the external ; or, that the internal is
that which is called the spiritual man, and the external that
which is called the natural man. Also, that the one is distinct
from the other, as heaven is from the world ; and likewise, that
all things which take effect, and exist, in the external or natural
man, so take effect and exist from the internal or spiritual.

93. Thus much respecting the correspondence between the
internal or spiritual man, and the external or natural : in what
follows we shall treat of the correspondence of the whole of
heaven with all the individual parts of man.

94. It has been shown, that the universal heaven is as one man, and that it is in form a man, and is therefore called the Grand Man. It has also been shown, that the angelic societies, of which heaven consists, are hence arranged in the same order as the members, organs, and viscera in man; so that there are some that have their station in the head, some in the breast, some in the arms, and some in every distinct part of those members (see above, n. 59—72). The societies, therefore, which are in any member in heaven, correspond to the same member in man. For instance: the societies which are there in the head, correspond to the head in man: those which are there in the breast, correspond to the breast in man: those that are there in the arms, correspond with the arms in man: and so with the rest. It is from that correspondence that man subsists; for man derives his subsistence solely from heaven.

95. That heaven is divided into two kingdoms, one of which is called the celestial kingdom and the other the spiritual kingdom, has been shown in a particular Section, above. The celestial kingdom in general corresponds to the heart and to all the parts related to the heart in the whole body: and the spiritual kingdom corresponds to the lungs, and to all the parts in the whole body related to that organ. The heart and lungs, also, constitute two kingdoms in man; for the heart reigns throughout his body by the arteries and veins, and the lungs by the nervous and motive fibres; both being concerned in every power he exercises, and in every action he performs. In the spiritual world of every man, which is called his spiritual man, there are also two kingdoms; one being that of the will, and the other that of the understanding. The will reigns by means of the affections of good, and the understanding by means of the affections of truth. These kingdoms also correspond to the kingdoms of the heart and the lungs in the body. The like obtains in the heavens. The celestial kingdom is the will-principle of heaven; and in that kingdom reigns the good of love; and the spiritual kingdom is the intellectual principle of heaven; and what reigns in that kingdom is truth. These are the things which correspond to the functions of the heart and lungs in man. It is in consequence of that correspondence, that the heart, in the Word, signifies the will, and also the good of love; and that the breath, which belongs to the lungs, signifies the understanding, and the truth of faith. Hence, also, it is, that it is usual to ascribe the affections to the heart; though that is not their seat, nor do they flow from thence.[2]

---

[2] Of the correspondence of the heart and lungs with the Grand Man, which is heaven, from experience, nn. 3883—3896. That the heart corresponds to those who dwell in the celestial kingdom, but the lungs to those who dwell in the spiritual kingdom, nn. 3885, 3886, 3887. That in heaven there is a pulse like that of the heart, and a respiration like that of the lungs, but more interior, nn. 3884, 3885, 3887. That the pulse of the heart is various there according to the states of love; and the respiration

96. The correspondence between the two kingdoms of heaven and the heart and lungs, is the most general correspondence between heaven and man. A less general one is that between heaven and the several members, organs, and viscera, of man ; the nature of which shall also be mentioned.

In the Grand Man, who is heaven, they that are stationed in the head, are in the enjoyment of every good above all others : for they are in the enjoyment of love, peace, innocence, wisdom, and intelligence ; and thence of joy and happiness. These have an influx into the head, and into whatever appertains to the head, with man, and corresponds thereto. In the Grand Man, who is heaven, they that are stationed in the breast, are in the enjoyment of the good of charity and faith : their influx, also, with man, is into the breast ; to which they correspond. But, in the Grand Man, or heaven, they that are stationed in the loins, and in the organs belonging to generation therewith connected, are they who are eminently grounded in conjugial love. They who are stationed in the feet, are grounded in the ultimate good of heaven, which is called spiritual-natural good. They who are in the arms and hands, are in the power of truth derived from good. They who are in the eyes, are those eminent for understanding. They who are in the ears are in attention and obedience. They in the nostrils, are those distinguished for perception. They in the mouth and tongue, are such as excel in discoursing from understanding and perception. They in the kidneys, are such as are grounded in truth of a searching, distinguishing, and castigatory character. They in the liver, pancreas, and spleen, are grounded in the purification of good and truth by various methods. So with those in the other members and organs. All have an influx into the similar parts of man, and correspond to them. The influx of heaven takes place into the functions and uses of the members ; and their uses, being from the spiritual world, invest themselves with forms by means of such materials as are found in the natural world, and so present themselves in effects. Hence there is a correspondence between them.

97. On this account it is, that by those same members, organs, and viscera, are signified, in the Word, such things as have just been mentioned ; for all things named in the Word have a signification according to their correspondence. Hence, by the head is signified intelligence and wisdom ; by the breast, charity ; by the loins, conjugial love ; by the arms and hands, the power of truth ; by the eyes, understanding ; by the nostrils, perception ; by the ears obedience ; by the kidneys, the

according to the states of charity and faith. nn. 3886, 3887, 3889. That the heart, in the Word, denotes the will, thus that what is from the heart is from the will. nn. 2930, 7542, 8910, 9113, 10,036. That the heart also, in the Word, signifies the love ; thus that what is done from the heart is done from the love, nn. 7542, 9050, 10,336.

purification of truth; and so with the rest.(³) Hence, also, it is
usual to say in familiar discourse, when speaking of an intelligent and wise person, that he has a head; when alluding to
one who is influenced by charity, that he is a bosom friend; of
a person eminent for perception, that he has a good nose (or a
sharp scent); of one distinguished for intelligence, that he is
sharp-sighted: of one possessing great power, that he has long
arms; of a person that speaks or acts from love, that he says or
does it from his heart. These, and many other sayings in common use, are derived from correspondence: for such forms of
speech enter the mind from the spiritual world, though the
speaker is not aware of it.

·98. That there exists such a correspondence between all
things belonging to heaven and all things belonging to man,
has been evinced to me by much experience—so much, indeed,
as to convince me of it as of a thing self-evident, and not liable
to any doubt. But to adduce all this experience here, is unnecessary, and, on account of its abundance, would be inconve-
nient. It may be seen in the *Arcana Cœlestia*, in the Sections
on Correspondences, on Representations, on the Influx of the
Spiritual World into the Natural, and on the Intercourse between the Soul and the Body.(⁴)

99. But although there is a correspondence between all things
that belong to man, as to his body, and all things that belong
to heaven, still man is not an image of heaven as to his external
form, but as to his internal. For the interiors of man are recipient of heaven, and his exteriors are recipient of the world:
in proportion, therefore, as his interiors receive heaven, the
man is, as to them, a heaven in miniature, formed after the
image of heaven at large: but in proportion as his interiors do
not thus receive, he is not such a heaven, and such an image.
Still his exteriors, which receive the world, may exist in a form
which is according to the order of the world, possessing various
degrees of beauty: for the causes of external beauty, which is
that of the body, are derived from a person's parents, and from

(³) That the breast, in the Word, signifies charity, nn. 3934, 10,081, 10,087. That
the loins and organs of generation, signify conjugial love, nn. 3021, 4280, 4462, 5050,
5051, 5052. That the arms and hands signify the power of truth, nn. 878, 3091, 4933—
4937, 6947, 7205, 10,019. That the feet signify the natural principle, nn. 2162, 3147,
8761, 3986, 4280, 4938—4952. That the eye signifies the understanding, nn. 2701,
4403—4421, 4523—4534, 6923, 9051, 10,569. That the nostrils signify perception, nn.
3577, 4624, 4625, 4748, 5621, 8286, 10,054, 10,292. That the ears signify obedience, nn.
2542, 3869, 4523, 4653, 5017, 7216, 8361, 8990, 9311, 9397, 10,061. That the reins or
kidneys, signify the examination and correction of truth, nn. 5380—5386, 10,032.
(⁴) Of the correspondence of all the members of the body with the Grand Man, or
heaven, generally and specifically, from experience, nn. 3021, 3624—3649, 3741—3750,
3883—3896, 4039—4055, 4218—4228, 4318—4331, 4403—4421, 4523—4534, 4622—4633,
4652—4660, 4791—4805, 4931—4953, 5050—5061, 5171—5189, 5377—5396, 5552—5573,
5711—5727, 10,030. Of the influx of the spiritual world into the natural world, or of
heaven into the world, and of the influx of the soul into all things of the body; from
experience, nn. 6053—6058, 6189—6215, 6207—6327, 6466—6495, 6598—6626. Of the
intercourse between the soul and body, from experience, nn. 6053—6058, 6189—6215,
6307—6327, 6466—6495, 6598—6626.

his formation in the womb, and it is afterwards preserved by the common influx which the body receives from the world; in consequence of which, the form of a person's natural man may differ exceedingly from that of his spiritual man. The form of certain persons, as to their spirit, has sometimes been shown me; and in some, having fair and handsome faces, I have seen it to be deformed, black, and monstrous, so that you would pronounce it an image of hell, not of heaven; whereas in some, not outwardly handsome, I have seen it to be beautiful, fair, and like that of an angel. The spirit, also, of a man, after death, appears the same as it had been in the body, while he lived, so clothed, in the world.

100. But correspondence reaches much further than to man; for there is a correspondence between all the heavens respectively. To the third or inmost heaven corresponds the second or middle heaven; and to the second or middle heaven corresponds the first or ultimate. To the first or ultimate heaven also correspond the forms of man's body, called its members, organs, and viscera. Thus the corporeal part of man is that in which heaven ultimately closes, and upon which, as on its base, it rests. But this arcanum will be more largely explained elsewhere.

101. But it is most necessary to be known, that all the correspondence which any thing has with heaven, is with the Lord's Divine Humanity; for heaven is from Him, and He is heaven, as has been shown in the Sections preceding: for unless the Divine Humanity entered by influx into all things belonging to heaven, and, by correspondences, into all things belonging to the world, there could be no such beings as either angels or men. Hence it further appears, why the Lord was made Man, and clothed His Divinity with Humanity from first to last: the reason was, because the Divine Humanity from which heaven subsisted before the coming of the Lord, was no longer adequate to the support of all things, because man, who is the base of the heavens, fell away, and destroyed the order according to which they were established. What, and of what nature the Divine Humanity was which existed before the Lord's coming, and what was the state of heaven at that time, may be seen in the extracts from the *Arcana Cœlestia* referred to at the end of the preceding chapter.

102. The angels are amazed when they hear that men are to be found who ascribe every thing to nature and nothing to the Divine Being; and who also believe that their body, which displays so many wonders of heavenly origin, is fashioned by nature; and still more, that man's rational faculty also is derived from the same source; although, if they would elevate their minds ever so little, they might see that such wonders are derived from the Divine Being, and not from nature; and that nature was only created to clothe what is spiritual, and to pre-

47

sent it in a corresponding form in the ultimate sphere of order. Such persons they compare to owls, which see in the dark, and not at all in the light.

THAT THERE IS A CORRESPONDENCE BETWEEN HEAVEN AND ALL THINGS BELONGING TO THE EARTH.

103. What correspondence is has been explained in the preceding Section; where it also was shown that all the parts of the animal body, both generally and individually, are correspondences. It follows in order to show now, that all things belonging to the earth, and in general, all things in the world, are correspondences.

104. All things that belong to the earth are divided into three general kinds, which are called so many kingdoms. There is the animal kingdom, the vegetable kingdom, and the mineral kingdom. The objects of the animal kingdom are correspondences in the first degree, because they live: those of the vegetable kingdom are correspondences in the second degree, because they only grow: and those of the mineral kingdom are correspondences in the third degree, because they do neither. Correspondences in the animal kingdom are animated creatures of various kinds, both such as walk and creep on the ground, and such as fly in the air; which it is needless to mention specifically, because they are well known. Correspondences in the vegetable kingdom are all such things as grow and flourish in gardens, woods, corn-fields, and meadows; which, likewise, it is unnecessary to name specifically, because they also are well known. Correspondences in the mineral kingdom are all metals, both the more noble and the more base, precious and common stones, and earths of various kinds; not excluding water. Besides these products of nature, those things also are correspondences which the industry of man prepares or manufactures from them for his own use; such as food of all kinds, garments, houses, public edifices, and similar objects.

105. The objects which are stationed above the earth, such as the sun, moon, and stars; also those that are seen in the atmosphere, such as clouds mists, rain, thunder, and lightning; all likewise are correspondences. Those which proceed from the sun, and his presence or absence, as light and shade, heat and cold, are also correspondences; together with those which thence exist successively; like the seasons of the year, which are called spring, summer, autumn, and winter; and the times of the day, or morning, noon, evening, and night.

106. In a word, all things that exist in nature, from its mi-

nutest parts to its greatest, are correspondences.(¹) The reason that they are correspondences is, because the natural world, with all that belongs to it, derives its existence and subsistence from the spiritual world; and both from the Divine Being. Subsistence is mentioned as well as existence, because every thing has its subsistence from the same source as its first existence, subsistence being perpetual existence; and because, also, nothing can exist from itself, but only from something prior to itself, and thus, originally, from the First Cause; from which, therefore. were it to be separated, it would utterly perish, and disappear.

107. Every object is a correspondent, which exists and subsists in nature from Divine Order. That which constitutes Divine Order is the Divine Good which proceeds from the Lord: it commences from Him; it proceeds from Him through the heavens in succession into the world, and is there terminated in ultimates. The things which exist in the world according to order are correspondences. All things there exist according to order, when they are good, and perfectly adapted to their intended use; for every thing good is such according to its use: its form has relation to truth, because truth is the form of good. Hence it is that all things in the whole world, and partaking of the nature of the world, which are in divine order, have relation to good and truth.(²)

108. That all things found in the world exist from a Divine Origin, and are clothed with natural elements so as to exist and perform their use in that sphere, and thus to be in correspondence, is manifest from every thing that is seen both in the animal and in the vegetable kingdom. In both are things which every one may see, if he thinks from an interior ground, are from heaven. To illustrate this, out of the innumerable instances that present themselves, a few shall be mentioned. To begin with some from *the Animal Kingdom.*

What wonderful knowledge is, as it were, inherent in every animal, is known to many. The bees know how to gather honey from flowers, to build cells of wax in which to lay it up in store, and thus to provide food for themselves and their associates against the coming winter. Their female lays her eggs, and the others wait upon her, and cover them up, to give birth to a new

(¹) That all things which exist in the world, and in its three kingdoms, correspond to heavenly things which exist in heaven; or that the things which exist in the natural world correspond to those which exist in the spiritual, nn. 1632, 1881, 2758, 2760—2763, 2987—3003, 3213—3227, 3483, 3624—3639, 4044, 4053, 4116, 4366, 4939, 5116, 5377, 5428, 5477, 9280. That by correspondences the natural world is conjoined to the spiritual world, n. 8615. That hence, universal nature is a theatre representative of the Lord's kingdom, nn. 2758, 2999, 3000, 3483, 3518, 4939, (8848,) 9280.

(²) That all things in the universe, both in heaven and in the world, which exist according to order, have relation to good and truth, nn. 2452, 3166, 4390, 4409, 5232, 7256, 10,122. And to the conjunction of both, that they have a real existence, n. 10,555.

generation. They live under a certain form of government, with which all in the hive are instinctively acquainted. They preserve the useful members of the community, and turn out the useless ones, depriving them of their wings. Not to mention other wonderful things; all which they derive from heaven, on account of their use; for their wax serves man for candles in all parts of the world, and their honey sweetens his food. What can surpass the wonders displayed in caterpillars, which are among the lowest productions of the animal kingdom? They know how to nourish themselves with the juice of the particular kinds of leaves suited to their nature, and, after completing this stage of their existence, to wrap themselves up in a covering, and deposit themselves, as it were, in a womb, and so to produce an offspring of their own kind. Some are first metamorphosed into nymphs and chrysalises, spin a ball of thread, and, when their toil is ended, are adorned with a different body, are decorated with wings, fly in the air as in their proper heaven, celebrate their marriages, lay their eggs, and provide for themselves a posterity. Besides these specific instances, all the fowls of the air in general know the food proper for their nourishment, and not only what it is, but also where it is to be found; they know how to form their nests, every species in a mode peculiar to itself, to lay their eggs in them, to sit on them, to hatch their young, to nourish them, and when to drive them away to take care of themselves. They also know what enemies they have to shun, and what friends to associate with; and all from their very infancy. Not to mention the wonders observable in their eggs themselves, in which are prepared, and arranged in due order, all things that are requisite for the formation and nourishment of the embryo chick. With innumerable things besides. What person who thinks from any degree of rational wisdom will ever pretend to say, that such instincts can proceed from any other origin than the spiritual world, to which the natural world serves for clothing what thence proceeds with a body, or for presenting in effect, that which is spiritual in its cause? The reason that the animals of the earth, and the fowls of the air, come into all this knowledge by birth, whereas man does not, whose nature, nevertheless, is so much superior to theirs, is, because animals exist in the order of their life, and have not been able to destroy that which is in them from the spiritual world, because they have no rational faculty. But with man, who thinks from the spiritual world, it is different. Because he has perverted in himself what he receives thence by a life contrary to order, which his rational faculty favors, he cannot but be born into mere ignorance; whence he is afterwards to be brought back, by divine means, into the order of heaven.

109. How the objects that are found in *the Vegetable Kingdom* exist in correspondence, may appear from many particulars.

As, for instance, that such minute seeds grow into trees, which put forth leaves, produce blossoms, and at last fruit, in which they deposit new seeds; and that these effects take place successively, and at last exist together in such admirable order, as is impossible to be described in few words. It would require volumes to do it justice; and still the interior arcana, which are in nearer connection with their uses, are such as science can never exhaust. Since these things also proceed from the spiritual world, or from heaven, which is in the form of a man (as shown above in its proper Section), every individual thing in that kingdom has also a certain relation to something that belongs to man; a fact which is known to some of the learned. That all things which exist in that kingdom also are correspondences, has been made evident to me by much experience. For when I have been in gardens, and have noticed the trees, fruits, flowers, and herbs, I have often perceived their correspondences in heaven, and have conversed with those in and about whom those correspondences existed, and have been instructed respecting whence they were and what was their quality.

110. But to know the spiritual things in heaven to which the natural things in the world correspond, is at this day possible to none except by instruction from heaven; because the science of correspondences is at this day utterly lost. I will, however, illustrate what is the nature of the correspondence between spiritual things and natural, by some examples.

The animals of the earth, in general, correspond to affections; the tame and useful animals corresponding to good affections, and the fierce and useless kinds to evil affections. In particular, oxen and bullocks correspond to the affections of the natural mind; sheep and lambs to the affections of the spiritual mind; and birds or winged creatures, according to their species, correspond to the intellectual faculties and exercises of both minds.[*] Hence it is that various animals, as oxen, bullocks, rams, sheep, she-goats, he-goats, and male and female lambs, also pigeons and doves, were employed in the Israelitish Church, which was a representative one, for holy uses, it being of them that the sacrifices and burnt-offerings consisted; for when so employed, they corresponded to certain spiritual things, and were understood in heaven according to their correspondences. Animals, also, according to their genera and species, actually are affections; the reason of which is, because they live; and nothing

[*] That animals, from correspondence, signify affections, the tame and useful animals good affections, and the savage and useless ones evil affections, nn. 45, 46, 142, 148, 246, 714, 715, 719, 2179, 2180, 3519, 9280: illustrated by experience from the spiritual world, nn. 3218, 5198, 9090. Of the influx of the spiritual world into the lives of beasts, nn. 1633, 3646. That oxen and bullocks, from correspondence, signify the affections of the natural mind, nn. 2180, 2566, 9391, 10,132, 10,407. What sheep signify, nn. 4169, 4809. What lambs, nn. 3994, 10,132. That winged animals signify things intellectual, nn. 40, 745, 776, 778, 866, 983, 991, 5149, 7441; with a variety according to their genera and species; from experience from the spiritual world, n. 3219.

can have life, except from affection, and according to it. Hence, likewise, it is, that every animal possesses an innate knowledge according to the affection of its life. Man, too, as to his natural man, is like the animals; wherefore, also, it is usual to compare him to them in common discourse. Thus a man of mild disposition is called a sheep or a lamb; a man of rough or fierce temper is called a bear or a wolf; a crafty person is termed a fox or a snake; and so in other instances.

111. There is a similar correspondence with the objects of the vegetable kingdom. A garden in general corresponds to heaven as to intelligence and wisdom; wherefore heaven is called (in the Word) the garden of God, and paradise([4]), and is also named by man, the heavenly paradise. Trees, according to their species, correspond to perceptions and knowledges of good and truth, from which are procured intelligence and wisdom. Therefore it was that the ancients, who were skilled in the science of correspondences, celebrated their sacred worship in groves([5]); and hence it is that, in the Word, trees are so often mentioned, and heaven, the church, and man, are compared to them, as to the vine, the olive-tree, the cedar, and others; and good works are compared to fruits. The various kinds of food, also, which are obtained from them, especially those from grain, correspond to affections of good and truth, because these sustain man's spiritual life, as earthly food sustains his natural life([6]). Hence bread, in general, corresponds to the affection of all good, because it supports life better than other aliments; and because by bread is meant all food whatever. On account of this correspondence, also, the Lord calls Himself the bread of life; and for the same reason loaves were applied to a sacred use in the Israelitish Church, being placed upon the table in the tabernacle and called the shew-bread: and hence, likewise, all the divine worship performed by sacrifices and burnt-offerings, was called bread. On account, also, of this correspondence, the most holy solemnity of worship in the Christian Church is the holy supper, the elements used in which are bread and wine([7]). From these few examples the nature of correspondence may be seen.

([4]) That a garden and a paradise, from correspondence, signify intelligence and wisdom, nn. 100, 108; from experience, n. 3220. That all things which correspond, signify also the same things in the Word, nn. 2896, 2987, 2989, 2990, 2991, 3002, 3225.
([5]) That trees signify perceptions and knowledges, nn. 103, 2163, 2682, 2722, 2972, 7692. That therefore the ancients celebrated divine worship in groves under trees, according to their correspondences, nn. 2722, 4552. Of the influx of heaven into the subjects of the vegetable kingdom, as into trees and plants, n. 3648.
([6]) That meats, from correspondence, signify such things as nourish spiritual life, nn. 3114, 4459, 4792, 4976, 5147, 5293, 5340, 5342, 5410, 5426, 5576, 5582, 5588, 5655, 5915, 6277, 8562, 9003.
([7]) That bread signifies all the good which nourishes the spiritual life of man, nn. 2165, 2177, 3478, 3735, 3813, 4211, 4217, 4735, 4976, 9323, 9545, 10,686. That the bread, which was on the table in the tabernacle, had a like signification, nn. 3478, 9545. That the sacrifices in general were called bread, n. 2165. That bread involves

112. How conjunction between heaven and the world is effected by correspondences, shall also be briefly explained.

The Lord's kingdom is a kingdom of ends, which are uses; or, what amounts to the same, is a kingdom of uses, which are ends. On this account, the universe was so created and formed by the Divine Being, as that uses might everywhere be invested with such coverings, as to be presented in act or effect, first, in heaven, and afterwards, in the world; and should thus be manifested by degrees, and in succession, even to the ultimates of nature. It hence is evident, that the correspondence between natural things and spiritual, or between the world and heaven, exists through uses, and that uses are what conjoin them ; also, that the forms with which uses are clothed, are correspondences, and mediums of conjunction, so far as they are forms of uses. In the natural world, and its three kingdoms, all things that exist according to divine order are forms of uses, or are effects formed *from* use *for* use; and thus they all are correspondences. In man, however, so far as he lives according to divine order, thus in the love of the Lord and his neighbor, his actions are uses in form, and are correspondences, by which he is conjoined with heaven. To love the Lord and the neighbor is, in general, to perform uses.(*) It is to be observed, further, that man is the being through whom the natural world is conjoined with the spiritual, or that he is the medium of such conjunction. For both the natural world and the spiritual world exist in him (see above, n. 57) : wherefore, so far as he is a spiritual man, he is a medium of such conjunction; but so far as he is only a natural man, and not also a spiritual man, he is not such a medium. But, nevertheless, the Divine influx continues to flow into the world, independently of the mediation of man, and even into the elements appertaining to him which are derived from the world; but not into his rational faculty.

113. As all things that exist according to divine order correspond to heaven, so all things that exist in contrariety to divine order correspond to hell. All those which correspond to heaven,

---

all food, n. 2165. Thus that it signifies all food, celestial and spiritual, nn. 276, 680, 2165, 2177, 3478, 6118, 8410.

(*) That all good has its delight from uses, and according to uses, and likewise its quality; hence, such as the use is, such the good, nn. 3049, 4984, 7038. That angelic life consists in the goods of love and of charity, thus in performing uses, n. 454. That nothing is regarded by the Lord, and thence by the angels, but the ends, which are uses, appertaining to man, nn. 1317, 1645, 5949. That the kingdom of the Lord is a kingdom of uses, thus of. ends, nn. 454, 696, 1103, 3645, 4054, 7038. That to serve the Lord is to perform uses, n. 7038. That all things in man, to every particular, are formed for use, nn. (3565,) 4104, 5189, 9297; and that they are formed from use; thus, that use is prior to the organic forms in man by which use is effected, because use exists from the influx of the Lord through heaven, nn. 4223, 4926. That the interiors of man also, which belong to his mind, as he grows up to maturity, are formed from use and for use, nn. 1964, 6815, 9297. That hence, man is of such a quality as are the uses appertaining to him, nn. 1568, 3570, 4054, 6571, 6935, 6938, 10,284. That uses are the ends, for the sake of which the actions are performed, nn. 3565, 4054, 4104. 4915. That use is the first and last, thus the all of man, n. 1964.

have relation to good and truth; but those which correspond to hell, have relation to evil and falsity.

114. Something shall now be offered respecting the science of correspondences, and its use.

It has been stated above, that the spiritual world, which is heaven, is conjoined with the natural world by correspondences; by which, therefore, man has communication with heaven. For the angels of heaven do not think from natural things, as man does: wherefore, when man is grounded in the science of correspondences, he may be in consort with the angels as to the thoughts of his mind, and so be conjoined with them as to his spiritual or internal man. In order that there might exist a conjunction between heaven and man, the Word was written by pure correspondences. All its contents, to the most minute particulars, are in such correspondence:([9]) wherefore, if man were skilled in the science of correspondences, he would understand the Word as to its spiritual sense, and would thence be enabled to obtain a knowledge of arcana, of which nothing is to be seen in the literal sense. For, in the Word, there is both a literal sense and a spiritual sense. The literal sense is composed of such ideas as exist in the world, but the spiritual sense of such as exist in heaven: and since the conjunction between heaven and the world is the result of correspondences, therefore a Word was given of such a kind, as that every particular contained in it, even to the minutest iota, should have its correspondence.([10])

115. I have been instructed from heaven, that the most ancient natives of our earth, who were celestial men, thought from correspondences themselves, and that the natural objects of the world, which they had before their eyes, served them as mediums for such contemplations; and that, as being of such a character, they enjoyed consociation with the angels, and held conversation with them; so that, through them, heaven was conjoined with the world. On this account, that period was called the golden age; respecting which it is related by ancient writers, that the inhabitants of heaven then dwelt with men, and conversed with them familiarly, as friends with their friends. But after those times, another race arose, who, as I have been informed, did not think from correspondences themselves, but from the science of correspondences; and that then also existed a conjunction of heaven with man, but not of so intimate a kind. The period when these flourished was called the silver age. Another race still succeeded, who possessed, indeed, a knowledge of correspondences, but did not think from the science of them,

([9]) That the Word was written by pure correspondences, n. 8615. That by the Word, man has conjunction with heaven, nn. 2899, 6943, 9896, 9400, 9401, 10,375, 10,432.

([10]) Respecting the spiritual sense of the Word, see the small work on the White Horse mentioned in the Apocalypse (now printed at the end of the *Doctrine of the New Jerusalem respecting the Sacred Scripture*).

by reason that they were only grounded in natural good, and not in the spiritual, like their predecessors. The period of these was called the age of brass (or copper). After these ages had passed away, man, I have been instructed, became, in succession, external, and at last corporeal; and that then the science of correspondences became utterly extinct, and with it, knowledge respecting heaven, and most things belonging to it. Their naming those ages from gold, silver, and brass (or copper),([11]) also had its ground in correspondence; for gold, by correspondence, signifies celestial good, being the good in which the most ancient race were grounded; but silver signifies spiritual good, being that which formed the character of the ancients who succeeded them: brass (or copper) signifies natural good, being that of their next posterity. But iron, from which the last age took its name, signifies hard truth without good.

OF THE SUN IN HEAVEN.

116. In heaven, the sun of this world is not to be seen, nor any thing which thence exists, the whole of which is natural. For nature commences from that sun, and whatever it produces is denominated natural. But that which is spiritual, in the sphere of which heaven exists, is above nature, and is entirely distinct from that which is natural; nor is there any communication between them, except by correspondences. The nature of the distinction between them may be comprehended from what was delivered above respecting degrees (n. 38); and the nature of the communication between them, from what is stated in the two preceding Sections respecting correspondences.

117. But although the sun of this world is not seen in heaven, nor any thing which exists from it; it nevertheless is true, that in heaven there is a sun, that there is light, that there is heat, and all things that are seen in the world, with innumerable others: only, they are not from the same origin: for all the things which exist in heaven are spiritual, whereas those in the world are natural. The sun of heaven is the Lord,* the light

---

([11]) That gold, from correspondence, signifies celestial good, nn. 113, 1551, 1552, 5658, 6914, 6917, 9510, 9874, 9881. That silver signifies spiritual good, or truth from a celestial origin, nn. 1551, 1552, 2954, 5658. That copper signifies natural good, nn. 425, 1551. That iron signifies truth in the ultimate of order, nn. 425, 426.

* This statement is not to be understood too strictly, as if the Lord Himself were that sun. It has been shown above, in a particular Section (nn. 78—86), that heaven is in the form of a man, because the Lord is in that form, or because "God is a Man" (n. 85): and it is stated below (n. 121), that "the Lord in person is *encompassed with the sun*," thus, is not that sun Himself. As to suppose this would be a dangerous error, the Author sometimes cautions the reader against falling into it; as in the following passage: "He Himself is not that sun; but divine love and divine wisdom, in their proximate emanation from Him, and round about Him, appear as a sun before

there is Divine Truth, and the heat there is Divine Good, which proceed from the Lord as a sun. It is from that origin that all things proceed which exist and appear in heaven. But the light and heat, with the things thence existing, in heaven, will be treated of in the following Sections; this Section shall be devoted to the sun which there shines. The reason that the Lord appears in heaven as a sun, is, because it is from Divine Love that all spiritual things exist, and, by means of the sun of the natural world, all natural things likewise. It is that Love which shines as a sun.

118. That the Lord actually appears in heaven as a sun, has not only been told me by the angels, but it has also, sometimes, been granted me to see. What, therefore, I have heard and seen of the Lord as a sun, I will here briefly describe.

The Lord appears as a sun, not in heaven, but far above the heavens; nor yet over head, or in the zenith, but before the faces of the angels, in a medium altitude. He appears at a great distance, in two situations, one before the right eye, and the other before the left. Before the right eye, He appears exactly like a sun, as if of the same sort of fire, and of the same magnitude, as the sun of this world : but before the left eye He does not appear as a sun, but as a moon, of similar but more brilliant whiteness, and of similar magnitude, with the moon of our earth ;* only it appears surrounded with many smaller moons, as it were, each of which is similarly white and brilliant. The reason that the Lord appears, with this difference, in two situations, is, because He appears to every one according to the nature of the party's reception of Him, thus differently to those who receive Him in the good of love and to those who receive Him in the good of faith. To those who receive Him in the good of love, He appears as a sun, fiery and flaming, according to their reception. These are the subjects of His celestial kingdom. But to those who receive Him in the good of faith, He appears as a moon, white and brilliant, according to their re-

the angels. Himself, in the sun, is a Man, our Lord Jesus Christ, both with respect to the all-originating Divinity, and with respect to the Divine Humanity."—(*True Christian Religion*, n. 25).—*N*.

* It is not to be supposed, from what is here said, that the Lord appears both as a sun and as a moon to the same angels; still less that, as a moon, he appears not more bright than the moon in the world. The two appearances are described as those of a sun and moon respectively, because they bear the same relation to each other as do those two natural luminaries; but, in reality, to those by whom the Lord is said to be seen as a moon, that moon is their sun, and is so denominated by the author in some of his other works. To the angels of the celestial kingdom, the Lord appears as a sun, of a glowing brightness, of which no conception can be formed by our natural ideas; and it is seen by them rather towards the right, or before the right eye: and to the angels of the spiritual kingdom he also appears as a sun, far exceeding in radiance the sun of this world, though, compared to the sun seen by the celestial angels, this sun is only as a moon; and it appears rather towards the left, or before the left eye of those who behold it. With this explanation in the mind, all that is said above, and in what follows, will be easily understood.—*N*.

ception. These are the subjects of His spiritual kingdom.(¹) The reason is, because the good of love corresponds to fire, whence fire, in the spiritual sense, is love; and the good of faith corresponds to light, and light, also, in the spiritual sense, is faith.(²) The reason that He appears before their eyes, is, because the interiors, which belong to the mind, see through the eyes; from the good of love through the right eye, and from the good of faith through the left.(³) For all things that are on the right side, both in angels and men, correspond to the good from which proceeds truth; and those on the left, to truth which is derived from good.(⁴) The good of faith is, in its essence, truth derived from good.

119. It is on this account, that, in the Word, the Lord, with respect to love, is compared to the sun, and with respect to faith, to the moon; and also that love, derived from the Lord and directed to Him, is signified by the sun, and faith, similarly derived and directed, by the moon; as in these places: "*The light of the moon shall be as the light of the sun, and the light of the sun shall be seven-fold, as the light of seven days*".—(Isa. xxx. 26.) "*When I shall put thee out, I will cover the heaven, and make the stars thereof dark: I will cover the sun with a cloud, and the moon shall not give her light. All the bright lights of heaven will I make dark over thee, and set darkness upon thy land.*"—(Ezek. xxxii. 7, 8.) "*The sun shall be darkened in his going forth, and the moon shall not cause her light to shine.*"—(Isa. xiii. 10.) "*The sun and moon shall be dark, and the stars shall withdraw their shining.—The sun shall be turned into darkness, and the moon into blood.*"—(Joel ii. 10, 31; iv. 15.) "*The sun became black as sackcloth of hair, and the moon became as blood: and the stars of heaven fell into the earth.*"—(Rev. vi. 12, 13.) "*Immediately after the tribulation of those days, the sun shall be darkened, and the moon shall not give her light, and the stars shall fall from heaven.*"—(Matt. xxiv. 29.) And in other places.

(¹) That the Lord appears in heaven as a sun, and that He is the sun of heaven, nn. 1053, 3636, 3643, 4060. That the Lord appears to those who dwell in the celestial kingdom, where love to Him is the ruling love, as a sun, and to those who dwell in the spiritual kingdom, where charity towards the neighbor and faith bear rule, as a moon, nn. 1521, 1529, 1530, 1531, 1837, 4060. That the Lord, as a sun, appears at a middle altitude before the right eye, and as a moon, before the left eye, nn. 1053, 1521, 1529, 1530, 1531, 3636, 3643, 4321, 5097, 7078, 7083, 7173, 7270, 8812, 10,809. That the Lord has been seen as a sun and as a moon by me, nn. 1531, 7173. That the Lord's Essential Divinity is far above His Divine Sphere in heaven, nn. 7270, 8760.

(²) That fire, in the Word, signifies love in each sense, nn. 934, 4906, 5215. That sacred or heavenly fire signifies divine love, nn. 934, 6314, 6832. That internal fire signifies the love of self and of the world, and every concupiscence which belongs to those loves, nn. 1861, 5071, 6314, 6832, 7575, 10,747. That love is the fire of life, and that the life itself is actually thence derived, nn. 4906, 5071, 6032, 6314. That light signifies the truth of faith, nn. (3395,) 3485, 3636, 3643, 3993, 4302, 4413, 4415, 9548, 9684.

(³) That the sight of the left eye corresponds to the truths of faith, and that the sight of the right eye corresponds to their goods, nn. 4410, 6923.

(⁴) That the parts and things which are on a man's right side have reference to good from which truth is derived; and that the parts and things on the left side have reference to truth derived from good, nn. 9495, 9604.

In these passages, by the sun is signified love, by the moon, faith, and by the stars, the knowledges of good and truth ;[5] which are said to be darkened, to lose their light, and to fall from heaven, when they exist no longer. That the Lord is seen in heaven as a sun, is also evident from His appearance when He was transfigured before Peter, James, and John; on which occasion it is related, that "*His face did shine as the sun*". (Matt. xvii. 2). When the Lord was thus seen by those disciples, they were withdrawn from the body, and were in the light of heaven. Hence it was, that the ancients, who belonged to the representative church, when in divine worship, turned their faces towards the sun in the east: and it is from them that the custom is derived of building churches with eastern aspect.

120. How immense, and of what nature the Divine Love is, may be inferred from comparing it with the sun of this world. From such comparison it will be seen, that it is of the most ardent description: in reality, if you can believe the assertion, its ardency is much greater than the heat of that sun. On this account, the Lord, as a sun, does not flow into heaven immediately, but the ardency of His love is tempered, by degrees, in the way. The tempering mediums appear like radiant belts around the sun ; in addition to which, the angels are veiled over with a thin suitable cloud, that they may not be injured by the influx.[6] Thus, also, the heavens are situated at distances from the sun proportioned to the angels' capacities of reception. The superior heavens, being grounded in the good of love, are nearest to the Lord as a sun: and the inferior heavens, being in the good of faith, are more remote from that sun: but they who are grounded in no good at all, like the inhabitants of hell, are very remote indeed, and this in proportion to the degree of their opposition to good.[7]

121. When, however, the Lord appears *in* heaven, which often occurs, he does not appear clothed with the sun, but in an angelic form, distinguished from the angels by the Divinity which is translucent from his countenance. For He is not there

---

[5] That constellations and stars, in the Word, signify the knowledges of good and truth, nn. 2495, 2849, 4697.

[6] The nature and degree of the divine love of the Lord illustrated by comparison with the fire of the sun of the world, nn. 6834, (6844,) 6849. That the divine love of the Lord is love towards all the human race, desiring to save them, nn. 1820, 1865, 2253, 6872. That the love proximately proceeding from the fire of the Lord's love does not enter heaven, but that it appears around the sun as radiant belts, n. 7270. That the angels also are veiled with a thin corresponding cloud, lest they should suffer injury from the influx of burning love, n. 6849.

[7] That the presence of the Lord with the angels is according to their reception of the good of love and of faith from Him, nn. 904, 4198, 4320, 6280, 6832, 7042, 8819, 9680, 9682, 9683, 10,106, 10,811. That the Lord appears to every one according to His quality, nn. 1861, 3235, 4198, 4206. That the hells are remote from the heavens in consequence of their inhabitants not being able to bear the presence of divine love from the Lord, nn. 4299, 7519, 7738, 7989, (8157,) 8306, 9327. That hence the hells are most remote from the heavens, and that this remoteness is the great gulf, nn. 9346, 10,187.

in person,--the Lord, in person, being always encompassed with
the sun; but He is in the presence of the angels by aspect.
For it is common, in heaven, for persons to appear as present in
the place on which the view is fixed, or in which it is terminated, although this may be very distant from the place in which
the persons thus seen actually are. This presence is called the
presence of the internal sight; which will be treated of hereafter.
The Lord has also been seen by me out of the sun, in an angelic
form, a little below the sun, at a great altitude. I have likewise
seen Him near, in a similar form, with a resplendent countenance: and once in the midst of a band of angels, as a flaming
beam of light.

122. The sun of the natural world appears to the angels as a
sort of mass of thick darkness opposite to the sun of heaven;
and the moon as a sort of mass of darkness opposite to the moon
of heaven: the reason is, because any thing fiery belonging to
the world corresponds to the love of self; and any thing luminous thence proceeding corresponds to falsity derived from that
love; and the love of self is diametrically opposite to Divine
Love, and the falsity thence derived is diametrically opposite to
Divine Truth; and, to the angels, whatever is opposite to Divine
Love and Divine Truth, is thick darkness. On this account, to
worship the sun and moon of the natural world, and to bow
down one's self to them, signifies, in the Word, to love one's
self, and the falsities which proceed from the love of self: wherefore it is said of such idolaters, that they should be cut off.(⁸)
(Deut. iv. 19; xvii. 3, 4, 5; Jer. viii. 1, 2; Ezek. viii. 15, 16, 18;
Rev. xvi. 8; Matt. xiii. 6.)

123. Since the Lord appears in heaven as a sun, by virtue of
the Divine Love which is in Him and proceeds from Him, all
the inhabitants of the heavens turn themselves constantly towards Him; those who belong to the celestial kingdom turning
towards Him as a sun, and those who belong to the spiritual
kingdom turning towards Him as a moon. But the inhabitants
of hell turn themselves towards that mass of thick darkness and
that mass of darkness which are opposite to the former, thus,
backwards from the Lord. The reason of this is, because all
who inhabit the hells are grounded in the love of self and of the
world, and thus are opposite to the Lord. Those who turn themselves towards that appearance of thick darkness which is in
lieu of the sun of the natural world, are those who inhabit the
hells at the back, and are called *genii;* but those who turn
themselves towards the appearance of darkness which is in lieu

(⁸) That the sun of the world does not appear to the angels, but, in its place, a dark
appearance at the back, opposite to the sun of heaven, or the Lord, nn. 7078, 9755.
That the sun, in the opposite sense, signifies the love of self, n. 2441. In which sense,
by adoring the sun is signified to adore those things which are contrary to heavenly
love, or to the Lord, nn. 2441, 10,584. That to those who reside within the hells, the
sun of heaven is thick darkness, n. 2441.

of the moon, are those who inhabit the hells in front, and are called spirits. It on this account that the inhabitants of the hells are said to be in darkness, and those of the heavens in light. Darkness signifies falsity derived from evil, and light signifies truth derived from good. The reason that they turn themselves in such directions, is, because all, in the other life, look towards the objects which reign in their interiors, thus, towards their loves; and the interiors of an angel or spirit fashion his face; and, in the spiritual world, the quarters are not determinate, as they are in the natural world, but they are determined by the direction of the faces of the inhabitants. Man, also, as to his spirit, turns himself in a similar way. A person who is immersed in the love of self and the world, turns himself backwards from the Lord; whereas one who is grounded in love to Him and his neighbor, turns himself towards Him. Of this, however, the man himself is not conscious; because he is living in the natural world, in which the quarters are determined by the rising and setting of the sun. As, however, this is a matter which can with difficulty be comprehended by man, it shall be illustrated in some following Sections, in which the Quarters, Space, and Time, in Heaven, shall be treated of.

124. Since the Lord is the Sun of heaven, and all things which are from Him look towards Him, He, also, is the Common Centre, from which proceed all direction and determination.([*]) Thus, likewise, all things beneath are in His presence and under His auspices; both those in heaven, and those on earth.

125. From what has now been stated, the truths advanced and shown in the preceding Sections respecting the Lord may be seen more clearly; namely, *That He is the God of Heaven* (nn. 2—6); *That His Divine Sphere constitutes Heaven* (nn. 7—12); *That the Divine Sphere of the Lord in Heaven is Love to Him and Charity towards the Neighbor* (nn. 13—19); *That there is a Correspondence between all things belonging to the World, and Heaven, and through Heaven with the Lord* (nn. 87—115); also, *That the Sun and Moon of the Natural World have such Correspondence* (n. 105).

OF LIGHT AND HEAT IN HEAVEN.

126. That there is light in the heavens cannot be conceived by those who only think from nature; and yet the light in the

---

([*]) That the Lord is the common centre, to which all things belonging to heaven turn themselves, n. 3633.

heavens is so great, as to exceed by many degrees the noonday light of the world. I have often seen it, even in the evening and in the night. In the beginning of my experience, I wondered when I heard the angels say that the light of the world is little better than shade compared with the light of heaven; but since I have seen it I can testify that it is so. Its whiteness and brightness are such as to surpass all description. The objects seen by me in the heavens were seen in that light; thus, far more clearly and distinctly than objects can be seen in the world.

127. The light of heaven is not natural like that of the world, but spiritual; for it proceeds from the Lord as a sun, and that sun is Divine Love: as shown in the preceding Section. That which proceeds from the Lord as a sun, is called in heaven Divine Truth. It is, however, in its essence, Divine Good united to Divine Truth. It is hence that the angels have light and heat; their light being from Divine Truth, and their heat from Divine Good. It may hence be manifest, that the light of heaven, and its heat also being from such an origin, are spiritual and not natural.([1])

128. The reason that Divine Truth is the angels' light is, because the angels are spiritual, and not natural. Spiritual beings see from their sun, and natural beings from theirs. Divine Truth is that from which the angels derive understanding, and understanding is their internal sight, which enters by influx into their external sight, and produces it. Hence, whatever objects appear in heaven from the Lord as a sun, appear in light.([2]) Such being the origin of light in heaven, it undergoes variations according to the angels' reception of Divine Truth from the Lord; or, what amounts to the same, according to the intelligence and wisdom in which the angels are grounded. It therefore is different in the celestial kingdom from what it is in the spiritual kingdom; and so, again, in every society of both. The light in the celestial kingdom appears as of flame, because the angels who dwell there receive light from the Lord as a sun: but the light in the spiritual kingdom is white, because the angels who dwell there receive light from the Lord as a moon. (See above, n. 118.) The light, also, is not the same in one society as in another. It likewise differs in each individual society; those who inhabit the centre enjoying more light, and those in the circumferences less. (See above, n. 43.) In one word: in the same degree as the angels are recipients of Divine Truth, or are grounded in intelligence and wisdom from the

([1]) That all light in the heavens is from the Lord as a sun, nn. 1053, 1521, 3195, 3341, 3636, 3643, 4415, 9548, 9684, 10,809. That the divine truth proceeding from the Lord appears in heaven as light, and causes all the light of heaven, nn. 3195, 3223, 5400, 8644, 9399, 9548, 9684.
([2]) That the light of heaven illuminates both the sight and the understanding of angels and spirits, nn. 2776, 3138.

Lord, they have light.(*)   On this account the angels of heaven are called angels of light.

129. Since the Lord in the heavens is Divine Truth, and Divine Truth is there the light, therefore, in the Word the Lord is called the Light, as is likewise every truth that proceeds from Him; as in these places: *Jesus said, "I am the light of the world: he that followeth Me shall not walk in darkness, but shall have the light of life."*—(John viii. 12.) *"As long as I am in the world, I am the light of the world."*—(Ch. ix. 5.) *"Jesus said,—Yet a little while is the light with you Walk while ye have the light, lest darkness come upon you. While ye have light, believe in the light, that ye may be the children of light.——I am come a light into the world, that whosoever believeth on Me should not abide in darkness."*—(Ch. xii. 35, 36, 46.) *"Light is come into the world, and men loved darkness better than light, because their deeds were evil."*—(Ch. iii. 19.) John said of the Lord, that *He "was the true light, which enlighteneth every man."*—(Ch. i. 9.) *" The people that sat in darkness saw great light; and to them that sat in the region and shadow of death, light is sprung up."*—(Matt. iv. 16.) *I will "give thee for a covenant of the people, for a light of the Gentiles."*—(Isa. xlii. 6.) *" I will give thee for a light of the Gentiles, that thou mayest be my salvation unto the end of the earth."*—(Ch. xlix. 6.) *"The nations of them that are saved shall walk in the light of it."*—(Rev. xxi. 24.) *" O send out thy light and thy truth: let them lead me."*—(Ps. xliii. 3.) In these and other passages the Lord is called the light, on account of the Divine Truth which proceeds from Him; and the truth itself is also denominated light. Since light exists in the heavens from the Lord as a sun, therefore, when he was transfigured before Peter, James, and John, *" His face did shine as the sun, and his raiment was white as the light,"* or *"became shining, exceeding white as snow, so as no fuller on earth could white them."*—(Matt. xvii. 2; Mark ix. 3.) The reason that the Lord's garments thus appeared, was because they represented the Divine Truth which exists from Him in the heavens. Garments, also, in the Word signify truths;(*) whence it is said in David, *" O Jehovah,—who coverest thyself with light, as with a garment."*—(Ps. civ. 2.)

130. That the light in heaven is spiritual, and that such light is Divine Truth, may also be concluded from the fact that man likewise enjoys spiritual light, and derives from it enlighten-

(*) That light is seen in heaven according to the intelligence and wisdom of the angels, nn. 1524, 1520, 1530, 3389. That the differences of light in the heavens are as many as are the angelic societies, since perpetual varieties as to good and truth, thus as to wisdom and intelligence, exist in the heavens, nn. 684, 690, 8241, 8744, 8745, 4414, 5598, 7236, 7833, 7836.

(*) That garments, in the Word, signify truths, because they invest good, nn. 1073, 2576, 5248, 5319, 5954, 9916, 9952, 10,536. That the garments of the Lord, when He was transfigured, signified the divine truth proceeding from His divine love, r.n. 9212, 9216.

ment, in proportion as he is grounded, from Divine Truth, in intelligence and wisdom. Man's spiritual light is the light of his understanding, the objects of which are truths; which that light arranges analytically into order, forms into reasons, and draws from them conclusions in series respecting the subjects of inquiry.(⁵) That it is by a real light that the understanding sees all this the natural man is not aware, because he does not see it with his eyes nor discern it in his thoughts: nevertheless, there are many who are acquainted with it, and who also distinguish it from the natural light which alone is enjoyed by those who only think naturally and not spiritually. They think only naturally who merely direct their view into the world, and ascribe all to nature; but they think spiritually who elevate their view to heaven, and attribute all to the Divine Being. That that which enlightens the mind is a true light, completely distinct from that which is called natural light, it has been frequently granted me to perceive, and to see also. I have been elevated into that light, more and more interiorly, by degrees; and in proportion to such elevation my understanding was enlightened, till at length I had a perception of things of which I before had none, and at last of such as I could not so much as comprehend in thought derived from natural light. I have sometimes been vexed at not being able so to comprehend them, although in heavenly light I had perceived them clearly and perspicuously.(⁶) Since there is a light appropriate to the understanding, it is usual to speak of that faculty in the same terms as of the eye; as when we say that it sees, and has light,—meaning, that it perceives; or that it is obscure, and in the dark,—meaning, that it does not perceive; with many similar phrases.

131. The light of heaven being Divine Truth, it also is Divine wisdom and intelligence; whence the same is meant by being elevated into the light of heaven, as by being elevated into intelligence and wisdom, and enlightened; wherefore the angels have light exactly in the same degree as they have intelligence and wisdom. Since the light of heaven is Divine wisdom, all, when seen in that light, are known at once as to their quality. The interiors of every one are displayed openly in his face, just

---

(⁵) That the light of heaven illuminates the understanding of man; and that, on this account, man is rational, nn. 1524, 3138, 3167, 4408, 6608, 8707, 912², 9399, 10,569. That the understanding is enlightened, because it is recipient of truth, ᵢ ᵤ. 6222, 6608, 10,661. That the understanding is enlightened so far as man receives truth in good from the Lord, n. 3619. That the understanding is of such a quality as are the truths derived from good, from which it is formed, n. 10,064. That the understanding has light from heaven, as the sight has light from the world, nn. 1524, 5114, 6608, 9128. That the light of heaven proceeding from the Lord, is always present with man, but that it only enters so far as man is grounded in truth derived from good, nn. 4060, 4214.

(⁶) That man, when he is elevated from the sensual principle, comes into a milder lumen, and at length into celestial light, nn. 6313, 6315, 9407. That there is an actual elevation into the light of heaven, when man is elevated into intelligence, n. 8190. How great a light has been perceived, when I have been withdrawn from worldly ideas, nn. 1526, 6608.

as they really are: and not the least particular can remain con
cealed. The interior angels, also, love to have all that is in
them made manifest, because they will nothing but what is
good. It is different with spirits below heaven, who do not will
what is good; on which account they are dreadfully afraid of
being looked at in the light of heaven: and, what is wonderful,
the inhabitants of hell, though they appear among themselves
as men, appear in the light of heaven as monsters, horrible in
countenance and horrible in person, the exact forms of their
own evil.([7])   Man also appears in a similar way, as to his
spirit, when looked at by angels: if he is good, he appears as a
man, beautiful according to the degree in which he is good: if
he is evil, he appears as a monster, deformed according to the
degree in which he is evil. It hence is clear, that in the light
of heaven all things are made manifest: they are so because the
light of heaven is Divine Truth.

132. Since, in the heavens, Divine Truth is light, all truths
whatever, be they found where they may, whether within an
angel or without him, whether within the heavens or without
them, shine, or give light. Truths without the heavens, however, do not shine like truths within them. Truths without the
heavens give a frigid light, like snow, that possesses no heat,
because they do not derive their essence from good, as do truths
within the heavens; wherefore also that frigid light, on the
illapse of light from heaven, disappears, and, if there is evil
beneath, is turned into darkness. This I have often witnessed;
with many other remarkable facts relating to shining truths;
the mention of which I omit.

133. Something shall now be stated respecting the heat of
heaven.

The heat of heaven, in its essence, is love. It proceeds from
the Lord as a sun: and that this is the Divine Love existing in
the Lord and proceeding from Him, has been shown in the previous Section. It hence is evident, that the heat of heaven is
spiritual, as well as its light, being both from the same origin.([8])
There are two things which proceed from the Lord as a sun,
Divine Truth and Divine Good. Divine Truth is displayed in
the heavens as light; and Divine Good as heat. Divine Truth
and Divine Good are, however, so united, that they are not two,
but one. Still, with the angels they are separated; there being
some angels who receive Divine Good more than Divine Truth,
and others who receive Divine Truth more than Divine Good.

([7]) That those who dwell in the hells, in their own light, which is like that of ignited charcoal, appear to themselves as men, but in the light of heaven as monsters, nn.
4531, 4533, 4674, 5057, 5058, 6605, 6626.
  ([8]) That there are two origins of heat, and likewise two origins of light, viz., the sun
of the world and the sun of heaven, nn. 3338, 5215, 7324. That heat from the Lord as
a sun is the affection which proceeds from love, nn. 3636, 3643. Hence, that spiritual
heat is, in its essence, love, nn. 2146, 3338, 3339, 6314.

They who receive more Divine Good are in the Lord's celestial kingdom; and they who receive more Divine Truth are in the Lord's spiritual kingdom. The most perfect angels are those that receive both in the same degree.

134. The heat of heaven, like its light, is everywhere various. It is different in the celestial kingdom from what it is in the spiritual kingdom; and also in every society of each. It not only differs in degree, but also in quality. It is more intense and pure in the Lord's celestial kingdom, because the angels there receive more Divine Good: it is less intense and pure in the Lord's spiritual kingdom, because the angels there receive more Divine Truth: and it differs, also, in every society, according to the state of reception in the inhabitants. There is also heat in the hells, but of an unclean nature.[*] The heat in heaven is what is meant by sacred and heavenly fire; and the heat of hell is what is meant by profane and infernal fire. By both is meant love; by heavenly fire, love to the Lord and love towards the neighbor, with every affection related to those loves; and by infernal fire, the love of self and the love of the world, with every concupiscence thereto related. That love is heat derived from a spiritual origin, is evident from the fact that there is increase of warmth according to increase of love; for a man is inflamed, and grows hot, according to the quantity and quality of his love, and its burning nature is manifested when it is assaulted. It is on this account, also, that it is customary to use such expressions as "being incensed," "growing hot," "burning," "boiling," and "taking fire," when speaking either of the affections belonging to the love of good, or of the concupiscences belonging to the love of evil.

135. The reason that the love proceeding from the Lord as a sun is felt in heaven as heat, is, because, from the Divine Good that proceeds from the Lord, the interiors of the angels are full of love; whence their exteriors, being heated from that source, have a sense of warmth. On this account it is, that in heaven, the heat and the love mutually correspond to each other, so that every one there enjoys such a degree and kind of heat as he does of love: as stated just above. The heat of the natural world does not at all enter heaven, because it is too gross, and is natural and not spiritual. With men, however, the case is different, because they exist both in the spiritual world and in the natural world at once: as to their spirit, they have warmth solely according to their loves; but as to their body, they derive it from both sources, both from the heat of their own spirit and from the heat of the world. The former flows into the latter, because they correspond to each other. The nature of the cor-

_____

[*] That there is heat in the hells, but of an unclean nature, nn. 1773, 2757, 3340. And that the odor thence arising is like odor from dung and excrement in the world, and, in the worst hells, is like that of corpses, nn. 814, 819, 820, 943, 954, 5394.

respondence between these two kinds of heat, may be conc.uded from observing the animals; for the passions of arimals, the chief of which is that of procreating an offspring of their own nature, burst forth, and operate, in proportion to the presence and afflux of heat from the sun of this world, which heat only prevails in the seasons of spring and summer. They are much deceived who imagine, that the influent heat of this world is what excites the passions of animals; for there is no influx of what is natural into what is spiritual, but only of what is spiritual into what is natural. This influx is according to divine order; to which order, the other influx would be contrary.[10]

136. Angels, like men, have understanding and will. The light of heaven constitutes the life of their understanding, because the light of heaven is Divine Truth, and thence Divine wisdom; and the heat of heaven constitutes the life of their will, because the heat of heaven is Divine Good and thence Divine love. The most essential life of the angels is derived from that heat; but not from the light, except so far as this has heat within it. That life is derived from heat, is manifest; for when heat is withdrawn, life perishes. It is similar with faith without love, or with truth without good: for truth, which is called the object of faith, is light; and good, which is the object of love, is heat.[11] These truths are seen more evidently when illustrated by the heat and light of the world, to which correspond the heat and light of heaven. By the heat of the world conjoined with its light, all things that grow on the surface of the earth receive life and flourish. This occurs in the seasons of spring and summer. But by the light separate from heat, nothing receives life and flourishes, but all things droop and die. This occurs in the season of winter, when heat is absent, though light remains. In consequence of that correspondence, heaven is called a paradise; because there, truth is conjoined with good, or faith with love, as light is with heat in the vernal season on earth. From these observations, the truth advanced in its proper Section above (nn. 13—19),—"That the Divine Sphere of the Lord in heaven is love to Him and charity towards the neighbor,"—may be more fully evident.

137. It is said in John, "*In the beginning was the Word, and the Word was with God, and the Word was God.——All things*

[10] That there is spiritual influx, and not physical; thus, that there is influx from the spiritual world into the natural, and not from the natural into the spiritual, n. 3219, 5119, 5259, 5427, 5428, 5477, 6322, 9110, 9111.

[11] That truths without good are not in themselves truths, because they have not life, for truths have all their life from good, n. 9603. Thus, that they are as a body without a soul, nn. 8180, 9154. That truths without good are not accepted of the Lord; n. 4368. What is the quality of truth without good, thus what is the quality of faith without love; and what the quality of truth derived from good, or the quality of faith derived from love, nn. 1949, 1950, 1951, 1964, 5830, 5951. That it comes to the same thing, whether we speak of truth or of faith, and of good or of love, since truth is the object of faith, and good is the object of love, nn. (2839) (4353,) 4097, 7178, 7628, 7624, 10,367.

were made by Him, ana without Him was not any thing made that was made. In Him was life: and the life was the light of men.——He was in the world, and the world was made by Him.——And the Word was made flesh, and dwelt among us, and we beheld His glory."—(Ch. i. 1, 3, 4, 10, 14). That it is the Lord who is meant by the Word, is evident, because it is said that the Word was made flesh: but what is specifically meant by the Word has not heretofore been known; wherefore it shall here be declared.

The Word here mentioned is the Divine Truth, which exists in, and proceeds from, the Lord :([12]) wherefore, also, it is here called the light; and that this is the Divine Truth, has been shown above in this Section. How all things were made and created by the Divine Truth, shall now be explained.

In heaven, all power belongs to Divine Truth, and there is none at all without it.([13]) It is from their reception of the Divine Truth that all the angels are denominated powers; and they actually are such, in proportion as they are recipients or receptacles of it. It is by this that they have power over the hells, and over all who put themselves in opposition; for a thousand enemies cannot there bear one ray of the light of heaven, which is Divine Truth. Since angels are angels by virtue of their reception of the Divine Truth, it follows that the whole of heaven has no other origin; for heaven is composed of the angels. That such immense power is inherent in Divine Truth, cannot be believed by those who have no other idea of truth than they have of thought, or discourse, which have no power in themselves, except so far as others act in obedience to what is spoken: but Divine Truth has power inherently in itself, and power of such a kind, that by it were both heaven and the world created, with all things that exist in each.

That such power exists inherently in Divine Truth, may be illustrated by two comparisons: namely, by the power of truth and good in man; and by the power of light and heat which proceed from the sun in the world.

By the power of truth and good in man. All things whatever that man performs, he does from his understanding and will. He acts from his will by good, and from his understanding by truth; for all things that exist in the will have relation

[12] That the term word, in the Sacred Scripture, signifies various things, viz., discourse, the thought of the mind, every thing which really exists; also, something; and in the supreme sense, the divine truth, and the Lord, n. 9987. That the Word signifies divine truth. nn. 2803, 2894, 4692, 5075, 5272, (7830,) 9987. That the Word signifies the Lord, nn. 2533, 2859.
[13] That it is the divine truth proceeding from the Lord which has all power, n. 6948, 8200. That all power in heaven belongs to truth derived from good, nn. 3091, 8563, 6344, 6423, 8304, 9643, 10,019, 10.182. That the angels are called powers, and that they likewise are powers, by virtue of the reception of divine truth from the Lord, n. 9639. That the angels are recipients of divine truth from the Lord, and that on this account they are frequently in the Word called gods, nn. 4295, 4402, 8301, 8192, 9160.

to good, and all things that exist in the understanding have re-'
lation to truth.([14]) From these, then, it is, that man puts his
whole body in motion, in which thousands of things rush at
once into action at the behest and pleasure of those principles.
It hence is evident, that the whole body is formed to be at the
disposal of good and truth; and, consequently, that it is formed
from good and truth.

*By the power of the heat and light which proceed from the
sun in the world.* All things in the world that grow, such as
trees, corn, flowers, grasses, fruits, and seeds, no otherwise de
rive existence, than by means of the heat and light of the sun.
It hence is evident what a productive power is inherent in those
elements: what then must that power be which is inherent in
Divine Light, which is Divine Truth, and in Divine Heat, which
is Divine Good; from which, as heaven derives its existence, so
also does the world? for the world exists through heaven, as
has been shown above.

From these considerations may appear how it is to be understood, that by the Word were all things made; and without it
was not any thing made that was made, and that the world also
was made by it; namely, that these works were produced by
the Divine Truth which proceeds from the Lord.([15]) It is on
this account, also, that, in the book of Genesis, mention is first
made of light, and afterwards of such things as depend on light
(ch. i. 3, 4). It also is from this cause, that all things in the
universe, both in heaven and in the world, have relation to good
and truth, and to their conjunction, in order to their possessing
any actual existence.

139.* It is to be observed, that the Divine Good and Divine
Truth which exist in the heavens from the Lord as a sun, are
not *in* the Lord, but *from* Him. *In* the Lord, there is only
Divine Love, which is the Esse, from which those principles
Exist. To Exist from Esse is what is meant by the expression,
to Proceed. This, likewise, may be illustrated by comparison
with the sun of the natural world: The heat and light which
exist in the world, are not *in* the sun, but are *from* it. *In* the
sun is nothing but fire; from which those elements exist and
proceed.

140. Since the Lord, as a sun, is Divine Love, and Divine
Love is Divine Good Itself, the Divine Emanation which proceeds from Him, and is His Divine Sphere in heaven, is called,

---

([14]) That the understanding is recipient of truth, and the will recipient of good, nn.
3623, 6125, 7503, 9800, (9930.) That therefore all things which are in the understanding have reference to truths, whether they actually are truths, or man only believes
them to be such; and that all things which are in the will have reference to goods, in
like manner, nn. 803, 10,122.

([15]) That the divine truth proceeding from the Lord is the only real existence, nn.
6880, 7004, 8200. That by the divine truth all things were made and created, nn. 2803,
2884, 5272, 7678.

* There is no n. 138 in the original.—*N.*

for the sake of distinction, Divine Truth ; although it is Divine Good united with Divine Truth. This Divine Principle is what is called the Holy Proceeding that emanates from Him.

ON THE FOUR QUARTERS IN HEAVEN.

141. In heaven, as in the world, there are four quarters, the east, the south, the west, and the north. These, in both worlds, are determined by their respective suns; in heaven, by the sun of heaven, which is the Lord; in the world, by the sun of the world: but still there are great differences between them.

The FIRST difference is, that in the world, that point is called the south, where the sun appears when at his greatest altitude above the earth; the north, where he is when in the opposite point below the earth; the east, where he rises at the equinoxes; and the west, where he then sets. Thus, in the world, all the quarters are determined from the south. But, in heaven, that point is called the east where the Lord appears as a sun; opposite, is the west; on the right, in heaven, is the south; and on the left is the north; and this continues, let them turn their face and body about as they may. Thus,. in heaven, all the quarters are determined from the east. The reason that the point where the Lord appears as a sun is called the east, is, because all the *origin* of life is from Him as a sun; and also, because, in proportion as heat and light, or love and intelligence,. are received by the angels from Him, the Lord is said to *arise* upon them.* This also is the reason that the Lord, in the Word, is called the east.([1])

142. ANOTHER difference is, that, with the angels, the east is always before their face, the west behind their back, the south on their right, and the north on their left. But this cannot, without difficulty, be comprehended in the world, because a man here turns his face towards any quarter, indifferently: wherefore it shall be explained.

The whole of heaven turns itself towards the Lord as its common centre; whence all the angels turn themselves in the same direction. That every thing on earth also tends to a common centre, is well known. But the direction which things have towards their centre in heaven differs from that which they have in the world in this respect: that, in heaven, it is the fore parts that are directed towards the common centre; whereas, in the

([1]) That the Lord, in the supreme sense, is the east, because he is the sun of heaven, which always is in its rising, and never setting, nn. 101, 5097, 9668.
* To enable the English reader to understand this sentence, he must be informed, that the Latin word for the east is *oriens*, derived from *orior*, to arise ; whence also is formed *origo*, the exact meaning of which is retained in our word "*origin*." The sense of the above will be clear to the English reader, if, wherever the term "east" occurs, he substitutes in his mind "the rising," which is the literal signification of the Latin word —*N.*

world, it is the lower parts. In the world, this tendency is called
the centripetal force, and also, gravitation. The interiors of
the angels, also, actually are turned forwards; and as the interiors exhibit themselves in the face, it is the face, there, which
determines the quarters.([2])

143. But that the angels have the east before their face, let
them turn their face and body about as they may, is a fact which
will be still more difficult of comprehension in the world; because, here, a man has every quarter before his face, as he turns
himself round: wherefore this also shall be explained.

Angels, like men, turn and incline their faces and bodies in
every direction; but still they always have the east before their
eyes. The changes of aspect of angels, occasioned by turning
round, are not like those of men; for they are from a different
origin. They appear, indeed, similar, but yet they are not.
The ruling love is the origin from which all determinations of
aspect proceed, both with angels and spirits. For, as just observed, their interiors are actually turned towards their common
centre, consequently, in heaven, towards the Lord as a sun:
wherefore, as their love is continually before their interiors, and
their face exists from their interiors, being the external form of
them, it follows that the love which reigns in them is continually
before their face. In the heavens, therefore, the Lord as a sun
is continually before them, since it is from Him that their love
is derived:([3]) and as the Lord Himself is present in His love
with the angels, it is He that causes them to look towards Him,
turn about as they may. These particulars cannot yet be further elucidated; but in the subsequent Sections, especially in
those on Representatives and Appearances in heaven, and on
Time and Space in heaven, they will be made more plainly intelligible.

That the angels constantly have the Lord before their face,
has been granted me to know by much experience, and also to
perceive myself. Whenever I have been in company with
angels, I was sensible of the Lord before my face; and although
He was not seen, still He was perceived in light. That such is
the fact, the angels, also, have frequently testified. Because
the Lord is constantly before the face of the angels, it is usual
to say in the world, respecting persons who believe in God, and

---

([2]) That all in heaven turn themselves to the Lord, nn. 9828, 10,130, 10,189, 10,420.
That, nevertheless, the angels do not turn themselves to the Lord, but the Lord turns
them to Himself, n. 10,189. That the presence of the angels is not with the Lord,
but the Lord's presence is with the angels, n. 9415.

([3]) That all in the spiritual world constantly turn themselves to their own loves;
and that the quarters there commence and are determined from the face, nn. 10,130,
10,189, 10,420, 10,702. That the face is formed to correspond with the interiors, nn.
4791—4805, 5695. That hence, the interiors shine forth from the face, nn. 3527, 4066,
4796. That the face makes one with the interiors with the angels, nn. 4796, 4797,
4799, 5695, 8249. Of the influx of the interiors into the face and its muscles, nn. 3631,
4800.

love Him, that they have Him before their eyes, and before their face, that they look to Him, and that they keep Him in view Man derives this mode of speaking from the spiritual world; for many phrases in human language come from thence, though men are not aware that such is their origin.

144. The existence of such a turning of the face to the Lord is one of the wonders of heaven. Many may be there together in one place, and one may turn his face and body in this direction, and another in that; and yet they all see the Lord before them, and each has the south on his right, the north on his left, and the west behind. Another of the wonders of heaven is this: that although the aspect of the angels is always directed towards the east, they nevertheless have also an aspect to the three other quarters: but their aspect towards these is from their interior sight, which is that of thought. Another, still, of the wonders of heaven is this: that it is not lawful for any one in heaven to stand behind another, so as to look at the back of his head; and that if this is done, the influx of good and truth which proceeds from the Lord suffers disturbance.

145. The mode in which the angels see the Lord differs from that in which the Lord sees the angels. The angels see the Lord through their eyes; but the Lord views the angels in the forehead. The reason that he views them in the forehead is, because the forehead corresponds to love; and the Lord, by love, flows into their will, and causes Himself to be seen by their understanding; to which the eyes correspond.([4])

146. But the quarters in the heavens which constitute the Lord's celestial kingdom, differ from the quarters in the heavens which constitute His spiritual kingdom, by reason that the Lord appears to the angels in His celestial kingdom as a sun, but to those in His spiritual kingdom as a moon. Where the Lord appears, is the east: and the distance between the sun and moon there is thirty degrees; whence there is the same difference in the position of the quarters. That heaven is divided into two kingdoms, which are called the celestial kingdom and the spiritual kingdom, may be seen in its proper Section, nn. 20—28. And that the Lord appears in the celestial kingdom as a sun, and in the spiritual kingdom as a moon, n. 118. Nevertheless, the quarters, in heaven, are not hereby rendered indistinct, because the spiritual angels cannot ascend to the celestial angels, nor these descend to them. (See above, n. 35.)

147. It hence is evident, what is the nature of the Lord's presence in the heavens,—that He is everywhere, and with

([4]) That the forehead corresponds to celestial love, and that therefore, by the forehead, in the Word, that love is signified, n. 9936. That the eye corresponds to the understanding, because the understanding is internal sight, nn. 2701, 4410, 4526, 9051, 10,569. Wherefore, to lift up the eyes and see, signifies to understand, to perceive, and to observe, nn. 2789, 2829, 3198 3202, 4083, 4086, 4339, 5684.

every one, in the good and truth which proceed from Him: consequently, that He dwells with the angels in what is His Own (as was stated above, n. 12). Their perception of the Lord's presence is seated in their interiors: from these, their eyes see; thus they see Him without themselves, because there is continuity [between the Lord as existing within them, and the Lord, as existing without them].* It may hence appear how it is to be understood, that the Lord is in them, and they in the Lord; according to His own words: "*Abide in Me, and I in you.*"—(John xv. 4.) "*He that eateth My flesh, and drinketh My blood, dwelleth in Me, and I in him.*"—(Chap. xvi. 56.) The Lord's flesh signifies Divine Good, and His blood, Divine Truth.(ᵇ)

148. All the inhabitants of the heavens have their habitations distinct according to the quarters. Towards the east and west dwell those who are grounded in the good of love,—towards the east, those who have a clear perception of it,—and towards the west, those who have but an obscure perception of it. Towards the south and north dwell those who are grounded in wisdom thence derived,—towards the south, those whose light of wisdom is clear,—and towards the north, those whose light of wisdom is obscure. The angels of the Lord's spiritual kingdom have their habitations arranged in the same order as those of His celestial kingdom, yet with a difference, according to the good of love and the light of truth from good, which they respectively enjoy. For the love that reigns in the celestial kingdom is love to the Lord, and the light of truth thence derived is wisdom; but in the spiritual kingdom it is love towards the neighbor, which is called charity; and the light of truth thence derived is intelligence, which is also called faith. (See above, n. 23.) They differ, likewise, as to the quarters; for the quarters in the one kingdom, and in the other, are thirty degrees apart; as stated just above (n. 146).

149. The angels also dwell among themselves in the same way, in every society in heaven: towards the east are those who enjoy a greater degree of love and charity; towards the west, those who have less; towards the south are those who enjoy more light of wisdom and intelligence; towards the north, those who have less. The reason that they dwell distinct in this manner, is, because every society is an image of heaven at large, and is, also, heaven on a smaller scale. (See above,

---

(ᵇ) That the flesh of the Lord signifies His Divine Humanity, and the divine good of His love, nn. 3813, 7850, 9127, 10,283. And that the blood of the Lord signifies the divine truth, and the holy principle of faith, nn. 4735, 6978, 7317, 7326, 7846, 7850, 7877, 9127, 9393, 10,026, 10,033, 10,152, 10,204.

* The words in brackets are added to complete the sense. Mr. Clowes has added, in his version, "between the eyes and the interiors." But that the sense intended is that given above, is plain from the author's immediately stating, that it explains the fact, that the Lord is **His people**, and they *in Him.*—N.

nn. 51—58.) The same order prevails in their assemblies. They fall into this order as a consequence of the form of heaven, by virtue of which every one knows his place. It is also provided by the Lord, that there should be some of all kinds in every society, in order that heaven, as to form, should be like itself everywhere: Nevertheless, the arrangement of heaven, viewed collectively, differs from that of a single society, as does the whole from a part: for all the societies situated towards the east excel those towards the west, and those towards the south excel those towards the north.

150. It is from this ground, that the quarters in the heavens signify such qualities as are found in those that inhabit them. Thus the east signifies love, and its good, enjoyed in clear perception, and the west, the same in obscure perception; the south, wisdom and intelligence in clear light, and the north, the same in obscure light. And as such things are signified by those quarters, the same are signified by them in the internal or spiritual sense of the Word ;(⁶) for the internal or spiritual sense of the Word is framed in perfect accordance with the things that exist in heaven.

151. The reverse has place with the inhabitants of the hells. Those who dwell there do not look towards the Lord as a sun or a moon, but they look backwards from Him, towards that mass of thick darkness which is in lieu of the sun of the natural world, and that mass of darkness which is in lieu of the moon of this earth; those who are called *genii* looking towards the former, and those who are called spirits towards the latter.(⁷) That the sun of the natural world, and the moon of this earth, do not appear in the spiritual world, but in lieu of that sun, a mass of thick darkness opposite to the sun of heaven, and in lieu of that moon, a mass of darkness opposite to the moon of heaven, may be seen above (n. 122). Thus the quarters, with those in hell, are opposite to the quarters of heaven. Their east is where that mass of thick darkness, and that mass of darkness, appear; their west is where the sun of heaven is : their south is on their right, and their north on their left. This also continues, however they may turn themselves about: nor can it possibly be otherwise; by reason that every tendency of their interiors, and every determination of aspect thence proceeding, turns to, and strives to be in, that direction. That the direction of the interiors and thence the actual determination of the aspect of all, in the other life, is according to their love, has been shown above (n. 143); and the love of those in the hells is the love of self and the world.

(⁶) That the east, in the Word, signifies love in clear perception, nn. 1250, 3708. The west, love in obscure perception, nn. 3708, 9653. The south, a state of light, or of wisdom and intelligence, nn. 1458, 3708, 5672. And the north, that state in obscurity, n. 3708.

(⁷) Who and of what quality those are that are called genii, and who and of what quality those are that are called spirits, nn. 947, 5035, 5977, 8593, 8622, 8625.

Those loves are what are signified by the sun of the natural world and the moon of this earth (see n. 122); and those loves, also, are opposite to love to the Lord and love towards the neighbor.[8] Hence it is that the infernals turn themselves back from the Lord towards those masses of darkness. The inhabitants of the hells, also, dwell according to their quarters; those who are grounded in evils from the love of self, dwelling from their east to their west; and those who are grounded in falsities of evil, from their south to their north. But of these, more will be said below, when treating of the hells.

152. When any evil spirit gains admission amongst the good, the quarters become so confounded, that the good scarcely know where their east is. This I have myself sometimes perceived to have occurred, and have also heard it mentioned by spirits, who were lamenting on account of it.

153. Evil spirits sometimes appear turned towards the quarters of heaven; at which time they possess the intelligence and perception of truth, but no affection of good. Hence, as soon as they turn back towards their own quarters, they again have no intelligence and perception of truth; and they then affirm, that the truths which they heard and had a perception of, were not truths, but falsities: they also desire that falsities should be truths. I have been informed, in regard to such turning, that, with the wicked, the intellectual faculty may be so turned, but not the will-faculty; and that this is provided by the Lord, in order that every one may be able to see and acknowledge truths, but that no one should receive them unless he is grounded in good, since it is good that receives truths, and not, by any means, evil. I have been further informed, that the same takes place with man, in order that it may be possible for him to be amended by means of truths; but that still no one is amended any further than as he is grounded in good. Also, that it is for the same reason, that man may, in like manner, be turned to the Lord; but that, if he is grounded in evil as to life, he immediately turns himself back again, and confirms in himself the falsities of his own evil in opposition to the truths which he understood and saw; and that this takes place when he thinks within himself from his own interior state.

OF THE CHANGES OF STATE EXPERIENCED BY THE ANGELS IN HEAVEN.

154. By the changes of state experienced by the angels, are meant their changes in respect to love and faith, and thence as to their wisdom and intelligence; thus, with respect to the

---

[8] That those who are immersed in the loves of self and of the world turn themselves back from the Lord, nn. 10,130, 10,189, 10,420, 10,702. That love to the Lord and charity towards the neighbor constitute heaven; whilst the love of self and the love

states of their life. The term "states" is applied to life, and to such things as belong to it; and as the angelic life is the life of love and faith, and thence of wisdom and intelligence, the term "states" is applied to these, and they are called states of love and faith, and states of wisdom and intelligence. How these states, with the angels, undergo changes, shall now be described.

155. The angels are not constantly in the same state as to love, nor, consequently, as to wisdom; for all the wisdom they enjoy is derived from love, and exists according to it. Sometimes they are in a state of intense love, and sometimes in a state of love not so intense. It decreases by degrees, from its greatest intensity to its least. When they are in the greatest degree of their love, they are in the light and heat of their life, or in their state of lucidity and enjoyment: but when they are in its least degree, they are in shade and in cold, or in their state of obscurity and non-enjoyment. From the last state they return to the first; and so on. These vicissitudes take place one after another, in succession, but admit of variety. These states succeed each other, like the variations of the states of light and shade, of heat and cold; or like the morning, noon, evening, and night, in every day in the world; which undergo perpetual varieties during the course of the year. There is also a correspondence between them; the morning corresponding to their state of love in its lucidity, the noon to their state of wisdom in its lucidity, the evening to their state of wisdom in its obscurity, and the night to a state when there is no love nor wisdom. But it is to be observed, that there are no states of life belonging to the inhabitants of heaven which correspond to night, but only some that correspond to the dawn which precedes the morning: night only finds its correspondence among the inhabitants of hell.([1]) It is in consequence of this correspondence that, in the Word, days and years signify states of life in general; heat and light, love and wisdom; morning, the first and supreme degree of love; noon, wisdom in its light; evening, wisdom in its shade; the dawn, the obscure state which precedes the morning; but night, the privation of all love and wisdom.([2])

156. As the states of the interiors of the angels, which relate

of the world constitute hell, because they are opposite, nn. 2041, 3610, 4225, 4776, 6310, 7366, 7369, 7490, 8232, 8678, 10,455, 10,741—10,745.

([1]) That in heaven, there is no state corresponding to night, but to the twilight which precedes morning, n. 6110. That twilight signifies a middle state between the last and the first, n. 10,134.

([2]) That the vicissitudes of states, as to illustration and perception, in heaven, are as the times of the day in the world, nn. 5672, 5962, (6310,) 8426, 9213, 10,605. That a day and a year in the Word, signify all states in general, nn. 23, 487, 488, 493, 893, 2788, 3462, 4850, 10,656. That morning signifies the beginning of a new state of love, nn. 7218, 8426, 8427, 10,114, 10,134. That evening signifies a state of closing light and love, nn. 10,134, 10,135. That night signifies a state of no love and faith, nn. 221, 709, 2353, 6000, 6110, 7870, 7947.

to their love and wisdom, undergo changes, so also do the states
of various things that are without them, and which appear before their eyes ; for the things without them put on an appearance according to those within them.　But what those things
are, and of what nature, will be described subsequently, in the
Section on Representatives and Appearances in Heaven.

157.　Every angel undergoes and passes through such changes
of state, and so does each society in general ; nevertheless, they
are not experienced by one exactly as by another, by reason
that they differ in love and wisdom ; for those who occupy the
centre are in a more perfect state than those who are stationed
in the circumferences, the diminution extending from the centre
to the last boundary of all.　(See above, nn. 23, 128.)　But to
describe all the differences would occupy too much space : suffice
it to say, that every one undergoes changes of state according
to the quality of his love and his faith.　Hence it happens, that
one is in his state of lucidity and enjoyment, while another is
in his state of obscurity and non-enjoyment, even in the same
society at the same time ; and that the same differences prevail
between one society and another ; and also, between the societies
of the celestial kingdom and those of the spiritual kingdom.　The
differences between those changes of state in general, are like
the variations of the state of the days in the several climates of
the earth ; in which it is morning with some when it is evening with others, and some experience warm weather while others
have cold ; and *vice versa.*

158.　I have been instructed from heaven why such changes of
state exist there.　The angels have told me that there are several
reasons for it.　The *First* is, that the enjoyment of life and of
heaven which they experience, resulting from the love and wisdom which they receive from the Lord, would by degrees be
thought little of, did they abide in it continually ; as is experienced by those who are perpetually surrounded by delightful
and agreeable objects without variety.　A *Second* Cause is, that
angels possess a *proprium** as well as men ; that this consists
in loving one's self ; that the inhabitants of heaven are all withheld from their *proprium*; and, so far as they are withheld from
it by the Lord, they are in the enjoyment of love and wisdom,

* It has been found impossible, by other translators of our Author, to avoid using
the Latin word *proprium*, as introduced by him, without attempting to translate it.
The word " selfhood" is sometimes employed as a rendering of it, and conveys the
most of what is intended by it.　It may, therefore, be properly used for it in other
works ; but in versions of the Author's own writings, it appears best to retain the
Latin word,—neither " selfhood," nor any other English word, answering to it exactly.
Proprium simply means, *what is one's own;* and when this is known to the reader, no
inconvenience can result from its use.　In time, no doubt, like *medium, decorum,
memorandum,* and other words of the same form (not to mention the innumerable
purely Latin words of other forms which are incorporated in our tongue), it will be
perfectly domesticated amongst us, and will then occasion no more unpleasantness to
English ears, or embarrassment to English understandings, than the Latin words alluded to do now.—*N.*

whereas, so far as they are not withheld from it, they are immersed in the love of self; and since every one loves his *proprium*, and this draws him away,([3]) therefore they experience · changes of state, or successive vicissitudes. A *Third* Cause is, that they may advance in perfection: for they are thus accustomed to be kept in the sense of love to the Lord, and to be withheld from the love of self; and also, that, by alternations of enjoyment and non-enjoyment, their perception and sense of good may become more exquisite.([4]) The angels said, further, that the Lord does not produce their changes of state, since the Lord, as a sun, is always flowing into them with an influx of heat and light, that is, of love and wisdom : but that the cause of those changes is in themselves, because they love their proprium, which continually draws them away. This they illustrated by a comparison drawn from the sun of the natural world; for this is not the cause of the changes of state as to heat and cold, light and shade, which occur every year and every day; for the sun stands motionless; but the changes are caused by the motion of the earth.

159. It has been shown me how the Lord appears to the angels of the celestial kingdom in their first state, how in their second, and how in their third. The Lord was at first seen as a sun, glowing and beaming with such splendor as it is impossible to describe; and I was informed, that it was thus that the Lord as a sun appears to the angels in their first state. There was afterwards seen a great dusky belt round the sun, in consequence of which the glowing and beaming appearance, which at first gave it such splendor, began to be dulled : and I was told, that the sun has that appearance in their second state. Afterwards, the belt appeared to become more dusky, and the sun, in consequence, less glowing; which process went on by degrees, till at last the sun became, apparently, quite white; and I was informed, that it appears to them in this way in their third state. After this, again, that white mass appeared to move to the left towards the moon of heaven, and to add itself to its light; upon which the moon shone with more brightness than usual : and it was stated to me, that that was the fourth state to the angels of the celestial kingdom, and the first to those of the spiritual kingdom, and that the changes of state in the two kingdoms thus proceed alternately in regard to each other; not, however, in the whole at once, but in one society after another; and also, that those vicissitudes do not return at stated periods, but occur

([3]) That the *proprium* of man consists in loving himself, nn. 694, 731, 4317, 5660. That the *proprium* must be separated, to the intent that the Lord may be present, nn. 1023, 1044. That it is also actually separated, when any one is held in good by the Lord, nn. 9334, 9335, 9336, 9447, 9452, 9453, 9454, 9983.
([4]) That the angels are perfecting to eternity, nn. 4803, 6648. That in heaven, one state is in no case altogether like another, and that hence is perpetual perfection, n. 10,200.

sooner or later, without their being aware of their approach.
The angels said, further, that the sun is not thus changed, and
does not make such progression, in itself, but that, nevertheless,
it appears to do so, according to the successive progressions of
states experienced by the angels, by reason that the Lord appears to every one according to the quality of his state; whence
the sun appears glowing to them when they are in an intense
state of love, and less glowing, and at last white, as their love
diminishes. They stated, likewise, that the quality of their
states was represented by the dusky belt, which induced on
the sun those apparent variations in respect to its flame and
light.

160. When the angels are in their last state, which is when
they have descended into their *proprium*, they begin to grow
sad. I have conversed with them while in this state, and have
witnessed that sadness. But they said, that they were in hopes
of soon returning into their former state, and thus, as it were,
of again returning into heaven; for it is heaven, to them, to be
withheld from their *proprium*.

161. There are also changes of state in the hells: but these
will be described below, when hell is treated of.

OF TIME IN HEAVEN.

162. Though all things in heaven have their successions and
progressions, as in the world, still the angels have no notion or
idea of time and space; and so completely destitute are they of
such notion and idea, that they do not even know what time and
space are. Time, in heaven, shall be treated of here; and space,
in its proper Section, below.

163. The reason that the angels do not know what time is,
notwithstanding all things occur, with them, in successive progression, as in the world, and so completely so that there is no
difference whatever, is this: In heaven, they have no years and
days, but changes of state; and where years and days exist,
there are times and seasons: but where changes of state exist
instead, there are states.

164. The reason that times or seasons exist in the world, is,
because, there, the sun, in appearance, passes from one degree
of the zodiac to another, and causes the times and seasons, as
they are called, of the year; and, moreover, revolves round the
earth, causing the times, as they are called, of the day; performing both revolutions at regular intervals. Not so the sun
of heaven. The sun does not, by successive progressions and
circumgyrations, produce years and days, but, in appearance,
changes of state, and these not at regular intervals (as shown in

the preceding Section). On this account, the angels cannot form any idea of time, but have, instead of it, an idea of state. (What state is, may be seen above, n. 154.)

165. Since the angels have no idea drawn from time, as men in the world have, neither have they any idea respecting time, or any thing relating to time. As to those things which are proper to time, the angels do not so much as know what they are; such as what a year is, what a month, a week, a day, an hour, to-day, to-morrow, yesterday. When angels hear these named by man (for a man always has angels adjoined to him by the Lord), they have, in lieu of them, a perception of state, and of such things as relate to state: thus the natural idea of man is turned into a spiritual idea with the angels. It is on this account that times or seasons, in the Word, signify states; and that the things proper to time, such as those named above, signify spiritual things that correspond to them.(¹)

166. The like occurs in regard to all things that exist from time, such as the four seasons of the year, which are called spring, summer, autumn, and winter; the four times of the day, which are called morning, noon, evening, and night; and the four ages of man, which are called infancy, youth, manhood, and old age; with all things else, which either exist from time, or follow in succession in the order of time. When man thinks of these things, he thinks from time, but an angel, from state; wherefore every thing derived from time which is included in those ideas with man, is turned, with an angel, into the idea of state. Spring and morning are turned into the idea of the state of love and wisdom, as these exist with angels when in their first state; summer and noon are turned into the idea of love and wisdom, as these exist in their second state; autumn and evening, such as they are in their third; but night and winter, into an idea of a state such as exists in hell. Hence it is that those times have, in the Word, such significations (see above, n. 155). It thus is evident, that the natural ideas which exist in the thoughts of man, become spiritual ones in the thoughts of the angels who are present with him.

167. Since the angels have no notion whatever of time, they have a different idea of eternity from that which men on earth have. By eternity, the angels have a perception of an infinite state—not of infinite time.(²) I was once engaged in thought respecting what eternity is; and I found that I could conceive,

---

(¹) That times, in the Word, signify states, nn. 2788, 2839, 3254, 3356, 4814, 4901, 4916, 7218, 8070, 10,133, 10,605. That the angels think without an idea of time and space, n. 3404. The reasons why, nn. 1274, 1382, 3356, 4882, 4901, 6110, 7218, 7381. What a year, in the Word, signifies, nn. 487, 488, 493, 893, 2906, 7828, 10,209. What a month, n. 3814. What a week, nn. 2044, 3845. What a day, nn. 23, 487, 488, 6110, 7680, 8426, 9213, 10,132, 10,605. What to-day, nn. 2838, 3998, 4304, 6165, 6984, 9939. What to-morrow, nn. 3998, 10,497. What yesterday, nn. 6983, 7114, 7140.

(²) That men have an idea of eternity with time, but the angels without time nn. 1382, 3404, 8325.

by the idea of time, what *to* eternity might be, namely, existence without end; but that I could not thus conceive what *from* eternity could be, nor, consequently, what God was engaged in before creation, from eternity. Falling, in consequence, into a state of anxiety, I was elevated into the sphere of heaven, and thus into the state of perception respecting eternity which is enjoyed by the angels. I then was enlightened to see, that eternity is not to be thought of from time, but from state, and that then a perception can be obtained of what *from* eternity is; which, accordingly, I then experienced.

168. The angels who converse with men, never speak by means of the natural ideas proper to man, all which are drawn from time, from space, from materiality, and from things analogous to these; but by means of spiritual ideas, all of which are drawn from states, and their various changes, within and without the angels. Nevertheless, the ideas of the angels, which are spiritual, when they enter into men by influx, are changed in a moment, and of themselves, into such natural ideas proper to man as perfectly correspond to their spiritual ones: but that such change takes place, is not known either to the angels or to the man. Such, also, is the nature of all the influx that flows into man from heaven. There were certain angels who were admitted more nearly into my thoughts than is usual, even into my natural thoughts, in which were many ideas drawn from time and space: but as they then understood nothing, they suddenly withdrew: after which I heard them conversing, and saying, that they had been in darkness. How complete is the ignorance of the angels in regard to time, it has been granted me *to* know by experience. A certain angel came from heaven who was of such a character, that he could be admitted, not only into spiritual ideas, but also into natural ideas, such as those of man; in consequence of which, I afterwards conversed with him, as one man does with another. At first, he did not know what that which I called time was; wherefore I was obliged to inform him how the sun appears to revolve round the earth, causing years and days: and that the years are thence divided into four seasons, and also into months and weeks; and the days into twenty-four hours; all which recur at stated intervals; and that such is the origin of times. On hearing this, he wondered, and said that he knew nothing of such matters, but that he knew what states are. In the course of our conversation, I also told him, that it is known in the world that there is no time in heaven; or that men talk, at least, as if they knew it; for they say when a person dies, that he has left the things of time, and that he has departed out of time; by which they mean, out of the world. I also remarked, that it is known to some that times, in their origin, are states, from the circumstance, that they depend entirely upon the states of the affections in which

the person is, being short to those who are in agreeable and cheerful states, long to those who are in disagreeable and melancholy ones, and variable in a state of hope and of expectation. On which account, the learned discuss what time and space are; and there even are some who know that time belongs to the natural man.

169. The natural man may imagine, that he would have no thoughts at all, if the ideas of time, of space, and of material things, were removed; for upon these ideas are founded all the thoughts which man can conceive.(³) But be it known to such a person, that the thoughts are bounded and contracted in proportion as they partake of time, space, and materiality; and that they are not bounded, but are extended, in proportion as they do not partake of those things, because the mind is so far elevated above things corporeal and worldly. It is hence that the angels derive their wisdom, and that it is such as is called incomprehensible, because it cannot be conceived by ideas that merely consist of such elements.

OF REPRESENTATIVES AND APPEARANCES IN HEAVEN.

170. A man who thinks from natural light alone, cannot comprehend that any thing in heaven can be like what exists in the world : the reason is, because, from that light, he has conceived and confirmed the notion, that angels are nothing but minds, and that minds are a sort of ethereal puffs of breath; and that, on this account, they have not the senses that man has; nor, consequently, any eyes; and that if they have no eyes, there can be no objects of sight: whereas the truth is, that angels have all the senses that man has, much more exquisite than his are; and that they also have light, by which they see, much brighter than the light by which man sees. That angels are men in most perfect human form, and enjoy every sense that man does, may be seen above, nn. 73—77. And that the light of heaven is much brighter than the light in the world, nn. 126—132.

171. What is the nature of the objects which appear to the angels in the heavens, cannot be described in few words; they are, however, in great part like those which exist on earth, except that they are more perfect in form, and more abundant in number. That such objects exist in the heavens, may be evident from those which were seen by the prophets; such as those belonging to the new temple and new earth shown to Ezekiel

(³) That man does not think without an idea of time; otherwise than the angels, n. 1404.

(chs. xl.—xlviii. of his prophecies), those shown to Daniel (see chs. vii.—xii. of his book), and those to John (see the Revelation, from beginning to end), and to others (mentioned both in the historical and prophetical books of the Word). They saw these objects when heaven was opened to them; and heaven is said to be opened when the interior sight is opened, which is that of a man's spirit; for objects in heaven cannot be seen with man's bodily eyes, but only with the eyes of his spirit. When it pleases the Lord, these eyes are opened; and man is then withdrawn from natural light, which he perceives by the senses of his body, and is elevated into spiritual light, which he perceives by his spirit. It was in this light that I beheld the objects that are in the heavens.

172. But although the objects which appear in the heavens are, in great part, like those which exist on earth, they still are not like them with respect to their essence; for those in the heavens derive their existence from the sun of heaven, and those on earth from the sun of this world. Those things which derive their existence from the sun of heaven are termed spiritual things: but those which derive their existence from the sun of this world are termed natural.

173. The objects which exist in the heavens do not exist in the same manner as do those on earth. In the heavens, all things have existence from the Lord according to their correspondence with the interiors of the angels. To the angels belong both interiors and exteriors. All things that exist in their interiors have relation to love and faith, thus to will and understanding, for the will and understanding are their receptacles: but things exterior correspond to their interiors. That things exterior correspond to things interior, may be seen above, nn. 87—115. This may receive illustration from what was advanced above respecting the heat and light of heaven, namely, that the angels enjoy heat according to the quality of their love, and light according to the quality of their wisdom. (See nn. 128—134.) It is the same with respect to all things else that appear to the senses of the angels.

174. Whenever it has been granted me to be in company with the angels, the objects in heaven were seen by me exactly as those in the world are, and were so completely perceptible, that I could not tell but that I was in the world, and in a royal palace. I have also conversed respecting them with the angels, as one man does with another.

175. As all objects which correspond to things interior also represent them, they are called, on this account, *Representatives:* and as they are varied according to the state of the interiors with the angels, they are termed, on this account, *Appearances;* notwithstanding the objects which appear before the eyes of the angels in the heavens, and which are perceived by

their senses, appear and are perceived in as lively a manner, as do those which appear and are perceived on earth by man; indeed, much more clearly, distinctly, and perceptibly. The appearances which exist from this origin in heaven, are called *real appearances*, because they exist in reality. There also are appearances which are not real, being such as do, indeed, appear, but do not correspond to their interiors.([1]) But these will be treated of hereafter.

176. To illustrate what is the nature of the objects which appear to the angels according to correspondences, I will only mention this single fact. To those who are distinguished for intelligence there appear gardens and paradises, full of trees and flowers of every kind. The trees in them are planted in most beautiful order, so combined as to form arbors, the entrance into which is by ornamental openings, and around which are walks; all disposed with such beauty as no language can describe. They who are distinguished for intelligence also walk about in them, and gather flowers, which they form into wreaths, with which they adorn little children. There also are species of trees and flowers there, such as never were seen, nor could exist, in the world. On the trees likewise, are fruits, according to the good of love in which those intelligent ones are grounded. They behold such objects, because a garden and paradise, and fruit-trees and flowers, correspond to intelligence and wisdom.([2]) That such things exist in the heavens is also known on earth, but only to such as are grounded in good, and have not extinguished in themselves the light of heaven by natural light and its fallacies: for they think and say, when meditating and speaking of heaven, that such things are there as *eye hath not seen, nor ear heard.*

([1]) That all things which appear amongst the angels are representative, nn. 1971, 3213—3227, 3342, 3475, 3485, 9481, 9543, 9576, 9577. That the heavens are full of representatives, nn. 1521, 1532, 1619. That the representatives are more beautiful as they are more interior in the heavens, n. 3475. That representatives in the heavens are real appearances, because from the light of heaven, n. 3485. That the divine influx is turned into representatives in the superior heavens, and thence also in the inferior heavens, nn. 2179, 3213, 9457, 9481, 9576, 9577. Things are called representatives which appear before the eyes of the angels in such forms as are in nature, thus such as are in the world, n. 9577. That internal things are thus turned into external, nn. 1632, 2987—3002. The nature of representatives in the heavens illustrated by various examples, nn. 1521, 1532, 1619—1625, 1807, 1973, 1974, 1977, 1980, 1981, 2299, 2601, 2761, 2762, 3217, 3219, 3220, 3348, 3350, 5198, 9090, 10,278. That all the things which appear in the heavens are according to correspondences, and are called representatives, nn. 3213—3216, 3342, 3475, 3485, 9481, 9574, 9576, 9577. That all things which correspond, represent also, and likewise signify, nn. 2896, 2987, 2988, 2989, 2990, 3002, 3225.

([2]) That a garden and paradise signify intelligence and wisdom, nn. 100, 108, 3220. What is meant by the garden of Eden and the garden of Jehovah, nn. 99, 100, 1588. Of paradisiacal scenes in the other life, and how magnificent they are, nn. 1122, 1622, 2296, 4528, 4529. That trees signify perceptions and knowledges, from which wisdom and intelligence are derived, nn. 103, 2163, 2682, 2722, 2972, 7692. That fruits signify the goods of love and charity, nr. 3146, 8690, 9337.

83

OF THE CLOTHES IN WHICH THE ANGELS ARE DRESSED.

177. Since angels are men, and live in society as men on earth do, it follows that they have clothes, houses, and other things of that nature; differing, however, from those of men on earth, by being more perfect, because angels exist in a more perfect state. For as the wisdom of angels so far exceeds that of men as to be called ineffable, so also does every thing which is perceived by them and appears to them; because all things which are perceived by the angels, and which appear to them, correspond to their wisdom. (See above, n. 173.)

178. The clothes, in which the angels are dressed, like other things connected with them, are in correspondence; and being in correspondence, they have a real existence. (See above, n. 175.) Their clothes correspond to their intelligence; wherefore all the inhabitants of heaven appear in dresses that accord with their intelligence; and as, in intelligence, one excels another, so one has better clothes than another. The most intelligent wear clothes that glow as if from flame, and some wear dresses that shine as if from light: the less intelligent have garments of clear or of opake white not shining; and the less intelligent still wear clothes of different colors; but the angels of the inmost heaven are naked.

179. Since the garments of the angels correspond to their intelligence, they also correspond to truth, since all intelligence is derived from the Divine Truth; whether, therefore, you say that the angels are clothed in accordance with their intelligence or in accordance with the Divine Truth as received by them, it amounts to the same. The reason that the dresses of some glow as from flame, or shine as from light, is, because flame corresponds to good, and light to truth derived from good :([1]) and the reason that the garments of some are of a clear or of an opake white not shining, or of different colors, is, because the Divine Good and Truth are less refulgent, and also are variously received among the less intelligent.([2]) White, also, both clear and opake, corresponds to truth,([3]) and colors to its varieties.([4]) The reason that, in the inmost heaven, the inhabitants

([1]) That garments, in the Word, signify truths, from correspondence, nn. 1073, 2576, 5319, 5554, 9212, 9216, 9952, 10,536. Because truths invest good, n. 5248. That a veil or covering signifies the intellectual principle, because the intellect is the recipient of truth, n. 6378. That bright garments of fine linen signify truths derived from the Divine Being, nn. 5319, 9469. That flame signifies spiritual good, and the light thence issuing, truth from that good, nn. 3222, 6832.

([2]) That angels and spirits appear clothed with garments according to the truths possessed by them, thus according to their intelligence, nn. 165, 5248, 5954, 9212, 9216, 9814, 9952, 10,536. That the garments of the angels in some cases possess splendor, and in some cases do not, n. 5248.

([3]) That brightness and whiteness, in the Word, signify truth, because derived from the light of heaven, nn. 3301, 3993, 4007.

([4]) That colors, in heaven, are variegations of the light there, nn. 1042, 1043, 1053, 1624, 3993, 4530, 4742, 4922. That colors signify various things which relate to intel-

are naked, is, because they are grounded in innocence, and in-nocence corresponds to nakedness.([5])

180. Since the angels wear clothes in heaven, they also appeared in clothes when they were seen in the world; as in the case of those who appeared to the prophets, and also of those who were seen at the Lord's sepulchre, *whose countenance was like lightning, and their garments white and shining* (Matt. xxviii. 3; Mark xvi. 5; Luke xxvi. 4; John xx. 12); with those seen by John in heaven, whose garments were of *fine linen, and white* (Rev. xix. 14; iv. 4). Intelligence being derived from the Divine Truth, therefore the Lord's garments, when he was transfigured, became glittering, and white as the light. (Matt. xvii. 2; Mark ix. 3; Luke ix. 29. That light is the Divine Truth proceeding from the Lord, may be seen above, n. 129.) It is on this account that garments, in the Word, signify truths, and intelligence derived from them, as in John: They "*who have not defiled their garments,—shall walk with Me in white, for they are worthy. He that overcometh, the same shall be clothed in white raiment.*"—(Rev. iii. 4, 5.) "*Blessed is he that watcheth, and keepeth his garments.*"—(Ch. xvi. 15.) And of Jerusalem, by which is meant the church that is grounded in truth,([6]) it is thus written in Isaiah: "*Awake, put on thy strength, O Zion; put on thy beautiful garments, O Jerusalem.*"— (Ch. lii. 1.) So in Ezekiel: "*I girded thee about with fine linen, and I covered thee with silk.—Thy raiment was of fine linen and silk.*"—(Ch. xvi. 10, 13.) And in many other places. A person, however, who is not grounded in truths, is said not to be clothed with a wedding-garment; as in Matthew: "*And when the king came in,—he saw there a man that had not on a wedding-garment: and he said unto him, Friend, how camest thou in hither not having a wedding-garment?—Cast him into outer darkness.*"—(Ch. xxii. 11, 12, 13.) By the house where the marriage was celebrated, is meant heaven and the church, on account of the conjunction of the Lord with them by His Divine Truth; wherefore, in the Word, the Lord is called the Bridegroom and Husband, and heaven and the church the bride and wife.

181. The garments of the angels do not merely appear as garments, but are such in reality. This is evident from these circumstances: that they not only see them, but also feel them;

---

ligence and wisdom, nn. 4530, 4922, 9466. That the precious stones in the Urim and the Thummim, according to their colors, signified all things of truth derived from good in the heavens, nn. 9865, 9868, 9905. That colors, so far as they partake of red-ness, signify good, and so far as they partake of white, signify truth, n. 9476.

([5]) That all who dwell in the inmost heaven are forms of innocence, and that there-fore they appear naked, nn. 154, 165, 297, 2736, 3887, 8375, 9960. That innocence is represented in the heavens by nakedness, nn. 165, 8375, 9960. That to the innocent and the chaste nakedness is no shame, because without offence, nn. 165, 213, 8375.

([6]) That Jerusalem signifies the church, in which is genuine doctrine, nn. 402, 3654, 9166.

that they possess many of them; that they put them off, and put them on; and that when they are not in use, they lay them by, and, when in use, take them again. That they wear different dresses, I have witnessed a thousand times. I inquired whence they obtained them; and they told me, from the Lord; that they receive them as gifts; and that they sometimes are clothed with them, without knowing, themselves, how it has been done. They said, also, that their garments are changed according to their own changes of state; and that, in their first and second states, their garments are shining and of a clear white, but, in their third and fourth states, are a little more dull; and that this, likewise, occurs from correspondence, because their changes of state are changes with respect to intelligence and wisdom. (On which, see above, nn. 154—161.)

182. Since every one in the spiritual world has clothes in accordance with his intelligence, thus in accordance with the truths from which his intelligence is derived, it follows that the inhabitants of the hells, being destitute of truths, do indeed appear in some sort of clothes, but such as are ragged, filthy, and disgusting, according to every one's insanity; nor can they wear any others. That they should have some sort of clothing is granted them by the Lord, that they may not appear naked.

OF THE HABITATIONS AND MANSIONS OF THE ANGELS.

183. Since in heaven there are societies, and the angels live as men do, it follows that they also have habitations, and that these are of different kinds according to every one's state of life; thus that those who are in a state of higher dignity have magnificent habitations, and those in lower, such as are not so magnificent. I have sometimes conversed with the angels respecting the habitations in heaven, and have observed that scarcely any person will believe, at the present day, that they have houses and mansions; some denying the fact, because they do not see them; some, because they are ignorant that angels are men; some, because they suppose the heaven of angels to be the heaven that they behold with their eyes above and around them; and as this appears to be empty space, and they suppose the angels to be merely ethereal forms, they conclude that they live in the ether. Besides, they cannot conceive how there can be, in the spiritual world, such objects as exist in the natural world, because they are in entire ignorance respecting what that which is spiritual is. The angels replied, that they are aware that such ignorance prevails at the present time in the world, and especially (what astonished them) within the church, where it possesses the intelligent much more than those

whom *they* call the simple. They said, further, that those who are in such ignorance might nevertheless know from the Word that angels are men, because such of them as have been seen were seen as men; as was the Lord also, who took with him the whole of His Humanity: and that it might likewise be known, since angels are men, that they have mansions and habitations, and do not, as some suppose in their ignorance, which the angels call insanity, flit about in the air, nor are mere puffs of wind, notwithstanding their being called "spirits."* The angels added, likewise, that they who form such notions might nevertheless comprehend the truth, as just stated, would they only think on the subject independently of their preconceived notions respecting angels and spirits; as is done when they do not first raise the question, *whether it is so*, and make this the immediate subject of their thoughts. For the idea is common to every one, that angels are in human form, and that they have dwellings, which they call the abodes of heaven, that are far more magnificent than the abodes of earth: but this idea, common to all, which is the result of an influx from heaven, is instantly annihilated when the question, *whether it is so*, is placed directly before the view, and is made the central object of the thoughts. This is chiefly done by the learned, who, by their self-derived intelligence, have shut heaven against themselves, and have closed the avenue by which its light might enter. The belief respecting the life of man after death undergoes the same fate. When a person speaks on this subject, not thinking at the time from his acquired learning respecting the soul, nor from the doctrine of its reunion with the body, he believes that he shall live after death as a man, and, if he has led a good life, in company with the angels; and that he shall then behold magnificent objects, and partake of transporting joys. But as soon as he reverts to the doctrinal notion of reunion with the body, or to the common hypothesis about the soul; and the thought occurs whether the soul is of such a nature, and thus the question is raised, *whether it is so;* his former idea is dissipated.

184. But it is better to adduce the evidence of experience. Whenever I have orally conversed with the angels, I have been with them in their habitations. These are exactly like the habitations on earth which are called houses, but more beautiful. They contain chambers, withdrawing-rooms, and bedchambers, in great numbers: they have courts to them, and are encompassed with gardens, flower-beds, and fields. Where the angels live together in societies, the habitations are contiguous, one adjoining another, and arranged in the form of a city, with streets, roads, and squares, exactly like the cities on our earth.

* It is to be remembered that the word for a spirit, in the ancient languages, like 'ghost" in our own, primarily signifies *breath*, or *wind.—N.*

It has also been granted me to walk through them, and to look about on all sides, and occasionally to enter the houses. This occurred to me when wide awake, my interior sight being open at the time.([1])

185. I have seen palaces in heaven, so magnificent as to surpass all description. The upper parts were refulgent, as if built of pure gold; and the lower parts, as if constructed of precious stones. Some palaces were more splendid than others. The inside was suitable to the outside; the apartments were ornamented with such decorations, that neither language nor science is adequate to the description of them. On the side which looked towards the south, were paradises, all the objects in which were similarly resplendent. In some places, the leaves of the trees were as if formed of silver, and the fruit as of gold: the flowers, as arranged in beds, presented, by their colors, the appearance of rainbows: and beyond the boundaries other palaces were seen, which terminated the view. Such is the architecture of heaven, that you would say you there behold the very art itself, and no wonder; for it is from heaven that that art is derived to men on earth. The angels said, that such objects as have been mentioned, and innumerable others still more perfect, are presented before their eyes by the Lord: but that, nevertheless, they impart more pleasure to their mind than to their eyes; because, in every particular, they behold correspondences; and, through those correspondences, things Divine.

186. Respecting these correspondences, I have also been informed, that not only the palaces and houses, but all things, to the most minute particulars, both within them and without them, correspond to the interior things which are in the angels from the Lord: that the house itself in general corresponds to their good, and all the objects within it to the various particulars of which their good is composed;([2]) and those without the house to their truths derived from good, and also, their perceptions and knowledges; and since those objects correspond to the goods and truths which they possess from the Lord, that they correspond to their love, and to their wisdom and intelligence thence derived, since love relates to good, wisdom to good and at the same time to truth, and intelligence to truth derived from good; and that since it is such things as these of which the angels have a perception when they view those

([1]) That the angels have cities, palaces, and houses, nn. 940, 941, 942, 1116, 1626, 1627, 1628, 1630, 1631, 4622.
([2]) That houses, with the things within them, signify those things appertaining to man which belong to his mind, thus to his interiors, nn. 710, 2233, 2331, 2559, 3128, 3538, 4973, 5023, 6105, 6690, 7353, 7848, 7910, 7929, 9150. Consequently, which relate to good and truth, nn. 2233, 2331, 2559, 4982, 7848, 7929. That inner rooms and bed-chambers signify interior things, nn. 3900, 5694, 7353. That the roof of a house signifies what is inmost, nn. 3152, 10,184. That a house of wood signifies those things which belong to good, and a house of stone, those things which belong to truth, n. 8720.

objects, they delight and affect their minds more than their eyes.

187. This makes it evident why the Lord declared .Himself to be the temple that was at Jerusalem(³) (John ii. 19, 21); and why the New Jerusalem was seen as if built of pure gold, her gates of pearls, and her foundations of precious stones (Rev. xxi.): it was because the temple represented the Lord's Divine Humanity; and the New Jerusalem signifies the church which is to be hereafter established; its twelve gates, truths leading to good; and its foundations, the truths upon which it is based.(⁴)

188. The angels of whom the Lord's celestial kingdom is composed, dwell, for the most part, in elevated situations, which appear like mountains composed of earthy substance. The angels who compose the Lord's spiritual kingdom dwell in situations not so elevated, which appear like hills. But the angels who occupy the lowest parts of heaven, dwell in places which appear like rocks composed of stones. These circumstances, also, exist from correspondence; for things interior correspond to things superior; and things exterior to things inferior.(⁵) It·is on this account that mountains, in the Word, signify celestial love; hills, spiritual love; and rocks, faith.(⁶)

189. There also are angels who do not live in societies, but separate, a house here, and a house there. These dwell in the central part of heaven; for they are the best of the angels.

190. The houses in which the angels reside are not built by manual labor, as houses are in the world, but are given them gratis by the Lord, according to the reception of good and truth by each. They also undergo some slight variations, according to the changes of the state of the interiors of their inhabitants. (Of which, see above, nn. 154—160.) All things whatever that the angels possess, they ascribe to the Lord as his gifts; and whatever they have need of, is bestowed upon them.

(³) That the house of God, in the supreme sense, signifies the Divine Humanity of the Lord, as to divine good, but the temple, as to divine truth; and, in the respective sense, heaven and the church as to good and truth, n. 3720.

(⁴) That Jerusalem signifies the church in which is genuine doctrine, nn. 402, 3654, 9166. That gates signify introduction to the doctrine of the church, and by doctrine into the church, nn. 2943, 4477. That a foundation signifies the truth, on which heaven, the church, and doctrine, are founded, n. 9643.

(⁵) That, in the Word, interior things are expressed by superior, and that superior things signify things interior, nn. 2148, 3084, 4599, 5146, 8325. That high signifies what is internal, and likewise heaven, nn. 1735, 2148, 4210, 4599, 8153.

(⁶) That in heaven there appear mountains, hills, rocks, valleys, and countries, altogether as in the world, n. 10,608. That on mountains dwell the angels who are in the good of love, on hills those who are in the good of charity, on rocks those who are in the good of faith, n. 10,438. That therefore by mountains, in the Word, is signified the good of love, nn. 795, 4210, 6435, 8327, 8758, 10,438, 10,608. By hills, the good of charity, nn. 6435, 10,438. By rocks, the good and truth of faith, nn. 8581, 10,580. That stone, of which a rock consists, in like manner signifies the truth of faith, nn. 114, 643, 1298, 3720, 6426, 8609, 10,376. Hence it is that by mountains is signified heaven, nn. 8327, 8805, 9420. And by the top of a mountain the supreme of heaven, nn. 9422, 9434, 10,608. That therefore the ancients celebrated holy worship on mountains, nn. 796, 2722.

OF SPACE IN HEAVEN

191. Although all things in heaven appear in place and in space, exactly as they do in the world, still the angels have no notion or idea of place and space. As this cannot but appear as a paradox, and it is a matter of great moment, I am desirous to place it in a clear point of view.

192. All progressions in the spiritual world are effected by changes of the state of the interiors, so that these progressions are no other than changes of state.([1]) In this manner, also, I have been conveyed by the Lord into the heavens, and also, to various earths in the universe; this being effected as to my spirit, my body still remaining in the same place.([2]) It is thus that all angels effect their progressions. Hence, with them, there are no distances; and if there are no distances, neither are there any spaces; but, instead of them, there are states, and their changes.

193. As it is thus that progressions are effected, it is evident, that approximations are similitudes as to the state of the interiors, and that removals are dissimilitudes. Hence, those are near each other who are in a similar state, and those are far apart whose state is dissimilar; and spaces in heaven are nothing but external states corresponding to internal ones. This is the only cause that the heavens are distinct from each other; as, also, the societies of every heaven, and all the angels in a society. This also is the cause that the hells are so completely separated from the heavens; for they are in a contrary state.

194. It is likewise from this cause, that, in the spiritual world, one person becomes present to another, provided, only, he intensely desires it; for he thus views the other in thought, and puts himself in his state. And, *vice versa*, that one person is removed from another in proportion as he holds him in aversion; and as all aversion proceeds from contrariety of affections and disagreement of thoughts, it hence results, that many who are there in one place, so long as they agree, appear to each other; whereas, as soon as they disagree, they disappear.

195. When, also, any one proceeds from one place to another,

([1]) That, in the Word, places and spaces signify states, nn. 2625, 2837, 3356, 3387, 7381, 10,580; from experience, nn. 1274, 1277, 1376—1381, 4321, 4882, 10,146, 10,580. That distance signifies the difference of the state of life, nn. 9104, 9967. That motion and changes of place, in the spiritual world, are changes of the state of life, because they originate in them, nn. 1273, 1274, 1275, 1377, 3356, 9440. In like manner journeyings, nn. 9440, 10,734; illustrated by experience, nn. 1273—1277, 5605. That hence, in the Word, to journey, signifies to live, and likewise a progression of life; in like manner, to sojourn, nn. 3335, 4554, 4585, 4882, 5493, 5605, 5996, 8345, 8397, 8417, 8420, 8557. That to go with the Lord, is to live with Him, n. 10,567.

([2]) That man, as to his spirit, may be led to a distance afar off by changes of state, whilst his body remains in its place; also, from experience, nn. 9440, 9967, 10,734. What is it to be brought by the spirit into another place, n. 1884.

whether in his own city, or in the courts, or the gardens, or to others out of his own society, he arrives sooner when he desires it, and later when he does not. The way itself is lengthened or shortened according to the strength of the desire, though it is the same all the while. This I have often witnessed, and have wondered at. From these facts it again is evident, that distances, and consequently spaces, exist with the angels altogether according to the states of their interiors; and such being the fact, that the notion and idea of space cannot enter their thoughts; although spaces exist with them equally as in the world.(*)

196. This may be illustrated by the thoughts of man: for neither are these connected with spaces, but those things on which he intently fixes his thoughts become to him as present. It is known, also, to him who reflects on it, that neither are spaces cognizable by the sight, otherwise than as discovered by intervening objects on the earth that he sees at the same time, or from his knowing that those objects are at such and such a distance. This occurs, because space is continuous, and in what is continuous, distance does not appear, except from the occurrence of objects that are not continuous. Still more is this the case with the angels, because their sight acts as one with their thought, and their thought with their affection; and because things near and remote appear such, and also undergo variations, according to the state of their interiors; as observed above.

197. It is on this account that, in the Word, by places and spaces, and by all the things that partake in any respect of space, are signified such things as relate to state. Such, therefore, is the case with distances, nearness, remoteness, ways, journeys, and sojournings; with miles and furlongs; with plains, fields, gardens, cities, and streets; with motions; with measures of various kinds; with length, breadth, height, and depth; and with innumerable other things: for most things which exist with man in his thoughts derived from the world, partake, in some way, of space and time. I will only mention what is signified in the Word by length, breadth, and height. In the world, long and broad, and high likewise, are predicated of objects which are such in respect to space: but in heaven, where the thoughts of the inhabitants do not partake of space, by length is understood a state of good, by breadth a state of truth, and by height, their distinctions in regard to degrees. (Respecting degrees, see above, n. 38.) The reason that those three dimensions have such significations, is, because heaven, in length, extends from east to west, which quarters are inhabited by those who are grounded more especially in the good of love; and breadth, in heaven, is its extension from south to north, which quarters are

(*) That places and spaces are presented visibly according to the states of the interiors of angels and spirits, nn. 5605, 9440, 10,146.

inhabited by those who are more particularly grounded in truth derived from good; and height, in heaven, denotes both good and truth, according to degrees. (See above, n. 148.) It is on this account that such things are signified by length, breadth, and height, in the Word. Thus, in Ezekiel (Chs. xl.—xlviii.), by the new temple and the new earth, with the courts, chambers, doors, gates, windows, and suburbs, which are described with their dimensions as to length, breadth, and height, is signified a new church, with the goods and truths to be enjoyed in it: why, else, should all those measures be enumerated? The New Jerusalem is described in the Revelation in a similar manner, in these words : "*And the city lieth four-square, and the length is as large as the breadth. And he measured the city with the reed, twelve thousand furlongs. The length and the breadth and the height of it are equal.*"—(Ch. xxi. 16.) Here, by the New Jerusalem, is signified a new church, whence by its dimensions are signified particulars belonging to the church; by its length being signified its good of love, by its breadth, its truth derived from that good, by its height, its good and truth as to their degrees, and by twelve thousand furlongs, all good and truth taken collectively; otherwise, what sense would there be in the statement, that its height was twelve thousand furlongs, the same as its length and breadth? That, in the Word, by breadth is signified truth, is evident in David : *Thou* "*hast not shut me up into the hand of the enemy ; thou hast set my foot in a large room ;*"—more literally, "*in a broad place.*"—(Ps. xxxi. 8.) "*I called upon Jehovah in distress*"—literally, "*out of a narrow place :*"—"*Jehovah answered me, and set me in a large place*"—literally, "*a broad place.*"—(Ps. cxviii. 5.) Not to mention other passages, as Isa. viii. 8 ; Hab. i. 6.

198. From these remarks it may be seen, that although spaces exist in heaven as well as in the world, still nothing is there reckoned by spaces, but by states; consequently, that spaces cannot there be measured, as is done in the world, but only be seen from, and according to, the state of the interiors of the inhabitants.[4]

199. The very first and most essential cause of all this is, that the Lord is present with every one according to his love and faith,[5] and that all things appear either near or remote according to His presence ; for it is by this that the situation of all things in the heavens is determined. By this, also, the angels have their wisdom ; for it is by this that they experience an extension of thoughts, and thereby a communication of all

---

[4] That, in the Word, length signifies good, nn. 1613, 9487. That breadth signifies truth, nn. 1613, 3433, 3434, 4482, 9487, 10,179. That height signifies good and truth as to degrees, nn. 9489, 9773, 10,181.

[5] That the conjunction and presence of the Lord with the angels are according to the reception of love and charity from Him, nn. 290, 681, 1954, 2658, 2886, 2888, 2889, 3001, 3741, 3742, 3743, 4318, 4319, 4524, 7211, 9128.

things that exist in the heavens. In oι.e word, it is through this that they think in a spiritual manner, and not in a natural manner, as men do.

OF THE FORM OF HEAVEN, ACCORDING TO WHICH THE CONSO-CIATIONS AND COMMUNICATIONS OF THE INHABITANTS ARE ARRANGED.

200. The nature of the form of heaven may in some measure appear from what has been shown in some preceding Sections; as, That heaven is like itself in its greatest forms and in its least (n. 72), whence every society is a heaven on a smaller scale, and every angel is a heaven in miniature (nn. 51—58): That as heaven collectively is as one man, so every society is as a man on a smaller scale, and every angel on the smallest (nn. 59—77): That in the midst dwell the most wise, and in the circumferences, by degrees, extending to the boundaries, those who are less wise; and that it is the same in every society (n. 43): and That those who are especially grounded in the good of love have their abodes in heaven, from the east to the west; and those who are especially grounded in truths derived from good, from the south to the north; and the same in every society (nn. 148, 149). All these arrangements take place according to the form of heaven; from which, therefore, a conclusion may be drawn respecting the nature of that form in general.[1]

201. It is of importance to know what is the nature of the form of heaven, because not only are all its inhabitants arranged in society according to that form, but, likewise, all communication takes place according to it, and thence, also, all diffusion of thoughts and affections, consequently, all the intelligence and wisdom of the angels. On this account, in proportion as any one exists in the form of heaven, thus, in proportion as he is a form of heaven, he is in the enjoyment of wisdom. Whether we speak of being in the form of heaven, or in the order of heaven, it amounts to the same; since the form of every thing results from its order, and is according to it.[2]

202. Something shall now be first offered, respecting what is meant by being in the form of heaven. Man was created after the image of heaven and the image of the world; his internal being created after the image of heaven, and his external after that of the world. (See above, n. 57.) Whether we say, "after

[1] That the universal heaven, as to all the angelic societies, is arranged by the Lord according to His divine order, inasmuch as the Divine Sphere of the Lord abiding with the angels constitutes heaven, nn. 3038, 7211, 9128, 9338, 10,125, 10,151, 10,157. Of the form of heaven, nn. 4040, 4041, 4042, 4043, 6607, 9877.

[2] That the form of heaven is according to divine order, nn. 4040—4043, 6607, 9877.

the image," or, " according to the form," it is the same thing. But as man, by the evils of his will, and by the falsities of his thought thence derived, has destroyed in himself the image, consequently the form, of heaven, and has introduced in their place the image and form of hell, his internal is closed from the time of his birth; which is the reason that man, differently from all kinds of animals, is born into mere ignorance. In order, therefore, that the image or form of heaven should be restored in him, he must be instructed in such matters as belong to order; for, as remarked above, according to the order is the form. The Word contains all the laws of Divine order, those laws being the precepts therein delivered; in proportion, therefore, as man becomes acquainted with these precepts, and lives according to them, his internal is opened, and the order or image of heaven is there formed anew. We now may see what is meant by being in the form of heaven: namely, that it consists in living according to the truths contained in the Word.[*]

203. So far as any one exists in the form of heaven, he actually is in heaven, and is, himself, a heaven in miniature (n. 57). Consequently, also, he is so far in the enjoyment of intelligence and wisdom: for, as stated above, every thought that belongs to his understanding, and every affection that belongs to his will, diffuse themselves into heaven in every direction, according to its form, and communicate in a wonderful manner with the societies that exist there; as do these, reciprocally, with him.[*] There are some who imagine that their thoughts and affections do not actually diffuse themselves around them, but are inclosed within them, because they see what they think inwardly in themselves, and not as a distant object. But this is a great mistake: for as the sight of the eye extends itself to remote objects, and is affected according to the order of the things which it beholds in such extended vision, so likewise, does man's interior sight, which is that of the understanding, extend itself in the spiritual world, although he is not sensible of it, for the reason explained above (n. 196). The

[*] That divine truths are the laws of order, nn. 2447, 7995. That man, so far as he lives according to order, thus so far as he is principled in good according to divine truths, becomes a man, nn. 4839, 6605, 6626. That man is the being into whom are collated all things of divine order, and that from creation he is divine order in a form, nn. 4219, 4220, 4223, 4523, 4524, 5114, 5368, 6013, 6057, 6605, 6626, 9706, 10,156, 10,472. That man is not born into good and truth, but into evil and falsity, thus into what is contrary to divine order; and that hence he is born into mere ignorance, and therefore it is necessary that he be born anew, that is, be regenerated, which is effected by divine truths from the Lord, that he may be inaugurated into order, nn. 1047, 2307, 2308, 3518, 3812, 8480, 8550, 10,283, 10,284, 10,286, 10,731. That the Lord, when He forms man anew, that is, regenerates him, arranges all things in him according to order, which is, into the form of heaven, nn. 5700, 6690, 9931, 10,303.

[*] That every one in heaven has communication of life, which may be called a diffusion into the angelic societies around, according to the quantity and quality of his good, nn. 8794, 8797. That thoughts and affections have such diffusion, nn. 2475, 6598–6613. That they are conjoined and disjoined according to the ruling affections, n. 4111.

only difference is, that the sight of the eye is affected in a natural manner, because by such things as exist in the natural world; whereas the sight of the understanding is affected in a spiritual manner, because by such things as exist in the spiritual world, all of which have relation to good and truth. The reason that man is not aware that such is the fact, is, because he is not aware that there exists a light which illuminates the understanding; although, were there not such a light, man would be absolutely unable to think at all. (Respecting that light, see above, nn. 126—132.) There was a certain spirit who thus imagined that he exercised thought from himself, consequently, without any diffusion of his thoughts beyond himself, or any communication, by such means, with societies existing without himself. To convince him that he was in error, the communication between him and the societies nearest to him was taken away; upon which he not only was deprived of thought, but fell down as if dead, only throwing his arms about like a new-born infant. After some time, the communication was restored; upon which he gradually, as the restoration was effected, returned into a state capable of thinking. Some other spirits, who witnessed this experiment, thereupon confessed that all thought and affection enter by influx, according to such communication; and, since all thought and affection thus enter, so, also, does the all of life; since the all of man's life consists in his capacity of thinking and being affected, or, what amounts to the same, in his capacity of exercising understanding and will.([5])

204. But it is to be understood, that intelligence and wisdom vary with every one, according to the nature of the communication that he experiences. Those whose intelligence and wisdom are formed of genuine truths and goods, have communication with societies according to the form of heaven: whereas those whose intelligence and wisdom are not formed of genuine truths and goods, but still of such as harmonize with genuine ones, have a communication that is interrupted, and is only kept up in an irregular manner, because not maintained with societies in such a series as the form of heaven exists in. But those who do not possess intelligence and wisdom, being immersed in falsities derived from evil, have communication with societies in

([5]) That there is only one single Life, from which all live, both in heaven and in the world, nn. 1954, 2021, 2536, 2658, 2886—2889, 3001, 3484, 3742, 5847, 6467. That that life is from the Lord alone, nn. 2886—2889, 3344, 3484, 4319, 4 12, 4524, 4882, 5986, 6325, 6468, 6469, 6470, 9276, 10,196. That it flows into angels, spirits, and men, in a wonderful manner, nn. 2886—2889, 3337, 3338, 3484, 3742. That the Lord flows in from His divine love, which is of such a nature, that what is His own He wills should be another's, nn. 3742, 4320. That for this reason, life appears as if it was in man, and not as if it were influent, nn. 3742, 4320. Of the joys of the angels, as perceived, and confirmed by what they told me, that they do not live from themselves, but from the Lord, n. 6469. That the wicked are not willing to be convinced that life enters by influx, n. 3743. That life from the Lord flows, also, into the wicked, nn. 2706, 3743, 4417, 10,196. But that they turn good into evil and truth into falsity; for according to man's quality, such is his reception of life; illustrated, nn. 4319, 4320, 4417.

hell. The extensiveness of the communication is in proportion
to the degree of confirmation. It is further to be understood,
that this communication with societies is not such as comes
manifestly to the perception of those who compose there, but is
a communication with their quality, that is, with the quality in
which they are grounded, and which proceeds from them.[6]

205. All in heaven are connected in society according to
spiritual affinities, which are those of good and truth in their
order. It is thus in heaven regarded as a whole: it is thus in
every society; and it is thus in every house. It is from this
cause that the angels who are grounded in good and truth of
similar quality recognize one another, as those related by con-
sanguinity and affinity do on earth, just as if they had known
each other from infancy. The goods and truths which constitute
intelligence and wisdom, are connected in the same manner
with every individual angel: they recognize each other in the
same manner; and as they recognize each other, so, also, do
they join themselves together.[7] From the same cause those
with whom truths and goods are conjoined according to the
form of heaven, see the consequences flowing from them in their
series, and have an extensive view of their coherence in all directions. Not so those with whom goods and truths are not
conjoined according to the form of heaven.

206. Such, in each heaven, is the form, according to which
the communication and diffusion of the thoughts and affections
of the angels exist, thus according to which they have intelligence and wisdom. But the communication between one heaven
and another, as between the third or inmost and the second or
middle, and between both these and the first or ultimate, is
different. But the communication between the different heavens
ought not to be termed communication, but influx. Respecting
this something shall now be offered. (That there are three
heavens, and that they are distinct from each other, may be
seen in its proper Section above, (nn. 29—40).

207. That there is not a communication between the different
heavens, but an influx from one into another, may be obvious
from their respective situations. The third or inmost heaven is
situated above, the second or middle heaven is below, and the
first or ultimate heaven is further below still. All the societies
of each heaven are arranged in a similar manner. Thus, for instance, in those societies that are located in elevated situations,
which appear like mountains (n. 188), those angels dwell on the

[6] That thought diffuses itself into the societies of spirits and of angels round
about, nn. 6600—6605. That still it does not move and disturb the thoughts of those
societies, nn. 6601, 6603.
[7] That good acknowledges its truth, and truth its good, nn. 2429 3101, 3102, 3161,
3179, 3180, 4358, 5407, 5835, 9637. That hence is the conjunction of good and of
truth, nn. 3834, 4096, 4097, 4301, 4345, 4353, 4364, 4368, 5365, 7623—7627, 7752—7762,
8530, 9258, 10,555. And that this is from the influx of heaven. n. 9079.

summits who belong to the inmost heaven; below them are those who belong to the second heaven; and below these, again, are those who belong to the ultimate heaven. A similar arrangement prevails everywhere, whether in elevated situations or not. A society of a superior heaven has no communication with a society of an inferior heaven, except by correspondences (see above, n. 100): and communication by correspondences is that which is called influx.

208. One heaven is conjoined with another, or a society of one heaven with a society of another, by the Lord alone, by influx, both immediately and mediately—immediately, from Himself, and mediately, through the superior heavens, in order, into the inferior.([8]) Since the conjunction of the heavens with each other by influx is the work of the Lord alone, it is most especially provided that no angel of a superior heaven should look down into a society of an inferior heaven, and converse with any of its inhabitants. As soon as he does so, the angel is deprived of his wisdom and intelligence. The cause of this, also, shall be stated. Every angel has three degrees of life, in the same manner as there are three degrees of heaven. Those who are in the inmost heaven have the third or inmost degree open, and the second and first shut: those who are in the middle heaven have the second degree open, and the first and third shut: and those who are in the ultimate heaven have the first degree open, and the second and third shut: as soon, therefore, as an angel of the third heaven looks down into a society of the second heaven, and converses with any one there, his third degree is closed, and, when this is closed, he is deprived of his wisdom, because this resides in his third degree, and he does not possess any in his second and first. This is what is meant by the Lord's words in Matthew: "*Let him that is on the house-top not come down to take any thing out of his house: neither let him that is in the field return back to take his clothes.*"—(Ch. xxiv. 18, 19.) And in Luke: "*In that day, he that is upon the house-top, and his stuff in the house, let him not come down to take it away: and he that is in the field, let him, likewise, not return back. Remember Lot's wife.*"—(Ch. xvii. 31, 32.)

209. There is no influx from the inferior heavens into the superior, because this would be contrary to order: the influx proceeds from the superior heavens into the inferior. The wisdom, also, of the angels of a superior heaven, exceeds that of the angels of an inferior heaven, in the proportion of ten thousand to one. This, also, is the reason, that the angels of an inferior heaven cannot converse with the angels of a superior heaven;

([8]) That there is immediate influx from the Lord, and mediate, by or through heaven, nn. 6063, 6307, 6472, 9682, 9683. That the Lord's influx is immediate into the most particular things of all, nn. 6058, 6474—6478, 8717, 8728. Of the Lord's mediate influx by or through the heavens, nn. 4067, 6982, 6985, 6996.

indeed, when they look in that direction, they do not see them: their heaven appears like something misty over their heads. The angels of a superior heaven can, however, see those who are in an inferior heaven, but are not at liberty to join in conversation with them, except with the loss of their wisdom; as stated above.

210. Neither the thoughts and affections, nor yet the discourse, of the angels of the inmost heaven, can possibly come to the perception of those in the middle heaven, because they so greatly transcend the capacity of the angels in that heaven. When, however, it is the Lord's good pleasure, a sort of flaming appearance proceeding thence is seen in the inferior heavens. So, the thoughts and affections, and discourses, of the angels in the middle heaven, cause a lucid appearance to be seen in the ultimate heaven, which sometimes assumes the form of a white or variously-colored cloud; and by the appearance of that cloud,—its ascent, descent, and form, is also known, in some degree, the subject of their conversation.

211. From these observations it may appear, of what nature is the form of heaven; namely, that in the inmost heaven it is the most perfect of all; that in the middle heaven, it also is perfect, but in an inferior degree; and, in the ultimate, in a degree still inferior; and that the form of one heaven derives its subsistence from that of another by an influx from the Lord. But the nature of communication by influx cannot be comprehended, without a knowledge of the nature of degrees of altitude, and of the difference between these degrees and those of longitude and latitude. What is the nature of both these kinds of degrees, may be seen above (n. 38).

212. The specific form of heaven, however, and the manner in which its motions and fluxions proceed, are subjects incomprehensible to the angels themselves: yet some idea of it may be presented, by considering the form of all the parts in the human body, as surveyed and investigated by a man of sagacity and wisdom. For it has been shown above, in proper Sections, that the whole of heaven is in form as one man (see nn. 59—72); and that all the parts that exist in man correspond to the heavens (nn. 87—102). How incomprehensible and inextricable that form is, may be concluded, though only in a general way, from the nervous fibres, by compagination of which all the parts, generally and individually, are formed. The nature of those fibres, and how their motions and fluxions proceed in the brain, cannot even be discerned by the eye; for they are there innumerable, and so folded together, that, taken collectively, they appear as a continuous soft mass; and yet all things, both generally and individually, which belong to the will and the understanding, flow, according to those innumerable complicated fibres, most distinctly into acts. How these fibres, again,

wreathe themselves together in the body, appears from the various collections of them called *plexus*—such as the cardiac plexus, those of the mesentery, and others. The same appears, also, from the knots of them called 'ganglions, into which enter many fibres from every province, mix themselves there together, and thence go forth again, differently combined, to the performance of their functions ;—a process which is repeated again and again. Not to mention similar wonders in every viscus, member, organ, and muscle. Whoever· surveys these things, and many other wonders there displayed, with the eye of wisdom, must be filled with amazement : and yet the wonders that the eye sees are comparatively few: those which the eye cannot see, as belonging to interior nature, are more marvellous still. That this form corresponds to the form of heaven, manifestly appears from the operation of all things that belong to the understanding and will in it and according to it : for whatever a man wills, descends spontaneously, according to that form, into act; and whatever he thinks, pervades those fibres from their origins to their terminations, whence he has sensation : and as this form is that of the thought and will, it is the form of intelligence and wisdom. This form it is which corresponds to the form of heaven ; whence it may be known, that such is the form according to which every affection and thought of the angels diffuses itself, and that they are in the possession of intelligence and wisdom in proportion as they exist in that form. That heaven derives this form from the Divine Humanity of the Lord, may be seen above (nn. 78—86). These facts are adduced, that it may also be known, that the heavenly form is of such a nature, that it never can be exhausted even as to the most general things belonging to it; and thus that it is incomprehensible to the angels themselves ; as observed above.

OF GOVERNMENTS IN HEAVEN

213. Since heaven is divided into societies, and the larger societies consist of some hundreds of thousands of angels (n. 50); and since all the members of one society are, indeed, grounded in similar good, but not in similar wisdom (n. 43) ; it necessarily follows, that, in heaven, there are governments also. For order is to be observed, and all things belonging to order are to be kept inviolable. But the governments in the heavens are various : they are different in the societies which constitute the Lord's celestial kingdom from what they are in the societies which constitute the Lord's spiritual kingdom : they differ, also,

according to the ministries discharged by each society. In the heavens, however, no other government exists than that of mutual love; and the government of mutual love is heavenly government.

214. The government in the Lord's celestial kingdom is called *Justice* or *Righteousness;* because all the subjects of that kingdom are grounded in the good of love, directed to the Lord, and derived from Him: and whatever is done from that good is called just or righteous. The government, there, is that of the Lord alone: He leads them, and instructs them in the matters relating to life. The truths, which are called those of judgment, are inscribed on their hearts: every one knows them, perceives them, and sees them :([1]) whence matters of judgment never are brought, there, into question, but only matters of justice or righteousness. Respecting these, the less wise interrogate the more wise, and these the Lord, and obtain answers. Their heaven, or their inmost joy, consists in living justly or righteously from the Lord.

215. The government in the Lord's spiritual kingdom is called *Judgment,* because the subjects of this kingdom are grounded in spiritual good, which is the good of charity towards the neighbor: and this good, in its essence, is truth ;([2]) and truth belongs to judgment, and good to justice or righteousness.([3]) These, also, are led by the Lord, but mediately (n. 208); wherefore they have governors over them, few or more according to the needs of the society to which they belong. They also have laws, according to which they are to regulate their social life. The governors administer all things according to the laws. Being wise, they understand them aright, and, in doubtful matters, they receive illustration from the Lord.

216. Since government from good, such as is exercised in the Lord's celestial kingdom, is called justice or righteousness, and government from truth, such as is established in the Lord's spiritual kingdom, is called judgment, therefore, in the Word, justice or righteousness, and judgment, are mentioned, where the subject treated of is heaven and the church; and by justice

---

([1]) That the celestial angels do not think and speak from truths, like the spiritual angels, since they are in the perception of all things relating to truths from the Lord, nn. 202, 597, 607, 784, 1121, 1387, 1398, 1442, 1919, 7680, 7877, 8780, 9277, 10,386. That the celestial angels say, of truths, Yea, yea, Nay, nay; but that the spiritual angels reason about them, whether the truth be so or not so, nn. 2715, 3246, 4448, 9166, 10,786; where the Lord's words are explained, "*Let your discourse be Yea, yea, Nay, nay; for whatsoever is more than this, cometh of evil* (Matt. v. 37).

([2]) That those who inhabit the Lord's spiritual kingdom are principled in truths, and those who inhabit the celestial kingdom, in good, nn. 863, 875, 927, 1023, 1043, 1044, 1555, 2256, 4328, 4493, 5113, 9596. That the good of the spiritual kingdom is the good of charity towards the neighbor; and that this good in its essence is truth, nn. 8042, 10,296.

([3]) That justice or righteousness, in the Word, is predicated of good, and judgment of truth; and that hence, to do justice and judgment, denotes, good and truth, nn. 2235, 9857. That great judgments denote the laws of divine order, thus divine truths, n. 7206.

or righteousness is signified celestial good, and by judgment, spiritual good, which latter, as just observed, in its essence, is truth; as in these places: "*Of the increase of his government and peace there shall be no end, upon the throne of David, and upon his kingdom, to order it, and to establish it with* JUDGMENT *and with* JUSTICE, *from henceforth even forever.*"—(Isa. ix. 7.) By David is here meant the Lord,([4]) and by his kingdom, heaven; as appears from this passage: "*I will raise unto David a righteous Branch, and a king shall reign and prosper, and shall execute* JUDGMENT *and* JUSTICE *in the earth.*"—(Jer. xxiii. 5.) "*Jehovah is exalted; for He dwelleth on high: He hath filled Zion with* JUDGMENT *and* RIGHTEOUSNESS."—(Isa. xxxiii. 5.) By Zion, also, are meant heaven and the church.([5]) "*I am Jehovah; who exercise loving-kindness, judgment, and righteousness, in the earth: for in these things I delight, saith Jehovah.*"—(Jer. ix. 24.) "*I will betroth thee unto Me forever: yea, I will betroth thee unto Me in* RIGHTEOUSNESS *and in* JUDGMENT."—(Hos. ii. 19.) "*O Jehovah,—thy righteousness is like the great mountains; thy judgments are a great deep.*"—(Ps. xxxvi. 5, 6.) "*They ask of Me the ordinances*"—literally, " *the* JUDGMENTS—*of* JUSTICE: *they take delight in approaching to God.*"—(Isa. lviii. 2.)

217. In the Lord's spiritual kingdom, the forms of government are various, being not the same in one society as in another. The varieties are in accordance with the ministries which the societies discharge; and these are in accordance with the offices of all the parts in man, to which they correspond. That these are various, is well known: for there is one office belonging to the heart, another to the lungs, another to the liver, another to the pancreas and spleen, and another, likewise, to every organ of sense. As these discharge different functions in the body, so, also, do the societies in the Grand Man, which is heaven; for there are societies which correspond to all those organs respectively. That there is a correspondence between all things belonging to heaven and all things belonging to man, has been shown in its proper Section above (nn. 87—102). But all the forms of government agree in this, that they all look, as their end, to the public good, and, in that good, to the good of every individual.([6]) This results from the fact, that all the

___

([4]) That by David, in the prophetical parts of the Word, is understood the Lord, nn. 1888, 9954.

([5]) That by Zion, in the Word, is meant the church, specifically the celestial church, nn. 2362, 9055.

([6]) That every man and society, also a man's country and the church, and, in a universal sense, the kingdom of the Lord, is our neighbor; and that to do good to them from the love of good, according to the quality of their state, is to love our neighbor; thus that their good, which is also the general good, and which is to be consulted, is our neighbor, nn. 6818—6824, 8123. That civil good, also, consisting in what is just, is our neighbor, nn. 2915, 4730, 8120, 8123. Hence, that charity towards the neighbor extends itself to all things, both generally and particularly, belonging to the life of man; and that to love good and to do good from the love of what is good and true, and also inhabitants of the universal heaven are under the guidance of the Lord, who loves them all, and, from his Divine Love, provides that there should exist a common good from which every individual should receive his particular good. Every individual, also, does receive good for himself, in proportion as he loves the common good: for so far as any one loves the community, he loves all the individuals who compose it; and since this is the love of the Lord Himself, he is loved by the Lord in the same proportion, and good results to himself.

218. From these observations it may appear, what is the character of the governors, and that they are such as are distinguished beyond others for love and wisdom, consequently, such as, from a principle of love, desire the good of all, and, from the wisdom by which, also, they are distinguished, know how to provide that the good they desire may be realized. Persons who are of this character do not domineer and command imperiously, but minister and serve; for to do good to others out of the love of good, is what is meant by serving, and to provide that such desired end may be realized, is what is meant by ministering. Neither do such account themselves greater than others, but less; for they put the good of the society and of their neighbor in the first place, and their own in the last; and that which is in the first place, is greater, and that which is in the last, is less. They nevertheless are in the enjoyment of honor and glory: they dwell in the centre of the society, in a more elevated situation than others, and inhabit magnificent palaces. They also accept this glory and that honor; not, however, for their own sake, but for the sake of securing obedience: for all in heaven know that that honor and that glory are conferred on them by the Lord, and that, therefore, they are to be obeyed. These are the things which are meant in these words of the Lord to his disciples: "*Whosoever will be chief among you, let him be your servant: even as the Son of man came not to be ministered unto, but to minister, and to give his life a ransom for many*."—(Matt. xx. 27, 28.) "*He that is the greatest among you, let him be as the younger; and he that is chief, as he that doth serve*."—(Luke xxii. 26.)

219. A similar government, in miniature, obtains, also, in every house. There is in each house a master, and there are domestics: the master loves the domestics, and the domestics love the master; the consequence of which is, that, out of love, they mutually serve each other. The master teaches how they should live, and prescribes what they should do; and the domestics obey, and perform their duties. To be of use is the delight of life among all. It hence is evident, that the Lord's kingdom is a kingdom of uses.

do what is just from the love of what is just, in every function and in all our dealings, is to love our neighbor, nn. 2417, 8121, 8124.

220. There are also governments in the hells, for if there were not, the inhabitants could not be kept in bonds. But the governments there are the opposites of those in the heavens. They all are such as are founded in self-love. Every one there desires to rule imperiously over others, and to attain pre-eminence. Such as do not favor their wishes, they hate, seek to be revenged on them, and treat them with cruelty; for such is the nature of self-love: wherefore the more desperately malignant are set over them; whom they obey from fear.(*) But of this, more below, where the hells are treated of.

OF DIVINE WORSHIP IN HEAVEN.

221. Divine Worship in the heavens is not unlike that on earth as to externals, but it differs as to internals. Angels, as well as men, have doctrines, preaching, and temples or churches. The *doctrines* all agree as to things essential; but those in the superior heavens are of more interior wisdom than those in the inferior heavens: The *preaching* is according to the doctrines: And as they have houses and palaces (nn. 183—190), so, also, they have temples or churches, in which the preaching is performed. Another reason why such things exist in heaven, is, because the angels are continually perfected in wisdom and love: for they have will and understanding as well as men, and the understanding is of such a nature as to be capable of advancing in perfection continually; and so, also, is the will; the understanding being perfected by the truths that belong to intelligence, and the will by the goods that belong to love.(¹)

222. But divine worship in the heavens does not consist, properly speaking, in frequenting the temples and hearing the preaching, but in the life of love, charity, and faith, according to their doctrines: the preaching in the temples only serves as means for obtaining instruction in matters relating to life. I have conversed with the angels on this subject, and have told them that it is imagined in the world, that divine worship con-

---

(*) That there are two kinds of rule, one grounded in the love of the neighbor, the other in the love of self, n. 10,814. That all things good and happy result from such government as is grounded in neighborly love, nn. 10,160, 10,614. That, in heaven, no one can exercise rule from the love of self, but that all are willing to minister; and that this is to exercise rule from neighborly love; and that hence they possess so great power, n. 5732. That all evils result from the exercise of rule grounded in the love of self, n. 10,038. That when the loves of self and of the world began to prevail, men were compelled for security to subject themselves to governments, nn. 7364, 10,160, 10,814.

(¹) That the understanding is recipient of truth, and the will of good, nn. 3623, 6125, 7503, 9300, 9930. That as all things have relation to truth and good, so the all of man's life has relation to the understanding and the will, nn. 803, 10,122. That the angels advance in perfection to eternity nn. 4803, 6648.

sists in nothing but going to church, hearing preaching, receiving the sacrament three or four times a year, and attending to the other rituals of worship as prescribed by the church; as also in giving time to prayer, and behaving devoutly on the occasion. The angels said, that these are externals which ought to be observed, but that they are of no use unless they proceed from an internal principle; and that such internal principle consists in a life according to the precepts which doctrine inculcates.

223. In order that I might know the nature of their assemblies in their temples, it has sometimes been granted me to enter, and to hear the preaching. The preacher stands in a pulpit on the east. In front of him sit those who are in the enjoyment, more than the rest, of the light of wisdom; and on the right and left of these sit those who have less. The seats are disposed like those of a circus, so that all are in view of the preacher. No one sits quite on either side of him, so as to be out of his sight. At the door, which is on the east side of the temple, at the left of the pulpit, stand the novitiates. It is not allowed for any one to stand behind the pulpit, for if any one does, the preacher is confused; as also occurs if any one in the congregation dissents from what he hears; wherefore, should this happen, he must turn away his face. The sermons are so replete with wisdom, that none that are heard in the world can be compared to them; for the preachers in the heavens are in the enjoyment of interior light. The temples in the spiritual kingdom appear as if constructed of stone, and, in the celestial kingdom, as of wood; because stone corresponds to truth, in which, more especially, the angels of the spiritual kingdom are grounded, and wood corresponds to good, which is the distinguishing characteristic of the angels of the celestial kingdom.([2]) In this latter kingdom, likewise, the sacred edifices are not called temples, but houses of God. In the celestial kingdom, the sacred edifices are not of a magnificent description; but in the spiritual kingdom they all possess magnificence, greater or less.

224. I have conversed with one of the preachers respecting the state of sanctity in which the hearers are when listening to the sermons in the temples. He said, that every one is in a state of piety, devotion, and sanctity, according to the state of the interior things belonging to him which relate to love and faith; for it is in these that sanctity, properly so called, resides, because these are the receptacles of the Divine Sphere proceeding from the Lord; and that he did not know what external sanctity, independent of those interior principles, could be.

([2]) That stone signifies truth, nn. 114, 643, 1298, 3720, 6426, 8609, 10,376. That wood signifies good, nn. 643 3720, 8354. That, on this account, the most ancient people, who were principled in celestial good, built their sacred edifices o. wood, n. 3720.

On reflecting on such separate external sanctity, he said, that probably it might be some feigned appearance of sanctity in outward form, either acquired by art, or assumed hypocritically; and that some spurious fire, proceeding from the love of self and of the world, might excite and display such an appearance.

225. All the preachers belong to the Lord's spiritual kingdom, and none of them to his celestial kingdom. The reason that they all belong to the spiritual kingdom is, because the angels of that kingdom are especially grounded in truths derived from good; and all preaching is performed from truths. The reason that none of them belong to the celestial kingdom is, because the angels of that kingdom are especially grounded in the good of love, from which they see and have a perception of truths, but do not speak of them. But notwithstanding the angels of the celestial kingdom have a perception of truths, and see them, still there is preaching among them, because they are thus enlightened in the truths which they know, and their perfection is advanced by many which they before did not know. As soon as they hear such, they also recognize them as truths, and thus receive a perception of them. The truths of which they have a perception, they also love, and by living according to them they incorporate them into their life. They likewise affirm, that to live according to truths is to love the Lord.[3]

226. All the preachers are appointed by the Lord, and thence possess the gift of preaching; nor are any others permitted to teach in the temples. They are called preachers, not priests; the reason of which is, because the priesthood of heaven is the celestial kingdom; for the priesthood signifies the good of love to the Lord; in which the subjects of that kingdom are grounded. So, the royalty of heaven is the spiritual kingdom; royalty, also, signifies truth derived from good; in which the subjects of that kingdom are grounded.[4] (See above, n. 24.)

227. The doctrines, according to which the preaching is framed, all regard life as their end, and none of them faith without life. The doctrine of the inmost heaven is more replete with wisdom than the doctrine of the middle heaven, and this is more replete with intelligence than the doctrine of the ultimate heaven. The doctrines, also, are adapted to the perceptions of the angels in each heaven. The essential point in all the doctrines is, to acknowledge the Lord's Divine Humanity.

[3] That to love the Lord and our neighbor, is, to live according to the Lord's precepts, nn. 10,143, 10,153, 10,310, 10,578, 10,645, 10,648.

[4] That priests represent the Lord as to divine good, kings as to divine truth, nn. 2015, 6148. That hence a priest, in the Word, signifies those who are principled in the good of love to the Lord; thus that the priesthood signifies that good, nn. 9806, 9809. That a king, in the Word, signifies those who are grounded in divine truth, thus the regal office signifies truth derived from good, nn. 1672, 2015, 2069, 4575, 4581, 4966, 5044.

OF THE POWER OF THE ANGELS OF HEAVEN.

228. That the angels possess power, is a thing which cannot be conceived by such as have no knowledge respecting the spiritual world and its influx into the natural world; for they imagine that the angels cannot have any power, because they are spiritual beings, so refined and rare, that they cannot even be seen with the eyes. But such as look interiorly into the causes of things are of a different opinion. These know, that all the power which is possessed by man, is derived from his understanding and will, since, without these, he could not move a particle of his body. Man's understanding and will are his spiritual man: and this actuates the body and its members just as it pleases; for what this thinks, the mouth and tongue speak, and what this wills, the body executes; to which, also, it gives force at pleasure. Man's will and understanding are governed by the Lord, through the instrumentality of angels and spirits; and as his will and understanding are thus governed, so, also, are all things belonging to his body, because these are derived from the former; and, if you will believe it, man cannot so much as take a step with his feet independently of the influx of heaven. That such is the fact, has been evinced to me by much experience: it has been given to the angels to move my steps, my actions, my tongue and speech, as they pleased, which they effected by an influx into my will and thought; and I found that, of myself, I had no power whatever. They afterwards told me, that every man is governed in this manner, and that he might know that it is so from the doctrine of the church, and from the Word; for it is usual for him to pray that God would send His angels, that they may lead him, may guide his steps, may teach him, and inspire what he should think and what he should speak; with more to that effect; although, when, without regard to doctrine, he thinks within himself, he speaks and thinks differently. These observations are made, that the nature of the power which the angels have with man may be known.

229. But the power of angels in the spiritual world is so great, that were I to relate every thing that has been witnessed by me on that subject, it would surpass all belief. If any thing there makes resistance, and is to be removed, because opposed to Divine order, they cast it down and overturn it by a mere effort of will, and by a look. I have seen mountains which were occupied by the wicked thus cast down and overthrown, and sometimes made to shake from one end to the other, as occurs in earthquakes. I have beheld rocks, also, split open in the middle down to the deep, and the wicked who were on them swallowed up. I have likewise seen some hundreds of thousands of evil spirits dispersed by them, and cast into hell. Numbers

avail nothing at all against them ; nor arts, nor cunning machinations, nor confederacies : they see through all, and dispel them
in a moment. (More may be seen on this subject in the work
On the Last Judgment and the Destruction of Babylon.) Such
is the power which the angels possess in the spiritual world.
That they also have similar power in the natural world, when it
is granted them to exercise it, is evident from the Word ; in
which we read that they have caused the utter destruction of
whole armies, and occasioned a pestilence of which seventy
thousand men died. Of the angel who produced the latter
calamity, it is written thus : "*And when the angel stretched out
his hand upon Jerusalem to destroy it, the Lord repented Him
of the evil, and said to the angel that destroyed the people, It is
enough: stay now thy hand.—And David—saw the angel that
smote the people.*"—(2 Sam. xxiv. 15, 16, 17.)   Not to mention
other cases. Since the angels possess such power, they are
denominated Powers ; and it is said in David, "*Bless Jehovah,
ye His angels, that excel in strength*,"—more literally, "*mighty
in strength.*"—(Ps. ciii. 20.)

230. But it is to be understood, that the angels have no power
at all of themselves, but that all the power they exercise they
derive from the Lord, and that the appellation of Powers only
belongs to them, so far as they are grounded in the acknowledgment that such is the fact. When any angel supposes that he
possesses power from himself, he instantly becomes so weak, as
to be unable to resist so much as one evil spirit. On this account, the angels attribute no merit whatever to themselves, and
are averse from receiving any praise or glory on account of any
thing done by them, all which they ascribe to the Lord.

231. It is the Divine Truth proceeding from the Lord to
which belongs all power in the heavens ; for the Lord, in
heaven, is Divine Truth in union with Divine Good (see above,
nn. 126—140) : and it is in proportion as the angels are in the
reception of the same, that they are Powers.(¹) Every one,
also, is his own truth and his own good, because every one is
of such a quality as are his understanding and will : and his
understanding is his understanding of truth, because all that
belongs to it is composed of truths ; and his will is his will of
good, because all that belongs to it is composed of goods ; for
whatever is the subject of a person's understanding or intelligence, he calls truth ; and whatever is the subject of his will,
he calls good. It hence results, that every one is his own truth
and his own good.(²) So far, therefore, as the truth which any

(¹) That all the angels are called powers, and that they are powers, by virtue of the
reception of divine truth from the Lord, n 9639. That angels are recipients of divine
truth from the Lord, and that, on this account, they are called gods in the Word
throughout, nn. 4295, 4402, 8301, 9160.
    ' That a man and an angel is his own good and his own truth, thus his own love

angel is, is truth from the Divine Being, and the good which he is, is good from the same source, he is a power, because so far the Lord is with him.　And since no one is grounded in good and truth that is exactly similar, or the same, with that of another (for in heaven, as in the world, the variety is endless, n. 20), it follows that no angel is in the possession of the same power as another.　The greatest power is enjoyed by those who constitute the arms in the Grand Man, or heaven, by reason that the angels who belong to that province are grounded in truths more than others, and there is an influx of good into their truths from the whole of heaven.　Thus, also, in individual men, the power of the whole man transfers itself into his arms, and, by them, the whole body exercises its force; on which account, in the Word, by the arms and hands is signified power.[3]　In heaven, there sometimes appears a naked arm stretched forth, which is of such power, that it could bruise to powder whatever comes in its way, even to a great stone in the ground; it once was advanced towards me; on which I had a perception, that it was able to pound my bones into minute fragments.

232. That all power resides in the Divine Truth which proceeds from the Lord, and that the angels have power in proportion as they are in the reception of the Divine Truth, has been shown above (n. 137).　The angels, however, are only in the reception of Divine Truth, in proportion as they are in the reception of Divine Good; for all power resides in truths derived from good, and none in truths without good; and, on the other hand, good has all its power by means of truths, and none without truths.　Power is the result of the conjunction of the two.　It is the same with respect to faith and love; for whether you mention truth, or faith, it amounts to the same, since all that is the object of faith is truth; and in the same manner, it amounts to the same, whether you mention good, or love, since all that is the object of love is good.[4]　How great is the power which the angels possess by means of truths derived from good, was also made manifest by this circumstance: that an evil spirit, only on being looked at by an angel, faints away, and no longer appears as a man; in which state he continues

and his own faith, nn. 10,298, 10,367.　That he is his own understanding and his own will, since the all of his life is thence derived, the life of good being of the will, and the life of truth being of the understanding, nn. 10,076, 10,177, 10,264, 10,284.

[3] Of the correspondence of the hands, the arms, and shoulders, with the grand man or heaven, nn. 4931—4937.　That by arms and hands, in the Word, is signified power, nn. 878, 3091, 4934, 4932, 6947, 10,019.

[4] That all power in the heavens belongs to truth derived from good, thus to faith grounded in love, nn. 3091, 3563, 6423, 8304, 9643, 10,019, 10,182.　That all power is from the Lord, because from Him is all the truth, which belongs to faith, and the good, which belongs to love, nn. 9327, 9410.　That this power is meant by the keys given to Peter, n. 6344.　That it is the divine truth proceeding from the Lord which has all power, nn. 6948, 82.10.　That this power of the Lord is what is understood by sitting at the right hand of Jehovah, nn. 3387, 4592, 4933, 7518, 7673, 8281, 9133.　That the right hand denotes power, n. 10,019.

till the angel turns away his eyes. The reason that such a phenomenon takes place by the aspect of the angel's eyes, is, because the sight of the angels is derived from the light of heaven, and the light of heaven is Divine Truth. (See above, nn. 126—132.) The eyes, also, correspond to truths derived from good.([5])

233. Since all power resides in truths derived from good, it follows, that there is no power whatever in falsities derived from evil.([6]) All the inhabitants of hell are grounded in falsities derived from evil; wherefore they have no power against truth and good. But what sort of power they possess among themselves, and what sort of power is exercised by evil spirits before they are cast into hell, will be described in a subsequent part of this work.

OF THE SPEECH OF THE ANGELS.

234. The angels converse together just as men do in the world, and talk, like them, on various subjects, such as their domestic affairs, those belonging to their state in society, matters of moral life, and those of spiritual life: there is no difference, except that the angels converse with more intelligence than men, because from a more interior ground of thought. It has often been granted me to be in company with them, and to converse with them as one friend does with another, and sometimes as one stranger with another; and as I was then in a state like their own, I could not tell but that I was conversing with men on earth.

235. The speech of angels is divided into words, just as the speech of men is: it is also both uttered and heard sonorously, just in the same manner; for they have mouth, tongue, and ears, exactly as man has. They likewise have an atmosphere, in which the sound of their speech is articulated; but the atmosphere is a spiritual one, such as is suited to angels, who are spiritual beings. The angels, also, breathe in their atmosphere, and pronounce their words by means of their breath; as men do in theirs.([1])

236. In the whole of heaven, all have one language: all understand each other, whatever society they belong to, whether

([5]) That the eyes correspond to truths derived from good, nn. 4403—4421, 4523—4534. 6923.
([6]) That falsities derived from evil have no power, because truth derived from good has all power, nn. 6784, 10,481.
([1]) That in the heavens there is respiration, but of an interior kind, nn. 3884, 3885; from experience, nn. 3884, 3885, 3891, 3893. That respirations are dissimilar there, and various, according to their states, nn. 1119, 3886, 3887, 3889, 3892, 3893. That the wicked cannot respire at all in heaven, and that if they come thither they are suffocated, n. 3894.

109

neighboring or remote. This language is not learned artifi
cially, but is inherent in every one; for it flows direct from their
affection and thought. The sound of their speech corresponds
to their affection, and the articulations of sound, composing the
words, correspond to the ideas of their thought proceeding from
their affection: and as their language corresponds to these, it,
likewise, is spiritual, being, in reality, audible affection and
speaking thought. Whoever attends to the subject may be
aware, that all thought proceeds from affection, which belongs
to love, and that the ideas of thought are various forms into
which the common affection is distributed; for no thought or
idea can possibly exist without affection, it being from this that
it derives its soul and life. On this account, the angels know
the character of any one merely by his speech, discerning the
quality of his affection by its sound, and that of his mind by
the articulations of its sound, or his words: and the wiser class
of angels can tell, on his uttering a few connected sentences, the
nature of his ruling affection; for it is to this that they principally attend. That every one has various affections, is well
known: for one kind of affection prevails with a man when he
is in a state of joy, another when in a state of grief, another
when in a state of clemency and compassion, another when in a
state of sincerity and truth, another when in a state of love and
charity, another when in a state of zeal or of anger, another when
in a state of pretence and deceit, another when in the ambitious
pursuit of honor and glory; and so on: yet the ruling affection
or love exists in them all; wherefore the wiser class of angels,
who perceive by a person's speech what is his ruling affection,
know, at the same time, all the states belonging to him. That
such is the fact, has been made known to me by much experience. I have heard angels laying open the life of a person on
only hearing him speak: they also affirmed, that they can discover all things belonging to a person's life by a few ideas of his
thoughts, because they thence discover his ruling love, in which
all things else are contained in their proper order; and that
man's Book of Life is nothing else.

237. The angelic tongue has nothing in common with human
languages, except with certain words, the sound of which is
derived from some affection; and then, what the angelic tongue
has in common with them, is not with the words themselves,
but with the sound of them; on which subject, something will
be offered hereafter. That the angelic tongue has nothing in
common with human languages, is evident from this fact, that
to utter one word of any human language, is, to the angels, impossible. The experiment was tried; but they were unable to
do it. For they are unable to utter any thing, but what is in
perfect accordance with their affection; whatever is not in such
accordance, is repugnant to their very life; for their life is that

ot their affection, and from this proceeds their speech. It has been tol.l me, that the primitive language of mankind on our earth, possessed agreement with that of the angels, because they derived it from heaven; and that the Hebrew language possesses such agreement in some particulars.

238. Since the speech of the angels corresponds to their affection, which belongs to their love, and the love that prevails in neaven is love to the Lord and love towards the neighbor (see above, nn. 13—19), it is evident how elegant and pleasing must be their discourse; for it not only affects the ears, but, also, the interiors of the mind, of those who hear it. There was a certain spirit, remarkable for hardness of heart, with whom an angel was speaking, and who, at length, was so affected by his discourse, that he burst into tears: he said that he could not help it, for what he heard was love itself speaking; and that he had never wept before.

239. The speech of the angels is also full of wisdom, because it proceeds from their interior thought, and their interior thought *is* wisdom, as their interior affection is love. In their speech, their love and wisdom are united; whence it is so full of wisdom, that they are able to express by a single word what man cannot in a thousand. The ideas of their thoughts, also, comprise such things, as man is not able to conceive, much less to utter by speech. It is on this account, that the things that have been heard and seen in heaven are said to be unspeakable, and such as eye hath not seen, nor ear heard. That they are so, has also been my privilege to know by experience. I have sometimes been admitted into the state which is proper to the angels, and have conversed with them; and, while in that state, I understood all that was said; but when I returned into my former state, and thus into the natural thought proper to man, and wished to recollect what I had heard, I was unable; for there were thousands of things which could not be brought down to the ideas of natural thought, thus which were not capable of being expressed, except, only, by variegations of the light of heaven, and, consequently, not at all by human words. The angels' ideas of thought, from which proceed their words, are, likewise, modifications of the light of heaven; and their affections, from which proceeds the sound of the words, are variations of the heat of heaven; because the light of heaven is Divine Truth or wisdom, and the heat of heaven is Divine Good or love (see above, nn. 126—140); and the angels derive their affection from the Divine love, and their thought from the Divine wisdom.(²)

240. As the speech of the angels proceeds immediately from

(²) That the ideas of the angels, from which they speak, are effected by wonderful variegations of the light of heaven, nn. 1646, 3343, 3993.

their affection, their ideas of thought, as observed above (n. 236), being various forms into which the common affection is distributed, they are able to express, in less than a minute, what man cannot do in half an hour. They also are able to give, in a few words, what, if put in writing, would fill several pages. This, likewise, has been evinced to me by much experience.([²]) The angels' ideas of thought, and the words of their speech, form a one, in the same manner as the efficient cause and the effect; for that which exists, in its cause, in their ideas of thought, is shown, in effect, in their words: which also is the reason that every word comprehends so many things within itself. All the particulars of the angels' thoughts, and thence all the particulars of their speech, when visibly exhibited, appear, likewise, as a rarified circumfluent undulation or atmosphere, comprising within it innumerable things in their proper order, which proceed from their wisdom, and which enter, and affect, the thought of another. The ideas of the thought of every one, whether angel or man, are rendered visible in the light of heaven, when the Lord sees fit.([⁴])

241. The angels who belong to the Lord's celestial kingdom make use of speech, in the same manner as the angels of the Lord's spiritual kingdom; only the celestial angels speak from a more interior ground of thought than the spiritual angels. The celestial angels, also, being grounded in the good of love to the Lord, speak from wisdom; and the spiritual angels, being grounded in the good of charity towards the neighbor, which in its essence is truth (n. 215), speak from intelligence; for wisdom proceeds from good, and intelligence from truth. On this account, the speech of the celestial angels is like a gentle stream, soft, and as it were continuous; but the speech of the spiritual angels is rather vibratory and discrete. The speech of the celestial angels, also, partakes greatly of the sound of the vowels U and O; but the speech of the spiritual angels, of the vowels E and I.* For vowels are signs of sounds, and in the sound resides the affection: for, as observed above (n. 236), the sound of

([²]) That the angels can express by their speech in a moment more than man can express by his in half an hour; and that they can also express such things as do not fall into the words of human speech, nn. 1641, 1642, 1643, 1645, 4609, 7089.

([⁴]) That there are innumerable things contained in one idea of thought, nn. 1008, 1869, 4946, 6613, 6614, 6615, 6617, 6618. That the ideas of the thought of man are opened in the other life, and presented visibly, as to their quality, by a living image, nn. 1869, 3310, 5510. What is the nature of their appearance, nn. 6201, 8885. That the ideas of the angels of the inmost heaven appear like flaming light, n. 6615. That the ideas of the angels of the ultimate heaven appear like thin bright clouds, n. 6614. The idea of an angel seen, from which issued a radiation towards the Lord, n. 6620. That the ideas of thought diffuse themselves widely into the angelic societies around, nn. 6598—6613.

* It is to be recollected, that the sound of E, here referred to, is that which is expressed, in English, by the close sound of A, or the sound of A in *fate;* and that the sound of I is that which we give to the vowel E. So, also, the sound described as that of U is what is more commonly expressed in English by double O, as in *choose.* The sound assigned to O is the same in all languages.—*N.*

the angels' speech corresponds to their affection, and the articulations of the sound, which are the words, correspond to their ideas of thought proceeding from their affection. The vowels do not belong to a language, but to the elevation of its words by sound to express various affections according to the state of every one; on which account, in the Hebrew language, the vowels are not written, and are, also, variously pronounced. The angels, hence, know the quality of a man in respect to his affection and love. The speech of the celestial angels, also, contains no hard consonants, and few transitions from one consonant to another, without the interposition of a word that begins with a vowel. It is on this account that, in the Word, there is such frequent use of the particle "*and*," as may be evident to those who read the Word in Hebrew, in which that particle has a soft expression, and always takes a vowel-sound before and after it. In the Word, as existing in that language, it may also in some degree be known, from the sound of the words themselves, whether they belong to the celestial class or to the spiritual class, consequently, whether they involve the signification of good or that of truth. Those which involve the signification of good partake much of the sound of U and O, and also, in some degree, of that of A; but those which involve the signification of truth, partake of the sound of E and I. Since the affections particularly display themselves in sounds, therefore in human oratory also, when treating of great subjects, such as heaven and God, such words are preferred as sound much of U and O : lofty musical sounds, likewise, are chosen, when employed on such themes : but when not treating on great subjects, other sounds are preferred. It is from this cause that the art of music has the power of expressing various kinds of affections.

242. In the speech of angels there is a species of musical concord, such as cannot be described.([5]) It results from the circumstance, that the thoughts and affections, from which the speech proceeds, pour themselves forth, and diffuse themselves around, according to the form of heaven; and it is according to the form of heaven that all are connected in societies, and that all communication is effected. That the angels are consociated together according to the form of heaven, and that their thoughts and affections proceed according to that form, may be seen above (nn. 200—212).

243. The same kind of speech as obtains in the spiritual world is inherent in every man, only it is seated in his interior intellectual part; but as, in man, it does not descend into words analogous to his affection, as it does with the angels, he is not aware that he possesses it. It is from this cause, however, that

---

([5]) That in angelic speech there is concord with harmonious cadence, nn. 1648, 1649, 7191.

when man enters the other life, he speaks the same language as
the spirits and angels who are there already, and that he understands it without a teacher.([6])   But on this subject, more will
be said below.

244. As stated above, all in heaven have one kind of speech:
it is, however, varied in this respect; that the speech of the
wiser class is more interior, and more fully replenished with
variations of affections and ideas of thoughts; whilst the speech
of the less wise is more exterior, and not so full of such contents;
and the speech of the simple is more exterior still, and consists,
from that cause, of words, from which the sense is to be gathered,
much as is done in the conversation of men.   There is also a
kind of speech by the face, terminating in something sonorous
modified by ideas.   There is another kind of speech, in which
representatives of heaven are mixed with the ideas, and consisting, also, of ideas made visible.   There is a kind of speech by
gestures corresponding to their affections, and representing the
same things as their words do.   There is a kind of speech by
the general principles of their affections and the general principles of their thoughts.   There is, likewise, a kind of thundering
speech.   Not to mention others.

245. The speech of evil and infernal spirits is in like manner
spiritual, because proceeding from their affections, but from evil
affections, and from filthy ideas thence derived, which are held
by the angels in utter aversion..   Thus the kinds of speech that
obtain in hell are opposite to those in heaven; whence the
wicked cannot bear the speech of angels, nor the angels the
speech of infernals.   The speech of hell affects the angels as a
bad odor does the nostrils.   The speech of hypocrites, who are
such as are able to feign themselves angels of light, is, as to the
words, similar to the speech of the angels, but as to the affections,
and the ideas of thought thence proceeding, it is diametrically
opposite; wherefore their speech, when its interior quality is
perceived, as it is by the wiser of the angels, is heard as the
gnashing of teeth, and strikes the hearer with horror.

OF THE SPEECH OF THE ANGELS WITH MAN.

246. When angels converse with man, they do not speak in
their own language, but in that of the man, or in other languages which he understands, but not in such as are unknown

([9]) That the faculty of spiritual or angelic speech, resides with man, although he is
ignorant of it, n. 4104.   That the ideas of the internal man are spiritual, but that man,
during his life in the world, perceives them naturally, because he then thinks in the
natural principle, nn. 10,236, 10,246, 10,550.   That man after death comes into his
interior ideas, nn. 3226, 3342, 3343, 10,568, 10,604.   That those ideas then form his
speech, nn. 2470, 2478, 2479.

to,him. The reason of this is, because when angels converse with man, they turn towards him, and conjoin themselves with him; the effect of which is, to bring both parties into a similar state of thought: and as the man's thought coheres with his memory, and his speech flows from it, both parties possess and use the same language. Besides, when an angel or spirit approaches a man, and by turning towards him comes into conjunction with him, he enters into all the man's memory, so completely, that he is scarcely aware that he does not know, of himself, all that the man knows, including the languages with which the man is acquainted. I have conversed with the angels on this phenomenon, and have remarked to them, that they might possibly suppose, that *they* were speaking with me in my native tongue, because it so appeared to them, whereas it was not they who thus spoke, but myself; and that this might be demonstrated from the fact, that angels cannot utter one word of any human language (n. 237); and because, also, the language of men is natural, whereas they are spiritual, and spiritual beings cannot utter any thing in a natural manner. The angels replied, that they were aware that their conjunction with a man, when conversing with him, is with his spiritual thought; but as this flows into his natural thought, and the latter coheres with his memory, it appears to them as if the man's language were their own, and all his knowledge likewise; and that this effect takes place, because it was the Lord's pleasure that such a conjunction, and as it were insertion of heaven into man, should exist with him: they added, however, that the state of man at this day is different, so that such a conjunction with angels no longer exists, but only with spirits who are not in heaven. I have also conversed on the same subject with spirits; but they would not believe that it is the man who speaks, but that it is they who speak in the man: they also insisted, that it is not the man who knows what he does, but they, and thus that all the man knows he derives from them. I endeavored to convince them, by many arguments, that they were mistaken: but it was all to no purpose. Who are meant by spirits, and who by angels, will be explained in a subsequent part of this work, where we shall treat of the world of spirits.

247. Another reason why angels and spirits conjoin themselves with man so closely as not to know but that all that belongs to the man is their own, is, because there exists such a conjunction between the spiritual and natural worlds with man, that they are as if they were one: but as man has separated himself from heaven, it has been provided by the Lord, that angels and spirits should be present with every man, and that he should be governed by the Lord through their instrumentality. It is on this account that there is so close a conjunction between them. It would have been otherw se if man had not separated himself from heaven;

for then he might have been governed by the Lord by the common influx from heaven, without having spirits and angels so particularly adjoined to him. But this subject will be particularly considered in a subsequent part of this work, when treating of the conjunction of heaven with man.

248. The speech of an angel or spirit, when addressed to a man, is perceived by him as sonorously as the speech of one man with another. It is not heard, however, by others who may be present, but only by the person spoken to; the reason of which is, that the speech of an angel or spirit flows first into the man's thought, and thence, by an internal way, into his organ of hearing, which it thus actuates from within; whereas the speech of one man with another flows first into the air, and thence, by an external way, into his organ of hearing, which it thus actuates from without. It hence is evident, that the speech with man of an angel or spirit, is heard in the man, and as it equally actuates the organs of hearing as speech from without does, that it sounds as audibly. That the speech of an angel or spirit flows down from within into the ear itself, was evinced to me by this fact: that it flows, also, into the tongue, and causes it slightly to vibrate, but not with any local motion, such as takes place when the sound of speech is articulated by the tongue into words by the man himself.

249. But to speak with spirits is at this day rarely granted, because it is dangerous :(¹) for the spirits then know that they are present with man, which they otherwise do not; and evil spirits are of such a nature, that they regard man with deadly hatred, and desire nothing more than to destroy him both soul and body. This effect actually is experienced by those who have much indulged in phantasies, going to the extreme of banishing the enjoyments suited to the natural man. Persons, also, who pass their life in solitude, sometimes hear spirits speaking to them, without its being attended with danger: but the spirits that are present with them are at intervals removed by the Lord, lest they should know that they are present with a man: for most spirits do not know that there is any other world than the one inhabited by them, nor, consequently, that there are men elsewhere; wherefore it is not allowable for the man to speak to them in return, for if he did, they would know this. Persons who think much upon religious subjects, and dwell upon them so incessantly as at length to see them, inwardly, as it were, in themselves, also begin to hear spirits speaking to them: for religious subjects of whatever kind, when a man, of his own accord, dwells upon them incessantly, and does not occasionally vary his meditations by attending to matters of business in the

(¹) That man is able to discourse with spirits and angels, and that the ancients frequently did so, nn. 67, 68, 69, 784, 1634, 1636, 7802. That in some earths, angels and spirits appear in a human form, and speak with the inhabitants, nn. 10,751, 10,752. But that in this earth, at this day, it is dangerous to discourse with spirits, unless man be principled in a true faith, and be led by the Lord, nn. 784, 9438, 10,751.

world, penetrate to the interiors, and there fix themselves, and take possession of the whole of the man's spirit; when they enter the spiritual world, and act upon the spirits who inhabit it. These, however, are visionaries and enthusiasts, who believe any spirit whom they hear speaking to them to be the Holy Spirit, although he is only an enthusiastic spirit. Spirits of this description see falsities as truths, and because they see them, they persuade themselves that they are truths, and infuse the same persuasion into those with whom they communicate by influx. As those spirits also began to persuade those whom they influenced to the commission of evils, and were obeyed when they did so, they were gradually removed. Enthusiastic spirits are distinguished from others by this peculiarity, that they believe themselves to be the Holy Spirit, and their dictates to be divine oracles. These spirits do not offer injury to the man with whom they communicate, because he pays them divine worship and honor. I, also, have sometimes conversed with spirits of this kind; when the nefarious principles and practices which they infused into their worshippers were discovered to me. They dwell together towards the left, in a desert place.

250. But to speak with angels of heaven is granted to none, but such as are grounded in truths originating in good, especially, in the acknowledgment of the Lord, and of the Divinity in His Humanity; this being the truth in which the heavens are established. For, as has been shown above, the Lord is the God of heaven (nn. 2—6); the Lord's Divine Sphere constitutes heaven (nn. 7—12); the Lord's Divine Sphere in heaven is love to Him and charity towards the neighbor, derived from Him (nn. 13—19); and the whole of heaven, viewed collectively, is in form as one man: as is also every society of heaven; and every angel is in a perfect human form; and they derive this distinction from the Divine Humanity of the Lord (nn. 59—86). Such being the case, it is evident, that to speak with angels is only possible to those, whose interiors are opened, by divine truths, to the Lord Himself; for it is into the interiors that the Lord enters by influx with man; and when the Lord thus enters, heaven enters also. The reason that divine truths open man's interiors, is, because man was so created, as to be an image of heaven as to his internal man, and an image of the world as to his external (n. 57); and the internal man is only opened by the Divine Truth proceeding from the Lord; for that is both the light, and the life, of heaven (nn. 126—140).

251. The influx of the Lord Himself, with man, flows into his forehead, and thence into the whole of his face; because the forehead of man corresponds to his love, and the face to all his interiors.(*) The influx, with man, of the spiritual angels, flows

(*) That the forehead corresponds to celestial love, and thence, in the Word, signifies that love, n. 9936. That the face corresponds to the interiors of man, which are of the

117

into his head in all directions, from his forehead and temples to all the parts which inclose the portion of the brain called the *cerebrum*, because that region of the head corresponds to intelligence. But the influx of the celestial angels flows into that part of the head which incloses the portion of the brain called the *cerebellum*, and which is named the *occiput*, reaching from the ears in all directions around from the back of the neck; for that region of the head corresponds to wisdom. The speech of the angels, when addressed to man, always enters by those ways into his thoughts; by noting which, I knew what angels they were with whom I have conversed.

252. Those persons who converse with angels of heaven, see, also, the objects that exist in heaven, because they see by the light of heaven, in which their interiors are. Through them, likewise, the angels behold the objects that exist on earth ;([3]) for, in such persons, heaven is conjoined with the world, and the world with heaven. For, as observed above (n. 246), when the angels turn themselves towards man, they conjoin themselves with him in such a manner, that they cannot tell but that every thing belonging to the man belongs to themselves; not only whatever he relates in conversation, but whatever he has seen and heard: the man, also, on his part, does not know, but that whatever enters by influx from the angels is his own. Such was the conjunction which existed between the angels of heaven and the most ancient inhabitants of this earth; on which account, those times are denominated the golden age. Because they acknowledged the Divine Being under a human form, thus, because they acknowledged the Lord, they conversed with the angels of heaven as with their own kindred, and the angels conversed reciprocally with them as with theirs; and, in them, heaven and the world formed a one. But, after those times, man gradually removed himself farther and farther from heaven, through loving himself in preference to the Lord, and the world in preference to heaven, whence he began to have a sense of the enjoyments of the love of self and the world separate from the enjoyments of heaven, and at last became ignorant of any other enjoyment. Then his interiors, which opened towards heaven, were closed, and his exteriors were opened towards the world: and when this is his state, a man is in possession of light with respect to all things belonging to the world, but is immersed in darkness in regard to all things belonging to heaven.

253. Since those times, it has been a rare thing for any one to converse with angels of heaven; but some have conversed

---

thought and affection, nn. 1568, 2988, 2989, 3681, 4796, 4797, 4800, 5165, 5168, 5695, 9306. That the face also is formed to correspond with the interiors, nn. 4791—4805, 5695. That hence the face, in the Word, signifies the interiors, nn. 1999, 2434, 3527 4066, 4796.

([3]) That spirits can see nothing which is in this solar world, by or through man, but that they have so seen through my eyes; with the reason thereof, n. 1880.

with spirits who were not in heaven. For man's interiors and exteriors are of such a nature, that they are either turned towards the Lord as their common centre (n. 124), or towards themselves, and thus away from the Lord. When turned towards the Lord, they are also turned towards heaven; and when towards self, they are also turned towards the world: and when this is their state, it is with difficulty that they can be elevated. They are, however, as far as possible, elevated by the Lord, by effecting a change of the love; which is accomplished by means of truths derived from the Word.

254. I have been informed how the Lord spoke with the prophets, by whose instrumentality the Word was written. He did not speak with them as He did with the ancient inhabitants of this globe, by an influx into their interiors, but by spirits sent to them, whom the Lord filled with His aspect, and so inspired the words which they dictated to the prophets. What these experienced, therefore, was not an influx, but a dictate; and as the words proceeded immediately from the Lord, every one of them is filled with a Divine principle, and they contain an internal sense, which is of such a nature, that the angels of heaven understand the words in a celestial and spiritual sense, while men understand them in a natural sense. In this way, the Lord has effected a conjunction between heaven and the world by means of the Word. How spirits are filled with Divinity by the Lord by aspect, has also been shown me. A spirit so filled with Divinity by the Lord, does not know, at the time, but that he is the Lord, and that what he speaks is Divine. This state continues till he has uttered what he is charged with; after which he perceives and acknowledges that he is only a spirit, and that he did not speak from himself, but from the Lord. Since such was the state of the spirits who spoke with the prophets, it is said by them, that Jehovah spoke; the spirits themselves, likewise, called themselves Jehovah; as may be seen, not only in the prophetical parts of the Word, but in the historical parts also.

255. That the nature of the conjunction of angels and spirits with man may be understood, it is permitted to relate some particulars worthy of being mentioned, by which the subject may be illustrated, and seen to be as described. When angels and spirits turn themselves towards a man, it appears to them that the man's language is their own, and that they possess no other: the reason is, because, at such time, they are in the knowledge and use of the man's language, and not of their own, of which, in that state, they have no recollection; but as soon as they turn themselves away from the man, they are in the knowledge and use of their own angelic and spiritual language, and know nothing whatever of the man's. The like has occurred to myself. When I have been in company with

angels, and in a state similar to theirs, I have conversed with
them in their language, and knew nothing whatever of my own,
which never came to my recollection: but as soon as I ceased
to be in their company, I was in the knowledge and use of my
own language again. It is also worthy of mention, that when
angels and spirits turn themselves towards a man, they can converse with him at any distance: they have also conversed with
me a long way off, and their speech sounded as loud as when
they were near: but when they turn themselves from the man,
and converse among themselves, not a syllable of their conversation is heard by him, though carried on close to his ear. It
was made manifest to me, from these facts, that all conjunction,
in the spiritual world, depends upon how the parties are turned
in respect to each other. It is further worthy of mention, that
a number of spirits can speak with a man together, and the
man with them. They send one of their party to the man with
whom they wish to converse, and this emissary spirit turns himself towards the man, and the rest of them towards that spirit,
thus concentrating their thought in him; to which he gives
utterance. That spirit does not know, at the time, but that he
is speaking from himself; nor do they, but that they are speaking from themselves. In this way, a conjunction of many with
one individual is effected; this also resulting from the manner
in which the parties are turned in regard to each other.([*])
But respecting these emissary spirits, who also are called subjects, and the communication effected through their instrumentality, more will be stated in the following pages.

256. It is not lawful for any angel or spirit to converse with
a man from his own memory, but only from that of the man.
For angels and spirits have memory as well as men; and if a
spirit were to speak with a man from his own memory, the man
would not know but that the things which then became the
subjects of his thoughts belonged to himself, although they belonged to the spirit. This case is like remembering a thing,
which, nevertheless, the man had never heard of, or seen. That
such is the fact, has been given me to know by experience.
This is the origin of the opinion held by some of the ancients,
that after some thousands of years they should return into their
former life, and into all its transactions, and that they actually
had so returned. They drew this conclusion from the circumstance, that there sometimes occurred to them what seemed to
be a remembrance of things, which, nevertheless, they had never
seen or heard. This appearance was produced by an influx of
spirits, from their own memory, into their ideas of thought.

([*]) That the spirits sent from societies of spirits to other societies are called subjects,
nn. 4403, 5856. That communications in the spiritual world are effected by such emissary spirits, nn. 4403, 5846, 5983. That a spirit, when he is sent out and serves for a
subject, does not think from himself, but from those by whom he was sent out, nn.
5985, 5986, 5987.

257. There also are certain spirits, called natural and corporeal spirits, who, when they approach a man, do not, like other spirits, conjoin themselves with his thought, but enter into his body, and take possession of all his senses, so as to speak by his mouth and act by his members; not knowing, at the time, but that all things belonging to the man belong to them. These are the spirits by whom men are possessed. But these spirits have been cast by the Lord into hell, and thus completely removed; on which account, such possessions do not now occur.(5)

OF WRITINGS IN HEAVEN.

258. Since angels have speech, and their speech is composed of words, it follows that they have writings also, and that they express the sentiments of their minds by writing as well as by speaking. There have sometimes been sent to me papers covered with writing; some of which were exactly like papers written by hand, and others like papers that had been printed, in the world: I also could read them in the same manner; but I was not permitted to draw from them more than a sentence or two; the reason of which was, because it is not according to Divine order for a man to be instructed from heaven by writings, but only by the Word, because it is only by the Word that communication and conjunction are effected between heaven and the world, thus, between the Lord and man. That papers written in heaven also appeared to the prophets, is evident from Ezekiel: *"And when I looked, behold, a hand was sent unto me; and, lo, a roll of a book was therein: and he spread it before me : and it was written within and without."*—(Ch. ii. 9, 10.) And in John: *"And I saw in the right hand of Him that sat on the throne, a book, written within and on the back side, sealed with seven seals."*—(Rev. v. 1.)

259. That there should be writings in heaven, was provided by the Lord for the sake of the Word. The Word, in its essence, is the Divine Truth, from which all the heavenly wisdom, enjoyed by men and by angels, is derived: for it was dictated by the Lord; and what is dictated by the Lord passes through all the heavens in order, and terminates with man.

---

(5) That external obsessions, or those of the body, do not exist at this day, as formerly, n. 1983. But that, at this day, internal obsessions, which are those of the mind, exist more than formerly, nn. 1983, 4793. That man is obsessed interiorly, when he has filthy and scandalous thoughts concerning God and his neighbor, and when he is only withheld from publishing them by external bonds, which relate to the fear of the loss of reputation, of honor, of gain, to the dread of the law, and to the loss of life, n. 5990. Of the diabolical spirits who chiefly obsess the interiors of man, n. 4793. Of certain diabolical spirits who are desirous to obsess the exteriors of man, but are shut up in hell, nn. 2752, 5990.

Thus originating and proceeding, it is accommodated both to the wisdom proper to angels, and to the intelligence enjoyed by men. From this cause it is, that the Word is possessed, also, by the angels, and that they read it just as men do on earth: from it, likewise, their tenets of doctrine are deduced; and from it, their sermons are composed (n. 221). It is the same Word; only its natural sense, which is our literal sense, does not exist in heaven, but its spiritual sense, which is its internal sense. (What is the nature of this sense, may be seen in the little work *On the White Horse mentioned in the Revelation.*)

260. There was once sent to me from heaven a bit of paper, on which were only written a few words in Hebrew characters; and it was stated, that every letter involved arcana of wisdom, these being contained in the inflections and curvatures of the letters, and thence also in the sounds. It hence was made evident to me what is meant by these words of the Lord: "*Verily, I say unto you, Till heaven and earth pass, one jot or one tittle shall in no wise pass from the law.*"—(Matt. v. 18.) That the Word is Divine as to every tittle, is also known in the church; but where its Divinity in every tittle lies, is not yet known; wherefore it shall be declared.

The writing in the inmost heaven consists of various inflected and circumflected forms; and those inflections and circumflections are disposed according to the form of heaven. By these, the angels express the arcana of their wisdom, including many that cannot be vocally uttered; and, what is wonderful, the angels know how to write in this manner without taking any pains to learn, or being taught by a master. It is inherent in them, as their speech itself is. (On which subject, see n. 236.) Thus this writing of theirs is heavenly writing. The reason that the knowledge of it is inherent in the angels, is, because the diffusion of their thoughts and affections, and thence the communication of their intelligence and wisdom, proceeds, in every instance, according to the form of heaven (see n. 201), whence their writing, also, flows into that form. It has been told me, that the most ancient inhabitants of this earth, before alphabetic writing was invented, had writing of this sort; and that this was transferred into the letters of the Hebrew language, all which, in ancient times, were inflected, and none of them had the square form in use at present. From this cause it is, that, in the Word, Divine things, and heavenly arcana, are contained in its very iotas, dots, and tittles.

261. This sort of writing, by characters of heavenly form, is in use in the inmost heaven, the inhabitants of which, in wisdom, excel all others. By those characters they express the affections, from which their thoughts flow, and follow in order according to the subject under consideration. On this account, those

writings involve arcana which no thought can exhaust. It has also been granted me to see such writings. But in the inferior heavens, such writings as these do not exist. The writings in these heavens are like those in the world, formed with similar letters: yet even these are not intelligible to man, being in the angelic tongue, which is of such a nature as to have nothing in common with human languages (n. 237); for by the vowels they express affections, by the consonants, the ideas of thought proceeding from those affections, and by the words composed of both, the meaning of the subject under consideration. (See above, nn. 236, 241.) This kind of writing also includes in a few words more than a man can express in several pages. Writings of this kind have likewise been seen by me. In the inferior heavens, they have the Word written in this manner; and, in the inmost heaven, they have it written by heavenly forms.

262. It is a remarkable fact, that, in the heavens, their writings flow naturally from their thoughts themselves, and are executed with such facility, that it is as if their thoughts threw themselves on the paper; nor does the hand ever pause for the selection of a word, because the words themselves, both when they speak and when they write, correspond to the ideas of their thought; and all correspondence is natural and spontaneous. There also are writings in the heavens, produced, without the intervention of the hand, from mere correspondence with the thoughts; but these are not permanent.

263. I have also seen writings obtained from heaven, which consisted of nothing but numbers, written in order and series exactly like writings composed of letters and words; and I was instructed, that this sort of writing is derived from the inmost heaven, and that their heavenly writing mentioned above (nn. 260, 261), takes the form of numbers among the angels of an inferior heaven, when thought, derived from that heavenly writing, flows down thither; and that that writing composed of numbers likewise includes arcana, some of which cannot be comprehended by the thoughts, nor expressed by words.([1]) For all numbers have their correspondence, and bear a signification according to such correspondence, just like words. There is, however, this difference: that numbers involve general ideas, and words particular ones; and since one general idea includes innumerable particular ones, it follows that the kind of writing composed of numbers includes more arcana than that composed of letters. From these facts it was made to me evident, that, in the Word, numbers signify things, as much as words do. (What

([1]) That all numbers, in the Word, signify things, nn. 482, 487, 647, 648, 755, 813, 1963, 1988, 2075, 2252, 3252, 4264, 4670, 6175, 9488, 9659, 10,217, 10,253. Shown from heaven, nn. 4495, 5265. That numbers multiplied signify similar things with the simple numbers, from which they result by multiplication, nn. 5291, 5335, 5708, 7973. That the most ancient people had heavenly arcana in numbers, forming a kind of computation of things relating to the church, n. 575.

the simple numbers, such as 2, 3, 4, 5, 6, 7, 8, 9, 10, 12, signify; and what the compound numbers, such as 20, 30, 50, 70, 100, 144, 1000, 10000, 12000, and others, may be seen in the *Arcana Cœlestia*, in the places where those numbers are treated of.) In that kind of writing in heaven, that number is always placed first, on which those that follow in the series depend as their subject; for that number is as an index, pointing out what subject is treated of; and from that first number, those which follow obtain their determination to that subject specifically.

264. Such persons as possess no knowledge respecting heaven, and are unwilling to form any idea of it but as of a mere atmospherical region, in which the angels flit about like intellectual minds destitute of the senses of hearing and sight, cannot possibly conceive that they have speech and writing; for they place the existence of every thing real in material nature. It nevertheless is true, that the objects which exist in heaven, exist as really as those in the world; and that the angels, who dwell there, possess every thing which can be of use, either for life, or for wisdom.

OF THE WISDOM OF THE ANGELS OF HEAVEN.

265. Of what nature is the wisdom of the angels of heaven, can with difficulty be comprehended: because it so much transcends the wisdom of men as to preclude all comparison; and that which transcends the wisdom of men, appears to them to have no existence. To describe it, also, some unknown truths must be adduced; and things unknown, before they become known, appear in the understanding like shadows, and thus conceal the subject in question, as to its intrinsic nature. These unknown truths, however, are such as may be known. and, when known, be comprehended, provided the mind take delight in such knowledge : for delight carries light with it, because it proceeds from love; and on those who love such things as belong to Divine and heavenly wisdom, light shines from heaven, and they receive illumination.

266. A conclusion may be formed as to the nature of the wisdom of the angels, from the circumstance, that they dwell in the light of heaven, and the light of heaven, in its essence, is the Divine Truth, or Divine Wisdom; which light simultaneously enlightens their internal sight, which is that of the mind, and their external sight, which is that of the eyes. (That the light of heaven is the Divine Truth, or Divine Wisdom, may be seen above, nn. 126—133.) The angels dwell, also, in the heat of heaven, which, in its essence, is the Divine Good, or Divine Love; from which they derive the affection of being wise, and the desire to be so. (That the heat of heaven is the Divine Good, or Divine Love, may be seen above, nn. 133—140.)

That the angels are in the enjoyment of wisdom, to such a degree that they might be called Wisdoms, absolutely, may be concluded from this fact: that all their thoughts and affections flow according to the form of heaven, which is the form of the Divine Wisdom ; and that their interiors, which receive wisdom, are framed after that form. (That the thoughts and affections of the angels flow according to the form of heaven, consequently, also, their intelligence and wisdom, may be seen above, nn. 201—212.) That the angels are in the enjoyment of super-eminent wisdom, may also be evident from this circumstance, that their speech is the speech of wisdom, since it flows imme-diately and spontaneously from their thought, as this does from their affection, so that their speech is thought and affection in an external form ; whence there is nothing to withdraw them from the Divine influx, nothing extraneous being present, such as, with man, intrudes into his speech from thoughts not con-nected with the subject. (That the speech of the angels is that of their thought and affection, may be seen above, nn. 234—245.) To exalt the wisdom of the angels ·to such excellence, this cir-cumstance, also, conspires : that all things which they see with their eyes, and perceive by their senses, are in concord with their wisdom, because they are correspondences ; and thence the objects which they behold are forms representative of such things as belong to wisdom. (That all the objects which appear in heaven are correspondences to the interiors of the angels, and are representations of their wisdom, may be seen above, nn. 170—182.) Besides, the thoughts of the angels are not bound-ed and confined by ideas derived from space and time, as the thoughts of men are ; for space and time are things proper to nature, and things proper to nature withdraw the mind from such as are spiritual, and deprive of extension the intellectual sight. (That the ideas of the angels derive nothing from space and time, and thus, compared with those of men, are free from limitation, may be seen above, nn. 162—169, and 191—199.) Neither are the thoughts of the angels drawn down to earthly and material subjects, nor interrupted by any cares about the necessaries of life ; consequently, they are not withdrawn by such matters from the delightful contemplation of wisdom, as are the thoughts of men in the world ; since they receive all things that they have need of gratis from the Lord : they are clothed gratis, they are fed gratis, and they are lodged gratis (see nn. 181, 190) ; and they are gifted, in addition, with what-ever can conduce to their enjoyment and pleasure, according to their reception of wisdom from the Lord. These statements are made, that it may be known whence the angels derive such exalted wisdom.[1]

[1] Of the wisdom of the angels, and that it is incomprehensible and ineffable, nn. 2795, 2796, 2802, 3314, 3404, 3405, 9004, 9176.

267. The reason that the angels are capable of receiving such exalted wisdom, is, because their interiors are open; and wisdom, like every other perfection, increases in ascending towards the interiors, thus, in proportion to the degree in which the interiors are open.(²) There exist, with every angel, three degrees of life, corresponding to the three heavens (see nn. 29—40): those in whom the first degree is open, dwell in the first or ultimate heaven; those in whom the second degree is open, inhabit the second or middle heaven; and those in whom the third degree is open, reside in the third or inmost heaven. The wisdom of the angels in the heavens proceeds according to these degrees; consequently, the wisdom of the angels of the inmost heaven immensely transcends that of the angels of the middle heaven, and the wisdom of these no less transcends that of the angels of the ultimate heaven. (See above, nn. 209, 210; and respecting the nature of the degrees, n. 38.) The reason that such distinctions exist, is because those things which are in a superior degree are particular, and those in an inferior are general, and things general are the continents of things particular. Things particular, in respect to things general, are as thousands or myriads to one; and so is the wisdom of the angels of a superior heaven, respectively, to that of the angels of an inferior heaven. The wisdom, however, of these last, transcends that of man in the same proportion. For man exists in the corporeal nature and its sensual organs and apprehensions, and the corporeal sensual organs and apprehensions of man are stationed in the lowest degree of all. It may hence be evident, what sort of wisdom is possessed by those who think from the suggestions of their sensual organs and apprehensions, or of those who are called sensual men; and it will be seen, that they are not in the enjoyment of wisdom at all, but only of a superficial kind of knowledge.(³) It is different, however, with those men whose

---

(²) That so far as man is elevated from things external towards interior things, he comes into light, and thus into intelligence, nn. 6183, 6313. That there is an actual elevation, nn. 7816, 10,330. That elevation from things external to things interior is like elevation out of a mist into light, n. 4598. That exterior things are more remote from the Divine Being as dwelling in man, wherefore they are respectively obscure, n. 6451. And likewise respectively inordinate, nn. 996, 3855. That interior things are more perfect, because nearer to the Divine Being, nn. 5146, 5147. That in what is internal there are thousands and thousands of things which appear as one general thing in what is external, n. 5707. That hence thought and perception are clearer in proportion as they are interior, n. 5920.

(³) That the sensual principle is the ultimate of the life of man, adhering to, and inhering in, his corporeal nature, nn. 5077, 5767, 9212, 9216, 9331, 9730. That he is called a sensual man who judges and concludes respecting all things from the senses of the body, and who believes nothing but what he can see with his eyes and touch with his hands, nn. 5094, 7693. That such a man thinks in externals, and not interiorly in himself, nn. 5089, 5094, 6564, 7693. That his interiors are closed, so that he sees nothing therein of spiritual truth, nn. 6564, 6844, 6845. In a word, that he is in gross natural light, and thus perceives nothing which belongs to the light of heaven, nn. 6201, 6310, 6564, 6844, 6845, 6598, 6612, 6614, 6622, 6624. That interiorly he is in contrariety to those things which relate to heaven and the church, nn. 6201, 6316, 6844, 6845, 6948, 6949. That those learned men become of such a character, who have confirmed themselves against the truths of the church, n. 6316. That sensual men are cunning and thoughts are elevated above their sensua. apprehensions; and still more so with those whose interiors are open to the actual light of heaven.

268. How great is the wisdom of the angels, may be evident from this circumstance; that, in the heavens, there is a universal communication, so that the intelligence and wisdom of one are communicated to another. Heaven, in short, is a communion of all things good. The reason is, because heavenly love is of such a nature, as to desire that whatever is its own should be another's: consequently, no one in heaven regards the good he possesses to be good in himself, unless it be also in others. This, likewise, is the origin of the happiness of heaven. The angels derive this tendency to impart whatever they possess to others, from the Lord, whose Divine Love is of this nature. That there exists such a communication in the heavens, is a truth which it has also been granted me to know by experience. Certain simple spirits were once taken up into heaven; and when they had entered, they entered, also, into the wisdom of the angels: they then understood such things as they before could not at all comprehend, and they said such things, as, in their former state, they could not possibly utter.

269. The nature of the wisdom of the angels cannot be described by words; it can only be illustrated by some general facts belonging to it. Angels can express in one word what man cannot do in a thousand; and besides this, there are comprised in one word of angelic language innumerable things, which cannot be expressed in the words of human language at all; for in every one of the words uttered by angels there are arcana of wisdom in continuous connection, beyond what human sciences can ever reach. Such things, also, as the angels do not fully express by the words of their discourse, they supply by the sound of it, in which is contained the affection belonging to the things spoken of in their proper order: for, as was observed above (nn. 236, 241), they express affections by the sounds, and the ideas of thought proceeding from those affections by the words; on which account it is, that the words heard in heaven are said to be unspeakable.* The angels can also recite, in a few words, the whole contents of any book, and they infuse into every word such contents, as elevate it to the expression of interior wisdom. For their speech is of such a nature, that its sounds harmonize with the affections, and every word with the ideas: the words, likewise, are varied in infinite ways, according to the series of the things which exist collectively in their thoughts. The interior angels, also, are able, from the tone of

malicious more than others, nn. 7693, 10,236. That they reason sharply and cunningly, but from the corporeal memory; in doing which they make all intelligence to consist, nn. 195, 196, 5700, 10,236. But that they reason from the fallacies of the senses, nn. 5084, 6948, 6949, 7693.

* 2 Cor. xii. 4.—*N.*

voice, coupled with a few words uttered by any one, to obtain a knowledge of the speaker's whole life; for from the sound variegated by the ideas in the words, they perceive his ruling love, in which are contained, as if written thereon, all the particulars of his life.(⁴) From these facts it is evident, what is the nature of the wisdom of the angels. Their wisdom, in comparison with human wisdom, is as a myriad to one; much as the moving forces of the whole body, which are innumerable, are to the action which results from them, though, to human sense, they appear as one; or as the thousands of parts of an object viewed by a perfect microscope, to the single obscure thing which they form to the naked eye. I will also illustrate the subject by an example. A certain angel gave a description, from his wisdom, of regeneration: he enumerated some of the arcana belonging to it, in their proper order, to the amount of some hundreds, and he filled every arcanum with ideas, in which were still more interior arcana. This he did from beginning to end; for he explained how the spiritual man is conceived anew, is carried, as it were, in the womb, is born, grows up, and is successively perfected. He said that he could multiply the number of arcana to several thousands; and that still those which he spoke of only related to the regeneration of the external man, and that those relating to the regeneration of the internal man would be innumerably more. From this and similar examples that I have heard from angels, it was made evident to me, how great is their wisdom, and how great, respectively, the ignorance of man; for he scarcely knows what regeneration is, and is not acquainted with any step of its progression while he is undergoing it.

270. The wisdom of the angels of the third or inmost heaven, and how far it exceeds the wisdom of the angels of the first heaven, shall now be treated of. The wisdom of the angels of the third or inmost heaven is incomprehensible, even to the inhabitants of the ultimate heaven: the reason is, because the interiors of the angels of the third heaven are open to the third degree, whereas the interiors of the angels of the first heaven are open only to the first degree; and all wisdom increases as it ascends towards the interiors, and is perfected according to the degree in which they are opened (nn. 208, 267). Since the interiors of the angels of the third or inmost heaven are open to

(⁴) That what governs, or has the universal dominion with man, exists in all the particulars of his life, thus in all the particulars of his affection and thought, nn. 4459, 5949, 6159, 6571, 7648, 8067, 8853—8858. That the quality of man is such as his governing love is, nn. 918, 1040, 8858; illustrated by examples, nn. 8854, 8857. That what reigns universally constitutes the life of the spirit of man, n. 7648. That it is his very will, his very love, and the end of his life; since what a man wills, he loves, and what he loves, he regards as an end, nn. 1317, 1568, 1571, 1909, 3796, 5949, 6936. That therefore man is of such a quality as his will is; or of such a quality as his governing love is; or of such a quality as the end of his life is, nn. 1568, 1571, 3570, 4054, 6571, 6934, 6938, 8856, 10,076, 10,109, 10,110, 10,284.

.he third degree, they have divine truths, as it were, inscribed on them. For the interiors of the third degree are disposed, more than the interiors of the second and first degree, in the form of heaven, and the form of heaven exists from the Divine Truth, consequently, according to the Divine Wisdom. It is from this cause that divine truths appear, to those angels, as if inscribed on their interiors, or as if inherent and innate. On this account, when they hear genuine divine truths, they immediately recognize and perceive them as such, and afterwards inwardly see them, as it were, in themselves. Since the angels of that heaven are of such a character, they never reason about divine truths, much less do they hold controversy about any truth, disputing whether it be so or not; nor do they know what is meant by believing or having faith; for they say, "What is faith? I perceive and see that the truth is so." They illustrate this by comparisons, such as these: To urge a person who sees the truth in himself to believe or have faith, would be, they say, as if a person who sees a house, with various objects in and around it, should tell his companion, that he must believe the house to be a house, and the other objects to be what he sees that they are: or as if, on seeing a garden, with trees and fruit in it, he should exhort the other to have faith that it is a garden, and that the trees and fruit are trees and fruit; although he sees them plainly with his eyes. On this account, those angels never mention faith, nor have the least idea of it; and therefore they never reason about divine truths, much less do they enter into controversy about any particular truth, disputing whether it be so or not.([5]) But the angels of the first or ultimate heaven have not divine truths thus inscribed on their interiors, by reason that, with them, only the first degree of life is open: they, consequently, reason about truths; and those who have recourse to reasoning, scarcely see any thing beyond the immediate object about which they reason, or go beyond the subject in debate further than to confirm it by certain arguments; and when they have so confirmed it, they say, that it is a point of faith, and must be believed. I have conversed with the angels on these subjects; when they said, that the difference between the wisdom of the angels of the third heaven, and that of the angels of the first heaven, is like that between what is lucid and what is obscure. They also compared the wisdom of the angels of the third heaven to an elegant palace, full of suitable furniture, standing in the midst of an extensive paradise, and sur-

---

(*) That the celestial angels are acquainted with innumerable things, and are immensely wiser than the spiritual angels, n. 2718. That the celestial angels do not think and speak from a principle of faith, like the spiritual angels, inasmuch as they are in the enjoyment of a perception from the Lord of all things relating to faith, nn. 202, 597, 607, 784, 1121, 1387, 1398, 1442, 1919, 7680, 7877, 8780, 9277, 10,336. That in regard to truths of faith, they say only, Yea, yea, or Nay, nay, but that the spiritual angels reason whether it be so, nu. 2715, 3246, 4448, 9166, 10,786, where the Lord's words are explained, "*Let your discourse be Yea, yea, Nay, nay*" (Matt. v. 37).

rounded with magnificent objects of various kinds; and they said that those angels, being grounded in truths of wisdom, are able to enter the palace and view its splendid contents, and also to walk about the paradises in every direction, and enjoy all their beauties. But it is different, they said, with those who reason about truths, and especially with those who dispute about them, and who, because they do not see truths by the light of truth, but either imbibe them from others, or from the literal sense of the Word not interiorly understood, insist that they must be believed, or that faith is to be had in them; after which they are unwilling to allow any interior view of them to be taken. Of these, the angels said, that they cannot approach the first threshold of the palace of wisdom, much less enter it, and walk about in its paradises, because they stand still at the first step of the way towards it; whereas they who are grounded in truths themselves, find no obstacle to their making progress without limit; for truths inwardly seen lead them wherever they go, and open wide fields before them; by reason that every truth is of infinite extent, and is in connection with numerous others. They said, further, that the wisdom of the angels of the inmost heaven chiefly consists in this, that they behold divine and heavenly things in every object they see, and, in a series of many objects together, such as are wonderful: for all the things that appear before their eyes have their proper correspondence. Hence, when they see, for example, palaces and gardens, their view does not terminate in the objects before their eyes, but they see, also, the interior things from which they originate, and to which, therefore, they correspond. These they behold, with all possible variety, according to the aspect which the objects present: consequently they see innumerable things, simultaneously, in their regular order and connection; and their minds derive such enjoyment from the view, that they seem to be carried out of themselves. (That all things which appear in the heavens correspond to the divine things which are present with the angels from the Lord, may be seen above, nn. 170—176.)

271. The reason that the angels of the third heaven are of such a character, is, because they are grounded in love to the Lord; and that love opens the interiors belonging to the mind to the third degree, and is the receptacle of all the elements of wisdom. It should be known, further, that the angels of the inmost heaven are, notwithstanding, being perfected in wisdom continually, and that this perfecting is differently effected with them, than it is with the angels of the ultimate heaven. The angels of the inmost heaven do not deposit divine truths in the memory, and, consequently, do not form of them any thing like a science, but, as soon as they hear them, they recognize them by perception, and commit them to life. This is the reason that

divine truths permanently abide with them, as if they were inscribed on their interiors; for what is committed to life, remains thus inherent. But it is different with the angels of the ultimate heaven. These first deposit divine truths in their memory and store them up among the things that they know: they afterwards bring them forth from this storehouse, and apply them to the perfecting of their understanding; and then, without any interior perception whether they are truths or not, they make them objects of their will, and commit them to life. Hence their state, respectively, is one of obscurity. It is worthy of mention, that the angels of the third heaven are perfected in wisdom by the way of hearing, not by that of sight. The truths which they hear by preaching do not enter their memory, but pass immediately into their perception and will, and are incorporated in their life; whereas the objects which these angels behold with their eyes, enter their memory, and on these they reason and converse. It was made manifest to me from these facts, that, with them, the way of hearing is the way of wisdom. This, also, is from correspondence; for the ear corresponds to obedience, and obedience belongs to the life; whereas the eye corresponds to intelligence, and intelligence has relation to doctrine.(⁶) The state, also, of these angels, is described in the Word throughout; as in Jeremiah: *"I will put my law in their inward parts, and write it in their hearts. They shall teach no more every man his neighbor, and every man his brother, saying, Know ye Jehovah: for they shall all know me, from the least of them unto the greatest of them, saith Jehovah."*—(Ch. xxxi. 33, 34.) And in Matthew: *"Let your communication be, Yea, yea; Nay, nay: for whatsoever is more than these, cometh of evil."*—(Ch. v. 37.) It is said that what is more than these cometh of evil, because it is not from the Lord: for the truths which are in the angels of the third heaven are from the Lord, because those angels are grounded in love to Him. Love to the Lord, in that heaven, consists in willing and doing Divine Truth; for the Divine Truth is the Lord in heaven.

272. In addition to the reasons above adduced, why the angels are capable of receiving such exalted wisdom, another is to be mentioned, which, in heaven, is the chief of all; it is, that they are free from self-love; for just in proportion as any one is free from that love, he is capable of attaining wisdom in regard to divine things. That love is what closes the interiors

---

(⁶) Of the correspondence of the ear and of hearing, nn. 4652—4660. That the ear corresponds to perception and obedience, and that hence it signifies those faculties, nn. 2542, 3869, 4653, 5017, 7216, 8361, 9311, 9397, 10,065. That it signifies the reception of truths, nn. 5471, 5475, 9926. Concerning the correspondence of the eye and of its sight, nn. 4403—4421, 4523—4534. That the sight of the eye, hence, signifies the intelligence which belongs to faith; and also signifies faith, nn. 2701, 4410, 4526, 6923, 9051, 10,569.

against the Lord and heaven, whilst it opens the exteriors, and turns them towards self. On this account, all with whom that love is dominant, are immersed in thick darkness in regard to the things of heaven, whatever light they may enjoy in regard to those of the world. The angels, on the contrary, being free from that love, are in the light of wisdom: for the heavenly loves in which they are grounded, which are love to the Lord and love towards the neighbor, open the interiors; by reason that those loves come from the Lord, and the Lord himself is in them. (That those loves constitute heaven in general, and form heaven with every one in particular, may be seen above, nn. 13—19.) Since heavenly loves open the interiors to the Lord, all the angels, in consequence, turn their faces towards the Lord (n. 142). For, in the spiritual world, the love turns the interiors of every one towards itself, and in the same direction as it turns the interiors, it also turns the face; for the face, there, acts as one with the interiors, being the external form of them. Since the love turns the interiors and the face towards itself, it likewise conjoins itself with them, love being spiritual conjunction; whence, also, it communicates with them all that it possesses. It is from this turning, and consequent conjunction and communication, that the angels derive their wisdom. (That all conjunction, in the spiritual world, depends upon the direction in which the inhabitants turn themselves, may be seen above, n. 255.)

273. The angels are being perfected in wisdom continually;[*] but still they never can attain such perfection, as to cause there to be any proportion between their wisdom and the Divine Wisdom of the Lord; for the Lord's Divine Wisdom is Infinite, whilst that of the angels is finite; and between Infinite and finite there can be no proportion.

274. Since wisdom perfects the angels, and constitutes their life; and since heaven with all its goods enters by influx into every one according to his wisdom—it follows that all the inhabitants of heaven must desire wisdom, and feel an appetite for it, much as a hungry man does for food. Knowledge, intelligence, and wisdom, are, likewise, spiritual nourishment, as food is natural nourishment; and they mutually correspond to each other.

275. The angels in one heaven, and those in one society of heaven, are not all in the enjoyment of similar degrees of wisdom. Those who are stationed in the centre are in the greatest degree of wisdom, and those in the circumferences, to the last boundary of all, are in less and less. The diminution of their wisdom in proportion to their respective distances from the centre, is like that of light verging towards shade. (See above, nn

[*] That the angels advance in perfection to eternity, nn. 4803, 6648.

13, 128.) They have light, also, in similar degrees; since the light of heaven is the Divine Wisdom, and every one dwells in right in proportion to his reception of that Wisdom. (Of the light of heaven, and its various reception, see above, nn. 126—132.)

OF THE STATE OF INNOCENCE OF THE ANGELS IN HEAVEN.

276. What innocence is and what its nature, is known to few in the world, and not at all to those who are immersed in evil. It appears, indeed, before men's eyes, displaying itself in the face, speech, and gestures, more especially of little children: but still what it consists in is not known, much less that it is the principle in which heaven inmostly abides with man. In order, therefore, that it may be understood, I will proceed regularly to treat, first of the innocence of infancy, next, of the innocence of wisdom, and finally, of the state of heaven, in regard to innocence.

277. The innocence of infancy, or of little children, is not genuine innocence, since it only exists in external form, and not in internal: and yet we may learn from it what the nature of innocence is; for it shines forth from their faces, from some of their gestures, and from their infantile prattle, and acts upon the affections of the observer. The reason is, because they have no internal thought; for they as yet do not know what either good and evil, or truth and falsity, are; and these are the elements from which thought exists. On this account, they have no prudence derived from *proprium*, no purpose and deliberate object, and, consequently, no end of an evil nature. They have no *proprium* acquired by the love of self and the world: they attribute nothing to themselves, and all things that they receive they refer to their parents: they are content and pleased with the few and trifling objects which are given them; they have no anxiety about food and clothing, and none about future events: they do not look to the world, and covet a multitude of its possessions: they love their parents, their nurses, and their infantile companions, with whom they innocently play: they suffer themselves to be led by those who have the care of them, whom they listen to, and obey. Such being their state, they receive all they are taught in the life; whence they acquire, without knowing how, becoming manners, speech, and the rudiment of memory and thought; for the reception and imbibing of all which, their state of innocence serves as a medium. This innocence, however, as observed above, is exter-

nal, being only of the body and not of the mind,([1]) their mind
being not yet formed : for the mind consists of understanding
and will, with thought and affection thence proceeding. It has
been told me from heaven, that little children are especially
under the Lord's auspices ; and that there is an influx from the
inmost heaven, where the state of innocence prevails, which
passes through their interiors, affecting them, in its transit,
with nothing but innocence ; that it is from this source that
innocence displays itself in their faces, and in some of their
gestures, and becomes apparent : and that this is what so inti-
mately affects their parents, and produces the peculiar emotion
called parental love.

278. The innocence of wisdom is genuine innocence, since it
is internal : for it belongs to the mind itself, consequently, to
the will itself, and to the understanding thence derived : and
when in these there is innocence, there also is wisdom, for they
are its seat. On this account it is said in heaven, that innocence dwells in wisdom, and that an angel possesses wisdom in
proportion as he possesses innocence. That such is the fact,
they confirm by these considerations : That those who are in a
state of innocence attribute nothing of good to themselves, but
regard every thing of the kind as gifts received, ascribing them
to the Lord : that they desire to be led by Him, and not by
themselves : that they love every thing that is good, and are
delighted with every thing that is true ; because they know and
perceive, that to love good, consequently to will and do it, is
to love the Lord, and to love truth is to love their neighbor :
that they live content with what is their own, whether little or
much, because they know that all receive as much as is good
for them, those for whom little is best receiving little, and those
for whom much is best receiving much ; and that they do not
know, themselves, what is best for them, this being only known
to the Lord, all whose providence regards things eternal. On
this account, also, they are not anxious about things future, and
call all such anxiety care for the morrow, which they define to
be grief for the loss, or for not receiving, of such things as are
not necessary for the uses of life. They never, in dealing with
their associates, have in view any end of an evil nature, but act
from principles of goodness, justice, and sincerity : to act with
an evil end in view they call cunning, which they shun as the
poison of a serpent, because it is diametrically contrary to innocence. Loving nothing more than to be led by the Lord, and

---

([1]) That the innocence of infants is not true innocence, but that true innocence
dwells in wisdom, nn. 1616, 2305, 2306, 8495, 4563, 4797, 5608, 9301, 10,021. That the
good of infancy is not spiritual good, but that it becomes so by the implantation of
truth, n. 3504. That, nevertheless, the good of infancy is a medium by which intelligence is implanted, nn. 1616, 3183, 9301, 10,110. That man, without the good of innocence infused in infancy, would be a wild beast, n. 3494. That whatsoever is imbibed
in infancy, appears natural, n. 3494.

ascribing all that they enjoy to the Lord, as gifts received from him, they are removed from their *proprium*, and in proportion as any are removed from this, the Lord enters by influx; on which account it is, that whatever they hear from Him, whether through the medium of the Word or through that of preaching, they do not lay by in the memory, but immediately obey it, that is, will and do it, the will itself being their memory. These, for the most part, have the appearance of simplicity in their external form, but, in their internal, are wise and prudent; and it is these who are meant by the Lord, when he says, "*Be ye wise as serpents, and harmless as doves.*"—(Matt. x. 16.) Such is the character of the innocence which is called the innocence of wisdom. Since innocence attributes nothing of good to self, but ascribes it all to the Lord—and since, consequently, it loves to be led by the Lord, and, on that account, is the receptacle of all good and truth, which are the constituents of wisdom—therefore man was so created, as, when an infant, to exist in innocence, though such as is external, and, when an old man, to be grounded in internal innocence, that by the former he may proceed to the latter, and from the latter may return into the former. On this account, also, when a man grows old, he diminishes in size, and becomes, as it were, an infant anew; only he is now as a wise infant, consequently an angel; for an angel is a wise infant, using the terms in an eminent sense. This is the reason that, in the Word, an infant or little child signifies one who is innocent,([2]) and an old man, a wise man in whom there is innocence.

279. The like takes place with every one who becomes regenerate. Regeneration is re-birth as to the spiritual man. The person who undergoes it is first introduced into the innocence of infancy, which consists in the acknowledgment that man has no knowledge of truth, nor ability to do good, from himself, but only from the Lord, and in desiring and seeking after truth and goodness solely for their own sake. They also are given him by the Lord, as he advances in age. He is led first into the knowledge of them, then, from knowledge, into intelligence, and finally, from intelligence, into wisdom. Innocence accompanies him all the way; which consists, as just observed, in the acknowledgment, that man has no knowledge of truth, nor ability to do good, from himself, but only from the Lord. Without this belief, and a perception of its truth, no one can receive any heavenly gift; and it is in this that the innocence of wisdom chiefly consists.

([2]) That by infants, in the Word, is signified innocence, n. 5608. And likewise by sucklings, n. 3183. That by an old man is signified a wise man, and, in the abstract sense, wisdom, nn. 3183, 6524. That man is so created, that in proportion as he verges to old age, he may become as an infant, and that then innocence may reside in wisdom, and that the man in that state may pass into heaven, and become an angel, nn. 3183, 5608.

280. Since innocence consists in being led by the Lord, and not by self, all the inhabitants of heaven are in the enjoyment of innocence ; for all who have a place in heaven love to be led by the Lord. For they know that to lead one's self is to be led by one's own *proprium*, and the *proprium* of man consists in loving himself, and he who loves himself does not submit to be led by another. On this account, so far as an angel is grounded in innocence, he is actually in heaven; that is, he is so far in the reception of the Divine Good and Divine Truth ; for to be in the reception of these is to be in heaven. In consequence of this, the heavens are distinguished according to their innocence. Those who inhabit the first or ultimate heaven, are grounded in innocence of the first or ultimate degree; those who belong to the second or middle heaven, in innocence of the second or middle degree ; but those who belong to the inmost or third heaven, in innocence of the third or inmost degree. These, therefore, may be said to be innocence itself, in relation to heaven at large; for, beyond all others, they love to be led by the Lord, as little children by their father; on which account, also, they receive the Divine Truth which they hear, whether it comes from the Lord immediately, or mediately by the Word and by preaching, directly in the will, enter on the practice of it, and thus commit it to the life. It is from this cause that their wisdom is so great, and so far exceeds that of the angels of the inferior heavens. (See nn. 270, 271.) Because these angels are of such a character, they dwell nearest to the Lord, from whom their innocence is derived : they also are separated from their *proprium*, so that they live, as it were, in the Lord. In outward form they appear simple, and, to the eyes of the angels of the inferior heavens, as little children, thus as of small stature. They also appear like such as do not possess much wisdom, though they are the wisest of the angels of heaven : for they know that they possess not an atom of wisdom from themselves, and that wisdom consists in the acknowledgment of this truth. They likewise are conscious, that what they know is as nothing in respect to what they do not know; and they affirm, that to know, acknowledge, and see this by perception, is the first step towards wisdom. Those angels, also, are naked, because nakedness corresponds to innocence.([3])

281. I have had much conversation with angels respecting innocence, and have been instructed by them that it is the *esse* of every thing good, and that, on this account, good is really good in proportion as there is innocence within it; consequently,

---

([4]) That all in the inmost heaven are forms of innocence, nn. 154, 2736, 3887. And that therefore they appear to others as infants, n. 154. That they are also naked, nn. 165, 8375, 9960. That nakedness is a mark of innocence, nn. 165, 8375. That spirits have a custom of testifying their innocence by putting off their clothes, and presenting themselves naked, nn. 8375, 9960.

that wisdom is really wisdom in proportion as it partakes of innocence; and that it is the same with love, charity, and faith.([4]) I have likewise been instructed by them, that this is the reason that no one can enter heaven without innocence; which is what is meant by the Lord, when he says, "*Suffer the little children to come unto me, and forbid them not: for of such is the kingdom of God. Verily I say unto you, Whosoever shall not receive the kingdom of God as a little child, shall not enter therein.*"— (Mark x. 14, 15; Luke xviii. 16, 17.) By little children in this passage, and in other parts of the Word, are meant such as are innocent. The state of innocence is also described by the Lord, but by pure correspondences, in Matt. vi. 25—34. The reason that good is really good in proportion as there is innocence within it, is, because all good is from the Lord, and innocence consists in being willing to be led by Him. I have been further instructed by the angels, that truth cannot be conjoined with good, nor good with truth, except by innocence as a medium. On this account, also, it is, that no angel can be an angel of heaven unless innocence be in him: for heaven does not reside in any one, until truth is conjoined in him with good; whence the conjunction of truth and good is called the heavenly marriage, and the heavenly marriage is heaven itself. I have been instructed, in addition, that love truly conjugial derives its existence from innocence, because it derives its existence from the conjunction of the good and truth in which two minds,—those of the husband and wife,—are established, and when that conjunction descends into a lower sphere, it displays itself under the form of conjugial love; for the married partners mutually love each other, in the same manner as their minds do. On this account, in conjugial love there is a playfulness, like that of infancy, and like that of innocence.([5])

282. Since innocence is the very *esse* of good as abiding in the angels of heaven, it is evident that the Divine Good proceeding from the Lord is innocence itself; for it is that good which flows into the angels, and affects the inmost recesses of their minds, and disposes and fits them for the reception of every good of heaven.

<hr />

([4]) That every good of love and truth of faith ought to have innocence in it, that it may be good and true, nn. 2526, 2780, 3111, 3994, 6013, 7840, 9262, 10,134. That innocence is the essential of what is good and true, nn. 2780, 7840. That no one is admitted into heaven unless he has something of innocence, n. 4797.

([5]) That love truly conjugial is innocence, n. 2736. That conjugial love consists in willing what the other wills, thus mutually and reciprocally, n. 2731. That those who are in the enjoyment of conjugial love dwell together in the inmost principles of their life, n. 2732. That there is a union of two minds, and thus that from love they are one, nn. 10,168, 10,169. That love truly conjugial derives its origin and essence from the marriage of good and truth, nn. 2728, 2729. Of certain angelic spirits, who have a perception whether there be a conjugial principle, from the idea of the conjunction of good and of truth, n. 10,756. That conjugial love is altogether circumstanced like the conjunction of good and of truth, nn. 1094, 2173, 2429, 2503, 3103, 3132, 3155, 8179, 3180, 4355, 5407, 5835, 9206, 9207, 9495, 9637. That therefore, in the Word, by marriage is understood the marriage of good and truth, such as exists in heaven, and such as should exist in the church, nn. 3132, 4434, 4835.

It is similar with little children, whose interiors are not only formed by the transflux of innocence from the Lord., but are also continually fitted and disposed for the reception of the good of celestial love: for the good of innocence acts from the inmost ground of all, it being, as already observed, the *esse* of every thing good. From these facts it may be obvious, that all innocence is from the Lord; on which account it is, that the Lord, in the Word, is called a Lamb, a lamb signifying innocence.(⁶) Since innocence is the inmost principle in every good of heaven, it has such a power of affecting the mind, that whoever is made sensible of it, as occurs on the approach of an angel of the inmost heaven, feels as if he were unable to contain himself; and seems, in consequence, to be seized and transported with such delight, that every delight belonging to this world appears as nothing in comparison. I speak this from experience.

283. All who are grounded in the good of innocence, are affected by innocence; and this in proportion to the degree in which it exists in themselves. But those who are not grounded in the good of innocence, are not affected by it. Consequently, all the inhabitants of hell are diametrically opposed to innocence: they do not even know what innocence is: nay, they are of such a nature, that in proportion as any one is innocent, they burn to do him injury; on which account, they cannot bear the sight of little children, and, as soon as they behold them, they are inflamed with a cruel desire to hurt them. It is manifest from these facts, that the *proprium* of man, and thence the love of self, is opposite to innocence; for all the inhabitants of hell are immersed in their *proprium*, and thence in the love of self.(⁷)

OF THE STATE OF PEACE IN HEAVEN.

284. No one who has not been in the actual enjoyment of the peace of heaven, can have any perception of what the peace is in which the angels exist. For man, so long as he remains in the body, cannot receive the peace of heaven, consequently, cannot have a perception of it, because the seat of his perceptions is in his natural man. In order to his having a perception of the peace of heaven, it is necessary that his state should be such, as to admit of his being elevated and withdrawn, as to his thought, from the body, and kept in the spirit, and being, when in the spirit, in company with angels. Since I have had a perception,

(⁶) That a lamb, in the Word, signifies innocence and its good, nn. 3994, 10,132.
(⁷) That the *proprium* of man consists in loving himself in preference to God, and the world in preference to heaven, and in making his neighbor of no account in respect to himself; thus that it consists in the love of self and of the world, nn. 694, 731, 4317, 5660. That the wicked are altogether opposed to innocence, so that they cannot endure its presence, n. 2126.

in this way, of the peace of heaven, I am enabled to describe it; not, however, as to its intrinsic nature, by words, because human words are not adequate to the subject; but only as to its nature in comparison with that composure of mind, which is enjoyed by those who are content in God.

285. The inmost elements of heaven are two; which are, innocence and peace. They are said to be the inmost, because they immediately proceed from the Lord. Innocence is that from which is derived every good of heaven; and peace is that from which is derived all the delight which good carries with it. All good has its delight; and each, both the good and the delight, is related to love; for what a man loves, he calls good, and feels as delightful. It hence follows, that those two inmost elements, innocence and peace, proceed from the Lord's Divine Love, and affect the angels from the inmost of their frame. That innocence is the inmost element of good, has been shown in the Section immediately preceding, which treats of the state of innocence of the angels of heaven; but that peace is the inmost element of the delight proceeding from the good of innocence, shall be now explained.

286. The origin of peace shall first be declared. Divine Peace exists in the Lord, resulting from the union, in Him, of the Essential Divinity and the Divine Humanity. The Divine Sphere of Peace that exists in heaven proceeds from the Lord, resulting from His conjunction with the angels of heaven; and, in particular, from the conjunction of good and truth in every angel. These are the origins of peace. It may hence be seen, that peace in the heavens, is the Divine Sphere that proceeds from the Lord, inmostly affecting with beatitude all the good which there exists: which beatitude, consequently, is the source of all the joy of heaven; and that this is, in its essence, the Divine Joy of the Lord's Divine Love, resulting from His conjunction with heaven, and with its every inhabitant. This joy, perceived by the Lord in the angels, and by the angels from the Lord, is peace. It is from this, by derivation, that the angels experience all that is blessed, delightful, and happy; or what is denominated heavenly joy.[1]

287. The origins of peace being from this source, the Lord is called the Prince of Peace, and says that peace is from Him, and is in Him: so, also, the angels are denominated angels of peace, and heaven the habitation of peace; as in these passages: "*Unto us a Child is born, unto us a Son is given: and the government shall be upon His shoulder: and His name shall be*

---

[1] That by peace, in the supreme sense, is meant the Lord, because from Him is peace; and, in the internal sense, heaven, because the inhabitants are in a state of peace, nn. 3780, 4681. That peace, in the heavens, is the Divine Sphere inmostly affecting with blessedness every good and truth there; and that it is incomprehensible to man, nn. 92, 3780, 5662, 8455, 8665. That divine peace resides in good, but not in truth without good, n. 8722.

called Wonderful, Counsellor, the Mighty God, the Everlasting Father, the PRINCE OF PEACE.*"*—(Isa. ix. 6.)   Jesus said, "PEACE *I leave with you: my* PEACE *I give unto you; not as the world giveth, give I unto you.*—(John xiv. 27.)   *" These things have I spoken unto you, that in me ye might have* PEACE.*"*—(Ch. xvi. 33.) *"Jehovah lift up his countenance upon you, and give you* PEACE.*"* —(Num. vi. 26.)   *" The ambassadors"*—more literally—" THE ANGELS OF PEACE *shall weep bitterly. The highways lie waste."* —(Isa. xxxiii. 7, 8.)   *"The work of righteousness shall be* PEACE. —*And my people shall dwell in a* PEACEABLE HABITATION"— more literally—" A HABITATION OF PEACE.*"*—(Ch. xxxii. 17, 18.) That Divine and heavenly peace is the peace which is meant in the Word, may also appear from other places where it is named. (As Isa. lii. 7, liv. 10, lix. 8; Jer. xvi. 5, xxv. 37, xxix. 11; Hag. ii. 9; Zech. viii. 12; Ps. xxxvii. 37; and elsewhere.)   Since peace signifies the Lord and heaven, and also heavenly joy and the delight that accompanies good, the salutations of ancient times, consisted in saying, *"Peace be unto you;"* as is also sometimes the case at the present day.   This form, likewise, the Lord confirmed, who said to the disciples when he sent them forth, *"Into whatsoever house ye enter, first say,* PEACE *be to this house; and if the son of* PEACE *be there, your* PEACE *shall rest upon it."*— (Luke x. 5, 6.)   The Lord Himself, likewise, when He appeared to the apostles, said to them, " PEACE *be unto you.*"—(John xx. 19, 21, 26.)   A state of peace is also meant in the Word, when it is said that *"Jehovah smelled an odor* of rest" (as in the original of Ex. xxix. 18, 25, 41; Lev. i. 9, 13, 17; ii. 2, 9; vi. 8, 14; xxiii. 12, 13, 18; Num. xv. 3, 7, 13; xxviii. 6, 8, 13; xxix. 2, 6, 8, 13, 36): by an odor of rest, in the celestial sense, is signified, the perception of peace.([2])   Since peace signifies the union of the Essential Divinity and the Divine Humanity in the Lord, and the conjunction of the Lord with heaven and with the church, and with all the inhabitants of heaven, together with all in the church who receive Him, therefore, in remembrance of these things, the sabbath was instituted, was named from rest or peace, and was the most holy representative of the church; and for the same reason, the Lord called Himself the Lord of the sabbath.([3])—(Matt. xii. 8; Mark ii. 27, 28; Luke vi. 5.)

([2]) That odor, in the Word, signifies the perceptivity of what is agreeable or disagreeable, according to the quality of the love and the faith, of which it is predicated, nn. 3577, 4626, 4628, 4748, 5621, 10,292. That an odor of rest, when applied to Jehovah, denotes a perception of peace, nn. 925, 10,054. That on this account, frankincense, incense, odors in oils and ointments, were made representative, nn. 925, 4748, 5621, 10,177.

([3]) That the sabbath, in the supreme sense, signified the union of the Essential Divinity, and the Divine Humanity in the Lord; in the internal sense, the conjunction of the Divine Humanity of the Lord with heaven and with the church; in general, the conjunction of good and truth, thus the heavenly marriage, nn. 8495, 10,356, 10,730. Hence, that resting on the sabbath day signified the state of that union, because then the Lord has rest, and by it there is peace and salvation in the heavens and in the earth; and, in the respective sense, the conjunction of the Lord with man, because then he has peace and salvation, nn. 8494, 8510, 10,860, 10,367, 10,870, 10,874, 10,668, 10,730.

288. Since the peace of heaven is the Divine Sphere that proceeds from the Lord inmostly affecting with beatitude the good which exists with the angels, it does not come manifestly to their perception, except by the delight of heart which they feel when in the enjoyment of the good of their life, and by the pleasure which they experience when they hear such truth as agrees with their good, together with the hilarity of mind of which they are sensible when they perceive the conjunction of such good and truth; nevertheless, it thence flows into all the acts and thoughts of their life, displaying itself under the form of joy, even in outward development. But peace differs in the heavens, with respect to its quality and quantity, according to the innocence of the inhabitants, since innocence and peace always go hand in hand; for, as observed above, innocence is that from which proceeds all the good of heaven, and peace is that from which proceeds all the delight which that good carries with it. It may hence be seen, that the same things as were stated in the preceding Section respecting the state of innocence in the heavens, may be repeated here respecting the state of peace; since innocence and peace are joined together, like good and the delight which attends it; for good is made sensible by the delight which attends it, and the nature of the delight is known by that of its good. Such being the case, it is evident, that the angels of the inmost or third heaven are in the enjoyment of the third or inmost degree of peace, because they are grounded in the third or inmost degree of innocence; and that the angels of the inferior heavens are in the enjoyment of a minor degree of peace, because grounded in a minor degree of innocence. (See above, n. 280.) That innocence and peace go together, like good and its attendant delight, is evident from the case of little children; who, being in the possession of innocence, are also in the enjoyment of peace; and being in the enjoyment of peace, all their thoughts and actions are full of playfulness. Peace, however, as existing with little children, is external; but internal peace, like internal innocence, is only to be found in wisdom; whence, also, it is found in the conjunction of good and truth, for it is from this origin that wisdom exists. Heavenly or angelic peace is also found in men, when they are in the enjoyment of wisdom derived from the conjunction of good and truth, and who thence feel themselves content in God: so long, however, as they live in the world, it lies concealed in their interiors; but when they leave the body, and enter heaven, it is revealed; for then the interiors are opened.

289. Since divine peace originates from the conjunction of the Lord with heaven, and, in every angel in particular, from the conjunction of good and truth, it follows, that when the angels are in a state of love, they are in a state of peace; for it is then that the conjunction of good with truth is effected in them.

(That the states of the angels undergo regular changes, may be seen above, nn. 154—160.) It is similar with man in the course of his regeneration: when the conjunction of good and truth takes place with him, which is chiefly effected after temptations, he comes into a state of delight originating in heavenly peace.([4]) This peace may be compared to the morning or dawn in the season of spring; at which time, the night being ended, and the sun rising, all the productions of the earth begin to live anew; the scent of the flowers, sprinkled with the dew which descends from heaven, is spread abroad; and, through the medium of the vernal temperature, fertility is imparted to the soil, and a serene pleasure is diffused through the human mind: all which effects take place, because the morning or dawn, in the season of spring, corresponds to the state of peace of the angels in heaven.([5]) (See n. 155.)

290. I have also conversed respecting peace with the angels; when I observed, that it is called peace in the world when wars and hostilities cease between kingdoms, and quarrels and dissensions between men; and that it is imagined that interna peace consists in repose of mind on the removal of cares, and especially in tranquillity and delight resulting from the success of our undertakings. But the angels said, that repose of mind, and tranquillity and delight, on the removal of cares and the success of our undertakings, appear like the offspring of peace, and yet are not, except with those who are grounded in heavenly good: for peace is never to be found except in that good; since peace flows from the Lord into the inmost part of their minds, whence it descends, and flows down into the lower parts, where it shows itself under the forms of repose of the rational mind, tranquillity of the natural mind, and joy thence resulting. But with those who are immersed in evil, no peace can exist.([6]) It appears, indeed, when things go as they wish, as if they experienced rest, tranquillity, and delight: but all this is external, and not at all internal: internally they are burning, all the while, with enmity, hatred, revenge, cruelty, and many other evil lusts; into which their external mind, also, rushes, breaking out into violence if not restrained by fear, as soon as they see any one who is not favorable to them. This is the reason that their delight dwells in insanity; whereas the delight of those who are grounded in good dwells in wisdom. The difference is as wide as that between hell and heaven.

([4]) That the conjunction of good and truth with the man who is regenerating, is effected in a state of peace, nn. 8696, 8517.
([5]) That the state of peace, in the heavens, is like the state of day-dawn and of spring, on earth, nn. 1726, 2780, 5662.
([6]) That the lusts which originate in the love of self and of the world, entirely take away peace, nn. 3170, 5662. That some make peace to consist in restlessness, and in such things as are contrary to peace, n. 5662. That there can be no peace, unless the lusts of evil are removed, n. 5662.

OF THE CONJUNCTION OF HEAVEN WITH THE HUMAN RACE.

291. It is known in the church, that all good is from God, and none at all from man, and that, consequently, no one ought to ascribe any thing good to himself as his own. It is also known, that evil is from the devil. They, therefore, who frame their language by the doctrine of the church, say, respecting persons who live well, and also respecting such as converse and preach piously, that they are led by God; and the contrary respecting persons who live ill and speak in an impious manner. None of these things could be so, had not man conjunction with heaven, and conjunction with hell; nor unless those conjunctions were formed with his will and with his understanding, since it is from these that the body acts, and the mouth speaks. The nature of that conjunction shall now be declared.

292. There are present with every man both good and evil spirits: by the good spirits his conjunction with heaven is effected, and by the evil, his conjunction with hell. Those spirits are inhabitants of the world of spirits, which is the intermediate region between heaven and hell, and which will be treated of specifically in the following pages. When those spirits come to a man, they enter into all his memory, and thence into all his thoughts; the evil spirits entering into those particulars of his memory and thoughts which are evil, but the good spirits into those which are good. The spirits are not at all aware that they are present with the man, but, while they are so, they imagine that all the particulars which belong to the man's memory and thoughts are their own: neither do they see the man, because the objects of our solar world do not fall within the sphere of their vision.[1] The greatest care is exercised by the Lord to prevent the spirits from knowing that they are present with a man; for if they knew it, they would speak with him, and then the evil spirits would destroy him; for evil spirits, being in conjunction with hell, desire nothing more ardently than to destroy man, not only as to his soul, that is, as to his faith and love, but as to his body also. It is otherwise when they do not speak with the man: they do not then know that they draw from him the subjects on which they think, and also those on which they converse with each other; for they draw the subjects on which they converse with each other from the man, but believe all the while that they are their own, and every one esteems and loves what is his own; in consequence

[1] That angels and spirits are attendant on every man, and that, by them, man has communication with the spiritual world, nn. 697, 2796, 2886, 2887, 4047, 4048, 5846—5866, 5976—5993. That man without spirits attendant on him cannot live, n. 5993. That man does not appear to spirits, nor spirits to man, n. 5862. That spirits can see nothing which is in our solar world, that is present to a man except to him with whom they speak, n. 1880.

of which the spirits are made to love and esteem the man, although they are not aware of it. That such a conjunction of spirits with man really exists, has been made so thoroughly known to me by the uninterrupted experience of many years, that there is nothing which I know more certainly.

293. The reason that spirits who communicate with hell are also adjoined to man, is, because man is born into evils of every kind, whence his first life is derived entirely from them; wherefore, unless spirits were adjoined to man of the same quality as himself, he could not live, nay, he could not be withdrawn from his evils and be reformed. On this account, he is held in his own life by evil spirits, and withheld from it by good spirits. Through the agency of the two, also, he is placed in equilibrium; and being in equilibrium, he has his liberty, and can be withdrawn from evils, and inclined to good, and good can also be implanted in him, which could not possibly be effected were he not in a state of liberty; nor could he be endowed with liberty, did not spirits from hell act on him on one side, and spirits from heaven on the other, the man standing in the middle. It has also been shown me, that man, so far as he partakes of his hereditary nature, and thus of self, would have no life, if it were not permitted him to be in evil; nor yet if he were not in a state of liberty; and further, that he cannot be driven to good by compulsion, and that what is infused by compulsion is not permanent; as also, that the good which man receives in a state of liberty is implanted in his will, and becomes as if it were his own :(*) and that these are the reasons why man has communication both with hell and with heaven.

294. The nature of the communication of heaven with good spirits, and of hell with evil spirits; and thence, the nature of the conjunction of heaven and hell with man; shall also be declared. All the spirits who are stationed in the world of spirits, have communication either with heaven or with hell, the evil with hell, and the good with heaven: heaven is divided into distinct societies; and so is hell: and every spirit belongs to one of those societies, and also subsists by the influx thence proceeding; whence he acts in unity with that society. It hence results, that as man is conjoined with spirits, so is he, likewise, either with heaven or with hell, and, in reality, with that particular society in one or the other, which is the native

---

(*) That all freedom is connected with love and affection, since what a man loves he does freely, nn. 2870, 3158, 8987, 8990, 9585—9591. As freedom is an adjunct of love, that it is an adjunct of man's life, n. 2873. That nothing appears as man's own but what is from freedom, n. 2880. That man ought to have freedom, to be capable of being reformed, nn. 1937, 1947, 2876, 2881, 3145, 3146, 3158, 4031, 8700. That, otherwise, the love of good and of truth cannot be implanted in man, and be appropriated apparently as his own, nn. 2877, 2879, 2880, 2888, 8700. That nothing is conjoined to man which is the result of compulsion, nn. 2875, 8700. That if man could be reformed by compulsion, all would be reformed, n. 2881. That what is of compulsion in reformation is hurtful, n. 4031. What states of compulsion are, n. 8392.

seat of his peculiar affection or of his peculiar love : for all the societies of heaven have their distinctions according to the affections of good and of truth ; and all the societies of hell according to the distinctions of evil and falsity. (See above, nn. 41—45, and 148—151.)

295. The spirits adjoined to a man are of such a quality, as he is himself as to affection or as to love ; only the good spirits are adjoined to him by the Lord, but the evil ones are invited by the man himself. The spirits present with man are, however, changed, according to the changes of his affections. Spirits of one class are with him in infancy, of another in childhood, of another in youth and manhood, and of another in old age. In infancy, those spirits are present with man who are distinguished for innocence, and who, consequently, communicate with the heaven of innocence, which is the inmost or third heaven : in childhood, those spirits are present who are characterized by the affection of knowing, and who, in consequence, communicate with the ultimate or first heaven : in youth and manhood, those are present who eminently cherish the affection of truth and good, and who thence are grounded in intelligence, consequently, who communicate with the second or middle heaven : but in old age, those spirits are present who are eminently grounded in wisdom and innocence, and who, consequently, communicate with the inmost or third heaven. This adjunction, however, is effected by the Lord, where the parties are such as are capable of being reformed and regenerated : but it is different with those who are not. To these, also, good spirits are adjoined, that they may be withheld by them from evil as much as possible : but their immediate conjunction is with evil spirits who communicate with hell, so that the spirits attached to them are of the same quality as are the men themselves. If they are lovers of themselves, or lovers of gain, or lovers of revenge, or lovers of adultery, similar spirits are present with them, and dwell, as it were, in their evil affections. These spirits, so far as the man cannot be restrained from evil by the good spirits, set him on fire, and, so far as their affection reigns in him, they adhere to him, and never recede. Thus is a wicked man conjoined with hell, and a good man with heaven.

296. The reason that man is governed by the Lord through the instrumentality of spirits, is, because he does not stand in the order of heaven. He is born into evils which are those of hell, thus into a state which is diametrically opposite to divine order ; consequently he has to be brought back into order ; and this can only be effected mediately, through the instrumentality of spirits. It would be different if man were born into good, which is according to the order of heaven : he would not then be governed by the Lord through spirits, but by order itself, consequently, by the common influx. Man is governed by this

10   145

influx as to those things which proceed from his thought and will into act, thus as to his speech and actions, for both the one and the other of these flow according to natural order: with these, therefore, the spirits that are adjoined to man have nothing in common. Animals, likewise, are governed by the common influx proceeding from the spiritual world; for animals exist in the order of their life, which they have not been able to pervert and destroy, because they have no rational faculty.(³) (What is the distinction between men and beasts, may be seen above, n. 39.)

297. As to what further concerns the conjunction of heaven with the human race, it is to be observed, that the Lord Himself enters by influx into every man according to the order of heaven; both into the inmost elements of his being, and into the last or ultimate, disposing him for the reception of heaven, and governing his ultimate powers from his inmost, and his inmost, at the same time, from the ultimate, and thus keeping all things belonging to him, to the minutest particulars, in connection. This influx of the Lord is called immediate influx; but the other, which is effected through spirits, is called mediate influx: the latter subsists through the former. The immediate influx, which is that of the Lord Himself, proceeds from his Divine Humanity, and flows into the will of man, and, through the will, into his understanding; thus it flows into the good existing in man, and, through his good, into his truth; or, what amounts to the same, into his love, and, through his love, into his faith: but it never proceeds in the reverse order; much less does it flow into faith that is without love, or into truth without good, or into an understanding that is not derived from the will. This Divine Influx is perpetual, and, by the good, is received in good, but not by the evil. By these, it is either rejected, or suffocated, or perverted; whence their life is an evil one; which, in a spiritual sense, is death.(⁴)

(³) That the distinction between men and beasts is, that men are capable of being elevated by the Lord to Himself, and of thinking about the Divine Being, of loving Him, thus of being conjoined to the Lord, whence they have eternal life; but it is otherwise with beasts, nn. 4525, 6323, 9231. That beasts are in the order of their life, and therefore they are born into things suitable to their nature; whereas man is not, who must therefore be introduced by things intellectual into the order of his life, nn. 637, 5850, 6323. That according to the common or general influx, thought, with man, falls into speech, and will into gestures, nn. 5862, 5990, 6192, 6211. Of the common or general influx of the spiritual world into the life of beasts, nn. 1633, 3646.

(⁴) That there is immediate influx from the Lord, and likewise mediate through the spiritual world, nn. 6063, 6307, 6472, 9682, 9683. That the immediate influx of the Lord is into the most particular of all things, nn. 6058, 6474—6478, 8717, 8728. That the Lord flows into the first elements, and at the same time into the last, in what manner, nn. 5147, 5150, 6473, 7004, 7007, 7270. That the influx of the Lord takes place into the good appertaining to man, and by or through good into truth; and not vice versa, nn. 5482, 5649, 6027, 8685, 8701, 10,153. That the life which flows in from the Lord varies according to the state of man and according to reception, nn. 2888, 5986, 6472, 7343. That, with the wicked, the good which flows in from the Lord is turned into evil, and the truth into what is false, from experience, nn. 3607, 4632. That the good and the truth thence derived, which continually flow from the Lord, are so far received, as evil and the falsity thence derived do not oppose, nn. 2411, 3142, 3147, 5828.

146

298. The spirits who are present with man, both those that are in conjunction with heaven and those that are in conjunction with hell, never enter into man with an influx from their own memory and the thought thence originating, for if they were to enter with an influx from their own thought, the man would not know but that their thoughts and reminiscences were his own. (See above, n. 256.) By their instrumentality, however, there enters into man, by influx, affection from heaven, which is that of the love of good and truth, and affection from hell, which is that of the love of evil and falsity. In proportion, therefore, as the affection of the man agrees with that which thus enters him by influx, it is received by him in his own thought, for the interior thought of man is in complete accord with his affection or love: but in proportion as it does not agree, it is not received by him. It hence is evident, since thought is not conveyed into man by the spirits, but only the affection of good and the affection of evil, that man has the power of choosing, because he has liberty; thus, that he has the power of receiving good in his thought, and of rejecting evil; for he knows what good and evil are, respectively, from the Word. What he receives in thought from affection, is, also, appropriated to him; but what he does not so receive, is not. From these observations, the nature of the influx into man of good from heaven, and of evil from hell, may evidently be seen.

299. It has also been granted me to know the origin of the anxiety, grief of mind, and interior sadness, called melancholy, with which man is afflicted. There are certain spirits who are not yet in conjunction with hell, being as yet in their first state, which will be described hereafter, when the world of spirits is treated of. They love undigested and malignant substances, such as those of food when it lies corrupting in the stomach. They consequently are present where such substances are to be found in man, because these are delightful to them; and they there converse with one another from their own evil affection. The affection contained in their discourse thence enters the man by influx; and if it is opposed to the man's affection, he experiences melancholy, sadness, and anxiety; whereas if it agrees with his affection, he becomes gay and cheerful. Those spirits appear near the stomach, some to the left, some to the right, some below, and some above, with different degrees of proximity and remoteness; thus they take various stations, according to the affections which form their character. That such is the origin of anxiety of mind, has been granted me to know and be assured of by much experience: I have seen those spirits, I have heard them, I have felt the anxieties arising from them, and I have conversed with them: they were driven away, and my anxiety ceased; they returned, and it returned; and I was sensible of its increase and decrease according to their approxima-

tion and removal. Hence was made manifest to me the or gin of the persuasion entertained by some, who do not know what conscience is by reason that they have none, when they attribute its pangs to a disordered state of the stomach.([5])

300. The conjunction of heaven with man is not like that of one man with another, but is a conjunction with the interiors which belong to his mind, thus with his spiritual or internal man. With his natural or external man, however, there is a conjunction by correspondences : the nature of which will be described in the next Section, in which the conjunction of heaven with man by means of the Word will be treated of.

301. That the conjunction of heaven with the human race, and of the human race with heaven, is of such a nature, that the one subsists from the other, will also be shown in the next Section.

302. Respecting the conjunction of heaven with the human race, I have conversed with angels : to whom I observed, that the members of the church say, indeed, that all good is from God, and that angels are present with man ; but that still, few believe that they are conjoined to man, much less that they reside in his thought and affection. The angels replied, that they know that such want of belief, connected, nevertheless, with such a mode of speaking, prevails in the world, especially (at which they wondered) within the church, where, notwithstanding, the Word exists, which imparts instruction respecting heaven, and respecting its conjunction with man; but that the conjunction, nevertheless, is of such a nature, that man cannot think the least in the world without having spirits adjoined to him, and that his spiritual life depends upon that fact. They declared the cause of this ignorance to be, that man fancies he lives of himself, without connection with the First Esse of life, and does not know that that connection is maintained through the heavens; although, if that connection were dissolved, he would instantly fall down dead. If man would believe, what is really the truth, that all good is from the Lord and all evil from hell, he would not claim merit for the good attached to him, nor would evil be imputed to him ; for then, in all the good which he thinks and does, he would look to the Lord, and all the evil which enters by influx would be rejected to hell

([5]) That those who have no conscience do not know what conscience is, nn. 7490, 9121. That there are some who laugh at conscience when they hear what it is, n. 7217. That some believe that conscience is nothing ; some, that it is something natural, which is sad and mournful, arising either from causes in the body, or from causes in the world ; some, that it is something peculiar to the vulgar, and occasioned by religion, n. 950. That there is a true conscience, a spurious conscience, and a false conscience, n. 1033. That pang of conscience is an anxiety of mind on account of what is unjust, insincere, and in any respect evil, which man believes to be contrary to God, and to the good of his neighbor, n. 7217. That they have conscience who are principled in love to God and in charity towards their neighbor, but not they who are not so principled, nn. 831, 965, 2380, 7490.

from whence it comes. But as man does not believe that there is any influx from heaven and from hell, and supposes, in consequence, that whatever he thinks, and whatever he wills, is in himself, and thence is from himself; he appropriates to himself the evil, and defiles the good which enters by influx with the notion of merit.

OF THE CONJUNCTION OF HEAVEN WITH MAN BY MEANS OF THE WORD.

303. Those who think from interior reason are able to see, that all things have a connection, by intermediate links, with the First Cause, and that whatever is not maintained in such connection, drops out of existence. For they know, when they reflect, that nothing can subsist from itself, but only from something prior to itself, and consequently, that all things subsist from a First Cause; and that the connection of any thing with something prior to itself, is like that of an effect with its efficient cause; for when the efficient cause is withdrawn from the effect, the effect is dissolved, and falls to nothing. Because the learned have thought in this manner, they have, consequently, seen and affirmed, that subsistence is perpetual existence; and thus, that since all things originally existed from the First Cause, they perpetually exist, that is, subsist, from the First Cause also. But what is the nature of the connection of every thing with that which is prior to it, and thus with the First Cause from Whom all things existed, cannot be stated in few words, because it includes much variety and diversity; further than that, in general, there is a connection of the natural world with the spiritual, and that this is the reason that there is a correspondence between all the objects that exist in the natural world and all that exist in the spiritual (respecting which correspondence, see nn. 103—115); and also, that there is a connection, and consequently a correspondence, between all things belonging to man and all things belonging to heaven (respecting which, see also above, nn. 87—102).

304. Man was so created, as to have both connection and conjunction with the Lord, but, with the angels of heaven, only consociation. The reason that he has not conjunction with the angels, but only consociation, is, because man, by creation, is like an angel as to the interiors, which belong to the mind: for man has a will similar to that of an angel, and an understanding similar to his; on which account, after death, man, if he has lived according to divine order, becomes an angel, and then enjoys a wisdom similar to that of the angels. When, therefore,

mention is made of the conjunction of man with heaven, what is meant is, his conjunction with the Lord and consociation with angels; for heaven is not heaven by virtue of any thing proper to the angels, but by virtue of the Divine Sphere of the Lord which constitutes it. (That the Divine Sphere of the Lord constitutes heaven, may be seen above, nn. 7—22.) Man, however, has this besides, which the angels have not,—that he not only exists in the spiritual world as to his interiors, but that he also exists at the same time in the natural world as to his exteriors. His exteriors, which exist in the natural world, are all things belonging to his natural or external memory, and which thence become the subjects of his thought and imagination; in general, his knowledges and sciences, with their delights and pleasures, so far as they savor of the world; together with many pleasures that belong to the sensual organs and faculties of the body; with which are to be reckoned, also, the senses, speech, and actions, themselves. All these, likewise, are the ultimate things, in which the Lord's divine influx terminates; for this never stops in the middle, but always goes on to its ultimates. From these facts it may evidently appear, that in man is placed the ultimate of Divine order, and that, being its ultimate, he is its basis and foundation. Since the Lord's Divine Influx does not stop in the middle, but always goes on to its ultimates, as just observed—and since the middle region through which it passes is the angelic heaven, and the ultimate has place in man; and since nothing unconnected can exist—it follows, that the connection and conjunction of heaven with the human race are of such a nature, that the one subsists from the other, and that it would fare with the human race without heaven, as with a chain on the removal of the staple from which it hangs; and with heaven without the human race, as with a house without a foundation.(¹)

305. But since man has broken this connection with heaven, by turning his interiors away from heaven towards the world and himself, through the love of self and the world, and thus has so withdrawn himself as no longer to serve as a base and foundation for heaven, a medium has been provided by the Lord

---

(¹) That nothing exists from itself, but from what is prior to itself, thus all things from the First Cause; and that they also subsist from Him who gave them existence; and that to subsist is perpetually to exist, nn. 2886, 2888, 3627, 3628, 3648, 4523, 4524, 6040, 6056. That divine order does not stop in the middle, but terminates in the ultimate, and the ultimate is man; thus that divine order terminates with man, nn. 634, (2853,) 3632, 5897, (6239,) 6451, 6465, 9216, (9217,) 9824, 9828, 9836, 9905, 10,044, 10,329, 10,335, 10,548. That interior things flow by successive order into external things, even to the extreme or ultimate, and that there, also, they exist and subsist, nn. 634, 6239, 6465, 9216, (9217.) That interior things exist and subsist in what is ultimate in simultaneous order, concerning which, nn. 5897, 6451, 8603, 10,099. That hence, all interior things are held together in connection from the First Cause by the last effect, n. 9828. That hence the First and the Last signify all things generally and particularly, thus, the whole, nn. 10,044, 10,329, 10,335. And that hence in ultimates there is strength and power, n. 9836.

to fill the place of such base and foundation, and to maintain, at the same time, the conjunction of heaven with man. This medium is the Word. (How the Word serves as such a medium, is largely shown in the *Arcana Cœlestia*. The passages may be seen collected together in the little work *On the White Horse mentioned in the Revelation*, and also in the Appendix to the work *On the New Jerusalem and its Heavenly Doctrine;* whence some references are adduced in the Notes below.) (²)

306. I have been instructed from heaven, that the most ancient natives of this globe enjoyed immediate revelation, because their interiors were turned towards heaven; and that there then existed, in consequence, a conjunction of the Lord with the human race. But that, after those times, such immediate revelation ceased, and there was given, instead of it, a mediate revelation by correspondences. For the divine worship of the people who then existed, consisted entirely of correspondent rites; whence the churches of those times are styled representative churches. For it was then known what correspondence and representation are, and that all the objects that exist on earth correspond to the spiritual existences belonging to heaven and the church; or, what amounts to the same, that they represent them; in consequence of which, the natural performances which composed their external worship served them as means for thinking spiritually, and thus in concert with the angels. After the science of correspondences and representations was obliterated, the Word was written, in which all the words, and the meanings of the words combined in sentences, are correspondences, and consequently contain a spiritual or internal sense, of which the angels have a perception. In consequence of this, when a man reads the Word, and understands it according to its literal or external sense, the angels understand it according to its spiritual or internal sense; for the

---

(²) That the Word in its literal sense is natural, n. 8783. By reason that what is natural is the ultimate, in which spiritual and celestial things, which are things interior, close, and on which they stand, as a house upon its foundation, nn. 9430, 9433, 9824, 10,044, 10,436. That the Word, in order to be of such a quality, is written by pure correspondences, nn. 1408, 1409, 1540, (1615,) 1659, 1709, 1783, 8615, 10,687. That the Word, being of such a quality in the sense of the letter, contains a spiritual and celestial sense, n. 9407. And that it is accommodated both to men and angels at the same time, nn. 1767—1772, 1887, 2143, 2157, 2275, 2333, 2395, 2540, 2541, 2547, 2553, 7331, 8862, 10,322. And that it is the medium for uniting heaven and earth, nn. 2310, 2495, 9212, 9216, 9357, 9396, 10,375. That the conjunction of the Lord with man is effected by the Word, through the medium of the internal sense, n. 10,375. That by all things contained in the Word, in every particular, conjunction is effected; and that hence the Word is wonderful above all other writings, nn. 10,632, 10,633, 10,634. That the Lord, since the Word has been written, speaks by it with men, n. 10,290. That the church, where the Word is, by which the Lord is known, is, in respect to those who are out of the church, where the Word is not, and the Lord is not known, as the heart and lungs in man in respect to the other parts of the body, which live from them as from the fountains of their life, nn. 637, 931, 2054, 2853. That the universal church on earth is, before the Lord, as one man, nn. 7396, 9276. Hence, unless there was a church where the Word is, and by it the Lord is known, in this earth, the human race would here perish, nn. 468, 637, 931, 4545, 10,452.

thoughts of angels are altogether spiritual, whereas those of men are natural; and though these two kinds of thoughts appear different, they nevertheless form a one, because they correspond to each other. Thus it is, that, after man removed himself from heaven, and broke the band which connected him therewith, a medium for the conjunction of heaven with man was provided by the Lord through the Word.

307. How conjunction between heaven and man is effected by means of the Word, I will illustrate by citing a few passages. In the Revelation, the New Jerusalem is described in these words: *"I saw a new heaven and a new earth: for the first heaven and the first earth were passed away.—And I, John, saw the holy city, new Jerusalem, coming down from God out of heaven.—And the city lieth four-square, and the length is as large as the breadth. And he measured the city with a reed, twelve thousand furlongs. The length and the breadth and the height of it are equal. And he measured the wall thereof, a hundred and forty and four cubits, according to the measure of a man, that is, of the angel. And the building of the wall of it was of jasper: and the city was pure gold, like unto clear glass. And the foundations of the wall of the city were garnished with all manner of precious stones.—And the twelve gates were twelve pearls:—and the street of the city was pure gold, as it were transparent glass."*—(Rev. xxi. 1, 2, 16—19, 21.) When a man reads these words, he only understands them in their literal sense; according to which the visible heaven and earth are to perish, a new heaven is to appear, and the holy city Jerusalem is to descend, and take its station upon a new earth; all the dimensions of which city will be such as are mentioned in the above description. But the angels present with the man understand the whole quite differently, apprehending spiritually what the man apprehends naturally. They, by a new heaven and new earth, understand a new church. By the city Jerusalem descending from God out of heaven, they understand the heavenly doctrine of that church, revealed by the Lord. By its length, breadth, and height, which are equal, each being twelve thousand furlongs, they understand all the goods and truths of that doctrine collectively. By its wall, they understand the truths which protect it. By the measure of the wall, a hundred and forty-four cubits, which is the measure of a man, that is, of the angel, they understand all those protecting truths considered collectively, and their quality. By the twelve gates, which were twelve pearls, they understand the truths which introduce; pearls, also, signify such truths. By the foundations of the wall, which were composed of precious stones, they understand the knowledges upon which that doctrine is founded. By the gold like unto clear glass, of which both the city and its street were formed, they understand the good of love, which imparts clear-

ness to doctrine and its truths. It is thus that the angels apprehend all these statements, quite differently, as is evident,
from man; and it is thus that the natural ideas of man pass
into spiritual ideas when they reach the angels. This is effected,
without the angels knowing any thing about the literal sense of
the Word, or about the new heaven and the new earth, the new
city of Jerusalem, its wall, the foundation of the wall, and its
dimensions: and yet the thoughts of the angels form a one with
the thoughts of man, because they correspond to them. They
form a one, much like the words of a speaker and the sense of
them as understood by the hearer, who does not attend to the
words, but only to their meaning. From this example it may
be seen, how a conjunction is effected between heaven and man
by means of the Word.

Let us take another example: *"In that day there shall be a
highway out of Egypt to Assyria; and the Assyrians shall
come into Egypt, and the Egyptians into Assyria; and the
Egyptians shall serve with the Assyrians. In that day shall
Israel be the third with Egypt and with Assyria, even a blessing
in the midst of the land: whom Jehovah of hosts shall bless,
saying, Blessed be Egypt my people, and Assyria, the work of
my hand, and Israel mine inheritance."*—(Isa. xix. 23, 24, 25.)
In what manner man thinks, and in what manner the angels,
when these words are read, will be evident from the literal sense
of the Word, and from its internal sense. From the literal
sense, man thinks that the Egyptians and the Assyrians are to
be converted to God, and accepted by Him, and to form one
body with the Israelitish nation: but the angels think, according to the internal sense, of the man of the spiritual church, who
in that sense is here described, and whose spiritual mind is Israel, whose natural mind is Egypt, and whose rational mind,
which is the intermediate, is Assyria.[3] Both these senses,
nevertheless, compose a one, because they correspond to each
other; whence, when the angels think spiritually, as just stated,
and man thinks naturally, also as just stated, there is a conjunction between them, almost like that of the soul and the body.
The internal sense of the Word is, likewise, its soul, and the
literal sense its body. Such is the nature of the Word throughout; whence it may be evident, that it is a medium of conjunction between heaven and man, and that its literal sense serves
as a base and foundation.

308. A conjunction is also effected, by means of the Word,
between heaven and the people who are beyond the limits of

[3] That Egypt and Egyptians in the Word, signify the natural principle, and the
scientific thence derived, nn. 4967, 5079, 5080 5095, 5160, 5799, 6015, 6147, 6252, 7855,
7648, 9391, 9340. That Assyria signifies the rational principle, nn. 119, 1186. That
Israel signifies the spiritual principle, nn. 5414, 5801, 5803, 5806, 5812, 5817, 5819, 5826,
5833, 5879, 5951, 6426, 6637, 6862, 6868, 7035, 7062, 7193, 7201, 7215, 7223, 7957, 8234,
8805, 9340.

the church, inhabiting countries where the Word is not known. For the Lord's church is universal, existing with all who acknowledge a Divine Being and live in charity; all of whom, likewise, are instructed by angels after their decease, and then receive divine truths.(*) (Respecting which subject, see the Section below, which treats of the Gentiles.) The church universal on earth, is, in the sight of the Lord, as one man, just as heaven is (of which, see above, nn. 59—72): but the church in which the Word is read, and the Lord, in consequence, is known, is like the heart and lungs in that man. That all the viscera and members of the whole body draw their life, by various derivations, from the heart and lungs, is well known; so, also, do those portions of the human race, which live without the church that is in possession of the Word, and which constitute the members of that man. The conjunction effected by means of the Word between heaven and those who live in remote countries, may also be compared to light, which is propagated from its centre in every direction around. In the Word is Divine Light, in which the Lord, with heaven, is present; and in consequence of His being thus present, even those at a distance are in the enjoyment of light. It would be very different if no Word existed. (These truths may receive further elucidation from what was stated above respecting the form of heaven, according to which the consociations and communications of the inhabitants are arranged, nn. 200—212.) This, however, is an arcanum which is capable of being comprehended by those who are in the enjoyment of spiritual light, but not by those who are only in natural light: for by those who are in the enjoyment of spiritual light, innumerable things are seen clearly, which, by those who are only in natural light, are not seen at all, or, if seen, only appear as one obscure object.

309. Had not a Word of such a nature been given on this earth, its natives would have been separated from heaven, and had they been separated from heaven, they would no longer have been rational beings; for the rational faculty of man derives its existence from the influx of the light of heaven. The natives of this earth, also, are of such a character, that they are incapable of receiving immediate revelation, and being in that way instructed respecting divine truths, like the inhabitants of other earths, of whom I have treated in a work expressly on that subject; for the natives of this earth are more immersed than those of others in worldly things, and consequently in their

(*) That the church specifically exists where the Word is, by which the Lord is known; thus, where divine truths from heaven are revealed, nn. 8857, 10,761. That the church of the Lord exists with all in the universal terrestrial globe, who live in good according to the principles of their religion, nn. 8263, 6637, 10,765. That all in every country, who live in good according to the principles of their religion, and acknowledge a Divine Being, are accepted of the Lord, nn. 2589—2604, 2861, 2863, 3263, 4190, 4197, 6700, 9256. And, besides, all infants wheresoever they are born, nn. 2289—2309, 4792.

external faculties; whereas it is the internal faculties which receive revelation; were it received by the external or es, truth would not be understood. That such is the character of the natives of this earth, is manifestly evident from those who live within the limits of the church, who, though they possess knowledge from the Word respecting heaven, hell, and the life after death, yet in heart deny their existence; and amongst whom are some who have sought to obtain the reputation of superior learning, and of whom it might therefore be supposed, that they possessed superior wisdom.

310. I have sometimes conversed respecting the Word with angels; when I observed, that it is despised by some on account of the simplicity of its style; and that nothing whatever is known respecting its internal sense, on which account it is not believed to contain such exalted wisdom concealed in its bosom. The angels replied, that although the style of the Word appears simple in the literal sense, it nevertheless is of such a nature, that nothing whatever can be compared with it for excellence, because that divine wisdom is concealed in it, not only in the meaning of every sentence, but in every word; and that that wisdom, in heaven, shines or gives light. They meant to say that it is the light of heaven, because it is Divine Truth; for Divine Truth, in heaven, gives light. (See above, n. 132.) They said, also, that without a Word of such a nature, no degree of the light of heaven would exist among the natives of our earth, nor could there be any conjunction between them and heaven; for it is in proportion as the light of heaven is present with man that such conjunction exists, and also, that revelation of Divine Truth is made to him by means of the Word. The reason that man is not aware that that conjunction is effected through the Word's having a spiritual sense corresponding to its natural sense, is, because the natives of this earth have no knowledge respecting the spiritual thought and speech of the angels, and are not aware that it differs from the natural thought and speech of men; and without knowing this, it is impossible to have any knowledge at all respecting what the internal sense of the Word is, nor, consequently, that such a conjunction is capable of being effected by means of that sense. The angels observed, further, that if man were aware of the existence of such a sense, and, when reading the Word, were to admit some knowledge of it to influence his thoughts, he would enter into interior wisdom, and into a still closer conjunction with heaven; because, by means of that sense, he would enter into ideas similar to those of the angels.

155

THAT ALL THE INHABITANTS OF HEAVEN AND OF HELL ARE DERIVED FROM THE HUMAN RACE.

311. It is utterly unknown in the Christian world, that all the inhabitants of heaven and of hell are derived from the human race; for it is imagined, that the angels were created such from the beginning, and that this was the origin of heaven; and that the devil, or Satan, was an angel of light, but that, becoming a rebel, he was cast down with his crew; and that this was the origin of hell. The angels are exceedingly astonished that such a belief should exist in the Christian world; and still more, that nothing should be known respecting heaven, although the existence of heaven is a primary article in the doctrines of the church. As, however, such ignorance prevails, the angels rejoice in heart that it has pleased the Lord now to reveal to mankind many particulars respecting heaven and also respecting hell, and by such means, as far as possible, to dispel the darkness, which is continually increasing, by reason that the church has come to its end. They therefore desire me to state from their lips, that there does not exist, in the universal heaven, a single angel who was created such from the first, nor any devil in hell who was created an angel of light and afterwards cast down thither; but that all the inhabitants, both of heaven and of hell, are derived from the human race; the inhabitants of heaven consisting of those, who, when in the world, had lived in heavenly love and faith, and the inhabitants of hell of those who had lived in infernal love and faith: and further, that all hell, taken collectively, is what is called the devil and Satan, the hell which is at the back,* and is inhabited by those who are called evil genii, being termed the devil, and the hell which is in front,* and is inhabited by those who are called evil spirits, being termed Satan.([1]) The nature, respectively, of both these hells, will be described in the following pages. The angels said, further, that the Christian world has formed such a belief respecting the inhabitants of heaven and hell, from certain passages of the Word only understood according to the literal sense, and not illustrated and explained by genuine doctrine drawn from the Word; although the literal sense of the Word, when not viewed by the light of genuine doctrine, draws

---

([1]) That the hells, taken together, or the infernals, taken together, are called the devil and Satan, n. 694. That those who have been devils in the world, become devils after death, n. 968.

* Here the Author is to be understood as speaking of the situation of things and places as they appear to the spectator in the spiritual world, and which always have the same aspect with respect to his body, as to right and left, behind and before, above and beneath, &c., wheresoever he is, or which way soever he turns see before, un. 123, 124.—H.

the mind aside into various opinions, which circumstance gives birth to ignorance, heresies, and errors.(²)

312. Another reason for the existence of this belief among the members of the church may also be mentioned; which is this: that they believe that no man will be admitted into either heaven or hell till the time of the last judgment; respecting which they have imbibed the opinion, that all visible objects will then perish, and be replaced by new ones; and that the soul will then return into its body, by virtue of which reunion, man will then live again as a man. This belief implies the other respecting angels created such from the beginning: for it cannot be believed that the inhabitants of heaven and of hell are all derived from the human race, while it is imagined that no man will be admitted into either till the end of the world. But that men might be convinced that such is not the fact, it has been granted me to enjoy the society of angels, and also to converse with the inhabitants of hell. This privilege I have now enjoyed for many years, sometimes from morning to evening without cessation; and I have thus received information respecting both heaven and hell. This also has been granted me, in order that the members of the church might no longer adhere to their erroneous belief respecting the resurrection at the period of the last judgment, and the state of the soul in the mean time; as also, respecting angels and the devil. This faith, being a belief of what is false, involves the mind in darkness, and, with persons who think on those subjects from self-intelligence, occasions doubt, and, finally, denial. For they say in their heart, how can the visible heavens, with such myriads of stars, and the sun and moon, be destroyed and dissipated? And how can the stars, which are larger than the earth, then fall from heaven upon it? And how can our bodies, though eaten by worms, consumed by putrefaction, and dispersed to all the winds, be gathered together again, to be reunited with their souls? Where is the soul in the mean time? and what sort of thing can it be, when without the senses which it had in the body? With many similar questions, the points referred to in which, being incomprehensible, cannot be objects of belief, and, with many, destroy all belief in the life of the soul after death, and respecting heaven and hell, and, together with these, respecting the other points which belong to the faith of the church. That they have had this destructive effect, is evident from those who

(²) That the doctrine of the church must be derived from the Word, nn. 8464, 5402, 5482, 10,763, 10,764. That the Word without doctrine is not understood, nn. 9025, 9409, 9424, 9430, 10,324, 10,431, 10,582. That true doctrine is a lamp to those who read the Word, n. 10,400. That genuine doctrine must be had from those who are in illustration from the Lord, nn. 2510, 2516, 2519, 9424, 10,105. That those who abide in the sense of the letter, without doctrine, never attain any understanding respecting divine truths, nn. 9409, 9410, 10,582. And that they are led away into many errors, n. 10,431. What is the difference between those who teach and learn from the doctrine of the church derived from the Word, and those who teach and learn from the literal sense alone, n. 9025.

say, Wh) has ever come to us from heaven, and assured us of its
existence? What is hell? is there such a place? What can it
be, for a man to be tormented in fire forever? What is the day
of judgment? has it not been expected for ages past, and has not
arrived yet? With similar observations, implying denial of the
whole. Lest, therefore, those who think in this manner, as is
customary with many who possess much worldly wisdom, and
on that ground are accounted men of erudition and learning,
should any longer disturb and seduce the simple in faith and
heart, and induce infernal darkness with respect to God, heaven,
eternal life, and other subjects which depend on these, my interiors, which are of the spirit, have been opened by the Lord, and
it has thus been given me to converse with all that ever I knew
while they lived in the body, after their decease. With some of
these I conversed for several days, with others for months, and
with others for a year. I have also conversed with such multi-
tudes of other deceased persons, that I should underrate their
number were I to reckon them at a hundred thousand; of whom
many were in the heavens, and many in the hells. I have conversed, too, with some, two days after their decease; whom I
told, that their friends were now preparing for their funeral, and
for the burial of their remains. They replied, that their friends
did well to put out of the way what had served them for a body
and its functions in the world; and they wished me to say, that
they were not dead, but alive, being now as really men as before,
having only migrated from one world into another; and that they
were not conscious of having lost any thing, because they were
living in a body, possessing the faculties of sense, the same as
before, and were also in the enjoyment of understanding and
will, as before; and that they had thoughts and affections,
sensations and desires, similar to what they had in the world.
Many of the newly deceased, when they see that they are living
as men, as before, and are in a similar state (for the first state
of every one's life after death is such as he was in while in the
world; but this is gradually changed with him, either into
heaven or into hell), are affected with new joy at finding themselves alive, and declare that they could not have believed it:
but they wonder exceedingly that they should have been in such
ignorance and blindness respecting the state of their life after
death; and still more, that the same should possess the members of the church, who, above all others in the whole terrestrial
globe, might be in the possession of light on those subjects.([8])

([*]) That in Christendom, at this day, few believe that man rises again immediately
after death, Preface to chap. xvi. Gen., and nn. 4622, 10,758; but that he shall rise again
at the day of the last judgment, when the visible world will perish, n. 10,595. The
reason why it is so believed, nn. 10,595, 10,758. That, nevertheless, man rises again
immediately after death, and that then he is a man in every respect, nn. 4527, 5006,
5078, 8939, 8991, 10,594, 10,758. That the soul which lives after death is the spirit of
man, which, in man, while in the world, is the man himself, and which, in the other

They then first discovered the cause of such blindness and igno-rance; which is, that external things, which are such as relate to the world and the body, have possessed and filled men's minds to such a degree, that they cannot be elevated into the light of heaven, and view the things belonging to the church farther than as matters of doctrine; for when corporeal and worldly things are so loved as they are at the present day; mere darkness flows from them into the mind, as soon as any one advances a step beyond what he has learned from doctrine.

313. Great numbers of the learned men who come from the Christian world, when they see themselves, after their decease, possessed of a body, clothed with garments, and dwelling in houses, as when they were in the world, are seized with amaze-ment; and when they recall to mind what they had thought respecting the life after death, respecting the soul, respecting spirits, and respecting heaven and hell, they feel ashamed, and confess that they had thought foolishly, and that the thoughts of those who held their faith in simplicity were much wiser than theirs. The state of the learned who had confirmed themselves in such notions, and who had ascribed every thing to nature, was investigated; and it was ascertained, that their interiors were completely closed, and only their exteriors open, so that they had not looked to heaven, but to the world, and thus, also, to hell. For so far as a person's interiors are open, he looks to heaven; but so far as they are closed, and only his exteriors are open, he looks to hell; for man's interiors are formed for the re-ception of all things belonging to heaven, and his exteriors for the reception of all things belonging to the world; and those who receive the world, and not heaven at the same time, receive hell.(*)

314. That the inhabitants of heaven are derived from the hu-man race, may also be evident from the fact, that the minds of angels and those of men are similar to each other. Both enjoy the faculty of understanding, perceiving, and willing: both are formed for the reception of heaven. For the human mind is ca-pable of wisdom equally with the angelic mind; but the reason that it does not enjoy wisdom in an equal degree in the world, is, because man is then invested with a terrestrial body, in which his spiritual mind thinks in a natural manner: whereas, when it is released from its connection with that body, it no longer thinks in a natural but in a spiritual manner; and when it thinks spir-

life, is in a perfect human form, nn. 322, 1880, 1881, 3633, 4622, 4735, 5888, 6054, 6605, 6626, 7021, 10,594; from experience, nn. 4527, 5006, 8939; from the Word, n. 10,597. What is meant by the dead seen in the holy city, Matt. xxvii. 53, n. 9229. In what manner man is raised from the dead, from experience, nn. 168—189. Concerning his state after resurrection, nn. 317, 318, 319. 2119, 5079. 10,596. False opinions concerning the soul and its resurrection, nn. 444, 445, 4527, 4622, 4658.

(*) That in man the spiritual and the natural world are conjoined, n. 6057. That the internal of man is formed after the image of heaven, but the external after the image of the world, nn. 3628, 4523, 4524, 6057, 8814, 9706, 10,156, 10,472.

itually, it embraces things incomprehensible and ineffable to **the** natural man, and thus enjoys the same wisdom as an angel. From these observations it may be seen, that the internal of man, which is called his spirit, is, in its essence, an angel[5] (see above, n. 57); and, when released from the terrestrial body, is in the human form, equally with an angel. (That an angel is in a perfect human form, may be seen above nn. 73—77). But when a man's internal is not open above, but only below, it is still, after its separation from the body, in a human form, but in such as is direful and diabolical; for it is unable to look upwards to heaven, but only downwards to hell.

315. He who is instructed in the nature of Divine Order, may also understand, that man was created to become an angel: for in him is placed the ultimate of order (see above, n. 304), in which may be formed a subject of heavenly and angelic wisdom, that may afterwards be renewed and multiplied. Divine Order never stops mid-way, and there forms a being without its ultimate; for it is not, there, in its fulness and perfection: but it goes on to the ultimate, and when it has arrived there, it commences the work of formation. It also, by means there brought together, renews itself, and goes on to further productions; which it accomplishes by the way of procreation. In the ultimate, consequently, is the seminary of heaven.

316. The reason that the Lord rose again, not only as to His spirit, but also as to His body, was, because, while He was in the world, He glorified the whole of His Humanity,—that is, made it Divine. For His soul, which He had from the Father, was the Essential Divinity; and His body was made the likeness of His soul, that is, of the Father; consequently, Divine also. Hence it was, that He, differently from any man, rose again as to both.[6] This, also, He made manifest to the disciples, who imagined, when they beheld Him, that they saw a spirit, by saying, *"Behold my hands and my feet, that it is I myself: handle Me, and see: for a spirit hath not flesh and bones, as ye see Me have"* (Luke xxiv. 37, 39): by which he indicated, that he was not only a Man as to His spirit, but as to His body also.

317. In order that it might be known that man lives after death, and goes either to heaven or to hell according to his life in the world, many things have been discovered to me respecting the state of man after death. These will be delivered, in order, in the following pages, when we treat of the World of Spirits.

(⁵) That there are as many degrees of life in man, as there are heavens, and that they are opened in man after death according to his life, nn. 8747, 9594. That heaven is in man, n. 8884. That men who live a life of love and charity have in them angelic wisdom, which at the time, is hidden, but that they come into it after death, n. 2494. That a man who receives the good of love and of faith from the Lord, is called, in the Word, an angel, n. 10,528.

(⁶) That man rises again only as to his spirit, nn. 10,593, 10,594. That the Lord alone rose again as to the body also, nn. 1729, 2083, 5078, 10,825.

OF THE STATE, IN HEAVEN, OF THE GENTILES, OR NATIVES OF
COUNTRIES NOT WITHIN THE LIMITS OF THE CHURCH.

318. It is a common opinion, that persons who are born out of
the limits of the church, and who are called Gentiles or Heathens,
cannot be saved, because they do not possess the Word, and thus
are ignorant of the Lord; and it is certain that, without the
Lord, there can be no salvation. Nevertheless, that salvation is
open to these also, is a truth which might be inferred from these
considerations alone: That the Lord's mercy is universal, or extends to every individual; that they are born men, as really as
those who are born within the church, who are but few in comparison; and that their being ignorant of the Lord is by no fault
of their own. Every person who thinks from a rational faculty
in any degree enlightened, may see clearly, that no man can be
born designedly for hell; since the Lord is Love itself, and His
Love consists in desiring the salvation of all. On this account
He provides, that all should be attached to some religion, and
should possess, by means of it, the acknowledgment of a Divine
Being, and interior life; since to live according to a religious
belief is to live interiorly; for a man then has respect to a Divine
Being, and so far as he does this, he does not look to the world,
but removes himself from the world, consequently, from the life
of the world, which is exterior life.(¹)
319. That Gentiles are saved as well as Christians, may be
known to those who are aware what it is that constitutes heaven
with man; for heaven is in man, and those who have heaven in
themselves, go to heaven after death. It is heaven in man to
acknowledge a Divine Being, and to be led by Him. The first
and chief essential of all religion consists in acknowledging a
Divine Being: and a religion which does not include this acknowledgment, is no religion at all. The precepts, also, of every
religion have respect to worship, or teach how the Divine Being
is to be worshipped, in order to render man acceptable to Him:
and when this is implanted in a man's mind, or in proportion as
it is an object of his will or of his love, he is led by the Lord.
It is known that the Gentiles live a moral life as well as Chris-

(¹) That the Gentiles are saved, equally with Christians, nn. 932, 1032, 1059, 2284,
2589, 2590, 3778, 4190, 4197. Of the lot of the Gentiles and people who are out of the
limits of the church in the other life, nn. 2589—2604. That the church is specifically
where the Word exists, by which the Lord is known, nn. 3857, 10,761. Nevertheless,
that those who are born where the Word exists, and where, by means of it, the Lord
is known, are not on that account of the church, but those who live a life of charity
and of faith, nn. 6637, 10,143, 10,153, 10,578, 10,645, 10,820. That the church of the
Lord exists with all in the universe who live in good according to their religious principles, and acknowledge the Divine Being; and that they are accepted of the Lord,
and go to heaven, nn. 2589—2604, 2861, 2863, 3263, 4190, 4197, 6700, 9256.

11   161

tians, and many of them better.   Men live a moral life, either
from regard to the Divine Being, or from regard to the opinion
of the people in the world; and when a moral life is practised
out of regard to the Divine Being, it is a spiritual life.   Both
appear alike in their outward form, but in their inward they are
completely different : the one saves a man, but the other does
not; for he that lives a moral life out of regard to the Divine
Being, is led by Him; but he who does so from regard to the
opinion of people in the world, is led by himself.

But this shall be illustrated by an example.   A person who
abstains from doing injury to his neighbor, because, to do so,
would be contrary to religion, consequently, contrary to the will
of the Divine Being, practises such abstinence from a spiritual
ground : whereas a person who merely abstains from doing injury to another out of fear of the law, of the loss of reputation,
honor, or gain, thus out of regard to self and the world, only
practises such abstinence from a natural ground, and is led by
himself.   The life of this person is natural in its quality; but
that of the former is spiritual.   The man whose moral life is of
a spiritual quality, has in himself heaven : but the man whose
moral life is only of a natural quality, has not.   The reason is,
because heaven enters by influx from above, and opens man's
interiors, and then, through his interiors, flows into his exteriors;
whereas the world enters by influx from below, and opens man's
exteriors, but not his interiors : for there cannot be any influx
from the natural world into the spiritual, but only from the
spiritual world into the natural; and consequently, if, when the
world flows into the exteriors, heaven is not received at the same
time, the interiors are closed.   From these observations may be
seen, who the persons are that receive heaven in themselves, and
who they are that do not.   Heaven, however, in one person, is
not the same in quality as it is in another.   It differs in every one
according to his affection of good, and of truth thence derived.
All who cherish the affection of good out of regard to the Divine
Being, love Divine Truth; for good and truth mutually love each
other, and desire to be in conjunction :([*]) on which account the
Gentiles, although they are not possessed of genuine truths while
in the world, receive them in the other life, by virtue of the love
in which they are grounded.

320.   There was a certain spirit from among the Gentiles, who,
when in the world, had lived in the good of charity according to
his religious persuasion, who happened to hear some Christian
spirits disputing about points of belief : for spirits reason with
one another much more fully and acutely than men do, especially

([*]) That between good and truth there is the resemblance of marriage, nn. 1904, 2173,
2508.   That in good and truth there is a perpetual tendency to conjunction, and that
good desires truth, and to be conjoined with it, nn. 9206, 9207, 9495.   In what manner
the conjunction of good and truth is effected, and in whom, nn. 8884, 8843, 4093, 4097,
4301, 4345, 4353, 4364, 4368, 5365, 7623—7627, 9258.

on subjects relating to good and truth. He much wondered at their contending so about them, observing, that he did not like to hear such disputes, for they were reasoning from appearances and fallacies. He instructed them by saying, If I am a good man, I am able to determine what sentiments are true from good itself: and such truths as I am not acquainted with, I have a capacity for receiving.

321. I have been instructed, by many examples, that the Gentiles who have passed a moral life, have lived in obedience and subordination, and in mutual charity according to their religious persuasion, and who thence have acquired some degree of conscience, are accepted in the other life, and are there instructed by the angels, with sedulous care, in the goods and truths of faith: and that, while under instruction, they behave themselves modestly, intelligently, and wisely, and easily receive truths, and have them incorporated in their minds: for they have not formed for themselves any principles of falsity opposed to the truths of faith, which would need to be first removed; much less, any scandalous notions against the Lord, as many Christians have, who cherish no other idea of Him than that of a common man. Not so the Gentiles; for when they hear that God was made man, and thus was manifested in the world, they immediately acknowledge it, and adore the Lord, observing, that God assuredly had manifested Himself, because He is the God of heaven and earth, and the human race is His work.(³) It is, indeed, a divine truth, that without the Lord there can be no salvation: but the way in which that truth is to be understood, is this: that there can be no salvation except from the Lord. There are, in the universe, numerous earths, and all full of inhabitants: scarcely any of them know that the Lord assumed Humanity in our planet; but nevertheless, as they adore the Divine Being under a Human Form, they are accepted and led by the Lord. (On which subject, see the little work, *On the Earths in the Universe.*)

322. Among Gentiles, as among Christians, there are both wise and simple; and that I might be made acquainted with the character of both, it was granted me to converse with both, sometimes for hours and days together. There are, however, no such wise men at the present day as existed in ancient times,

(³) The difference between the good in which the Gentiles are principled, and that in which Christians are principled, nn. 4189, 4197. Of the truths appertaining to the Gentiles, nn. 3263, 3778, 4190. That the interiors cannot be so closed with the Gentiles, as with Christians, n. 9256. That neither can so thick a cloud exist with the Gentiles, who live according to their religious principles in mutual charity, as with the Christians who live in no charity, the reasons, nn. 1059, 9256. That the Gentiles cannot profane the holy things of the church like Christians, because they are not acquainted with them, nn. 1327, 1328, 2051. That they are afraid of Christians on account of their lives, nn. 2596, 2597. That those who have lived well, according to their religious principles, are instructed by the angels, and easily receive the truths of faith, and acknowledge the Lord, nn. 2049, 2595, 2598, 2600, 2601, 2603, 2861, 2863, 3263.

163

more particularly in the Ancient Church, which extended over a great part of the Asiatic world, whence religion emanated, and was diffused through many Gentile nations. That I might know of what quality they were, it was granted me to converse with some of them familiarly.

I found myself in company with a person, who had formerly been one of those, who possessed superior wisdom, and was also, on that account, known in the literary world. I conversed with him on various subjects; and it was given me to believe that he was Cicero. As I knew that he had been a wise man, my discourse with him was respecting wisdom, intelligence, order, the Word, and finally, the Lord. Respecting wisdom, he observed, that there is no wisdom, but such as relates to life; and that nothing else can deserve the name. Respecting intelligence, that it proceeds from the former. Respecting order, that it comes from the Supreme God; and that to live in that order, is to be wise and intelligent. As to the Word, when I read to him a passage from the prophets, he was very much delighted, especially on finding that every individual name and word signified interior things; and he was exceedingly surprised, that the learned of the present day should not take pleasure in such a study. I manifestly perceived that the interiors of his thought or mind were open. He said that he could not attend longer, because he had a perception of something more holy than he could bear,—so interiorly was he affected. Our conversation at length turned on the subject of the Lord; when I remarked, that he was born a man, but was conceived of God: that he put off the maternal humanity and put on the Divine Humanity; and that it is He who governs the universe. To these observations he replied, that he knew many things respecting the Lord, and that he apprehended, in his own way, that, if the human race was to be saved, it was impossible but that what I had stated must be the truth. Certain wicked Christians, however, injected various scandalous suggestions; but to these he paid no attention, observing, that their conduct was not to be wondered at, since, in the life of the body, they had imbibed unbecoming notions on those subjects, and that, before these were removed, they could not admit the considerations which confirm the truth, as those can who are ignorant of it altogether.

323. It has also been granted me to converse with some others who lived in ancient times, and who then belonged to the class of those who were eminent for wisdom. They at first appeared in front at some distance. From that station they were able to perceive the interiors of my thoughts, and thus fully to discern many things belonging to them; and from one idea of thought they were able to discern the whole series to which it belonged, and to fill it with delightful conceptions

of wisdom, combined with beautiful representations. I thence perceived, that they were of the class of such as were eminent for wisdom; and I was told, that they were some of the ancients. They then drew nearer; and on my reading a passage of the Word, they were exceedingly delighted. The nature of their delight and pleasure was perceived by me, and it chiefly arose from the circumstance, that all they heard from the Word, even to the most minute particular, was representative and significative of things celestial and spiritual. They stated, that in their days, when they lived in the world, their mode of thinking and speaking, and of writing, also, was of this kind, and that to render it such was the aim of their wisdom.

324. But as to the Gentiles of the present day, they are not of this wise character, but many of them are simple-hearted persons. Such of them, however, as have lived in mutual charity receive wisdom in the other life; respecting whom it may be proper to mention one or two instances.

Once when I was reading chapters xvii. and xviii. of Judges, respecting Micah, whose graven image, teraphim, and Levite, were taken from him by the sons of Dan, there was present a spirit from among the Gentiles, who, when he lived in the body, had worshipped a graven image. On listening attentively to the relation of what was done to Micah, and of the grief that he felt for the loss of his graven image, he, also, was seized with grief, and was affected by it to such a degree, that he scarcely knew, through the interior pain that he experienced, what he was thinking of. His grief was perceived by me; and it was perceived at the same time, that there was innocence in all his affections. Some Christian spirits were present, who observed the transaction, and wondered that the worshipper of a graven image could be moved with so great an affection of compassion and innocence. Certain good spirits afterwards entered into conversation with him; who remarked, that a graven image ought not to be worshipped, and that, as a human being, he was able to understand that such is the truth; but that, independently of his graven image, he ought to think of God the Creator and Governor of the universe, including both heaven and earth; and that that God is the Lord. When this was said to him, I was enabled to perceive the interior affection of his adoration, which was communicated to me, and was of a far more holy character than prevails among Christians. It may hence be evident, that the Gentiles enter heaven far more easily than the Christians of the present day: according to these words of the Lord in Luke: "*And they shall come from the east and from the west, and from the north and from the south, and shall lie down in the kingdom of God: and, behold, there are last who shall be first, and there are first who shall be last.*"—(Ch. xiii. 29, 30.) For in the state in which he then was, he was in a capacity for imbibing all the doctrines of faith, and for receiving them with interior affection: he possessed the compassion which is an attribute of love, and in his ignorance was included innocence; and where these are present, all the doctrines of faith are received as if spontaneously, and their reception is accompanied with joy. He was afterwards admitted among the angels.

325. One morning there was heard at a distance a certain company singing in concert, and from the attendant representations it was made known to me that they consisted of natives of China; for they presented the figure of a he-goat clothed with wool, and of a cake made of millet, and an ebony spoon, together with the idea of a floating city. They expressed a desire to come nearer to me; and when they did so, they said that they wished to be with me alone, that they might unbosom their thoughts. But they were told that they were not alone, and that others were present who were displeased at their wishing to be alone, although they were strangers. On perceiving their displeasure, they began to consider, whether they had trespassed against their neighbor, and whether they had claimed any thing for themselves which was the property of others (for all thoughts in the other life are communicated to those around). It was given me to perceive the agitation of their minds: it included an acknowledgment that they might possibly have done them injury, with shame on that account, combined with a mixture of other commendable affections; whence it was known that they were possessed of charity. I soon afterwards entered into conversation with them, and at last spoke with them respecting the Lord. When I called him Christ, I perceived in them a degree of repugnance; but the reason of this was discovered, and it was found that they had brought it with them out of the world, because they knew that Christians led worse lives than they did, and that they were void of charity. But when I simply called him the Lord, they exhibited an interior emotion. They were afterwards informed by angels, that the Christian doctrine insists on love and charity more than any other in the world; but that those who live according to it are few. There are some Gentiles, who, when they lived in the world, knew, by conversation and report, that Christians lead wicked lives, practising adultery, hatred, contention, drunkenness, and other crimes, which these Gentiles abhorred, as being contrary to their religious principles. These, in the other life, are more timid than others in receiving the truths of faith. They are instructed, however, by the angels, that the Christian doctrine, and the true Christian faith, teach quite different conduct; but that the professors of Christianity live far less according to their doctrine than is usual with Gentiles. When they perceive the correctness of these statements, they receive the

truths of faith, and worship the Lord; but they are longer before they do so than others.

326. It is customary for the Gentiles who have adored some god under the form of an image or statue, or have worshipped a graven idol, to be introduced, on entering the other life, to certain spirits who are substituted in the place of their gods or idols; which is done for the purpose of divesting them of their phantasies; and when they have remained with those spirits for some days, they are withdrawn. Those, also, who have worshipped deceased men, are sometimes introduced to the objects of their veneration, or to others who personate them: thus many of the Jews are introduced to Abraham, Jacob, Moses, and David: but when they find that human nature, in them, is the same as in others, and that they can give them no help, they are ashamed, and are transferred to their own place according to their life. Of all the Gentiles, the Africans are most esteemed in heaven; for they receive the goods and truths of heaven more easily than others. They particularly desire to be called obedient, but not faithful: Christians, they say, may be called faithful, because they possess the doctrine of faith; but themselves not so, unless they receive that doctrine, or, as they express themselves, are able to receive it.

327. I have conversed with some who belonged to the Ancient Church, or the church which existed after the flood, and which then extended through many kingdoms, as Assyria, Mesopotamia, Syria, Ethiopia, Arabia, Lybia, Egypt, Philistia including Tyre and Sidon, and the Land of Canaan on both sides of Jordan.(⁴) Those with whom I conversed, while in the world, had possessed knowledge respecting the Lord as being to come, and had been instructed in the goods of faith, but had nevertheless fallen away, and had become idolaters. They were in front towards the left, in a dark place, and in a state of misery. Their speech was in sound like a pipe having but one note, and was almost destitute of rational thought. They said that they had been in that place for many ages, and that they are occasionally taken out of it to act as servants to others for the performance of some uses of a mean description. From observing

---

(⁴) That the first and most ancient church on this earth was that which is described in the first chapters of Genesis; and that that church, above all others, was a celestial church, nn. 607, 895, 920, 1121, 1122, 1123, 1124, 2896, 4493, 8891, 9942, 10,545. What is the quality of the members of that church in heaven, nn. 1114—1125. That there were various churches after the flood, which are called ancient churches, concerning which, nn. 1125, 1126, 1127, 1327, 10,355. What was the quality of the members of the ancient church, nn. 607, 895. That the ancient churches were representative churches, nn. 519, 521, 2896. That the ancient church had a Word, but that it is lost, n. 2897. What was the quality of the ancient church when it began to decline, n. 1123. The difference between the most ancient church and the ancient one, nn. 597, 607, 640, 641, 765, 784, 895, 4493. That the statutes, the judgments, and the laws, which were commanded in the Jewish church, were in part like those which were in the ancient church, nn. 4288, 4449, 10,149. That the Lord was the God of the most ancient church, and likewise of the ancient, and that He was called Jehovah, nn. 1343, 6846.

the state of these, I was led to think of that of many Christians, who, though not idolaters outwardly, are such inwardly, being worshippers of self and the world, and denying the Lord in their hearts; and to consider what sort of lot awaits them in the other life.

328. That the Lord's church is spread through the whole terrestrial globe, consequently, is universal, and that it includes all who have lived in the good of charity according to their religious belief; and also, that the church that is in possession of the Word, by means of which the Lord is known, is, to those who live beyond its limits, as the heart and lungs in man, from which all the viscera and members of the body derive life, with variety according to their forms, situations, and combinations, may be seen above, n. 308.

OF INFANTS OR LITTLE CHILDREN IN HEAVEN.

829. It is the belief of some, that only those infants or little children that are born in the church go to heaven, but not those who are born out of it: and the reason which they assign is, that children born in the church are baptized, and are initiated by baptism into the faith of the church. But such persons are not aware, that heaven is not imparted to any one by baptism, nor faith either: for baptism is only instituted as a sign and memorial that man is to be regenerated, and that it is possible for those to be regenerated who are born in the church, since the church possesses the Word, in which are contained the divine truths by means of which regeneration is effected, and in the church the Lord is known, by whom it is accomplished.([¹]) Be it known, therefore, that every infant or little child, let him be born where he may, whether in the church or out of it, whether of pious or of wicked parents, is received when he dies by the Lord, and is educated in heaven; where he is instructed according to Divine Order, and is imbued with affections of good, and, through them, with knowledge of truth; and that afterwards, as he is perfected in intelligence and wisdom, he is introduced into heaven, and becomes an angel. Every person who thinks from reason may be aware, that no one is born for hell, but all for heaven, and that if a man goes to hell the blame is his own, but that no blame can attach to infants or little children.

([¹]) That baptism signifies regeneration from the Lord by the truths of faith derived from the Word, nn. 4255, 5120, 9088, 10,239, 10,386, 10,387, 10,388, 10,392. That baptism is a sign that man belongs to the church where the Lord is acknowledged, from whom regeneration is derived; and where the Word exists, containing the truths of faith, by which regeneration is effected, nn. 10,386, 10,387, 10,388. That baptism does not confer faith nor salvation, but that it testifies that those who are regenerated will receive them, n. 10,891.

330. When infants depart this life, they are still infants in the other, having a similar infantile mind, a similar innocence in ignorance, and a similar tenderness in all respects. They are only in the first initiatory state for enabling them to become angels: for infants are not angels already, but become so. Every one who departs out of this world resuscitates in a state of life similar to that in which he was before, an infant in the state of infancy, a boy in the state of boyhood, and a youth, man, and old man, in the state of youth, manhood, and old age, respectively: but the state of every one is afterwards changed. The state of infants, however, excels that of the other ages in this respect, that they are in a state of innocence, and that evil is not yet rooted in them by actual life; and such is the nature of innocence, that all things belonging to heaven can be implanted in it; for innocence is the receptacle of the truth of faith and of the good of love.

331. The state of infants in the other life far surpasses that of infants in the world, because they are not invested with a terrestrial body, but with one like those of the angels. The terrestrial body in itself is heavy or dull. It does not receive its first sensations and first motions from the interior or spiritual world, but from the exterior or natural; on which account, infants in the world must learn to walk, to use their limbs, and to talk; and even the senses, as those of sight and hearing, must be opened in them by use. Not so in the other life. There, being spirits, they immediately begin to act according to their interiors. They walk without previous practice, and talk with the same readiness; only they speak, at first, from common or general affections, not yet perfectly distinguished into ideas of thought: but they are speedily initiated into these also; and the reason that this is so easily effected is, because their exteriors are homogeneous to their interiors. (That the speech of angels flows from affections variegated by ideas of thought, so that their discourse is in perfect conformity with their thoughts from affection, may be seen above, un. 234—245.)

332. As soon as infants are resuscitated, which takes place immediately after their decease, they are carried up into heaven, and are committed to the care of angels of the female sex, who, in the life of the body, had been influenced by a tender love for little children, and, at the same time, by love for God. As these angels had, while in the world, loved all infants with a tenderness like that of their mothers, they receive the little ones committed to their charge as if they were their own; and the infants, on their part, from an inherent inclination, love them in return as their mothers. Every one has as many infants under her care, as, from spiritual maternal love, she desires. This heaven appears in front, over against the forehead, directly in the line or radius in which angels look to the Lord: it is there situated,

because all infants are under the immediate auspices of the Lord. They also receive an influx from the heaven of innocence, which is the third heaven.

333. Infants differ in their genius; some being of the genius by which the spiritual angels are distinguished, and some of the genius by which the celestial angels are distinguished. The infants who are of the celestial genius appear on the right in that heaven, and those who are of the spiritual genius on the left. In the Grand Man, which is heaven, all infants are in the province of the eyes, those who are of the spiritual genius being in the province of the left eye, and those who are of the celestial genius in the province of the right; the reason of which is, because the Lord appears to the angels who are in the spiritual kingdom before the left eye, and to those who are in the celestial kingdom before the right eye. (See above, n. 118.) From the circumstance, that, in the Grand Man or heaven, infants are in the province of the eyes, it also is evident, that they are under the immediate view and auspices of the Lord.

334. In what manner infants are educated in heaven, shall also be briefly stated. They learn of their governess to talk. Their first speech is only a sound expressive of affection; but this becomes by degrees more distinct, as ideas of thought enter into it; for ideas of thought derived from their affections constitute all the speech of angels. (On which subject, see its proper Section above, nn. 234—245.) Into their affections, which all proceed from innocence, are first insinuated such things as appear before their eyes, and are of a delightful nature; and as these are from a spiritual origin, such things as belong to heaven flow into them at the same time; by which the interiors of the children are opened, and they thus are continually advanced in perfection. After this first period is completed, they are transferred to another heaven, where they are instructed by masters. And so they advance.

335. Infants are chiefly instructed by representatives suited to their respective genius; and these are so beautiful, and at the same time so full of wisdom from an interior ground, as to surpass belief. Thus is intelligence insinuated into them by degrees, such as derives its life from good. Two representatives, which it was granted me to behold, I am at liberty to mention; from which a conclusion may be drawn respecting the others. They first represented the Lord ascending out of the sepulchre, and at the same time the union of his Humanity with his Divinity; which was performed in so wise a manner as to surpass all the wisdom of men, though in a manner innocently infantile at the same time. They also presented an idea of a sepulchre, but not, simultaneously, an idea of the Lord, except so remotely, that it was scarcely to be perceived that it was the Lord, otherwise than, as it were, afar off; because the idea of a sepulchre

includes something funereal, which they thus removed. They afterwards cautiously admitted into the sepulchre a sort of atmospheric production, but appearing like a subtile aqueous substance; by which they represented, still with a decent removal of every thing unbecoming, spiritual life in baptism. I afterwards saw represented by them the Lord's descent to them that were in prison, and his ascent with them to heaven, all performed with incomparable prudence and piety. What was truly infantile, they let down soft, tender, and almost invisible threads, to lift up the Lord with in his ascent. Through all the operation, they were possessed by a holy fear, lest the least part of the representation should border upon any thing that did not include a spiritual and celestial essence. Not to mention other representatives in use among them, and by which, as by sports suited to the minds of little children, they are conducted into the knowledges of truth and the affections of good.

336. The nature of their tender intellect, has also been shown me. When I was praying in the words of the Lord's Prayer, and they entered at the time into the ideas of my thought by an influx from their intellectual faculty, it was perceptible that their influx was so tender and soft us almost to be that of affection alone; and it was at the same time observable, that their intellectual faculty was open even from the Lord; for what flowed from them was as if it flowed through them. The Lord, also, flows most especially into the ideas of infants from inmost principles, for nothing has closed their ideas, as is the case with adults; no principles of falsity exist to shut their minds against the intelligence of truth, nor is there the life of evil to shut them against the reception of good, and thus against the reception of wisdom.

From these facts it may be evident, that infants do not enter upon the angelic state immediately after death, but that they are introduced into it successively by means of the knowledges of good and of truth; and that this is effected according to all heavenly order. For the most minute particulars of their genius are known to the Lord; wherefore, according to all, even the most particular, impulses of their inclination, they are led to receive the truths of good, and the goods of truth.

337. How all things are insinuated into them by such delightful and agreeable means as are suitable to their genius, was likewise shown me. It was granted to me to see little children most elegantly clothed, having about their breasts wreaths of flowers shining with the most agreeable and heavenly colors, and others about their tender arms. Once, also, I saw some little children with their governesses, in company with some maidens, in a paradisiacal garden most beautifully adorned, not so much by the trees that grew in it, as by espaliers as of laurel, and thus by porticoes, with paths leading towards its interior recesses.

The children were clothed in the manner mentioned above; and upon their approach, the clusters of flowers that overshadowed the entrance beamed forth a cheerful brightness. It may hence appear what delights attend them; and also, that they are introduced, by means of objects and scenes most agreeable and delightful, into the goods of innocence and charity; which goods are continually insinuated by those delightful and agreeable objects by the Lord.

338. By a mode of communication usual in the other life, it has been shown me what sort of ideas little children have when they behold any objects. All, even to the most minute, were as if they were alive; whence, in all the minutiæ of their ideas of thought, life is included. It was also perceived by me, that little children in the world have ideas nearly similar when engaged in their playful amusements; for they do not yet possess reflection, like that of adults, to show them what is inanimate.

339. It has been stated above, that infants are either of the celestial or of the spiritual genius. The distinction between them is very obvious. Those who are of the celestial genius think, speak, and act, with more softness than those of the spiritual genius, so that scarcely any thing appears but something of a flowing character, derived from the love of good directed to the Lord, and towards other little children. Those of the spiritual genius, on the other hand, do not think, speak, and act, with such softness, but something of a fluttering and vibratory character, so to speak, manifests itself in every thing that they say and do. It also is apparent from the indignation which they exhibit; and by other signs.

340. Many may imagine, that infants remain such in heaven, and exist as infants among the angels. Those who are ignorant what an angel is, may be confirmed in this opinion from the images sometimes seen in churches, in which angels are represented as little children. But the real fact is quite different. Intelligence and wisdom are the attributes which constitute an angel; and so long as infants are not yet possessed of these, they are, indeed, associated with angels, but they are not angels themselves. They first become angels, when they become intelligent and wise; and, what I was surprised at observing, they then no longer appear as children, but as adult persons; for they then are no longer of an infantile genius, but of the more adult genius belonging to angels. This maturity is inherent in intelligence and wisdom themselves. The reason that infants, as they are perfected in intelligence and wisdom, appear of more adult stature, thus as youths and young men, is, because intelligence and wisdom are real spiritual nourishment[2]; thus, the

(2) That spiritual food is science, intelligence, and wisdom, thus the good and truth from which those things are derived, nn. 3114, 4459, 4792, 5147, 5293, 5340, 5342, 5410, 5426, 5576, 5582, 5588, 5655, 8562, 9003. Hence, that food, in a spiritual sense, is every thing which comes forth from the mouth of the Lord, n. 681. That bread signifies all

same things as nourish their minds, nourish also their bodies: which is the result of correspondence, the form of the body being nothing but the external form of the interiors. It is to be observed, that infants who grow up in heaven, do not advance beyond the first period of juvenile manhood, in which they remain to eternity. That I might know this fact with certainty, it has been granted to me to converse with some who had been educated as infants in heaven, and had there grown up: also, with some when they were infants, and afterwards with the same when they had become young men; and I heard from their own lips what had been the course of their life from one age to the other.

341. That innocence is the receptacle of all things constituent of heaven, and thus that the innocence of infants is a plane for all the affections of good and truth, may be evident from what has been stated above (nn. 276—283) respecting the innocence of the angels in heaven. It was there shown, that innocence consists in being willing to be led by the Lord and not by self; consequently, that man is in the enjoyment of innocence, just in proportion as he is removed from his *proprium:* and just in proportion as any one is removed from his own *proprium,* he is in the Lord's *Proprium,* which is what is called the Lord's righteousness and merit. But the innocence of infants is not genuine innocence, because, as yet, it is without wisdom. Genuine innocence is wisdom; for in proportion as a person is wise, he loves to be led by the Lord; or, what amounts to the same, in proportion as any person is led by the Lord, he truly is wise. Infants, therefore, are led from external innocence, which is what they possess at first, and which is called the innocence of infancy, to internal innocence, which is the innocence of wisdom. This wisdom is the end of all their instruction and advancement; wherefore, when they arrive at the innocence of wisdom, the innocence of infancy, which had served them in the mean time as a plane, is conjoined to them. The nature of the innocence of infants was represented to me, by something that appeared as of wood, nearly destitute of life, but which is animated as the children are perfected by knowledges of truth and affections of good. The nature of genuine innocence was afterwards represented by a most beautiful infant, full of life, and naked. For those eminently innocent ones who inhabit the inmost heaven, and thus are nearest to the Lord, appear to the sight of the other angels just like infants, and some of them naked, because innocence is represented by the nakedness which does not inspire shame, as we read of the first man and his wife in paradise (Gen. ii. 25); wherefore, also, when they fell from their state of inno-

food in general, therefore it signifies every good, celestial and spiritual, nn. 276, 680. 2165, 2177, 3478, 6118, 8410. The reason is, because those things nourish the mind, which belongs to the internal man, nn. 4459, 5293, 5576, 6277, 8410.

cence, they blushed for their nakedness, and hid themselves.
(Ch. iii. 7, 10, 11.) In one word: the wiser angels are, the more
innocent they are; and the more innocent they are, the more
they appear to themselves as little children. It is on this account, that infancy, in the Word, signifies innocence. (See
above, n. 278.)

342. I have conversed with angels respecting infants, inquiring
whether they were pure from evils, because they have no actual
evil, like adults. But I was informed, that they are equally the
subjects of evil(*); but that they, like all the angels, are withheld
from evil, and held in good, by the Lord; and that this is done
so effectually, that it appears to them as if they were in good of
themselves. Lest, therefore, infants who have grown up in heav-
en should entertain a false opinion of themselves, imagining that
the good which attaches to them is self-derived, and is not communicated from the Lord, they sometimes are let into the evils
which they have received hereditarily, and are left in them, till
they know, acknowledge, and believe, the truth on the subject.
There was a spirit, the son of a certain king, who had died when
an infant, and had grown up in heaven, who entertained the
opinion just mentioned. He was therefore let into the life of
evils that was innate in him; when I perceived, by the sphere
of his life, that he had a disposition to exercise command over
others, and that he regarded adulteries as of no account; these
being evils that he derived hereditarily from his parents: but
after he was brought to the acknowledgment that he was of
such a nature, he was again taken up among the angels with
whom he was living before. No one, in the other life, ever
suffers punishment for hereditary evil, because this is not his
own, and thus it is by no fault of his own that he is of such a
nature; but what he is punished for is actual evil, which is his
own; thus he suffers punishment for so much of his hereditary
evil as he has made his own by actual life. When infants who
have grown up in heaven are let into the state of their hereditary
evil, it is not that they may be punished for it, but that they may
learn that, of themselves, they are nothing but evil, and that they
are withdrawn from the hell which adheres to them, and taken to

(*) That all men whatsoever are born into evils of every kind, insomuch that their *proprium* is nothing but evil, nn. 210, 215, 731, 874, 875, 876, 987, 1047, 2307, 2308, 3518, 3701, 3812, 8480, 8550, 10,283, 10,284, 10,286, 10,732. That man, therefore, must be re-born, that is, regenerated, n. 3701. That the hereditary evil of man consists in loving himself above God, and the world above heaven, and in making no account of his neighbor in comparison with himself, except only for the sake of himself, thus in re-garding himself alone; so that it consists in the love of self and of the world, nn. 694, 731, 4317, 5660. That from the love of self and of the world, when those loves pre-dominate, come all evils, nn. 1307, 1308, 1321, 1594, 1691, 3413, 7255, 7376, (7480,) 7488, 8318, 9335, 9348, 10,038, 10,742. Which evils are contempt of others, enmity, hatred, revenge, cruelty, deceit, nn. 6667, 7372, 7373, 7374, 9348, 10,038, 10,742. And that from these evils comes all that is false, nn. 1047, 10,283, 10,284, 10,286. That those loves rush forward so far as the reins are given them, and that the love of self aspires even to the throne of God, nn. 7375, 8678.

heaven, by the mercy of the Lord; and that they have a place in heaven, not by their own merit, but by the Lord's bounty; for which reason, they should not boast of themselves to others on account of the good which is attached to them, since to do so were as contrary to the good of mutual love as it is to the truth of faith.

343. Many times, when a number of infants have been present with me in choirs, whilst they were still in quite an infantile state, I heard from them a sound as of something tender and unarranged, so that they did not yet act as one, as they do afterwards when in a more adult state: and, what surprised me, the spirits present with me could not refrain from inciting them to speak. A desire of this kind is innate in spirits. But it was always observable, that the infants manifested repugnance, being not willing to speak when thus incited. I have often perceived their refusal and repugnance, which were attended with a certain species of indignation; and when some liberty of speaking was given them, they said no more than *that it was not so.* I was informed, that the temptation of little children is of this kind, and that it is permitted in order that they may learn, not only to resist what is false and evil, but also not to think, speak, and act, from another, and, consequently, not to allow themselves to be led by any other than the Lord alone.

344. From what has been adduced may be seen, the nature of the education of infants in heaven; namely, that they are introduced by the intelligence of truth and the wisdom of good into the angelic life, which consists in love to the Lord and mutual love, both including innocence. But how contrary is the education of children, as practised by many on earth, may appear from this example. Being in the streets of a great city, I saw some little boys fighting: a crowd gathered round, that enjoyed the sight with great pleasure; and I was informed that the parents themselves excited their little offspring to engage in such battles. The good spirits and angels who beheld the transaction through my eyes, were so shocked at it, that I could perceive their horror, especially at the circumstance, that parents should stir up their children to such practices. They said, that parents thus extinguish, in earliest years, all the mutual love, and all the innocence, which are infused into little children by the Lord, and initiate them into hatred and revenge; consequently, that they thus studiously exclude their children from heaven, where nothing prevails but mutual love. Let those parents, therefore, who wish well to their children, beware of such practices.

345. The nature of the difference between those who die when infants, and those who die in adult age, shall also be stated. They who die in adult age, have, and carry with them, a plane acquired from the terrestrial and material world. This plane

consists of their memory, and its corporeal-natural affection. This plane, after death, is fixed, and then remains quiescent; but it still serves as an ultimate plane for their thought, for the thought flows into it. It hence results, that according to the quality of that plane, and according to the manner in which the rational mind corresponds with its contents, is the quality of the man after death. But infants who have died such, and have been educated in heaven, have not such a plane, but instead of it, a spiritual-natural one; because they derive nothing from the material world and the terrestrial body, wherefore they cannot be in such gross affections and thence in such gross thoughts; for they derive all from heaven. Besides, infants are not aware that they were born in the world, but suppose themselves to have been born in heaven; consequently, they do not know what any birth is but the spiritual birth, which is effected by knowledges of good and truth, and by intelligence and wisdom, by virtue of which it is that a man is a man; and as these are from the Lord, they believe, and love to believe, that they are the children of the Lord Himself. But, notwithstanding, the state of men who grow up on earth may become equally perfect with the state of infants who grow up in heaven, provided they remove corporeal and earthly loves, which are those of self and the world, and receive spiritual loves in their place.

OF THE WISE AND THE SIMPLE IN HEAVEN.

346. It is generally believed, that the wise will enjoy glory and eminence in heaven beyond what falls to the lot of the simple, because it is said in Daniel, "*They that are* [*wise,* more literally] *intelligent shall shine as the brightness of the firmament, and they that turn many to righteousness, as the stars, for ever and ever.*"—(Ch. xii. 3.) But few are aware who are here meant by the intelligent, and by those who turn many to righteousness. It is commonly supposed, that those who are called men of erudition and learning are the persons alluded to, especially such as have been teachers in the church, and have excelled others in doctrine and preaching; and, more especially still, those among them who have converted many to the faith. All such as these are believed, in the world, to be the intelligent: but the above words relate to those who are regarded as intelligent in heaven; and those just mentioned do not belong to the number, unless their intelligence be heavenly intelligence; the nature of which shall be here explained.

347. Heavenly intelligence is interior intelligence, arising from the love of truth, unconnected with any regard either to

glory in the world or to glory in heaven, but only to truth itself for its own sake, with which they are affected and delighted in their inmost soul. They who are affected and delighted with truth itself, are also affected and delighted with the light of heaven ; and they who are affected and delighted with the light of heaven, are likewise affected and delighted with the Divine Truth, yea, with the Lord himself: for the light of heaven is the Divine Truth, and the Divine Truth is the Lord in heaven. (See above, nn. 126—140.) This light only enters into the interiors of the mind, which are formed for its reception; and as it enters, it also affects them, and imparts delight; for whatever enters by influx from heaven, and is received, carries in its bosom enjoyment and pleasure. From this source is the genuine affection of truth, which is the affection of truth for its own sake. Those who are in possession of this affection, or, what amounts to the same, of this love, are in the possession of heavenly intelligence, and shine, in heaven, as with the brightness of the firmament. The reason that they so shine is, because the Divine Truth, wherever it exists in heaven, shines or gives light (see above, n. 132); and the firmament of heaven signifies, by correspondence, that interior intellectual principle, as existing both with angels and with men, that is in the light of heaven. But those who cherish the affection of truth either with a view to glory in the world or to glory in heaven, cannot shine in heaven, because they are not delighted and affected with the light of heaven, but only with the light of the world, which, in heaven, is mere darkness :([1]) for their own glory is what is predominant in their minds, this being the end which they have in view; and when his own glory is the end in view, the man has respect, in the first place, to himself, and only regards the truths which tend to promote his glory as means to that end, and as servants for his use. For whoever loves divine truths for the sake of his own glory, regards himself in them, and not the Lord; whence he turns away his eyes, or the sight of his understanding and faith, from heaven to the world, and from the Lord to himself. Such persons, consequently, are in the light of the world, but not in the light of heaven. These appear in external form, or in the sight of men, equally intelligent and learned with those who are in the light of heaven, by reason that they speak in a similar manner, and sometimes in external appearance with more wisdom, because they are ex-

---

([1]) That the light of the world is for the external man, the light of heaven for the internal, nn. 3222, 3223, 3337. That the light of heaven flows into natural light, and that the natural man is so far wise, as he receives the light of heaven, nn. 4302, 4408. That from the light of the world, which is called natural light, the objects which are in the light of heaven cannot be seen, but *vice versa*, n. 9755. Wherefore those who are in the light of the world alone do not perceive those things which are in the light of heaven, n. 3108. That the light of the world is thick darkness to the angels, nn. 1521, 1783, 1880.

cited by self-love, and have learned to make a feigned display
of heavenly affections; but still in internal form, in which they
appear in the sight of angels, they are totally different. From
these observations may in some measure be seen, who they are
that are meant by the intelligent that shall shine in heaven
with the brightness of the firmament: but who are meant by
those who turn many to righteousness, who shall shine as the
stars, shall now be shown.

348. By those who turn many to righteousness are meant
those who are wise; and, in heaven, those are called wise who
are eminently grounded in good, and those are there eminently
grounded in good, who admit divine truths immediately into
the life. For when divine truth is incorporated in the life, it
becomes good; for it becomes the object of the will and love,
and whatever is the object of the will and love is called good.
These, therefore, are denominated wise, for wisdom belongs to
the life; but those are denominated intelligent, who do not
immediately admit divine truths into the life, but first into the
memory, whence they are afterwards drawn forth, and committed to life. In what manner, and to what extent, these
two classes of persons differ in the heavens, may be seen in the
Section which treats of the two kingdoms of heaven, the celestial kingdom and the spiritual kingdom (nn. 20—28); and in
that which treats of the three heavens (nn. 29—40). Those who
dwell in the Lord's celestial kingdom, thus, those who dwell in
the third or inmost heaven, are called the righteous, because
they attribute nothing of righteousness to themselves, but all to
the Lord. The Lord's righteousness, in heaven, is the good
which proceeds from Him.(*) These, then, are the persons who
are here meant by those who turn many to righteousness. They
are the same as those of whom the Lord says, "*The righteous
shall shine as the sun in the kingdom of their Father*" (Matt.
xiii. 43): the reason of its being said that they shall shine as
the sun, is, because they are grounded in love to the Lord derived from the Lord; and that that love is meant by the sun,
has been shown above (nn. 116—125). The light, also, which
shines around them, has a flaming appearance, and the ideas of
their thought partake of a flaming quality, by reason that they
receive the good of love immediately from the Lord as the Sun
in heaven.

349. All who have procured for themselves intelligence and
wisdom in the world, are accepted in heaven, and become

(*) That the merit and righteousness of the Lord are the good which rules in heaven,
nn. 9486, 9986. That a righteous and justified person is one to whom the merit and
righteousness of the Lord are ascribed; and that he is unrighteous who has his own
righteousness and self-merit, nn. 5069, 9263. What is the quality of those in the other
life, who claim righteousness to themselves, nn. 942, 2027. That justice or righteousness, in the Word, is predicated of good, and judgment of truth; hence to do justice
and judgment, is to do what is good and true, nn. 2235, 9857.

angels, every one according to the quality and quantity of his intelligence and wisdom. For whatever a man has acquired to himself in the world, remains, and he carries it with him after death: it is then also increased, and filled up, but only within the degree of his affection and desire for good and truth, but not beyond that degree. Those who had but little of such affection and desire, receive but little, but still as much as they are able to receive within that degree; but those who had much affection and desire receive much. The actual degree of the ·affection and desire, serves as a measure, which is filled full; whence more is given to those whose measure is large, and less to those whose measure is small. The reason of this is, because love, to which belong affection and desire, receives all that agrees with itself; whence love and reception are co-extensive. This is meant by the Lord's words when he says, "*Whosoever hath, to him shall be given, and he shall have more abundance.*"—(Matt. xiii. 12.) "*Good measure, pressed down, and shaken together, and running over, shall men give into your bosom.*"—(Luke vi. 38.)

350. All are received in heaven who have loved truth and good for their own sake. They, therefore, who have loved them much, are those who are called the wise; and they who have loved them but little, are those who are called the simple. In heaven, the wise dwell in much light; but the simple, in less; every one according to the degree of his love for good and truth. To love truth and good for their own sake, is, to will them and do them; for they who will them and do them are those that love them; but not they who will and do them not. The former, also, are those that love the Lord, and are loved by Him; for good and truth are from the Lord; and such being the case, He is in them; whence, also, He dwells with those who receive good and truth in their lives by willing and doing them. Man, likewise, regarded in himself, is nothing but his own good and truth, by reason that good is the object of his will, and truth of his understanding, and the quality of the man is such as is that of his will and understanding; from which fact it is evident, that man is loved by the Lord, just in proportion as his will is formed by good, and his understanding by truth. To be loved by the Lord also means, to love the Lord: for love is reciprocal, and to him who is loved, it is granted by the Lord to love in return.

351. It is supposed in the world, that they who possess much knowledge, whether relating to the doctrines of the church and to the Word, or to the sciences, see truths more interiorly and acutely than others, and thus are more intelligent and wise; and such persons imagine the same respecting themselves. But what true intelligence and wisdom are, what spurious, and what false, shall be here declared.

True intelligence and wisdom consist in seeing and perceiving what is true and good, and thence what is false and evil, and in accurately distinguishing the one from the other, by intuition and interior perception. Every man possesses interiors and exteriors, or interior and exterior principles or faculties, his interiors being those which belong to the internal or spiritual man, and his exteriors those which belong to the external or natural man : and according as his interiors are formed, and act as one with his exteriors, is the man's mental sight and perception. The interiors of man can only be formed in heaven; but his exteriors are formed in the world. When the interiors are formed in heaven, their contents then flow into the exteriors which are derived from the world, and form them to correspondence, that is, to act as one with themselves; and when this is accomplished, the man sees and perceives things from an interior ground. In order that the interiors may be formed, the only means are, that the man should look to the Divine Being and to heaven; for, as just observed, the interiors are formed in heaven: and man looks to the Divine Being when he believes in His existence, and likewise, that all truth and good, and consequently all intelligence and wisdom, come from that Source; and he believes in the Divine Being, when he is willing to be led by Him. It is in this way, and in no other, that the interiors of man are opened. The man who is grounded in that faith and in a life according to it, enjoys the power and capacity of becoming intelligent and wise: but in order to his becoming such actually, it is necessary for him to acquire a knowledge of many things, not only such as relate to heaven, but also such as relate to the world. Those relating to heaven are to be learned from the Word, and from the church; and those relating to the world, from the sciences. In proportion as a man makes such acquisitions, and applies them to life, he becomes intelligent and wise; for in the same proportion his interior sight, which is that of the understanding, and his interior affection, which is that of the will, are perfected The simple of this class are they, whose interiors have been opened, but have not been much cultivated by spiritual, moral, civil, and natural truths; these have a perception of truths when they hear them, but they do not see them in themselves: but the wise of this class are they, whose interiors have not only been opened, but have also been cultivated: these both see truths in themselves, and have a perception of them. From these observations it may be evident, what true intelligence and wisdom are.

352. Spurious intelligence and wisdom consist in not seeing and perceiving what is true and good, and thence what is false and evil, from an interior ground, but in only believing that to be true and good, or false and evil, which is so pronounced by others, and in afterwards confirming it as such. They who do

not see what is true from truth itself, but from the dictate of another, may as easily embrace and believe falsity as truth, and may also afterwards confirm it so as to appear to be truth; for whatever is confirmed puts on the appearance of truth, and there is nothing whatever which may not be confirmed. The interiors of these persons are only open from below, but their exteriors are open to the extent of their confirmations: consequently, the light by which they see is not the light of heaven, but the light of the world, which is called natural light: for in this light falsities may appear lucid like truths, nay, when they are confirmed, may shine with brilliance; but not in the light of heaven. Of this class, the less intelligent and wise are those who have greatly confirmed themselves in their assumed opinions; but the more intelligent and wise are those who have done this but little. From these observations it may be evident what spurious intelligence and wisdom are. But in this class are not to be included those, who, in childhood, have supposed the sentiments to be true which they have heard from their masters, provided, when they grow up and think from their own understanding, they do not tenaciously adhere to those sentiments, but desire truth, and from such desire seek after it, and when they find it, are interiorly affected by it: such persons, because they are affected by truth for its own sake, see it to be truth before they confirm it as such.([3]) This shall be illustrated by an example. A conversation arose among certain spirits, as to whence it is that animals are born into all the knowledge suitable to their respective natures, whereas man is not: and it was observed, that the reason is, because animals exist in the order of their life, but man does not, wherefore he is to be brought into that order by means of knowledges and sciences; whereas, if man were born into the order of his life, which is to love God above all things and his neighbor as himself, he would be born into intelligence and wisdom, and thence, also, into a belief of every truth, so far as knowledges were present to make him acquainted with them. The good spirits saw this immediately, and perceived that it was so, solely by the light of truth: but the spirits who had confirmed themselves in faith alone, and had thence cast aside love and charity, could not understand it; because the light of confirmed falsity had obscured, with them, the light of truth.

353. False intelligence and wisdom are all such as do not include the acknowledgment of a Divine Being, for all those who do not acknowledge a Divine Being, but nature instead,

<hr>

([3]) That wisdom consists in seeing and perceiving whether a thing be true before it is confirmed, but not in confirming what is said by others, nn. 1017, 4741, 7012, 7680, 7950. That to see and to perceive whether a thing be true before it is confirmed, is only possible for those who are affected with truth for the sake of truth, and for the sake of life, n. 8521. That the light of confirmation is natural light and not spiritual; and that it is sensual light, which has place even with the wicked, n. 8780. That all things, even falsities, may be confirmed, so as to appear like truths, nn. 2482, 2490, 5033, 6865, 8521.

think from the corporeal-sensual principle or nature, and **are** merely sensual men, how much soever they may be esteemed in the world as men of erudition and learning.([4]) Their erudition does not ascend beyond such objects as appear in the world before their eyes, which they retain in their memory, and contemplate in almost a material manner; although they are the same sciences as serve the truly intelligent for the formation of their understanding. By the sciences are meant the various kinds of experimental knowledge, such as physics, astronomy, chemistry, mechanics, geometry, anatomy, psychology, philosophy, history, both that of kingdoms or nations and of literature, criticism, and languages. Neither do those leaders in the church who deny a Divine Being, elevate their thoughts beyond the sensual apprehensions which belong to the external man. They regard the Word, and whatever relates to it, only as others do the sciences, not making them subjects of thought, or of any intuition, proceeding from an enlightened rational mind. The reason is, because their interiors are closed, as are also their exteriors that are nearest to the interiors. These are closed, because such persons have averted themselves from heaven, and have turned the faculties which were capable of looking in that direction, and which, as observed above, are the interiors of the human mind, the contrary way: the consequence of which is, that they are not able to see what is true and good, these being to them in darkness, while falsity and evil are in light. Nevertheless, sensual men are able to reason, and some of them more adroitly and acutely than other persons: but only from the fallacies of the senses confirmed by their scientific acquisitions; and because they possess this skill in reasoning, they also believe themselves to be wiser than others.([5]) The fire which inflames their reasonings with its affection, is the fire of the love of self and of the world. These are the characters who are the subjects of false intelligence and wisdom, and who are meant by the Lord when he says in Matthew, "*They seeing see not, and hearing they*

([4]) That the sensual nature is the ultimate of the life of man, adhering to, and inhering in, his corporeal nature, nn. 5077, 5767, 9212, 9216, 9331, 9730. That he is called a sensual man, who judges and concludes all things from the senses of the body, and who believes nothing but what he sees with his eyes and touches with his hands, nn. 5094, 7693. That such a man thinks in his outermost faculties, and not interiorly in himself, nn. 5089, 5094, 6564, 7693. That his interiors are closed, so that he sees nothing of divine truth, nn. 6564, 6844, 6845. In a word, that he is in gross natural light, and thus perceives nothing which is derived from the light of heaven, nn. 6201, 6310, 6564, 6844, 6845, 6598, 6612, 6614, 6622, 6624. That therefore he is inwardly opposed to all those things which belong to heaven and the church, nn. 6201, 6316, 6844, 6845, 6948, 6949. That the learned, who have confirmed themselves against the truths of the church, are sensual men, n. 6316. The quality of the sensual man is described, n. 10,236.

([5]) That sensual men reason acutely and cunningly, since they make all intelligence to consist in speaking from the corporeal memory, nn. 195, 196, 5700, 10,236. But that they reason from the fallacies of the senses, nn. 5094, 6948, 6949, 7693. That sensual men are cunning and malicious more than others, nn. 7692, 10,236. That such were called by the ancients serpents of the tree of knowledge, nn. 195, 196, 197, 6398, 6949, 10,313.

hear not, neither do they understand."—(Ch. xiii. 13.)   And in
another place : "*Thou hast hid these things from the wise and
prudent, and hast revealed them unto babes.*"—(Ch. xi. 25.)

354. It has been granted me to converse with many of the
learned after their departure out of the world, including some
of the highest reputation, who are celebrated for their writings
through the whole literary world; and some who are not so
celebrated, but who, nevertheless, had their minds stored with
hidden wisdom. Those of the former class, who in heart had
denied a Divine Being, how much soever they had confessed him
with their lips, were become so stupid, that they could scarcely
understand any truth relating to civil affairs, much less any
spiritual truth. I perceived, and saw too, that their interiors
belonging to the mind were so closed as to appear black (in the
spiritual world, such things are made objects of sight); and thus
that they could not endure any ray of heavenly light, and, consequently, could not admit any influx from heaven. The blackness, with which their interiors appeared to be invested, was
greatest, and extended farthest, in those who had confirmed
themselves against the existence of a Divine Being by scientific
considerations supplied by their erudition. In the other life,
such persons receive every thing false with delight, imbibing it
as a sponge does water; whilst they repel every thing true, as a
bony elastic surface repels what falls on it. I have also been
told, that the interiors of those who have confirmed themselves
against a Divine Being, and in favor of mere nature, are actually
ossified : their head, likewise, appears like a callous substance,
as if made of ebony, which reaches even to the nose—a sign that
they no longer possess any perception. Those who are of this
character are immersed in whirlpools, which appear like bogs,
where they are whirled about by the phantasies into which their
false notions are turned. The infernal fire which torments them
is their thirst for glory and renown; from which thirst they assault one another, and, from their infernal heat, torture those who
do not worship them as deities; and thus, by turns, they torture
each other. Into such insanities and horrors is turned all worldly
erudition, when not made interiorly receptive of light from heav-
en, by the acknowledgment of a Divine Being.

355. That the learned of this class are of such a quality in the
spiritual world, when they go thither after death, may be concluded from this circumstance alone : that then all things that
are deposited in the natural memory, and are immediately in
connection with the sensual organs and faculties of the body, as
are such scientific acquirements as are mentioned above, are
quiescent, and only the rational conclusions which had been
deduced from them there serve for the materials of thought and
speech. Man carries with him, indeed, all his natural memory,
but the things contained in it are not, there, under his view, and

do not present themselves to his thoughts, as they did while he lived in the world. Nothing can he thence take out, and bring forth into spiritual light, because it contains nothing which belongs to that light. But the rational or intellectual conclusions or ideas which man has acquired for himself from the sciences while he lived in the body, agree with the light of the spiritual world; whence it results, that just in proportion as a man's spirit has been made rational by means of knowledges and sciences in the world, is he rational when separated from the body: for then the man is a spirit; and the spirit is that which thinks while he lives in the body.(6)

356. Those, on the other hand, who, by means of knowledges and sciences, have procured for themselves intelligence and wisdom, being those who have applied them all to uses of life, and at the same time have acknowledged a Divine Being, have loved the Word, and have lived the spiritual-moral life described above (n. 319); to these the sciences have served for means of becoming wise, and also, of corroborating the principles of faith. The interiors belonging to the minds of these were perceived by me, and seen too, as if transparent with light, and of a white, flaming, or azure color, like that of pellucid diamonds, rubies, and sapphires; and that they had this appearance, according to the extent to which they had derived confirmations from the sciences in favor of the existence of a Divine Being, and in favor of divine truths. True intelligence and wisdom appear under such forms when exhibited to view in the spiritual world; and they derive the appearance from the light of heaven, which is the Divine Truth proceeding from the Lord, from which all intelligence and wisdom are derived. (See above, nn. 126—133.) The planes for the reception of that light, in which the variegations, like those of colors, exist, are the interiors of the mind; and confirmations of divine truths by means of such objects as exist in nature, thus such as are treated of in the sciences, produce those variegations.(7)   For

---

(6) That matters of external knowledge, which may be called scientifics, belong to the natural memory, which man possesses in the body, nn. 5212, 9922. That man carries with him after death all the natural memory, n. 2475: from experience, nn. 2481—2486. But that he cannot then bring any thing forth from that memory, as in the world, for several reasons, nn. 2476, 2477, 2749.

(7) That most beautiful colors appear in heaven, nn. 1053, 1624. That colors in heaven are derived from the light there, and that they are its modifications or variegations, nn. 1042, 1043, 1053, 1624, 3993, 4530, 4922, 4742. Thus that they are the appearances of truth derived from good, and signify such things as belong to intelligence and wisdom, nn. 4530, 4922, 4677, 9466.

Extracts from the ARCANA CŒLESTIA *respecting the Sciences.*

That man ought to be imbued with sciences and knowledges, since by them he learns to think, afterwards to understand what is true and what is good, and at length to grow wise, nn. 129, 1450, 1451, 1453, 1548, 1802. That scientifics* are the first grounds on which

* For convenience, this word is retained, because, though not usual in the English language, there is no other single word that will express the Author's meaning; and because, on this account, it has been generally adopted in the translation of the *Arcana Cœlestia*, and of his other works. It is applied by the Author, not only to what are termed, in the customary use of the term as an adjective in English, *scientific subjects*, but to all matters of knowledge of an external kind, such as abide in the memory as matters of fact, but are not seen in intellectual light, or viewed by rational intuition.—*N.*

the interior mind of man takes a view of the stores in his natural memory, and such things as it finds there that can be applied in confirmation, it sublimates, as it were, by the fire of heavenly love, separates them from gross appendages, and purifies them even into spiritual ideas. That such a process takes place, is

is built and founded the life of man, both civil, moral, and spiritual, and that they are learned for the sake of use as an end, nn. 1489, 8310. That knowledges open the way to the internal man, and afterwards conjoin that man with the external according to uses, nn. 1563, 1616. That the rational principle is born by means of sciences and knowledges, nn. 1895, 1900, 3086. Yet not by knowledges themselves, but by the affection of the uses derived from them, n. 1895.
That there are scientifics which admit divine truths, and others which do not admit them, n. 5213. That empty scientifics ought to be destroyed, nn. 1489, 1492, 1499, 1580. That empty scientifics are those which have for their end, and which confirm, the loves of self and of the world, and which withdraw from love to God and love towards the neighbor; because such scientifics close the internal man, so that man afterwards cannot receive any thing from heaven, nn. 1563, 1600. That scientifics are the means of growing wise, and the means of becoming insane, and that by them the internal man is either opened or closed, and thus the rational principle is either cultivated or destroyed, nn. 4156, 8628, 9922.
That the internal man is opened and successively perfected by scientifics, if man has good use for an end, especially a use which respects eternal life, n. 3086. That in this case, scientifics, which reside in the natural man, are met by spiritual and celestial things from the spiritual man, which adopt such as are suitable, n. 1495. That the uses of heavenly life in this case are extracted, purified, and elevated, from the scientifics which reside in the natural man, by the internal man, from the Lord, nn. 1895, 1896, 1900, 1901, 1902, 5871, 5874, 5901. And that incongruous and opposing scientifics are cast aside, and exterminated, nn. 5871, 5886, 5889.
That the sight of the internal man calls forth from the scientifics of the external man no other things than what accord with its love, n. 9394. That beneath the sight of the internal man, those things which belong to the love are in the centre, and appear in clearness; but those things which do not belong to the love are at the sides, and appear in obscurity, nn. 6068, 6085. That suitable scientifics are successively implanted in man's loves, and as it were dwell in them, n. 6325. That man would be born into intelligence, if he were born into love towards his neighbor; but as he is born into the love of self and of the world, he is born in total ignorance, nn. 6323, 6325. That science, intelligence, and wisdom, are offsprings of love to God, and of love towards the neighbor, nn. 1226, 2049, 2116.
That it is one thing to be wise, another thing to understand, another to know, and another to do; but that still, with those who possess spiritual life, they follow in order, and exist together in doing, or in deed, n. 10,331. That also it is one thing to know, another to acknowledge, and another to have faith, n. 896.
That scientifics, which belong to the external or natural man, reside in the light of the world; but that truths, which have been made truths of faith and of love, and have thus gained life, reside in the light of heaven, n. 5212. That the truths which have gained spiritual life, are comprehended by natural ideas, n. 5510. That spiritual influx proceeds from the internal or spiritual man into the scientifics which are in the external or natural man, nn. 1940, 8005. That scientifics are the receptacles, and as it were, the vessels, of the truth and good which belong to the internal man, nn. 1469, 1496, 3068, 5489, 6004, 6023, 6052, 6071, 6077, 7770, 9922. That scientifics are, as it were, mirrors, in which the truths and goods of the internal man appear as in an image, n. 5201. That they there abide together as in their ultimate, nn. 5373, 5874, 5886, 5901, 6004, 6023, 6052, 6071.
That influx is spiritual and not physical, that is, that there is influx from the internal man into the external, thus into the scientifics of the latter, but not from the external into the internal; thus not from the scientifics of the former into the truths of faith, nn. 3219, 5119, 5259, 5427, 5428, 5478, 6322, 9110, 9111. That from the truths of the doctrine of the church, which are derived from the Word, the principle from which to set out is to be drawn, and those truths are first to be acknowledged, and that afterwards it is allowable to consult scientifics, n. 6047. Thus that it is allowable for those who are grounded in an affirmative principle respecting the truths of faith, to confirm them intellectually by scientifics, but not for those who are in a negative principle, nn. 2568, 2588, 6047. That he who refuses to believe divine truths unless he be persuaded by scientifics, will never believe them, nn. 2094, 2832. That to enter into the truths of faith from scientifics is contrary to order, n. 10,236. That those who do so become infatuated as to those things which belong to heaven and the church, nn.

unknown to man whilst he lives in the body, because he there thinks both spiritually and naturally at the same time, and what he thinks spiritually he is not conscious of, but only of what he thinks naturally; whereas, when he comes into the spiritual world, he is not conscious of any thing that he thought naturally in the world, but only of what he thought spiritually: such is his change of state.

From these facts it is manifest, that man is made spiritual by means of knowledges and sciences, and that these are the mediums of becoming wise,—only, however, to those, who, both in faith and in life, have acknowledged the Divine Being. Such persons, also, are accepted in heaven more than others, and are among those who there dwell in the centre (see n. 43), as being

128, 129, 140. That they fall into falsities of evil, nn. 232, 233, 6047. And that in the other life, when they think on spiritual subjects, they become like persons intoxicated, n. 1072. What their further quality is, n. 196. Examples illustrating that things spiritual cannot be comprehended, if entered into by scientifics, nn. 233, 2094, 2196, 2203, 2209. That many of the learned are more insane in spiritual things than the simple, by reason that they are immersed in a negative principle, and confirm this by scientifics, which they have continually and in abundance before their view, nn. 4760, 8629.

That those who reason from scientifics against the truths of faith, reason sharply, because from the fallacies of the senses, which are engaging and persuasive, since it is with difficulty that they can be dispersed, n. 5700. What and of what quality the fallacies of the senses are, nn. 5084, 5094, 6400, 6948. That those who understand nothing of truth, and likewise those who are immersed in evil, can reason about the truths and goods of faith, and yet not understand them, n. 4214. That merely to confirm a dogma is not the part of an intelligent person, but to see whether it be true or not, before it is confirmed, nn. 4741, 6047.

That sciences are of no avail after death, but what a man has imbibed in his understanding and life by means of sciences, n. 2480. That still all scientifics remain after death, but that they are quiescent, nn. 2476—2479, 2481—2486.

That the same scientifics, with the evil, are falsities, because they are applied to evils, and with the good, are truths, because they are applied to good, n. 6917. That scientific truths, with the evil, are not truths, howsoever they may appear as truths when they are spoken, because inwardly in them there is evil, n. 10,331.

What is the quality of the desire of knowing, which spirits have, an example, n. 1978. That with the angels there is an immense desire of knowing and of growing wise, since science, intelligence, and wisdom are spiritual food, nn. 8114, 4459, 4792, 4976, 5147, 5293, 5340, 5342, 5410, 5426, 5576, 5582, 5588, 5655, 6277, 8562, 9003. That the science of the ancients was the science of correspondences and representations, by which they introduced themselves into the knowledge of spiritual things; but that that science at this day is altogether obliterated, nn. 4844, 4749, 4964, 4965.

Spiritual truths cannot be comprehended, unless the following universals be known: I. That all things in the universe have reference to good and truth, and to the conjunction of both, in order to their possessing any real existence; thus, to love and faith, and their conjunction. II. That man possesses an understanding and will, and that the understanding is the receptacle of truth, and the will of good; and that all things have reference to those two faculties appertaining to man, and to their conjunction, as all things have reference to truth and good, and their conjunction. III. That there is an internal man and an external, and that they are as distinct from each other as heaven and the world; and yet that they ought to make one, in order that man may be truly a man. IV. That the light of heaven is that in which the internal man is, and the light of the world that in which the external man is, and that the light of heaven is divine truth itself, which is the source of all intelligence. V. That there is a correspondence between the things which exist in the internal man and those which exist in the external, and that hence they appear in all cases under another aspect, insomuch that they are not discerned except by the science of correspondences. Unless these and several other things be known, no ideas can be conceived and formed of spiritual and celestial truths except such as are incongruous; and thus scientifics and knowledges, which belong to the natural man, without those universals, can be of little service to the rational man for understanding and improvement. Hence it is evident how necessary scientifics are.

in the light more than others. These are the intelligent and wise in heaven, who shine with the brightness of the firmament, and who shine as the stars. But the simple, there, are those who have acknowledged the Divine Being, have loved the Word, and have lived a spiritual-moral life, but with whom the interiors belonging to the mind have not been much cultivated by knowledges and sciences. The human mind is like ground, which acquires a quality according to the pains bestowed on its cultivation.

OF THE RICH AND THE POOR IN HEAVEN.

357. Various opinions exist respecting the reception of people in heaven. Some imagine, that the poor are received there, but not the rich; others, that rich and poor are admitted alike; others, that the rich cannot be accepted, unless they relinquish their possessions, and put themselves on a level with the poor: and all confirm their respective opinions by the Word. But they who make any difference between the rich and the poor in regard to their capability of admission into heaven, do not understand the Word. The Word, in its inward recesses, is spiritual, but in its letter it is natural; whence they who only apprehend the Word as to its literal sense, and not, in any degree, as to its spiritual sense, cannot but fall into error on many subjects, and especially respecting the rich and the poor; as when they suppose, that it is as difficult for the rich to go to heaven as it is for a camel to go through the eye of a needle, and that it is easy to the poor merely because they are poor, it being said, " *Blessed be ye poor ; for yours is the kingdom of God.*"—(Luke vi. 20.) But they who know any thing of the spiritual sense of the Word, think differently, being aware that heaven is designed for all who live a life of faith and love, whether they be rich or poor. But who are meant in the Word by the rich, and who by the poor, will be shown in what follows. From much conversation with the angels, and from living in society with them, I have had opportunity of knowing with certainty, that the rich obtain admission into heaven as easily as the poor; and that no man is excluded from heaven merely because he abounded in this world's goods, and no man is received there merely because he was without them. There are in heaven both rich and poor; and there are many of the rich who are in stations of greater glory and happiness than the poor.

358. It is proper to mention by way of preface, that a man may acquire riches, and accumulate wealth, as far as opportunity is given him, provided it is not accomplished by the exercise of cunning and c: wicked arts; that he may eat and drink daintily,

provided he does not make his life to consist in such enjoyments; that he may have a handsome house and furniture, so far as is suitable to his situation in life; that he may converse with others as others do, may frequent places of amusement, and talk about worldly affairs; and that he has no need always to wear an air of devotion, going with a sad and sorrowful countenance, and walking with his head bowing down, but may appear good-humored and cheerful; and that neither is he obliged to give his property to the poor, any further than affection leads him to do so; in one word, that he may live, in external form, just as a man of the world does: and that these things will not prevent his going to heaven, provided, in the inward recesses of his mind, he thinks respecting God in a becoming manner, and deals sincerely and justly with his neighbor. For man is such in quality as are his affection and thought, or his love and faith: all things that he does in externals thence derive their life, for to act is to will, and to speak is to think, because a man acts from his will and speaks from his thought. On this account, when it is said in the Word, that man will be judged according to his deeds and rewarded according to his works, the meaning is, that he will be judged and rewarded according to the thought and affection from which his deeds or works proceeded, or which were included in them; for without these, the actions are of no moment, and the character of the actions is precisely that of the thought and affection from which they are performed.([1]) It hence is evident, that the external of man goes for nothing, but that the internal is all, from which the external proceeds. Let us take an illustration. Suppose a person to act sincerely, and to abstain from defrauding another, merely because he is afraid of the law, of the loss of character, and thence of honor and gain, but who, if that fear did not restrain him, would defraud others as much as he could; thus, in his thought and will is fraud, and yet his deeds, in their external form, appear sincere: such a person, being insincere and fraudulent interiorly, has hell within him. On the other hand, suppose a person to act sincerely, and to abstain from defrauding another, because to do otherwise would be to sin against God and against his neighbor: this person, if he had

---

([1]) That it is very frequently said in the Word, that man shall be judged, and that he shall be recompensed, according to his deeds and his works, n. 3934. That by deeds and works, in such passages, are not meant deeds and works in the external form, but in the internal; since good works in the external form are done also by the wicked, but in the external and at the same time in the internal form, only by the good, nn. 3934, 6073. That works, like all acts, derive their *esse* and *existere*, and their quality, from the interiors of man, which are those of his thought and will, since they thence proceed; wherefore, such as the interiors are, such are the works, nn. 3934, 6911, 10,331. Thus, such as the interiors are in regard to love and faith, nn. 3934, 6073, 10,331, 10,333. That thus, works contain those principles, and are them in effect, n. 10,331. Wherefore, for a man to be judged and recompensed according to his deeds and works, denotes, according to those principles, nn. 3147, 3934, 6073, 6911, 10,331, 10,333. That works, so far as they respect self and the world, are not good, but only so far as they respect the Lord and a man's neighbor, n. 3147.

opportunity to defraud another, still would not do it: his thought and will are regulated by conscience; thus, he has heaven within him. In external form, the deeds of both appear similar; but in internal, they are totally different.

359. Since a man may live, in external form, as others do; may acquire riches, keep a plentiful table, be elegantly lodged and attired according to his condition and occupation, may enjoy pleasurable and cheerful scenes and objects, and undertake worldly engagements for the sake of occupation and business, and in order that his life, both of mind and body, may be kept in a sound state, provided he interiorly acknowledges the Divine Being and cherishes good-will to his neighbor; it is evident, that it is not so difficult to enter the way to heaven as many suppose. The only difficulty is, to be able to resist the love of self and of the world, and to prevent it from being predominant; for this is the root of all evils.(*) That it is not so difficult as many suppose, is taught by these words of the Lord : "*Learn of Me ; for I am meek and lowly of heart ; and ye shall find rest unto your souls. For My yoke is easy, and My burden is light.*"— (Matt. xi. 29, 30.) The reason that the Lord's yoke is easy, and His burden light, is, because, so far as a man resists the evils that spring from the love of self and of the world, he is led by the Lord, and not by himself; and the Lord afterwards resists those evils in man, and removes them.

360. I have conversed after death with some, who, while on earth, renounced the world, and gave themselves up to an almost solitary life, that by the abstraction of their thoughts from worldly concerns, they might be incessantly engaged in pious meditations; believing that this was the way to enter the path to heaven. But these, in the other life, are found to have acquired a melancholy disposition : they despise others who are not like themselves, and are indignant at not obtaining a happier lot than others, believing that they have deserved it ; neither have they any concern about others ; and they avert themselves from offices of charity, though it is by these that conjunction is maintained with heaven. They desire heaven more than others do ; but when they are raised to where the angels are, they cause anxieties, which disturb the felicities of the angels ; wherefore they are separated from their society ; after which they betake themselves to desert places, where they follow a similar life to that which they led in the world. Man can only be formed for heaven by means of the world. It is there that ultimate effects have their station, into which the affection of every one is to be deter-

(*) That all evils are derived from the love of self and of the world, nn. 1307, 1308, 1321, 1594, 1691, 3418, 7255, 7376, 7480, 7488, 8318, 9335, 9348, 10,038, 10,742. Which are, contempt of others, enmity, hatred, revenge, cruelty, deceit, nn. 6667, 7372, 7373, 7374, 9348, 10,038, 10,742. That man is born into those loves, thus that in them are his hereditary evils, nn. 694, 4317, 5660.

mined·; for unless the affection puts itself forth, or effuses itself into acts, which is done in a numerous society, it is suffocated, and, at last, so completely, that the man has no longer any respect to his neighbor, but only to himself. It hence is manifest, that the life of charity towards the neighbor, which consists in doing what is just and right in all our dealings and occupations, leads to heaven ; but not a life of piety without the former :(³) consequently, that the exercises of charity, and the increase of the life of charity by their means, can only have existence so far as a man is engaged in occupations of business ; and that they cannot have existence, so far as he removes himself from such occupations. Of those who have done so, I will now speak from experience. Many of those who had employed themselves in the world in trade and merchandise, and also had become rich by these pursuits, are in heaven ; but fewer of those who attained rank and wealth by filling offices in the state ; and the reason is, because the latter, by the gain they had made, and by the honors conferred upon them, for dispensing justice and equity, and also by conferring posts of profit and honor on others, were induced to love themselves and the world, and through this, to remove their thoughts and affections from heaven, and turn them to themselves. For so far as a man loves himself and the world, and respects himself and the world in every thing, he alienates himself from the Divine Being, and removes himself from heaven.

361. The lot of the rich who go to heaven is of such a nature, that they find themselves in the possession of opulence beyond others. Some of them dwell in palaces, all the interior and furniture of which shine as with gold and silver ; and they have abundance of every thing that can promote the uses of life. They do not, however, in the smallest degree, place their hearts on these things, but on the uses themselves : these they behold in clearness, and as if in the light ; but the gold and silver they see obscurely, and as if, respectively, in the shade. The reason is, because, in the world, they had loved uses, and gold and silver only as means, and instruments of service. Thus uses themselves are refulgent in heaven ; the good of use shining like gold, and truth of use like silver.(⁴) According to the quality, there

(³) That charity towards a man's neighbor consists in doing what is good, just, and right, in all our dealings and in every employment, nn. 8120, 8121, 8122. Hence, that charity towards a man's neighbor extends itself to all things, both general and particular, which he thinks, wills, and does, n. 8124. That a life of piety without a life of charity is of no avail, but with it is profitable for all things, nn. 8252, 8253.

(⁴) That all good has its delight from use, and according to use, nn. 3049, 4984, 7038 ; and also its quality ; consequently, such as the use is, such is the good, n. 3049. That all the happiness and delight of life result from uses, n. 997. In general, that life is the life of uses, n. 1964. That angelic life consists in the goods of love and charity, thus in performing uses, n. 452. That the Lord, and from Him the angels, regard only the ends respected by man, which ends are uses, nn. 1817, 1645, 5844. That the kingdom of the Lord 's a kingdom of uses, nn. 454, 696, 1103, 3645, 4054, 7038. That to fore, of the uses which such persons had performed in the world, is that of their opulence in heaven, and of their enjoyment and happiness. Good uses consist in a man's providing for himself and his family the necessaries of life; in desiring abundance for the sake of his country, and also of his neighbor, to whom a rich man can do good in many ways, which a poor man cannot; and because he is thus enabled to withdraw his mind from a life of idleness, which is a pernicious life, since, in idleness, man, from the evil inherent in him, is prone to indulge bad thoughts. These uses are good, so far as they have in them a Divine Principle; that is, so far as man looks in them to the Divine Being and to heaven, and places his own good in those uses, and only in wealth as a subordinate good, tending to promote the former.

362. But the lot of those rich men who have not believed in a Divine Being, and have rejected from their mind the things belonging to heaven and the church, is quite contrary. These are in hell, surrounded by filth, misery, and destitution. Such are the things into which riches are turned when they are loved as an end; and not only the riches are so changed, but also the uses to which they have been applied, and which were, either that their possessors might follow in every thing the bent of their inclinations, indulge in voluptuous enjoyments, and be able, more abundantly and freely, to give their mind to flagitious practices; or else, to exalt themselves over others, whom they despise. These riches, and these uses, seeing they have nothing in them of a spiritual, but only what is of an earthly nature, turn to filth. For a spiritual principle contained in riches and the uses of them, is like the soul in the body, and like the light of heaven in moist ground: without it, they rot, like a body without a soul, and like moist ground without the light of heaven. These are the persons whom riches seduce, and who are withdrawn by them from heaven.

363. The ruling affection or love of every man remains with him after death, and is not extirpated to eternity. The reason of this is, because the spirit of a man is altogether such as his love is; and, what is an arcanum, the body of every spirit and angel is the external form of his love, perfectly corresponding to its internal form, which is that of his natural and rational mind. Hence it is that spirits are known as to their quality by their countenance, their gestures, and their speech; and man would be known in the same manner, as to his spirit, while he lives in the world, had he not learned to put on, in his countenance, his gestures, and his speech, appearances which do not belong to him. From these facts it may be seen with certainty, that man remains to eternity, such as is his predominant affection or love.

serve the Lord is to perform uses, n. 7038. That all have a quality according to the quality of the uses which they perform, nn. 4054, 6815; illustrated, n. 7038.

It has been granted me to converse with some who lived seventeen centuries ago, and whose lives are known from the writings of that age; and it was ascertained, that they are still led by the love which prevailed in them then. It may hence also appear with certainty, that the love of riches, and of the uses to be performed by riches, remains with every one to eternity, and continues to be completely of the same quality as had been acquired in the world. There is, however, this difference; that riches, with those who had employed them for good uses, are turned into enjoyments according to those uses; whereas riches, with those who had employed them for bad uses, are turned into filth; with which also, they are then delighted; much as, in the world, they had been delighted with riches for the sake of the bad uses to which they applied them. The reason that they are then delighted with filth, is, because the foul voluptuous pleasures and flagitious practices, which were the uses to which they applied them,—and avarice likewise, which is the love of riches without regard to any use,—correspond to filth. Spiritual filth is nothing else.

364. As for the poor, they do not go to heaven on account of their poverty, but on account of their life. His life follows every one, whether he be rich or poor. There is no special grace for one any more than for another :([5]) he is received who has lived well, and he is rejected who has lived ill. Besides, poverty seduces and withdraws a man from heaven, as much as wealth does. Among the poor are great numbers who are not content with their lot, who covet many things, and who believe riches to be real blessings ;([6]) on which account, not obtaining them, they are incensed, and form bad thoughts of the Divine Providence. They also envy others their advantages; and, besides, they are equally ready to defraud others when they find opportunity, and equally live in debasing voluptuous pleasures. Not so the poor who are content with their lot, who are industrious and diligent in their calling, who love work better than idleness, and who deal sincerely and faithfully; living, at the same time, a Christian life. I have sometimes conversed with some of those, who belonged to the class of peasants and common people, who, while they lived in the world, had believed in God, and had done what was just and right in their callings. Being grounded in an affection for knowing the truth, they asked what charity and faith are; because, in the world, they had heard much about faith,

([5]) That there is no such thing as immediate mercy, but that mercy is mediate, that is, is shown to those who live according to the Lord's precepts; because, from a principle of mercy, He leads men continually in the world, and afterwards to eternity, nn. 8700, 10,659.
([6]) That dignities and riches are not real blessings, wherefore they are given to the wicked as well as to the good, nn. 8939, 10,775, 10,776. That real blessing is the reception of love and of faith from the Lord, and thereby conjunction, for thence comes eternal happiness, nn. 1420, 1422, 2846, 3017, 3408, 3504, 3514, 3530, 3565, 3584, 4216, 4981, 8939, 10,495.

and, in the other life, much about charity. It was, therefore, told them, that charity is every thing that relates to life, and faith is every thing that relates to doctrine; consequently, that charity consists in willing and doing what is just and right in all our dealings, and faith in thinking justly and rightly : and that faith and charity are mutually conjoined, like doctrine and a life according to it, or like thought and will; and that faith becomes charity, when a man also wills and does what he justly and rightly thinks; on the accomplishment of which, they are no longer two, but one. All this they well understood, and rejoiced at the information, observing that, when in the world, they could not comprehend, how believing could be any thing else than living.

365. From these facts it may appear with certainty, that both rich and poor go to heaven alike, and the one as easily as the other. The reason that it is imagined that the poor are admitted easily, and the rich with difficulty, is, because the Word has not been understood, where it makes mention of the rich and the poor. By the rich are there meant, in the spiritual sense, those who abound in the knowledges of good and truth, thus who belong to the church, which is in possession of the Word; and by the poor, those who are destitute of such knowledges, but yet desire them, thus, who live in countries beyond the limits of the church, where the Word does not exist. By the rich man who was clothed in purple and fine linen, and who was cast into hell, is meant the Jewish nation, which, as possessing the Word, and thence abounding in the knowledges of good and truth, is called a rich man. By garments of purple are also signified knowledges of good, and by garments of fine linen, knowledges of truth.(7) But by the poor man who lay at his gate, and desired to be fed with the crumbs which fell from the rich man's table, and who was carried by angels into Abraham's bosom, are meant the Gentiles, who did not possess the knowledges of good and truth, but yet desired them.—(Luke xvi. 19—31.) By the rich men who were called to a great supper, and excused themselves, is also meant the Jewish nation; and by the poor men who were introduced in their place, are meant the nations that were not within the church.—(Luke xii. 16—24.) Who are meant by the rich man, of whom the Lord said, "*It is more easy for a camel to go through the eye of a needle, than for a rich man to enter into the kingdom of God*" (Matt. xix. 24), shall also be explained. By a rich man are there meant the rich in both senses, both the natural and the spiritual. In the natural sense, the rich are those who abound in wealth, and set their heart upon it: but, in the spiritual sense, they are those who abound in knowledges

(7) That garments signify truths, thus knowledges, nn. 1073, 2576, 5319, 5954, 9212, 9216, 9952, 10,536. That purple signifies celestial good, n. 9467. That fine linen signifies truth from a celestial origin, nn. 5319, 9469, 9744.

and sciences, for these are spiritual riches, and who desire, by means of them, to introduce themselves, by self-derived intelligence, into the things belonging to heaven and the church. As this is contrary to divine order, it is said that it is easier for a camel to pass through the eye of a needle: for in the spiritual sense, by a camel is signified the principle of knowledge and science in general, and by the eye of a needle, spiritual truth.(*) That such things are signified by a camel and the eye of a needle, is not known at the present day, because hitherto the science has not been disclosed, which teaches what is meant, in the spiritual sense of the Word, by the expressions employed in its literal sense. In every particular of the Word there is contained a spiritual sense; and a natural sense also; for, in order that conjunction might be effected between heaven and the world, or between angels and men, after immediate conjunction had ceased, the Word was written by pure correspondences, according to the relation between natural things and spiritual. It hence is evident, who are specifically meant by the rich man in the above cited passage. (That by the rich are meant in the Word, in its spiritual sense, those who possess the knowledges of good and truth, and, by riches, those knowledges themselves, which also are real spiritual riches, may be seen from various passages: as Isaiah x. 12—14, xxx. 6, 7, xlv. 3; Jerem. xvii. 3, xlvii. 7, l. 36, 37, li. 13; Dan. v. 2, 3, 4; Ezek. xxvi. 7, 12, xxvii. 1-—end; Zech. ix. 3, 4; Ps. xl. 13; Hos. xii. 9; Rev. iii. 17, 18; Luke xiv. 33; and elsewhere. And that by the poor in the spiritual sense, are signified those who do not possess the knowledges of good and truth, and yet desire them, may be seen from Matt. xi. 5; Luke vi. 20, 21, xiv. 21; Isa. xiv. 30, xxix. 19, xli. 17, 18; Zeph. iii. 12, 18. All these texts may be seen explained in the *Arcana Cœlestia*, n. 10,227.)

OF MARRIAGES IN HEAVEN.

366. Since the inhabitants of heaven are from the human race, whence consequently the angels who occupy it are of both sexes;

(*) That a camel, in the Word, signifies the principle of knowledge and of science in general, nn. 3048, 3071, 3143, 3145. What is meant by needle-work, and working with a needle; and hence, what by a needle, n. 9688. That to enter into the truths of faith from scientifics is contrary to divine order, n. 10,236. That those who do so become infatuated as to those things which belong to heaven and to the church, nn. 128, 129, 130, 232, 233, 6047. And that in the other life, when they think about spiritual things, they become like persons intoxicated, n. 1072. What further is their quality, n. 196. Examples to illustrate that spiritual things cannot be comprehended, if entrance to them be made by scientifics, nn. 233, 2094, 2196, 2203, 2209. That from spiritual truth it is allowable to enter into the scientifics which belong to the natural man; but not *vice versa*, because spiritual influx into the natural principle takes place, but not natural influx into the spiritual principle, nn. 3219, 5119, 5259, 5427, 5428, 5478, 6322, 9110, 9111. That the truths of the Word and of the church ought first to be acknowledged, and afterwards it is allowable to consult scientifics, but not *vice versa*, n. 6047.

and since it was ordained from creation that the woman should be for the man, and the man for the woman, thus that the one should be the other's; and since the love that it should be so is innate in both; it follows, that there are marriages in the heavens as well as on earth. Marriages in the heavens, however, greatly differ from marriages on earth. What, therefore, is the nature of marriages in the heavens, in what they differ from marriages on earth, and in what they agree, shall here be shown.

367. In the heavens, marriage is the conjunction of two into one mind; the nature of which conjunction shall be first explained. The mind consists of two parts, one of which is called the understanding, and the other the will. When those two parts act in unity, they are then called one mind. In heaven, the husband acts as that part which is called the understanding, and the wife as that which is called the will. When this conjunction, which exists in the interiors, descends into the inferior parts that belong to the body, it is perceived and felt as love; and the love thus felt is conjugial* love. From these truths it is evident, that conjugial love derives its origin from the conjunction of two individuals into one mind. This is termed, in heaven, dwelling together; and it is said of such, that they are not two, but one. Therefore, in heaven, two married partners are not called two, but one angel.([1])

368. That there should exist such a conjunction of the husband and wife in their inmost parts, which belong to their minds, results from creation itself. For the man is born to be under the influence of intellect, thus, to think from the understanding; but the woman to be under the influence of will, thus, to think from the will. This also is evident from the inclination, or connate

([1]) That it is unknown at this day what and whence conjugial love is, n. 2727. That conjugial love consists in willing what the other wills, thus mutually and reciprocally, n. 2731. That those who are grounded in conjugial love dwell together in their inmost principles of life, n. 2732. That there is a union of two minds, and thus that from love they become one, nn. 10,168, 10,169. For the love of minds, which is spiritual love, is union, nn. 1394, 2057, 3939, 4018, 5807, 6195, 7081—7086, 7501, 10,180.

* This word, *conjugial*, is not in common use in the English language, which has adopted *conjugal* instead. Both are originally Latin, in which language they are written *conjugialis*, and *conjugalis*. Though both the Latin words are equally classical, our Author, when speaking of what he denominates "conjugial love," has confined himself to the use of the former. Only a very few instances of the use of the latter occur in all his works; and then, as generally appears most probable, by error of the press. The reason of his preference is doubtless to be found in their etymology. *Conjugialis* is derived, through *conjugium* (*marriage*, and *conjux,—a married partner*), from *conjungo*, which signifies to *conjoin;* whereas *conjugalis* is from *conjugo*, which signifies *to yoke together*. Now as a yoke carries with it the idea of compulsion and domination, which is abhorrent from all that our Author teaches of the genuine nature of marriage love; whilst the idea of conjunction is in perfect harmony with it; it can be no matter of surprise that he preferred the term *conjugialis* to *conjugalis*. As, also, the original radical ideas remain in the words when anglicized by lopping off their termination, most of our Author's translators have preferred to adopt the appropriate, though unusual word, *conjugial*, instead of the less appropriate, though common word, *conjugal*. The superior softness of the former in sound, also, renders it more suitable in application to such a subject as *Conjugial Love*. For these reasons, the word *conjugial* is retained in the present translation.—*N*.

disposition, of each; and likewise from their form. From their
disposition, it is seen, that the man acts from reason; but the
woman from affection: and from their *form*, that the face of
the man is more rough and less beautiful, his speech of deeper
tone, and his body more robust; whilst the face of the woman
is smoother and fairer, her tone of voice more tender, and her
body more delicate. There is a similar difference between the
understanding and the will, or between thought and affection;
and also between truth and good, and between faith and love;
for truth and faith have relation to the understanding, and good
and love to the will. It is on this account, that, in the Word,
by a youth and man, in the spiritual sense, is meant the understanding of truth, and by a virgin and woman, the affection of
good; and also, that the church, by virtue of her affection for
good and truth, is called a woman and a virgin; and further,
that all who are grounded in the affection of good are called
virgins; as in Rev. xiv. 4.([2])

369. Every one, whether man or woman, enjoys understanding
and will; but still, in the man, the understanding predominates,
and in the woman, the will; and the character of the human
being is determined by the predominating faculty. In marriages
in the heavens, however, there is not any domination exercised
by one party over the other; for the will of the wife is also that
of the husband, and the understanding of the husband is also
that of the wife; because the one loves to will and to think as
the other does, and thus, to do so mutually and reciprocally; the
result of which is, their conjunction into one. This conjunction
is actual; for the will of the wife enters into the understanding
of the husband, and the understanding of the husband into the
will of the wife, more especially when they look each other in
the face: for, as has often been stated above, in the heavens
there is a communication of thoughts and affections; and more
especially does this exist between married partners, because they
mutually love each other. From these statements may be seen,
what is the nature of that conjunction of minds which constitutes
marriage, and produces conjugial love, in the heavens; namely,
that it consists in the one partner's willing or desiring that whatever is his or hers should be the other's, and in the reciprocal
existence of such will or desire.

370. It has been told me by the angels, that just in proportion
as two married partners are united in such conjunction, they are

([2]) That young men, in the Word, signify the understanding of truth, or one that is
intelligent, n. 7668. That men (*viri*) have a like signification, nn. 158, 265, 749, 915,
1007, 2517, 8134, 3236, 4823, 9007. That a woman signifies the affection of good and of
truth, nn. 568, 8160, 6014, 7837, 8994: also the church, nn. 252, 253, 749, 770: and that
a wife also signifies the same, nn. 252, 253, 409, 749, 770; with what difference, nn. 915,
2517, 3236, 4510, 4823. That husband and wife, in the supreme sense, are predicated
of the Lord and of his conjunction with heaven and the church, n. 7022. That a virgin signifies the affection of good, nn. 3067, 3110, 3179, 3189, 6731, 6742: and also the
church, nn. 2362, 3081, 3963, 4638, 6729, 6775, 6778.

in the enjoyment of conjugial love, and at the same time, and in the same proportion, of intelligence, wisdom, and happiness. The reason of this is, because the Divine Truth and the Divine Good, which are the sources of all intelligence, wisdom, and happiness, principally flow into conjugial love, and consequently, conjugial love is the actual plane for receiving the divine influx, for this reason, that it is, at the same time, the marriage of truth and good. For as it is a conjunction of understanding and will, it is also a conjunction of truth and good; since the understanding receives the Divine Truth, and also is formed by truths, and the will receives the Divine Good, and is also formed by goods : for what a man wills, is, to him, good, and what he understands, is, to him, truth : whence it amounts to the same thing, whether we say, the conjunction of understanding and will, or whether we say, the conjunction of truth and good. The conjunction of truth and good constitutes an angel, together with his intelligence, wisdom, and happiness; for an angel is such, in proportion as good is conjoined in him with truth, and truth with good; or, what amounts to the same, an angel is such, in proportion as love is conjoined in him with faith, and faith with love.

371. The reason that the Divine Sphere proceeding from the Lord flows principally into conjugial love, is, because that love descends from the conjunction of good and truth; for, as just observed, whether we say, the conjunction of the understanding and the will, or, the conjunction of good and truth, it amounts to the same thing. The conjunction of good and truth derives its origin from the Lord's Divine Love towards all the inhabitants of heaven and earth. From the Divine Love proceeds the Divine Good; and the Divine Good is received by angels and by men in divine truths. The only receptacle of good is truth ; on which account, nothing that proceeds from the Lord and from heaven can be received by any one who is not in possession of truths. In proportion, therefore, as truths are conjoined in man with good, the man himself is conjoined with the Lord in heaven. Here, then, is the actual origin of conjugial love ; consequently, that love is the actual plane of the Divine Influx. This is the reason that, in heaven, the conjunction of good and truth is called the heavenly marriage, and that, in the Word, heaven is compared to a marriage, and is actually so called ; and that the Lord is termed the bridegroom and husband, and heaven, together with the church, the bride and wife.(³)

(³) That love truly conjugial derives its origin, cause, and essence, from the marriage of good and truth; thus, that it is from heaven, nn. 2728, 2729. Of the angelic spirits, who have a perception whether there be a conjugial principle, from the idea of the conjunction of good and truth, n. 10,756. That conjugial love is circumstanced altogether like the conjunction of good and truth, nn. 1904, 2173, 2429, 2508, 3101, 3102, 3155, 3179, 3180, 4358, 5407, 5835, 9206, 9495, 9637. In what manner the conjunction of good and truth is effected, and with whom, nn. 3834, 4096, 4097, 4301, 4345, 4353, 4364, 4368, 5365, 7623—7627, 9258. That it is not known what love truly conjugial is, except by those who are established in good and truth from the Lord, n. 10,171. That in the

872. Good and truth conjoined in an angel or a man are not two but one; since good, then, belongs to truth, and truth to good. This conjunction is like that which exists, when a man thinks what he wills, and wills what he thinks; for then the thought and the will constitute a one, thus one mind; for the thought forms, or presents in a form, that which the will desires, and the will infuses into it delight. This, also, is the reason, that two married partners are not, in heaven, called two, but one angel. It is this, likewise, which is meant by these words of the Lord: "*Have ye not read, that He who made them from the beginning made them a male and a female, and said, For this cause shall a man leave father and mother, and shall cleave to his wife, and they two shall be one flesh? Wherefore they are no more two, but one flesh. What, therefore, God hath joined together, let not man put asunder.——All men cannot receive this saying, save they to whom it is given.*"—(Matt. xix. 4, 5, 6, 11; Mark x. 6—9; Gen. ii. 24.) What is here described, is the heavenly marriage in which the angels live, and, at the same time, the marriage of good and truth; and by man's being forbidden to put asunder what God hath joined together, is meant, that good is not to be separated from truth.

873. From these truths may now be seen, whence love truly conjugial proceeds; namely, that in those who are united in marriage, it is first formed in the mind, and that it descends thence, and is derived into the body; where it is perceived and felt as love. For whatever is felt and perceived in the body derives its origin from man's spiritual part, since it proceeds from his understanding and will. These constitute the spiritual man; and whatever descends from the spiritual man into the body, there shows itself under another form, but still remaining similar and unanimous; as is the case with the soul and the body, and with the cause and the effect. (As may be manifest from what was stated and shown in the two Sections on Correspondence.)

874. I once heard an angel describing love truly conjugial, and its heavenly delights, to this effect: That it is the Divine Sphere of the Lord in heaven, which is the Divine Good and the Divine Truth, united in two individuals, but in such a manner, as not to be two, but one. He said, that two married partners, in heaven, are that love in form, because every one is his own good and his own truth, both with respect to his mind and his body; for the body is the effigy of the mind, being formed after its likeness. He inferred from this, that the Divine Being is effigied in two individuals who are united in love truly conjugial; and, since the Divine Being is effigied in them, that heaven is so likewise, since the universal heaven is the Divine Good and Divine Truth

Word, by marriage is signified the marriage of good and truth, nn. 3132, 4434, 4835. That in love truly conjugial is the kingdom of the Lord and heaven, n. 2787.

proceeding from the Lord; whence it is that all the elements of heaven are inscribed on that love, with beatitudes and enjoyments beyond the power of computation. He expressed the number by a word which involved myriads of myriads. He wondered that the members of the church should know nothing of this subject, although the church is the Lord's heaven upon earth, and heaven is the marriage of good and truth. He said that he was astounded at the thought, that adultery is practised within the church more than out of it, and is even confirmed as allowable, although the delight of it, in the spiritual sense, and thence in the spiritual world, is, in itself, nothing but the delight of the love of falsity conjoined with evil; which is infernal delight; being diametrically opposite to the delight of heaven, which is that of the love of truth conjoined with good.

375. Every one knows, that two married partners, who love each other, are interiorly united, and that the essential thing in marriage is the union of minds. From this truth it may be known, that such as is, inherently, the character of their minds, such is that of their union, and, also, such is that of the love existing between them. The mind is solely formed by truths and goods: for all things that exist in the universe have reference to good and truth, and also to their conjunction: whence it results, that the union of minds is altogether such in quality as are the goods and truths by which they are formed: consequently, that the union of minds that are formed by genuine truths and goods is the most perfect. It is to be observed, that no two things mutually love each other more than truth and good; on which account, from that love descends the love truly conjugial.(*) Falsity and evil also love each other; but this love is changed into hell.

376. From what has now been stated respecting the origin . conjugial love, a conclusion may be drawn as to who are in the enjoyment of it, and who are not. It may be seen, that those are in the enjoyment of conjugial love, who, by the reception of divine truths, are grounded in Divine Good; and that conjugial love is more genuine, so far as the truths, which are conjoined with good, are more genuine. It also follows, since all the good which is conjoined with truths is from the Lord, that no one can be in the enjoyment of the love truly conjugial, unless he acknowledges the Lord and his Divinity; for without that acknowledgment, the Lord cannot enter by influx, and be conjoined with the truths that are possessed by man.

377. From these remarks it is evident, that those are not in the

<hr/>

(*) That all things in the universe, both in heaven and in the world, have reference to good and truth, nn. 2451, 3166, 4390, 4409, 5232, 7256, 10,122. And to the conjunction of both, n. 10,555. That between good and truth there is a marriage, nn. 1094, 2173, 2503. That good loves, and from love desires, truth, and its conjunction with itself, and that hence they are in a perpetual tendency to conjunction, nn. 9206, 9207, 9495. That the life of truth is from good, nn. 1589, 1997, 2579, 4070, 4096, 4097, 4736, 4757, 4884, 5147, 9667. That truth is the form of good, nn. 3049, 3180, 4574, 9154. That truth is to good as water to bread, n. 4976.

enjoyment of conjugial love who are immersed in falsities, and not at all those who are immersed in falsities grounded in evil. With those, also, who are immersed in evil and thence in falsities, the interiors, which belong to the mind, are closed, wherefore there cannot exist any origin of conjugial love there: but below those interiors, in the external or natural man separate from the internal, there exists a conjunction of falsity and evil, which is called the infernal marriage. It has been granted me to see the nature of the marriage that exists between persons who are immersed in falsities of evil, and which is called the infernal marriage. They talk with each other, and also are connected from an impulse of lasciviousness; but they inwardly burn against each other with deadly hatred, which is so great as to surpass all description.

378. Neither can conjugial love exist between two persons of different religions, because the truth of the one does not agree with the good of the other, and two dissimilar and discordant elements cannot make one mind out of two; on which account, the origin of their love does not partake of any thing of a spiritual nature. If they live together in concord, it is only from natural causes.(*) On this account, in the heavens, marriages are contracted between parties who belong to the same society, because these are grounded in similar good and truth; but not between parties who belong to different societies. (That all in heaven who are in the same society are grounded in similar good and truth, and differ from those who are in other societies, may be seen above, nn. 41, et seq.) This, also, was represented among the Israelites by their contracting marriages within their own tribes, and, specifically, within their own families, and not out of them.

379. Neither can love truly conjugial exist between one husband and several wives: for this destroys its spiritual origin, which consists in the formation of one mind out of two; consequently, it destroys the interior conjunction, which is that of good and truth, from which the very essence of conjugial love is derived. The marriage of a man with more than one wife, is like an understanding divided among several wills; and like a man who is attached, not to one church, but to several; in which case his faith is drawn different ways, till it becomes none at all. The angels affirm, that to have a plurality of wives is utterly contrary to Divine Order; and that they know this from several causes, among which, this is one: That as soon as they entertain the thought of marriage with more than one wife, they lose all sense of internal beatitude and heavenly happiness, and immediately become like persons intoxicated, because good is then disjoined in them from its own truth: and as the interiors that belong to their minds fall

(*) That marriages between those who are of different religions are unlawful, on account of the non-conjunction of similar good and truth in the interiors, n. 8998.

Into such a state on the mere thought of such a thing with any intention, they perceive clearly, that marriage with more than one wife would shut their internal, and, in place of conjugial love, would introduce the love of lasciviousness, which is a love that withdraws from heaven.(*) They say, further, that man with difficulty comprehends this, because there are few who are grounded in genuine conjugial love; and they who are not, know nothing whatever of the interior delight which is inherent in that love, but only of the delight of lasciviousness, which is turned into what is undelightful after persons of this character have lived a little time together; whereas the delight of love truly conjugial not only lasts till old age in the world, but also becomes the delight of heaven after death, and is then filled with interior enjoyment, which is perfected to eternity. They stated, also, that the beatitudes of the love truly conjugial might be enumerated to the extent of several thousands, not one of which is known to man, nor can be comprehended by any individual who is not grounded in the marriage of good and truth derived from the Lord.

380. The love of domination to be exercised by one party over the other completely banishes conjugial love and its heavenly delight: for, as observed above, conjugial love, and the delight belonging to it, consist in the circumstance, that the will of one is that of the other, and that such is their state mutually and reciprocally. The love of domination destroys this; for the ruling party would have his or her will alone to be in the other, and none of the other's reciprocally in him or her; whence there is nothing mutual between them, no communication of any love and its delight with the other, and no reciprocal interchange; although such communication and interchange, with the conjunction thence resulting, are what constitute that interior delight, called beatitude, which exists in real marriage. The love of domination utterly extinguishes this beatitude, and with it, every thing celestial and spiritual belonging to that love, even to the abolishing of all knowledge of its existence; and if such persons were told of it, they would regard it as so contemptible, that on the mere mention of beatitude from such a source, they would either laugh or fly in a passion. When one party wills or loves what the other does, both enjoy liberty, for all liberty is the offspring of love: but where domination is assumed, neither enjoys liberty: one party is confessedly a slave; and so is the

(*) As husband and wife ought to be one, and to dwell together in the inmost ground of their life; and as they together constitute one angel in heaven; therefore love truly conjugial cannot exist between one husband and several wives, nn. 1907, 2740. That to marry more wives than one at the same time is contrary to divine order, n. 10,887. That no marriage can exist but between one husband and one wife, is clearly perceived by those who dwell in the Lord's celestial kingdom, nn. 865, 3246, 9961, 10,172. The reason is, because the angels there are in the marriage of good and truth, n. 3246. That the Israelitish nation were permitted to marry several wives, and to adjoin concubines to wives, but Christians are not so permitted; the reason was, because that nation were in externals without internals, but Christians may be in internals, thus in the marriage of good and of truth, nn. 3246, 4837, 8809.

ruling party too, because led as a slave by the lust of domination. This, however, he cannot at all conceive, because he does not know what the liberty of heavenly love is. From what has been advanced above respecting the origin and essence of conjugial love, however, it may be known, that just in proportion as domination enters, the minds of the parties are not united, but divided. Domination subjugates; and the mind that is subjugated has afterwards no will at all, or else a contrary will: if there is no will, there is also no love; if a contrary will, instead of love, there is hatred. The interiors of those who live in such a marriage, are in such mutual collision and combat, as ever exists between two opposites, however their exteriors may be restrained and kept quiet for the sake of peace. The collision and combat of their interiors display themselves openly after death. Then, for the most part, they meet; when they fight like hostile champions, mutually inflicting injuries as if they would tear each other to pieces: for they then act according to the state of their interiors. It has sometimes been granted me to behold their battles and mutual injuries; when I saw that, in some, they were full of revenge and cruelty. For, in the other life, the interiors of every one are set at liberty, and are no longer held under restraint by external considerations, connected with reasons that operate in the world: for every one is then seen to be such in quality as he interiorly is.

381. There exists, with some, a certain resemblance of conjugial love, which, nevertheless, is not conjugial love, where the parties are not grounded in the love of good and truth, but is a love appearing like it, grounded in various causes; as, for instance, that they may be waited upon in the house; that they may live in security, or in tranquillity, or in idleness; or that they may be nursed in sickness and old age; or to have their children, whom they love, taken care of. With some, it is a state of constraint, occasioned by fear of the other party, or for their reputation, or of injuries: and with some it is induced by lasciviousness. Conjugial love differs, also, in the two married partners themselves: it may exist, more or less, in one, and little, or not at all, in the other; and as it may differ so widely, heaven may await the one, and hell the other.

382. Genuine conjugial love prevails in the inmost heaven, because the angels of that heaven are eminently grounded in the marriage of good and truth; and also, are eminently in the enjoyment of innocence. The angels of the inferior heavens are also in the enjoyment of conjugial love, but only so far as they are grounded in innocence: for conjugial love, regarded in itself, is a state of innocence; wherefore, between married partners who are grounded in conjugial love, there exist heavenly delights, which, as presented before their minds, are almost similar to such sports of innocence as are practised among little children;

for there is nothing which does not impart delight to their minds; since heaven, with its joy, flows into all the minutiæ of their life. On this account, conjugial love is represented in heaven by the most beautiful objects. I have seen it represented by a virgin of inexpressible beauty, encompassed by a bright cloud. It has been told me, that all the beauty that adorns the angels in heaven is derived from conjugial love. The affections and thoughts which proceed from it are represented by *auræ* or atmospheres of the brightness of diamonds, and sparkling as with carbuncles and rubies; all attended with delightful sensations affecting the interiors of the angels' minds. In one word, heaven represents itself in conjugial love; because heaven, with the angels, consists in the conjunction of good and truth; and this conjunction constitutes conjugial love.

382.* Marriages in heaven differ from marriages on earth in this respect. Besides their other uses, marriages on earth are ordained for the procreation of offspring; but not in heaven; but there, in lieu of the procreation of offspring, there is a procreation of good and truth. The reason that this procreation there takes the place of the former, is, because marriage, in heaven, is the marriage of good and truth, as has been shown above; in which marriage, the supreme objects of love are good and truth, and their conjunction; wherefore these are what are propagated by marriages in heaven. It is on this account, that by nativities and generations, in the Word, are signified spiritual nativities and generations, which are those of good and truth; by mother and father being signified the truth conjoined with good which procreates; by sons and daughters, the truths and goods which are procreated; and by sons-in-law and daughters-in-law, the conjunctions of these; and so in other instances.([7]) From these facts it is evident, that marriages in heaven are not like marriages on earth. In the heavens, nuptials are spiritual, and are not to be called nuptials, but conjunctions of minds originating in the marriage of good and truth; but on earth they are nuptials, because they are not only of the spirit, but also of the flesh: and as there are no nuptials in heaven, the two married partners are not there called husband and wife, but, from the idea which the angels have of the conjunction of two minds into one, each is called by a word which signifies, what is each other's mutually

---

([7]) That conceptions, births, nativities, and generations, signify spiritual conceptions, &c., which are those of good and truth, or of love and faith, nn. 613, 1145, 1155, 2020, 2584, 3860, 8868, 4070, 4668, 6239, 8042, 9325, (10,197). That hence, generation and nativity signify regeneration and re-birth by faith and love, nn. 5160, 5598, 9042, 9845. That a mother signifies the church as to truth, thus also the truth of the church; a father, the church as to good, thus also the good of the church, nn. 2691, 2717, 3703, 5589, 8897. That sons signify the affections of truth, thus truths, nn. 489, 491, 533, 2623, 3373, 4257, 8649, 9807. That daughters signify the affections of good, thus goods, nn. 489, 490, 491, 2362, 3963, 6729, 6775, 6778, 9055. That a son-in-law signifies truth associated to the affection of good, n. 2389. That a daughter-in-law signifies good associated to its truth, n. 4813.

* This number is repeated in the original.

and reciprocally. From these observations may be known how the Lord's words respecting nuptials (Luke xx. 35, 36) are to be understood.*

383. In what manner marriages are entered into in the heavens, it has also been granted me to see. Throughout heaven, those whose characters are similar are connected together in society, and those whose characters are dissimilar are parted asunder. Every heavenly society consists of angels of similar dispositions : like are drawn to like, not of themselves, but of the Lord. (See above, nn. 41, 43, et seq.) In the same manner, conjugial partners, whose minds are capable of being conjoined into one, are drawn to each other; whence, at first sight, they love each other from their inmost soul, see themselves to be each other's conjugial partner, and engage in marriage. Hence all marriages in heaven are made by the Lord alone. They also hold a sacred festival on the occasion, which is celebrated in a numerous assembly ; the festivities differing in different societies.

384. Marriages on earth, because they are the seminaries of the human race, and of the angels of heaven also (for, as has been shown in its proper Section, the inhabitants of heaven are from the human race); because, likewise, they proceed from a spiritual origin, that is, from the marriage of good and truth; and since, in addition, the Lord's Divine Proceeding principally flows into conjugial love; are most holy in the estimation of the angels of heaven; and, on the other hand, adulteries, as being contrary to conjugial love, are regarded by them as profane. For as, in marriages, the angels behold the marriage of good and truth, which constitutes heaven, so, in adulteries, they behold the

* The Author here makes a distinction between *marriage* and *nuptials*, which cannot easily be made in English. We have no word in English to express the entering into the state that he calls *nuptials*, but that which also expresses the entering into the state that he denominates *marriage*. Thus the expressions used in the English version of the passage of Luke to which he refers, and which, he intimates, relate to the state of *nuptials*, not that of real *marriage*, are "marry," and "given in marriage." In Latin, the terms are generally rendered "nubunt," and "tradere in nuptias." The last word is that from which we have our *nuptials*. As, then, in the passage of Luke, and the corresponding passages of Matthew and Mark, only carnal unions are spoken of, our Author here applies the Latin word there used to express them, and which is anglicized into *nuptials*, to carnal unions only; of which, as he observes, there can be none in heaven. (The word *nuptials*, however, in English, is commonly applied only to the *marriage-solemnities*, not to the *marriage-state*; and its Latin original is so used by our Author, in other parts of his works.) In Latin, there are three other words which signify the *marriage-state*;—*matrimonium*, *connubium*, and *conjugium*; the last of which is the term almost everywhere used by our Author,—doubtless because, including in its etymological signification the idea of *conjunction*, which the others do not, it is best adapted to convey the spiritual ideas which he always has in view.
For the further elucidation of this subject, including ample proofs that such marriages as are meant by our Author do exist in heaven, and that the Lord's answer to the Sadducees, contained in the passage above referred to in Luke, and the corresponding passages in Matthew and Mark, only relates to merely carnal connections, which, of course, cannot have place in heaven, it perhaps may be allowable, because useful, to refer to the work, by the writer of this note, entitled, "*An Appeal in behalf of the Views of the Eternal World and State, and the Doctrines of Faith and Life, held by the New Church*," &c. ; in Sect. VI. of which, all the objections that have been raised upon this subject, and against our Author's representations of heaven and hell in general, are fully considered.—*N.*

marriage of falsity and evil, which constitutes hell. On this account, when they only hear adultery mentioned, they turn themselves away; which also is the reason, that when man commits adultery with delight, heaven is shut against him; and when heaven is closed to him, he no longer acknowledges the Divine Being, nor any thing belonging to the faith of the church.(*) That all the inhabitants of hell are in opposition to conjugial love, was given me to perceive from the sphere thence exhaling, which was like a perpetual effort to dissolve and violate marriages; from which it was made evident, that the delight which reigns in hell is the delight of adultery, and that the delight of adultery is also the delight of destroying the conjunction of good and truth, which is what constitutes heaven. It hence follows, that the delight of adultery is an infernal delight completely opposite to the delight of marriage, which is a heavenly delight.

385. There were certain spirits, who, from habit acquired in the life of the body, infested me with peculiar ingenuity. They effected it by a gentle, and, as it were, undulatory kind of influx, such as is usually that of well-disposed spirits; but I perceived that it included cunning and similar vices, to captivate and deceive. At length I entered into conversation with one of them, who, I was informed, when he lived in the world, had been a general officer; and as I perceived that a lascivious tendency lurked in his ideas of thought, I conversed with him on the subject of marriage. I used the spiritual sort of speech accompanied by representatives, which fully express the sense intended, with many accompaniments, in a moment. He said, that when he lived in the body, he had accounted adulteries as nothing. But it was given me to reply, that adulteries are wicked, although they appear to such as himself, from the delight that they took in them, and from the persuasion thence inspired, not to be of such a nature—in fact, to be allowable. I observed, that he might be convinced of their wickedness by the consideration, that marriages are the seminaries of the human race, and thence, also, of the kingdom of heaven, and therefore on no account to be violated, but to be esteemed holy; as also, from the consideration, which he ought to be aware of, as being in the other life, and in a state of perception, that conjugial love descends from the Lord through heaven, and that from this love, as its parent, is derived mutual love, which is the strengthening bond of heaven; and, in addition, from the fact, that when adulterers only approach to the

<hr/>

(*) That adulteries are profane, nn. 9861, 10,174. That heaven is closed against adulterers, n. 2750. That those who have perceived delight in adulteries, cannot enter into heaven, nn. 539, 2733, 2747, 2748, 2749, 2751, 10,175. That adulterers are unmerciful, and without a religious principle, nn. 824, 2747, 2748. That the ideas of adulterers are filthy, nn. 2747, 2748. That in the other life they love filth, and are in such hells, nn. 2755, 5394, 5722. That by adulteries, in the Word, are signified the adulterations of good, and by whoredoms the perversions of truth, nn. 2466, 2729, 3399, 4865, 8904, 10,648.

vicinity of heavenly societies, they are made sensible of their own stench, and cast themselves headlong down towards hell. I further observed, that at least he might know, that to violate marriages is contrary to the divine laws, and to the civil laws of all states, as well as contrary to the genuine light of reason, because it is contrary to all order, both divine and human: with more to the same effect. But he replied, that he had no such thoughts, while in the life of the body. He wished to reason as to whether it was so. But he was told, that truth does not admit of reasonings, for they favor the delights of the reasoner, thus his evils and falsities; and that he ought first to think of the considerations that had been advanced, because they were true: It was also urged upon him, from that principle so well known in the world,—that no one ought to do to another what he would not like another to do to him,—to consider, if any one had deceived in that manner his own wife, whom he loved, as every man loves his wife in the beginning of their marriage, whether, speaking while he was incensed with anger on the occasion, he would not himself have expressed detestation of adultery, and, being a man of strong mind, would not have confirmed himself more than others in the belief of its criminality, even to the extent of condemning it to hell.

386. It has been shown me, in what manner the delights of conjugial love advance in their progress towards heaven, and the delights of adultery in their progress towards hell. The progression of the delights of conjugial love towards heaven, was effected by entering into beatitudes and felicities continually more numerous till they become innumerable and ineffable; and the more interiorly they advanced, into still more innumerable and ineffable ones, till they reached the very beatitudes and felicities of the inmost heaven, or the heaven of innocence; and all with the most perfect freedom: for all freedom proceeds from love, and thus the most perfect freedom from conjugial love, that being heavenly love itself. But the progression of adultery was towards hell, and, by degrees, to the lowest of all, where nothing exists but what is direful and horrible. Such is the lot which awaits adulterers after their life in the world. By adulterers are meant those who find what is delightful in adulteries and what is not delightful in marriage.

OF THE OCCUPATIONS OF THE ANGELS IN HEAVEN.

387. The occupations that exist in the heavens cannot be enumerated, nor specifically described, but only admit of something being stated respecting them of a general nature; for they are innumerable, and vary, also, according to the offices of the

various societies   Every society discharges its peculiar office:
for as the societies are distinctly arranged according to the goods
by which they are distinguished (see above, n. 41), they are also
arranged according to the uses which they perform; since the
goods which prevail with all the inhabitants of heaven are goods
in act, which are uses. Every one, there, performs some use;.
for the Lord's kingdom is a kingdom of uses.([1])

388. There are in heaven, as on earth, various administrations:
for there exist there ecclesiastical affairs, civil affairs, and domestic
ones. That there exist there ecclesiastical affairs, is manifest
from what was stated and shown above respecting Divine Worship, nn. 221—227. That there exist there civil affairs, is plain
from what was advanced respecting Governments in Heaven,
nn. 213—220. And that there exist there domestic affairs, from
what has been detailed respecting the Habitations and Mansions
of the Angels, nn. 183—190; and respecting Marriages in
Heaven, nn. 366—380. It hence follows, that many occupations
and administrations exist within every heavenly society.

389. All things in heaven are instituted according to Divine
Order, which is everywhere maintained by administrations discharged by angels; such affairs as relate to the general good or
use being administered by the wiser angels, and such as relate
to any particular good or use by those less wise; and so pro-
gressively. Those who discharge them are arranged in subordination, exactly as the uses themselves are subordinated in the
arrangements of Divine Order. It hence results, that dignity is
attached to every occupation according to the dignity of its use.
No angel, however, arrogates the dignity to himself, but ascribes
it all to the use; and as the use is the good which he performs,
and all good is from the Lord, he gives it all to the Lord. He,
therefore, who thinks of honor as due to himself and thence to
the use performed by him, and not to the use performed by him
and thence to himself, cannot fill any office in heaven; because
he looks away from the Lord, regarding himself in the first place
and use in the second. When use is mentioned, the Lord is
meant, also; since, as just observed, use is good, and good is
from the Lord.

390. From these observations may be inferred what is the
nature of the subordinations that exist in heaven; namely; that
in proportion as any one loves, esteems, and honors, any use,
he also loves, esteems, and honors, the person to whom that use
is adjoined: and also, that the person is loved, esteemed, and
honored, in proportion as he does not arrogate the use to him-

---

([1]) That the kingdom of the Lord is a kingdom of uses, nn. 454, 696, 1103, 3645, 4054,
7038. That to serve the Lord is to perform uses, n. 7038. That, in the other life, all must
perform uses, n. 1103. Even the wicked and infernal; but in what manner, n. 696.
That all are such as are the uses which they perform, nn. 4054, 6815; illustrated, n.
7038. That angelic blessedness consists in the goods of charity, thus in performing
uses, n. 454.

self, but ascribes it to the Lord; for it is in this proportion that
he is wise, and that the uses which he performs are performed
from a good principle.   Spiritual love, esteem, and honor, are
nothing but love, esteem, and honor for use in the person who
performs it; and the honor of the person is derived from the use,
and not that of the use from the person.   He, also, who looks at
men under the influence of spiritual truth, regards them in no
other manner: for he sees that one man is like another, whether
stationed in great dignity or in little, the difference being solely in
their wisdom; and wisdom consists in loving use, consequently,
in loving the good of our fellow-citizens, of the society to which
we belong, of our country, and of the church.   Love to the Lord,
also, consists in the same, since all the good which constitutes
the good of use is from Him: and so, likewise, does love towards
our neighbor, since the good that is to be loved in our fellow-citizen, in our society, in our country, and in the church, and which
is to be done to them, is our neighbor.(*)

391. All the societies in the heavens are distinctly arranged
according to the uses which they minister, since they are distinctly arranged according to the various kinds of good in which
they are grounded (as stated above, nn. 41, *et seq.*); and those
goods are goods in act, or goods of charity, which are uses.
There are societies, whose occupations consist in having the care
of infants.   There are other societies whose occupation it is to
instruct and educate them as they grow up.   There are others,
that, in like manner, instruct and educate boys and girls that
have acquired a good disposition from the education they had
received in the world, and who thence go to heaven.   There are
others, that teach the simple good who come from the Christian
world, and lead them into the way to heaven.   There are others,
that discharge the same office to the various classes of Gentiles.
There are others, that protect novitiate spirits, who are such as
are newly arrived from the world, from the infestations proceeding from evil spirits.   There are some angels, also, who attend
upon those who are in the lower earth; and there are some who
are present with those in hell, who so restrain their violence, as
to prevent them from torturing each other beyond the prescribed
limits.   There likewise are some who attend upon those who are
being resuscitated from the dead.   In general, the angels of

(*) That to love one's neighbor is not to love his person, but to love that which appertains to him, and which constitutes him, nn. 5025, 10,336. That those who love the
person, and not what appertains to the man, and which constitutes him, love equally
an evil man and a good man, n. 3820: and that they do good alike to the evil and to
the good, when yet to do good to the evil is to do evil to the good, which is not to love
the neighbor, nn. 3820, 6703, 8120. The judge who punishes the evil that they may
be amended, and to prevent the good being contaminated and injured by them, loves
his neighbor, nn. 3820, 8120, 8121. That every man and society, also a man's country
and the church, and, in a universal sense, the kingdom of the Lord, are one's neighbor; and that to do good to them from the love of good according to the quality of
their state, is to love one's neighbor; thus their good, which is to be consulted, is
one's neighbor, nn. 6818—6824, 8123.
208

every society are sent on missions to men, to guard them, and to withdraw them from evil affections and the thoughts thence originating, and to inspire them with good affections, so far as they will freely receive them; and by means of such good affections, they also govern the deeds or works of men, removing, as far as possible, evil intentions. When the angels are present with men, they dwell, as it were, in their affections, and are near to the man, in proportion as he is grounded in good derived from truths; but are more remote, in proportion as he is remote from good in his life.(³) But all these occupations of the angels are functions performed by the Lord through them as instruments; for the angels do not discharge them of themselves, but from the Lord. It is on this account, that by angels in the Word, in its internal sense, are not meant angels, but some attribute or function of the Lord; and it is from the same cause that angels, in the Word, are called gods.(⁴)

392. These occupations of the angels are their general ones; but to every angel is assigned his own in particular. For every general use is composed of innumerable others, that are called mediate, ministering, and subservient uses. All and each of these are co-ordinated and subordinated according to Divine Order, and, taken together, they constitute and perfect the gen eral use, which is the common good.

393. Those are appointed to ecclesiastical offices in heaven, who, while in the world, had loved the Word, and, from desire, had sought in it for truths, not with a view to honor and gain, but with a view to the uses of life, both of themselves and of others. These, according to their love and desire of use, are there in the enjoyment of illumination, and of the light of wisdom; which, also, they acquire from the Word as it exists in heaven, where it is not natural in its form, as in the world, but spiritual. (See above, n. 259.) These discharge the office of preachers; and in heaven, according to Divine Order, those fill the superior stations, who excel the others in wisdom derived from illumination. Those fill civil offices, who, while in the world, had loved their country and the common good more than their private advantage, and had done what was just and right from the love of justice and rectitude. So far as these, from the desire of their love, had inquired into the laws of justice,

and had become intelligent in consequence, they possess a capacity for administering offices in heaven; and they administer, accordingly, such offices as belong to that station or degree
which corresponds with their intelligence, which is then in the
same degree as their love for the common good. There are,
moreover, in heaven, so many offices and administrations, and
so many kinds of employment also, that they cannot be enumerated on account of their abundance, those in the world being
but few respectively. All the inhabitants, how numerous soever, feel delight in their works and labors derived from the
love of use, and no one performs them from the love of self or
of gain. Neither is any one influenced by the love of gain for
the sake of his living, since all the necessaries of life are given
them gratis : they are lodged gratis, they are clothed gratis, and
they are fed gratis. From all these facts it is evident, that they
who have loved themselves and the world more than they have
loved to be of use, have no inheritance in heaven : for his own
love or affection remains with every one after his life in the
world, nor is it extirpated to eternity. (See above, n. 363.)

394. Every one in heaven has his proper work to perform according to correspondence, the correspondence not being with
the work, but with the use of any one's work (see above, n.
112); and all things that exist have their correspondence. (See
n. 106.) When any one in heaven is engaged in his occupation,
or in some work corresponding to the use of his occupation, he
is in a state of life altogether similar to that in which he was,
when so engaged, in the world ; for what is spiritual and what
is natural act as one by correspondences. There is, however,
this difference ; that the delight which he now feels is of a more
interior kind, because he is in a spiritual state of life, which
is an interior kind of life, and is therefore more receptive of
heavenly beatitude.

OF HEAVENLY JOY AND HAPPINESS.

395. What heaven and heavenly joy are, is scarcely known
to any one at the present day. They who have reflected either
on the one or on the other, have conceived so general and gross
an idea of them, as hardly amounts to any idea at all. I have had
excellent opportunities of knowing what notions are entertained
on these subjects, from the spirits who pass from the world into
the other life ; for when left to themselves, as if they were still
in the world, they think in the same manner. The reason that
men do not know what heavenly joy is, is founded in the circumstance, that they who have reflected on it, have formed their
conclusions respecting it from the external joys that are proper

to the natural man, and have been ignorant of what the internal or spiritual man is, and, consequently, of what constitutes the enjoyment and beatitude thereto belonging; wherefore, should they be told, by such as are in the enjoyment of spiritual and internal delight, what, and of what nature, heavenly joy is, they would not comprehend it. The information, to be understood, would require the presence of ideas which to them are unknown, and would, consequently, rank among the things which the natural man would reject. Nevertheless, every one may be aware, that when a person leaves the external or natural man, he comes into the internal or spiritual man; from which circumstance it may be known, that heavenly delight is an internal and spiritual delight, not an external and natural one; and that, as being internal and spiritual, it is of a more pure and exquisite nature, and has a power of affecting the interiors of man, which are those of his soul or spirit. From these considerations alone, every one may conclude, that a man experiences such delight in the other life, as had been that of his spirit in this; and that the delight of the body, which is called carnal pleasure, is, respectively, not heavenly. For that which exists in the spirit of man, when he leaves the body, remains with him after death; for man then lives as a spirit.

396. All delights flow from love; for what a man loves, he feels delightful; and no one can experience delight from any other origin. The delights of the body or the flesh all flow from the love of self and the love of the world, which also are the sources of concupiscences and of their pleasures: but the delights of the soul or of the spirit all flow from love to the Lord and love towards the neighbor, which also are the sources of the affections of good and truth, and of interior enjoyments. These loves, with their delights, enter by influx from the Lord and from heaven by an internal way, and thus come from above, and affect the interiors; but the former loves, with their delights, enter by influx from the flesh and from the world by an external way, and thus come from beneath, and affect the exteriors. In proportion, therefore, as those two loves of heaven are received, and their affecting influence is experienced, the interiors, which belong to the soul or spirit, are opened, and their aspect is turned away from the world towards heaven; but in proportion as those two loves of the world are received, and their affecting influence is experienced, the exteriors are opened, which are those of the body and the flesh, and their aspect is turned from heaven towards the world. As these loves, of either kind, enter by influx and are received, their delights enter at the same time, the delights of heaven flowing into the interiors, and the delights of the world into the exteriors; for, as just observed, all delight is the offspring of love.

397. Heaven in itself, is of such a nature, as to be full of de-

lights, so completely, that, viewed in itself, it is nothing but beatitude and delight. For the Divine Good proceeding from the Lord's Divine Love constitutes heaven, both in general, and in particular, with every inhabitant; and the Divine Love consists in willing the well-being and happiness of all, from inmost grounds, and in full .perfection. On this account, whether you mention heaven, or heavenly joy, it is all one.

398. The delights of heaven are ineffable, and they are also innumerable: but innumerable as they are, not one of them can be either known or believed by a person who only has a relish for the delights of the body or of the flesh; because, as just observed, the aspect of the interiors of such a person is turned away from heaven towards the world, and thus they look backwards. For a person who is wholly immersed in bodily or carnal pleasures, or, what amounts to the same, in the love of self and of the world, feels no delight but in honor, in gain, and in the voluptuous pleasures of the body and the senses; and these so extinguish and suffocate interior delights, which are those of heaven, as to destroy all belief in their existence. Such a person, therefore, would be exceedingly astonished, were he only told that any delights can exist when those of honor and gain are removed; and still more, were he informed, that the delights of heaven, which succeed in place of the former, are innumerable, and of such a nature, that the delights of the body and the flesh, which are chiefly those of honor and gain, cannot be compared to them. The reason is now evident, why it is not known what heavenly joy is.

399. How great the delight of heaven is, may appear from this circumstance alone; that it is delightful to all who are there to communicate their enjoyments and beatitudes to each other; and all the inhabitants of heaven being of this character, it is plain how immense the delight of heaven must be: for there exists, in the heavens, a communication of all with every individual, and of every individual with all (as is shown above, n. 268). Such communication flows from the two loves of heaven, which, as has been stated, are love to the Lord and love towards the neighbor; and it is the nature of these loves to communicate their delights to others. The reason that love to the Lord is of such a nature, is, because the Lord's love is the love of communicating all that He has to all His creatures; for He desires the happiness of all: and a similar love prevails in the individuals who love Him, because the Lord is in them. It is from this ground that the angels mutually communicate their delights to each other. That love towards the neighbor is of such a nature also, will be seen in what follows. From these observations it may appear, that it is the nature of those loves to communicate their delights. Not so the loves of self and of the world. The love of self abstracts and takes away all their delight from others,

and appropriates it to self, for it enterta ns good will to self alone; and, under the influence of the love of the world, men would have their neighbor's possessions to be their own. Thus it is the nature of these loves to destroy the delights enjoyed by others: when those who are under their influence communicate, it is for the sake of themselves, not of others; and thus, as regards others, except so far as the delights of those others are present with, or resident in, themselves, they do not communicate, but destroy. That the loves of self and of the world, when they have the supremacy, are of such a nature, it has often been granted me to perceive by actual experience. Whenever any spirits, who had been immersed in these loves while they lived as men in the world, came near me, my sense of delight receded and vanished; and it has also been told me, that if such spirits only approach any heavenly society, the delight of those who compose it is diminished, precisely according to the degree of their presence: and, what is wonderful, the evil spirits are then in the enjoyment of their delight. The nature of the state of the spirit of such a man while in the body, was thence made evident to me; for it is then similar to what it is after his separation from the body; namely, that he longs for, or covets, the enjoyments or goods of others, and that, so far as he obtains them, he feels delight himself. From these facts may be seen, that it is the nature of the loves of self and of the world to destroy the joys of heaven; consequently, that they are diametrically opposite to the heavenly loves, the nature of which is, to communicate their joys.

400. It is, however, to be observed, that the delight experienced by those who are immersed in the loves of self and of the world, when they approach to any heavenly society, is the delight of their own lust; and is, consequently, diametrically opposite to the delight of heaven. They come into the delight of their own lust on the privation and removal of heavenly delight among those in the heavenly society. Not so when such privation and removal do not take place: then they cannot approach, because, so far as they do, they are seized with distress and pain; on which account, they seldom venture to go near. This, also, it has been granted me to know by many experimental observations, of which I will mention a few particulars.

The spirits who have recently passed from the world into the other life desire nothing more earnestly than to be admitted into heaven. This is the wish of almost all, supposing that, to enjoy heaven, nothing more is necessary than to be admitted and received within its precincts. Desiring it so earnestly, they are led, in consequence, to some society of the ultimate heaven. On approaching the first threshold of that heaven, those who are immersed in the love of self and of the world begin to be distressed, and to be so inwardly tortured, that they feel hell in themselves rather than heaven; wherefore they cast their selves headlong down, and find no rest till they are in hell among their like. It has also frequently happened, that such spirits desired to know what heavenly joy is, and, when they heard that it is seated in the interiors of the angels, wished to have it communicated to themselves. This was done accordingly; for whatever a spirit who is not yet either in heaven or in hell desires, is granted him, if conducive to any good purpose. On the communication being made, however, they began to feel torture, which prevailed to such a degree, that they did not know into what posture to squeeze their bodies through the violence of the pain: I saw them thrust their heads down to their feet, and cast themselves on the ground, where they writhed about in orbicular convolutions after the manner of a serpent; the whole being produced by their interior anguish. Such was the effect of the delight of heaven upon those who cherish the delights proceeding from the love of self and of the world: the reason is, because those loves and the loves of heaven are perfect opposites; and when one opposite acts upon the other, such pain is the result. Since, also, the delight of heaven enters by an internal way, and flows into a delight which is the reverse of itself, it violently bends the interiors, which are the seat of the latter delight, the contrary way, thus into a direction opposite to their own; and this is what produces such torments. The ground of the contrariety is, that, as stated above, love to the Lord and love towards the neighbor desire to communicate all they possess to others, for this constitutes their delight; whereas the love of self and the love of the world desire to abstract what they possess from others, and to appropriate it to themselves; and so far as they succeed in doing so, they are in the enjoyment of their delight.

From these facts may also be known, what is the cause of the separation between hell and heaven. All the inhabitants of hell, when they lived in the world, had been immersed in the mere delights of the body and the flesh, derived from the love of self and of the world; whereas all the inhabitants of heaven, when they lived in the world, had been attached to the delights of the soul and the spirit, derived from love to the Lord and love towards the neighbor. These loves being contraries, heaven and hell are, consequently, in complete separation from each other; and to such an extent is the separation carried, that a spirit in hell dares not so much as put forth thence a finger, nor raise out of it the top of his head; for on his doing either the one or the other ever so little, he feels torture and anguish. This, likewise, I have often witnessed.

401. A man who is immersed in the love of self and of the world, feels, so long as he lives in the body, the delight proceeding from them, and finds enjoyment, also, in all the pleasures

which thence derive their origin. But a man who is grounded in love to God and in love towards his neighbor, does not, so long as he lives in the body, manifestly feel the delight proceeding from them, and from the good affections which thence derive their origin, but only a sense of beatitude that is almost imperceptible, because it lies hidden and stored up in his interiors, and is veiled over by the exteriors that belong to the body; whilst it is deadened, also, by the cares of the world. But the states of the two classes are completely changed after death. Then, the delights of the love of self and of the world are turned into painful and direful sensations, being such as are called hell-fire; and, occasionally, into filthy and vile objects corresponding to those pleasures; which, however, (wonderful to relate!) are then delightful to them. But the obscure delight, and almost imperceptible sense of beatitude, which abode in those in the world who were grounded in love to God and in love towards their neighbor, are then turned into the delight of heaven, which is rendered perceptible and sensible in all manner of ways. For that beatitude which lay hidden and stored up in their interiors while they lived in the world, is then revealed, and is brought forth to manifest sensation; for they are then in the spirit, and that delight was the delight of their spirit.

402. All the delights of heaven are conjoined with uses, and are inherent in them, because uses are the good works of love and charity, in the practice of which the angels live; on which account, every one enjoys delights of such a nature as are the uses he performs, and in a degree proportioned to his affection for use. That all the delights of heaven are delights of use, may also appear with certainty from a comparison drawn from the five bodily senses in man. To every sense is given a delight according to its use: the sight has its proper delight, and the hearing its proper delight; and so have the smell, the taste, and the touch. The sight draws its delight from the beauties of color and form; the hearing, from harmonious sounds; the smell, from agreeable odors; and the taste, from savory viands. The uses which all the senses, respectively, perform, are known to those who investigate the subject, and more fully to those who are acquainted with their correspondences. The sight has such a delight attached to it, on account of the use which it performs to the understanding, which is the internal sight. The hearing is attended by such a delight, on account of the use which it administers both to the understanding and to the will, by affording the means of hearkening and attention. The smell has such a delight connected with it, on account of the use which it contributes both to the brain and to the lungs. The taste is united with such a delight, on account of the use which it renders to the stomach, and thence to the whole body, by disposing it to take nourishment. The conjugial delight, which is a purer and more

exquisite delight of touch, surpasses all the others on account of its use, which is the procreation of the human race, and thence of the angels of heaven. These delights are rendered inherent in those organs of sense by an influx from heaven, where every delight is the delight of use, and exists according to it.

403. There were some spirits who imagined, from having imbibed such an opinion in the world, that heavenly happiness consists in a life without occupation, and in being waited on, while taking their ease, by others. But they were told, that happiness could not possibly consist in resting, unoccupied; for if it did, every one would desire to take away the happiness of others to promote his own; and when all desired to do so, none could obtain their desire. It was observed to them further, that such a life would not be an active but an idle one, the subjects of which would fall into a state of torpor; whereas, as they might easily know, without activity of life there cannot be happiness of life, and that, in an active life, rest from occupation is only resorted to for the sake of recreation, that the person might return, with fresh vigor, to the activity of his life. It was afterwards shown them by numerous evidences, that the angelic life consists in performing the good works of charity, which are uses, and that the angels find all their happiness in use, from use, and according to it. In order that they who had the idea that heavenly joy consists in living without occupation, inhaling eternal joy in a state of idleness, might be made ashamed of such notions, it was given them to perceive what the nature of such a life is; when they were convinced that it is of a most melancholy description, and that, all joy thus perishing, they would feel for it, in a little time, only disgust and loathing.

404. Some spirits who thought themselves better informed than others, observed, that their belief, in the world, had been that heavenly joy consists in nothing else but praising and glorifying God, and that such was the active life of heaven. But they were told, that praising and glorifying God, is not such an active life as is meant by that expression; and, besides, that God has no need of being praised and glorified; but that His will is, that His subjects should perform uses, and thus do the good works which are called the goods of charity. Those spirits, however, could not conceive any idea of heavenly joy, but of slavery instead, as connected with the good works of charity. But the angels testified, that the performance of those works is attended with the most perfect freedom, being done from interior affection, and conjoined with unspeakable enjoyment.

405. Nearly all who enter the other life imagine, that a similar hell, or a similar heaven, awaits every one who goes to either; when, nevertheless, the truth is, that there are infinite varieties and diversities in each, and that neither a hell nor a heaven altogether similar is ever allotted to one person as to another; just

216

as there never is found one man, spirit, or angel, exactly like another, not even in the face. When I only thought of two being exactly similar or equal to each other, the angels were shocked at the idea, observing, that every thing that is a one, or a whole, is formed by the harmonious accordance of various parts, and that the one or whole is such in quality as that accordance is: and that it is in this manner that every society of heaven forms one whole, and that all the societies of heaven form one whole collectively; which effect is produced by the Lord alone, through love as the medium.(¹) Uses in the heavens exist, in like manner, with all possible variety and diversity, and the use of one angel is never exactly similar and the same as the use of another; consequently, neither is his capacity of enjoyment. Much more are the delights of every one's use innumerable, all which are similarly various, but still joined together in such an order as mutually to regard each other; just as do the uses of every member, organ, and viscus, in the body, and, still more, those of every vessel and fibre in each member, organ, and viscus; all of which, both collectively and individually, are so connected together, as to regard their own good in another, and, consequently, the good of each in all, and of all in each. From this universal and individual mutual regard, they act as one.

406. I have often conversed with spirits who had newly come from the world respecting the state of eternal life. I observed, that it was important for them to know, who is the Lord of the kingdom into which they had entered, what is the nature of His government, and what its form; for as nothing is more necessary for travellers in the world, on passing into another kingdom, than to know who and of what character is the king, what the nature of his government, and other particulars relating to that kingdom; much more was it necessary to possess such knowledge in the kingdom in which they now were, in which they were to live to eternity. They ought, therefore, to know, that the Lord is the king who governs heaven, and the whole universe, since He who governs the one, governs the other; thus that the kingdom in which they now were is the Lord's, and that the laws of this kingdom are eternal truths, all which are founded in that primary law, that its subjects are to love the Lord above all things, and their neighbor as themselves; and in fact, that now, if they wished to be like the angels, they ought to go still farther, and love their

(¹) That every whole consists of various things, and hence receives form, and quality, and perfection, according to the quality of their harmony and agreement, nn. 457, 3241, 8003. That there is an infinite variety, and in no case is any one thing the same with another. nn. 7236, 9002. In like manner, in the heavens, nn. 5754, 4005, 7236, 7833, 7836, 9002. That hence, all the societies in the heavens, and every angel in a society, are distinct from each other, because in various good and use, nn. 690, 3241, 3519, 3804, 3986, 4067, 4149, 4263, 7236, 7833, 7986. That the divine love of the Lord arranges all into a heavenly form, and conjoins them so that they are as one man, nn. 457, 3986, 5598.

neighbor more than themselves. On hearing these observations, they could make no answer, because they had heard something to the same effect in the life of the body, but did not believe it. They wondered that such love should exist in heaven, and how it could be possible for any one to love his neighbor better than himself. But they were informed, that all things good increase immensely in the other life: and that man's life, while in the body, is of such a nature that he cannot advance farther than to love his neighbor as himself, being immersed in corporeal impediments; but when these are removed, such love becomes purer, and at length like that of the angels, which consists in loving their neighbor more than themselves. For, in heaven, it is delightful to do good to another, and is not delightful to do good to one's self, unless with a view to its becoming another's, consequently, for the sake of another; and this is what is meant by loving one's neighbor more than one's self. It was told them, that the possible existence of such love may be concluded with certainty in the world, from the fact, that some, under the influence of conjugial love, have preferred death, rather than suffer their conjugial partner to be injured; and from the love of parents towards their children, which is such, that a mother would rather encounter starvation herself, than see her infant want food. The same, it was also observed, may be inferred from the existence of sincere friendship, under the influence of which, there are persons who encounter dangers for their friends; and even from the friendship of civility and pretence, which endeavors to emulate such as is sincere, and which induces men to offer the best they have to those for whom they profess a regard, and to make profession of such regard with their lips, though they do not feel it in their heart. Finally, the possible existence of such love was urged from the nature of love itself, its very nature being such, as to find its joy in serving others, not for one's own benefit, but for theirs. But these observations could not be comprehended by those, who loved themselves more than others, and who, in the life of the body, had been greedy after lucre. Least of all could they be understood by misers.

407. A certain spirit, who, in the life of the body, had been in a station of superior power, retained the desire to exercise authority in the other life. But he was told that he was now in another kingdom, which is eternal, and that his authority had died in the world; and that where he was now, no one is esteemed except according to the good and truth, and to the share of the Lord's mercy, of which he is in the enjoyment by virtue of his life in the world. It was observed to him, further, that this kingdom is like those on earth, where people are esteemed for their wealth, and for the favor which they possess with the prince; only the wealth, here, is good and truth, and favor with the prince is the Lord's mercy, which every man experiences according to the character

of his life in the world: and that if he wished to exercise author ity in any other manner, he was a rebel, being now in the king- dom of another Sovereign. On hearing these remarks, he was ashamed.

408. I have conversed with some spirits, who imagined heaven and heavenly joy to consist in being great. But they were told, that the greatest in heaven is he who is the least; for he is called the least who possesses no power or wisdom, and is willing to possess no power or wisdom from himself, but from the Lord. He who in this way is the least, has the greatest happiness; and since he has the greatest happiness, it follows that he is the greatest; for he thus has, from the Lord, power to do all things, and wisdom above all others. What is being the greatest except being the happiest? for to be happiest is what the powerful seek through power, and the rich through riches. It was further told them, that heaven does not consist in desiring to be the least with a view of being the greatest, for he who does this, pants and lusts to be greatest all the while; but it consists in desiring, from the heart, good for others more than for one's self, and in serving them with a view to their happiness, not from any selfish aim of obtaining remuneration, but out of love.

409. Real heavenly joy, such as it is in its essence, cannot be described, because it resides in the inmost recesses of the life of the angels, and thence in all the minutiæ of their thought and affection, and by derivation from these, in all the minutiæ of their speech, and in all the minutiæ of their actions. It is as if their interiors were completely unbound, and set open for the reception of delight and beatitude, which are diffused through every fibre, and thus through the whole frame; whence the per- ception and sensation of them is such as cannot be described : for that which begins in the inmost recesses of all, flows into all the parts, even to the most minute, which thence take their rise, and propagates itself, with continual augmentation, towards the exteriors. Good spirits who are not yet in the perception of that delight, because they are not yet taken up to heaven, on perceiv- ing it flowing from an angel by the sphere of his love, are filled with such delight, that they fall, as it were, into a delicious swoon. This has often occurred to those, who desired to know what heav- enly joy is.

410. There also were certain spirits who desired to know what heavenly joy is, and to whom, therefore, it was granted to have a perception of it to that degree, beyond which they were unable to bear any more. What they perceived, however, was not the joy of angels: it scarcely amounted to the smallest degree of angelic joy; as was granted me to perceive by its being com- municated to me. It was so slight as almost to partake of some- thing rather frigid; and yet they called it most heavenly, it being the inmost joy of which they were receptive. It was proved to

219

me by this circumstance, not only that there are various degrees of the joys of heaven, but also, that the inmost joy of one degree scarcely approaches to the last or middle of another, and further, that when any one receives that which is the inmost to him, he is in the enjoyment of his proper heavenly joy; and that he cannot bear any more interior degree of it, but would find it painful.

411. Certain spirits, not evil ones, fell into a state of repose like that of sleep, and were thus translated, as to the interiors that belonged to their minds, into heaven: for spirits, before their interiors are opened, may be translated into heaven, and instructed respecting the felicity of its inhabitants. I saw them in this state of repose for about half an hour; after which they relapsed into their exteriors in which they had been before, retaining, however, the recollection of what they had seen. They related, that they had been among the angels in heaven, and that they had there seen and perceived amazing objects, all shining as with gold, silver, and precious stones, presenting admirable forms, which were varied in a wonderful manner. They added, that the angels did not take delight in the external things themselves, but in those that they represented, which were things divine, unspeakable, and of infinite wisdom: and that these were the source of their joys; not to mention other things innumerable, not a ten thousandth part of which can be expressed by human languages, nor fall into ideas which partake, in any degree, of materiality.

412. Nearly all who enter the other life are ignorant of what heavenly beatitude and happiness are, because they have no knowledge respecting what, and of what nature, internal joy is, forming their conceptions of it solely from corporeal and worldly gayeties and joys. What they are ignorant of, therefore, they regard as nothing; although corporeal and worldly joys are of no account, respectively. In order, therefore, that the welldisposed, who know not what heavenly joy is, may know and understand it, they are first led to paradisiacal scenes that surpass every idea that imagination could form. They now suppose that they have come into the heavenly paradise; but they are instructed, that this is not, in reality, heavenly happiness. It is therefore granted them to experience interior states of joy, to the inmost of their capacity for perceiving them. They are afterwards led into a state of peace, to the inmost degree that is capable of being opened in them: when they confess, that nothing of its nature can be expressed by words, nor conceived in imagination. Finally, they are brought into a state of innocence, also to the inmost sense of it of which they are capable. Hence it is granted them to know, what spiritual and celestial good truly is.

413. But in order that I might know what, and of what nature, heaven and heavenly joys are, it has frequently, and for a long time together, been granted me by the Lord to have a perception

of the delights of heavenly joys: I thus am able, indeed, to say, that I know what they are, because I have had actual experience of them; but I am totally unable to describe them. Merely, however, that some idea of them may be formed, a few observations shall be offered.

Heavenly joy is an affection of delights and joys innumerable, which compose together a certain common whole, in which common whole, or common affection, are included the harmonies of innumerable affections, which do not come distinctly, but only obscurely, to the perception, because the perception is of the most common or general kind. It nevertheless was granted me to perceive, that innumerable things were included in it, so arranged that they cannot possibly be described. Those innumerable things are such as flow from the order of heaven. Such is the order that prevails in all the individual and most minute particulars of the affection, which are only presented to the mind, and come to the perception, as one most common or general whole, according to the capacity of the person who is their subject. In a word, infinite things, in a form of most perfect order, are contained in every common whole; and there is nothing among them which does not live, and exert an affecting influence; all, in fact, doing so from the inmost recesses: for it is from the inmost recesses that all heavenly joys proceed. I perceived, also, that the joy and delight came as it were from the heart, diffusing themselves most gently through all the inmost fibres, and thence into the collections of fibres, with such an inmost sense of enjoyment, that every fibre felt as if it were nothing but joy and delight, and every thing capable of perception and sensation thence felt, in like manner, all alive with happiness. The joy that belongs to the pleasures of the body, compared with these joys, is like a gross and pungent clot of matter, compared with a pure and most gentle breath of refined air, or *aura*.* I observed, that when I wished to transfer all my delight into another person, there followed a new influx of delight, more interior and more full than the former; and that in proportion to the amount that I desired to impart, was the amount of that which flowed in: and I perceived that this was from the Lord.

414. They who dwell in heaven, are continually advancing towards the vernal season of life, and the more thousands of years they live there, the more delightful and happy is the state of spring to which they attain; and this goes on to eternity, with continual increments, according to the progressions and degrees of their love, charity, and faith. Those of the female sex who

---

* *Aura* is a term employed by the Author throughout his writings, to express an atmosphere of the third or highest degree of purity. For he considers the atmospheres, both in the spiritual and in the natural world, to consist of three degrees, to the lowest of which, being the only one perceptible to the senses, he gives the name of air (*aër*), to the middle, that of ether (*æther*), and to the third or supreme, that of *aura.—N.*

had died old women, quite worn out with age, but who had lived in faith in the Lord, in charity towards their neighbor, and in happy conjugial love with their husband, come more and more, in the course of years, into the flower of youth, accompanied with such beauty, as surpasses every idea of beauty ever perceptible to the sight. Goodness and charity are what model their form, presenting in it the likeness of themselves, and causing the delight and beauty of charity to shine forth from every individual feature of their face, so as to make them the very forms of charity. They have been beheld by some, who were overwhelmed with amazement at the sight. The form of charity, which is seen to the life in heaven, is of such a nature, that charity itself is both that which produces it, and that which is effigied in it; and, in fact, so completely is this the case, that the whole angel, but especially his face, is as it were charity, which both manifestly appears, and is perceived. The form, when viewed, is that of beauty unspeakable, affecting with charity the very inmost life of the mind. In one word, in heaven, to grow old is to grow young. They who have lived in love to the Lord and in charity towards their neighbor, become, in the other life, such forms, and such beauties. All the angels are such forms, in inexhaustible variety: and of these is heaven composed.

OF THE IMMENSITY OF HEAVEN.

415. That the Lord's heaven is immense, may appear from many things which have been stated and shown in the preceding sections; especially from the fact, that the inhabitants of heaven are derived from the human race (see above, nn. 311—317), and not only from that portion of the human race who are born within the limits of the church, but also from that portion of mankind who are born beyond those limits (see nn. 318—328); thus, that it is composed of all who have lived in good from the first origin of this earth. How great a multitude of men exists in the whole of this terrestrial globe, may be concluded by any one who knows any thing about the quarters, countries, and kingdoms of this earth. He who makes the calculation will find, that men die, in this earth, to the number of several thousands every day, and thus, in a year, to the amount of some myriads or millions; and that this has been going on from the first ages, since which there have intervened some thousands of years; and that they all, on their decease, have passed, and are still continually passing, into the spiritual world. How many, however, of these, have become, and now become, angels, it is impossible to say: but I have been told that, in ancient times, there were very many, because men

then thought more interiorly and more spiritually, and thence were in the enjoyment of heavenly affection; but not so many in the succeeding ages, because man, in progress of time, became more external, and began to think more in a natural manner, and thence to be immersed in earthly affection. From these facts it may appear, in the first place, that the extent of heaven, as filled with natives of this earth alone, must be great.

416. That the Lord's heaven is immense, may appear from this fact alone; that all infants or little children, whether born in the church or out of it, are adopted by the Lord, and become angels; the number of whom amounts to a fourth or fifth part of the whole of the human race on this earth. That every infant or little child, wheresoever born, whether in the church or out of it, and whether of pious or of wicked parents, is received, if he dies, by the Lord, is educated in heaven, is instructed according to divine order, and imbued with affections of good, and, through them, with knowledges of truth, and afterwards, as he is perfected in intelligence and wisdom, is introduced into heaven and becomes an angel; may be seen above (nn. 329—345). It may easily, therefore, be concluded, how great a multitude of angels of heaven has existed from them alone, from the beginning of creation to the present time.

417. How immense is the Lord's heaven, may appear with certainty from the fact, that all the planets that are visible to the sight in our solar system, are so many earths; and that, besides these, there are innumerable others in the universe, all full of inhabitants. I have treated of these in a particular work, *On the Earths in the Universe;* from which I will make the following extract:

" That there are numerous earths, with men upon them, who after death become spirits and angels, is a fact well known in the other life; for it is there granted to every one who desires it from the love of truth and thence of use, to converse with the spirits of other earths, and thus to be assured of the existence of a plurality of worlds, and to be instructed, that the human race is not the offspring of one earth alone, but of earths innumerable. I have often conversed on this subject with spirits from our earth, and have observed, that a man of intellectual capacity may learn, from many things with which he is acquainted, that there are numerous earths, and men upon them. He may infer from reason, that such great bodies as' are the planets, some of which surpass this earth in magnitude, are not empty masses, only created to be whirled along and to travel round the sun, and to shed their little ray of light upon a single earth; but that they must be designed for uses far more excellent than this. Whoever believes, as every one ought to believe, that the Divine Being created the universe for no other end than to give existence to the human race, and thence to heaven, **the** human race being the seminary of heaven, cannot but believe also, that there are men wherever there is an earth. That the planets which, as being within the limits of our solar system, are visible before our eyes, are earths, may manifestly be inferred from the fact, that they are bodies of earthy matter, as is evident from their reflecting the light of the sun, and, when viewed through a telescope, not appearing like stars glowing with flame, but like earths variegated with lights and shadows; and also from this, that, in the same manner as our earth, they are carried round the sun, and travel through the path of the zodiac, whence they have their years, and the seasons of the year, spring, summer, autumn, and winter; and that, besides, in the same manner as our earth, they revolve about their axis, whence they have their days, and the times of the day, morning, noon, evening, and night; in addition to which, some of them have moons, which are called their satellites, which move around them in stated periods, as the moon does round our earth; and the planet Saturn, because his distance from the sun is very great, is encompassed by a great luminous ring, which gives much though reflected light to that earth. Who that is acquainted with these facts, and thinks under the influence of reason, will pretend to say, that these are empty bodies? I have observed, moreover, when in conversation with spirits, that man may readily believe that there are more earths in the universe than one, when he considers that the starry heaven is so immense, and the stars in it so innumerable, every one of which, in its place, or in its system, is a sun, and like the sun of our world, but varying in magnitude. Whoever rightly considers this, must conclude, that all that immense apparatus cannot but be a means provided for the existence of a certain end, and that end the final end of creation; which is, the existence of a heavenly kingdom, in which the Divine Being may dwell with angels and men. For the visible universe, or the sky above us, lighted up with stars so innumerable, which are so many suns, is only a means provided for the existence of earths, and that men might exist upon them, out of whom might be formed a heavenly kingdom. From these facts the rational man cannot do otherwise than think, that so immense a means, provided for so great an end, was not created with a view to the production of the human race from one earth alone. What would this be for the Divine Being, who is Infinite, to whom thousands, yea, myriads of earths, all full of inhabitants, would be but little, indeed, scarcely any thing? There are certain spirits whose sole study is to acquire knowledges, because in these alone they feel delight, and to whom, therefore, for that object, it is permitted to travel about, and even to pass beyond the bounds of this solar system into the systems belonging to other suns. These have informed me, that there not only are earths, inhabited by men, in this solar system, but beyond it also, in the starry heavens, in immense numbers. These spirits are from the planet Mercury. It has been calculated, that if there were a million of earths in the universe, and in every earth three hundred millions of men; and if two hundred generations existed in the period of six thousand years; and if a space of three cubic ells were allotted to every man or spirit—all of that number, men or spirits, collected into one body, would not fill the space that this earth does, and indeed, little more than the space occupied by a satellite of one of the planets. This would be a space in the universe so small as to be almost invisible; for it is with difficulty that a satellite is distinguished by the naked eye. What would this be for the Creator of the universe, to whom the whole universe, filled in this manner, would not be sufficient? for He is Infinite. I have conversed on these subjects with the angels, who observed, that they had a similar idea of the paucity of the human race in respect to the Infinity of the Creator; but that, nevertheless, they do not think from spaces, but from states; and that, according to their ideas, earths to the number of as many myriads as can possibly be conceived, would still be absolutely nothing to the Lord."

Respecting the earths in the universe, with their inhabitants, and the spirits and angels who come from them, the work above named may be consulted. The facts it relates were revealed and shown to me, in order that it might be known, that the Lord's heaven is immense, and that the whole of it is peopled from the human race; and also, that our Lord is everywhere acknowledged as the God of heaven and earth.

418. That the Lord's heaven is immense, may also be evident from this consideration: That heaven, viewed collectively, is in form as one man, and actually corresponds to all the parts, even to the most particular, that exist in man; and that this correspondence can never be completely filled up, since it is not only a correspondence with all the individual members, organs, and viscera of the body in general, but also, particularly and individually, with all and each of the minute viscera and organs included within the former, yea, with the individual vessels and fibres; and not with these only, but also with the organic substances which interiorly receive the influx of heaven, whence man possesses interior activities subservient and conducive to the activities of his mind. For whatever exists interiorly in man, exists in forms, which are substances; and whatever does not exist in substances as its subjects, is nothing at all. All these have correspondence with heaven (as may be seen in the Section on the Correspondence between all things of Heaven and all things of Man, nn. 87—102). This correspondence can never be filled up entirely, since the more angelic societies there are, corresponding to one member, the more perfect does heaven become; for, in the heavens, all perfection increases as the num-

15   225

bers do. The reason that, in the heavens, perfection increases as the numbers do, is, because all have one end in view, and all unanimously look to that end. That end is, the common good; and when this is the governing object, every individual derives good from the common good, and, from the good of every individual, good is derived to the community. This takes place, because the Lord turns all who dwell in heaven towards Himself (see above, n. 123), and thus causes them to be one in Himself. That the unanimity and concord of many, especially when derived from such an origin, and combined in such a bond, must be productive of perfection, every one may discover, if he views the subject from some measure of enlightened reason.

419. It has been granted me to behold the extent of the heaven that is inhabited, and also of that which is not inhabited; when I saw that the extent of heaven which is not inhabited is so vast, that, even if there existed myriads of earths, and in every earth as great a multitude of men as in ours, it could not be filled to eternity. (On which subject, also, see the work *On the Earths in the Universe*, n. 168.)

420. That heaven, instead of being so immense, is of little extent, is an opinion entertained by some from certain passages of the Word understood according to their literal sense; as from those in which it is said, that only the poor are received in heaven: that none but the elect can be accepted; that only those belonging to the church can be admitted, and not those without it; that it is only for those for whom the Lord intercedes; that it will be closed when full, and that the time for this is predetermined. Such persons are not aware, that heaven will never be closed; that there is not any time for such closing predetermined, nor are its inhabitants limited to any definite number; that those are called the elect who are grounded in the life of good and truth;[1] and those the poor who are not possessed of the knowledges of good and truth, and yet desire them; who also, by virtue of that desire, are called them that hunger.[2] Those who have conceived the opinion of the small extent of heaven through not having understood the Word, have no other idea, than that heaven is confined to one spot, where all its inhabitants compose one assembly; when, nevertheless, heaven consists of innumerable societies. (See above, nn. 41—50.) They also have no other

[1] That those are the elect who are established in the life of good and truth, nn. 3755, 3900. That there is not any election nor reception into heaven of mere mercy, as is generally understood, but according to life, nn. 5057, 5058. That the Lord's mercy is not immediate, but mediate, that is, is shown to those who live according to His precepts, whom, from a principle of mercy, He leads continually in the world, and afterwards to eternity, nn. 8700, 10,659.

[2] That by the poor, in the Word, are understood those who are spiritually poor, that is, who are in ignorance of truth, but still desire to be instructed, nn. 9209, 9253, 10,227. That they are said to hunger and thirst, which is to desire the knowledges of good and of truth, by which there is introduction into the church and heaven, nn. 4958, 10,227.

idea, than that heaven is bestowed on every one by immediate mercy, and thus that nothing more is required for its enjoyment, than to be let in, and received, of mere favor. They do not understand, that the Lord, of His mercy, leads every one who receives Him, and that those receive Him who live according to the laws of Divine Order, which are the precepts of love and faith; and that to be thus led by the Lord, from infancy to the end of a man's life in the world, and afterwards to eternity, is the mercy which is meant by that mode of speaking. Be it known, therefore, to such, that every man is born for heaven; and that he is received in heaven who receives heaven in himself while in the world, and he is excluded who does not.

227

OF THE WORLD OF SPIRITS,

AND

OF THE STATE OF MAN AFTER DEATH.

WHAT THE WORLD OF SPIRITS IS.

421. The world of spirits is not heaven, nor yet hell, but is a place or state intermediate between the two. Thither man first goes after death; and having completed the period of his stay there, according to his life in the world, he is either elevated into heaven, or cast into hell.

422. The world of spirits is a place intermediate between heaven and hell; and it also is the intermediate state of man after death. That it is an intermediate place, was made evident to me by the fact, that the hells are beneath it, and the heavens above it; and that it is an intermediate state, by the fact, that a man, so long as he is there, is not, as yet, either in heaven or in hell. The state of heaven, as existing with man, is the conjunction, in him, of good and truth; and the state of hell is the conjunction, in him, of evil and falsity. When, in the man, now a spirit,* good is conjoined with truth, he passes into heaven, because, as just remarked, that conjunction is heaven, as existing with him. But when, in the man, now a spirit, evil is conjoined with falsity, he passes into hell, because that conjunction is hell as existing with him. These conjunctions are effected in the world of spirits, since man is then in an intermediate state. It is much the same, whether we say, the conjunction of the understanding and the will, or, the conjunction of truth and good.

423. Something shall here be first premised respecting the conjunction of the understanding and the will, and its resemblance to the conjunction of good and truth; since that con-

---

* The Author here uses the expression *homo-spiritus*,—"man-spirit," as one word. It is applied by him to the spirit of a man who has newly entered the spiritual world, when he is, as yet, in his *externals*, much of what belonged to him as a man in the world, adhering to him still. But as the expression "man-spirit," sounds very harsh in English, and the Latin words, thus combined, are used by the Author but a very few times, they are in every instance, in this translation, rendered as above,—"man, now a spirit," except at n. 552, where, for the reason stated in a note at that place, a somewhat different rendering was unavoidable.—*N.*

228

junction is effected in the world of spirits. Man possesses an understanding, and he possesses a will. The understanding receives truths, and is formed from them; and the will receives goods, and is formed from them; on which account, whatever a man concludes in his understanding, and thence thinks, he calls true, and whatever he wills, and thence thinks, he calls good. Man is able to think from his understanding, and thence to apprehend, what is true, and also what is good; but still he does not so think from his will, unless he both wills it to be so, and acts accordingly. When he makes it an object of will, and acts, in consequence, according to it, it resides both in his understanding and in his will, consequently, in the man himself. For the understanding alone does not constitute the man, neither does the will alone, but the understanding and the will together: what, therefore, is in both, is in the man himself, and is appropriated to him. What is only in the understanding, is indeed present with the man, but is not in him. It is only an object of his memory, and a matter with which he is acquainted therein deposited,—a thing of which he is able to think when he is not retired within himself, but is drawn out of himself in company with others; consequently, he is able to speak and reason respecting it, and can assume feigned affections and gestures according to it.

424. It is provided that man should be able to think from the understanding, without thinking at the same time from the will, in order that he might be capable of being reformed. For man is reformed by means of truths, and truths, as just observed, are objects of the understanding. Man is born into all evil as to his will, whence, of himself, he wills good to none but to himself alone: and whoever wills good to himself alone, takes pleasure in the misfortunes that befall others, especially when they tend to his own advantage: for he desires to appropriate to himself the goods of all others, whether consisting in honors or in wealth, and, so far as he accomplishes it, he is inwardly pleased. In order that this state of the will may be amended and reformed, it is given to man to be able to understand truths, and by means of them to subdue the affections of evil which spring from the will. It is on this account that man is enabled to think truths from the understanding, and also to speak them, and to do them; but still he cannot think them from the will, before he is such in quality, as to will and do them from himself, that is, from his heart. When man is such in quality, the truths which he thinks from his understanding are objects of his faith, and the truths which he thinks from his will are objects of his love; wherefore faith and love then enter into conjunction in him, as his understanding and will do.

425. In proportion, therefore, as truths, as being objects of the understanding, are conjoined with goods. as being objects

of the will; thus, in proportion as a man wills truths and thence does them; he has in himself heaven; since, as stated above, the conjunction of good and truth is heaven. But in proportion as falsities, as being objects of the understanding, are conjoined with evils, as being objects of the will, a man has in himself hell; since the conjunction of falsity and evil is hell. In proportion, however, as truths, as being objects of the understanding, are not conjoined with goods, as being objects of the will, the man is in an intermediate state. Almost every man, at the present day, is in such a state, as to be acquainted with truths, and from such acquaintance, and also from the understanding, to think them, and either to do much of what they require, or little, or nothing; or else, to act in opposition to them from the love of evil, and thence from the belief of falsity. In order, therefore, that such a man may be fitted either for heaven or for hell, he, after death, is first translated into the world of spirits, where the conjunction of good and truth is effected for those who are to be elevated into heaven, and the conjunction of evil and falsity for those who are to be cast into hell. For it is not allowable for any one in heaven, nor for any one in hell, to have a divided mind, that is, to make one thing the object of his understanding, and another the object of his will; but that which is the object of any one's will must also be that of his understanding, and that which is the object of his understanding must also be that of his will. In heaven, therefore, every one, the object of whose will is good, must have truth as the object of his understanding: and in hell, every one, the object of whose will is evil, must have falsity as the object of his understanding. On this account, in the world of spirits, falsities, with the good, are removed, and truths are given them suitable and conformable to their good: and truths are removed with the evil, and falsities are given them suitable and conformable to their evil. From these statements may be evident, what the world of spirits is.

426. The world of spirits contains a great number of inhabitants, because it is the region in which all first assemble, and where all are examined, and are prepared for their final abode. Their stay there is not limited to any fixed period: some do but just enter it, and are presently either taken up to heaven or cast down to hell: some remain there only a few weeks; and some for several years, but never more than thirty. The varieties in the length of their stay depend upon the correspondence, or non-correspondence, between their interiors and their exteriors. But in what way a man, in that world, is led from one state into another, and is prepared for his final abode, will be stated in the following Sections.

427. As soon as men, after their decease, enter the world of spirits, they are accurately distinguished by the Lord into classes.

The wicked are immediately connected by invisible bonds with the society of hell, in which they had been, as to their governing love, while in the world: and the good are immediately connected, in a similar way, with the society of heaven, in which they had been, while in the world, as to their love, charity, and faith. But notwithstanding they are thus distinctly classed, all meet in that world, and converse together, when they desire it, who had been friends and acquaintances in the life of the body; especially wives and husbands, brothers and sisters. I saw a father conversing with his six sons, all of whom he recognized; and many others conversing with their relations and friends: but as they were different in disposition, resulting from their course of life in the world, after a short time they were parted. But those who go from the world of spirits to heaven, and those who thence go to hell, afterwards neither see nor know each other any more, unless they are similar in disposition, and similar in love. The reason that all who had been acquainted see one another in the world of spirits, and not in heaven nor in hell, is, because, while they inhabit the world of spirits, they are brought into states similar to those which they experienced in the life of the body, passing from one into another; but afterwards, all are brought into a permanent state, similar to that of the governing love; and then, one individual only knows another from the similitude of his love; for similitude conjoins, and dissimilitude parts asunder (as shown above, nn. 41—50).

428. As the world of spirits is an intermediate state between heaven and hell, as these exist in man, so is it also an intermediate place. Beneath are the hells, and above are the heavens. All the hells are closed in the direction of that world, the only openings being through holes and clefts like those of rocks, and through chasms of wide extent; all which are guarded, lest any one should come out except by permission; which, however, is sometimes granted, when any urgent necessity requires it; as will be explained hereafter. Heaven, likewise, is securely shut in on all sides, nor is any approach open to any heavenly society, except by a narrow way, the entrance of which is also guarded. Those outlets and these entrances are what are called, in the Word, the gates and doors of hell and of heaven.

429. The world of spirits appears like a valley lying between mountains and rocks, here and there sinking and rising. The doors and gates leading to the heavenly societies do not appear, except to those who are prepared for heaven; nor can they be found by any others. To every society there is one entrance from the world of spirits, beyond which there is one path, but which, as it ascends, is parted into several branches. Neither do the gates and doors leading to the hells appear to any but those who are about to enter them. To such, they then are opened; when there appear dusky and seemingly sooty caverns, tending ob-

liquely downwards to a great depth, where, again, there are several doors. Through those caverns are exhaled horrible stenches and foul smells; which good spirits shun, because they excite in them aversion, but evil spirits seek, because they yield them delight; for as every one, in the world, takes delight in his own evil, so, after death, is he delighted with the stench to which his evil corresponds. Such persons may be compared, in this respect, to birds and beasts of prey, such as ravens, wolves, and swine, which, on scenting the stench proceeding from carrion and dung, fly or run eagerly to the spot. I once heard a certain spirit uttering a loud cry as if seized with inward torture, when he caught the scent of an exhalation that emanated from heaven; and I saw the same spirit rendered composed and joyful, by the stench of an exhalation that emanated from hell.

430. There also exist with every man two gates, one of which opens towards hell, and is opened to the evils and falsities thence proceeding; and the other opens towards heaven, and is opened to the goods and truths which flow from thence. In those who are immersed in evil and thence in falsity, the gate of hell is open, and only a few rays of light from heaven enter by influx through chinks, as it were, above: through which influx, man receives the ability to think, to reason, and to converse. But in those who are grounded in good and thence in truth, the gate of heaven is open. For there are two ways which lead to man's rational mind; a superior or internal way, by which enter good and truth from the Lord; and an inferior or external way, by which enter evil and falsity from hell. The rational mind of man is stationed in the centre, to which the two ways tend: whence, in proportion as light is admitted into it from heaven, the man is rational; but in proportion as that light is not admitted, he is not rational, how much soever he may appear to himself to be so. These facts are stated, that the nature of the correspondence of man with heaven and with hell, may also be known. His rational mind, while in the course of its formation, corresponds to the world of spirits; whatever is above it corresponds to heaven, and whatever is below it to hell. The parts above it are opened, and those below it are shut against the influx of evil and falsity, with those who are prepared for heaven: but the parts below it are opened, and those above it are shut against the influx of good and truth, with those who are prepared for hell. The latter, in consequence, cannot do otherwise than look beneath them, that is, to hell; and the former cannot do otherwise than look above them, that is, to heaven. To look above is to look to the Lord, He being the common centre to which all things belonging to heaven look; but to look beneath is to look away from the Lord to the opposite centre, to which all things belonging to hell look and tend. (See above, nn. 123, 124.)

431. By spirits, when mentioned in the preceding pages, are meant the sojourners in the world of spirits; but by angels, the inhabitants of heaven.

THAT, AS TO HIS INTERIORS, EVERY MAN IS A SPIRIT.

432. Whoever rightly considers the subject, may be aware, that the body does not think, because it is material; but that the soul does think, because it is spiritual. The soul of man, respecting the immortality of which so much has been written, is his spirit; for this is immortal as to every thing that belongs to it; and this it is that thinks in the body. For the spirit is a spiritual existence, and that which is spiritual receives that which is spiritual, and lives in a spiritual manner; and to live in a spiritual manner is to exercise thought and will. All the rational life, therefore, which appears in the body, belongs to the spirit, and nothing whatever of it to the body. For the body, as just observed, is material, and materiality, which is what is proper to the body, is a thing added, and almost, as it were, adjoined, to the spirit, in order that the spirit of man might live, and perform uses, in the natural world; all the objects of which are material, and, in themselves, void of life. Now, since that which is material does not live, but only that which is spiritual, it may appear with certainty, that whatever lives in man, is his spirit, and that the body only serves it mechanically, just as an instrument serves a living motive force. It is usual to say, indeed, respecting an instrument, that it acts, moves, or strikes; but to suppose that these powers belong to the instrument, and not to him who acts, moves, or strikes, by it, is a fallacy.

433. Since every thing that lives in the body, and, by virtue of such life, acts and feels, is solely of the spirit, and nothing of it whatever is of the body; it follows, that the spirit is the real man; or, what is much the same, that man, regarded in himself, is a spirit. It also follows, that the spirit exists in a form similar to that of the body: for whatever lives and feels in man belongs to his spirit: and there is nothing in him whatever, from the crown of his head to the sole of his foot, which does not live and feel; wherefore, when the body is separated from his spirit, which is called dying, the man continues to be a man, and lives still. I have heard from heaven, that some who die, while they lie upon the bier, before they are resuscitated, actually think in their cold body, and are not conscious but what they are alive still, except with the difference, that they cannot move a single material particle, all these belonging to the body alone.

434. Man cannot exercise thought and will at all, unless there be a subject, which is a substance, from and in which he exerts

233

those faculties. Whatever is imagined to exist, and yet to be destitute of a substantial subject, is nothing. This may be known from the circumstance, that man cannot see, without an organ which is the subject of his sight, nor hear, without an organ which is the subject of his hearing. Without these, sight and hearing are nothing whatever, and can have no existence. It is the same with thought, which is internal sight; and with apprehension, which is internal hearing: unless these existed in, and from, substances, which are organic forms, and are the subjects of those faculties, they could not exist at all. From these truths it may appear with certainty, that the spirit of a man is equally in a form, and *that* the human form; and that it equally possesses senses, and organs of sense, when it is separate from the body, as when it was in it; and that the whole of the life of the eye, and the whole of the life of the ear,—in one word, the whole of the sensitive life that man enjoys, does not belong to his body, but to his spirit; for his spirit dwells in them, and in the most minute particulars that enter into their composition. It is from this cause, that spirits see, hear, and feel, as well as men do; only, after their separation from the body, they do not exercise those senses in the natural world, but in the spiritual. The reason that the spirit exercises sensation in a natural manner while in the body, is, because it then acts through the material nature which is added to it; but even then it enjoys sensation, at the same time, in a spiritual manner, by the exercise of thought and will.

435. These truths are mentioned, in order that the rational man may be convinced, that man, viewed in himself, is a spirit, and that the corporeal frame, which is added to him for the sake of the functions he has to exercise in the natural and material world, is not the man, but only an instrument that is wielded by his spirit. But confirmations of an experimental kind are preferable, because rational arguments transcend the capacity of many, and, by those who have confirmed themselves in the opposite opinion, are made to appear doubtful by reasonings drawn from the fallacies of the senses. It is usual for those who have confirmed themselves in the contrary opinion to think, that beasts, also, have life and sensation, and thus, that they too have a spiritual nature, similar to that of men; which nevertheless, with them, dies with the body. The spiritual nature, however, of beasts, is not of the same kind as the spiritual nature of man. For man has (what beasts have not) an inmost degree or region of the soul, into which the Divine Being enters by influx, elevates it to Himself, and thus conjoins it with Himself. It is from this cause that man, differently from beasts, is able to think of God, and of the divine things that belong to heaven and the church, and to love God from and in those things, and thus to be conjoined to Him; and whatever is capable of being

conjoined to the Divine Being, is incapable of being dissipated; whereas, whatever is not capable of being conjoined to the Divine Being, is dissipated unavoidably. That inmost degree or region of the soul, which man has, and which beasts are without, was treated of above (n. 39); and I will here repeat what was there stated, because, it is of importance that the fallacies that have been embraced through ignorance of the difference between man and beasts, should be dispersed; and those fallacies prevail with many, who, through the want of knowledges on the subject, and through not having their understanding opened, are incapable of forming rational conclusions respecting it for themselves. The passage alluded to is as follows: "I will here mention a certain arcanum respecting the angels of the three heavens, which never before entered the mind of any one, because no man has hitherto understood the doctrine of degrees. (On, which see n. 38.) There is in every angel, and also in every man, an inmost and supreme degree, or a certain inmost and supreme region of the soul, and faculty of reception, into which the Divine Sphere of the Lord first or proximately flows, and from which it regulates the other interior receptive faculties, which follow in succession, according to the degrees of order. This inmost or supreme region of the soul may be called the Lord's entrance to angels and men, and his most immediate dwelling-place in them. It is owing to his having this inmost or supreme abode for the Lord, that man is man, and is distinguished from the brute animals, which do not possess it. It is by virtue of this, that man, differently from animals, with respect to all the interiors, or the faculties belonging to his internal and external mind, is capable of being elevated by the Lord to himself, of believing in him, of being affected with love to him, and thus of seeing him; and is capable of receiving intelligence and wisdom, and of conversing in a rational manner; and it is also by virtue of this, that man lives to eternity. But the arrangements and provisions that are made by the Lord in this inmost region, do not come manifestly to the perception of any angel, because they are above his sphere of thought, and transcend his wisdom."

436. That, as to his interiors, man is a spirit, has been granted me to know by much experience, the whole of which, were I to adduce it, would fill many sheets. I have conversed with spirits as a spirit, and I have conversed with them as a man in the body; and when I conversed with them as a spirit, they were not aware but that I was a spirit myself; and they saw that I was in human form, as they were. It was thus that my interiors appeared before them; for, when I conversed with them as a spirit, my material body did not appear.

437. That, as to his interiors, man is a spirit, may appear with certainty from the fact, that after his body is separated

from him, as occurs when he dies, he still continues to live a man as before. That I might be fully convinced of this truth, it has been granted me to converse with almost all whom I ever knew when they lived in the body, with some for a few hours, with some for weeks and months, and with some for years. This was granted me, chiefly to the end, that I might be assured of the truth myself, and that I might testify it to others.

438. To what has already been stated, may be added, that every man, even while he lives in the body, is, as to his spirit, in society with spirits, although he is not conscious of it; a good man being, through them as mediums, in an angelic society, and a bad man in an infernal society; and that he passes into the same society after death. This has often been declared and shown to those, who, after death, came among spirits. The man does not indeed appear in that society as a spirit, while he lives in the world, by reason that he then thinks in a natural manner: but persons who think abstractedly from the body, being then in the spirit, do sometimes appear in their own society. On those occasions, however, they are accurately distinguished by the spirits who dwell there from the others; for they walk about in meditation, do not speak, and do not look at the other spirits, behaving as if they did not see them; and as soon as any spirit accosts them, they vanish.

439. To illustrate the truth, that, as to his interiors, man is a spirit, I will relate, from experience, what it is for a man to be withdrawn from the body, and what it is to be carried of the spirit into another place.

440. With respect to the first, that is, being withdrawn from the body, it is effected thus: The person is brought into a certain state, which is intermediate between sleeping and waking. When he is in this state, he cannot possibly know but that he is wide awake. All the senses are as active as when the body is perfectly awake, not only the senses of sight and hearing, but (what is wonderful) that of touch also, which is then more exquisite than it ever can be when the body is awake. In this state, likewise, spirits and angels are seen in complete reality; they also are heard to speak, and (what is wonderful) are felt by touch, scarcely any thing of the body being then interposed between them and the person who beholds them. This is the state, of which it is said, by those who have experienced it, that they were *absent from the body*, and that *whether they were in the body or out of the body they could not tell.** I have only been let into this state three or four times, merely that I might know the nature of it, and might be assured, likewise, that spirits and angels enjoy all the senses, and that man, as to his spirit, does so too, when he is withdrawn from the body.

* As the Apostle Paul, 2 Cor. xii. 2, 8.—*N.*

441. As to the other state,—that of being carried of the spirit into another place,—it has been shown me, by actual experience, but only twice or thrice, what is its nature, and how it is effected. I will mention a single instance. Walking through the streets of a city, and through fields, and being at the time in conversation with spirits, I was not aware but that I was awake, and in the use of my sight, as at other times. I thus walked on without mistaking the way, being, at the same time, in vision, beholding groves, rivers, palaces, houses, men, and other objects. But after walking thus for hours, I suddenly returned into my bodily sight, and discovered that I was in a different place. Being exceedingly astonished at this, I perceived that I had been in the state experienced by those, of whom it is said, that they were *carried of the spirit to another place.** While it continues, the length of the way is not reflected on, though it were many miles; nor the time occupied in the journey, though it were many hours or days; nor is there any sense of fatigue. The person is also led, without mistaking the road, through ways that he did not know, to the place of his destination.

442. But these two states of man, which are states belonging to him when he is in his interiors, or, what amounts to the same, when he is in the spirit, are extraordinary ones, and were only shown me that I might know the nature of them, the existence of such states being known in the church. But to converse with spirits, and to be among them as one of themselves, has been granted me when fully awake as to the body; and the privilege has now been continued to me for many years.

443. That, as to his interiors, man is a spirit, may be further confirmed from the facts advanced and explained above, where it was shown that the inhabitants of heaven and hell are all from the human race (nn. 311—317).

444. By the proposition, that, as to his interiors, man is a spirit, is meant, that he is a spirit as to every thing belonging to his thought and will; for these are actually the interior things which cause a man to be a man; and which make him such a man, in quality, as he is as to those faculties.

OF MAN'S RESUSCITATION FROM THE DEAD, AND ENTRANCE INTO ETERNAL LIFE.

445 When the body is no longer capable of discharging its functions in the natural world, corresponding to the thoughts and affections of its spirit, which are derived from the spiritual world, the man is said to die. This occurs, when the respiratory motions of the lungs, and the systolic motions of the heart, cease.

---

* As was experienced by Philip (Acts viii. 39), and was common with the prophets. (1 Kings xviii. 12; 2 Kings ii. 16).—*N.*

Nevertheless, the man does not die, but is only separated from the corporeal frame which was of use to him in the world : the man himself lives. It is affirmed, that the man himself lives, because a man is not such by virtue of his body, but by virtue of his spirit; since it is the spirit in man that thinks, and thought, together with affection, is what makes him a man. It hence is evident, that man, when he dies, only passes out of one world into another. On this account, death, in the Word, in its internal sense, signifies resurrection, and the continuation of life.(¹)

446. The inmost communication of the spirit with the body takes place with the respiration, and with the motion of the heart, the thought communicating with the respiration, and the affection that belongs to love with the heart;(²) wherefore, when those two motions cease in the body, the separation immediately ensues. Those two motions,—the respiratory motion of the lungs and the systolic motion of the heart,—form the bonds, on the rupture of which the spirit is left by itself; and the body, being now destitute of the life of its spirit, grows cold, and putrefies. The reason that the inmost communication of the spirit of man with his body takes place with the respiration and with the heart, is, because all the vital motions depend on these, not only in the body generally, but in every part.(³)

447. Man's spirit, after the separation, remains a little time in the body, but not longer than till the total cessation of the motion of the heart; which takes place sooner or later according to the nature of the disease of which the man dies. With some, the motion of the heart continues a long while after the body is apparently dead, but with others, not so long. As soon as this motion ceases, the man is resuscitated: but this is effected by the Lord alone. By resuscitation is meant, the withdrawing of the spirit of man from his body, and its introduction into the spiritual world; which is commonly called resurrection. The reason that a man's spirit is not separated from his body before the motion of the heart has ceased, is, because the heart corresponds to the affection that belongs to the love, which is the very life of man; for it is from love that every one derives the vital heat :(⁴) wherefore so long as this motion* continues, that corre-

---

(¹) That death, in the Word, signifies resurrection, since, when man dies, his life is still continued, nn. 3498, 3505, 4618, 4621, 6036, 6222.

(²) That the heart corresponds to the will, thus likewise to the affection which belongs to the love; and that the respiration of the lungs corresponds to the understanding, thus to the thought, n. 3888. That the heart, in the Word, hence signifies the will and love, nn. 7542, 9050, 10,336. And that the soul signifies understanding, faith, and truth ; hence, from the soul and from the heart, signifies, from the understanding, faith, and truth, and from the will, love, and good, nn. 2930, 9050. Of the correspondence of the heart and lungs with the Grand Man or heaven, nn. 3883—3896.

(³) That the pulse of the heart and the respiration of the lungs prevail in the body throughout, and flow mutually into every part, nn. 3887, 3889, 3890.

(⁴) That love is the *esse* of man's life, n. 5002. That love is spiritual heat, and that thence originates the actual vitality of man, nn. 1589, 2146, 4906, 7081—7086, 9954, 10,740. That affection is the continuous derivation of love, n. 3938.

* The word in the original is here *conjunctio;* but that this has been written or printed by mistake for the very different word *motus,* appears evident from the whole

238

spondence continues, and, consequently, the life of the spirit in the body.

448. In what manner resuscitation is effected, has not only been related to me, but has also been shown me by actual experience. I was myself made the subject of that experience, in order that I might fully know how the great change is accomplished.

449. I was brought into a state of insensibility as to the bodily senses, and thus nearly into the state of dying persons; the interior life, nevertheless, remaining entire, together with the faculty of thought, that I might observe, and retain in my memory, the particulars of the process that I was about to undergo, being such as are experienced by those who are being resuscitated from the dead. I perceived that the respiration of the body was almost taken away, the interior respiration, which is that of the spirit, remaining conjoined with a slight and tacit respiration of the body. There was opened, in the first place a communication with the Lord's celestial kingdom as to the pulsation of the heart, because that kingdom corresponds to the heart in man.([5]) Angels belonging to that kingdom were also seen, some at a distance, and two sitting near my head. By their means, all affection proper to myself was taken away; but thought and perception still continued. I was in this state for some hours. The spirits who were around me then withdrew, supposing that I was dead. There was also perceived an aromatic odor, like that of an embalmed corpse; for when celestial angels are present, the effluvium of the corpse is perceived as an aromatic perfume,* on smelling which, spirits are unable to approach. By this means, also, evil spirits are driven away from the spirit of a man, when he is first introduced into eternal life. The angels who sat at my head did not speak, but only communicated their thoughts with mine. When their thoughts, thus communicated, are received, the angels know that the man's spirit is in such a state, as to be capable of being drawn out of the body. The communication of their thoughts was effected by directing the aspect of their countenances on mine; for it is by this means that communications of thoughts are produced in heaven. As thought and perception remained with me, in order that I might know and remember how resuscitation is

context. It is not the cessation of the conjunction between the spirit and the body that the Author is immediately treating of, but the *cause* of the cessation of that conjunction; which he affirms to be, by the termination of the correspondence between them, through the cessation of the motion of the heart.—*N.*

([5]) That the heart corresponds to the Lord's celestial kingdom, and the lungs to His spiritual kingdom, nn. 3635, 3886, 3887.

* This may serve to explain what many readers have met with, as related by authors of good credit, concerning certain persons of eminent piety, who are said to have died in the *odor of sanctity*, from the fragrancy that issued (in appearance) from their bodies after death.—*H.*—To this the author of the present translation can add, that he has himself known at least one undeniable instance of the kind.—*N.*

accomplished, I perceived that those angels first examined what my thoughts were, to see if they were similar to those of dying persons, which are usually engaged about eternal life; and that they wished to keep my mind occupied with such thoughts. It was told me afterwards, that a man's spirit is kept in the last thoughts that he had when his body was expiring, till he returns to the thoughts that flow from the general or governing affection that possessed him in the world. It was particularly given me to perceive, and to feel, also, that there was a drawing, and, as it were, a pulling out, of the interiors belonging to my mind, thus of my spirit, from the body; and it was told me, that this proceeded from the Lord, and that it is this which effects the resurrection.

450. The celestial angels who thus minister to the resuscitated person, do not leave him, because they love every one; but if the spirit is such in quality that he cannot longer continue in the company of celestial angels, he feels a desire to depart from them. When he does so, angels of the Lord's spiritual kingdom come to him, by whom the use of light is given; for, previously, he saw nothing, but only exercised his thoughts. It was also shown me how this is done. Those angels seemed to unroll, as it were, the coat of the left eye towards the nose, that the eye might be opened, and the faculty of sight imparted. It appears to the spirit as if such an operation were actually performed; but it is only an appearance. After the coat of the eye has seemed to be thus drawn off, a lucid but indistinct appearance is observed, like that which, on first awaking from sleep, a man sees through his eye-lids before he opens them. This indistinct lucid appearance, as seen by me, was of a sky-blue color: but I was afterwards informed, that there are varieties in the color, as seen by different persons. After this, there is a sensation as if something were gently drawn off the face; and when this operation is completed, the resuscitated person is introduced into a state of spiritual thought. That drawing off of something from the face, is likewise, however, only an appearance; and by it is represented the passing from the state of natural thought into the state of spiritual thought. The angels use the utmost caution lest any idea should proceed from the resuscitated person but such as partakes of love. All this being done, they tell him, that he is now a spirit. After the spiritual angels have imparted to the new-born spirit the use of light, they render him all the kind offices which, in that state, he can possibly desire, and instruct him respecting the things that exist in the other life, as far as he is capable of comprehending them. But if the resuscitated person is not of such a character as to be willing to receive instruction, he desires to withdraw from the company of those angels. The angels, notwithstanding, do not leave him, but he separates himself from

their society : for the angels love every one, and desire nothing more than to perform kind offices to all, to give them instruc- tion, and to take them to heaven; in which consists their supreme delight. When the spirit has thus separated himself from the society of the angels, he is taken charge of by good spirits, who, while he remains in their company, also do him all sorts of kind offices. If, however, his life in the world had been of such a nature that he cannot abide in the company of the good, he likewise desires to be away from them. This conduct he repeats during a shorter or longer period of time, and in fewer or more instances, till he becomes associated with such spirits as completely agree with his life in the world : in their company, he finds his own life; and, what is wonderful, he then pursues a similar course of life to that which he had led in the world.

451. But this commencing state of man's life after death does not continue more than a few days : but how he is afterwards led on from one state to another, and at last either into heaven or into hell, will be related in the following Sections; for with this process, also, I have been made acquainted by abundant experience.

452. I have conversed with some on the third day after their decease; when the process had been completed that is described just above, nn. 449, 450. Three of these had been known to me in the world; to whom I related, that preparations were now being made for the burial of their body. I happened to say, for *their* burial; on hearing which, they were struck with a sort of stupor, and declared, that they were alive, but that their friends might commit to the grave what had served them for a body in the world. They afterwards wondered exceedingly, that, when they lived in the body, they did not believe there was such a life after death ; and they were especially astonished that, within the church, almost all are possessed by a similar incredulity. Those who, while in the world, had not believed in any life of the soul after the life of the body, on finding them- selves to be living after death, are exceedingly ashamed : but those who had confirmed themselves in the denial of it, are con- nected in society with their like, and are separated from those who had maintained the belief of it. For the most part, they are attached, by an invisible bond, to some infernal society; for such characters have also denied the Divine Being, and have held in contempt the truths of the church. For just in proportion as any one confirms himself against the eternal life of his own soul, he also confirms himself against all things that belong to heaven and to the church.

16   241

THAT MAN, AFTER .DEATH, IS IN PERFECT HUMAN FORM.

453. That the form of man's spirit is the human form; or that the spirit is a man even with respect to form; may be evident from what has been offered in several Sections above, especially from those in which it was shown, that every angel is in a perfect human form (nn. 73—77); that, as to his interiors, every man is a spirit (nn. 432—444); and that the angels in heaven are from the human race (nn. 311—317). This may be seen still more clearly from the fact, that a man is a man by virtue of his spirit, and not by virtue of his body; and that the corporeal form is added to the spirit according to the form of the latter, and not conversely: for the spirit is clothed with a body according to its own form. It is owing to this circumstance, that the spirit of a man acts on all the parts, even to the most minute, of the body, and this so universally, that any part which is not acted upon by the spirit, or in which the spirit is not active, does not live. That such is the fact, every one may be aware of from this circumstance alone, that the thought and will actuate all the parts of the body, both collectively and individually, so completely at their pleasure, that there is nothing which does not respond to their behests; and if there should be any thing which does not so respond, it is no part of the body, and, as being void of a living principle, is cast out from it. Now thought and will belong to the spirit of man, not to his body. The reason that the spirit, in human form, does not appear to men after its separation from the body, nor yet the spirit that is in another man, is, because the organ of sight belonging to the body, or the bodily eye, so far as the sphere of its vision is in the world, is material, and what is material can see nothing but what is material, whilst what is spiritual sees what is spiritual; wherefore, when the material substance of the eye is shut out from, and deprived of its correspondence with, its spiritual substance, spirits appear in their own form, which is the human; and not only such spirits as are in the spiritual world, but also the spirit that is in another person while he is yet in his body.

454. The reason that the form of the spirit is the human, is, because man, as to his spirit, was created according to the form of heaven; for all things belonging to heaven, and to its order, are collated into those belonging to the mind of man;(¹) from which circumstance it is, that he possesses the faculty of receiv-

(¹) That man is the being into whom are collated all things of divine order, and that, from creation, he is divine order in form, nn. 4219, 4220, 4223, 4523, 4524, 5114. 5808, 6013, 6057, 6605, 6626, 9706, 10,156, 10,472. That so far as man lives according to divine order, in the other life he appears as a man, perfect and beautiful, nn. 4839, 6605, 6626.

ing intelligence and wisdom. Whether you say, the faculty of receiving intelligence and wisdom, or, the faculty of receiving heaven, it amounts to the same thing. All this may evidently appear from what has been shown above respecting the light and heat of heaven (nn. 126—140); respecting the form of heaven (nn. 200—212); and respecting the wisdom of the angels (nn. 265—275); and in the Sections in which it is shown, that heaven, as to its form, is, both in the whole and in its parts, as a man (nn. 59—77); and this by derivation from the Lord's Divine Humanity, from which proceeds both heaven and its form (nn. 78—86).

455. All the statements that have now been advanced, a rational man will be able to understand, for he is able to view things from the chain of causes, and from truths flowing in their own order; but a person who is not a rational man will not understand them. For this, there are several reasons: the chief of which is, that he is not willing to understand them, because they contradict his false notions, which he has made his truths: and he who, on this account, is not willing to understand them, has closed the way against the influx of heaven into his rational faculty. Still, however, that way is capable of being opened, provided the will do not resist. (See above, n. 424.) That a man is capable of understanding truths, and becoming truly rational, provided he be but willing, has been demonstrated to me by much experience. Often have I beheld evil spirits, who had become irrational through having, when in the world, denied the Divine Being and the truths of the church, and having confirmed themselves in such denial, turned, by a divine force, towards those who were in the enjoyment of the light of truth. They then comprehended those truths, as the angels do, confessed them to be truths, and acknowledged that they comprehended them all. But as soon as they relapsed into themselves, and turned to the love which was that of their own will, they comprehended nothing, and affirmed the direct contrary. I have also heard some infernal spirits say, that they knew and perceived that what they did was evil, and that what they thought was false, but that they could not resist the delight of their love, or could not act against their will, and that this was what directed their thoughts, causing them to see evil as good, and falsity as truth. It was thus made evident, that those who are immersed in falsities derived from evil, are capable of understanding truths, and thus of being rational, but that they are not willing; and that the reason why they are not willing is, because they have loved falsities in preference to truths, since falsities agreed with the evils in which they were sunk. Loving and willing amount to the same thing; since what a man wills, he loves, and what he loves, he wills. Since the state of men is such, that they are capable of understanding truths provided

they be but willing, it has been permitted me to confirm spiritual truths, which are those belonging to heaven and to the church, by rational considerations. This has been granted, to the end that the false notions, which, with many, have closed the rational faculty, might, by such rational considerations, be dispersed, and thus, in some little measure, their eyes be opened. For it is permitted to all who are grounded in truths, to confirm spiritual truths by rational considerations. Who could ever understand the Word, from reading it in its literal sense, unless he viewed the truths contained in it from an enlightened rational faculty? From what cause, but the want of so viewing it, have so many heresies arisen from the same Word?[2]

456. That the spirit of a man, after its separation from the body, is itself a man, and similar in form, has been proved to me by the daily experience of many years. I have seen them, I have heard them speak, and I have talked with them, thousands of times: and our conversation has sometimes been on this very subject,—that men in the world do not believe spirits to be men also, and that those who do believe it are accounted by the learned as simpletons. The spirits were grieved at heart that such ignorance should still continue in the world, and especially in the church. They said that this negative belief had emanated principally from the learned, who had thought respecting the soul from their corporeal-sensual apprehensions, from which they had conceived no other idea of it than as a mere thinking principle, which, when regarded as destitute of any subject, in and by virtue of which it could have an actual existence, is like a sort of volatile breath of pure ether, which cannot but be dissipated when the body dies. As, however, the church, on the authority of the Word, believes in the immortality of the soul, they could not but ascribe it to some vital faculty, like that of thought, though they deny it any sensible faculty, such as is enjoyed by man, till it should again be united to the body. On this opinion is founded the common doctrine of the resurrection, and the belief that such reunion will take place on the arrival of the last judgment. To this it is owing, that, when any one thinks about the soul from the common doctrine, and, at the same time, from the above-named hypothesis respecting its nature, he does not at all comprehend that the soul is the spirit, and that this is in the human form. In addition to which, scarcely any one, at the present day, is aware

[2] That we ought to begin with the truths of doctrine of the church, which are derived from the Word, and first acknowledge those truths; and that afterwards it is allowed to consult scientifics, n. 6047. Thus that it is allowed those who are in an affirmative principle concerning the truths of faith, to confirm them rationally by scientifics, but it is not allowable for those who are in a negative principle, nn. 2568, 2588, 4760, 6047. That it is according to divine order from spiritual truths to enter rationally into scientifics, which are natural truths, and not from the latter into the former; because spiritual influx into natural things takes place, but not natural or physical influx into things spiritual, nn. 3219, 5119, 5259, 5427, 5428, 5478, 6322, 9110, 9111.

of what the spiritual nature is, and still less that any human form can belong to spiritual existences, as all spirits and angels are. To this it is owing, that almost all who pass out of this world into the other, wonder exceedingly to find themselves alive, and that they are men equally as before; that they can see, hear, and speak; that their body possesses the sense of feeling as before; and that there is no discernible difference whatever. (See above, n. 74.) But when they cease to wonder at themselves, they begin to wonder that the church should possess no knowledge whatever about the state of men, as being such, after death, nor, consequently, respecting heaven and hell; although, notwithstanding, all persons who have ever lived in the world, have passed into the other life, and are there living as men. As likewise, they wondered that this was not made manifest to man by means of visions, it being an essential arti cle in the faith of the church, they were informed from heaven, that this might indeed have been done, for nothing is more easy, when the Lord sees good; but that, nevertheless, those who have confirmed themselves in false notions contrary to these truths, would not believe them, even were they themselves to be made the subjects of such ocular demonstration. They were informed, further, that it is dangerous to confirm any thing by visions to persons who are grounded in falsities; for they would, in con- sequence, first believe what was so confirmed to them, and would afterwards deny it, and thus would profane the truth it- self; for first to believe truths, and afterwards to deny them, is to commit profanation; of which those who are guilty, are thrust down into the deepest and most grievous of all the hells.([3]) The danger of this is what is meant by the Lord's words: "*He hath blinded their eyes, and hardened their heart; that they should not see with their eyes, nor understand with their heart, and be converted, and I should heal them.*"—(John xii. 40.) And that those who are confirmed in falsities would still not believe, is taught in these words: "*Abraham saith unto the rich man in hell, They have Moses and the prophets;*

([3]) That profanation consists in the commixing of good and evil, also of what is true and what is false, with man, n. 6348. That none can profane truth and good, or the holy things of the Word and the church, but those who first acknowledge them, and especially if they live according to them, and afterwards recede from the faith, deny them, and live to themselves and the world, nn. 593, 1008, 1010, 1059, 3398, 8399, 3898, 4289, 4601, 10,284, 10,287. If man, after repentance of heart, relapses into his former evils, that he is guilty of profanation, and that in such case his latter state is worse than his former, n. 8894. That those cannot profane holy things, who have not acknowledged them; still less those who do not know them, nn. 1008, 1010, 1059, 9188, 10,284. That the Gentiles, who are out of the church, and have not the Word, cannot profane it, nn. 1327, 1328, 2051, 2081. That, on this account, interior truths were not discovered to the Jews, since if they had been discovered and acknowledged, that people would have profaned them, nn. 3398, 3399, 6963. That the lot of profaners in the other life is the worst of all, because the good and truth, which they have ac- knowledged, remain, and likewise the evil and falsity, and, because they cohere, the life is rent asunder, nn. 571, 582, 6348. That therefore the utmost provision is made by the Lord to prevent profanation, nn. 2426, 10,384.

*let them hear them. And he said, Nay, father Abraham: but
if one went unto them from the dead, they would repent. And
he said unto him, If they hear not Moses and the prophets,
neither will they be persuaded though one rose from the dead."*
—(Luke xvi. 29, 30, 31.)

457. The spirit of a man, when first he enters the world of
spirits, which takes place soon after his resuscitation, described
in the last Section, is similar in countenance, and in the tone of
his voice, to what he was in the world. The reason is, because
he is then in the state of his exteriors, and his interiors are not
yet laid open. This is the first state of man after death. But
afterwards his countenance is changed, and becomes quite different; being rendered similar to his governing affection or
love, which is that in which the interiors belonging to his mind
had been grounded while in the world, and which had reigned
in his spirit while this was in the body. For the face of a man's
spirit differs exceedingly from that of his body; the face of his
body being derived from his parents, but that of his spirit from
his affection, of which it is the image. Into this his spirit
comes, after his life in the body, when his exteriors are removed,
and his interiors are revealed. This is the third state of man
after death. I have seen some who were recently come from the
world, whom I knew by their face and tone of voice; but I did
not know them when I saw them afterwards. Those who had
been grounded in good affections were then seen with beautiful
faces; but those who had been immersed in evil affections, with
ugly ones: for the spirit of man, regarded in itself, is nothing
but his affection; of which the external form is the face. Another
reason of the change of countenance is, because it is not allowable
for any one, in the other life, to feign affections that are not his
own, nor, by consequence, to put on looks that are contrary to his
love. All persons, be they who they may, are there brought
into such a state, as to speak as they think, and to show, in
their countenance and gestures, what are the inclinations of
their will. From these causes it results, that the faces of all
become the forms and images of their affections; whence it also
happens, that all who knew each other in the world, know each
other, likewise, in the world of spirits; but not in heaven, nor
in hell.(*) (As was observed above, n. 427.)

458. The faces of hypocrites are changed more tardily than
those of others, by reason that, through practice, they have con-

(*) That the face is formed to correspondence with the interiors, nn. 4791—4805,
5695. Concerning the correspondence of the face and its looks with the affections of
the mind, nn. 1568, 2988, 2989, 3631, 4796, 4797, 4800, 5165, 5168, 5695, 9306. That,
with the angels of heaven, the face makes one with the interiors which belong to the
mind, nn. 4796—4799, 5695, 8250. That on this account, the face, in the Word, signifies the interiors which belong to the mind, that is, which belong to the affection and
thought, nn. 1999, 2434, 3527, 4066, 4796, 5102, 9306, 9546. In what manner the influx
from the brain into the face has been changed in a successive course of time, and with
it the face itself, as to correspondence with the interiors, nn. 4326, 8250.

tracted a habit of settling their interiors so as to imitate good affections; whence, for a long time, they appear not unbeautiful; but since they are gradually divested of that assumed imitation, and the interiors belonging to their minds are settled according to the form of their own affections, they afterwards become more ugly than others. Hypocrites are such persons as talked like angels, but interiorly acknowledged nothing but nature, and thus denied the Divine Being, and, consequently, the things belonging to heaven and the church.

459. It is to be observed, that the human form of every one after death is more beautiful, in proportion as he had more interiorly loved divine truths, and had lived according to them : for the interiors of every one are both opened and formed according to that love and life; on which account, the more interior is the affection, so much the more conformable to heaven, and, consequently, so much the more handsome, is the countenance. It is owing to this, that the angels who dwell in the inmost heaven are so exceedingly beautiful; they being forms of celestial love. But those who had loved divine truths more externally, and thus had more externally lived according to them, are less beautiful; for only their exteriors shine forth from their face, and interior heavenly love is not translucent through them, consequently, not the form of heaven such as it intrinsically is. There appears something respectively obscure emanating from their countenance, not animated by the trans-lucence of interior life. In a word; all perfection increases as it ascends towards the interiors, and decreases as it descends towards the exteriors; and beauty does the same. I have seen faces of angels of the third heaven, which were so beautiful, that no painter, with all the resources of his art, could impart such brightness to his colors, as should equal a thousandth part of the light and life which appeared in those countenances. But the faces of angels of the ultimate heaven, may, in some degree, be equalled by a painter.

460. I will, in the last place, communicate a certain arcanum, which has hitherto been known to none. It is this : that every thing good and true that proceeds from the Lord, and constitutes heaven, is in the human form; and that it is so, not only in the whole, and on the greatest scale, but in every part, and in the smallest: and that this form exercises an affecting influence on every one who receives good and truth from the Lord, and im-parts the human form to every inhabitant of heaven, according to the degree of his reception. It is owing to this, that heaven is similar to itself both in general and in particular; and that the human form is that of the whole, of every society, and of every angel; as shown in four Sections above. (From n. 59 to n. 86.) To which may be made this addition : that the human form exists also in the angels, in every minutia of thought, that

247

is derived from celestial love. But this arcanum can with difficulty come within the comprehension of any man; though it enters with clearness into the understanding of angels, because they dwell in the light of heaven.

––––––––––

THAT MAN, AFTER DEATH, IS POSSESSED OF EVERY SENSE, AND OF ALL THE MEMORY, THOUGHT, AND AFFECTION, THAT HE HAD IN THE WORLD; AND THAT HE LEAVES NOTHING BEHIND HIM BUT HIS TERRESTRIAL BODY.

461. That when a man passes from the natural into the spiritual world, as he does when he dies, he takes with him all things belonging to him as a man except his terrestrial body, has been proved to me by manifold experience. For when he enters the spiritual world, or the life after death, he is in a body, as he was in the world: to all appearance, there is no difference whatever, because there is none that he can discover either by touch or by sight. But his body is now spiritual in its nature, and thus is separated or purified from the terrestrial particles: and when what is spiritual touches and sees what is spiritual, the effect to the sense is exactly the same, as when what is natural touches and sees what is natural. On this account, when man has become a spirit, he does not know, by consciousness, that he is not still in the body in which he was when in the world; consequently, he does not know by consciousness, that he has died. The man, now a spirit, enjoys every sense, both internal and external, that he possessed in the world. He sees, as before; he hears and speaks, as before; he smells, likewise, and tastes, and feels when he is touched, as before; he longs, also, he desires, he wishes, he thinks, he reflects, he is affected, he loves, he wills, as before: and a person who takes pleasure in study, reads and writes, as before. In a word, a man's transit from one life into the other, or from one world into the other, is like a journey from one place into another; and he takes with him all things that he possesses in himself as a man; so that it cannot be said that a man after death, his death being only that of his terrestrial body, has lost any thing that belonged to himself. He also carries with him his natural memory: for every thing that he ever heard, saw, read, learned, or thought, from his earliest infancy to the last day of his life, he still retains. The natural objects, however, which are contained in his memory, not being capable of being reproduced in a spiritual world, remain quiescent, just as they do with a man in the world when he does not think of them: but, notwithstanding, they are reproduced when the Lord sees good. But respecting this memory, and its state after death, more will be

related presently. A sensual man cannot at all believe that the state of man after death is of such a nature, because he does not comprehend how it can be: for a sensual man cannot do otherwise than think in a natural manner, even on spiritual subjects; wherefore, whatever he does not perceive by the senses, or does not see with the eyes, and feel with the hands, of his body, he affirms to have no existence; as we read of Thomas, in John xx. 25, 27, 29. (What is the character of the sensual man, may be seen above, n. 267, and in the references there made.)

462. Still, however, the difference between the life of a man in the spiritual world, and his life in the natural world, is great, both with respect to the external senses and their affections, and to the internal senses and their affections. The inhabitants of heaven have much more exquisite senses,—that is, they see and hear much more exquisitely,—and they also think with much more wisdom, than they did when they were in the world. For they see by the light of heaven, which exceeds, by many degrees, the light of the world (see above, n. 126); and they hear through a spiritual atmosphere, which also, in purity, by many degrees, excels the atmosphere of the earth (see n. 235). The difference between these external senses, as they exist in angels and in men, is like the difference, in the world, between a clear sky and a dark mist; or like that between noon-day light and evening shade. For the light of heaven, being the Divine Truth, enables the sight of the angels to perceive and to distinguish the minutest objects. Their external sight, also, corresponds to their internal sight, or that of their understanding; for, with the angels, the one species of sight flows into the other, so as to cause them to act as one; to which is owing their great keenness of sight. In the same manner, likewise, their hearing corresponds to their perception, which is a faculty belonging to the understanding and the will in combination; in consequence of which, they distinguish, both in the tone of voice and in the words of a person speaking, the most minute particulars of his affection and thought, perceiving in the tone all relating to his affection, and in the words all relating to his thought. (See above, nn. 234—245.) But the other senses, in the angels, are not so exquisite as are those of sight and hearing; by reason that these are conducive to their advancement in intelligence and wisdom, which the others are not. Were the other senses as exquisite as these, they would take away the light and delight of their wisdom, and would introduce the delight of the pleasures connected with the body and the various appetites, which, so far as they prevail, obscure and debilitate the understanding; as actually takes place with men in the world, who become dull and stupid in regard to spiritual truths, in proportion as they indulge in the pleasures of taste, and in the blandishments connected

with the sense of touch which soothe the body. That the interior senses of the angels of heaven, which are those of their thought and affection, are more exquisite and perfect than they were in the world, may also appear from what was stated and shown in the Section on the wisdom of the angels of heaven (nn. 265—275). As to the difference between the state of the inhabitants of hell and their state in the world, this, also, is great: for in proportion to the greatness of the perfection and excellence of the external and internal senses in the angels of heaven, is that of their imperfection in the inhabitants of hell. But the state of these will be treated of hereafter.

462.* That man takes with him from the world all his memory, has been shown me by many proofs; on which subject numerous things worthy of being mentioned have been seen and heard by me; some of which I will relate. There were some who denied the crimes and enormities which they had committed in the world; wherefore, lest they should be supposed to be innocent, these were all laid open, and were recited in order, from their own memory, from the first period of their life to the last: they consisted, chiefly, of adulteries and whoredoms. There were some who had practised deception upon others by wicked arts, and who had committed robberies: their tricks and thefts were also enumerated in their order, though scarcely any of them had been known in the world, except to themselves alone. They also acknowledged them, because they were made manifest as if in broad daylight, together with all the thoughts, intentions, pleasures, and fears, which occupied their minds on the several occasions. There were some who had taken bribes, and made a trade of their judicial functions: these crimes were in like manner brought to light from their own memory, from which they were all recited, from the first day of their entering on their office to the last. All the particulars appeared, both as to the amount of the bribe and its nature, with the time, and the state of their mind and intention at the moment: all rushed to their recollection, and were displayed to the view of those present. The several transactions were many hundreds in number. This was done with several, and (what was wonderful) their memorandum books, in which they had noted down the particulars, were opened and read before them, page by page. Some were brought to a similar judgment who had enticed virgins to submit to be dishonored, or had violated the chastity either of maids or of matrons; when all the circumstances were brought forth and recited from their memory: the very faces of the virgins and women were also exhibited, as if they were present, together with the places, the words that passed between them, and the state of their

* This number is repeated in the original.—N.

minds : and all was displayed as suddenly, as when a scene is unfolded to the view. Such exposures sometimes were continued for several hours. There was a certain spirit who had accounted as nothing the evil of backbiting others. I heard his backbitings and defamations, with the very words he employed, recited in order; the persons respecting whom, and those to whom, he had uttered them, being discovered at the same time : all were brought forth, and vividly exhibited, together; and yet, in every instance, his practices had been carefully concealed by him while he lived in the world. There was one who had deprived a relation of his inheritance by a fraudulent pretext : he, too, was similarly convicted and judged ; and, what was wonderful, the letters and papers which had passed between them were read in my hearing, and I was informed that not a word was wanting. The same person, also, not long before his death, had clandestinely murdered his neighbor by poison ; which was brought to light in this manner : He was seen to dig a hole under ground, out of which, when dug, a man came forth, like one coming out of a grave, who cried out to him, "What hast thou done to me?" All the particulars were then revealed ; how the poisoner had conversed with him in a friendly manner, and had then given him the fatal cup ; together with what he had thought previously, and what happened afterwards : all which being brought to light, he was condemned to hell. In a word, all the criminal practices, the wicked deeds, the robberies, the deceptions, the artifices, of which he had been guilty in the world, are laid open to every evil spirit, being brought forth from his own memory ; and thus he is convicted ; nor is there any room for denial, since all the circumstances appear together. I also heard the particulars, when, from the memory of a certain spirit inspected and examined by the angels, every thing that he had thought for a month, day after day, was recited, all without the least mistake ; the particulars being recalled, just as he was engaged in them, on those days. From these examples it may evidently appear, that man carries all his memory with him into the other world, and that nothing is so concealed in this world, as not to be made manifest after death ; and that, too, in the presence of many witnesses ; according to these words of the Lord : "*There is nothing covered that shall not be revealed : neither hid, that shall not be known. Therefore, whatsoever ye have spoken in darkness, shall be heard in the light ; and that which ye have spoken in the ear in closets, shall be proclaimed upon the house-tops.*"—(Luke xii. 2, 3.)

463. When a man's actions are brought before him after death, the angels to whom the duty of making the inquiry is assigned, look into his face ; and then the examination proceeds through his whole body, beginning from the fingers of both hands. As I wondered what this could be for, it was discovered

to me. Al the particulars of a man's thought and will are inscribed on his brain; for there they exist in their first principles. Thence, also, they are inscribed on his whole body; because all things belonging to his thought and will proceed thither from their first principles, and are there terminated, as being there in their ultimates. This is the reason, that whatever things proceeding from a man's will and thence from his thought are inscribed on his memory, are not only inscribed on the brain, but also on the whole man, and there exist in order, according to the order of the parts of the body. It was hence made evident to me, that man is such in the whole, as he is in his will and in his thought thence derived, so that a bad man is his own evil, and a good man is his own good.([1]) From these facts may also be evident, what is to be understood by man's book of life, which is spoken of in the Word: the meaning of it is, that all things belonging to every one, both his actions and his thoughts, are inscribed on the whole man, and that they appear as if read out of a book, when they are called forth from his memory, and as if seen in effigy, when the spirit is viewed in the light of heaven.

To these statements I will add a certain memorable circumstance respecting the memory of man as remaining after death; by which I was assured, that not only general things, but also the most particular, which have once entered the memory, abide there, and are never obliterated. I saw some books, with writing in them, such as exist in the world; and I was informed, that they were taken from the memory of their authors, and that not a single word was wanting, that was contained in the books as written by those persons in the world: I was told at the same time, that, in this manner, the most minute particulars of all, contained in another person's memory, could be called forth from it, even such as he, in the world, had forgotten. The reason was discovered also; which is, that man has both an external memory and an internal one, the external memory being that of his natural man, and the internal memory that of his spiritual man; and that every individual thing that a man has thought, willed, spoken, or done, together with every thing that he has heard or seen, is inscribed on his internal or spiritual memory ;([2]) and further, that whatever is there written is never

---

([1]) That a good man, spirit, and angel, is his own good and his own truth; that is, that he is wholly such as his good and truth are, nn. 10,298, 10,367. The reason is, because good forms the will, and truth the understanding, and the will and understanding form the all of the life appertaining to a man, to a spirit, and to an angel, nn. 3332, 3625, 6065. In like manner it may be said, that every man, spirit, and angel, is his own love, nn. 6872, 10,177, 10,284.

([2]) That man has two memories, an exterior one and an interior one, or a natural one and a spiritual, nn. 2469—2494. That man does not know that he has an interior memory, nn. 2470, 2471. How much the interior memory excels the exterior n. 2478. That the things contained in the exterior memory are in the light of the world, but the things contained in the interior are in the light of heaven, n. 5212. That it is from the interior memory that man is enabled to think and speak intellectually and rationally, erased, because it is inscribed, at the same time, on the spirit itself, and on the members of his body, as stated just above; and thus that the spirit has acquired a form according to the thoughts and acts of his will. I am aware that these facts will appear like paradoxes, and will, therefore, with difficulty be believed; but, nevertheless, they are true. Let not, therefore, any man imagine, that there is any thing which he has thought in his own breast, or has done in secret, that can be hidden after death; but let him be assured, that all and each will then be manifest as in open day.

464. Although man has his external or natural memory in him after death, the merely natural things contained in it are not reproduced in the other life, but, instead, such spiritual things as are adjoined to those natural things by correspondences. These, however, when exhibited to view, appear in a form precisely similar to that which the natural things had in the natural world: for all objects that appear in the heavens appear similar to those in the world, although, in their essence, they are not natural, but spiritual. (As is shown in the Section on Representatives and Appearances in Heaven, nn. 170—176.) But the external or natural memory, so far as its contents partake of materiality, of time and space, and of whatever else is proper to nature, does not serve the spirit for the same use as it had done in the world. For man in the world, when he thinks from the external sensual part of his mind, and not at the same time from the internal sensual or intellectual part, thinks naturally and not spiritually; but in the other life, being then a spirit in a spiritual world, he thinks spiritually and not naturally. To think spiritually, is to think intellectually or rationally. It is owing to this, that the external or natural memory, as to the material part of its contents, is then quiescent, and those parts of its contents only come into use, which man has acquired by means of the former, and has invested with a rational character. The reason that the external memory, as to such part of its contents as are of a material nature, is quiescent, is, because such things cannot be reproduced; for spirits and angels speak from the affections, and from the thought thence originating, belonging to their minds; on which account, they cannot give utterance to any thing that does not agree with these. (As may appear from what is stated respecting the speech of the angels, both among themselves and with man, in two Sec-

n. 9394. That all the things, including every particular, which a man has thought, has spoken, has done, and which he has seen and heard, are inscribed on the interior memory, nn. 2474, 7398. That that memory is the book of his life, nn. 2474, 9386, 9841, 10,505. That in the interior memory are the truths which have been made truths of faith, and the goods which have been made goods of love, nn. 5212, 8067. That those things which have acquired habit, and have been made things of the life, and thereby obliterated in the exterior memory, are in the interior memory, nn. 9394, 9723, 9841. That spirits and angels speak from the interior memory, and hence that they have a universal language, nn. 2472, 2476, 2490, 2493. That languages in the world belong to the exterior memory, nn. 2472, 2476.

tions above, nn. 234—257.) From this cause, in proportion as a
man has become rational in the world by means of an acquaintance with languages and sciences, he is rational after death; but
not at all in proportion to the mere extent of his acquaintance
with those languages and sciences. I have conversed in the
other life with many, who, in the world, were regarded as men
of learning, on account of their knowledge of the ancient languages, such as Hebrew, Greek, and Latin, but who had not
cultivated their rational faculty by the information contained in
the books written in those languages; and some of them were
found to be as simple as those who were acquainted with no
language but their own; whilst others were absolutely stupid·
and yet a conceited persuasion remained with them, as if they
were wiser than others. I have conversed with some who imagined in the world, that a man's wisdom is in proportion to the
stores in his memory, and who had therefore crammed their
memory with a great number of things, and conversed almost
solely from it, and thus not from themselves, but from others,
without having at all improved their rational faculty by what
their memory contained. Some of these were quite stupid;
others were mere idiots, not at all comprehending any truth so
as to see whether it was a truth or not, and eagerly embracing
any falsities that were propounded as truths by such as call
themselves men of learning: for such persons are not able to
see, for themselves, whether any thing propounded as true be so
or not, and, consequently, can apprehend nothing rationally that
they hear from others. I have also conversed with some, who,
in the world, had written a great deal, embracing scientific
matters of all kinds, and who had thus acquired a reputation
for learning through a great part of the world. Some of these
could, indeed, reason about truths, debating whether they were
such or not; and some, when turned towards those who enjoyed
the light of truth, could understand that they were truths; but
still they were not willing to understand them; wherefore they
denied them again, when they sunk into their own falsities and
thus into themselves. There were others who were as ignorant
as the unlettered vulgar. Thus they differed one from another,
according as, by the scientific works which they had written or
copied, they had cultivated their rational faculty. But those
who had been opposed to the truths of the church, and had
occupied their thoughts with mere matters of science, by means
of which they had confirmed themselves in falsities, had not
cultivated their rational faculty, but only the faculty of reasoning.
This, in the world, is supposed to be rationality; but it is a faculty
with which rationality has no connection, being a mere talent for
confirming as true whatever a man pleases, and, from preconceived principles and from fallacies, seeing falsities as truths, but
not truths themselves. Such persons can never be brought to
254

recognize truths as being such; because truths cannot be seen, as to their real nature, from falsities, though falsities may be so seen from truths.   The rational faculty of man is like a garden and flower bed, or like a fallow field : the memory is the ground : scientific truths and knowledges are the seeds.   As the light and heat of the sun are what make the natural earth and seeds productive, and without these there can be no germination : so, unless the light of heaven, which is Divine Truth, and the heat of heaven, which is Divine Love, be admitted into the mind, there can be no growth there : it is to these, alone, that the rational faculty owes its existence.   The angels grieve exceedingly that so great a proportion of the learned ascribe all things to nature, and have thence so closed the interiors belonging to their minds, as not to be able to see any thing of truth by the light of truth, which is the light of heaven.   In the other life, therefore, they are deprived of the faculty of reasoning, that they may not, by reasonings, diffuse falsities among the simple good, and so seduce them.   They also are banished into desert places.

465.   There was a certain spirit who was angry at not remembering many things with which he was acquainted in the life of the body, grieving over the pleasure that he had lost, with which he used to be greatly delighted.   But he was told that he had not lost any thing, but still was acquainted with all that ever he knew, including every particular : but that, in the world in which he now was, he was not allowed to bring such matters forward, and that he ought to be satisfied with being able to think and speak much better and more perfectly than before, without immersing his rational faculty, as he used to do, in gross, obscure, material, and corporeal things, which were of no use in the kingdom into which he had now entered.   It was also told him, that he now possessed every thing that could promote the uses of eternal life, and thus that he could not enjoy beatitude and happiness in any other manner; consequently, that it was mere ignorance to imagine, that, in the kingdom in which he now was, intelligence was lost with the removal and quiescence of the material contents of the memory; the fact in reality being, that in proportion as the mind is capable of being withdrawn from the sensual things that belong to the external man or to the body, it is elevated to things spiritual and celestial.

466.   Of what quality are the two memories, is sometimes, in the other life, exhibited to view, in such forms as are only there to be seen; for many things are there rendered objects of sight, which, among men, can only be conceived in idea.   The exterior memory is there presented, in appearance, like a callus, and the interior like a medullary substance, such as exists in the human brain; and from the appearance of them both is communicated a knowledge of the character of the parties to whom they belong. With those who, in the life of the body, had solely labored to store

the memory, and thus had not cultivated the rational faculty, the callosity appears hard, and as if inwardly interspersed with tendons. With those who had filled the memory with falsities, it appears hairy and rough; which appearance is occasioned by the things contained in the memory being such an unarranged mass. With those who had labored in storing the memory for the gratification of self-love and the love of the world, it appears as if the fibres were glued together and ossified. With those who wished to penetrate into divine arcana by scientific attainments, especially by what is called in the schools philosophy, and would not believe them till they should be persuaded by such means, the memory appears dark; the darkness being of such a nature as to absorb the rays of light, and to turn them into darkness. With those who had practised deceit and hypocrisy, it appears of a hard bony nature, like ebony, which reflects the rays of light. But with those who had been grounded in the good of love and in the truths of faith, such a callus does not appear, because their interior memory transmits the rays of light into their exterior, in the objects or ideas of which, as in their basis or ground, the rays are terminated, and find in them delightful receptacles. For the exterior memory is the last thing in order; in which, therefore, things spiritual and celestial gently terminate and dwell, when they find in it such contents as are good and true.

467. Men while living in the world, if grounded in love to the Lord and in charity towards their neighbor, have attached to them, and within them, intelligence and wisdom. These, however, are stored up in the inmost recesses of their interior memory, and can never appear, even to themselves, till they put off the corporeal elements. Then their natural memory is laid asleep, and they awake into their interior memory, and finally, by degrees, into such as belongs to the angels.

468. How the rational faculty may be cultivated, shall also be briefly declared. Genuine rationality consists of truths, and not of falsities: that which consists of falsities is not rationality. Truths are of three kinds: there are civil truths, moral truths, and spiritual truths. Civil truths relate to matters of law, and such as concern the forms of government in states; in general, to what belongs there to justice and equity. Moral truths relate to such matters as belong to the life of every one with respect to society and his intercourse with others; in general, to sincerity and uprightness, and specifically, to the virtues of every kind. But spiritual truths relate to such matters as belong to heaven and the church; and, in general, to good, which is the object of love, and to truth, which is the object of faith. There are, in every man, three degrees of life (see above, n. 267): and the rational faculty is opened to the first degree by means of civil truths, to the second degree by means of moral truths, and to the third by means of spiritual truths. But it is to be observed, that the

rational faculty is not formed and opened merely by a man's being acquainted with those truths, but by his living according to them: by living according to them is meant, his loving them from a spiritual affection; and by loving them from a spiritual affection is meant, loving what is just and equitable because it is just and equitable; what is sincere and upright because it is sincere and upright; and what is good and true because it is good and true: whereas to live according to them and love them from corporeal affection, is to love them for the sake of one's self, of one's own reputation, honor, or gain. In proportion, consequently, as a man loves those truths from corporeal affection, he does not become rational: for then, the truths are not what he loves, but himself, to whom they are serviceable, as servants are to their masters: and when truths are used merely as servants, they do not enter into the man, and open any degree of his life, not so much as the first; but they only reside in his memory, as matters of external knowledge under a material form; where they conjoin themselves with the love of self, which is corporeal love. From these facts it may appear, how man becomes rational; and that he is made rational to the third degree by the spiritual love of good and truth, which are the constituents of heaven and of the church; to the second degree, by the love of sincerity and uprightness; and to the first degree, by the love of justice and equity. These two latter loves are also rendered spiritual, by the spiritual love of good and truth; for this enters into them by influx, joins itself with them, and forms in them, as it were, its own countenance.

469. Spirits and angels possess memory, equally with men. Whatever they hear, see, think, will, or do, remains with them, and their rational faculty is continually cultivated by these means; a process which goes on to eternity. It is owing to this, that spirits and angels are perfected in intelligence and wisdom, by means of the knowledges of truth and good, equally with men. That spirits and angels have memory, is a fact that it has also been granted me to know by much experience. I have seen, when they have been in company with other spirits, that all the things that they had thought or done, whether in public or in private, were called forth from their memory: and I have seen, also, that those who have been grounded in any degree of truth, in consequence of having lived in simple good, were imbued with knowledges, and through them with intelligence, and were afterwards taken up into heaven. But it is to be observed, that none are imbued with knowledges and through them with intelligence, except to the extent of the degree of affection for good and truth which had been opened in them in the world, but not beyond it. For with every spirit and angel remains the same affection, both as to quantity and to quality, as he had possessed in the world. This is afterwards perfected by impletion or filling up, a process which goes on to eternity: for there is nothing which cannot be filled

17   257

up to eternity; since every thing admits of being infinitely varied, and thus of being enriched, consequently, multiplied and rendered fruitful, by various means. No end can be assigned to any thing that is good, because it proceeds from Him who is Infinite. (That spirits and angels are continually perfected in intelligence and wisdom by knowledges of truth and good, may be seen in the Sections on the Wisdom of the Angels of Heaven, nn. 265—275; on the State in Heaven of the Gentiles, or Natives of Countries not within the limits of the Church, nn. 318—328; and on Infants or Little Children in Heaven, nn. 329—345. And that this is accomplished to the extent of the degree of affection for good and truth which had been opened in them in the world, but not beyond it, n. 349.)

THAT MAN AFTER DEATH IS, IN QUALITY, SUCH AS HIS LIFE HAD BEEN IN THE WORLD.

470. That his own life remains with every one after death, is known to every Christian from the Word; for it is therein declared, in many places, that man shall be judged and rewarded according to his deeds and according to his works. Every one, also, who thinks under the influence of good, and of real truth, has no other idea, than that he who has lived well will go to heaven, and he who has lived ill will go to hell. Those, however, who are immersed in evil, are unwilling to believe that their state after death will be according to their life in the world; but they think, especially when on a sick bed, that heaven is awarded to every one of the pure mercy of the Lord, let his life have been what it may; and that it is given to men according to their faith; which such persons separate from life.

471. That man will be judged and rewarded according to his deeds and according to his works, is declared in the Word in many places, of which I will here adduce some. "*The Son of man shall come in the glory of his Father, with his angels; and then he shall reward every man according to his works.*"— (Matt. xvi. 27.) "*Blessed are the dead that die in the Lord, from henceforth: Yea, saith the Spirit; that they may rest from their labors: and their works do follow them.*"—(Rev. xiv. 13.) "*I will give unto every one of you according to your works.*"—(Rev. ii. 23.) "*I saw the dead, small and great, stand before God; and the books were opened:——and the dead were judged out of those things which were written in the books, according to their works. And the sea gave up the dead that were in it; and death and hell delivered up the dead that were in them; and they were judged every man according to their works.*"—(Rev. xx. 12, 13.) "*Behold, I come quickly; and my reward is with me, to give*

every man according as his work shall be."—(Rev. xxii. 12.) " *Whosoever heareth these sayings of mine, and doeth them, I will liken him unto a wise man, that built his house upon a rock.——And every one that heareth these sayings of mine, and doeth them not, shall be likened unto a foolish man, that built his house upon the sand.*"—(Matt. vii. 24, 26.) "*Not every one that saith unto me, Lord, Lord, shall enter into the kingdom of heaven; but he that doeth the will of my Father who is in heaven. Many will say unto me in that day, Lord, Lord, have we not prophesied in thy name? and in thy name have cast out devils? and in thy name have done many wonderful works? And then I will profess unto them, I never knew you: depart from me, ye that work iniquity.*"—(Matt. vii. 21, 22, 23.) "*Then shall ye begin to say, We have eaten and drunk in thy presence, and thou hast taught in our streets. But he shall say, I know you not whence ye are; depart from me, all ye workers of iniquity.*"— (Luke xiii. 26, 27.) "*I will recompense them according to their deeds, and according to the works of their own hands.*"—(Jerem. xxv. 14.) "*Thine eyes are upon all the ways of the sons of men, to give every one according to his ways, and according to the fruit of his doings.*"—(Jerem. xxxii. 19.) "*I will punish them for their ways, and reward them their doings.*"—(Hos. iv. 9.) "*Like as the Lord of hosts thought to do unto us, according to our ways, and according to our doings, so hath he dealt with us.*"—(Zech. i. 6.) Whenever the Lord foretells the last judgment, he mentions nothing but works, and declares that those who have done good works shall enter into life eternal, and those who have done evil works into damnation. (See Matt. xxv. 32—46: not to mention many other places, in which the subject treated of is man's salvation or condemnation.) That the works and deeds constitute man's external life, and that by them is made manifest what is the quality of his internal life, is evident.

472. But by deeds and works are not merely meant deeds and works as they appear in their external form, but as they appear internally. Every one knows, that every deed or work proceeds from the will and thought of the doer; for otherwise they would be mere motions, such as are performed by automatons and images. The deed or work, then, viewed in itself, is nothing but an effect, which derives its soul and life from the will and thought from which it is performed; and so completely is this the case, that the deed or work is the will and thought in their effect, and is, consequently, the will and thought in their external form. It hence follows, that such as are, in quality, the will and thought which produce the deed or work, such, also, is the deed or work itself; and that if the thought and will are good, the deeds or works are good; and if the thought and will are evil, the deeds and works are evil, notwithstanding, in their external form, they may appear like the former. A thousand men may act in a

259

similar manner, or perform similar deeds,—so similar, in fact, that, as to their external form, it shall scarcely be possible to distinguish one from the others,—and yet, viewed in themselves, every one of them is dissimilar, because proceeding from a dissimilar will. Let us take, as an example, a man's acting sincerely and justly with his neighbor. One person may act sincerely and justly with his neighbor, with the view of appearing to be a sincere and just man, out of regard to himself and his own honor: another may do the same, out of regard to the world and to gain; a third, for the sake of obtaining reward, and to set up a claim of merit; a fourth, from motives of friendship; a fifth, out of fear of the law, and of the loss of reputation, and, consequently, of office or business; a sixth, to draw over another to his own side, though his cause may be a bad one; a seventh, in order to deceive; and others may do it from other motives still. Now the deeds of all these, though good in appearance, since it is good to act sincerely and justly with our neighbor, are nevertheless, evil; because they are not done out of regard to sincerity and justice, or because the doers love these virtues, but out of regard to self and the world, these being what the doers love; and to the love of these, sincerity and justice are made to act as servants, like domestic servants to their master, whom the master despises and dismisses when they are serviceable to him no longer. Those, also, act sincerely and justly with their neighbor, in a manner which, in external form, presents a similar appearance, who do it from the love of sincerity and justice. Of these, some act from the truth of faith, or out of obedience, because it is so commanded in the Word; some from the good of faith, or under the influence of conscience, because from a principle of religion; some from the good of charity towards their neighbor, because his good ought to be consulted; some from the good of love to the Lord, because good ought to be done for its own sake, consequently, sincerity and justice ought to be practised for their own sake likewise; and such persons love these principles because they come from the Lord, and because the Divine Sphere proceeding from the Lord has in them a residence, in consequence of which, those goods, viewed in their absolute essence, are divine. The deeds or works of all these persons are interiorly good; on which account, they are exteriorly good, also: for, as just observed, deeds or works are precisely such in quality, as are the thought and will from which they proceed, and, independently of these, they are not deeds and works at all, but mere inanimate motions. From these truths may evidently appear, what is meant by deeds and works in the Word.

473. Since deeds and works are the products of will and thought, they also are the products of love and faith, and, consequently, are such in quality as the love and faith are: for whether you speak of man's love, or of his will, it amounts to

the same thing; and so it does whether you speak of his faith or of his deliberate thought; since what a man loves, he also wills, and what he believes, he also thinks. If a man loves what he believes, he wills it too, and, as far as he is able, he does it. Every one may know, that love and faith reside in man's will and thought, and do not exist out of them; since the will is that which is enkindled by love, and the thought is that which is enlightened in matters relating to faith; on which account, none but those who are able to think wisely are enlightened, and they, according to such illumination, both think truths, and will them; or, what amounts to the same, both believe truths, and love them.(¹)

474. But it is to be observed, that it is the will that constitutes the man, and only the thought so far as it proceeds from the will; and that the deeds or works proceed from both. Or, what amounts to the same, that it is love that constitutes the man, and only faith so far as it proceeds from love; and that the deeds or works proceed from both. It follows, that the will or love is the man himself; since every thing that proceeds, belongs to that from which it proceeds. To proceed, is to be brought forth and presented in a suitable form, in order that it may appear and be apprehended.(²) From these truths may evidently be seen, what faith is separate from love; that, in reality, it is not faith at all, but only a matter of superficial knowledge, possessing within it no spiritual life. It may equally be seen, what a deed or work is without love; that, in reality, it is not a living deed or work, but a dead one, having in it an appearance of life imparted by the love of evil and a faith in what is false. This appearance of life is what is called spiritual death.

(¹) That as all things in the universe, which exist according to order, have reference to good and truth, so, with man, they have reference to will and understanding, nn. 803, 10,122. The reason is, because the will is recipient of good, and the understanding is recipient of truth, nn. 3332, 3623, 5232, 6065, 6125, 7503, 9300, 9995. It amounts to the same thing, whether we speak of truth or faith, because faith is of truth and truth is of faith; and it amounts to the same thing, whether we speak of good or of love, because love is of good and good is of love, nn. 4353, 4997, 7178, 10,122, 10,367. Hence it follows, that the understanding is recipient of faith, and the will of love, nn. 7179, 10,122, 10,367. And since the understanding of man is capable of receiving faith in God, and the will capable of receiving love to God, it follows that man is capable of being conjoined with God in faith and love, and he who is capable of being conjoined with God in love and faith can never die, nn. 4525, 6323, 9231.

(²) That the will of man is the very *esse* of his life, because it is the receptacle of love or good; and that the understanding is the *existere* of life thence derived, because it is the receptacle of faith or truth, nn. 3619, 5002, 9282. Thus that the life of the will is the principal life of man, and that the life of the understanding proceeds thence, nn. 585, 590, 3619, 7342, 8885, 9282, 10,076, 10,109, 10,110. In like manner as light from fire or flame, nn. 6032, 6314. Hence it follows that man is man by virtue of his will, and of his understanding thence derived, nn. 8911, 9069, 9071, 10,076, 10,109, 10,110. Every man is loved and esteemed by others according to the good of his will, and of his understanding thence derived; for he is loved and esteemed who wills well and understands well, and he is rejected and despised who understands well and does not will well, nn. 8911, 10,076. That man, also, after death, remains such as his will is and his understanding thence derived, nn. 9069, 9071, 9386, 10,153. Consequently, that man, after death, remains such as his love is and his faith thence derived, and that the things which belong to faith, and not at the same time to his love, then vanish, because they are not in the man, and thus are not the man's, nn. 553, 2364, 10,153.

475. It is to be observed, further, that in the deeds or works the whole man is included, and that his will and thought, or his love and faith, which constitute his interiors, are not complete, till they exist in deeds or works, which constitute his exteriors: for these are the ultimates in which the former terminate, and without which the former are things not terminated, which as yet, do not exist, and thus, as yet, are not in the man. To think and to will, without doing when there is opportunity, are like a flaming substance shut up in a close vessel, by which it is extinguished; or like seed cast on the sand, which does not germinate, but perishes with all its prolific nature: whereas to think and to will, when they result in doing, are like a flaming substance in the open air, which diffuses heat and light all around; or like seed sown in the ground, which grows into a tree or flower, and continues to exist. Every one may know, that to will, and not to do, when there is opportunity, is in reality not to will; and that for a man to love good, and not to do it, when the means are afforded, is in reality not to love it; consequently, that it is only thinking that he wills and loves, and thus is only thought separate from will or love; which soon vanishes, and comes to nothing. Love and will are the very soul of deeds and works; and this forms itself a body in the sincere and just actions that the man performs. The spiritual body, or the body of a man's spirit, has no other origin; that is, it is formed of no other things than those which the man performs from his love or will. (See above, n. 463.) In one word, all things that belong to a man and to his spirit are included in his deeds or works.(*)

476. From these statements may now appear with certainty, what is meant, by the life which remains with man after death; that, in reality, it is his love and his faith thence derived, not only as existing potentially, but also as existing in act: consequently, that it consists of his deeds or works; since these contain within them all things belonging to the man's love and faith.

477. What remains with man after death, is his governing love; nor is this ever changed to eternity. Every man is the subject of many loves; but still, they all have reference to his governing love, and make with it a one, or, taken altogether, compose it. All things belonging to the will which agree with the governing love, are called loves, because they are loved.

(*) That interior things successively flow into exterior, even into the extreme or ultimate, and that there they exist and subsist, nn. 634, 6451, 6465, 9216. That they not only flow-in, but also form in the ultimate what is simultaneous, in what order, nn. 5897, 6451, 8603, 10,099. That hence all interior things are held together in connection, and subsist, n. 9828. That deeds or works are the ultimates, containing interior things, n. 10,331. Wherefore to be recompensed and judged according to deeds and works is to be recompensed and judged according to all things belonging to the love and faith, or to the man's will and thought, because these are the interior things contained in them, nn. 3147, 3934, 6073, 8911, 10,331, 10,338.

These loves are both interior and exterior: there are some which are in immediate connection with the governing love, and some whose connection is of the mediate kind : there are some which are nearer to it, and some which are more remote: but all serve its purposes in various ways. Taken collectively, they constitute, as it were, a kingdom, and are arranged with man in such order; although the man is totally ignorant of their possessing such an arrangement. It is, however, in some degree made manifest to him, in the other life; for it is according to their arrangement that the diffusion of his thought and affection around him is there regulated, that diffusion being directed into heavenly societies, if his governing love is composed of the loves of heaven, but into infernal societies, if his governing love is composed of the loves of hell. (That all the thought and affection of spirits and angels have diffusion into the societies around, may be seen above, in the Section on the Wisdom of the Angels of Heaven; and in that on the Form of Heaven, according to which the Consociations and Communications of the Inhabitants are arranged.)

478. But the truths which have hitherto been advanced, only affect the thought of the rational man : that they may also be rendered apprehensible to the senses, I will adduce some experimental facts, by which the same truths may be illustrated and confirmed. I will show then, FIRST: That Man, after Death, is his own Love, or his own Will: SECONDLY: That, in quality, Man remains to eternity such as he is with respect to his will or governing Love: THIRDLY: that the Man whose Love is celestial and spiritual, goes to Heaven: but that the Man whose Love is corporeal and worldly, destitute of such as is celestial and spiritual, goes to Hell: FOURTHLY: That Faith does not remain with Man, if not grounded in heavenly Love: FIFTHLY: That what remains with Man is Love in Act; consequently, his Life.

479. I. *That Man, after Death, is his own Love, or his own Will.* This has been testified to me by abundant experimental evidence. The whole of heaven is divided into societies according to the differences of the love of good ; and every spirit who is elevated to heaven and becomes an angel, is led to the society in which his love prevails, and when he comes thither, he is as if he were at home, or as if living in the house in which he was born. Of this the angel has a perception ; and he there is connected in society with other angels that are similar to himself. When he goes thence, and comes to some other place, he always is sensible of a certain inward resistance, and he is affected with a desire to return to his like, and thus to his own governing love. It is thus that the inhabitants are connected together in societies in heaven. The like occurs in hell; where, also, the inhabitants are connected together in societies accord-

ing to the loves that are the opposites of heavenly ones. (That heaven is constituted of innumerable societies; and hell, likewise; and that they all are distinctly arranged according to the differences of their love, may be seen above, nn. 41—50, and nn. 200—212.) That man, after death, is his own love, may also appear evidently from the fact, that then those things are removed, and in a manner taken away from him, which do not make one with his governing love. If he is good, all things that are discordant, or that disagree with his good, are removed, and in a manner taken away, and he is thus let into his own love. The like is done if he is evil. The difference is, that truths are taken away from the wicked, and falsities from the good; a process which does not terminate, till every one is made his own love. This is effected, when a man, now a spirit, is brought to his third state, which will be treated of in a subsequent Section. When this is accomplished, the spirit constantly turns his face to his own love, which he has perpetually before his eyes, let him turn himself about as he may. (See above, nn. 123, 124.) All spirits may be led wherever it is wished, provided they be held fast in their governing love; nor are they able to resist the attraction, how perfectly soever they may know that it is exercised upon them, and how firmly soever they may think that they will resist it. The experiment has often been tried, whether they could do any thing in opposition to it; and it was found, that to attempt it was in vain. Their love is like a chain or a cord, bound, as it were, around them, by which they may be drawn along, and to extricate themselves from which is out of their power. The like occurs in the world: their own love leads men also, and by means of it they are led by others: much more is this the case when they become spirits; for then it is not allowable for any one to make a show, in appearance, of any different love, and to assume, in pretence, what is not his own. That a man's spirit is his governing love, is made evident, in the other life, in every company: for so far as any one acts or speaks in agreement with the love of another, the latter appears wholly present, wearing an expanded, cheerful, lively countenance: but so far as any one acts or speaks in opposition to another's love, his countenance begins to change, to become obscure, and not to appear; and at length he disappears wholly, as if he had not been there. I have often wondered at this phenomenon, because nothing of the kind can take place in the world: but it was told me, that a similar phenomenon does occur with the spirit that is within a man; for when this turns itself away from another, it no longer remains in his sight. That the spirit is his own governing love, was also made evident by this circumstance: that every spirit eagerly seizes, and appropriates to himself, all things that agree with his love: and rejects, and separates from himself, all things that do not so agree.

The love of every one is like the spongy and porous wood of a tree, which imbibes such fluids as promote its vegetation, and rejects all others. It is also like animals of every kind, which know their proper aliments, and seek after such as agree with their nature, while they show aversion for such as do not. For every love desires to be nourished by its own aliments,—evil love by falsities, and good love by truths. It has sometimes been given me to observe, that certain simple good spirits wished to instruct evil ones in truths and goods, but that the latter fled far away from the proffered instruction, and when they came to their proper companions, embraced with great pleasure such falsities as were suitable to their love. I have also had opportunities given me for observing, that when good spirits were conversing among themselves respecting truths, other good spirits that were present listened with desire for information; whereas some evil spirits that were present also, paid no attention whatever to the conversation, and behaved as if they did not hear it. There appear, in the world of spirits, various ways, some of which lead to heaven, and some to hell, each conducting to some particular society. The good spirits enter no other ways than those which lead to heaven, and to the society in which the good of their own love prevails; nor do they see the ways which tend in any other direction: whereas evil spirits enter no other ways than those which lead to hell, and to that society of hell in which the evil of their own love prevails; nor do they see the ways that tend in any other direction; and if they do, they still are not willing to walk in them. Such ways, in the spiritual world, are real appearances, which correspond either to truths or to falsities; wherefore this is the signification of ways, when mentioned in the Word.([4]) By these experimental evidences are confirmed the truths before advanced from reason; that every man, after death, is his own love, and his own will. The will is mentioned, because the actual will of every one is his love.

480. II. *That, in quality, Man remains to Eternity, such as he is with respect to his Will, or governing Love.* This, also, has been confirmed to me by much experimental evidence. It has been granted to me to converse with some who lived two thousand years ago, whose life was known to me, because described in history: and it was ascertained, that they are still like what they then were, and are exactly of the character assigned to them in the description, being similar with respect to their love, from and according to which their life had been

---

([4]) That a way, a path, a road, a street, a broad street, signify truths which lead to good; and also, falsities which lead to evil, nn. 627, 2333, 10,422. That to sweep a way denotes to prepare for the reception of truths, n. 3142. That to make a way known, when concerning the Lord, denotes to instruct in truths which lead to good, n. 10,565.

framed. There were others with whom it was granted me to
converse, who lived seventeen centuries ago, who also were
known to me from history; others who lived four centuries
ago; others who lived three; and so on downwards: and it was
discovered, that a similar affection to that which governed them
in the world, reigned in them still; there being no other difference, than that their delights were turned into such things as
are correspondent. It has been told me by the angels, that the
life of the governing love is never changed with any one to
eternity, since every one is his own love; on which account, to
change it in a spirit, were to deprive him of his life, or to
extinguish him altogether. They also stated what is the cause
of this; which is, that man, after death, is no longer capable of
being reformed by means of instruction, as he is in the world,
because the ultimate plane, which consists of natural knowledges and affections, is then quiescent, and is incapable of being
opened, as not being spiritual (see above, n. 464); and that the
interiors, which belong to the internal and external mind, rest
upon that plane, like a house upon its foundation; on which
account it is, that man remains to eternity such as the life of
his love had been in the world. The angels wonder exceedingly
that man should not be aware, that every one is such in quality
as his governing love is; and that many should believe, that
they may be saved by immediate mercy, and by faith alone, of
whatever character they may have been as to life; also, that
they are not aware that the Divine Mercy operates by means,
consisting in being led by the Lord, both in the world, and
afterwards to eternity; and that those are led by mercy who do
not live in evil. They also are surprised that men should not be
aware, that faith is the affection of truth proceeding from heavenly love, the Author of which is the Lord.

481. III. *That the Man whose Love is celestial and spiritual
goes to Heaven; but that the Man whose Love is corporeal and
worldly, destitute of such as is celestial and spiritual, goes to
Hell.* Respecting this, I was enabled to arrive at certainty,
from all whom I have seen taken up into heaven, on the one
hand, and cast into hell, on the other. Those who were taken
up into heaven were in the enjoyment of a life grounded in
celestial and spiritual love; whereas those who were cast into
hell were sunk in a life grounded in love corporeal and worldly.
Heavenly love consists in a man's loving good, sincerity, and
justice, for their own sakes, and, from such love, in doing them:
whence such persons are in the enjoyment of the life of good,
sincerity, and justice, which is the heavenly life. Those who
love those principles for their own sakes, and who practise them,
or realize them in their life, also love the Lord above all things,
because those excellences proceed from Him: they likewise
love their neighbor, because those excellences are the neighbor

whom we are required to love.([5]) But corporeal love consists in a man's loving good, sincerity, and justice, not for their own sakes, but out of regard to himself, because by them as means, he seeks after réputation, rank, and gain. Such persons, in good, sincerity, and justice, do not regard the Lord and their neighbor, but themselves and the world, and feel delight in fraud'; and good, sincerity, and justice, when practised with fraudulent motives, are evil, insincerity, and injustice; which are the things' that such persons love in the former. Since his loves are what, in this manner, determine the quality of the life of every one, all, as soon as they enter the .spiritual world after death, are examined as to what quality they are of, and are connected, by invisible bonds, with those who are grounded in similar love ; those who are grounded in heavenly love being in this manner connected with the inhabitants of heaven, and those who are immersed in corporeal love with the inhabitants of hell. After having completed their first and second states, the two classes are separated, so as neither to see nor know each other any more : for every one becomes his own love, not only as to his interiors, which belong to the mind, but also as to his exteriors, which are those of his face, body, and speech. Thus every one becomes the image of his own love, even in external appearance. Those who are forms of corporeal love, appear dull, dusky, black, and ugly : whereas those who are forms of heavenly love, appear lively, bright, fair, and 'beautiful : for the two classes are utterly unlike each other in their minds and thoughts. Those who are forms of heavenly love, are, also, intelligent and wise : whereas those who are forms of corporeal love, are stupid and like idiots. When an inspection is granted of the interiors .and exteriors of the thought and affection of those who are in the enjoyment of heavenly love, their interiors appear to wear the resemblance of light, and those of some, the resemblance of flaming light; while their exteriors exhibit various beautiful colors, like those of the rainbow ; whereas the interiors of those who are sunk in corporeal love, appear like

([5]) That the Lord, in the supreme sense, is our neighbor, because He ought to be loved above all things ; but that to love the Lord is to love that which is from him, because He himself is in every thing which is from Himself; thus, it is to love what is good and true, nn. 2425, 3419, 6706, 6711, 6819, 6823, 8123. That to love what is good and true, which is from Him, is to live according to those principles, and that this is to love the Lord, nn. 10,143, 10,153, 10,310, 10,336, 10,578, 10,645. That every man, and society; also, a man's country and the church; and, in the universal sense, the kingdom of the Lord ; are our neighbor; and that to do them good from the love of good, according to the quality of their state, is to love the neighbor; thus their good, which is to be consulted, is our neighbor, nn. 6818—6824, 8123. That moral good, also, which is sincerity, and civil good, which is justice, are our neighbor; and that to act sincerely and justly from the love of sincerity and justice is to love one's neighbor, nn. 2915, 4730, 8120—8123. Hence that charity towards the neighbor extends itself to all things belonging to the life of man, and that to do what is good and just, and to act sincerely from the heart, in every occupation, and in all our dealings, is to love one's neighbor, nn. 2417, 8121, 8124. That the doctrine received in the ancient church was the doctrine of charity, and that hence they had wisdom, nn. 2417, 2385, 3419, 3420, 4344, 6628.

something black, because they are closed; and those of some have a dusky fiery appearance, this being the appearance of the interiors of those who interiorly cherish malignant deceit; whilst their exteriors exhibit frightful colors, melancholy to behold. It is to be borne in mind, that the interiors and the exteriors belonging both to the internal and the external mind, are, in the spiritual world, when the Lord sees good, rendered objects of sight.* Those who are immersed in corporeal love, see nothing in the light of heaven, that light being to them thick darkness: whereas the light of hell, which is like that proceeding from ignited charcoal, is to them like clear light. In the light of heaven, also, their interior sight is darkened, to such an extreme, that they become insane; wherefore they flee from it, and hide themselves in dens and caverns, of a depth proportioned to the falsities grounded in evil that possess their minds; whilst, on the contrary, those who are grounded in heavenly love, the more interiorly or eminently they enter into the light of heaven, the more clearly do they see all things, and the more beautiful do the objects appear to them; whilst they apprehend truths more intelligently and wisely in the same proportion. Those who are immersed in corporeal love, cannot possibly live in the heat of heaven, the heat of heaven being heavenly love; but only in the heat of hell, which is the love of exercising cruelty upon those who do not favor them. Contempt of others, enmity, hatred, revenge, are the delights of that love; and when they are in the exercise of these, they are in the enjoyment of their life; being utterly ignorant of what it is to do good to others from good itself, and for the sake of good itself; but only knowing what it is to do good from evil, and for the sake of evil. Neither can those who are sunk in corporeal love so much as breathe in heaven. As soon as any evil spirit is taken thither, he pants for breath, like a person in the agonies of death. On the other hand, those who are grounded in heavenly love, breathe the more freely, and live more fully, in proportion as they are more interiorly in heaven. From these facts it may be evident, that celestial and spiritual love constitutes heaven with man, because, on that love, all the constituents of heaven are inscribed: whereas corporeal and worldly love, destitute of such as is celestial and spiritual, constitutes hell with man, because, on those loves are inscribed all the constituents of hell. It manifestly follows, that the man whose love is celestial and spiritual, goes to heaven; but that the man whose love is corporeal and worldly, destitute of such as is celestial and spiritual, goes to hell.

482. IV. *That Faith does not remain in Man, if not grounded in heavenly Love.* This has been made manifest to me by so much experimental evidence, that if I were to recite all that I

* See above, n. 466.—*N.*

have seen and heard relating to this subject, it would fill a volume. This I can testify, that no faith whatever exists, nor can any be imparted, with those who are immersed in corporeal and worldly love destitute of such as is celestial and spiritual; and that what passes for such is a mere superficial knowledge, or persuasion, that the faith professed is truth, because it serves to promote the objects of their love. Many, also, of those who imagined themselves to have been possessed of faith, were brought to those who really were so; and when a communication with them was opened, the former perceived that they had no faith at all. They also confessed, afterwards, that merely believing the truth, and the Word, does not constitute faith, but loving truth from heavenly love, and willing and doing it from interior affection. It was also shown, that their persuasion, which they called faith, was only like the light of winter, during which season, there being no heat in the light, all the objects on earth lie torpid, locked up in frost, and buried in snow; on which account, no sooner is the light of their persuasive faith, as existing with them, stricken by the rays of the light of heaven, than it is not only extinguished, but actually becomes like thick darkness, in which no one can see himself: whilst their interiors are so darkened at the same time, that they cannot understand any thing whatever, and at last become insane with falsities. For this reason, all the truths which such persons had been acquainted with, derived from the Word and from the doctrine of the church, and had called the truths of their faith, are taken away from them, and they are imbued, instead, with every falsity that agrees with the evil of their life; for all are let into their own loves, and, at the same time, into the falsities that agree with those loves. After this, they hate truths, hold them in aversion, and thus reject them, because truths are repugnant to the falsities of evil in which they are immersed. This I am able to testify, from all the experience I have had respecting the concerns of heaven and of hell, that all those who have made profession of faith alone as their doctrine, and have been immersed in evil as to life, are in hell. I have seen them cast thither to the number of many thousands. (On which subject, see the treatise *On the Last Judgment, and the Destruction of Babylon.*)

483. V. *That what remains with Man, is Love in act; consequently, his Life.* This follows as a conclusion from all the experimental evidence that has now been adduced, and from the truths advanced above respecting deeds and works. Love in act, is work and deed.

484. It is to be observed, that all works and deeds are matters belonging to the moral and civil life, and, consequently, that they have respect to sincerity and uprightness, and to justice and equity. Sincerity and uprightness are virtues belonging to the moral life; and justice and equity are virtues belonging to

the civil life. The love from which they are practised is either heavenly or infernal. The works and deeds of moral and civil life are heavenly, if they are performed from heavenly love; for whatever is done from heavenly love is done from the Lord, and whatever is done from the Lord, is good. Whereas the deeds and works of moral and civil life are infernal, if they are performed from infernal love; for whatever is done from this love, which is the love of self and the world, is done from man himself; and whatever is done from man himself, is, in itself, evil; for man regarded in himself, or as to his *proprium*, is nothing but evil.(°)

THAT THE DELIGHTS OF THE LIFE OF EVERY ONE ARE TURNED, AFTER DEATH, INTO CORRESPONDENT ONES.

485. That the governing affection or dominant love remains with every one to eternity, has been shown in the preceding Section: that the delights of that affection or love are turned into correspondent ones, is to be shown now. By being turned into correspondent ones, is meant, into such spiritual delights as correspond to the natural ones. That they are turned into spiritual delights, may evidently appear from the fact, that man, so long as he lives in his terrestrial body, exists in the natural world; but after he has left that body, he enters the spiritual world, and puts on a spiritual body. (That the angels exist in perfect human form, as do men, also, after death; and that the bodies with which they are then invested are spiritual ones, may be seen above, nn. 73—77, and 453—460. And for what is meant by the correspondence between spiritual things and such as are natural, see nn. 87—115.)

486. All the delights which man enjoys are those of his governing love: for man feels nothing as delightful but what he loves; consequently, what he feels as most delightful is what he loves most of all. Whether you say, his governing love, or, what he loves most of all, it amounts to the same thing. Those delights are various; in general, there are as many as there are

---

(°) That the *proprium* of man consists in loving himself in preference to God, and the world in preference to heaven, and in making light of his neighbor in comparison with himself; thus that it consists in the love of self and of the world, nn. 694, 731, 4317. That it is this *proprium* into which man is born, and that it is dense evil, nn. 210, 215, 731, 874, 875, 876, 987, 1047, 2307, 2308, 3518, 3701, 3812, 8480, 6550, 10,283, 10,284, 10,286, 10,732. That from the *proprium* of man cometh not only all that is evil, but likewise all that is false, nn. 1047, 10,283, 10,284, 10,286. That the evils, which come from the *proprium* of man, are contempt of others, enmity, hatred, revenge, cruelty, deceit, nn. 6667, 7370, 7373, 7374, 9348, 10,038, 10,742. That so far as the *proprium* of man bears rule, the good of love and the truth of faith are either rejected, or suffocated, or perverted, nn. 2041, 7491, 7492, 7643, 8487, 10,455, 10,742. That the *proprium* of man is hell with him, nn. 694, 8480. That the good which man does from the *proprium*, is not good, but is in itself evil, n. 8480.

governing loves; consequently, there are as many delights as there are men, spirits, and angels: for the governing love of one is never in all respects similar to that of another. It is owing to this, that the face of one person is never exactly similar to that of another; for the face, in every one, is the image of his mind, and, in the spiritual world, is the image of his governing love. The delights of every one in particular are also of infinite variety; nor is one delight of any individual, ever in all respects similar to, or the same with, another; and this is true, both in regard to those delights which occur in succession one after another, and to those which exist together, one simultaneously with another. No one delight that is the same as another can ever exist. Nevertheless, these delights that exist specifically with every individual, have reference to the one love belonging to him, which is, his governing love; for they compose it, and, consequently, make one with it. In the same manner, all delights in general have reference to one universally governing love; which, in heaven, .is the love of the Lord; and, in hell, the love of self.

487. What, and of what nature, are the spiritual delights, into which the natural delights of every one are turned after death, can only be known from the science of correspondences. This teaches in general, that no natural thing can exist, which has not its corresponding spiritual one: and it also teaches, in particular, what, and of what nature, the corresponding thing is. On this account, a person skilled in that science, may know, and become acquainted with, his own state after death, provided he is acquainted with his own love, and knows what station it occupies in that universally governing love, to which all loves have reference; as observed just now. But it is impossible for those who are immersed in the love of self to be acquainted with their governing love; because they love whatever is their own, and call their evils goods, denominating, at the same time, the falsities which favor their evils, and by the help of which they confirm them, truths. Nevertheless, if they please, they may learn it from others who are wise; for such persons see things which they themselves do not see. Those, however, refuse to be taught, who are so wholly engrossed by the love of self, as to reject all admonition proffered by the wise. But those who are grounded in heavenly love, accept instruction, and on being brought into the evils into which they were born, see them to be such by the truths which they have learned; for these make evils manifest. Every one may, from such truth as originates in good, see evil and its falsity; but no one can, from evil, see good and truth: the reason is, because falsities grounded in evil are darkness, and actually correspond to darkness; on which account, those who are immersed in falsities grounded in evil are like blind men, who cannot see objects placed in the light; and they ac-

tually flee from such objects, as owls do.([1])   On the other hand, truths from good are light, and actually correspond to light (see above, nn. 126—134): on which account, those who are grounded in truths originating in good, are persons who see, and who have their eyes open; and they distinguish between the things that belong to the light, and those that belong to the shade.   In regard to these truths, also, it has been granted me to receive confirmation by experimental evidence.   The angels in heaven both see and perceive the evils and falsities which sometimes rise up in themselves; as well as the evils and falsities in which those spirits are immersed, who, while yet in the world of spirits, are connected by invisible bonds with the hells: whereas those spirits themselves are unable to see their own evils and falsities. What the good of heavenly love is, what conscience, what sincerity and justice (unless as practised for self-advantage), what it is to be led by the Lord; those spirits cannot conceive: they affirm that such things have no existence, and thus that they are not worth attending to. · These statements are made to induce man to examine himself, and learn from his delights what his love is, and, in consequence, so far as he understands the science of correspondences, what will be the state of his life after death.

488. In what manner the delights of every one's life are turned after death into correspondent ones, may indeed be known from the science of correspondences; but as that science has not yet been made public, I will throw some degree of light on the subject by a few facts of experience.   All who are immersed in evil, and who have confirmed themselves in falsities against the truths of the church,—especially those who have rejected the Word— shun the light of heaven, and betake themselves to places under ground, which, viewed at their apertures, appear very dark, and to the holes of rocks; and there conceal themselves: the reason of which is, because they have loved falsities, and have hated truths; for such places under ground, and the holes of rocks,([2]) correspond to falsities; as does darkness likewise;* whereas light corresponds to truth.   It is agreeable to them to dwell in such places, and·disagreeable to reside in the open fields.   The like is done by those, who took delight in laying snares clandestinely, and in secretly contriving deceitful machinations.   These also abide in those underground places, and enter into chambers so

---

([1]) That darkness, in the Word, from correspondence signifies falsities, and thick darkness, the falsities of evil, nn. 1839, 1860, 7688, 7711.   That the light of heaven is thick darkness to the evil, nn. 1861, 6832, 8197.   That the inhabitants of the hells are said to be in darkness, because in the falsities of evil, concerning whom, nn. 3340, 4418, 4531.   That the blind, in the Word, signify those who are in falsities, and are not willing to be instructed, nn. 2383, 6990.

([2]) That a hole and cleft of a rock, in the Word, signifies an obscure and false principle of faith, n. 10,582.   Because a rock signifies faith from the Lord, nn. 8581, 10,580; and a stone the truth of faith, nn. 114, 643, 1298, 3720, 6426, 8609, 10,376.

* That the above is the sense intended, is obvious; but, in the Latin original, *tum falsa, tenebris,* is erroneously printed, for *tum tenebræ, falsis.*   The mistake was not corrected in either of the former translations.—*N.*

dark, that they cannot so much as see each other; in the corners
of which they whisper into one another's ears. This is what the
delight of their love is turned into. Those who have studied the
sciences, with no other end in view than to be esteemed men of
learning, and have not cultivated their rational faculty by means
of them, but who took delight in storing their memory, out of the
self-conceit which possessed them on account of such attainments,
love sandy places, preferring them to fields and gardens; the
reason of which is, that sandy places correspond to such studies.
Those who have possessed an acquaintance with the doctrines of
their own and other churches, without having applied any thing
that they knew to life, choose for their residence rocky situations,
and dwell among heaps of stones; shunning cultivated regions,
because they regard such places with aversion. Those who have
ascribed every thing to nature, and those who have attributed all
to their own prudence, and who, by various artifices, have raised
themselves to honors and have gained wealth, devote themselves,
in the other-life, to magical arts, which are abuses of Divine Order; and find, in these, the greatest delight of their life. Those
who have applied divine truths to promote their own loves, and
thus have falsified them, love urinous substances and places,
because these correspond to the delights of such love.(*) Those
who have been sordid misers, dwell in cellars, and love the filth
of swine, and such nidorous exhalations as proceed from indi-
gested substances in the stomach. Those who have passed their
life in mere pleasures, have lived delicately, and have indulged
their palate and appetite, loving such enjoyments as the chief
good of life, love, in the other life, dunghills and privies, which
then become delightful to them: the reason of which is, because
such pleasures are spiritual filth. They shun places that are
clean, and free from filth, because these are disagreeable to them.
Those who have taken delight in adulteries, reside in brothels,
all the objects in which wear the aspect of mean and squalid
wretchedness. These places they love, and shun chaste houses,
on coming near to which they faint away. Nothing is more delightful to them than to cause breaches of the marriage-union.
Those who have lusted for revenge, and who have thence acquired
a savage and cruel nature, love cadaverous substances, or the
places where they exist; and they also dwell in hells of that
description. And so in other cases.

489. But the delights of the life of those, who, in the world,
have lived in heavenly love, are turned into corresponding objects,
such as are seen in the heavens, which derive their existence from
the sun of heaven, and from the light thence proceeding. That
light exhibits to view such objects, as inwardly include things
divine. The objects that are rendered apparent from this source,
affect the interiors which belong to the minds of the angels, and

(*) That the defilements of truth correspond to urine, n. 5390.

18   273

the exteriors which belong to their bodies at the same time. As the Divine Light, which is the Divine Truth proceeding from the Lord, flows into their minds, which are opened by heavenly love, it also exhibits, in externals, such objects to view, as correspond to the delights of their love. (That the objects which appear to the sight in heaven, correspond to the interiors of the angels, or to those which belong to their faith and love, and thence to their intelligence and wisdom, has been shown in the Section which treats of Representatives and Appearances in Heaven, nn. 170—176; and in that on the Wisdom of the Angels of Heaven, nn. 265—275.) Since we have entered on the confirmation of this matter from experimental evidence, to illustrate the truths, drawn from the causes of things, previously advanced respecting it, I will also mention some facts respecting the heavenly delights, into which natural delights, as existing with those who, in the world, live in heavenly love, are turned. Those who have loved divine truths, and the Word, from interior affection, or from an affection for truth itself, in the other world dwell in the light, in elevated situations, which appear like mountains, where they are continually surrounded by the light of heaven : they do not know what darkness is, such as prevails at night in the world : and they also live in the temperature of spring. When they look around, they behold fields and crops of corn; together with vineyards. In their houses, all the objects shine as if set with precious stones. To look through the windows is like looking through pure pieces of crystal. These are the delightful things presented to their sight : but these same things are interiorly delightful, in consequence of their correspondence with heavenly divine things; for the truths derived from the Word, which they have loved, correspond to crops of corn, vineyards, precious stones, windows, and crystals.[*] Those who have immediately applied the doctrinal truths of the church, drawn from the Word, to life, dwell in the inmost heaven, where they are in the enjoyment, beyond others, of the delight of wisdom. These, in all the objects around them, behold things divine : they do, indeed, see the objects, but the divine things corresponding to them flow immediately into their minds, filling them with a beatitude which runs through all their sensations. From this cause, all the objects before their eyes, as it were laugh, sport, and are alive. (Respecting these, see above, n. 270.) Those who have loved the sciences, and who, by means of them, have cultivated their rational faculty, whence they have procured for themselves intelligence, and who, at the same time, have acknowledged the Divine Being, find the pleasure that they

---

[*] That a crop of corn, in the Word, signifies a state of reception and of increase of truth derived from good, n. 9294. That a standing crop signifies truth in conception, n. 9146. That vineyards signify the spiritual church, and the truths of that church, nn. 1069, 9139. That precious stones signify the truths of heaven and the church transparent from good, nn. 114, 9863, 9865, 9868, 9873, 9905. That a window signifies the intellectual principle, which belongs to the internal sight, nn. 655, 658, 8391.

took in sciences, and their rational delight, turned, in the other life, into a spiritual delight, which is that of the knowledges of good and truth. They dwell in gardens, in which appear flower-beds and lawns divided into beautiful compartments, and surrounded by rows of trees forming piazzas and walks. The trees and flowers are varied every day. The view of the whole imparts delight to their minds in general, which the varieties in particular continually renew: and as the objects correspond to things divine, and those who behold them are grounded in the science of correspondences, they are perpetually replenished with new knowledges, by which is perfected their spiritual-rational faculty. They experience these delights, because gardens, flowers, lawns, and trees, correspond to sciences and knowledges, and to the intelligence thence procured.(⁵) Those who have ascribed every thing to the Divine Being, and have regarded nature as being respectively dead, merely subserving spiritual ends, and who have confirmed themselves in that belief, dwell in heavenly light; and all the objects which appear before their eyes, derive, from that light, the property of being transparent. In that transparency, they behold innumerable variegations of light, which their internal sight, in a manner, immediately imbibes: and they derive from them perceptions of interior delight. The objects which appear in their houses, are as if made of diamonds, in which similar variegations of light are displayed. It has been told me, that the walls of their houses are as if built with crystal, consequently, are transparent also, and that there appear in them floating forms representative of heavenly things; which likewise are attended with similar variety. The reason of all this is, because such transparency corresponds to an understanding enlightened by the Lord, the shades being removed which result from faith of a natural kind and from the love of natural things. Such are the things, with an infinity of others, respecting which it has been said, by those who had been in heaven, that they had seen things that eye never saw; and, from a perception communicated to them of the divine things that flow forth from the former, that they had heard things that ear never heard. Those who have not acted in a clandestine manner, but have been willing that all their thoughts should be open, so far as the forms of life in civil society would permit, appear, in heaven, because they had thought nothing but what was sincere and just from a Divine Source, with countenances that shine with light, and in consequence of that light, all their affections and thoughts appear in their countenances, as in their proper form; and their speech and actions are, in a manner, the effigies of their affections.

(⁵) That a garden, a grove, and paradise, signify intelligence, nn. 100, 108, 3220. That therefore the ancients celebrated holy worship in groves, nn. 2722, 4552. That flowers and flower-beds signify scientific truths and knowledges, n. 9553. That herbs, grasses, and grass-plots signify scientific truths, n. 7571. That trees signify perceptions and knowledges, nn. 103, 2163, 2682, 2722, 2972, 7692.

These are, in consequence, loved more than others. When they speak, their face is somewhat obscured; but when they have ended, the same things as they spoke appear all together in their face, fully presented to view. All the objects, likewise, which exist around them, since they correspond to their interiors, have such an appearance, that it is clearly perceived by others what they represent and signify. Such spirits as have taken delight in acting clandestinely, on seeing these ingenuous ones at a distance, shun their presence, and appear to themselves to glide away from them, like serpents. Those who have accounted adulteries as horribly wicked, and have lived in the chaste love of marriage, are, more than others, in the order and form of heaven, and thence possess consummate beauty, and remain perpetnally in the flower of their age. The delights of their love are ineffable, and go on increasing to eternity. For all the delights and joys of heaven flow into that love, because it descends from the conjunction of the Lord with heaven and the church, and, in general, from the conjunction of good and truth; which conjunction constitutes heaven itself, both as existing in the grand whole, and with every angel in particular. (See above, nn. 366—386.) Their external delights are such as cannot be described in the words of any human language. But the facts that have now been related respecting the correspondences of delights, as existing with those who are grounded in heavenly love, are, respectively, but few.

490. From these statements may be known, that the delights of all are turned, after death, into correspondent ones, the love itself remaining, nevertheless, to eternity; such as conjugial love, the love of justice, of sincerity, of good, and of truth, the love of sciences and knowledges, the love of intelligence and wisdom, and the rest. Delights are the results which flow from the love, like streams from their fountain. These, also, are permanent: but they are elevated to a superior degree, when, from natural ones, they pass into such as are spiritual.

OF THE FIRST STATE OF MAN AFTER DEATH.

491. There are three states which man undergoes after death, before he passes either into heaven or into hell. The first state is one in which he is yet in his exteriors: the second state is that in which he is in his interiors: and the third state is that of his preparation. These states are undergone by him in the world of spirits. There are some, however, who do not pass through these states, but who, immediately after death, are at once either carried up into heaven or cast down into hell. Those who are immediately carried up into heaven, are such as have

been regenerated, and so prepared for heaven, in the world. Those who have been so regenerated and prepared, as to have nothing to do but to cast off the mere defilements of nature with the body, are carried by angels into heaven at once: I have seen some translated in this manner directly after the hour of death. But those who, interiorly, have been ill-intentioned, though exteriorly, in appearance, good, thus, who have filled their malignity with deceit, and have employed goodness as a means of deception, are immediately cast into hell. I have seen some of this character cast into hell immediately after death: one, who was a most deceitful person, went with his head downwards and his feet upwards; and others in different ways. There also are some, who, immediately after death, are banished into caverns, and are thus separated from those who tarry in the world of spirits: they are afterwards taken out of those caverns, and are again sent into them, alternately: they consist of such persons as, under a cover of civility, had dealt maliciously with their neighbor. But both these and the former are but few, in respect to those who are detained in the world of spirits, and who are there prepared, according to Divine Order, for heaven, or for hell.

492. With respect to the first state, which is a state in which the party is still in his exteriors: it is that into which man comes immediately after death. Every man possesses, as to his spirit, both exteriors and interiors. The exteriors of his spirit are those, by means of which he adapts his body, while in the world, especially his face, his speech, and his behavior, for living in society with others. But the interiors of his spirit are those which are proper to his will, and to his thought thence proceeding: which seldom are suffered to appear in his face, his speech, and his behavior. For man is accustomed, from his infancy, to put on the appearance of friendship, benevolence, and sincerity, and to conceal the thoughts of his proper will; whence he acquires the habits of moral and civil life in his externals, whatever may be his character in his internals. In consequence of this habit, a man scarcely has any acquaintance with his own interiors, and does not reflect upon them.

493. The first state of a man after death is similar to what it had been in the world; because he is then still in his externals. His countenance is similar, his speech is similar, and his disposition is similar; with, consequently, his moral and civil life. In consequence of this, he is not aware but that he is still in the world, if he does not advert to the things which occur to him, and to what was told him by the angels when he was first resuscitated; who then informed him that he was now a spirit. (See n. 450.) Thus the one life passes into the other; and death is only the actual transit.

494. Since the spirit of a man who has recently entered the

other life after the conclusion of his life in the world, is of this description, it follows that he is then recognized by his friends, and by all whom he knew when they and he were in the world: for other spirits recognize him, not only by his countenance and speech, but also by the sphere of his life, on coming near him. Whenever, in the other life, any one thinks of another, he also, in thought, sets his countenance before him, with many of the circumstances of his life; and when he does this, the person he is thinking of appears present before him, as if he had been sent for, and called. This phenomenon occurs in the spiritual world, because there exists in that world, a communication of thoughts, and there are no spaces there, such as those in the natural world. (See above, nn. 191—199.) It is owing to this, that all, on their first entering the other life, are recognized by their friends, relations, and all to whom they were in any way known, and that they enter into conversation, and afterwards are connected together in society, according to the intimacy of their friendship or acquaintance in the world. I have frequently heard those who came from the world rejoice on seeing their friends again; whilst these rejoiced, on their part, that their friends had come to them. This is a common occurrence; that one married partner meets the other; when they congratulate each other on the occasion. They also remain together, for a longer or shorter time, according to the delight that had attended their dwelling together in the world; but nevertheless, if the bond of their connection had not been love truly conjugial, which consists in the conjunction of minds under the influence of heavenly love, after remaining together for some time they are separated. But if the minds of the two parties had been mutually discordant, and interiorly felt aversion for each other, they break out into open enmity, and sometimes actually fight: notwithstanding which, they are not separated, before they enter on the second state, to be treated of in the next Section.

495. As the life of recently separated spirits is not unlike their life in the natural world, and they have brought with them no knowledge respecting what their state of life would be after death, nor respecting heaven and hell, except what they had learned from the literal sense of the Word, and from sermons founded on that sense; the consequence is, that, after wondering at finding themselves in a body, and in the enjoyment of all the senses that they had in the world, and at beholding similar objects, they are seized with a desire to know what is the nature of heaven, and what the nature of hell, and where they are situated. They are therefore instructed, by friends, respecting the state of eternal life: they are also conducted about to various places, and to various companies: some are taken into cities, and into gardens and paradises, usually, to magnificent scenes; because such things are pleasing to their externals, in which they

at present are. They are also, by turns, led to remember the thoughts which they entertained, in the life of the body, respecting the state of their soul after death, respecting heaven, and respecting hell, till they feel indignant that they should have been in such complete ignorance on these subjects, and that such ignorance should exist respecting them in the church. Almost all are anxious to know whether they shall go to heaven: and most believe that they shall, because, when in the world, they had led a moral and civil life; not reflecting, that both the bad and the good lead a similar life in externals, each doing good to others in a similar manner, going to church, listening to sermons, and uttering prayers; and not being at all aware, that external actions, and the externals of worship, avail nothing, but only the internal principles from which the external performances proceed. Out of some thousands, scarcely one is to be found who knows what internal things are, and that it is in these that man possesses heaven and the church; still less, that external actions are such in quality, as are the intentions and thoughts, inclusive of the love and faith, from which they proceed: and when they are instructed on these subjects, they do not comprehend how thinking and willing can be of any consequence, but regard as every thing, the speaking and doing. Of this description are most of those, who at this day enter the other life from the Christian world.

496. They are examined, however, by good spirits, as to their quality; which is done in various ways; since, in this first state, the bad utter truths, and do good deeds, as well as the good. This they do from the cause explained above; which is, that they have equally led a moral life in external form, because they had lived under regular governments, and had been subject to the laws there established; and because, by such a course of life, they had sought after the reputation of justice and sincerity, and to conciliate the favor of others, and had thus been raised to honor, and had gained wealth. Evil spirits, however, are distinguished from good ones by this circumstance especially; that they eagerly attend to what is said on external subjects, and but little to what is said on internal ones, which are the truths and goods of heaven and the church. They hear, indeed, what is addressed to them on these subjects, but not with attention and joy. They are also distinguished by this; that they frequently turn themselves towards certain quarters, and, when left to themselves, walk in the ways which tend in those directions. By their turning towards certain quarters, and walking in certain ways, is known the nature of the love which leads them.

497. All the spirits who arrive from the world, are, indeed, attached, by invisible bonds, to some specific society in heaven, or to some specific society in hell. This attachment, however, only affects their interiors; and no one's interiors are open so

long as he is in his exteriors, these covering and hiding them, especially with such as are the subjects of interior evil. Afterwards, however, when they come into the second state, the interiors manifestly appear; for their interiors are then laid open, and their exteriors are laid asleep.

498. This first state of man after death lasts, with some, for some days, with others, for some months, and with others, for a year; but it seldom continues for more than a year with any one: the duration is longer or shorter, in each instance, according to the agreement or disagreement of the party's interiors with his exteriors. For, with every one, the exteriors and the interiors must act as one, and must correspond to each other. It is not allowable for any one, in the spiritual world, to think and will in one way, and to speak and act in another. Every one must there be the express image of his own affection, or of his own love; consequently, such as he is in his interiors, such must he be in his exteriors also: wherefore the exteriors of a spirit are first stripped off, and reduced to such order as to serve as a corresponding plane to his interiors.

OF THE SECOND STATE OF MAN AFTER DEATH.

499. The second state of man after death is called the state of his interiors, because he is then let into the interiors which belong to his mind, or to his will and thought, and his exteriors, in which he was in his first state, are laid asleep. Any person who pays attention to the life of man, and to his conversation and actions, may be aware, that every one possesses exteriors and interiors, or exterior and interior thoughts and intentions. He may be aware of this from these circumstances: every one who lives in civil society, thinks of others according to what he has heard and understood respecting them either from report or conversation; still he does not speak with them according to his thoughts, but treats them with civility; though they may be bad characters. That this is practised, is especially obvious from the case of pretenders and flatterers, who speak and act quite differently from what they think and will; and from that of hypocrites, who talk about God, about heaven, about the salvation of souls, about the truths of the church, about the good of their country, and about their neighbor, as if they spoke under the influence of faith and love; although, in their heart, they believe nothing of what they say, and love none but themselves. From these facts it may be evident, that there exist two classes of thought, the one exterior and the other interior, and that people speak from their exterior thought, while, in their interior, their sentiments are different; and that those two classes of

ought are separate from one another; for special care is taken
t at the interior should not flow into the exterior, and in any
w iy appear. Man is so formed by creation, as that his interior
thought should act as one with his exterior by correspondence;
an.l it actually does so in those who are grounded in good; for
they think nothing but what is good, and they speak accordingly.
But with those who are immersed in evil, the interior thought
does not form a one with the exterior; for they think what is
evil, and say what is good. With these, there is an inversion of
order; for good, as existing with them, is without, and evil is
within; on which account, evil rules over good, and subjects the
latter to itself like a slave, that it may serve it as an instrument
for obtaining its ends, which are such as are regarded by their
love. Such an end being contained within the good that they
say and do, it is evident, that, in them, good is not good, but is
infected with evil, how much soever, in its external form, it
may appear as good before those who are not acquainted with
the interiors of the doers of it. Not so with those who are
grounded in good. With these, there is no inversion of order
but, from their interior thought, good flows into their exterior, and thus into their speech and their actions. This is the
order into which man was created: for when men are in this
order, their interiors are in heaven, and in the light which there
shines; and as the light of heaven is the Divine Truth proceeding from the Lord, it is, consequently, the Lord in heaven (see
nn. 126—14v); whence those who dwell in it are led by the
Lord. These truths are advanced, that it may be known that
every man has interior thought and exterior thought, and that
these are distinct from each other. When thought is mentioned,
the will also is meant, thought being derived from will; for
without will, it is impossible to think. From these observations
it is evident, what is the state of the exteriors, and what the state
of the interiors, belonging to man.

500. When mention is made of the will and the thought, by
the will is also meant affection and love, with all the enjoyment
and pleasure which are connected with them; because affection
and love have reference to the will as their subject, since what
a man wills, he also loves, and feels delightful and pleasurable;
and, conversely, what a man loves, and feels delightful and
pleasurable, he also wills. But by the thought is then meant,
also, every thing by which he confirms his affection or love: for
thought is nothing but the form of the will, and is provided in
order that what a man wills may appear in the light. This form
is produced by various rational analyses, which derive their origin from the spiritual world, and properly belong to man's spirit.

501. It is to be observed, that man is entirely such in quality
as he is with respect to his interiors, and not such as he is with
respect to his exteriors separately from the former. The reason

of this is, because the interiors belong to his spirit, and the life of man is the life of his spirit, it being thence that the body lives: on which account, also, such as man is, in quality, as to his interiors, such he remains to eternity. But the exteriors, since they appertain also to the body, are separated from him after death, and those things derived from them which adhere to the spirit, are laid asleep, and only serve as a plane for the interiors; as was shown above, when treating of the memory of man that remains after death. Hence it is evident, what things are a man's own, or properly belong to him, and what things are not his own, or do not properly belong to him. With the evil, all such things as belong to their exterior thought, from which they speak, and to their exterior will, from which they act, are not their own, or do not properly belong to them; but only such as belong to their interior thought and will.

502. After the completion of the first state, treated of in the preceding Section, which is that of the exteriors, the man, now a spirit, is let into the state of his interiors, or into the state of his interior will and of the thought thence proceeding, in which he had been in the world, when, being left to himself, he thought freely and without restraint. He lapses into this state unconsciously; much as he does in the world, when he draws in the thought next to his speech, or that from which speech proceeds, towards his interior thought, and abides in the latter. When therefore the man, now a spirit, is in this state, he is at home in himself, and is in his very life: for to think freely from the affection properly belonging to him, is the very life of man, and is the man himself.

503. A spirit, in this state, thinks from his actual will, consequently from his actual affection, or from his actual love: and then his thought forms a one with his will, so completely, that he scarcely appears to be thinking, but only willing. It is nearly the same when he speaks; but there is this difference, that he speaks with a degree of fear lest the thoughts of his will should go forth naked: for this reserve has become a habit of his will, acquired by living in civil society in the world.

504. All men whatsoever are let into this state after death, because it is the proper state of their spirit. The former state is such as that of the man was, as to his spirit, when he was in company; and his state, then, is not properly his own. That this state, or the state of his exteriors, in which man first exists after death, and which was treated of in the preceding Section, is not properly his own, may evidently appear from many circumstances: such as this: that spirits not only think, but also speak, from their own affection; for it is from this that their speech proceeds. (As may be evident from what was stated and shown in the Section on the Speech of the Angels, nn. 234—245.) The man thought in a similar manner when in the world, when he

thought within himself; for he did not then think from the speech of his body, but only saw the things which the body uttered; and many more, within a minute of time, than he could afterwards deliver by speech in half an hour. That the state in which man is in his exteriors is not properly his own, or that of his spirit, is also evident from this circumstance; that when, during his life in the world, he is in company, he speaks according to the laws of moral and civil life, and his interior thought governs his exterior, as one person governs another, to prevent it from transgressing the limits of decorum and propriety. It is also evident from this circumstance; that when a man thinks within himself, he also considers how he must speak and act so as to please, and to obtain friendship, good-will, and favor; and this he does by modes foreign to what is natural to him; and, consequently, he speaks differently from what he would do, if he spoke from the immediate dictates of his own will. From these facts it is evident, that the state of his interiors into which the spirit is let, is the state properly belonging to him; and thus, also, is the state which properly belonged to him, while he lived as a man in the world.

505. When a spirit is in the state of his interiors, it manifestly appears of what quality the man was, in himself, when in the world; for he then acts from his *proprium*, or from what is properly his own, whether bad or good. He who, when he lived in the world, was interiorly grounded in good, then acts rationally and wisely, in fact, more wisely than he did in the world, because he is released from his connection with the body, and thus, from his connection with earthly things, which obscured, and, in a manner, cast a cloud over the wisdom that he interiorly possessed. But he who, when he lived in the world, was grounded in evil, then acts foolishly and insanely, in fact, more insanely than he did in the world, because he is now in a state of freedom, and under no restraint. For when he lived in the world he was sane in externals, and, by their means, assumed the feigned character of a rational man; wherefore, when his externals are stripped off from him, his insane phantasies are exposed. A bad man, who, in externals, puts on the semblance of a good man, may be compared to a vase exteriorly bright and polished, and covered with a lid, within which are concealed filthy matters of every kind; according to the Lord's declaration: "*Ye are like unto whited sepulchres, which indeed appear beautiful outward, but are within full of dead men's bones, and of all uncleanness.*" —(Matt. xxiii. 27.)

506. All who, in the world, have lived in a state of good, and have acted under the influence of conscience,—who are those who have acknowledged the Divine Being and have loved divine truths, and especially those who have applied them to life,— appear to themselves, when let into the state of their interiors,

283

like persons who, after having been asleep, become broad awake:
and like persons who pass out of the shade into the light. They
also think from the light of heaven, and thus from interior
wisdom; and they act from a principle of good, and thus from
interior affection. Heaven, likewise, flows into their thoughts
and affections with a sense of interior beatitude and delight,
such as, previously, they had no idea of: for they now have
communication with the angels of heaven. They now, also,
acknowledge the Lord, and worship Him from, their very life;
for they are in their own proper life, when they are in the state
of their interiors; as stated just above (n. 505). They likewise
acknowledge and worship Him from freedom, for freedom is
attendant on interior affection. They thus, also, recede from the
state of external sanctity, and come into that of internal sanctity,
in which real worship truly consists. Such is the state of those,
who have led a Christian life according to the commandments
delivered in the Word. But the state of those, who, in the world,
have lived in evil, and who have had no conscience, and have
thence denied the Divine Being, is the diametrical contrary.
For all who live in evil, in their own interior selves deny the
Divine Being, how much soever they may imagine, when in
their externals, that they do not deny but acknowledge Him:
for to acknowledge the Divine Being, and to live in evil, are
incompatible opposites. In the other life, those who are of such
a character, when they come into the state of their interiors,
appear, to those who hear their conversation and observe their
actions, like persons infatuated: for, under the influence of their
evil lusts, they break out into nefarious excesses, such as contempt
of others, mockery, railing, hatred, revenge, and the contriving
of deceitful devices, which some of them plot with such cunning
and malice, that it can scarcely be believed that any thing like it
can interiorly exist in any man. For in the state in which they
then are, they are free to act according to the thoughts of their
will, being separated from their exteriors, which, in the world,
coerced and restrained them. In one word, they are destitute of
rationality; because the rational faculty which they exercised in
the world, had not had its seat in their interiors, but only in their
exteriors; and yet they then appear to themselves to be wise
beyond all others. Being such in quality, therefore, when they
are in this second state, they are occasionally remitted, for a
short time, into the state of their exteriors, with a remembrance
of what their actions had been while they were in the state of
their interiors. Some are then ashamed of themselves, and confess that they had been insane: some are not ashamed: and
some are angry that they are not allowed to remain continually
in the state of their exteriors. But to these it is shown, what
sort of persons they would be if they could remain continually
in this state; for they would then endeavor to perform similar

nefarious deeds in a clandestine manner, and, by appearances of goodness, of sincerity, and of justice, would seduce the simple in heart and faith, and would also destroy themselves totally; for the conflagration which raged in their interiors would at length seize their exteriors also, and would consume the whole of their life.

507. When spirits are in this second state, they openly and completely show what sort of persons they had inwardly been in the world, and they actually make public what they then had done and said in secret: for, external considerations no longer restraining them, they openly say similar things, and also endeavor to perform similar actions, without any fear, as in the world, for their reputation. They also are then led into many states belonging to their former evils; that it may appear to angels and good spirits what sort of beings they are. Thus, things hidden are laid open, and things secret are uncovered; according to the words of the Lord: *"There is nothing covered, that shall not be revealed; neither hid, that shall not be known. Therefore, whatsoever ye have spoken in darkness, shall be heard in the light; and that which ye have spoken in the ear in closets, shall be proclaimed upon the house-tops."*—(Luke xii. 2, 3.) And again: *"I say unto you, That every idle word that men shall speak, they shall give an account thereof in the day of judgment."*—(Matt. xii. 36.)

508. What sort of beings the wicked are, in this state, cannot be described in a few words, because every one is then insane according to his own lusts, and these are various; wherefore I will only adduce some specific instances, from which a judgment may be formed as to the rest. Those who have supremely loved themselves, and, in the offices and occupations they have discharged, have only regarded their own honor, having performed uses, not for the sake of the uses themselves, and because they took delight in them, but with a view to their own reputation, and that they, for doing them, might be more highly esteemed than others, and thus might receive delight from the fame of their honor; these, when in this second state, are more stupid than others; for in proportion as any one loves himself, he is removed from heaven; and in proportion as he is removed from heaven, he is also removed from wisdom. But those who have been immersed in self-love, and have been cunning at the same time, and had raised themselves to honors by artful practices, connect themselves in society with the worst of all, and learn magical arts, which are abuses of Divine Order, by which they injure and infest all who do not pay them honor. They contrive snares, they cherish hatred, they burn with revenge, and they lust to exercise cruelty upon all who do not submit to them. They rush into the perpetration of all these crimes, so far as the malignant crew favors their endeavors; and at last they meditate how

they can climb up to heaven, and destroy it, or be worshipped there as gods. To such excesses is their madness carried. Those of this class who had been of the Roman Catholic religion, are more insane than the rest: for they are possessed with the notion, that heaven and hell are subject to their power, and that they are able to remit people's sins at pleasure. They arrogate to themselves every divine attribute, and call themselves Christ. The persuasion which possesses them that all this is true, is so strong, that, where the influx of it enters, it disturbs people's minds, and induces darkness that even causes pain. These spirits are much alike, in both states, but in the second they are destitute of rationality. (Respecting their insanities, and their lot after they have passed through this state, some particulars are related in the work on the *Last Judgment and the Destruction of Babylon.*) Those who have ascribed the creation to nature, and, as the result, have denied the Divine Being in their heart, though not with their lips, and, consequently, all things belonging to heaven and the church, connect themselves, in this state, in society with those who are like themselves, and call any one God who excels the others in cunning, actually worshipping him with divine honors. I have seen a number of such spirits collected in a meeting, worshipping a magician, debating about nature, and conducting themselves so insanely, that they might be taken for beasts under the human form: yet there were some among them who, in the world, had occupied stations of high rank; and some who had possessed the reputation of being learned and wise men. And so with other classes. From these few examples a judgment may be formed, as to what sort of persons those are, in whom the interiors, which belong to the mind, are shut in the direction of heaven, as they are in all who have not received any influx from heaven through the acknowledgment of the Divine Being, and through the life of faith. Every one may judge from himself what sort of person he would be, if of this character, were he at liberty to act without any fear of the law or of the loss of his life, and in freedom from external bonds, such as fear lest he should suffer in his reputation, and lest he should be deprived of honor, gain, and the pleasures derived from them. Nevertheless, the insanity of such spirits is restrained by the Lord, to prevent it from rushing beyond the limits of use; for use is performed even by every one of this description. In them, good spirits see what evil is, and what is its nature, and what sort of a being man would be were he not led by the Lord. It is also a use, that similar evil spirits should by them be gathered together, and separated from the good; and also, that the truths and goods which the evil have made a show of, and have falsely assumed in externals, should be taken from them, and that they should be led into the evils of their own life, and into the falsities of their evil, and so be prepared for hell. For no one goes to hell, until he is both immersed in his own evil and in the falsities proper to it; since it is not allowable, there, for any one to have a divided mind, or to think and speak one thing and to will another. Every evil spirit must there think what is false derived from evil, and must speak from such falsity, doing both from his will, consequently, from his own proper love, and its delight and pleasure; as he did in the world, when he thought in his spirit; that is, as he thought within himself, when he thought from his interior affection. The reason of this is, because the will is the man himself, and not the thought, except in proportion as it is derived from the will; and the will is man's absolute nature or disposition, so that to be let into his will is to be let into his own nature or disposition, and into his own life also, for man acquires a nature according to his life: and man remains, after death, of such a nature as he has procured for himself by his life in the world; which, with the evil, can then no longer be amended and changed by means of the thought or understanding of truth.

509. As evil spirits, when they are in this second state, rush into crimes of every kind, it happens that they are frequently and severely punished. In the world of spirits, there are punishments of many kinds: nor is any respect there had to persons, whether the individual to be punished had been in the world a king or a servant. All evil carries with it punishment: they are combined together; in consequence of which, whoever is in the commission of evil, is also immersed in the punishment of evil. Nevertheless, no one there suffers punishment for crimes which he had committed in the world, but only for the crimes which he commits there. It amounts, however, to the same thing, whether it be said that the wicked are punished for their crimes committed in the world, or for the crimes which they commit in the other life; since every one, after death, returns into his own life, and thus into similar evils; because man is then such in quality as he had been in the life of his body. (See above, nn. 470—484.) The reason that they are punished is, because the fear of punishment is, in this state, the only means by which their evils can be subdued: neither exhortation, instruction, nor yet fear of the law and for their reputation, are any longer of any avail; because the party now acts from his nature, which cannot be coerced, or broken, except by punishments. On the other hand, good spirits are never punished, notwithstanding their having committed evils in the world: for their evils do not return; and it has also been given me to know, that their evils were of a different kind or nature from those of the wicked: because they did not, in committing them, act of set purpose in opposition to truth, nor from a bad heart, any further than what adhered to them from the hereditary nature derived from their parents, into which they had been carried by the influence of blind pleasure, when they were in their externals separate from their internals.

510. Every one goes to his own society, in which his spirit was while he was in the world: for every man, as to his spirit, is conjoined to some society, either of hell or of heaven; a bad man being conjoined to a society of hell, and a good man to a society of heaven. (That every one returns, after death, to his own society, may be seen above, n. 438.) To this society the spirit is led by successive steps, till, at last, he enters into it. An evil spirit, when he is brought into the state of his interiors, is turned by degrees towards his own society, and at length he looks directly to it, before this state is completed; and when it is, the evil spirit casts himself, of his own accord, into the hell, where such as are like himself have their abode. When actually casting himself down, he appears at a distance like a person falling perpendicularly, with his head downwards and his feet upwards: the reason of which appearance is, because he is in inverted order, having loved infernal things and rejected heavenly ones. Some of the evil, while in this second state, occasionally enter their hells, and come out again; but they do not, at such times, appear to fall headlong, as they do when fully divested of every thing tending to keep them out. The very society in which they were as to their spirit while in the world, is also shown to them, while they are in the state of their exteriors, that they may know that they were in hell even while in the life of the body; although they were not then in a similar state with those who are in hell itself, but in a similar state with those who are in the world of spirits; the state of whom, respectively to that of those who are in hell, will be explained in the following Sections.

511. The separation of evil spirits from good spirits is effected in this second state. For in the first state they remain together; because, while a spirit is in his externals, he behaves much as he did in the world, in which the bad have intercourse with the good, and the good with the bad. Not so when the spirit is brought into his interiors, and is left to his own nature or will. The separation of the good from the evil is effected in various ways. They are usually carried round to those societies, with which they had had communication by good thoughts and affections in their first state, and, consequently, to such as they had induced to believe, by external appearances, that they were not evil. For the most part, they are carried round in an extensive circle, and it is everywhere shown to the good spirits of what quality they are in themselves. On seeing this, the good spirits turn themselves away; and as they do so, the evil spirits also, who are being carried round, have their faces turned away from them, and directed towards the quarter where the infernal society is located, into which they are about to enter. Not to mention other modes of effecting the separation, of which there are many.

OF THE THIRD STATE OF MAN AFTER DEATH:

Which is the State of Instruction provided for those who go to Heaven.

512. The third state of man, or of his spirit, after death, is the state of instruction. This state is provided for those who go to heaven and become angels; but is not experienced by those who go to hell, because these cannot be instructed. The second state of the latter, is, therefore, the third also; which ends in their being turned completely towards their own love, and, of course, towards the society in hell whose love is similar. When this is effected, they will and think from that love; and as that love is an infernal one, they then will nothing but what is evil, and think nothing but what is false, these being delightful to them, because they are the objects of their love: and they reject, in consequence, every thing good and true, which, because such things were serviceable to their love as means for obtaining its ends, they had previously adopted. But the good are led on from the second state to a third, which is that of their preparation for heaven by means of instruction: for no one can be prepared for heaven, except by the knowledges of good and truth, consequently, not without instruction; since no one can know what spiritual good and truth are, nor what evil and falsity, which are their opposites, are, except by instruction. What civil and moral good and truth are, which are called justice and sincerity, may be known in the world; for, in the world, there are civil laws, which teach what justice is, and there are social intercourses, in which man learns to live according to moral laws, all which have reference to sincerity and uprightness: but spiritual good and truth are not learned from the world, but from heaven. What they are, may indeed be known from the Word, and from the doctrines of the church as drawn from the Word; but still they cannot enter into the life, unless the man, as to the interiors which belong to his mind, be in heaven. Man is in heaven, when he acknowledges the Divine Being, and at the same time acts with justice and sincerity, on the ground that he ought to do so because it is commanded in the Word; for he then practises justice and sincerity out of regard to the Divine Being, and not with regard to himself and the world as ends. But no one can act thus, without having first been instructed in such truths as these: That there is a God; that there are a heaven and a hell; that there is a life after death; that God is to be loved by man above all things, and his neighbor as himself; and that the things revealed in the Word are to be believed, because the Word is divine. Without the knowledge and acknowledgment of these truths, man cannot think spiritually; and without thought re-

19   289

specting them, he does not will them: for what a man is not acquainted with, he cannot think of, and what he does not think of, he cannot will. When, therefore, these truths are objects of a man's will, heaven, by influx, enters into him; that is, the Lord, through heaven, flows into his life; for He flows into his will, and through this into his thought, and through both into his life; for all the life of man is from his will and thought. From these observations it is evident, that spiritual good and truth are not learned from the world, but from heaven: and that none can be prepared for heaven except by means of instruction. In proportion, also, as the Lord enters by influx into any one's life, He instructs him; for He so far enkindles his will with the love of knowing truths, and so enlightens his thought as to enable him to know them; and in proportion as these effects are produced, the man's interiors are opened, and heaven is implanted in them; and, still further, a divine and heavenly principle flows into the sincere actions that belong to his moral life, and into the just actions that belong to his civil life, and imparts to them a spiritual nature: since he then does them from a Divine Source, because out of regard to the Divine Being. The sincere and just actions, being those of the moral and civil life, which a man does from such an origin, are themselves effects of spiritual life; and the effect derives all that is in it from its efficient cause; since such as the cause is, such is the effect also.

513. The instructions are administered by the angels of many societies, especially those that are stationed in the northern and southern quarters, those angelic societies being eminently grounded in intelligence and wisdom derived from the knowledges of good and truth. The places of instruction are situated towards the north, and are of various descriptions, being arranged and distinguished according to the genera and species of heavenly goods, in order that every individual may have instruction imparted to him according to his own genius and his faculty of reception. These places extend in all directions there, to a considerable distance; and the good spirits who are to be instructed, are guided to them by the Lord, after the completion of their second state in the world of spirits. All, however, do not go to them: for such as have received instruction in the world, were also there prepared for heaven, and are taken to heaven by another route. Some of these go to heaven; immediately after death; some, after a short stay in the company of good spirits, among whom the grosser things connected with their thoughts and affections, which they had derived from the possession of honor and riches in the world, are removed, and their purification is thereby effected: some first undergo a divesting process, for the removal of such things adhering to them as are uncongenial with heaven. This process is accomplished in places under

the soles of the feet, which are called the lower earth: where some undergo severe sufferings. These are such as have confirmed themselves in falsities, and yet have lived a good life: for falsities, when confirmed, inhere tenaciously; and yet, till they are dispersed, truths cannot be seen, and, consequently, cannot be received.*

514. All who are received into the places of 'instruction dwell in distinct classes; for, individually, they are all connected, by invisible bonds, with the societies of heaven to which they will go: consequently, as the heavenly societies are arranged according to the form of heaven (see above, nn. 200—212), so, also, are the places where the instructions are administered: on which account, when those places are viewed from heaven, they appear like a heaven on a smaller scale. They extend, lengthwise, from east to west, and, breadthwise, from south to north: but the breadth is less, in appearance, than the length. The general arrangement of them is this. In front are those who died when infants or little children, and had been educated to the period of early youth in heaven; who, after having passed their infantile state under their governesses, are brought here by the Lord, and receive instruction. Behind these are the places where those are instructed who died at an adult age, and who had been grounded in an affection for truth derived from good in the world. Be-

---

* The divesting processes, usually termed, in other translations of the Author's works, vastations, and the modes in which they are performed, are treated of in the *Arcana Cœlestia*, in various passages, references to which may be seen below.([1])—*N.*

([1]) That divesting processes are accomplished in the other life; that is, that those who go thither from the world undergo such processes, nn. 698, 7122, 7474, 9793. That the well-disposed undergo a divesting process as to falsities, and the ill-disposed as to truths, nn. 7474, 7541, 7542. That, with the well-disposed, such processes are also undergone for the putting off of the earthly and worldly defilements, which they had contracted whilst they lived in the world, nn. 7186, 9763. And that evils and falsities may be removed, and thus place may be given for the influx of goods and truths out of heaven from the Lord, together with the faculty of receiving them, nn. 7122, 9331. That they cannot be elevated into heaven until such things are removed, because they oppose and do not agree with heavenly things, nn. 6928, 7122, 7186, 7541, 7542, 9763. That thus, likewise, those are prepared, who are to be elevated into heaven, nn. 4728, 7090. That it is dangerous for any to be admitted into heaven, before they are prepared, nn. 537, 538. Of the state of illustration, and of joy, experienced by those who come out of the divesting process, and are elevated into heaven; and of their reception there, nn. 2699, 2701, 2704. That the region where these processes are undergone is called the lower earth, nn. 4728, 7090. That that region is under the soles of the feet, surrounded by the hells; its quality is described, nn. 4940—4951, 7090. From experience, n. 699. What the hells are, which infest and induce the divesting process more than the rest, nn. 7317, 7502, 7545. That those who have infested the well-disposed, and brought them under the divesting processes, are afterwards afraid of them, shun them, and hold them in aversion, n. 7768. That those infestations and divesting processes are accomplished in different manners, according to the adherence of evils and falsities; and that they continue according to their quality and quantity, nn. 1106—1113. That some are willing to undergo the divesting process, n. 1107. That some have it induced on them by fears, n. 4942. Some, by infestations from their own evils which they have done in the world, and from their own falsities which they have thought in the world, whence arises anxieties and pangs of conscience, n. 1106. Some, by spiritual captivity; which is ignorance and interception of truth conjoined with the desire of knowing truths, nn. 1109, 2694. Some, by sleep; some, by a middle state between wakefulness and sleep, n. 1108. That those who have placed merit in works, appear to themselves to cut wood, n. 1110. Others in other ways, with much variety, n. 699.

hind these, again, are such as had professed the Mahomedan religion, and who, while in the world, had led a moral life, and had acknowledged one Divine Being, and the Lord, as the Great Prophet. These, when they withdraw from Mahomed, on finding that he can render them no help, approach to the Lord, worship Him, and acknowledge His Divinity; and are then instructed in the Christian religion. Behind these, more to the north, are the places of instruction for the various classes of Gentiles, who, when in the world, had led a good life, in conformity with their religion, and who had thus acquired a species of conscience, and had practised justice and uprightness, not so much out of obedience to the laws of their country, as to the laws of their religion, in the belief that these ought to be sacredly observed, and in no way to be violated by their actions. All these, on being instructed, are easily brought to acknowledge the Lord, because they have it impressed upon their heart, that God is not invisible, but is visible under a Human Form. These surpass the others in number. The best of them are from Africa.

515. But all are not instructed in the same manner, nor by angels of similar heavenly societies. Those who had been educated from their infancy in heaven, are instructed by angels of the interior heavens, because they had not imbibed falsities from false principles of religion, nor defiled their spiritual life by gross adhesions derived from a regard to honors and riches in the world. Those who had died at an adult period of life, are, for the most part, instructed by angels of the ultimate heaven, these angels being more adapted to their state than the angels of the interior heavens, since the latter are grounded in interior wisdom, which such spirits have not, as yet, a capacity for receiving. But the Mahomedans are instructed by angels who had originally been of that religion, but had been converted to Christianity. The various classes of Gentiles, also, are instructed by angels who had been such as themselves.

516. All instruction is there administered from doctrine drawn from the Word, and not from the Word independently of doctrine. Christians are instructed from the doctrine received in heaven, which agrees in every particular with the internal sense of the Word. The others, or the Mahomedans and the Gentiles, are instructed from doctrines adapted to their comprehension, which only differ from the doctrine of heaven in the circumstance, that, in them, the spiritual life is taught through the medium of a moral life, in harmony with the good tenets of their religion, from which they had formed their life in the world.

517. The modes of imparting instruction in the heavens differ from those practised on earth in this respect, that the knowledges are not impressed on the memory, but on the life; for the memory of the spirits resides in their life, since they receive and

imbibe every thing that agrees with their life, but do not receive, much less imbibe, any thing that does not; the reason of which is, because spirits are affections, and exist in a human form such as that of their affections. Such being their nature, the affection for truth, with a view to the uses of life, is inspired into them continually. For the Lord provides that every one should love the uses which are suited to his genius : this love is also rendered more intense by the hope of becoming an angel: and since all the uses regarded in heaven have reference to the common use, which is the good of the Lord's kingdom, which in that world is their country; and since all particular and private uses are excellent just in proportion as they more nearly and fully have respect to that common use; it follows, that all the particular and private uses, which are innumerable, are good and heavenly. On this account, the affection of truth is conjoined in every one with the affection for use, so completely, as to act as one : by means of which, truth is implanted in use, so that the truths which they learn are truths of use. It is thus that angelic spirits are instructed, and are prepared for heaven. The affection for truth suitable to the use which they are to perform, is insinuated into them by various means, most of which are unknown in the world; especially by representatives of uses, which are produced in the spiritual world in a thousand ways, accompanied with such delightful and pleasant sensations, as to penetrate the spirit, from his interiors, which belong to his mind, to his exteriors, which belong to his body, and thus to affect the whole of him. A spirit is thus rendered, in a manner, his own use: in consequence of which, when he enters his own society, into which he is initiated by this course of instruction, he is in the enjoyment of his life when he is in the performance of his use.(*) From these observations it may be evident, that knowledges, which are external truths, do not cause any one to go to heaven, but the life, which is the life of uses, implanted by means of those knowledges.

518. There were some spirits, who, from the thoughts they had entertained in the world, had persuaded themselves, that they should go to heaven, and be admitted in preference to others, because they had been men of learning, and had possessed a large stock of knowledge derived from the Word, and from the doctrines of their churches ; on which ground they fancied that they were wise, and were meant by those of whom it is said,

(*) That every good has its delight from uses, and according to uses, and likewise its quality; whence such as the use is, such is the good, nn. 3049, 4984, 7038. That the angelic life consists in the goods of love and charity, thus in performing uses, n. 454. That nothing appertaining to man is regarded by the Lord, and thence by the angels, out ends, which are uses, nn. 1317, 1645, 5949. That the kingdom of the Lord is a kingdom of uses, nn. 454, 696, 1108, 3645, 4054, 7038. That to serve the Lord is to perform uses, n. 7038. That man has a quality according to the quality of the uses appertaining to him, nn. 1568, 3570, 4054, 6571, 6935, 6938, 10,284.

that "*they shall shine like the brightness of the firmament, and as the stars.*"—(Dan. xii. 3.) They were examined, to ascertain whether their knowledges were seated in their memory, or in their life. Those who had been grounded in a genuine affection for truth,—or for truth regarded with a view to uses unconnected with corporeal and worldly considerations, which are, intrinsically, spiritual uses,—were, after they had been instructed, received into heaven. It was then given them to know, what it is that shines in heaven, and that, in fact, it is the Divine Truth, which is the light of heaven, embodied in use, which is the plane that receives the rays of that light, and turns them into splendors of various colors. But as for those in whom the knowledges which they possessed only resided in the memory, and who had only acquired by them a faculty of reasoning about truths, and of confirming the notions that they had assumed as first principles, and which, though false, after having been confirmed, were seen by them as truths; these persons, not having been in any degree of the light of heaven, entertain the persuasion, grounded in the self-conceit which for the most part adheres to such sort of intelligence, that they were more learned than others, and should therefore go to heaven, where they should be waited upon by angels as their servants. On this account, in order that they might be withdrawn from their infatuated persuasion, they were taken up to the first or ultimate heaven, to be introduced into some angelic society. But when they were only in the entrance, on receiving the influx of the light of heaven, their eyes began to be darkened, and their understanding to be confused, and they began to pant for breath like persons at the point of death: and when they perceived the heat of heaven, which is heavenly love, they began to feel inward torture. They were, consequently, cast down; after which they were instructed, that knowledges are not what constitute an angel, but the life acquired by means of them; since knowledges, regarded in themselves, are extraneous to heaven; but the life acquired by them is within it.

519. After the spirits, by means of instructions imparted in the places above mentioned, have been prepared for heaven,—which is effected in a short time, because they are in the enjoyment of spiritual ideas, which embrace many things at once,—they are clothed with angelic garments, which for the most part are white, as if made of fine linen. They are then guided to a way which leads upwards to heaven, and are put under the care of the angels who guard it; after which they are taken in charge by other angels, and are introduced into various societies, where they meet with many delightful things: and, finally, every one is guided to his own society by the Lord. This also is done by leading them through various ways, and occasionally through some that wind about greatly. No angel is acquainted with the

ways through which they are led, these being known only to the Lord. When they arrive in their own society, their interiors are opened; and as these are constituted like those of the angels who live in that society, they are immediately recognized, and are received with joy.

520. To these statements I will add a remarkable particular respecting the ways which lead from those places to heaven, and by which the novitiate angels are introduced. They are eight in number, two leading from each place of instruction, one of which ascends in an easterly direction, and the other towards the west. Those who go to the Lord's celestial kingdom, are introduced by the eastern way; but those who go to His spiritual kingdom, by the western. The four ways which lead to the Lord's celestial kingdom, appear as if ornamented with olive-trees and fruit-trees of various kinds; but those which lead to His spiritual kingdom, appear as if ornamented with vines and laurels. This originates in correspondence; because vines and laurels correspond to the affection for truth, and its uses; whilst olive-trees and fruit correspond to the affection for good, and its uses.

THAT NO ONE ATTAINS HEAVEN BY AN ACT OF IMMEDIATE MERCY.

521. Those who have no accurate information respecting heaven and the way thither, and respecting the life of heaven as it exists with man, are of opinion, that reception in heaven depends solely upon an act of mercy, which is performed for those who have faith, and for whom the Lord makes intercession; or, that it is nothing but admission out of grace or favor; consequently, that all men, without exception, might be saved if it were the Lord's pleasure; and some imagine, that all the inhabitants of hell might be saved also. But such persons are entirely unacquainted with the nature of man, being not aware that, in quality, he is wholly such as his life is, and that his life is such as his love is, not only as to his interiors, which belong to his will and his understanding, but as to his exteriors also, which belong to his body; and that his corporeal frame is only the external form in which his interiors produce themselves in effect; the result of which is, that the whole man is his own love. (See above, n. 363.) They likewise are not aware, that the body does not live of itself, but from its spirit, and that the spirit of a man is actually his affection, and his spiritual body is nothing else than the affection of the man in a human form, such as he also appears in after death. (See above, nn. 453—460.) So long as these truths

are unknown, a man may be induced to believe, that salvation is
nothing but an act of the Divine Good-pleasure, which is called
mercy, and grace.

522. But it shall first be declared what the Divine Mercy is.
Divine Mercy is the pure mercy of the Lord, displayed towards
all the human race for their salvation. It is also continually
present with every man, and never recedes from any one; so
that every one who possibly can be saved, is saved. But no one
can possibly be saved, except by divine means; which are those
revealed by the Lord in the Word. Divine means are what are
called divine truths. These teach how man must live, in order
that he may be saved. The Lord, by them as means, leads man
to heaven; and, by them as means, implants in him the life of
heaven. This the Lord does for all. But He cannot implant
the life of heaven in any one, unless he abstain from evil; for
evil is an obstacle in the way. In proportion, therefore, as man
abstains from evil, the Lord leads him, by divine means, out of
pure mercy; and this He does from his infancy to the end of his
life in the world, and afterwards to eternity. This is the Divine
Mercy which is meant. From these observations it is evident,
that the Lord's mercy is pure mercy, but not immediate mercy,
or mercy unconnected with means; by which is meant, a mercy
that saves all of mere good-pleasure, let them have lived how
they may.

523. The Lord never does any thing contrary to order, because
He is Order Itself. The Divine Truth proceeding from the Lord
is what constitutes order; and divine truths are the laws of order,
according to which it is that the Lord leads man. To save man,
then, by immediate mercy, or mercy without means, is contrary
to Divine Order; and what is contrary to Divine Order, is contrary to the Divine Being Himself. Divine Order is heaven as
existing with man: this man has perverted in himself by a life
contrary to the laws of order, which are divine truths: he is
brought back into that order by the Lord, out of pure mercy, by
means of the laws of order: and in proportion to the degree of
his restoration, he receives heaven within him; and he who has
heaven within him, goes to heaven after death. Hence it is
again evident, that the divine mercy of the Lord is pure mercy,
but not immediate mercy.(¹)

(¹) That the Divine Truth proceeding from the Lord is the source of order, and that
the Divine Good is the essential of order, nn. 1728, 2258, 8700, 8988. That hence the
Lord is order, nn. 1919, 2011, 5110, 5703, 10,336, 10,619. That divine truths are the
laws of order, nn. 2447, 7995. That the universal heaven is arranged by the Lord
according to His divine order, nn. 8038, 7211, 9128, 9338, 10,125, 10,151, 10,157. That
hence the form of heaven is a form according to divine order, nn. 4040—4043, 6607,
9877. That so far as man lives according to order, thus so far as he is principled in
good according to divine truths, he receives heaven in himself, n. 4839. That man is
the being into whom are collated all things of divine order, and that from creation he
is divine order in form, because he is its recipient, nn. 4219, 4220, 4223, 4523, 4524, 5114,
5658, 6013, 6057, 6605, 6626, 9706, 10,156, 10,472. That man is not born into what is

524. If man could be saved by immediate mercy, all would be saved, including even the inhabitants of hell: nay, there would not be any such place as hell. For the Lord is Mercy Itself, Love Itself, and Good Itself: wherefore, to say that He can immediately save all, and does not, is to speak against His Divine Nature. It is known from the Word, that the Lord wills the salvation of all, and the damnation of no one.

525. Most of those who enter the other life from the Christian world, carry with them the belief, that they are to be saved by immediate mercy: for this is the object of their supplications. But when such have been examined, it was discovered, that they believed, that, to attain heaven, nothing more was necessary than mere admission, and that all who were once let in, enter on the full fruition of heavenly joy: being utterly ignorant of what 'heaven is, and what heavenly joy. It was therefore told them, that the Lord refuses heaven to no one, and that they might be admitted, if they wished it, and might also stay there as long as they pleased. Those who wished it were admitted accordingly: but as soon as they arrived at the first threshold, and felt the heat of heaven breathe upon them,—such heat being the love in which the angels are grounded, and received the influx of the light of heaven, which is the Divine Truth,—they were seized with such anguish of heart, that they experienced infernal torment rather than heavenly joy; horror-struck by which, they cast themselves headlong down. They thus were convinced, by lively experience, that heaven cannot be bestowed upon any one of immediate mercy.

526. I have sometimes conversed on this subject with angels; to whom I observed, that most persons in the world who live in evil, when talking with others respecting heaven and eternal life, constantly affirm, that entrance into heaven consists in nothing but being admitted out of mercy alone: and that those more especially believe this, who make faith the only medium of salvation. For these, from the first principle of their religion, pay no regard to the life, and to the deeds of the love which compose the life, nor, consequently, to any other means by which the Lord implants heaven in man, and renders him receptible of heavenly joy: and as they thus reject every actual medium as requisite for the purpose, they, as the necessary consequence of their first

good and true, but into what is evil and false, thus not into divine order, but into what is contrary to order, and that hence it is that he is born into mere ignorance; and that on this account it is necessary that he be born anew, that is, be regenerated, which is effected by divine truths from the Lord, that he may be brought back into order, nn. 1047, 2307, 2308, 3518, 3812, 8480, 8550, 10,233, 10,284, 10,286, 10,731. That the Lord, when he forms man anew, that is, regenerates him, arranges all things appertaining to him according to order, which is, into the form of heaven, nn, 5700, 6690, 9931, 10,303. That evils and falsities are contrary to order, and that still those who are principled in those things are ruled by the Lord, not according to order, but from order, nn. 4839, 7877, 10,778. That it is impossible for a man, who lives in evils, to be saved by mercy alone, because this is contrary to divine order, n. 5700.

principle, lay it down as an axiom, that man goes to heaven of mercy alone,—God the Father, as they believe, being moved to such mercy by the intercession of the Son. To this the angels replied, that they knew that such a dogma necessarily follows from the assumed principle of salvation by faith alone; and as that dogma is the head of the rest, and, it not being true, no light from heaven can flow into it, that it is the source of the ignorance in which the church at this day is immersed respecting the Lord, respecting heaven, respecting the life after death, respecting heavenly joy, respecting the essence of love and charity, and, in general, respecting good, and its conjunction with truth; and consequently respecting the life of man, what is its origin, and what its nature; although no one possesses life from thought alone, but from his will and the deeds thence performed, and only so far from the thought as the thought partakes of the will; and consequently no one possesses life by his faith, except so far as his faith partakes of love. The angels grieve that those parties should not know that faith alone cannot exist with any one, because faith, independent of its origin, which is love, is only superficial knowledge, and, with some, a sort of confident persuasion, which puts on the semblance of faith (see above, n. 482); though this persuasion is not seated in the man's life, but is extrinsic to his life, being separated from the man if it does not cohere with his love. They said, further, that those who hold such a principle respecting the essential medium of salvation with man, cannot do otherwise than believe in immediate mercy; since they perceive by natural light, and also by ocular evidence, that separate faith does not constitute man's life, because they who lead a bad life can think in the same manner, and induce on themselves the same persuasion: which is the reason that it is believed, that the bad may be saved as well as the good, provided they only, at the hour of death, speak with confidence of the Lord's intercession, and of mercy as procured by that intercession. The angels declared, that they had never yet seen any one, who had lived wickedly, received into heaven by an act of immediate mercy, how much soever, when in the world, he might have spoken from such trust or confidence; as in a more eminent sense is meant by faith. On being asked whether Abraham, Isaac, Jacob, and David, with the apostles, had not been received into heaven of immediate mercy, they replied, Not one of them; and they affirmed, that every one of them had been received according to his life in the world; and that they knew where they were; and that they were not there held in more esteem than others. They observed, that the reason why they are mentioned with honor in the Word, is, because, in the internal sense, by them was meant the Lord; by Abraham, Isaac, and Jacob, the Lord as to His Divinity and His Divine Humanity; by David, the Lord as to His Divine

298

Royalty; and by the apostles, the Lord as to divine truths. They said, further, that they do not at all think about those persons when the Word is read by man, because their names do not enter into heaven; but instead of them, they have a perception of the Lord; as just stated; and that, consequently, in the Word, as it exists in heaven (respecting which, see above, n. 259), those individuals are nowhere mentioned; because that Word is the internal sense of the Word which exists in the world.(¹)

527. That it is impossible to implant the life of heaven in those who have led an opposite life in the world, I am able to testify from much experience. There were some who imagined that they should easily receive divine truths after death, on hearing them from angels, and should believe them, and, in consequence, should live in a different manner, and thus be capable of being received in heaven. But the experiment was tried on great numbers; only, however, on such as had held that opinion; to whom the trial was permitted, in order that they might be convinced, that there can be no repentance after death. Some of those on whom the trial was made, understood the truths they heard, and seemed to receive them; but no sooner did they turn towards the life of their love, than they rejected them, and even spoke against them. Some rejected them instantly, being unwilling so much as to hear them. Some were desirous that the life of the love contracted by them in the world should be taken from them, and the angelic life, or the life of heaven, infused in its place. This, also, by permission, was done for them: but when the life of their love was taken away, they lay as if dead, no longer possessing the use of any of their faculties. From these and other modes of experiment, the simple good were instructed, that no one's life can possibly be changed after death, and that to transmute an evil life into a good one, or the life of an infernal into that of an angel, is utterly impracticable: since every spirit is, from head to foot, such in quality as his love is, consequently, such as his life is; and to metamorphose this into an opposite one, were to destroy the spirit altogether. The angels declare, that it were easier to change a bat into a dove, or an owl into a bird of paradise, than

(¹) That by Abraham, Isaac, and Jacob, in the internal sense of the Word, is meant the Lord, as to the Essential Divinity and the Divine Humanity, nn. 1893, 4615, 6098, 6185, 6276, 6804, 6347. That Abraham is unknown in heaven, nn. 1834, 1876, 3229. That by David is meant the Lord as to His Divine Royalty, nn. 1888, 9954. That the twelve apostles represented the Lord as to all things belonging to the church, thus belonging to faith and love, nn. 2129, 3354, 3488, 3858, 6397. That Peter represented the Lord as to faith, James as to charity, and John as to the works of charity, nn. 3750, 10,087. That by the twelve apostles sitting on twelve thrones, and judging the twelve tribes of Israel, is signified, that the Lord will judge according to the truths and goods of faith and love, nn. 2129, 6397. That the names of the persons and the places mentioned in the Word do not enter heaven, but are turned into things and states; and that neither, in heaven, can the names be uttered, nn. 1876, 5225, 8516, 10,216, 10,282, 10,432. That the angels also think abstractedly from persons, nn. 8343, 8985, 9007.

to change an infernal spirit into an angel of heaven. (That man, in quality, remains after death, such as his life had been in the world, may be seen above in its proper Section, nn. 470—484.) From these facts it may now appear with certainty, that no one can be received into heaven by an act of immediate mercy.

THAT IT IS NOT SO DIFFICULT TO LIVE THE LIFE WHICH LEADS TO HEAVEN, AS IS COMMONLY SUPPOSED.

528. Some imagine, that to live the life which leads to heaven, which is called a spiritual life, is a difficult matter, because they have heard that a man must renounce the world, must deprive himself of what are called the lusts of the body and the flesh, and must live in a spiritual manner. By this they understand, that they must reject worldly things, which chiefly consist in riches and honors; must be continually intent on pious medita-tions respecting God, salvation, and eternal life; and must spend their life in prayer, and in the reading of the Word and books of piety. This is what they conceive to be meant, by renouncing the world, and living to the spirit and not to the flesh. But that the truth on the subject is very different, has been granted me to know by much experience, and from my conversation with angels; from which I have learned, that, in fact, those who renounce the world, and live to the spirit, in this way, acquire a melancholy sort of life, which is not capable of receiving the joys of heaven; and his own life remains with every one hereafter. I have thus been assured, on the contrary, that in order to a man's receiving the life of heaven, it is neces-sary for him to live in the world, engage in its duties and busi-ness ; and that, by living a moral and civil life, he then receives spiritual life ; and that there is no other way by which the spir-itual life can be formed in man, or his spirit be prepared for heaven. For to live an internal life and not an external one at the same time, is like living in a house which has no founda-tion ; which, in process of time, either sinks into the ground, or cracks and splits to pieces, or totters till it falls.

529. If a rational view and examination be taken of the life of man, it will be found that it is threefold ; that is, that there is a spiritual life, a moral life, and a civil life, all distinct from each other. For there are men who live a civil life, but not a moral and spiritual one : there are others who live a moral life, and yet not a spiritual one : and there are others who live a civil life, a moral life, and a spiritual life, all at once. The last class are those who lead the life of heaven ; but the two others are those who only lead the life of the world separate from the life of heaven. From these truths it may evidently appear, in

the first place, that the spiritual life is not unconnected with the natural life, or the life of the world, but that there is a conjunction between them like that between the soul and the body, and that to separate them would be like living in a house without a foundation, as just observed. Moral and civil life form the actual result of the spiritual life; for to will well belongs to the spiritual life, and to do well belongs to the moral and civil life; and without this, the spiritual life consists in nothing but thinking and speaking, from which the will withdraws, because it has no basis to rest on; and yet the will is the essential spiritual constituent of man.

530. That it is not so difficult to live the life which leads to heaven as is commonly supposed, may be seen from the following considerations. Who is there that is not able to lead a moral and civil life, when every one is initiated into it from his infancy, and knows how to practise it by his living in the world? Every one, also, does actually lead such a life, whether he be a bad man or a good one:* for who is there that does not wish to be reputed a sincere and just man? Almost all externally practise sincerity and justice, so perfectly as to appear as if they were sincere and just in their heart, or acted from real sincerity and justice. The spiritual man ought to do the same, and is able to do it as easily as the natural man; only there will be this difference; that the spiritual man believes in the Divine Being, and acts sincerely and justly, not merely because civil and moral laws require it, but out of regard to the divine laws, because these require it also. A man who, when he acts, thinks of the divine laws, has communication with the angels of heaven, and in proportion as he so thinks and acts, he enters into conjunction with them; and in this way his internal man is opened, which, viewed in itself, is the spiritual man. When a man is in this state, he is adopted and led by the Lord, although he is not conscious of it; and then, in practising the sincerity and justice which belong to the moral and civil life, he acts from a spiritual origin; and to practise sincerity and justice from a spiritual origin, is to do so from actual sincerity and justice, or to practise them from the heart. The justice and sincerity of such a person appear, in their external form, exactly like the same virtues as practised by natural men, and even by those who are evil and infernal; but in their internal form they are totally different. For the evil only act sincerely and justly out of regard to themselves and the world; wherefore, were they not afraid of the law and its penalties, and of the loss of character, honor, gain, or life, they would act with the utmost in-

---

* It will be observed, that, throughout this Section, the author is not treating of those who are openly wicked, but of such as, though inwardly wicked, are outwardly good: his object being to show, that even the wicked can lead good moral and civil lives, and, consequently, that all are able to live spiritual lives also.—*N.*

sincerity and injustice ; for they have no fear of God, nor of any
divine law, and, consequently, have no internal bond to restrain
them ; wherefore, were it not for the external bonds, just mentioned, they would defraud, rob, and plunder others, to the utmost of their ability, and would take delight in such practices.
That such is their character inwardly, manifestly appears from
those who are like them in the other life, where every one is
stripped of his externals, and has his internals opened, in which
he afterwards lives to eternity (see above, nn. 499—511); for
then, being free from external restraints, which, as just stated,
consist in fear of the law, and of the loss of character, honor,
gain, or life, they behave insanely, and laugh at sincerity and
justice.   But those who have acted sincerely and justly out of
regard to the divine laws, when stripped of their externals and
left in their internals, behave wisely, because they are in conjunction with the angels of heaven, by communication from
whom they receive their wisdom.   From these facts it may now
first appear evident, that the spiritual man can act as the natural man does, in the affairs of civil and moral life, provided
only, as to his internal man, or as to his will and thought, he
be in conjunction with the Divine Being.   (See above, nn. 358,
359, 360.)

531. The laws of spiritual life, the laws of civil life, and the
laws of moral life, are also delivered in the ten commandments
of the Decalogue ; the laws of spiritual life being delivered in
the first three,* the laws of civil life in the next four, and the
laws of moral life in the last three.   In external form, the
merely natural man lives according to all these commandments
in the same manner as the spiritual man does : for he worships
the Divine Being in similar manner, he goes to church, he
listens to the sermon, and he settles his countenance in a devo-
tional form : he does not commit murder, he does not commit
adultery, he does not steal, he does not bear false witness, and
he does not defraud his neighbors of their goods.   But he only
acts thus out of regard to himself and to the world, or to keep
up appearances.   In internal form, the same individual is the
exact opposite of what he appears in externals.   As in his heart
he denies the Divine Being, in his worship he plays the hypocrite, and, when he is left to himself and his own thoughts, he
laughs at the holy things of the church, believing that they only
serve to keep the simple multitude under restraint.   Such a person, in consequence, is completely separated from heaven ; on

---

* It is to be remembered, that the division of the commandments followed by our
Author, is that adopted in the Roman Catholic and Lutheran Churches ; in which the
first commandment includes the first and second of the Church of England division ;
and the last of the Church of England division is divided into two.   Thus the first
three, as mentioned above, are what are commonly reckoned, in this country, the first
four ; the four next, are what are commonly called the fifth, sixth, seventh, and eighth
and the three last are those commonly accounted the ninth and the tenth.—N.

which account, not being a spiritual man, neither is he truly a moral man nor a civil man. For although he does not commit murder, he hates every one who opposes him, and burns with revenge inspired by such hatred : from which cause, were he not prevented by civil laws, and by external bonds, which are fears, he would commit murder ; and as he continually desires this, it follows that he is continually a murderer. So, although he does not commit adultery, still, since he believes it to be allowable, he is a perpetual adulterer; for he does commit it as far as he can, and as often as he can do it with impunity. So, although he does not steal, still, as he lusts after the goods of others, and does not esteem frauds and wicked artifices to be contrary to what is lawful, he continually plays the thief in his mind. His conduct is similar with regard to the precepts of moral life, which are those that relate to not bearing false witness, and not coveting the goods of others. Such, in quality, is every man who denies the Divine Being, and has not any conscience derived from religion. That all such persons are of this character, manifestly appears from those like them in the other life, when, their externals being removed, they are let into their internals ; for then, being separated from heaven, they act in unity with hell ; on which account, they are connected in society with its inhabitants. Not so those who in heart have acknowledged the Divine Being, and who, in the actions of their life, have had respect to the divine laws, and have acted according to the three first commandments of the Decalogue as well as the others.' When these are let into their internals, on their externals being taken away, they are wiser than they were in the world. With them, to come into their internals, is like passing out of shade into light, out of ignorance into wisdom, and out of a sorrowful life into a happy one; because they are in the Divine Sphere proceeding from the Lord, and, consequently, in heaven. These particulars are stated, in order that it may be known what a difference there is between these two classes of persons, though they have led similar lives in the world.

532. Every one may know, that the thoughts flow and take a tendency according to the intentions, or towards that to which the man directs them : for the thought is man's internal sight, which is like the external sight, in being turned and fixed on the object to which it is bent and directed. If, therefore, the internal sight, or the thought, is turned towards the world, and is fixed upon it, it follows that the thought becomes worldly : if it is turned to self, and to self-honor, that it becomes corporeal; but if towards heaven, that it becomes heavenly : whence it follows, also, that if it is turned towards heaven, it is elevated ; if towards self, that it is withdrawn from heaven, and immersed, in the corporeal nature ; and if towards the world, that it is also

303

deflected from heaven, and is spent upon the objects that are before the eyes. Man's love is what produces the intention, and determines his internal sight, or his thought, towards its objects; consequently, the love of self determines the thought towards self and selfish objects; the love of the world towards worldly objects; and the love of heaven towards heavenly ones. From these truths may be known, when a man's love is known, in what sort of state are the interiors that belong to his mind; or that the interiors of a man who loves heaven, are elevated towards heaven, and are open above; and that the interiors of a man who loves the world and himself, are closed above and open exteriorly. From which it may be concluded, that if the superior parts or faculties belonging to the mind are closed above, the man can no longer see the objects belonging to heaven and the church, and that then these, to him, are enveloped in darkness; and objects that are in darkness are either denied or are not understood. It is owing to this, that those who supremely love themselves and the world, having the superior parts or faculties of their mind closed, in heart deny divine truths, and if they at all speak about them from the memory, they still do not understand them; for they regard them in the same way as they regard things worldly and corporeal. Such being their state, nothing occupies their minds but what enters through the senses of the body, and in nothing else do they take delight. Among the things which thus enter are many that are filthy, obscene, profane, and direfully wicked; nor can their external mind be withdrawn from such things, because no influx can take place into their internal mind from heaven, since this, as just observed, is closed above. The intention of man, which is what determines the direction of his internal sight, or thought, is his will; for what a man wills, he also intends, and what he intends, engages his thoughts: if, therefore, his intention is directed towards heaven, thither, also, is his thought determined, and with it his whole mind, which, in consequence, is in heaven; whence, he afterwards views the objects of the world as below him, as a person does who looks from the roof of a house. Owing to this, a man with whom the interiors which belong to his mind are open, is able to see the evils and falsities which adhere to him, because these are seated in a region below that of his spiritual mind; but, on the contrary, a man whose interiors are not open, cannot see his own evils and falsities, because he is immersed in them, and is not elevated above them. From these facts may be concluded, from what origin a man possesses wisdom, and from what origin he is possessed by insanity; and also, what sort of a being he will prove after death, when he finds himself left at liberty both to will and think, and to act and speak, according to his interiors. These facts are stated, also, that it may be known, how different a sort

304

of person one man may be interiorly from another, how like him soever he may exteriorly appear.

533. That it is not so difficult to live the life which leads to heaven as is commonly supposed, is now evident from the fact, that all that is necessary for a man to do, when any thing is suggested to him which he knows to be insincere and unjust and his mind is inclined towards it, is, to think that it must not be done, because it is contrary to the divine commandments. If a man accustoms himself to think in this manner, and acquires, by practice, a sort of habit of it, he is, by little and little, brought into conjunction with heaven. Now in proportion as a man is brought into conjunction with heaven, the superior parts or faculties belonging to his mind are opened : in proportion as these are opened, he sees what insincerity and injustice are : and in proportion as he sees them, they are capable of being removed from him; for it is impossible for any evil to be removed till after it is seen. This is a state into which man has the ability of entering from freedom : for who cannot think, from freedom, in the manner just mentioned? But when he has entered into it, the Lord works in him for the production of every thing that is good, and causes him not only to see evils, but also to reject them from his will, and finally to hold them in aversion. This is meant by the Lord's words, "*My yoke is easy, and my burden is light.*"—(Matt. xi. 30.) But it is to be observed, that the difficulty of thinking in this manner, and also that of resisting evils, increases, in proportion as man commits evils from actual will; for so far as he does this, he accustoms himself to them, till at length he does not see them, and at last he comes to love them; when, influenced by the delight inspired by love, he makes excuses for them, confirms them by fallacies of all kinds, and calls them allowable and good. But this is what takes place with those who, on first arriving at adult age, rush into evils as if regardless of all restraint, and at the same time reject divine things from their heart.

534. A representation was once made to me of the way which leads to heaven, and of that which leads to hell. A broad way was seen, tending towards the left, or towards the north; and there appeared many spirits who were passing along it. At a distance was perceived a stone of considerable magnitude, at which the broad way terminated. Beyond that stone, two ways went off, one towards the left, and the other, in the opposite direction, towards the right. The way which went towards the left was narrow or straight, leading through the west to the south, and so into the light of heaven; but that which turned off to the right was broad and spacious, leading obliquely downwards towards hell. All the spirits were seen, at first, going in the same way, till they came to the great stone where the two ways parted off; but when they arrived there, they were sepa-

rate.l. The good turned off to the left, and entered the straight way which led to heaven. But the evil did not see the stone which stood where the ways parted off, but fell over it, and were hurt; and when they got up, they ran along the broad way on the right, which tended towards hell. It was afterwards explained to me what all these particulars signified. By the first way, which was broad, and in which both good and bad walked along together, conversing with one another like friends, because no difference was apparent between them to the sight, were represented those who, in externals, live sincerely and justly alike, and who are not to be known, by their appearance, from each other. But the stone which parted the two ways, or the stone at the corner, against which the evil fell, and from which they afterwards ran along the way leading to hell, was represented the Divine Truth, which is denied by those who look towards hell; and in the supreme sense, by the same stone was signified the Lord's Divine Humanity. But those who acknowledged the Divine Truth, and the Lord's Divinity at the same time, were conducted along the way which led to heaven. From these representations it was further evinced to me, that both the bad and the good lead the same life in externals, or walk in the same way, and the one class as easily as the other; but, nevertheless, that those who acknowledge the Divine Being from their heart, and especially those within the church who acknowledge the Lord's Divinity, are conducted to heaven; whereas those who do not, are conducted to hell. The thoughts of man that proceed from his intention or will, are represented, in the other life, by ways. In appearance, also, ways are there seen, in complete accordance with such thoughts from intention; and every one, likewise, walks in them according to his thoughts which proceed from intention. In consequence of this, spirits may be known, as to what their quality is, and their thoughts, by the ways in which they walk. From these facts, also, it was made evident, what is meant by these words of the Lord: *"Enter ye in at the strait gate: for wide is the gate, and broad is the way, that leadeth unto destruction; and many there are who go in thereat: because strait is the gate, and narrow is the way, that leadeth unto life; and few there are who find it."*—(Matt. vii. 13, 14.) It is declared that the way which leads to life is narrow, not because to walk in it is difficult, but because there are few that find it; as is mentioned. From that stone seen at the corner, where the wide and common way terminated, and from which two other ways were seen tending to opposite quarters, was shown what is signified by these words of the Lord: *"What is this then that is written, The stone which the builders rejected, the same is become the head of the corner? Whosoever shall fall upon that stone, shall be broken."*—(Luke xx. 17, 18.) The stone signifies the Divine Truth; and the

stone (or rock) of Israel, the Lord as to His Divine Humanity; the builders, are the members of the church: the head of the corner, is the place where the two ways part off: to fall and be broken, is to deny and perish.([1])

535. It has been granted to me to converse with some in the other life, who had retired from the business of the world, in order to devote themselves to a pious and holy life; and with some who had afflicted themselves in various ways, because they imagined, that this was the way to renounce the world, and to subdue the lusts of the flesh. But the greater portion of such persons, having by these practices contracted a melancholy sort of life, and removed themselves from the life of charity, which can only be acquired by living in the world, cannot be connected in society with the angels, because the life of the angels is a cheerful one, in consequence of the beatitude which they inwardly experience, and consists in doing good deeds, which are the works of charity. Besides, those who have adopted a life of retirement from worldly business, are inflamed with the notion of their merits, and are continually urgent to be admitted into heaven, because they think of heavenly joy as the reward due to their merit; being utterly ignorant of what heavenly joy is. When, in consequence, they are admitted among the angels, and into a perception of their joy, which is unconnected with any notion of merit, and consists in the practice and open performance of duties and kind offices, and in the beatitude arising from the good which they do by such means, they are filled with astonishment, like persons who witness things quite contrary to what they expected: and being not capable of receiving that joy, they depart, and are connected in society with those who are like themselves, in consequence of having led a similar life in the world. But as to those who had lived in external sanctity, being continually in places of worship and putting up prayers there, and who had practised self-mortification, thinking all the while of themselves, as being, on these accounts, more worthy than others of being esteemed and honored, and of being, at last, reputed after death as saints; these, in the other life, are not in heaven, because they had done all these things solely with a view to themselves. Some of them, having defiled divine truths with the love of self, in which they had immersed them, are so insane, as to think themselves gods; on which account, they have their lot, among those whose character is like their own, in hell. Some of them are full of cunning and deceit, and have their lot in the hells of the deceitful: these are persons who had assumed such appearances in external form, as, by artful and cunning means, to induce the common people to believe

([1]) That stone, or a stone, signifies truth, nn. 114, 643, 1298, 3720, 6426, 8609, 10,376. That therefore the law was inscribed on tables of stone, n. 10,376. That the stone of Israel denotes the Lord as to divine truth and as to His Divine Humanity, n. 6426.

that a divine sanctity resided in them. Many of the Roman Catholic saints are of this description. With some of these it has been granted me to converse: when their life was manifestly described to me, such as it had been in the world, and such as it became afterwards.

These statements have been made, that it may be known, that the life which leads to heaven is not a life of retirement from the world, but passed in the world; and that a life of piety independent of the life of charity, which can only be acquired in the world, does not lead to heaven; but that the life which leads to heaven is the life of charity, which consists in acting sincerely and justly in every occupation, in every business, and in all our dealings, from an interior and thus heavenly origin; and that such an origin is inherent in such a life, when a man acts sincerely and justly because the divine laws require him to do so. Such a life is not difficult; whereas the life of piety independent of the life of charity, is difficult: and yet this life leads away from heaven, as much as it is commonly supposed to lead to it.(*)

(*) That a life of piety without a life of charity is of no avail, but with the latter is of advantage in every respect, nn. 8252, 8253. That charity towards one's neighbor consists in doing what is good, just, and right, in all our dealings, and in every employment, nn. 8120, 8121, 8122. That charity towards the neighbor extends itself to all the things, even to the most particular, which a man thinks, wills, and acts, n. 8124. That a life of charity is a life according to the Lord's precepts, n. 8249. That to live according to the Lord's precepts is to love the Lord, nn. 10,143, 10,153, 10,310, 10,578, 10,648. That genuine charity is not meritorious, because it proceeds from interior affection, and from the delight thence resulting, nn. (2340,) 2371, (2400,) 3887, 6388—6393. That man after death remains of such a quality, as was his life of charity in the world, n. 8256. That heavenly blessedness flows from the Lord into the life of charity, n. 2363. That no one is admitted into heaven by thinking only, but by willing and doing good at the same time, nn. 2401, 3459. That unless the doing of good is conjoined with willing good and with thinking good, there is no salvation, nor any conjunction of the internal man with the external, n. 8987.

308

OF HELL.

536. When treating above respecting heaven, it has every where been shown that the Lord is the God of Heaven (see, specifically, nn. 2—6) ; and thus that the whole government of the heavens is that of the Lord. Now as the relation which heaven bears to hell, and that which hell bears to heaven, is such as exists between two opposites, which mutually act against each other, and the result of whose action and reaction is a state of equilibrium, in which all things may subsist : therefore, in order that all and every thing should be maintained in equilibrium, it is necessary that He who governs the one should also govern the other. For unless the same Ruler were to restrain the assaults made by the hells, and to keep down the insanities which rage in them, the equilibrium would be destroyed, and with it the whole universe.

537. But some preliminary observations on equilibrium shall here be offered. It is well known, that when two things mutually act against each other, and when the reaction and resistance of the one are equal to the action and impulse of the other, no surplus force remains to either, there being the same power on both sides ; and that, in this situation, each may be guided by a third agent at pleasure : for when the force of the two is neutralized by their equal opposition, the force of the third does every thing, and acts with as much facility as if there were no opposition at all. There is such an equilibrium between hell and heaven : but it is not an equilibrium like that between two persons engaged in personal conflict, the strength of each of whom is equivalent to that of the other : but it is a spiritual equilibrium, which is that of falsity pressing against truth, and of evil against good : for falsity grounded in evil continually exhales from hell, and truth grounded in good continually exhales from heaven. It is this spiritual equilibrium that causes man to enjoy freedom in thinking and willing. For whatever a man thinks and wills has reference either to evil and the falsity proceeding from it, or to good and the truth which comes from that source : consequently, when he is placed in that equilibrium, he enjoys the liberty of either admitting and receiving evil and its falsity from hell, or good and its truth from

309

heaven. Every man is maintained in this equilibrium by the Lord, because he governs both—heaven as well as hell. But why man, by means of such an equilibrium, is maintained in this liberty, and why evil and falsity are not taken away from him, and good and truth infused into him, by Divine Power, will be explained in its proper Section below.

538. It has often been granted me to perceive the sphere of falsity originating in evil exhaling from hell. It was like an incessant effort to destroy every thing good and true, combined with anger, and a sort of raving madness, at not being able to effect it: there was, especially, an effort to destroy the Divine Sphere proceeding from the Lord, because every thing good and true comes from Him. But there was perceived, as proceeding from heaven, a sphere of truth originating in good, by which the mad fury of the effort ascending from hell was held in check. The result is equilibrium. This sphere from heaven was perceived to be from the Lord alone, though it appeared to come from the angels in heaven. The reason that it was perceived to come from the Lord alone, and not from the angels, is, because every angel in heaven acknowledges that there is nothing of good and truth originating in himself, but that it is all from the Lord.

539. All power, in the spiritual world, belongs to truth, originating in good, and none whatever is possessed by falsity originating in evil. The reason that all power resides in truth originating in good, is, because the actual Divine Sphere in heaven is Divine Good and Divine Truth; and all power belongs to the Divine Being. The reason that no power whatever is possessed by falsity originating in evil, is, because all power resides in truth originating in good; and in falsity originating in evil there exists nothing of truth originating in good. The result is, that all power is in heaven, and none at all in hell. For every one in heaven is grounded in truths originating in good, and every one in hell is immersed in falsities originating in evil: since no one is admitted into heaven, until he is grounded in truths originating in good, nor is any one cast down into hell until he is immersed in falsities originating in evil. (That such is the fact, may be seen in the Sections that treat of the first, second, and third states of man after death, nn. 491—520. And that all power resides in truth derived from good, may be seen in the Section on the Power of the Angels of Heaven, nn. 228—233.)

540. Such, then, is the equilibrium between heaven and hell. The inhabitants of the world of spirits exist in that equilibrium, because the world of spirits is intermediate between heaven and hell. From the same cause, all men in the natural world are maintained in the same equilibrium; for men in the natural world are governed of the Lord through the medium of spirits

in the world of spirits; a subject that will be treated of in its proper Section below. Such an equilibrium could not be maintained, did not the Lord govern both,—heaven as well as hell, and regulate the effort on each side: otherwise, falsities originating in evil would attain the preponderance, and would influence the simple good who dwell in the ultimate circumferences of heaven, who might be more easily perverted than the angels themselves : on the accomplishment of which, the equilibrium would perish, and together with it, the freedom enjoyed by men.

541. Hell, like heaven, is divided into societies, and, in fact, into as many as there are in heaven : for every society in heaven has a society opposite to it in hell; which is provided for the preservation of the equilibrium. But the societies in hell are distinctly arranged according to the various kinds of evil with the falsities thence originating ; because the societies in heaven are distinctly arranged according to the various kinds of good and the truths which are thence derived. That every kind of good has an evil opposite to it, and every kind of truth its opposite falsity, may be known from the circumstance, that neither would be any thing without relation to its opposite ; and that from its opposite is known what it is in kind, and what in degree; and that this is the cause of all perception and sensation. On this account, it is continually provided by the Lord, that every society of heaven should have its opposite in some society of hell, and that there should be an equilibrium between them.

542. Since hell is divided into as many societies as heaven is, it follows, that there are as many distinct hells as there are societies of heaven : for as every society of heaven is a heaven on a smaller scale (see above, nn. 51—58), so, on a smaller scale, every society of hell is a hell. Since, therefore, there are, in general, three heavens, it follows, that there are, in general, three hells: a lowest hell, which is opposite to the inmost or third heaven; a middle hell, which is opposite to the middle or second heaven ; and an upper one, which is opposite to the ultimate or first heaven.

543. In what manner the hells are governed by the Lord, shall also be briefly explained. In general, the hells are governed by the general afflux of Divine Good and Divine Truth proceeding from the heavens, by which the common or general effort flowing from the hells is restrained and held in check ; and also by the special afflux proceeding from every heaven, and from every society of heaven. In particular, the hells are governed by angels, to whom is assigned the office of inspecting the hells, and keeping down the insanities and disturbances which prevail in them. Sometimes, also, angels are sent thither, and regulate them when actually present. But, in general, all the inhabitants of hell are governed by their fears. Some are governed by fears that had been implanted in them while

311

they lived in the world, and which still retain an influence; but as these are not sufficient, and also gradually lose their force, they are governed by fears of punishment: and it is chiefly by these that they are deterred from committing evils. The punishments which they undergo are of many sorts, slighter or more grievous according to the nature of the evils to be restrained. For the most part, the more malignant spirits, who excel the others in cunning and artifice, and are able to keep them in obedience and slavery by punishments and the terrors thus inspired, are set over the rest: but these governors themselves dare not go beyond the bounds prescribed to them. It is necessary to be known, that the only means of restraining the violence and furious madness of the inhabitants of hell, is by the fear of punishment: there is no other whatever.

544. It has hitherto been supposed in the world, that there is a certain individual devil who rules over the hells; and that he was created an angel of light, but afterwards became a rebel, and was cast, with his crew, into hell. The reason that such a belief has prevailed is, because mention occurs in the Word of the devil and Satan, and also of Lucifer, and the Word has been understood, in those passages, according to the literal sense: whereas the truth is, that by the devil and Satan is there signified hell; by the devil being meant that hell which is at the back, and which is inhabited by the worst sort of spirits, who are called evil genii; and by Satan, the hell which is in front, the inhabitants of which are not so malignant, and who are called evil spirits: whilst by Lucifer are signified such as belong to Babel or Babylon, who are those who pretend to extend their authority over heaven itself. That there is not any individual devil to whom the hells are subject, is also evident from the circumstance, that all the inhabitants of the hells, like all the inhabitants of the heavens, are derived from the human race (see above, nn. 311—317); and that those who have gone thither, from the beginning of creation till the present time, are myriads of myriads in number, every one of whom is such a devil in quality, as he had made himself, while he lived in the world, by confirming himself against the Divine Being. (Respecting these subjects, see above, nn. 311, 312.)

THAT NO ONE IS CAST INTO HELL BY THE LORD; BUT THAT THE SPIRIT DOES IT HIMSELF.

545. The opinion has prevailed with some, that God turns away his face from man, rejects him, and casts him into hell; and that he is full of anger against him on account of the evil of which he is guilty: and some go still further, affirming that

God punishes man, and brings evil upon him. Those who hold this opinion confirm themselves in it by the literal sense of the Word, in which such statements occur; not being aware, that the spiritual sense of the Word, which explains the literal sense, is very different, and that, consequently, the genuine doctrine of the church, which is derived from the spiritual sense of the Word, inculcates different sentiments : for this teaches, that God never turns away his face from man, never rejects him, never casts any one into hell, and never is angry.(¹) This, also, every one whose mind is in a state of illumination, perceives, when he reads the Word, from this consideration alone, that God is Good Itself, Love Itself, and Mercy Itself; and that Good Itself cannot possibly do evil to any one; nor can Love Itself and Mercy Itself possibly cast man away from them, because this would be contrary to the very essence of mercy and love, and, of consequence, contrary to the Divine Nature Itself. Those, therefore, who think from an enlightened mind, clearly perceive, when they read the Word, that God never turns Himself away from man, and, as He never turns Himself away from man, that He deals with him from a principle of goodness, of love, and of mercy ; or, in other words, that He desires his good, that He loves him, and that He has mercy upon him. Consequently, they see also, that when such statements as are above alluded to, occur, they conceal within them a spiritual sense, according to which those expressions are to be explained, which, in the literal sense, are employed in accommodation to man's capacity, and which speak according to his first and general ideas.

546. Those who enjoy illumination, see, further, that good and evil are two opposites, which are as contrary as heaven and hell, and that all good comes from heaven, and all evil from hell ; and as the Divine Sphere proceeding from the Lord constitutes heaven (see above, nn. 7—12), that, from the Lord, nothing but good flows into man, and, from hell, nothing but evil ; and, consequently, that the Lord is continually withdrawing man from evil, and leading him to good ; but that hell is continually leading him into evil. Unless man stood between both, he would not possess any thought, nor any will, still less any liberty, nor any choice ; for man enjoys all these in consequence of the equilibrium between good and evil : if, therefore, the Lord were to turn Himself away from him, and leave him to evil alone, he would no longer be a man. From these truths

<hr />

(¹) That anger and wrath, in the Word, are attributed to the Lord, but they appertain to man, and that it is so expressed, because it so appears to man when he is punished and condemned, nn. 5798, 6997, 8284, 8483, 8875, 9306, 10,431. That evil also is attributed to the Lord, when yet from the Lord nothing but good can come, nn. 2447, 6078, 6992, 6997, 7533, 7632, 7877, 7926, 8227, 8228, 8632, 9306. Why it is so expressed in the Word, nn. 6073, 6992, 6997, 7643, 7632, 7679, 7710, 7926, 9282, 9009, 9128. That the Lord is pure mercy and clemency, nn. 6997, 8875.

it is evident, that the Lord enters by influx, with good, into every man, into the bad man as well as into the good; but with this difference; that, with the bad man, His operation consists in continually withdrawing him from evil; and with the good man, in continually leading him to good; and that the cause of this difference lies with the man himself, because he is the recipient.

547. From these observations it may appear with certainty, that it is by influence from hell that man does evil, and by influence from the Lord that he does good. But as man believes, that whatever he does, he does from himself, the consequence is, that the evil which he does adheres to him as his own. It hence follows, that the cause of his own evil lies with man, and not at all with the Lord. Evil as existing with man, is hell, as existing with him : for whether you say evil or hell, it amounts to the same thing. Now since the cause of his own evil lies with man himself, it follows, that it is he who casts himself into hell, and not the Lord; and so far is the Lord from leading man into hell, that He delivers from hell, so far as the man does not will and love to abide in his own evil. But the whole of man's will and love remains with him after death (see above, nn. 470—484): whoever wills and loves evil in the world, wills and loves the same evil in the other life; and he then no longer suffers himself to be withdrawn from it. It hence results, that the man who is immersed in evil, is connected by invisible bonds with hell: he also is actually there as to his spirit : and, after death, he desires nothing more earnestly than to be where his evil is. It follows that the man, after death, casts himself into hell; and that this is not done by the Lord.

548. In what manner this takes place, shall also be stated. When a man enters the other life, he is first taken under the care of angels, who render him all kind offices, converse with him respecting the Lord, respecting heaven, and respecting the angelic life, and instruct him in subjects relating to truth and to good. If, however, the man, who is now a spirit, is one of those, who, while in the world, were acquainted, indeed, with such matters, but in heart denied or despised them, he desires, after some conversation, to be rid of their company, and actually seeks how to depart ; on perceiving which, the angels leave him. After joining several other companies, he is at last associated with those who are immersed in the same evil as himself. (See above, nn. 445—452.) When this is effected, he averts himself from the Lord, and turns his face towards the hell with which he had been connected while in the world ; being the hell which is the abode of those who are immersed in a similar love of evil. From these facts it is evident, that the Lord draws every spirit towards Himself by means of His angels, and also by an influx from heaven ; but that the spirits who are grounded in evil

strenuously resist, and, in a manner, tear themselves away from the Lord: for they are drawn along by their own evil, and consequently by hell, as with a rope; and as they are thus drawn along, and, from the love of evil, are willing to follow, it is evident that they freely cast themselves into hell. That such is the fact, cannot be believed in the world, in consequence of the idea of hell commonly entertained; nor in the other life, to the eyes of those who are not in hell, does the actual process appear otherwise than in agreement with the common idea. But it does not so appear to those who undergo it: for they enter hell of their own accord, and those who enter it from an ardent love of evil, appear as if they were thrown in a perpendicular direction, with their head downwards and their feet upwards. It is owing to this appearance, that it seems as if they were cast down into hell by the Divine Power: on which subject more will be stated below. (See n. 574.) From these statements it may now be seen, that the Lord does not cast any one into hell, but that every one who goes there does it himself; and that he not only does so while he lives in the world, but after death likewise, when he becomes a spirit among other spirits.

549. The reason that the Lord cannot, from His Divine Essence, which is Good, Love, and Mercy, deal in the same manner with every man, is, because evils, and the falsities grounded in them, stand as obstacles in the way, and not only dull His divine influx, but reject it entirely. Evils and their falsities are like black clouds, which place themselves between a man's eye and the sun, and take away the sunshine and the serenity of the day. The sun, however, still continues in the perpetual effort to dissipate the obstructing clouds: for he remains behind them, and operates upon them for their dispersion; and, till this can be effected, he transmits a degree of shady light to the eye of man by various indirect passages. A similar state of things exists in the spiritual world: but there, the sun is the Lord, and his Divine Love (see above, nn. 116 - 140); the light is the Divine Truth (see above, nn. 126—140), black clouds, are falsities originating in evil; and the eye is the understanding. In proportion as any one there is immersed in falsities originating in evil, he is encompassed by such a cloud, the blackness and density of which are according to the degree of his evil. From this comparison may be seen, that the Lord is perpetually present with every one, but that He is received in different ways.

550. Evil spirits in the world of spirits are severely punished, in order that they may be deterred by such punishments from the commission of crimes. It also appears as if their sufferings were inflicted by the Lord: but still, not the least of the punishments which they undergo comes from the Lord, but all of it

from evil itself. For evil is so combined with its punishment, that to separate them is impossible. The infernal crew desire and love nothing better than to do injury, especially to inflict punishment and torture on others : and they also do injury to, and inflict punishment on, every one, who is not protected by the Lord. When therefore evil is done by any one from an evil heart, since evil casts away from itself all protection from the Lord, infernal spirits fall upon the person who is guilty of it, and punish him. This may in some measure be illustrated by crimes and their punishments in the world, where, also, they are combined together. The laws prescribe for every crime its punishment; in consequence of which, whoever commits the crime, also incurs the penalty. The only difference is, that, in the world, the crime may be concealed; whereas this is impossible in the other life. From these truths it may appear with certainty, that the Lord brings evil on no one, and that the case, in this respect, is the same as occurs in the world : for there, the cause of the punishment of a criminal neither lies in the king, nor in the judge, nor in the law; since neither of these was the cause of the crime committed by the malefactor.

THAT ALL THE INHABITANTS OF THE HELLS ARE IMMERSED IN EVILS, AND IN FALSITIES THENCE PROCEEDING, ORIGINATING IN SELF-LOVE AND THE LOVE OF THE WORLD.

551. All the inhabitants of the hells are immersed in evils and in falsities derived from them ; and there is no one there who is grounded in evils, and at the same time in truths. Most bad characters in the world are acquainted with spiritual truths, which are those belonging to the church, having learned them in childhood, and, at a later period, from sermons and from reading the Word, and having afterwards spoken of them from such acquired knowledge. Some, also, have led others to believe that they were Christians in heart, because they knew how to speak from truths with pretended affection, and to deal sincerely as if under the influence of spiritual fidelity : but such of these as interiorly thought in opposition to the truths from which they spoke, and only abstained from the practice of the evils that were agreeable to their thoughts out of regard to the laws of their country, and to their own reputation, honor, and gain, are all, in heart, evil, and are only grounded in truths and goods as to their body, not as to their spirit. In the other life, there-fore, when the externals of such persons are stripped off, and the internals belonging to their spirits are revealed, they are immersed altogether in evils and falsities, and do not retain any of the truths and goods which they had professed and appeared

to practise; and it is made manifest, that those truths and goods only resided in their memory, being entertained there like any common matters with which they were acquainted, and that, when they were in conversation, they thence drew them forth, and put on the semblance of good affections, as if under the influence of spiritual love and faith. When such persons are let into their internals, and consequently into their evils, they can no longer utter truths, but only falsities; because they speak from evils, and to utter truths from evils is a thing impossible, since the spirit is then nothing but his own evil, and what proceeds from evil is falsity. Every evil spirit is reduced to this state, before he is cast into hell. (See above, nn. 499—512.) This is called being divested of truths and goods;(¹) and the divesting process consists in nothing but in the party's being let into his internals, thus into the *proprium* of his spirit or into his spirit itself. (Respecting these, also, see above, n. 425.)

552. When a man after death is brought to this state, he is no longer a spirit resembling in his state a man,* as he is in his first state, treated of above (nn. 491—498), but is truly a spirit: for one who is truly a spirit has a face and personal form corresponding to his internals, which belong to his mind, and, consequently, has an external form, that is the type or effigy of his internals. Such is the state of a spirit, after he has completed the first and second states, treated of above. Consequently, it is then known, as soon as he is seen, what sort of a spirit he is, not only by his countenance, but by his person; and also by his speech, and by his gestures. As, likewise, he is now in his intrinsic identity, he cannot abide anywhere, but where those like himself dwell. For, in the spiritual world, there is a complete communication of affections and of the thoughts thence originating; on which account a spirit is conducted, as if of himself, because from his own affection and its delight, to those who are like him; indeed, he also turns himself in that direction, because he then inhales his own life, or draws his breath freely; which he cannot do when he turns another way. It is to be remembered, that communication with others takes place in the spiritual world according to the direction in which a spirit turns his face, and that he perpetually has those before his face who are grounded in the same love as himself; a cir-

(¹) That the evil, before they are cast down into hell, are devastated as to truths and goods, and that when these are taken away from them, they are carried of themselves into hell, nn. 6977, 7039, 7795, 8210, 8232, 9330. That the Lord does not devastate them, but that they devastate themselves, nn. 7643, 7926. That every evil has in it a principle of falsity, wherefore those who are immersed in evil, are also immersed in falsity, although some of them do not know it, nn. 7577, 8094. That those who are in evil, cannot but think what is false, when they think from themselves, n. 7437. That all who are in the hells speak falsities from evil, nn. 1695, 7351, 7352, 7357, 7892, 7689.

* The term here used in the original is *homo-spiritus*,—"a man-spirit," as mentioned in the note above, p. 228: but as it cannot here be translated, as in every other instance, "man, now a spirit," it is rendered as above, which seems exactly to express the author's meaning.—*N.*

cumstance which continues, let him turn his body about as he may. (See above, n. 151.) It is owing to this, that all internal spirits turn themselves back from the Lord towards those masses of thick darkness and of darkness, which, in the spiritual world, occupy the places of the sun and the moon of the natural world; whereas all the angels of heaven turn themselves towards the Lord, as the sun and as the moon of heaven. (See above, nn. 123, 143, 144, 151.) From these facts it may now appear with certainty, that all the inhabitants of the hells are immersed in evils and in the falsities thence proceeding: and also, that they are turned in the direction of their own loves.

553. All the spirits in the hells, viewed in any degree of the light of heaven, appear in the form belonging to their own evil: for every one is then the effigy of his own evil, because, in every one, the interiors and the exteriors act in unity, the interiors visibly exhibiting themselves in the exteriors, which consist of the face, the body, the speech, and the gestures. They thus, as to their quality, are recognized at sight. In general, there are forms expressive of contempt of others, and of menace against those who do not pay them respect: there are forms expressive of hatred of various kinds: there are forms expressive of revenge, also of various kinds. Through those forms their ferocious and cruel passions shine forth from their interiors. When, however, others praise them, treat them with respect, and worship them, their face draws in its savage expression, and shows an appearance of gladness arising from the delight thus imparted. All those forms, as they actually appear, cannot be described in a few words, for no one of them is the same as another: only, among those spirits who are characterized by a similar evil, and who reside, in consequence, in the same infernal society, there exists a common likeness, from which, as a plane giving birth to varieties, the faces of all the individuals belonging to the society possess a certain resemblance to each other. In general, their faces are shocking, and appear void of life, like those of corpses. Those of some are black: those of others are fiery, like little torches: those of others are deformed with pimples, blotches, and ulcers: and with many, no face appears at all, but instead of it a hairy or bony mass; and with some, nothing but grinning teeth. Their bodies, also, are monstrous in shape, and their speech sounds as if full of anger, of hatred, or of revenge: for every one speaks from his own falsity, and in a tone expressive of his own evil. In one word: they all are images of their own hell. As to hell itself, it has not been granted me to see of what form it is in the whole: it has only been told me, that as the universal heaven, viewed collectively, is as one man (see nn. 59 —67), so the universal hell, viewed collectively, is as one devil, and may also be exhibited to view in the shape of one devil. (See above, n. 544.) But as to the forms which belong to hells

ın particular, or .nfernal societies, these it has often been granted me to behold: for at the apertures leading to them in the world of spirits, which are called the gates of hell, there generally appears a monster, which represents the common form of those within. The outrageous passions of the inhabitants are also represented by shocking and direful appearances, the particulars of which I forbear to mention. But it is to be observed, that the infernal spirits appear in such forms only when viewed in the light of heaven: but among themselves they appear like men; which is provided of the Lord's divine mercy, that they may not appear as loathsome to each other as they do to the angels. This appearance, however, is a fallacy: for as soon as a ray of the light of heaven is let in upon them, their human forms are turned into monstrous ones, such as they intrinsically are, and as are described above; for in the light of heaven, every thing appears as it intrinsically is. For this reason, among others, they flee from the light of heaven, and cast themselves into their own gross light, which is like that emitted from ignited charcoal, and, in some places, like that of burning brimstone: but this light is also turned into absolute darkness, when any ray of light flows in upon it from heaven. It is on this account that the hells are said to be immersed in thick darkness and in darkness; and that thick darkness and darkness signify falsities originating in evil, such as prevail in hell.

554. From an inspection of the monstrous forms belonging to the spirits in the hells, all of which, as just stated, are forms of contempt of others, and of menace against those who do not treat them with honor and respect; together with forms of hatred and revenge against those who do not favor them; it was made evident to me, that they all, in general, are forms of self-love and the love of the world, and that the evils, of which in particular they are the forms, derive their origin from those two loves. It has also been told me from heaven, and proved to me by much experimental evidence, that those two loves,—self-love and the love of the world,—reign in the hells, and also constitute them: whereas love to the Lord and love towards the neighbor reign in the heavens, and also constitute them: and that the two former loves, which are the loves of hell, and the two latter, which are the loves of heaven, are diametrically opposite to each other.

555. I at first wondered how it was, that self-love and the love of the world should be so diabolical, and that those who are immersed in them should be such monsters to look upon; because, in the world, people reflect but little on self-love, but only upon that puffed up state of mind displayed externally which is called pride, which, as being obvious to the sight, is alone supposed to constitute self-love. Besides, such self-love as does not so exalt itself, is believed, in the world, to be the fire of life, by which a man is excited to aspire to offices and to perform

uses, and that unless he looked to the honor and glory to be thus acquired, his mind would become torpid. Who, they say, ever performed any honorable, useful, or memorable deed, but with a view to be celebrated and honored by others, or in the minds of others? And whence, they ask, does this arise, but from the ardor of his love for glory and honor,—consequently, for himself? The consequence of this mode of thinking is, that it is not known in the world, that self-love, viewed in itself, is the love that reigns in hell, and that it constitutes hell as existing in man. Such, however, being the fact, I will first describe what self-love is: and I will show afterwards, that all evils, and the falsities which originate from them, spring from that love.

556. Self-love consists in entertaining good-will for one's self alone, and for no others, not even for the church, for one's country, or for any society of men, except with a view to one's self: also, in doing them good only with a view to one's own fame, honor, and glory. Unless a person influenced by self-love sees these in the uses he performs for them, he says in his heart, What matters it? Why should I do it? and, What shall I get by it? and so omits it. It hence is evident, that a person who is immersed in self-love, neither loves the church, nor his country, nor any society that he belongs to, nor any use, but himself alone. His delight is only that of the love of himself; and since the delight which proceeds from love constitutes a man's life, it follows that his life is the life of himself: and the life of self is life proceeding from the *proprium* of man; whilst the *proprium* of man, viewed in itself, is nothing but evil. He who loves himself, also loves those who belong to him, who, in particular, are his children and descendants, and, in general, all who act in unity with him, whom he calls his friends. To love these, is also to love himself; for he regards them, as it were, in himself, and himself in them. Among those whom he calls his friends, are also included all who praise, honor, and pay their court to him.

557. What is the nature of self-love, may evidently appear from a comparison of it with heavenly love. Heavenly love consists in loving, for their own sake, the uses, or the good works, which a man performs to the church, to his country, to the society of persons to which he belongs, and to his fellow-citizens: for this is to love God and to love his neighbor, since all uses and all good works are from God, and are, at the same time, the neighbor that is to be loved. But he who loves these uses and good works for the sake of the advantage resulting to himself from his doing them, only loves them as he does the domestics of his family, because they render him service: whence it follows, that he who is immersed in self-love, would have the church, his country, societies of men, and his fellow-citizens, serve him, and not that he should serve them. He places himself above them, and them below himself. It hence results, that in

320

proportion as any one immerses himself in self-love, he removes himself from heaven, because he removes himself from heavenly love.

558. But further: In proportion as any one is grounded in heavenly love, which consists in loving uses and good works, and in a man's being affected with delight of heart when he performs them for the sake of the church, of his country, of the society of men with whom he is connected, and of his fellow-citizen, he is led by the Lord; since in that love the Lord Himself resides, and He is the Author of it. But in proportion as any one is grounded in self-love, which is that of performing uses and good works with a view to himself alone, he is led by himself; and in proportion as any one is led by himself, he is not led by the Lord: whence it also follows, that in proportion as any one loves himself, he removes himself from the Divine Presence, and, consequently, from heaven. For a man to be led by himself, is to be led by his *proprium*, and the *proprium* of man is nothing but evil: for it is his hereditary evil nature, which consists in loving himself in preference to God, and the world in preference to heaven.(*) Man is let into his *proprium*, and consequently into his hereditary evils, as often as, in the good works which he may do, he has regard to himself: for he then looks from those good works to himself, and not from himself to the good works; on which account, he sets up, in such good works, the image of himself, and not any image of the Divine Being. That such is the fact, has also been proved to me by experimental evidence. There are certain evil spirits, whose places of abode are in the intermediate quarter between the north and the west, under the heavens, who possess the art of drawing well-disposed spirits into their *proprium*, and consequently into evils of various kinds; which they accomplish thus: They draw them into thoughts respecting themselves; either operating openly for this purpose, by praises and ascriptions of honor; or clandestinely, by influencing their affections till they become determined towards themselves. In proportion as they accomplish their object, they turn away the faces of the well-disposed spirits from heaven; and, in the same degree, they darken their understanding, and call forth evils from their *proprium*.

558*. That self-love is opposite to love towards the neigh-

(*) That the *proprium* of man which he derives hereditarily from his parents, is nothing but dense evil, nn. 210, 215, 731, 876, 987, 1047, 2307, 2308, 3518, 3701, 8812, 8480, 8550, 10,283, 10,284, 10,286, 10,732. That the *proprium* of man consists in loving himself in preference to God, and the world in preference to heaven, and in making light of his neighbor in comparison with himself, except only for the sake of himself; thus that it consists in loving himself; consequently, that it is the love of self and of the world, nn. 694, 731, 4317, 5660. That all evils flow from the love of self and of the world, when they predominate, nn. 1307, 1308, 1321, 1594, 1691, 3413, 7255, 7376, (7480,) 7488, 8318, 9335, 9348, 10,038, 10,742. Which are, contempt of others, enmity, hatred, revenge, cruelty, deceit, nn. 6667, 7372, 7374, 9348, 10,038, 10,742. And that in these evils every false principle originates, nn. 1047, 10,283, 10,284, 10,286.

bor, may be seen from the origin and essence of both. The
love of the neighbor, as existing in those who are immersed in
the love of themselves, begins with themselves. It is their
maxim, that a man's nearest neighbor is himself; and so, each
taking himself as the centre, it proceeds to all those who make
one with him, diminishing as it goes further off, according to the
degree in which the various individuals are connected, by love,
with himself; whilst all beyond this connection are accounted
as nothing, and those who are opposed to them and to their evils,
as enemies, be they, in character, what they may, whether wise
or upright, sincere or just. But spiritual love towards the
neighbor begins with the Lord, and from Him as its centre
proceeds to those who have conjunction with Him by love and
faith, extending to all according to the quality of love and
faith existing in them. (^{8}) It hence is evident, that the love of
the neighbor that begins with man, is opposite to the love
towards the neighbor that begins with the Lord; and that the
former proceeds from evil, because it proceeds from the *proprium* of man; whereas the latter proceeds from good, because
it proceeds from the Lord, who is Good Itself. It is evident,
also, that the love of the neighbor which proceeds from man
and his *proprium*, is a corporeal love; whereas the love towards
the neighbor which proceeds from the Lord, is a heavenly love.
In one word: self-love, with the man who is led by it, constitutes
the head, and heavenly love constitutes the feet, on which he
stands; but, if the latter does not serve him, it does not even
constitute the feet, but is trampled under them. It is owing to
this, that those who are cast into hell, appear to drop perpendicularly, with their head downwards towards hell, and their
feet upwards towards heaven. (See above, n. 548.)

559. Self-love is also of such a nature, that in proportion as
the reins are given to it,—that is, in proportion as external bonds
are removed, which consist in fear of the law and its penalties,

---

(*) That those who do not know what it is to love their neighbor, suppose that every
man is our neighbor, and that good is to be done to every one who is in need of assistance, n. 6704: and they likewise believe, that every one is nearest neighbor to himself, and thus that neighborly love begins from self, n. 6933. That those who love
themselves above all things, thus with whom self-love prevails, reckon also the commencement of neighborly love from themselves, n. 6710. In what manner every one
is his own nearest neighbor explained, nn. 6933—6938. But those who are Christians,
and love God above all things, reckon the commencement of neighborly love from the
Lord, because He is to be loved above all things, nn. 6706, 6711, 6819—6824. That
the distinctions of the relationship of neighbor are as many, as the distinctions of good
derived from the Lord; and that good ought to be done with discrimination towards
every one according to the quality of his state, and that this is a branch of Christian
prudence, nn. 6707, 6709, 6710, 6818. That those distinctions are innumerable; and
that on this account the ancients, who were acquainted with what is meant by a neighbor, reduced the exercises of charity into classes, and marked them with their respective names; and that hence they knew in what respect every one was their neighbor,
and in what manner good was to be done to every one prudently, nn. 2417, 6625, 6705,
7259—7262. That the doctrine received in the ancient churches was the doctrine of
charity towards the neighbor, and that hence they had wisdom, nn 2417. 2385, 3419,
8420, 4844, 6629.

and of the loss of character, of honor, of gain, of employment, or of life, it pursues its career, till at last it not only desires to rule over the whole terrestrial globe, but over the whole of heaven, and over the Divine Being Himself. It never knows any limit or end. This tendency lurks within every one who is immersed in self-love; although it does not appear before the world, where the above-mentioned bonds hold it in. But that such is the fact, no one can fail to see who observes the actions of potentates and kings, who have no such restraints and bonds to withhold them, and who invade the territories of others, and subjugate provinces and kingdoms, as far as success attends their enterprises, and aspire after unlimited power and glory. The same fact is more evident still from the Babylon of modern times, which extends its domination over heaven, and has transferred all the Lord's divine power to itself, and continually lusts to go further. Such persons, when, after death, they enter the other life, are utterly opposed to the Divine Being, and to heaven, and enlist themselves on the side of hell. (Respecting which, see the work *On the Last Judgment, and the Destruction of Babylon.*)

560. Represent to yourself a society composed of such characters, all of whom love themselves alone, and no others, further than as they make one with themselves : and you will perceive that their love is no other than that which exists among robbers, who, so far as their associates act in conjunction with themselves, embrace them and call them their friends; but who, so far as any do not act in conjunction with themselves, but reject their domination, fall upon them, and slay them. If the interiors of such characters, or their minds, are examined, it will appear, that they are full of mortal hatred against each other, and that, in heart, they laugh at all justice and sincerity, and also at the Divine Being, whom they reject as of no account whatever. This will still better appear from the societies consisting of such in the hells, which will be described below.

561. The interiors belonging to the thoughts and affections of those who supremely love themselves, are turned towards themselves and towards the world, and thus are turned away from the Lord and from heaven. In consequence of this, they are possessed by evils of every kind, and the Divine Sphere cannot enter them by influx ; for as soon as ever it does, it is immersed in their thoughts respecting themselves, and is thus defiled, and is at the same time infused into the evils which arise from their *proprium*. It is from this cause, that all such characters, in the other life, look back from the Lord, towards that mass of thick darkness which there occupies the place of the sun of the natural world, and which is diametrically opposite to the sun of heaven, which is the Lord. (See above, n.

323

123.) Thick darkness, also, signifies evil; and the sun of the natural world signifies self-love.[4]

562. The evils which possess those who are immersed in the love of themselves, are, in general, contempt of others, envy, enmity against those who do not side with them, hostility on that account, hatred of various kinds, revenge, cunning, deceit, unmercifulness, and cruelty. As to religion, they not only entertain contempt for the Divine Being, and for divine things, which are the truths and goods of the church, but they feel anger against them; and this, when the man becomes a spirit, is also turned into hatred; when he not only cannot bear to hear of those things themselves, but also burns with hatred against all who acknowledge and worship the Divine Being. I have conversed with a certain spirit, who, when in the world, had been possessed of great power, and had loved himself in a greater degree than is usual. This spirit, when he only heard mention made of the Divine Being, and especially when the Lord was mentioned, was so filled with hatred arising from anger, that he burnt with the desire to destroy Him, as he would murder a man. This same spirit, when he was left to his love without restraint, also desired to be the devil himself, that, from his self-love, he might continually infest heaven. This, also, is the desire of many who are of the Roman Catholic religion, when they find, in the other life, that the Lord has all power, and themselves not any.

563. There appeared to me some spirits in the western quarter towards the south, who said that, when in the world, they had been in stations of great dignity, and that they deserved to be preferred to others, and to command them. They were examined by the angels, to ascertain what their character intrinsically was; and it was found, that, in discharging the duties of the offices which they had filled in the world, they had not had regard to uses, but to themselves, and thus that they had preferred themselves to uses. But as they intensely desired, and were urgently solicitous, to be set over others, it was granted to them to take a place among some, whose office it was to consult about matters of superior importance: when it was perceived, that they were unable to attend at all to the business that was being considered, or to see things interiorly in themselves, and that, in their speeches, they did not regard the use of the matter in question, but some use connected with themselves; and further, that they wished to act from their arbitrary pleasure, according to personal favor. They were therefore dismissed from that function, and left to seek employment for

---

[4] That the sun of the world signifies the love of self, n. 2441. In which sense, by adoring the sun is signified to adore those things which are contrary to heavenly love, and to the Lord, nn. 2441, 10,584. That the sun growing hot denotes the increasing concupiscence of evil, n. 8487.

t. emselves elsewhere. They went on, therefore, further into the western quarter, and were occasionally received upon trial; but they were everywhere told, that they thought of nothing but themselves, and of no matter of business except with a view to themselves; consequently, that they were stupid, and were only like corporeal-sensual spirits. On which account, wherever they went, they were soon sent away again. After some time, I saw them reduced to the greatest destitution, so as to ask for alms. From these facts it was evinced, that those who were immersed in the love of themselves, how wisely soever, from the fire of that love, they may seem to speak in the world, still only speak from their memory, and not from any rational light; on which account, in the other life, where the contents of the natural memory are no longer permitted to be reproduced, they are more stupid than others; the reason of which is, that they are separated from connection with the Divine Being.

564. There are two kinds of dominion, the one being that of love towards the neighbor, and the other that of the love of one's self. These two kinds of dominion are, essentially, diametrical opposites. He who exercises rule under the influence of love towards his neighbor, entertains good-will to all, and loves nothing more than to be of use, and, consequently, to serve others. By serving others, is meant, to entertain good-will to others, and to perform uses, whether it be to the church, or to one's country, or to one's society, or to a fellow-citizen. This constitutes such a person's love; and this is the delight of his heart. Such a person, also, when he is raised to stations of dignity that elevate him above others, is glad of it; not, however, on account of the dignity, but because he is then enabled to perform uses in greater abundance, and of a higher order. Such is the dominion that prevails in the heavens. But he who exercises rule under the influence of the love of himself, entertains good-will to none, but to himself alone: the uses which he performs are done out of regard to his own honor and glory, which are the only uses that he deems worth attention. When he serves others, it is with the view, that he himself may be served, honored, and permitted to bear rule: he is a candidate for stations of dignity, not on account of the good which he may perform in them to his country and the church, but that he may be in the enjoyment of pre-eminence and of glory, and thence of the delight of his heart. The love of bearing rule also remains with every one after the close of his life in the world. To those who have exercised it under the influence of love towards their neighbor, it is also entrusted in the heavens; but then, it is not they that bear rule, but the uses which they love; and when uses bear rule, the Lord rules. Whereas those who, when in the world, exercised rule under the influence of the love of themselves, are, after ending their life in the world,

in hell, where they are vile slaves. I have seen great potentates, who, when in the world, had exercised rule under the influence of the love of themselves, cast among those of the meanest class in hell, and some of them among those who there inhabit receptacles of excrement.

565. But as to the love of the world, this is not opposite to heavenly love in the same degree as the love of one's self is, because so great evils are not concealed within it. The love of the world consists in desiring to obtain the goods of others for one's self by any sort of artifice, in setting the heart on riches, and in suffering the world to withhold and withdraw the mind from spiritual love, which is love towards one's neighbor, and, of consequence, from heaven and from the Divine Being. But this love has many forms. There is the love of wealth for the sake of being raised to honors, these being the only objects that are loved. There is the love of honor and dignities for the sake of gaining wealth. There is the love of wealth for the sake of the various uses to be obtained from it, in procuring things with which people are delighted in the world. There is the love of wealth for wealth alone; which is the love of misers. And so on. The end for the sake of which wealth is sought, is called its use; and the end, or the use, is that, from which the love derives its quality. For the love is such in quality, as is the end for the sake of which it is entertained. All other things connected with it serve it as means.

WHAT IS MEANT BY THE FIRE OF HELL, AND WHAT BY THE GNASHING OF TEETH.

566. What is meant by the everlasting fire, and what by the gnashing of teeth, which are said in the Word to be experienced by the inhabitants of hell, have as yet been scarcely known to any one. The reason is, because people have thought materially respecting the things mentioned in the Word, not being acquainted with its spiritual sense; in consequence of which, by fire, some have understood material fire; some, torture in general; some, remorse of conscience; and some have supposed that the expression is only used to strike men with terror, that they might be deterred from the commission of crimes. So, by the gnashing of teeth, some have understood the literal act; and some, only a sense of horror, such as is experienced when grinding of the teeth is heard. But whoever is acquainted with the spiritual sense of the Word, may conclude what is meant by everlasting fire, and what by the gnashing of teeth. In every expression, and in every sentence or collection of expressions,

used in the Word, is contained a spiritual sense: for the Word, in its bosom, is spiritual, and what is spiritual cannot be otherwise expressed, so as to come to the apprehension of men, than in a natural manner, because man is an inhabitant of the natural world, and thinks from the objects which there exist. What, therefore, is meant by that everlasting fire, and what by that gnashing of teeth, which wicked men come into the experience of after death, or which are suffered by their spirits, which then exist in the spiritual world, shall be here declared.

567. There are two origins of heat,—one from the sun of heaven, which is the Lord, and the other from the sun of the world. The heat which proceeds from the sun of heaven, which is the Lord, is spiritual heat, which, in its essence, is love (see above, nn. 126—140): but the heat which proceeds from the sun of the world, is natural heat, which, in its essence, is not love, but something which renders service to spiritual heat, or love, by affording it a receptacle. That love, in its essence, is heat, may be evident from the fact, that both the mind and the body grow warm on the presence of love, and according to the degree of the love, and to its quality; an effect which is experienced by man in winter as well as in summer. The same is evident from the heating of the blood. That natural heat, which has existence from the sun of the world, renders service to spiritual heat by affording it a receptacle, is evident from the heat of the body, which is produced by the heat of the spirit, and stands, in a manner, in its place; especially from the effect of the vernal and summer heat on all kinds of animals, on the arrival of which they annually renew their loves: not, indeed, that that heat inspires them with love, but because it disposes their bodies for the reception of the heat which also flows into them from the spiritual world; for the spiritual world flows into the natural world, as the cause does into the effect. He who imagines that natural heat produces the loves of animals, is greatly deceived: for there is an influx of the spiritual world into the natural, but not of the natural world into the spiritual; and all love, being a thing belonging to the life itself, is spiritual. He, likewise, who imagines, that any thing exists in the natural world independently of an influx from the spiritual world, is equally deceived; for what is natural neither exists nor subsists but from what is spiritual. The subjects of the vegetable kingdom, also, bud forth by an influx from the spiritual world: and the natural heat which prevails in the seasons of spring and summer, only disposes the seeds into their natural forms, by expanding and opening them, so as to admit the influx from the spiritual world to act as the cause of their germination. These facts are adduced that it may be known that there are two kinds of heat, which are spiritual heat and natural heat: and that spiritual heat proceeds from the sun of heaven, but natural heat

from the sun of the world; and that the influx of the former into the latter, followed by their co-operation, produces the effects which appear before our eyes in the world.([1])

568. Spiritual heat, as existing with man, is the heat of his life; for, as observed just above, in its essence it is love. This is the heat which is understood by fire in the Word; love to the Lord, and love towards the neighbor, by heavenly fire; and self-love, and the love of the world, by infernal fire.

569. The fire of hell, or infernal love, comes from the same origin as the fire of heaven, or heavenly love; that is, from the sun of heaven, or the Lord: but it is rendered infernal by those who receive it. For all influx from the spiritual world is varied according to its reception, or according to the forms into which it flows; just as occurs with the heat and light proceeding from the sun of the natural world. When this heat flows into nurseries of trees and flowers, it produces vegetation, and draws forth agreeable and sweet odors; whereas the same heat, flowing into excrementitious and cadaverous substances, produces putrefaction, and draws forth abominable smells and stenches. So, the light proceeding from the same sun, produces, in one object, beautiful and pleasing colors; and in another, ugly and disagreeable ones. It is the same with the heat and light that proceed from the sun of heaven, which is love. When that heat or love flows into principles of good, as existing with good men and good spirits, and with angels, it renders their goods fruitful; whereas when it flows into bad men or spirits, the effect produced is contrary; for their evils either suffocate it or pervert it. So, also, the light of heaven, when it flows into truths of good, imparts intelligence and wisdom; whereas, when it flows into falsities of evil, it is there turned into insanities and phantasies of various kinds. Thus its effects, in every instance, are according to its reception.

570. Since infernal fire, or the fire of hell, is the love of self and of the world, it includes, also, every lust belonging to those loves; lust being love in its continuous state; for what a man loves or lusts after, when he obtains it, he feels as delightful; and man experiences heart-felt delight from no other origin. Infernal fire, or the fire of hell, is, therefore, the lust and delight, which spring, as their origins, from those two loves. The evils belonging to those loves are, contempt of others, enmity and hostility against those who are not on one's own side, envy, hatred, and revenge; with the ferocity and cruelty which spring from those passions. In regard to the Divine Being, they are denial and consequent contempt, with derision and revilement of the

([1]) That there is an influx of the spiritual world into the natural world, nn. 6053—6058, 6189—6215, 6307—6327, 6466—6495, 6598—6626. That there is an influx also into the lives of animals, n. 5850. And likewise into the subjects of the vegetable kingdom, n. 3648. That this influx is a continual effort to act according to divine order, n. 6211 at the end.

holy things which belong to the church; which, after death, when the man is a spirit, are turned into anger and hatred against them. (See above, n. 562.) And as those evils contin ually breathe the destruction and slaughter of those whom the persons immersed in them account as their enemies, and against whom they burn with hatred and revenge, the delight of their life consists in desiring to destroy and kill them, and so far as this is beyond their power, in desiring to injure, hurt, and rage against them. These are the things which are meant by fire, in the Word, where the wicked and the hells are treated of; some passages from which I will here adduce by way of confirmation : *"Every one is a hypocrite and an evil doer, and every mouth speaketh folly.——For wickedness burneth as the fire, it shall devour the briars and thorns, and shall kindle the thickets of the forest, and they shall mount up like the lifting up of smoke. ——And the people shall be as the fuel of fire: no man shall spare his brother."*—(Isaiah ix. 17, 18, 19.) *"I will show won- ders in the heavens and in the earth, blood, and fire, and pillars of smoke. The sun shall be turned into darkness."*—(Joel ii. 30, 31.) *"The land thereof shall become burning pitch. It shall not be quenched night nor day ; the smoke thereof shall go up for ever."*—(Isaiah xxxiv. 9, 10.) *"Behold, the day cometh, that shall burn as an oven ; and all the proud, and all that do wickedly, shall be stubble, and the day that cometh shall burn them up."*—(Mal. iv. 1.) *"Babylon—is become the habitation of demons.—And they cried when they saw the smoke of her burning.——And her smoke rose up for ever and ever."*—(Rev. xviii. 2, 18 ; xix. 2.) *"He opened the bottomless pit, and there arose a smoke out of the pit, as the smoke of a great furnace ; and the sun and the air were darkened by reason of the smoke of the pit."*—(Ch. ix. 2.) *"Out of their mouth issued fire, and smoke, and brimstone: and by these was the third part of men killed ; by the fire, and by the smoke, and by the brimstone."*— (Rev. ix. 17, 18.) *"If any man worship the beast, the same shall drink of the wine of the wrath of God, which is poured out without mixture into the cup of His indignation ; and he shall be tormented with fire and brimstone."*—(Ch. xiv. 9, 10.) *"The fourth angel poured out his vial upon the sun ; and power was given unto him to scorch men with fire. And men were scorched with great heat."*—(Ch. xvi. 8, 9.) *"They were cast into a lake of fire burning with brimstone."*—(Ch. xix. 20 ; xx. 14, 15 ; xxi. 8.) *"Every tree that bringeth not forth good fruit shall be hewn down, and cast into the fire."*—(Matt. iii. 10 ; Luke iii. 9.) *"The Son of man shall send forth his angels, and they shall gather out of his kingdom all things that offend, and them who do iniquity ; and shall cast them into the furnace of fire."* —(Matt. xiii. 41, 42, 50.) *"Then shall he say unto them on the left hand, Depart from me, ye cursed, into everlasting fire, pre-*

pared for the devil and his angels."—(Ch. xxv. 41.) *They shall
be " cast into everlasting fire,—into hell-fire ;"——" where their
worm dieth not, and the fire is not quenched.*"—(Ch. xviii. 8, 9;
Mark ix. 43—48.) *The rich man in hell said to Abraham, "I
am tormented in this flame.*"—(Luke xvi. 24.) In these, and in
several other passages, by fire is meant the lust which arises out
of self-love and the love of the world ; and by the smoke thence
issuing is meant falsity originating from evil.

571. Since the lust of committing the crimes which originate
in self-love and the love of the world is meant by the fire of hell ;
and since that lust prevails in all the inhabitants of the hells
(see the preceding Section) ; the consequence is, that, when the
hells are opened, there is seen a fiery appearance accompanied
with smoke, such as attends conflagrations of buildings, or what
are called " fires ;" a dense fiery appearance being seen to proceed from the hells in which self-love reigns, and a flaming appearance from the hells in which reigns the love of the world.
But when the hells are shut, that fiery appearance is not seen,
but, instead of it, an appearance like a dark mass of condensed
smoke. Nevertheless, the same sort of fire continues to rage
within; as is rendered perceptible by the heat which exhales
from them ; which, in some instances, is like that proceeding
from the burnt ruins after a fire, in others, like that of a heated
furnace, and in others, like the moist heat of a hot bath. When
this heat flows into a man, it excites in him lusts, and, in the
wicked, hatred and revenge ; whilst it renders the diseased
insane. Such fire, or such heat, is felt by those who are possessed by the loves just mentioned, because, as to their spirits,
they are attached by invisible bonds, even while they live in
the body, to the hells in which those loves reign. It is, however, to be observed, that the inhabitants of hell do not actually
live in fire, but that the fire is an appearance; for they do not
feel any sense of being burnt, but only such a heat as they experienced in the world. The appearance of fire arises from correspondence; for love corresponds to fire; and all things that
appear in the spiritual world, appear according to correspondences.

572. It must be kept in mind, that that fire, or the heat of
hell, is turned into intense cold, when heat flows into it from
heaven; upon the occurrence of which, the infernal inhabitants
shiver like persons seized with a cold fever, and feel inward
torture at the same time. The reason of this is, because they
are utterly opposed to the Divine Being ; and the heat of heav-
en, which is Divine Love, quenches the heat of hell, which is
self-love, and extinguishes, at the same time, the fire of their
life; in consequence of which, they feel such severe cold, with
the shivering produced by it, and inward torture at the same
time. They also, at those times, are immersed in utter dark-

ness, whence they experience infatuation, and darkening of mind. This, however, occurs but seldom; only when their outrageous efforts increase beyond measure, and require to be quelled.

573. As by the fire of hell is to be understood all the lust of doing evil flowing from self-love, by the same is also meant torment, such as exists in the hells. For the lust flowing from that love, is, in those who are inflamed by it, the lust of doing injury to all who do not honor, respect, and pay court to them; and, in proportion to the anger which they thence conceive against such individuals, and to the hatred and revenge inspired by such anger, is their lust of committing outrages against them. Now when such a lust rages in every one in a society, and they have no external bonds to keep them under restraint, such as the fear of the law, and of the loss of character, of honor, of gain, and of life, every one, under the influence of his own evil, attacks another, and, so far as he is strong enough, subjugates him, subjects the rest to his own authority, and exercises ferocious outrages, with delight, upon all who do not submit to him. This delight is inseparably attendant upon the love of tyrannous rule, so that they accompany each other by equal steps; for in enmity, envy, hatred, and revenge, which are the evils of that love, as has before been stated, the delight of doing injury exists inherently. All the hells are societies of this description: on which account, every spirit, in every society, cherishes hatred in his heart against every other; and, under the influence of such hatred, breaks out into savage outrages against him, as far as he is able to inflict them. These outrages, and the torments so occasioned, are also meant by hell-fire; for they are the effects of the lusts which there prevail.

574. It has been shown above (n. 548), that an evil spirit casts himself into hell of his own accord: it shall therefore be briefly explained, how this is, notwithstanding there exist in hell such torments. From every hell there exhales a sphere of the lusts which prevail in those who inhabit it. When this sphere is perceived by any one in whom the same lust prevails, he feels affected at his heart, and filled with delight: for lust and its delight form a one, since what any one lusts after, is to him delightful. In consequence of this, the spirit turns himself towards the place from which the sphere proceeds, and, from the heartfelt delight with which it inspires him, desires to go • thither. He is not as yet aware that such torments exist there; and those who know it, still desire to go there: for, in the spiritual world, no one can resist his lust; for his lust belongs to his love, and his love to his will, and his will to his nature; and every one, there, acts from his nature. When, in consequence of this, a spirit of his own accord, or of his own free

motion, comes to his own hell, and enters it, he is at first
received in a friendly manner; which makes him believe that
he has found his true friends. This, however, only lasts a few
hours. During that interval, trials are made upon him, to discover what degree of cunning, and consequent power, he possesses. When this is ascertained, they begin to infest him;
which they do in various ways, rendering the infestations
gradually more sharp and violent. This is effected by intro-
ducing him more and more interiorly and deeply into hell: for
in proportion as any one is more interiorly and deeply introduced into hell, the more malignant are the spirits by whom he
finds himself surrounded. After having practised upon him
these infestations, they begin to torture him with cruel punishments; which they continue, till he is reduced to the condition
of a slave. But as rebellious commotions are there of continual
occurrence, since every one there wishes to be the greatest, and
burns with hatred against the others, new insurrections again
break out. Thus one scene is changed into another: in consequence of which, those who had been made slaves are taken
out of their thraldom, to assist some new devil to subjugate the
others; when those who do not submit, and obey the new tyrant
at his nod, are again tortured in various ways. This goes on
continually. Such torturings are the torments of hell, which
are called hell-fire.

575. As for the gnashing of teeth, this is the continual disputing and combating of different falsities, and, by consequence, of those who entertain them, with each other; combined with contempt of others, enmity, derision, mockery, and
revilement; which also break out into butcherly assaults of
various kinds: for every one fights for his own false persuasion,
and calls it the truth. These disputings and combatings are
heard without those hells as gnashings of teeth; and they also
are turned into actual gnashings of teeth, when truths flow into
them from heaven. In those hells all have their abode, who
have acknowledged nature and denied the Divine Being; the
deeper hells being inhabited by those who have confirmed
themselves in such acknowledgment and denial. Such characters, being unable to receive a ray of the light of heaven, and,
consequently, to see any truth inwardly in themselves, are, for
the most part, corporeal-sensual in quality, who are such as believe nothing but what they can see with their eyes and touch
with their hands: in consequence of which, all the fallacies of
the senses are accounted by them to be truths; and it is from
these that they maintain their disputations. It is on this account,
that their disputations are heard as gnashings of teeth: for, in
the spiritual world, all falsities have a grating sound, like the
gnashing of teeth; and the teeth correspond to the ultimate
things in nature, and also to the ultimate things in man, which

are his corporeal-sensual organs and faculties.(3) That there exists, in the hells, the gnashing of teeth, is stated in various passages of the Word. (As in Matt. viii. 12; xiii. 42, 50; xxii. 13; xxiv. 51; xxv. 30; Luke xiii. 28.)

OF THE PROFOUND WICKEDNESS, AND DIREFUL ARTS, OF INFERNAL SPIRITS.

576. The superior excellence of spirits, in comparison with men, may be seen and comprehended by every one, who thinks interiorly, and knows any thing of the operations of his own mind: for, in his mind, a man can weigh, unravel, and form conclusions upon, more subjects, in the space of a minute, than he can express in writing or speech in half an hour. From this instance it is evident, how far man excels himself when he is in his spirit; and, consequently, when he becomes a spirit; for the spirit is that which thinks, and the body is that by which the spirit expresses its thoughts in speech or writing. It is owing to this, that the man who, after death, becomes an angel, enters into the enjoyment of an intelligence and wisdom that are ineffable in respect to the intelligence and wisdom which he enjoyed while he lived in the world: for while he lived in the world, his spirit was bound to his body, and existed, by means of this connection, in the natural world; in consequence of which, all that he then spiritually thought, flowed into natural ideas, which are respectively common, gross, and obscure. Innumerable things that are seen by spiritual thought, cannot be received by natural ideas at all: and those which they do receive are involved in dense shades arising from the cares of the world. Not so when the spirit is released from the body, and comes into its own spiritual state; which is effected, when it passes out of the natural world into the spiritual, which is its proper home. That the state of the spirit then, as to its thoughts and affections, is immensely superior to its former state, is evident from what has now been observed. It is from this cause that the thoughts of the angels embrace things ineffable and inexpressible, and, consequently, such as cannot possibly enter into the natural thoughts of men: and yet, every angel was born a man, and has lived as a man; when he did not seem to himself to possess more wisdom than was enjoyed by other men like himself.

(3) Of the correspondence of the teeth, nn. 5565—5568. That those correspond to the teeth who are merely sensual, and have scarce any thing of spiritual light, n. 5565. That a tooth, in the Word, signifies the sensual nature, which is the ultimate of the life of man, nn. 9052, 9062. That gnashing of teeth, in the other life, proceeds from those, who believe that nature is every thing, and the Divine Being nothing, n. 5568.

577 HELL.

577. In the same degree that wisdom and intelligence prevail in the angels, do profound wickedness and cunning prevail in infernal spirits. The two cases are exactly similar; since the spirit of a man, when released from the body, is occupied by his own good or his own evil, an angelic spirit by his own good, and an infernal spirit by his own evil. For every spirit is his own good or his own evil, because he is his own love; as has frequently been stated and shown above. As, therefore, an angelic spirit thinks, wills, speaks, and acts, from his own good, so does an infernal spirit from his own evil; and to think, will, speak, and act from his own evil, is to do so from all the particulars included in his evil. It was different while he lived in the body; for the evil of a man's spirit is then restrained by the bonds in which every man is held by the law, by his regard to gain, to honor, and to his character, and the fear of losing them; on which account the evil of his spirit cannot then break out, and manifest itself according to its intrinsic nature. Besides, the evil of a man's spirit then lies veiled over and wrapped up in external probity, sincerity, and justice, and in the external affection for truth and goodness, of which the man makes a verbal profession, and puts on an appearance for the sake of the world: under the mask of which his evil lies so concealed, and so buried in obscurity, that he is scarcely aware himself that so much profound wickedness and cunning exist in his spirit, nor consequently, that he is, in himself, such a devil, as he becomes after death, when his spirit enters into itself, and into its own nature. But then, such profound wickedness manifests itself, as to surpass all belief. Thousands of wicked things then burst out of the evil itself; among which are some that are of such a nature, that they cannot be described by the words of any language. Of what kinds they are, has been granted me to know, and also to apprehend, by many experimental evidences; because it has been granted me by the Lord to be in the spiritual world as to my spirit, and in the natural world as to my body, at the same time. This I am able to testify, that their profound wickedness is such, that scarcely one instance of it, out of thousands, admits of being described. I can testify, also, that unless man were protected by the Lord, it would be utterly impossible for him to be saved from hell: for there are present with every man both spirits from hell and angels from heaven (see above, nn. 292, 293), and the Lord cannot protect a man, unless he acknowledges the Divine Being, and lives the life of faith and charity; for otherwise he averts himself from the Lord, and turns towards the infernal spirits; by whom he is imbued, as to his spirit, with profound wickedness, similar to their own. Nevertheless, man is continually withdrawn by the Lord from the evils, which, by being connected in society with spirits, he applies and, as it were, draws to himself: and if he cannot be withdrawn from

334

them by internal bonds, which are those of conscience, of which he is not receptive if he denies the Divine Being, still he is restrained by external ones, which, as already stated, consist in fear of the law and its penalties, and of the loss of gain, and the privation of honor and reputation. Such a man may, indeed, be withdrawn from evils by the delights of his own loves, and by the fear of losing and being deprived of those delights, but he cannot so be drawn to goods of a spiritual order; for when he is drawn towards these, he meditates cunning and deceitful artifices, pretending and feigning to do good, sincere, and just actions, with a view of persuading others that he is of such a character, and thus of deceiving them. This cunning adds itself to the evil of his spirit, and gives it form, causing it to be of the same nature with itself.

578. The worst of all are those, who have been possessed by the evils originating in self-love, and who have, at the same time, in their interior selves, acted from deceit: for deceit enters more deeply than any other evil into the thoughts and intentions, and infects them with poison, by which it destroys all man's spiritual life. Most of these dwell in the hells at the back, and are called genii: their delight is to make themselves invisible, and to flit about others like phantoms, covertly infusing evils into them, which they scatter about as vipers do their poison. These undergo direful torments beyond others. But those who were not deceitful, and not so eaten up by malignant cunning, and yet were possessed by the evils originating in self-love, also dwell in the hells at the back, but not in such deep ones. Those, on the other hand, who have been possessed by the evils originating in the love of the world, are in the hells in the front, and are called spirits. The evils by which these are constituted, are not of such a kind,—that is, they are not such evils of hatred and revenge,—as form the character of those who are possessed by the evils originating in the love of self, in consequence of which they do not possess such profound wickedness and cunning; on which account, also, their hells are more mild.

579. It has been granted me to know by experience what profound wickedness belongs to those who are called genii. Genii do not operate upon, and flow into, the thoughts, but into the affections. These they perceive, and trace by scent, as hounds trace their game in the forest. Where they perceive good affections to exist, they in a moment turn them into evil ones, by drawing and bending them in a wonderful manner, through the delights of the party on whom they operate; which they do so clandestinely, and with such malignant art, that the party has no consciousness of the operation; for they exercise the most dextrous caution lest any idea on the subject should enter his thoughts, because this would discover them. They take their station, in regard to the man upon whom they operate, beneath

the occiput. These genii consist of those who, when they were men in the world, deceitfully captivated the minds of others, by drawing and persuading them by the delights of their affections or lusts. But these genii are prevented by the Lord from acting upon any man of whose reformation there is any hope: for such is their nature, that they not only are able to destroy man's conscience, but also to call forth his hereditary evils, which otherwise remain concealed. In order, therefore, that man may not be drawn into these evils, it is provided by the Lord that those hells should be kept quite shut: and when any man who is a genius of the same kind comes after death into the other life, he is instantly cast into their hell. Those genii, also, when they are inspected as to their deceit and cunning, appear like vipers.

580. What profound wickedness belongs to infernal spirits, may appear from their direful arts; which are so abundant, that only to enumerate them would fill a book, and to describe them would require several volumes. But nearly all those arts are unknown in the world. *One kind* has reference to abuses of correspondences: *a second*, to abuses of the ultimates of Divine Order: *a third*, to the communication and influx of thoughts and affections, by means of turning towards the subject of the operation, of fixing the sight upon him, and of operating through spirits at a distance from themselves, and through emissaries sent forth from themselves: *a fourth*, to operations by means of phantasies: *a fifth*, to ejections out of themselves, by which their presence is produced in a different place from that in which they are in the body: *a sixth*, to pretences, persuasions, and lies. The spirit of a bad man, when released from the body, comes into the knowledge of these arts of himself; for they are inherent in the nature of his evil, by which he is then possessed. In the hells, by the practice of these arts, the inhabitants torment one another. As, however, all these arts, except those which consist in pretences, persuasions, and lies, are unknown in the world, I am unwilling here specifically to describe them, both because they would not be comprehended, and because of their direful nature.

581. The reason that torments are permitted by the Lord to exist in the hells, is, because evils cannot otherwise be there restrained and subdued. The only means of restraining and subduing them, and of keeping the infernal crew in bonds, is, the fear of punishment. No other method is possible. And without the fear of punishment and torture, evil would rush into deeds of furious madness, and the whole universe would be dispersed: as a kingdom on earth would be, in which there was no law, or no penal sanctions to enforce it.

OF THE APPEARANCE, SITUATION, ANL PLURALITY, OF THE HELLS.

582 In the spiritual world, or in the world inhabited by spirits and angels, similar objects appear as in the natural world, or that inhabited by men; so similar, indeed, that, as to their outward aspect, there is no difference between them. There appear in the spiritual world plains and mountains, hills and rocks, with valleys between them: there also appear waters, and many other things that are seen on the earth. But, notwithstanding, all these things proceed from a spiritual origin; on which account, they are visible to the eyes of spirits and angels, but not to those of men, because men reside in a natural world; and spiritual beings see the objects which proceed from a spiritual origin, and natural beings see those which proceed from a natural origin. This is the reason that a man cannot possibly behold with his eyes the things in the spiritual world, unless the privilege is accorded him of being in the spirit, or until he has passed through death, when he becomes a spirit himself; nor, on the other hand, can an angel or a spirit see any thing in the natural world, unless he be present with a man who enjoys the privilege of conversing with angels or spirits: for the eyes of man are adapted to receive the light of the natural world, whereas the eyes of angels and spirits are adapted to receive the light of the spiritual world; and yet the eyes of both are, to appearance, exactly alike. · That the spiritual world is so. constituted, is a thing which the natural man cannot comprehend; least of all can the sensual man, who is a person that believes nothing but what he sees with his bodily eyes and touches with his bodily hands; and, consequently, who only believes the impressions that he has imbibed by his sight and touch, from which impressions it is that he thinks, in consequence of which, his thoughts are material, and not spiritual. Since there is such a resemblance between the spiritual world and the natural world, a man who has entered the former after death, is scarcely aware, that he is not still in the world in which he was born, and out of which he has departed: for which reason, death is there described as a translation out of one world into another like it. (That there is such a resemblance between the two worlds, may be seen above, in the Section on Representatives and Appearances in Heaven, nn. 170—176.)

583. In the more elevated situations in the spiritual world, are the heavens; in the low ones, is the world of spirits; and beneath both these are the hells. The heavens do not appear to the spirits in the world of spirits, except when their interior sight is opened: sometimes, however, they appear as mists, or as white clouds. The reason that they are not otherwise seen, is, because the angels of heaven are in a more internal state, as to intelligence and wisdom, than the spirits in the world of

spirits, and thus are above their sight. The spirits, however, who dwell in the plains and valleys, see each other : but when a separation has taken place between them, which is effected when they are let into their interiors, the evil spirits can no longer see those that are good, though these can see the evil ; but they turn themselves away from them, and when spirits do this they become invisible to those from whom they avert themselves. But the hells do not appear, because they are closed : only the entrances to them, called their gates, are seen, when they are opened to admit spirits of similar character to those within. All the gates leading to the hells open from the world of spirits : and none of them from heaven.

584. There are hells everywhere, both under the mountains, hills, and rocks, and under the plains and valleys. Those apertures or gates leading to the hells which are under the mountains, hills, and rocks, appear to the sight like the holes and fissures of rocks, some of them stretching far in breadth and amplitude, some confined and narrow, and most of them rugged. All, when looked into, appear dark and dusky ; but the infernal spirits, who are within them, find themselves in a sort of light resembling that emitted from ignited charcoal. Their eyes are adapted to receive that light, in consequence of their having, while they lived in the world, been in darkness, with respect to divine truths, in consequence of denying them, and having been apparently in light, with respect to falsities, in consequence of affirming them ; owing to which, the sight of the eyes of their spirit had acquired such a formation. From this cause, also, the light of heaven, to them, is thick darkness ; so that when they go out of their caves, they see nothing. From these facts it appeared to me most evident, that man comes into the light of heaven, in proportion as he acknowledges the Divine Being, and confirms with himself the things belonging to heaven and the church ; and that he comes into the thick darkness of hell, in proportion as he denies the Divine Being, and confirms in himself such persuasions as are contrary to the things belonging to heaven and the church.

585. Those apertures or gates leading to the hells which are situated under the plains and valleys, have different appearances to the sight. Some are like those which are under the mountains, hills, and rocks ; some are like caves and caverns ; some are like great chasms and whirlpools ; some are like bogs ; and some are like stagnant pools of water. All are covered over, and are not open, except when evil spirits from the world of spirits are cast in. When they are open, an exhalation proceeds from them, either like fire attended with smoke, such as appears in the air where houses are on fire,—or like flame without smoke, —or like soot, such as issues from a chimney on fire,—or like a mist and thick cloud. I have heard, that the infernal spirits do

not see, nor feel those fires, smokes, or mists, because, when they are immersed in them, they are as if in their own atmosphere, and thus in the delight of their life; which arises from the circumstance, that those objects correspond to the evils and falsities by which they are possessed; for fire corresponds to hatred and revenge, smoke and soot to falsities originating in those evils, flame to the evils of self-love, and mists and thick clouds to the falsities originating in them.

586. It has also been granted me to look into the hells, and to see what sort of places they are internally; for, when the Lord pleases, the sight of a spirit or angel who is above, can penetrate to the bottom, and examine what sort of objects they contain, notwithstanding their being covered over. It has been granted me, also, to look into them in this manner. Some hells appeared to the sight like caverns or caves in rocks, tending inwards, and afterwards obliquely or perpendicularly downwards. Some appeared to the sight like coverts and dens, such as are occupied by wild beasts in forests. Some, like vaulted caverns and hidden chambers, such as are seen in mines, with caves tending towards the lower regions. Most of the hells are threefold. In the upper parts they appear within quite dark, because those dwell there who are immersed in the falsities of evil; but the lower parts appear as if on fire, because they are inhabited by those who are immersed in evils themselves: for darkness corresponds to the falsities of evil, and fire to evils themselves: and in the deeper hells reside those who have acted from evil, but more internally; in the less deep, those who have so acted more externally; and those who do this, act from the falsities of evil. In some hells are seen what appear like the ruins of houses and cities produced by fires, in which the infernal spirits dwell, and in which they conceal themselves. In the milder hells are seen what appear like rude cottages, in some places arranged contiguously, in the manner of a city, with lanes and streets; and within these houses are infernal spirits, who are engaged in continual altercations, displays of enmity, beatings, and efforts to tear each other to pieces; while in the streets and lanes are committed robberies and depredations. In some hells are mere brothels, which are disgusting to behold, being full of all sorts of filth and excrement. There are also dark forests, in which infernal spirits prowl about like wild beasts; and in which, likewise, are subterraneous caves, into which they flee when they are pursued by others. There also are deserts, where all is sterile and sandy; with, in some places, rugged rocks with caverns in them; and in others, huts. Into these desert places, those are cast out from the hells who have suffered the last extremes; chiefly those who, when in the world, were more cunning than others in plotting and contriving artifices and deceit. Their last state is such a life.

587. With respect to the situation of the hells specifically, this can be known to none, not even to the angels in heaven, but only to the Lord. Their situation, generally, however, is known from the quarters in which they are found. For the hells, like the heavens, are distinctly arranged according to the quarters; and, in the spiritual world, the quarters are determined according to the various loves. All the quarters, in heaven, begin from the Lord as the Sun, who is the East; and as the hells are opposite to the heavens, their quarters begin from the opposite one, that is, from the west. (On this subject, see the Section on the four Quarters in Heaven, nn. 141—153.) On this account, the hells in the western quarter are the worst and the most horrible of all, becoming successively more and more so, by degrees, in proportion as they are more and more remote from the east. These hells are inhabited by those who, when in the world, had been full of self-love, and, consequently, full of contempt of others, and of enmity against those who did not side with them, and, at the same time, full of hatred and revenge against those who did not treat them with respect and make their court to them. In the most remote parts of these hells are those who had been of the Roman Catholic religion, as it is called, and who then wished to be worshipped as gods, and who, in consequence, burnt with hatred and revenge against all who refused to acknowledge their power over the souls of men, and over heaven. They are still actuated by the same mind, that is, by the same hatred and revenge, against those who oppose them, as they were in the world: it is their supreme delight to commit savage outrages; but this is turned, in the other life, upon themselves: for in their hells, of which the western quarter is full, every one rages like a madman against every other who does not allow him to be possessed of divine power. (For further particulars, see the work *On the Last Judgment, and the Destruction of Babylon.*) But how the hells in that quarter are arranged, cannot be known, further, than that the most direful of those of that genus are at the sides, bordering on the northern quarter, and the less direful are towards the south. Thus the direful nature of the hells diminishes as they proceed from the northern quarter to the southern; as it also does, by degrees, towards the east. Towards the east dwell those who had been full of self-conceit, and did not believe in the Divine Being, but who, nevertheless, had not been influenced by such hatred and revenge, nor such deceit, as those whose abodes are in the deeper regions of the western quarter. In the eastern quarter, there are not, at this day, any hells; those which were there having been transferred to the fore part of the western quarter. In the northern and southern quarters there are many hells: they are inhabited by those, who, when they lived on earth, had been full of the love of the world, and, from that origin, of evils of various kinds, such as enmity,

340

hostility, theft, robbery, craft, avarice, and unmercifulness. The worst hells of this genus are in the northern quarter, and the milder are in the southern. Their direful nature increases, in proportion as they are nearer to the western quarter, and also, as they are more remote from the south ; and it diminishes, in proportion as they approach the eastern quarter, and also, as they approach the southern. Behind the hells that are in the western quarter, there are dark forests, in which malignant spirits prowl about like wild beasts : and it is the same behind the hells in the northern quarter. But behind the hells in the southern quarter are the deserts, mentioned just above. Thus much may suffice to be said respecting the situation of the hells.

588. With respect to the plurality of the hells, they are as many in number as are the societies of angels in the heavens, because every heavenly society has an infernal society corresponding to it in the way of opposition. That the heavenly societies are innumerable, and all distinctly arranged according to the goods of love, of charity, and of faith, has been shown above (in the Section on the Societies of which Heaven consists, nn. 41—50 ; and in that on the Immensity of Heaven, nn. 415—420) ; and it is the same with the infernal societies, which are arranged according to the differences of the evils opposite to those goods. Every evil includes infinite varieties, the same as every good. That such is the fact, will not be comprehended, by those who only have a simple idea respecting every evil, as respecting contempt, respecting enmity, respecting hatred, respecting revenge, respecting deceit, and respecting others of the like nature : but be it known to them, that every one of those evils contains so many specific differences, and every one of these, again, so many other specific or particular differences, that a volume would not suffice to enumerate them all. The hells are so distinctly arranged in order, according to the differences of every evil. that nothing more orderly and distinct can be conceived. It may hence be evident, that the hells are innumerable, one being near another, or remote from it, according to the differences of their evils, general, specific, and particular. There are also hells beneath hells. Some communicate with others by intervening passages, and more by exhalations ; the communications being regulated precisely according to the affinities between one genus or species of evil and the others. How great is the number of the hells, was also granted me to know from the fact, that there are hells under every mountain, hill, and rock, and under every plain and valley, and that the hells extend under them in length, in breadth, and in depth. In one word : the whole of heaven, and the whole of the world of spirits, are, in a manner, excavated beneath : and under them is a continuous hell. Thus much may suffice to be said respecting the plurality of the hells.

OF THE EQUILIBRIUM BETWEEN HEAVEN AND HELL.

589. All things must be balanced in equilibrium, in order that any thing may be capable of existing. Without equilibrium, there is no action and reaction; for equilibrium is the balance between two forces, one of which acts, and the other reacts: the state of rest which results from equal action and reaction being what is called equilibrium. In the natural world, an equilibrium is maintained in all and in every thing belonging to it; and in general, in the atmospheres themselves, in which the inferior parts react and resist, in the same ratio as the superior parts act and press upon them. In the natural world, also, there is an equilibrium between heat and cold, between light and shade, and between dryness and moisture; the medium temperature being their equilibrium. There is likewise an equilibrium in all the subjects of the several kingdoms of nature, which are three, the mineral kingdom, the vegetable kingdom, and the animal kingdom; for without an equilibrium maintained in those kingdoms, nothing could exist or subsist. Everywhere there is, as it were, an effort acting on one side, and another reacting on the other. All existence, or every effect, is produced in equilibrium: and it is produced in this way; that one force acts, and another suffers itself to be acted upon; or that one force flows in with acting, and the other receives it, and yields to it, in a suitable manner. In the natural world, that which acts, and that which reacts, are called a force, and an effort; but in the spiritual world, that which acts, and that which reacts, are called life, and will. Life is there a living force, and will is a living effort; and the equilibrium itself is called liberty or freedom. Spiritual equilibrium, therefore, or freedom, exists and subsists between good acting on one part, and evil reacting on the other; or else, between evil acting on one part, and good reacting on the other. With the good, the equilibrium is between good as the agent and evil as the reagent; but, with the evil, between evil as the agent and good as the reagent. The reason that spiritual equilibrium is that between good and evil, is, because the whole of man's life has reference to good and to evil, of which his will is the receptacle. There is also an equilibrium between truth and falsity; but this is dependent upon that between good and evil. The equilibrium between truth and falsity is like that between light and shade, which operate upon the subjects of the vegetable kingdom in proportion as they have in them heat and cold: for that light and shade produce nothing of themselves, but that heat operates by them, is evident from the fact, that the light and shade in the season of winter, are similar to the light and shade in the season of spring. Comparison is made between truth and falsity and light and shade, on account of their corre-

spondence; for truth corresponds to light, falsity to shade, and heat to the good of love. Spiritual light, also, is truth, spiritual shade is falsity, and spiritual heat is the good of love. (On which subject, see the Section on Light and Heat in Heaven, nn. 126—140.)

590. There is a perpetual equilibrium between heaven and hell. From hell there continually exhales and ascends the effort of doing evil; and from heaven there continually exhales and descends the effort of doing good. In that equilibrium exists the world of spirits, which is stationed in the midst between heaven and hell. (See above, nn. 421—431.) The reason that the world of spirits is placed in that equilibrium, is, because every man, after death, first enters the world of spirits, and is there kept in a state similar to that in which he was in the world; which could not be accomplished, did not the most perfect equilibrium there prevail: for by means of this, all are explored as to their quality, being left there to their liberty, such as they enjoyed while in the world. Spiritual equilibrium, as existing with men and spirits, is freedom or liberty; as stated just above. (N. 589.) Of what description is every one's freedom, is known to the angels in heaven by the communication of his affections and of the thoughts originating in them; and is rendered apparent to the sight of angelic spirits by the ways in which the parties walk. Spirits that are good walk in the ways which tend towards heaven; whereas spirits that are evil walk in the ways which tend towards hell. In that world, ways actually appear; which is the reason that, in the Word, ways signify the truths which lead to good, and, in the opposite sense, the falsities which lead to evil. It is from this origin, also, that going, walking, and journeying, signify, in the Word, progressions of life.[1] It has often been granted me to see those ways, and to observe spirits going and walking in them freely, according to their affections and the thoughts thence proceeding.

591. The reason that evil continually exhales and ascends from hell, and good continually exhales and descends from heaven, is, because there is a spiritual sphere encompassing every one, and which issues and exudes from the life of his affections and consequent thoughts.[2] As such a sphere of his life issues from every individual, it follows, that such a sphere also issues

[1] That to journey, in the Word, signifies progression of life; in like manner, to go, nn. 3335, 4375, 4554, 4585, 4882, 5493, 5605, 5996, 8345, 8397, 8417, 8420, 8557. That to go, and to walk, with the Lord, denotes to receive spiritual life, and to live with Him, n. 10,567. That to walk denotes to live, nn. 519, 1794, 8417, 8420.

[2] That a spiritual sphere, which is a sphere of life, flows forth and issues from every man, spirit, and angel, and encompasses them, nn. 4464, 5179, 7454, 8630. That it flows forth from the life of their affections and thoughts, nn. 2489, 4464, 6206. That spirits are known as to their quality, at a distance, from their spheres, nn. 1048, 1053, 1316, 1504. That spheres from the evil are contrary to spheres from the good, nn. 1695, 10,187, 10,312. That these spheres extend themselves far into angelic societies, according to the quality and quantity of good, nn. 6598—6613, 8063, 8794, 8797. And into infernal societies according to the quality and quantity of evil, nn. 8794, 8797.

from every society of heaven, and from every society of hell; and, consequently, from all those societies together; that is, from the whole of heaven, and from the whole of hell. The reason that there is an influx from heaven of good, is, because all its inhabitants are grounded in good: and the reason that there is an influx from hell of evil, is, because all its inhabitants are immersed in evil. All the good which flows from heaven, proceeds from the Lord; for the angels who inhabit the heavens are all withheld from their own *proprium* and kept in the Lord's *Proprium*, which is Good Itself: whereas the spirits that inhabit the hells are all immersed in their own *proprium;* and the *proprium* of every one is nothing but evil, and, as being nothing but evil, is hell.([*]) From these facts it may be evident, that the equilibrium in which the angels in the heavens and the spirits in the hells are kept, is not like that which exists in the world of spirits. The angels in the heavens find their equilibrium in the measure of good in which they had been willing to be grounded, or in which they had lived, while they were in the world; and, consequently, in the degree in which they had held evil in aversion: whereas the spirits in hell find their equilibrium in the measure of evil in which it had been their will to be immersed, or in which they had lived, while in the world; and thus, consequently, in the degree in which, in heart and spirit, they had been opposed to good.

592. Unless the Lord governed both the heavens and the hells, no equilibrium could be preserved; and if there were no equilibrium, neither heaven nor hell could exist; for all things in the universe, that is, both in the natural world and in the spiritual, maintain their stations by equilibrium. That such is the fact, every rational man can perceive: suppose a preponderance on one side, and no resistance on the other, would not both perish? So would it be in the spiritual world, if good did not react against evil, and perpetually restrain its insurrections; and did not the Divine Being solely do this, heaven and hell would perish, and with them the whole human race. I use the expression, "Did not the Divine Being solely do this," because the *proprium* of every one, whether angel, spirit, or man, is nothing but evil (see above, n. 591); on which account, no angels and spirits can possibly resist the evils that continually exhale from the hells, because, from their *proprium*, they all tend towards hell themselves. From these facts it is evident, that unless the Lord alone governed both the heavens and the hells, there could not possibly be salvation for any one. Besides, all the hells act as one force, since evils are connected together in the hells as goods are in the heavens; and to resist all the hells, which are

([*]) That the *proprium* of man is nothing but evil, nn. 210, 215, 731, 874, 875, 876, 987 1047, 2307, 2308, 3518, 3701, 3812, 8480, 8550, 10,283, 10,284, 10,286, 10,732. That the *proprium* of man is hell appertaining to him, nn. 694, 8480.

unnumerable, and which act simultaneously against heaven, and against all its inhabitants, is possible to nothing but that Divine Power alone, which solely proceeds from the Lord.

593. The equilibrium between the heavens and the hells is diminished and increased, on the one side or on the other, according to the number of new-comers who respectively enter into heaven and hell, who amount to many thousands a day. To know and perceive which way the balance inclines, and to regulate and equalize it with perfect exactness, is not within the power of any angel, but of the Lord alone. For the Divine Sphere proceeding from the Lord is omnipresent, and everywhere sees where any thing is in danger; whereas an angel only sees what is near him, and cannot so much as perceive, within himself, what is passing in his own society.

594. How all things are arranged in the heavens and in the hells, so that all the inhabitants, both collectively and individually, should be maintained in their equilibrium, may in some measure appear from what has been advanced and shown above respecting the heavens and the hells: as, that all the societies of heaven are distinctly arranged, in the most perfect order, according to the varieties of good, and their genera and species; and all the societies of hell according to the varieties of evil, and their genera and species; and that under every society of heaven there is a society of hell, corresponding to it in the way of opposition, from which opposite correspondence results an equilibrium between them; on which account it is perpetually provided by the Lord, that the infernal society situated beneath a heavenly society should not become the stronger; and, so far as it begins to do so, it is restrained by various means, and is reduced to the proper proportion required for the equilibrium. These means are various, of which only a few shall be mentioned. Some of them have reference to a stronger presence of the Lord; some, to the stricter communication and conjunction of one or more societies with others; some, to the ejection of the supernumerary infernal spirits into the deserts; some, to the transferring of some of them from one hell into another; some, to the regulation of the inhabitants of the hells, which is effected in various ways; some, to the concealing of certain hells under denser and grosser coverings; and also to the letting of them down to greater depths. Not to mention other means employed, including those which are provided in the heavens which are over them. These facts are adduced, that it may in some measure be perceived, that the Lord alone provides, that there should be everywhere maintained an equilibrium between good and evil, and thus between heaven and hell, for on such equilibrium is founded the preservation of all in heaven, and of all on earth.

595. It is to be observed, that the hells continually assault heaven, and endeavor to destroy it; and that the Lord contin-

ually protects the heavens, withholding its inhabitants from the evils which proceed from their proprium, and keeping them in the good which proceeds from Him. It has often been granted me to perceive the sphere which flows from the hells, which wholly consisted of a sphere of efforts to destroy the Divine Sphere proceeding from the Lord, and, consequently, heaven. I have also sometimes perceived the ebullitions of certain hells, which were efforts to emerge and to destroy. On the contrary, the heavens never assault the hells; for the Divine Sphere proceeding from the Lord is a perpetual effort to save all; and as those who inhabit the hells cannot be saved, because they are immersed in evil and are in opposition to the Lord's Divine Operation, what is done with them is, that, as far as possible, their insurrections are quelled, and their fierce outrages are restrained, that they may not exercise them on one another beyond the permitted bounds. This is effected accordingly, by innumerable means, involving Divine Power.

596. There are two kingdoms into which the heavens are divided, called the celestial kingdom and the spiritual kingdom. (Respecting which, see above, nn. 20—28.) In the same manner, there are two kingdoms into which the hells are divided. One of these is opposite to the celestial kingdom, and the other is opposite to the spiritual kingdom. That which is opposite to the celestial kingdom is situated in the western quarter, and its inhabitants are called genii; but that which is opposite to the spiritual kingdom is situated in the northern and southern quarters, and its inhabitants are called spirits. All who dwell in the celestial kingdom are grounded in love to the Lord; and all who inhabit the hells opposite to that kingdom are immersed in the love of self: whereas all who dwell in the spiritual kingdom are grounded in love towards the neighbor; and all who inhabit the hells opposite to that kingdom are immersed in the love of the world. It was made evident to me by this circumstance, that love to the Lord and the love of self are the opposites of each other; and that it is the same with love towards the neighbor and the love of the world. It is incessantly provided by the Lord, that no efflux should be directed from the hells opposite to the Lord's celestial kingdom towards the angels who dwell in His spiritual kingdom; for if this were to be permitted, the spiritual kingdom would perish. (The reason of which may be seen above, nn. 578, 579.) These are the two general equilibriums, which are perpetually preserved from infringement by the Lord.

346

THAT MAN IS IN THE ENJOYMENT OF FREEDOM THROUGH THE EQUILIBRIUM THAT IS MAINTAINED BETWEEN HEAVEN AND HELL.

597. The equilibrium between heaven and hell has been treated of in the preceding Section; and it has there been shown, that it is an equilibrium between the good which proceeds from heaven, and the evil which proceeds from hell; and that, consequently, it is a spiritual equilibrium, which, in its essence, is freedom or liberty. The reason that spiritual equilibrium is, in its essence, freedom or liberty, is, because it is an equilibrium between good and evil, and between truth and falsity, which are spiritual things: wherefore, the power of willing either good or evil, and of thinking either truth or falsity, and of choosing the one in preference to the other, is the liberty of which we are here treating. This liberty is given to every man by the Lord, nor is it ever taken away from him. In its origin, indeed, it does not

Extracts from the ARCANA CŒLESTIA, *on the Freedom or Liberty of Man, on Influx, and on the Spirits by whom Communications are effected.*

ON FREEDOM OR LIBERTY. That all freedom is attendant on love or affection, since what a man loves, this he does freely, nn. 2870, 3158, 8987, 8990, 9585—9591. As freedom is attendant on love, that it is the life of every one, n. 2873. That nothing appears as a man's own, but what is from freedom, n. 2880. That there is heavenly freedom and infernal freedom, nn. 2870, 2873, 2874, 9589, 9590

That heavenly freedom is attendant on heavenly love, or on the love of what is good and true, nn. 1947, 2870, 2872. And as the love of good and of truth is from the Lord, that freedom essentially consists in being led of the Lord, nn. 892, 905, 2872, 2886, 2890, 2891, 2892, 9096, 9586, 9587, 9589, 9590, 9591. That man is introduced into heavenly freedom by the Lord through reason, nn. 2874, 2875, 2882, 2892. That man, in order to be capable of being regenerated, ought to have freedom, nn. 1937, 1947, 2876, 2881, 3145, 3146, 3158, 4031, 8700. That otherwise the love of good and of truth cannot be implanted in man, and appropriated to him apparently as his own, nn. 2877, 2879, 2880, 2888. That nothing is conjoined to man in a state of compulsion, nn. 8700, 2875. That if man could be reformed by compulsion, all would be saved, n. 2881. That compulsion, in reformation, is hurtful, n. 4031. That all worship from freedom is real worship, but not that which is from compulsion, nn. 1947, 2880, 7349, 10,097. That repentance ought to be done in a free state, and that what is done in a state of compulsion is of no avail, n. 8392. States of compulsion, what, n. 8392.

That it is granted to man to act from freedom of reason, that good may be provided for him; and that on this account man possesses the freedom of thinking and also of willing what is evil, and likewise of doing it, so far as the laws do not forbid, n. 10,777. That man is held by the Lord between heaven and hell, and thus in equilibrium, that he may be in possession of freedom, for the sake of his reformation, nn. 5982, 6477, 8209, 8907. That what is inseminated in freedom remains, but not what is inseminated in compulsion, n. 9588. That on this account, freedom is never taken away from any one, nn. 2876, 2881. That no one is compelled by the Lord, nn. 1937, 1947.

That a man may compel himself from a principle of freedom, but cannot be compelled, nn. 1937, 1947. That a man ought to compel himself to resist evil, nn. 1937, 1947, 7914. And likewise to do good as from himself, still acknowledging that it is from the Lord, nn. 2883, 2891, 2892, 7914. That man has a stronger freedom in temptation-combats in which he conquers, since he then forces himself more interiorly to resist; although it appears otherwise, nn. 1937, 1947, 2881.

That infernal freedom consists in being led by the loves of self and of the world, and their concupiscences, nn. 2870, 2873. That the inhabitants of hell know no other freedom, n. 2871. That heavenly freedom is as distant from infernal freedom, as heaven is from hell, nn. 2873, 2874. That infernal freedom, which consists in being led by the loves of self and of the world, is not freedom, but slavery, nn. 2884, 2890; since slavery consists in being led of hell, nn. 9586, 9589, 9590, 9591.

belong to man, but to the Lord, it being from the Lord; but, nevertheless, it is given to man, together with life, as his own : and it is given him to this end,—that he may be capable of being reformed and saved; for without liberty or freedom there can be no reformation and salvation. Every one who takes any rational view of things may see, that man is at liberty to think either ill or well, sincerely or insincerely, justly or unjustly ; and also, that he is at liberty to speak and to act well, sincerely, and justly, but is withheld from speaking and acting ill, insincerely, and unjustly, by spiritual, moral, and civil laws, by which his external is kept in bonds. From these facts it is evident, that the spirit of man, which is that which thinks and wills, is in the enjoyment of liberty ; but that his external, which is what speaks and acts, is not, except in conformity with the above-mentioned laws.

598. The reason that man would not be capable of being reformed, unless he were in the enjoyment of liberty, is, because he is born into evils of all kinds. These must be removed, in order that he may be saved: and they cannot be removed, unless he sees them in himself, and acknowledges them ; and afterwards ceases to will them, and at length holds them in aversion. It is then that they are first removed. This

On Influx. That all things which man thinks, and which he wills, enter by influx; from experience, nn. 904, 2886, 2887, 2888, 4151, 4319, 4320, 5846, 5848, 6189, 6191, 6194, 6197, 6198, 6199, 6213, 7147, 10,219. That man's capacity of viewing things, of thinking, and of forming analytical conclusions, is from influx, nn. 1285, 4319, 4320. That man could not live a single moment, if influx from the spiritual world were taken away from him; from experience, nn. 2888, 5849, 5854, 6321. That the life which flows in from the Lord varies according to the state of man, and according to reception, nn. 2069, 5986, 6472, 7343. That with the evil, the good which flows-in from the Lord is turned into evil, and truth into what is false, from experience, nn. 3642, 4632. That the good and truth, which continually flow-in from the Lord, are so far received, as they are not opposed by what is evil and false, nn. 2411, 3142, 3147, 5828.

That all good flows-in from the Lord, and all evil from hell, nn. 904, 4151. That man believes at this day that all things are in himself, and are from himself, when yet they enter by influx, and he may know this from the doctrinal tenet of the church, which teaches that all good is from God, and all evil from the devil, nn. 4249, 6193, 6206. But if man believed according to the doctrinal tenet, he would not then appropriate evil to himself, nor would he make good his own, nn. 6206, 6324, 6325. How happy the state of man would be, if he believed that all good flows into him from the Lord, and all evil from hell, n. 6325. That those who deny heaven, or know nothing about it, are ignorant that there is any influx from thence, nn. 4322, 5649, 6193, 6479. What influx is, illustrated by comparisons, nn. 6467, 6480, 9407.

That the all of life flows-in from the first Fountain of Life, because it is from that Source, and that it flows-in continually, thus from the Lord, nn. 3001, 3318, 3337, 3338, 3344, 3484, 3619, 3741, 3742, 3743, 4318, 4319, 4320, 4417, 4524, 4882, 5847, 5986, 6325, 6468, 6469, 6470, 6479, 9276, 10,196. That influx is spiritual, and not physical, thus that influx takes place from the spiritual world into the natural, and not from the natural into the spiritual, nn. 3219, 5119, 5259, 5427, 5428, 5477, 6322, 9110, 9111. That influx takes place through the internal man into the external, or through the spirit into the body, and not contrariwise, because the spirit of man is in the spiritual world, and the body in the natural, nn. 1702, 1707, 1940, 1954, 5119, 5259, 5779, 6322, 9110. That the internal man is in the spiritual world, and the external in the natural world, nn. 978, 1015, 3679, (4459,) (4523,) (4524,) 6057, 6309, 9701—9709, 10,156, 10,472. That it appears as if influx took place from the externals appertaining to man into the internals, but that it is a fallacy, n. 3721. That with man there is influx into the things of his rational faculty, and through these into scientifics, and not contrariwise, nn. 1495, 1707, 1940. What is the nature of the order of influx, nn. 775, 880, 1096, 1498, 7270. That could not be accomplished, unless man possessed in himself good as well as evil; for he is capable, from good, of seeing evils, but not, from evil, of seeing goods. The spiritual goods which man is capable of making objects of his thoughts, he learns, from his infancy, by reading the Word and hearing sermons; and he learns moral and civil goods by living in the world. This is the first reason why man ought to be in the enjoyment of liberty. Another is, that nothing is appropriated to man, but what he does from an affection that is proper to his love: other things may indeed enter his mind, but no further than into his thought: nothing else enters into his will: and what does not enter into the will, also, does not become his own: for the thought draws its materials from the memory, but the will from the life itself. Nothing that man ever does or thinks is free, but what proceeds from his will, or, what is the same thing, from an affection belonging to his love. Whatever a man wills or loves, he does freely; in consequence of which, a man's liberty, and the affection which is that of his love or of his will, are one: on which account, therefore, man must be in the enjoyment of freedom, in order that he may be capable of being affected by truth and good, or of loving them, and that they may become, in consequence, as if they were his own. In one word, whatever does not gain admission to man in a state of freedom, does not remain in him, because it is not an object of his love or of his will: and whatever is not an object of a man's love or will does not belong to his spirit: for the *esse* of the spirit of man is his love or will. We use the terms, " his love or will," because what a man loves, he also wills. These then are the reasons that a man cannot be reformed, except he be in a state of liberty. (Further particulars respecting man's liberty or freedom may be seen in the *Arcana Cœlestia*, in the places referred to in the extracts inserted above, p. 347.)

599. In order that man may be in a state of liberty, as necessary to his being reformed, he is connected, as to his spirit, with heaven and with hell: for spirits from hell, and angels from heaven, are attendant on every man. By the spirits from hell, man is held in his evil; but by the angels from heaven, he is held in good by the Lord. Thus he is preserved in spiritual equilibrium, that is, in freedom or liberty. (That angels from

tncre is immediate influx from the Lord, and likewise mediate through the spiritual world or heaven, nn 6068, 6307, 6472, 9682, 9683. That the Lord's influx flows into the good appertaining to man, and through the good into the truth, but not contrariwise, nn. 5482, (5649,) 6027, 8685, 8701, 10,153. That good gives the faculty of receiving it flux from the Lord, but not truth without good, n. 8321. That nothing is injurious which flows into the thought, but what flows into the will, since the latter is appropriated to man, n. 6803.

That there is a general or common influx, n. 5850. That it is a continual effort to act according to order, n. 6211. That this influx flows into the lives of animals, n. 5850. And likewise into the subjects of the vegetable kingdom, n. 3648. That, also, according to the general or common influx, thought falls into speech, and will into actions and gestures, with man, n. 5862, 5990, 6192, 6211.

heaven, and spirits from hell, are adjoined to every man, may be seen in the Section on the Conjunction of Heaven with the Human Race, nn. 291—302.)

600. It is to be observed, that the conjunction of man with heaven, and with hell, is not, immediately, with heaven and hell themselves, but mediately, through spirits inhabiting the world of spirits. It is these spirits who are adjoined to man, and not any from hell or from heaven themselves. Through evil spirits, abiding in the world of spirits, man has conjunction with hell; and through good spirits, abiding there also, he has conjunction with heaven. It is on this account, that the world of spirits has its station in the intermediate region between heaven and hell: and is the seat of the actual equilibrium between them (That the world of spirits is intermediate between heaven and hell, may be seen in the Section on the World of Spirits, nn. 421—431; and that that world is the seat of the actual equilibrium between heaven and hell, in the Section immediately above, nn. 589—596.) From these facts it is evident, whence it is that man is in the enjoyment of freedom or liberty.

601. Something further shall be stated respecting the spirits that are adjoined to man. An entire society may have communication with another society, or with any individual, be he where he may, by the mission of an emissary spirit. The spirit thus commissioned is denominated "a subject of many." It is the same with the conjunction of a man with societies in heaven, and with societies in hell, by spirits adjoined to him belonging to the world of spirits. (Respecting these "subjects," see, also, the *Arcana Cœlestia*, in the places referred to below.)

602. In the last place, something shall be mentioned respecting that inherent conviction, which man possesses, respecting his life after death, as a result of the influx which he receives from heaven. There were certain spirits belonging to the simple populace, who had lived, in the world, in the good of faith, who were brought into a state similar to that in which they had been when in the world. This can be effected with any one, when the Lord gives permission. It was then shown what idea they had entertained respecting the state of man after death. They said, that certain persons of intelligence had asked them in the world, what they thought respecting their soul after their life in the world; to which they replied, that they did not know what the soul is. Upon this the intelligent persons asked them, what their belief was respecting their state after death; to which they answered that they believed that they should live as spirits.

On SUBJECTS. That spirits sent forth from societies of spirits to other societies, also to other spirits, are called subjects, nn. 4403, 5856. That communications in the other life are effected by such emissary spirits, nn. 4403, 5856, 5983. That a spirit, who, being sent forth, serves for a subject, does not think from himself, but from those by whom he is sent forth, nn. 5985, 5986, 5987. Several particulars concerning those spirits, nn. 5988, 5989.

The interrogators then inquired, what faith they entertained respecting a spirit; when they said, that it is a man. Upon being asked how they knew this ; they replied, that they knew it, because it was so. Upon which those intelligent persons wondered that such faith should be possessed by the simple, and not by them. It was thence made evident, that every man who is in conjunction with heaven, has an inherent conviction that he is to live after death. This inherent conviction comes from no other origin than an influx from heaven, that is, through heaven from the Lord, conveyed through the medium of the spirits who are adjoined to man from the world of spirits. It is enjoyed by those who have not extinguished their freedom of thinking, by principles previously assumed, and confirmed in various ways, respecting the soul of man ; such as affirm it to be either pure thought, or some animated principle, the seat of which they seek for in the body : when, nevertheless, the truth is, that the soul is nothing but the life of man, but the spirit is the man himself, and the terrestrial body, which he carries about in the world, is only an instrument, by means of which the spirit, which is the man himself, acts in the natural world, in a manner suited to the nature of that world.

603. The particulars which have been delivered in this work respecting heaven, the world of spirits, and hell, will appear obscure to those who take no pleasure in acquiring a knowledge of spiritual truths ; but they will appear clear to those who take pleasure in that acquirement; and especially to those, who cherish an affection of truth for its own sake,—that is, who love truth because it is truth. For every thing that is loved enters with light into the ideas of the mind : and this is eminently the case, when that which is loved is truth : for all truth dwells in light.

INDEX TO THE PASSAGES OF SCRIPTURE CITED N THE FOREGOING WORK.

GENESIS.

Chap.	Verses.	Num.
i.	3, 4	137
ii.	24	372
ii.	25	341
iii.	7, 10, 11	341

EXODUS.

xxix.	18, 25, 41	287

LEVITICUS.

i.	9, 13, 17	287
ii.	2, 9	287
vi.	8, 14	287
xxiii.	12, 13, 18	287

NUMBERS.

vi.	26	287
xv.	3, 7, 13	287
xxviii.	6, 8, 13	287
xxix	2, 6, 8, 13, 36	287

DEUTERONOMY.

iv.	19	122
xviii.	3, 4, 5	122

JUDGES.

xvii. & xviii.		324

2d SAMUEL.

xxiv.	15, 16, 17	229

352

2d KINGS.

Chap.	Verses.	Num.
vi.	17	76

PSALMS.

xxxi.	9	197
xxxvi.	6, 7	216
xxxvii.	37	287
xl.	13	365
xliii.	3	129
ciii.	20	229
civ.	2	129
cxviii.	5	197

ISAIAH.

viii.	8	197
ix.	7	216
ix.	5, 6	287
ix.	17, 18	570
x.	12, 13, 14	365
xiii.	10	119
xiv.	30	365
xix.	23, 24, 25	307
xxix.	19	365
xxx.	26	119
xxx.	6, 7	365
xxxii.	17, 18	287
xxxiii.	5	216
xxxiii	7, 8	287
xxxiv	9, 10	570
xli.	17, 18	365
xlii.	6	129
xlv.	3	365
xlix.	6	129
lii.	1	180
lii.	7	287
liv.	13	25
liv	10	287
lviii	2	216
lix.	8	287

INDEX

HEAVEN AND HELL.

The Figures refer to the numbers of the paragraphs.

ABRAHAM.—In the Word, Abraham, Isaac, and Jacob, denote the Lord as to His Divine, and His Divine Human, 526.

ACTION AND REACTION.—In the natural world, that which acts, and that which reacts, are called force, and also endeavor or effort: but in the spiritual world that which acts and that which reacts are called *life* and *will*. Life in that world is a living force, and will is a living effort, 589.

ACTIVITY.—Moral and civil life is the activity of spiritual life, 529.

ADMINISTRATIONS.—There are in heaven, as on earth, various administrations, ecclesiastical, civil, and domestic, 388.

ADULTERIES.—In the Word, adulteries signify the adulterations of good and truth, 384, 385. Heaven is closed against adulterers: they are unmerciful, and without a religious principle, 384.

ADULTS.—The difference between those who die infants and those who die *Adults*, 345.

AFFECTION is the *continuous* principle of love, 447, *note*. Thought, together with affection, constitute the man, 445. The genuine affection of truth is the affection of truth for its own sake, 347. Affection is spiritual, and corporeal, 468. Affection of use, 517. Affections are various with every one, 236. See *Thought*.

AFFINITIES.—All relationships and affinities, in heaven, are from good, and according to its agreements and differences, 46, *note*.

AFRICANS.—In heaven the Gentiles are more numerous than all the rest, the best of them are from Africa, 514, 326.

AGE.—Concerning the four Ages of gold, silver, copper, and iron, 115.

ANCIENT, the most, 87, 115, 252, 260, 268, 306, 323.

ANCIENTS, the, 87, 115, 119, 249, 323, 415. Elevation and abstraction from sensual principles was known to the Ancients, 74, *note*. They frequently conversed with spirits and angels, 249, *note*.

AND.—Why this particle so often occurs in the Word, 241.

ANGELS, 7–12, 17. Celestial angels, 21, 25, 31, 188, 214, 270, 271. Spiritual, 21,

25, 31, 214, 241, 270. Difference between celestial and spiritual angels, 25. Spiritual-natural, and celestial-natural, angels, 31. Angels of light, wherefore so called, 128. Why they are called gods and powers, 137, *note*. Internal and external angels, 32. Intermediate, 27, 55. Interior, 22, 23, 80. Exterior, 22. Superior, 22, 23, 267. Inferior, 22, *note*, 80, 267, 270. How angels speak with men, 168, 246, and following. Angels with infants, children, and men, 391. Perfected to eternity, 158, *note*. The angels think without an idea of time and space, 165, *note*. Admitted into natural thoughts, 168. Ascent of angels into a superior heaven, and descent into an inferior heaven, 35. They turn themselves to man, 246. Angels employed to examine the spirits of men after death, 462,* 463. Seated near the head of those who die, 449. Represented in churches, sculptured or painted, 74. How angels see the Lord, and how the Lord sees them, 145. The most perfect angels, 133, 189. Their power, 228–233. They have cities, palaces, houses, 184, 185. Their employments, 387–393. Their thoughts and affections, 266. Their offices towards men who come into the other life, 391, *note*. Their beauty, 80. Their interiors and exteriors, 173. There is not a single angel who was originally created such, all are from the human race, 311. Every angel is heaven in its least form, 51–58. Every angel is in a perfect human form, 73–77. By angels, in the Word, is meant something of the Lord, or something Divine from the Lord, 8, 391. The Lord, in the Word, is called an angel, 52. An entire angelic society is so called, 52. A man who receives the good of love and faith from the Lord is called an angel, 314. See *Changes of State, Habitations, Houses, Speech, Wisdom, Innocence, Garments*.

ANGER.—Why, in the Word, anger is attributed to the Lord, 545, *note*.

ANIMALS.—Difference between man and brute animals, 39, 108, 202, 296, 353, 435. Animal kingdom, 104, 108, 110. Influx of the spiritual world into the lives of animals, 110, *note*, 296, 567. Animals correspond to affections, tame and useful animals to good affections, savage and useless animals to evil affections, 110.

ANXIETY.—Whence anxiety originates with man, 299.

APOSTLES, the twelve, represented the Lord as to all things of the Church, 526, *note.*

APPEARANCES, concerning, in heaven, 170–176. Real appearances, 175. Appearances which are not real, 175.

APPEARANCES OF THE DIVINE.—The Divine has always appeared under the Human Form, 84. Under this Form the Ancients saw Him, 82, 84, 87.

APPREHENSION is internal hearing, 484.

APPROXIMATIONS in the spiritual world are similitudes of the states of the interiors, 193, 195.

ARCANA, concerning the good and truth which proceed from the Lord, 460. Concerning the body of every spirit and angel, 368.

ARCHITECTURE, beauty of the, in heaven; the architectural art is itself from heaven, 185.

ARM, the, signifies power, 231.

ARMS signify the power of truth, 96, *note,* 97, 231. Naked arm, 231. In the Grand Man, they who are in the province of the arms are in the power of truth from good, 96.

ARTICULATIONS OF SOUND.—See *Sound of Speech.*

ARTS, direful, of infernal spirits, 576–581.

ASHUR OR ASSYRIA, signifies the rational principle, 307.

ATMOSPHERE.—The angels have an atmosphere in which the sound of their speech is articulated, and in which they breathe, but it is a spiritual atmosphere, 235, 462.

AUTUMN corresponds to wisdom in its shade, 166, 155.

AVARICE, which is the love of riches without regard to use, corresponds to filth, 363.

BAPTISM signifies regeneration from the Lord by the truths of faith derived from the Word, 329, *note.* Baptism is a sign that man is to be regenerated, 329. Baptism confers neither faith nor salvation, 329, *note.*

BEASTS signify affections, 110. Beasts are in the order of their life, 296. The spiritual principle of beasts is not the same quality as the spiritual principle of man, 435. See *Animals.*

BEAUTY of the body does not imply beauty of the spirit, 99, 131, 459.

BED-CHAMBERS.—See *Inner Rooms.*

BEES.—Wonderful labors of the bees, 108.

BELIEF in the Divine Being. Man believes in the Divine Being when he is willing to be led by Him, 351.

BELTS, radiant, around the sun of heaven, 120. Dusky belt round the sun of heaven, 159.

BIRTH, spiritual, is effected by knowledges of good and truth, and by intelligence and wisdom, by virtue of which man is man, 345.

BLESSEDNESS, angelic, consists in the goods of charity, thus in performing uses, 387, *note.*

BLESSINGS, real, and blessings not real, 364, *note.*

BLIND, the, in the Word, signifies those who are in falses, and are not willing to be instructed; 487, *note.*

BLOOD OF THE LORD, the, signifies divine truth and the holy principle of faith, 147, *note.*

BODY.—It is from the spirit of man that the body lives, 76, *note.* The whole body has been formed for obedience to good and truth, 187. Whatever is felt and perceived in the body derives its origin from man's spiritual principle, that is to say, from his understanding and will, 373; but it is from the exterior or natural world that the body receives its first sensations and first motions, 381. When man dies he only leaves behind his terrestrial body, and nothing more, 461. To be withdrawn from the body, 439, 440. To be in the body of the Lord, 81.

BOOK OF LIFE, man's. By this book, which is spoken of in the Word, is signified that all his actions and all his thoughts are inscribed on the whole man, and appear, when called forth from the memory, as though they were read from a book, and as though seen in effigy when the spirit is viewed in the sight of heaven, 463. 286. In the spiritual world there are books similar to those in the world, 463, 462.* See *Memory.*

BORN AGAIN, to be. Man must be reborn—that is, regenerated, 342.

BRAIN, the. Every particular of man's thought and will are inscribed on the brain, 463.

BREAD signifies all the good which nourishes the spiritual life of man, 111. The bread which was on the table in the Tabernacle, had a like signification, 111, *note.* Bread involves all food, and thus it signifies all food, celestial and spiritual, 111, 340.

BREADTH, by, is understood a state of truth, 197, 198, *note.*

BREAST, the, signifies charity, 97. In the Grand Man, they who are in the province of the breast are in the good of charity and faith, and flow into the breast of man, to which they correspond, 96.

BRIDE AND BRIDEGROOM.—In the Word, the Lord is called the Bridegroom, and the Church the Bride, 180.

BRIGHT, that which is, corresponds to truth, and in the Word signifies truth, 179.

BULLOCK, signifies the affections of the natural mind, 110.

CAMEL, a, signifies the principle of knowledge and science in general, 365.

CARE for the morrow, what it is, 278.

CARRIED, to be. What it is to be carried by the spirit to another place, 441, 192, 439.

CATERPILLARS.—Marvellous transformation of caterpillars, 108.

CEDAR, the, 111. A. C. 886.

CENTRE.—The Lord is the common centre, towards which all the angels turn themselves, 124, 142.

CEREBELLUM, the.—That part of the head which covers the *cerebellum* corresponds to wisdom, 251.

CEREBRUM, the.—That part of the head which covers the *cerebrum* corresponds to intelligence, 251.

CHANGES of place in the spiritual world are nothing but changes of state, 192, 195.

CHANGES of state, concerning, with the angels in heaven, 154–161. In the spiritual world, changes of place are changes of the state of life, 192, *note.*

CHARITY is every thing which relates to life, it consists in willing and doing what is just and right in every work, 364. A life of charity is a life according to the Lord's commandments, 535. Genuine charity is not meritorious, 535. *Charity towards the neighbor extends itself to the minutest things which a man thinks, wills, and does,* 217, 481, 535, *note ;* it consists in doing what is good, just, and right, in every act and in every employment, 360, 535, *note.*

CHINESE, 325.—See *Gentiles.*

CHRIST.—The Lord was thus named in the world, from the Divine Spiritual, 24. See *Jesus.*

CHURCH, the Ancient, is that which existed after the flood and extended through many kingdoms, 327. In the ancient church they had a Word, but it is lost, 327, *note.* Doctrine in the ancient church was the doctrine of charity, 481, *note,* 558.

CHURCH, the, is the Lord's heaven upon earth, 57. The church is within man, and not out of him, 57. The church at large consists of men in whom the church is, 57, *note.* The church of the Lord is universal, and includes all who acknowledge a Divine Being and live in charity, 308. It is spread over the whole globe, 328. The universal church on earth is before the Lord as one man, 305, *note.* The church specifically exists where the Word is, and where the Lord is known by the Word, 308, 318. Still they who are born where the Word is, and where the Lord is known, are not members of the church on that account, but they who live a life of charity and faith, 318. Unless there was a church on the earth where the Word is, and where the Lord is known by the Word, the human race here would perish, 305, *note.* If good were the characteristic and essential of the church, and not truth without good, the church would be a one, 57. *note.* All churches make one church before the Lord by virtue of good, 57, *note.*

CHURCH, the most ancient, on earth, is described in the first chapter of Genesis, and was, above all others, celestial, 327, *note.*

CICERO.—Conversation between Swedenborg and Cicero, 322.

CITIES.—The habitations of the angels are contiguous, and arranged in the form of a city, 184.

CLEFT OF THE ROCK, the, signifies an obscure and false principle of faith, 488, *note.*

CLIMATES.—With the angels, the differences in the changes of state are, in a general point of view, like the variations of the state of the day in different climates on the earth, 157.

CLOUDS, in the Word, signify the Word in the letter, or the sense of its letter, 1, *note.*

COHABITATION.—In heaven, the conjunction of two into one mind, is called cohabitation, 367, *note.*

COLORS in heaven are variegations of light, 179, *note.* They signify various things which relate to intelligence and wisdom, 179, *note,* 356. So far as they partake of redness, colors signify good, and so far as they partake of white, they signify truth, 179, *note.*

COMING OF THE LORD, the, is His Presence in the Word, and revelation thence, 1.

COMMUNICATION.—In heaven there is a communication of all goods, 49, 199, 200–212, 268; and of the thoughts of all, 2. There is a communication of all with each, and of each with all, 399. Communication with others in the spiritual world depends upon the aspect of the face, 552. There is an inmost communication of the spirit, in the respiration and the motion of the heart, 446.

COMMUNION.—Heaven is a communion of all goods, 268, 73.

COMPULSION. — Nothing is conjoined to man which is of compulsion, 293, *note.* What is of compulsion in reformation is hurtful, 293, *note.*

CONCEPTIONS signify spiritual concentions, which are those of good and truth, 382,* *note.*

CONCUPISCENCES all flow from the love of self and the love of the world, 396.

CONFIRMED, to be.—Whatever is confirmed puts on the appearance of truth, and there is nothing which cannot be confirmed, 352.

CONJOINED, to be.—That which is capable of being conjoined to the Divine cannot be dissipated, 435.

CONJUNCTION of heaven with the human race, 291–302. Conjunction of heaven with man by the Word, 303–310, 205, 208, 254, 319, 423, 424. Conjunction of heaven with the world by correspondences, 112. Conjunction of angels and spirits with man, 255, 246, 247, 369. Conjunction of the understanding and the will, 423. Actual conjunction of the husband and wife into one, 369. The conjunction of good and truth is heaven, and the conjunction of evil and the false is hell, 425.

CONNECTION, there is a, of all things by intermediates with the First, and whatever

the spiritual world originate solely in differences of the state of the interiors, 42, 192, 195, 197.

DIVINE, the, is One, and this Divine One is in the Lord, 2. A Divine which is not perceptible by any idea, cannot be an object of faith, 3. The Divine of the Lord makes heaven, 7–12. The Divine of the Lord in heaven is love to Him, and charity towards the neighbor, 13–19. A visible Divine, an invisible Divine, 79, 80. The Divine celestial, Divine spiritual, and Divine natural, 31.

DIVINE, the essential, of the Lord is far above His Divine in heaven, 118, *note.* The soul, which the Lord had from the Father, was the very Divine Itself, 316.

DIVINE GOOD, the, is the heat of heaven which proceeds from the Lord as a Sun, 117, 127, 133, 139. The Divine Good which proceeds from the Lord constitutes the Divine Order, 107.

DIVINE HUMAN, the.—See Extracts from the *A. C.* concerning the Lord, and concerning His Divine Human, p. 86. Also n. 78–86, 101.

DIVINE LOVE, it is, which shines as a Sun in heaven, 117, 127. The nature and intensity of the Divine Love, 120. The Divine Love which is the Lord as a Sun, is the *Esse* from which the Divine Good and Divine Truth in the heavens exist, 139. The Divine Love of the Lord is love towards all the human race, desiring to save them, 120, *note.*

DIVINE TRUTH, the, is the Divine proceeding from the Lord, 13, 140. It is the light which proceeds from the Lord as a Sun, 117, 122, 127, 128, 139, 133. All things were made and created by the Divine Truth, 137. Divine Truth is the Lord in heaven, 271.

DOCTRINE, the, of the Church must be derived from the Word, 311, *note.* The Word without doctrine is not understood, for true doctrine is a lamp to those who read the word, 311, *note.* Genuine doctrine must be had from those who are in illustration from the Lord, 311, *note.* The doctrine received from heaven is in perfect agreement with the internal sense of the Word, 516. Doctrine in the Ancient Church was the doctrine of charity, and hence that Church had wisdom, 481, *note.* The doctrines in heaven are adapted to the perceptions of the angels in each heaven, 221, 227. The essential of all heavenly doctrine is the acknowledgment of the Divine Human of the Lord, 227.

DOMINION.—There are two kinds of dominion, the one springs from love towards the neighbor, the other from self-love, 564. Dominion of one married partner over another, 380.

DOTS.—Whence it is that the very dots, iotas, and minutest parts of the Word contain heavenly arcana and things Divine, 260.

DOVES correspond to intellectual things, 110.

DRUNKEN.—As soon as the angels think of marriage with more than one, they are alienated from internal blessedness and heavenly felicity, and they become like drunken men, because good is disjoined in them from its own truth, 379.

DUNGHILLS.—They who pass their lives in mere pleasure, living delicately, and indulging in the pleasures of the table, so as to account them the highest good of life, love and delight in dunghills in the other life, 488.

DURATION of the first state of man after death, 498. Duration of the abode of man in the world of spirits, 426.

EARS, the, signify obedience, 97. In the Grand Man, those who are in the province of the ears are in attention and obedience, 96. The ear corresponds to perception and obedience, and also the reception of truths, 271.

EARTH, the, signifies the Church, 307. The lower earth, its situation, 513, 591. Concerning the Earths in the Universe, they are innumerable, 417. Their inhabitants adore the Divine Being under a Human Form, 321.

EAST, the.—In heaven, that quarter is called the east where the Lord appears as a Sun, 141. The Lord, in the supreme sense, is the East, 141. The East signifies love and its good in clear perception, 148, 149. In hell, they who are in the evils which spring from self-love, dwell from the East to the West, 151.

EDIFICES, why the sacred, of the most ancient people were of wood, 223, *note.* In the celestial kingdom, the sacred edifices are not called churches, but houses of God, 223.

EDUCATION of children in heaven, 384–344. In what respect it differs from that of children on earth, 344.

ELECT, they are the, who are in the life of good and truth, 420.

EFFECTS derive all their quality from their efficient cause, for such as the cause is, such is the effect, 512.

EGYPT AND EGYPTIAN in the Word signify the natural principle, and the scientific thence derived, 307, *note.* The science of correspondences flourished in Egypt, 87, *note.*

ELEVATION of the understanding into the light of heaven, 130, 131. There is an actual elevation of the understanding into the light of heaven, when man is elevated into intelligence, 130, *note.*

EMPLOYMENTS, concerning the, of the angels in heaven, 387–394.

END, no, can be assigned to any good thing, because it springs from the Infinite, 469. False opinions concerning the end of the world, 312.

ENDS.—Nothing is regarded by the Lord, and thence by the angels, but ends, which are uses, 112.

ENLIGHTENED, to be, is to be elevated into the light of heaven, 131. The understanding is enlightened because it is recipient of truth, and it is enlightened so far as man receives truth in good from the Lord, 130, *note*.

ENTHUSIASTS.—Who they are who become enthusiasts, and why they become such, 249.

ENTRANCE, concerning the, of man into eternal life, 445–452.

EQUILIBRIUM, concerning the, between heaven and hell, 589–596. Equilibrium is the balance of two forces, of which one acts, and the other reacts, 589. The safety of all in heaven and earth is founded on equilibrium, 594. The world of spirits is the especial seat of equilibrium, 600. The equilibrium between the heavens and the hells is diminished or increased, according to the number of spirits who enter them, 593.

ERRORS.—Those who are in the sense of the letter without doctrine are led away into many errors, 311, *note*.

ESSE.—The Divine Itself was the Esse of the Lord's Life, p. 86. The will of man is the very Esse of his life, 26, 447, 474.

ESSENTIAL, the, of order, is the Divine Good, 77, *note*, 523. It is an essential of the Church to acknowledge the Divine of the Lord and His union with the Father, p. 86. The essential of all heavenly doctrine is the acknowledgment of the Divine Human of the Lord, 227. Innocence is the essential of what is good and true, 281.

EVENING signifies a state of closing light and love, 155, 166. It corresponds to a state of wisdom in its shade, 155.

EVIL comes from the proprium of man, 484. All evils are derived from the love of self and the world, they are contempt of others, enmities, hatred, revenge, cruelty, deceit, 359, *note*. The hereditary evil of man consists in loving himself more than God, and the world more than heaven, and in making no account of his neighbor in comparison with himself, except only for the sake of himself, which is to love himself; so that it consists in the loves of self and the world, 342, *note*. Every evil brings its own punishment along with it, since evil and punishment are joined together, 509. Man is the cause of his own evil, and not the Lord, 547. Why, in the Word, evil is attributed to the Lord, when yet nothing can proceed from the Lord but good, 545. Every evil has a false principle within it, and therefore they who are in evil are also in the false, although some of them do not know it, 551.

EXIST, to.—Nothing can exist from itself, but from something prior to itself, consequently all things exist from a First, which is the very Esse of the life of all things, 9, 37, 304. With the Lord, the Existere of life, proceeding from the Esse, was the Human which went forth from the Divine itself, p. 86. With man, the Existere of life proceeding from the Esse is the understanding, 474.

EXTENSION, difference between, in heaven, and extension in the world, 85.

EXTERIORS, the, of the spirit enable man to adapt the body, and especially the face, speech, and manners, to the society in which he lives in the world, 492. Exterior things are more remote from the Divine in man, and therefore respectively obscure and confused, 267, *note*. See *Interiors*.

EYE, the, signifies the understanding; because the understanding is the internal sight, 97, 145. The sight of the eye signifies intelligence which is of faith, and also faith itself, 271.

EYE OF A NEEDLE, the, signifies spiritual truth, 365.

EYES, the, correspond to the understanding, 145. They correspond to truths derived from good, 232, *note*. In the Grand Man, those who are in the province of the eyes excel in understanding, 96. The reason why all infants in heaven are in the province of the eyes, 333. To lift up the eyes and to see, signifies to understand, to perceive, and to observe, 145.

FACE, the, is formed to correspondence with the interiors, 143. With the angels the face makes one with the interiors of the mind, 143, 457. It is the form of their affections, 47. The face of the spirit of man differs exceedingly from that of his body, 457. The face of the body is derived from his parents, but the face of the spirit is derived from the affection, and is the image of it, 457. In the Word, the face corresponds to the interiors of man, which are of the thought and affection, 251, 457.

FAITH is the light of truth; it is derived from charity, 148. Faith is every thing which relates to doctrine, and consists in thinking justly and rightly, 364. Faith separate from love is not faith, but mere science void of spiritual life, 474. Faith does not remain with man, unless it springs from heavenly love, 482. Mere belief in the truth and in the Word is not faith, but to love truth from heavenly love, and to will and do it from interior affection, is faith, 482.

FALSE PRINCIPLE, every, originates in evils, and springs from the love of self and the world, 342, 558.

FEET signify the natural principle, 97. In the Grand Man, they who are in the province of the feet, are in the ultimate good of heaven, which is called spiritual natural good, 96.

FIBRES, concerning nervous, in the human body, 212, 413.

FIELDS signify things analogous which pertain to state, 197.

FIRE, in the Word, signifies love, either heavenly or infernal. Sacred and celestial fire signifies Divine Love, and infernal fire, the loves of self and of the world, 18, 118, 134. Concerning infernal fire, 566–575.

FIRST, the, and the Last, signify all things in general and every particular thing, 304.

HOUSES IN HEAVEN, concerning, 184, 180. Houses, and the things which they contain, signify those things in man which are of his mind; that is, his interior, consequently, which relate to good and truth, 186, *note*. A *house of wood* signifies what is of good, and a *house of stone*, what is of truth, 186, *note*. The *House of God*, in the supreme sense, signifies the Divine Human of the Lord, as to Divine Good, and in the respective sense, heaven and the church as to good and truth, 187, *note*, 223. The house where the marriage was celebrated signifies heaven and the church, on account of the Lord's conjunction with them by His Divine Truth, 180.

HUMAN RACE, Heaven and Hell are from the, 311-317. The human race is the seminary of heaven, 417.

HUNDRED AND FORTY-FOUR, a, denotes all truths and goods in the complex, 78, *note*, 307.

HUNGER, to, signifies to desire the knowledge of good and truth, 420.

HUNGRY.—In the Word, those are called *hungry* who are not in the knowledges of good and truth, but who still desire them, 420.

HUSBAND.—Why the Lord, in the Word, is called husband, 180. Husband is predicated of the Lord, and of His conjunction with heaven and the church, 368, *note*. Husband signifies the understanding of truth, 368.

IDEA.—There are innumerable things contained in one idea of thought, 240, *note*. The ideas of thought are various forms into which the common affection is distributed, for no thought or idea can exist without affection; it is their soul and life, 236. The natural ideas of man are turned into spiritual ideas with the angels, 165. When angelic ideas, which are spiritual, flow in with man, they are turned in an instant, and of themselves, into natural ideas proper to man, to which they exactly correspond, 168. The ideas of the internal man are spiritual, but man during his life in the world perceives them naturally, because he then thinks in the natural principle, 243, *note*. After death man comes into his interior ideas, and those ideas then form his speech, 243, *note*.

IGNORANT.—Why man is born entirely ignorant, 108.

IMAGE.—In the other life every one becomes the visible image of his own love, even in externals, 481.

IMMENSITY OF HEAVEN, concerning the, 415-418.

INDUSTRY, HUMAN.—Whatever the industry of man prepares for his own use are correspondencies, 104.

INFANCY.—The spirits who attend on infancy are characterized by innocence; those which attend on childhood are distinguished by the affection of knowing, 295. The good of infancy is not spiritual good, but it becomes so by the implantation of truth,

277, *note*. Whatever is imbibed in infancy appears natural, 277, *note*.

INFANTS IN HEAVEN, concerning, 4, 329-345. They grow up there, 4; those who are of a spiritual character are in the province of the left eye of the Grand Man, and those who are of a celestial character are in the province of the right eye, 338, 339. Every object appears to them to be alive, 338. Temptation of infants, 343. In heaven they do not advance beyond early youth, but remain in that state to eternity, 340. Character of little children upon earth, 277. Those who die infants, wherever they are born, are accepted by the Lord, 308, *note*. In the Word, an infant signifies one who is innocent, 278.

INFINITE.—There is no proportion between what is infinite and what is finite. 273.

INFLUX.—See p. 608. Extracts from the *A. C.* concerning influx. See also n. 26, 37. 110, 112, 135, 143, 207, 208, 209, 277, 282, 296, 297, 298, 304, 319, 485, 455, 549, 567.

INHERENT.—See 74, 82, 260, 602.

INMOST.—In every man there is an inmost or supreme degree, by which he is distinguished from brute animals, and into which the Divine of the Lord first flows, and elevates man to Himself, 39, 485.

INNOCENCE is the receptacle of the truth of faith, and of the good of love, 330. Of the state of innocence of the angels in heaven, 276-283. Innocence with them is the very esse of all good, 282. Concerning the innocence of little children, 277. The innocence of infants is the plane of all the affections of good and truth, 341. The innocence of infants is not true innocence, because true innocence dwells in wisdom, 277. Genuine innocence is wisdom, 341.

INSPIRATION.—In what manner the Lord spoke with the prophets, by whom the Word was given, 254.

INSTRUCTION, concerning the state of, provided for those who go to heaven, 512-590.

INSTRUCTRESSES, concerning the, of children in the other life, 332, 337.

INTELLIGENCE.—The Divine Intelligence is the light of heaven, 131. Heavenly intelligence is interior intelligence, arising from the love of truth for the sake of truth, 347. Intelligence consists in receiving truth from the Lord, 80; and also in seeing and perceiving what is true and what is false, and in accurately distinguishing the one from the other, by intuition and interior perception, 351. What spurious intelligence consists in, 352. The nature of false intelligence, 353. Intelligence and wisdom constitute the man, 80. See *Wisdom*.

INTELLIGENT.—Who are meant by the intelligent, 347, 348, 356.

INTENTION springs from love, and therefore man's love determines his internal sight or thought towards its objects, 532.

INTERIORS, the, of the spirit, are of his own will and its derivative thought, 492. Interior things flow by successive order into external things, even to the extreme or ultimate, and there they exist and subsist, 304, *note*, 475. Their existence and subsistence in ultimates is in simultaneous order, hence all interior things are held together in connection from the First by the Last, 304, *note*, 475. The quality of man, as determined by his interiors, remains to eternity the same, 501. See also 80, 33, 38, 143, 173, 267, 313, 351, 444, 481.

IOTA, why every, of the Word contains heavenly arcana and things Divine, 260.

IRON signifies truth in the ultimate of order, 115, *note*.

ISAAC.—In the Word, Abraham, Isaac, and Jacob denote the Lord as to His Divine, and His Divine Human, 526.

ISRAEL signifies the spiritual principle, 307. The *stone* or *rock* of Israel denotes the Lord as to Divine Truth and as to the Divine Humanity, 534.

JACOB.—In the Word, Abraham, Isaac, and Jacob denote the Lord as to His Divine, and His Divine Human, 526.

JAMES represented the Lord as to charity, 526, *note*.

JEHOVAH.—The Lord was the God of the most ancient church, and also of the ancient, and He was called Jehovah, 327, *note*.

JESUS.—The Lord was called Jesus, in the world, from the Divine Celestial, 24. See *Christ*.

JERUSALEM is the Lord's church, 73. It signifies the church in which there is genuine doctrine, 180, 187.

JERUSALEM, The New, signifies the church which is to be established hereafter, 187. It signifies the New Church, 197. By the city of Jerusalem coming down from God out of heaven, is understood the heavenly doctrine revealed by the Lord, 307.

JOHN represented the Lord as to the works of charity, 526, *note*.

JOURNEY, to, signifies to live, and also a progression of life; to walk with the Lord, is to live with Him, 192, *note*, 520.

JOY, concerning heavenly, 395-415. When any one receives the inmost of his own joy, he is in his own heavenly joy, and cannot enjoy a more interior joy, because it would be painful to him, 410.

JUDGE, the, who punishes the evil that they may be amended, and to prevent the good being contaminated and injured by them, loves his neighbor, 390, *note*.

JUDGED, to be, according to man's deeds and works, is to be judged according to the interiors, 358; that is to say, according to the will and thought, or love and faith, which are his interiors, 475.

JUDGMENT.—In the Word, judgment is predicated of truth, 64, 215, 348. Great judgments denote laws of the Divine order, which are Divine truths, 215, *note*. By judgment is signified spiritual good, which in its essence is truth, 216.

JUST.—What is done from the good of

love to the Lord, is called just, 214. A justified person is one to whom the merit and righteousness of the Lord are ascribed, 348.

JUSTICE, in the Word, is predicated of good, 64, 215, 348. The justice of the Lord is the good which proceeds from the Lord and which rules in heaven, 348. Justice signifies celestial good, 216. To do justice and judgment denotes good and truth, 215, 348.

KEYS, the, given to Peter, signify the power derived from the Lord by faith, 232.

KIDNEYS, the, signify the examination and correction of truth, 97. In the Grand Man, they who are in the province of the kidneys excel in truth, which examines, distinguishes, and corrects, 96.

KINGDOM.—Heaven is distinguished into two kingdoms, 20-28. The celestial and the spiritual kingdom, 21. The celestial kingdom corresponds to the heart, and to all things which belong to the heart in the whole body; and the spiritual kingdom belongs to the lungs, and to all things which belong to them in the whole body, 95. Concerning these two kingdoms, see 133, 146, 148, 188, 213-215, 217, 223, 225, 241. Priestly kingdom, and regal kingdom, 24. The kingdom of the Lord is a kingdom of uses, 219, 361, 387.

KINGS, in the Word, signify those who are in Divine truth; they represent the Lord as to Divine truth, 226, *note*.

KNOWLEDGES, regarded in themselves, are out of heaven, but the life acquired by them is in heaven, 518.

LANGUAGE, angelic.—The universal heaven is of one language; this language is not taught there, but is implanted in every one, 236. It has nothing in common with human language, 237, 261. Spirits and angels speak from the interior memory, and I once they have a universal language, but languages in the world belong to the exterior memory, 463, *note*. The primitive language of mankind on earth was in agreement with angelic language, because they had it from heaven, and the Hebrew tongue agrees with it in some particulars, 237. They who, in the Grand Man, are in the province of the tongue, are in discourse from understanding and perception, 96.

LAMBS correspond to the affections of the spiritual mind, 110. A lamb, in the Word, signifies innocence and its good, 282.

LAST, the, 31, 304. See *the First*.

LAST JUDGMENT.—Erroneous belief concerning the last judgment, 1, 312.

LAURELS correspond to the affection of truth and its uses, 520.

LAWS OF ORDER, the, are Divine Truths, 57, 202. The laws of spiritual, civil, and moral life, are delivered in the Ten Commandments of the Decalogue, 531.

LETTERS, Hebrew, their form, 260, 241.

LEARNED.—False beliefs amongst the learned, 74, 183, 312, 518

man is the very *esse* of his life, and the understanding is the existere thence derived, 61. All things of Divine Order were collated into man, and he is from creation Divine Order and form, and thence a heaven in miniature, 30, 57, 202, 454. His internal man was formed after the image of heaven, and his external after the image of the world, 30, *note*, 57, 313. In man the spiritual and natural world are conjoined, 313. Man is born into evil and the false, and thus into what is contrary to Divine order, consequently he is born in utter ignorance, and therefore it is necessary that he should be born again, or regenerated, 202, *note*, 523. Every man is a spirit as to his interiors, 432–444. Man viewed in himself is a spirit, and the corporeal frame which is annexed to him, for the sake of performing functions in the natural and material world, is not the man, but only an instrument for the use of his spirit, 435. Angels and spirits are attendant on every man, and by them he has communication with the spiritual world, 292, *note*. Man cannot live without attendant spirits, 292. They are not visible to him, nor is he visible to them, 292. Spirits can see nothing which is in our solar world, except what belongs to him with whom they speak, 292, *note*. The spirits who are adjoined to man are of the same quality as he is himself, as to affection or love, 295. The quality of a man's uses is the quality of the man, 112, *note*. All things of man and of man's spirit are in his deeds or works, 475. Man after death is in a perfect human form, 453–460. At death he leaves nothing behind him but his terrestrial body, 461–469. When man passes from one life into the other, or from one world into the other, it is like passing from one place to another, 461. Man after death is equally man as before, 456. He is such as his life has been in the world, 470–484. He is his own love and his own will, 479. He remains after death, to eternity, of the same quality as his will or ruling love, 480. The reason why man, after death, is no longer capable of being reformed by instruction, as he is in the world, 480. The man who is in celestial and spiritual love goes to heaven, and he who is in corporeal and worldly love, without celestial and spiritual love, goes to hell, 481. Faith does not remain with man, unless it springs from heavenly love, 482. Love in act, which is the very life of man, remains after death, 483. Every man, as to his spirit, is in society with spirits, though during his life in the world he does not appear as a spirit in their society, but they who think abstractedly from the body sometimes appear in their own society, 438. Man is in freedom by virtue of the equilibrium between heaven and hell, 597–600. If man really believed the truth, that all good is from the Lord, and all evil from hell, he would not take merit to himself on account of his good; nor would evil be imputed to him, 302. In the Word, man

366

(vir) signifies the understanding of truth, or those who are intelligent, 368, *note*.

MAN, the Grand.—The universal heaven, viewed collectively, resembles one Man, and is therefore called the Grand Man, 59 See also 94, 96, 217, 333.

MANHOOD.—Those spirits which attend on youth and manhood are in the affection of truth and good, and communicate with the second, or middle heaven, 295.

MAN-SPIRIT, 422, 456, 461. Difference between man-spirit and spirit, 552.

MARRIAGE, by, in the Word is understood the marriage of good and truth which exists in heaven, and should be in the Church, 281, *note*. Concerning marriages in heaven, 366–386. The manner in which they are contracted in heaven, 383. The infernal marriage is the conjunction of the false and evil, 377.

MASTER.—In heaven the Master loves the servants, and the servants love the Master, 219. Children are instructed by masters, 334.

MATERIALITY, which is proper to the body, is added, and almost as it were adjoined to the spirit, in order that the spirit of man may live and perform uses in the natural world, because all things in this world are material, and in themselves void of life, 60, 432. That which is material sees nothing but what is material, and that which is spiritual sees what is spiritual, 453.

MEANS of Salvation are Divine Truths. These truths teach man how to live in order to be saved, 522.

MEASURE denotes the quality of a thing as to good and truth; 73, 307, 349.

MEMORY.—Man has two memories, one exterior and the other interior; the things contained in the exterior memory are in the light of the world, but the things contained in the interior memory are in the light of heaven. Every thing which man speaks or does, and every thing which he sees and hears, is inscribed on the interior memory; this memory is the book of man's life. Those things which have become habitual, and have been made matters of life, are obliterated in the exterior memory, but remain in the interior memory, 463, *note*. Man takes all his memory with him when he quits the world, 462.* The external or natural memory is in man after death, but it is quiescent, and nothing which man imbibed by means of material things is any longer active, except what he has made rational by reflective application to use, 464. See also 461, 466, 467, 469.

MERCY.—That no one goes to heaven, by an act of unconditional mercy, 521–527. Heaven is not granted from unconditional mercy, but according to the life; and the all of that life, by which man is led of the Lord to heaven, is from mercy, 54, *note*, 420. If heaven were granted from immediate mercy, it would be granted to all, 54, *note*, 524. There is no such thing as immediate mercy, but mercy is mediate, and is exercised towards those who live accord-

REGENERATION is re-birth as to the spiritual man, 279. How it is effected, 279. Described by an angel, 269.

RELATIONSHIPS in heaven are from good, and according to its agreements and differences, 46.

RELIGIOUS SUBJECTS. — Dangers which they incur who occupy themselves exclusively with religious subjects, 249.

REMOVALS, in the spiritual world, are dissimilitudes as to the state of the interiors, 193.

REPENTANCE.—After-death repentance is not possible, 527.

REPRESENTATIVES IN HEAVEN, concerning, 170–176. Things are called representative which appear before the eyes of the angels in such forms as are in nature, and internal things are thus turned into external, 175, note. Examples of representatives, 385.

RESPIRATION, the, of the lungs, prevails in the body throughout, and flows into every part, 446. In heaven there is a respiration like that of the lungs, but more interior, 95, note. The respiration there is various, according to states of charity and faith, 95, note, 235. See Pulse.

RESURRECTION, or resuscitation of man from the dead, concerning the, 445–452. Resuscitation is the withdrawing of the spirit from the body, and its introduction to the spiritual world, 447. Erroneous belief concerning the resurrection, 456. How the resurrection is effected, 449, 450. Man rises again only as to his spirit, but the Lord alone rose as to His body also, 316. Man rises again immediately after death, and is then in every respect a man, 312.

REVELATION.—The most ancient people had immediate revelation, but with those who succeeded them there was a mediate revelation by correspondences, 306. Why the men of this earth are incapable of receiving immediate revelation, 309.

RICH IN HEAVEN, concerning the, 357–365. By the rich, mentioned in the Word, are understood, in the spiritual sense, those who abound in the knowledges of good and truth, and who are thus within the church, where the Word is, 365.

RICHES are not real blessings, and therefore they are given to the wicked as well as to the good, 364, note. Spiritual riches are knowledges and sciences, 365.

RIGHT HAND, the, denotes power, 252, note. The things which are on man's right side have reference to good from which truth is derived, 118, note.

RIGHTEOUS PERSON, a, is he to whom the merit and righteousness of the Lord are ascribed, 348.

ROAD, a, signifies the truth which leads to good, and also the false which leads to evil, 479.

ROCK signifies faith proceeding from the Lord, 488, 188.

ROOMS, inner, signify interior things in man, 186, note.

ROYALTY signifies truth derived from good, 226.

SABBATH, the, in the supreme sense signifies the union of the essential Divine with the Divine Human of the Lord; in the internal sense, the conjunction of the Divine Human of the Lord with heaven and the church; and in general the conjunction of good and truth, thus the heavenly marriage, 287, note. Hence to rest on the Sabbath-day signifies a state of that union, and in the respective sense, the conjunction of the Lord with man, because then he has peace and salvation, 287.

SANDY PLACES correspond to the study of sciences from no other end than to acquire reputation, 488.

SATAN denotes the hell which is in front, the inhabitants of which are called evil spirits, 544. See Devil and Lucifer.

SCIENCES. — What are meant by the sciences, 353. See also extracts from the A. C. concerning the sciences, page 357. Concerning the science of correspondences, 87–102, 114, 115, 487, 488. How far the science of correspondences excels all other sciences; it was the chief science among the ancients, but is now obliterated; it flourished with the Orientals and in Egypt, 87, note.

SCIENTIFICS belong to the natural memory which man has in the body, 355, note. See extracts from the A. C. concerning the sciences, page 357.

SEVENTY-TWO denotes all truths and goods in the complex, 73.

SEERS, 76, 487.

SENSE OF THE WORD.—The literal sense of the Word consists of such things as are in the world, but the spiritual sense of such things as are in heaven, and the former is in correspondence with the latter, 114. In all and each of the things of the Word there is an internal or spiritual sense, 1, note. The internal sense of the Word is its soul, and the literal sense is its body, 307.

SENSUAL PRINCIPLE, the, is the ultimate of the life of man, and it adheres to, and inheres in his corporeal principle, 267, 353. He is called a sensual man who judges and concludes about all things from the senses of the body, and who believes nothing but what he can see with his eyes and feel with his hands. Sensual men reason sharply and cunningly, but it is from the corporeal memory in which they place all intelligence; they are more cunning and malicious than others, 267, note, 353, 461. See also 18, 74.

SEPARATION.—When and how the separation of good and evil spirits is effected, 511.

SERPENTS OF THE TREE OF SCIENCE.—Sensual men were so called by the ancients, 353. See Sensual.

SERVANTS.—See Master.

SHEEP signify affections of the spiritual mind, 110.

SIGHT OF THE EYE, the, signifies the intelligence which is of faith, and also faith itself. 271, note. The sight of the left eye corresponds to the truths of faith, and the sight of the right eye to their goods, 118, *note*. Internal sight is that of the thought, 85, 144; or of the understanding, 203, 462. The objects of the spiritual world are seen by man, with the eyes of the spirit, when he is withdrawn from the natural light of the bodily senses, 76, 171. The sight of the spirit is interior sight, 171.

SILVER signifies spiritual good, or truth from a celestial origin, 115.

SIMILITUDE conjoins, and dissimilitude disjoins, 427. Similitude brings spirits together, 42. Concerning similitudes, see 16, 47, 72, 582.

SIMPLE IN HEAVEN, concerning the, 846–856. Concerning the simple. See 74, 82, 86, 183, 268, 312, 313, 322, 464.

SMELL.—Concerning this sense, see 402, 462.

SMOKE corresponds to the falses which proceed from hatred and revenge, 585.

SOCIETIES.—Heaven consists of innumerable societies, 41–50. Every society is heaven in a less form, 51–58. Every society in the heavens resembles one man, 68–72. Every society in heaven has a society opposite to it in hell, 541, 588. Every man as to his spirit is conjoined with some society either of heaven or of hell; a wicked man is conjoined with a society of hell, and a good man with a society of heaven, 510. Every one after death comes into his own society, in which his spirit was when he lived in the world, 510.

SOCINIANS, the, are out of heaven, 8; their interiors are closed, 83.

SOLITARY.—Concerning those who in the world gave themselves up to an almost solitary life; how they are in the other life, 360, 585, 249.

SON-IN-LAW, a, signifies truth associated to the affection of good, 382,* *note*.

Sons signify the affections of truth, and thus truths, 382.*

SEOT corresponds to the falses which are derived from hatred and revenge, 585.

SOUL, the, of man is his spirit, for this is altogether immortal, 432, 602. False ideas which prevail regarding the soul, 183, 312, 456. In the Word, the soul signifies understanding, truth, and faith, 446, *note*.

SOUND OF ANGELIC SPEECH corresponds to affection, and the articulations of sound, which are words, to the ideas of thought derived from affection, 236, 241, 260, 269.

SOUTH, the, signifies wisdom and intelligence in clear light, or a state of light, or of wisdom and intelligence, 150. In the heavens, they who are in the clear light of wisdom dwell in the south, 148, 149. In hell, they who are in the falses of evil dwell from the south to the north, 151.

SPACE IN HEAVEN, concerning, 191–199. The angels have no spaces, but instead of spaces they have states and their changes, 192. Spaces in heaven are merely external states corresponding to internals, 193. They appear visible according to the states of the interiors of angels and spirits, 195.

Spaces in the Word signify states of life, 192, *note*.

SPEECH OF ANGELS, concerning the, 284–245. Concerning the speech of angels with man, 246–257. Spiritual or angelic speech is latent in man, although he is ignorant of it, 243, *note*. After death the interior ideas of man form his speech, 243, *note*. Man is able to converse with spirits and angels, and the ancients frequently did so; but on this earth it is dangerous to discourse with spirits now, unless man is principled in a true faith, and led by the Lord, 249, *note*.

SPHERE.—A spiritual sphere, which is a sphere of life, flows forth and diffuses itself from every man, spirit, and angel, and encompasses him: this sphere flows from the life of the affections, and thence of the thoughts, 17, 49, 591. Concerning spiritual spheres, see also, 384, 574, 591.

SPIRIT.—Every man is a spirit as to his interiors, 432–444. The spirit is the man himself, for the body lives from the spirit, 76. Conjunction of spirits with man, 292. Evil spirits, good spirits, 453. The form of man's spirit is the human form, 453. Spirits who are in the spiritual world, and also the spirits of men while they are alive in the body, become visible in their own form, 453. Men who think abstractedly from the body sometimes appear in the society of spirits, and are visible to them, 438. Enthusiastic spirits, 249. Emissary spirits, 255. Natural and corporeal spirits, 257. Infernal spirits, 123, 151.

SPIRITUAL.—Those things are called spiritual which exist from the sun of heaven, 172. That which is spiritual sees what is spiritual, 453. What is spiritual cannot be revealed to man except in a natural manner, 566. When spiritual beings touch and see spiritual things, the effect is exactly the same to the sense as when natural beings touch and see natural things, 461. It is allowable to enter from spiritual truth into the scientifics which are of the natural man, but not *vice versa*; because the spiritual flows into the natural, but the natural does not flow into the spiritual, 865, *note*.

SPLEEN, the, corresponds to the purification of good and truth, 96, 217.

SPRING signifies the first and highest degree of love, 166, 155.

STARS signify, in the Word, the knowledges of good and truth, 1, 105, 119.

STATES are predicated of life, and of those things which relate to life—states of love and faith, states of wisdom and intelligence, 155. Of the first state of man after death, 491–498. Of the second state, 499–511. Of the third state, 457, 512–520. See *Changes*.

STONE signifies the truth of faith, 188, 223, 488, 534.

STONES, precious, signify the truths and goods of heaven, and the church transparent from good, 489, 179, 307.

STREET, a, signifies truths which lead to good; and also falses which lead to evil, 479, *note*.

STYLE OF THE WORD, concerning the, 310.

SUBJECTS.—The spirits sent from societies of spirits to other societies are called subjects, 255, *note.* See page 339. Collection of extracts from *A. C.* concerning the spirits by whom communication is effected.

SUBSIST, to.—Nothing can subsist from itself; every thing subsists from a cause prior to itself, thus, finally from the First, from which, when separated, it vanishes away and perishes altogether, 106. To subsist, is to exist perpetually, 9, 304.

SUBSISTENCE is perpetual existence, 9, 37, 106, 303.

SUBSTANCES.—Whatever exists interiorly in man, exists in forms which are substances; and what does not exist in substances as its subjects, is nothing, 418. Whatever is supposed to exist without a substantial subject is nothing, 434.

SUCCESSIONS.—All things in heaven have their successions and progressions as in the world, 162, 163, 191.

SUN IN HEAVEN, concerning the, 116–125. The sun, in the Word, signifies the Lord as to love, and thence love to the Lord, 1, *note*, 119. In the opposite sense it signifies the love of self; in which sense, by adoring the sun is signified to worship those things which are contrary to heavenly love, or to the Lord, 122, 561.

SUPREME.—In every angel, and also in every man, there is an inmost or supreme degree, into which the divine of the Lord first or proximately flows, and which may be called his especial dwelling-place in them, 39.

SWEDENBORG.—It was permitted him to associate with angels, and to converse with them as one man with another, and to see the things which are in the heavens as well as those which are in the hells, 1, 174, 184. To converse with them as a friend, and sometimes as a stranger, 234; sometimes with one alone, and sometimes with many in company, when he was in the exercise of every bodily sense, and in a state of clear perception, 74. To converse with spirits, and to be with them as one of them when fully awake, 442. To converse with spirits who belonged to the ancient church, 327; with others who lived 2000 years ago, with some who lived 1700 years ago, with others who lived 400 and 300 years ago, and with others who lived more recently, 480; with some on the third day after their decease, 452; with almost all the deceased whom he knew in the life of the body, 487. To converse with spirits as a spirit, and to converse with them as a man in the body, 436. To be conducted by the Lord into the heavens, and to various earths in the universe, but as to the spirit only, whilst the body remained in the same place, 192. To be in the spiritual world as to the spirit, and at the same time in the natural world as to the body, 577; to be withdrawn from the body, 46, 440. To be brought nearly into the state of dying persons, that he might know how resuscitation is effected,

449, 450. Through his eyes spirits have seen that which is in our world, 252. Concerning Swedenborg, see also 69, 109, 118, 132, 228, 229, 312, 441, 456, and elsewhere.

TASTE.—See, concerning this sense, 402, 462.

TEMPLE, the, represented the Divine Human of the Lord, 187. Concerning temples in heaven, 221, 224. Whence the custom of building churches with an eastern aspect is derived, 119.

TENDENCY or DIRECTION.—There is a universal tendency to a common centre on earth, 142. In what the tendency in heaven differs from the tendency on earth, 142. The direction of the interiors of all who are in the other life is according to their love, 151.

THEATRE.—Universal nature is a theatre representative of the Lord's kingdom, 106, *note.*

THIEVES.—They are called thieves who rob the Lord of what is his, 10.

THINK, to.—They think naturally who look to the world only and attribute all things to nature; but they think spiritually who look to heaven, and attribute all things to the Divine, 130. To think spiritually is to think intellectually or rationally, 464. To think freely from his own real affection is the very life of man, and is the man himself, 502. The great majority of spirits from the Christian world at this day do not comprehend how thinking and willing can be of any consequence, and regard speaking and acting as every thing, 495.

THIRST, to, denotes to desire the knowledges of good and truth, 420.

THOUGHT is internal sight, 484, 532. Thought is nothing but the form of the will, or the medium by which man wills what may appear in the light, 500. Thought, together with affection, constitute the man, 445. Thought and will are of the spirit of man, and not of the body, 453. There are two kinds of thought with man, the one exterior and the other interior, 499. The interior thought of man is in perfect agreement with his affection or love, 298. Thought derives from affection its soul or life, 236. Thought falls into speech with man according to general influx, 296. Extension of the thoughts, 199, 201, 203, 204. Worldly thought, corporeal thought, heavenly thought, 532. See *Affection.*

THRONE OF THE LORD, the, signifies heaven, and particularly the spiritual kingdom of the Lord, 8, 24.

TIMES, in the Word, signify states, 165. Concerning time in heaven, 162–169. The angels think without an idea of time and space, 165, *note.* Man does not think without an idea of time, 169, *note.* Men have an idea of eternity with time, but the angels without time, 167, *note.* Times in their origin are states, 168. Why there are times in the natural world, 164, 168.

TO-DAY signifies eternity (*æternum*), 165, *A. C.* 8998. See *Yesterday, To-morrow.*

INDEX.

To-MORROW signifies eternity, 165, *note*, *A. C.* 3998. See *Yesterday* and *To-day*.

TOOTH, in the Word, signifies the sensual principle, which is the ultimate of the life of man, 575.

TOP OF A MOUNTAIN, the, signifies the supreme of heaven, 188.

TORMENTS.—What infernal torments are, 573, 574. Why the Lord permits torments in hell, 581. Torments which evil spirits experience when they approach heaven, or enter therein, 54, 354, 400.

TOUCH, concerning the sense of, 402, 462.

TREES.—In the Word, trees signify perceptions and knowledges, from which come intelligence and wisdom, 111, 176, 489. Fruit trees correspond to the affections of good and its uses, 520.

TRIBES signify all truths and goods in the complex, thus all things of faith and love, 1.

TRINE or TRINITY, the Divine.—A Trinity or Divine Trine may be conceived of in one person, and thus one God, but not in three persons, page 87. Such a Divine Trinity in the Lord is acknowledged in heaven, 2. The Trine in the Lord is the Divine Itself, which is called the Father, the Divine Human which is called the Son, and the Divine Proceeding which is called the Holy Spirit; this Divine Trine is One, page 87.

TRUMPET, a, signifies divine truth in heaven, and revealed from heaven, 1, *note*.

TRUTH, the, does not admit of reasonings, 385. Truth is the form of good, 107, 875. The life of truth is from good, 875. That is called truth which is of the memory, and thence of the thought, 26. All truth is turned into good, and implanted in the love, as soon as it enters the will, 26. Every truth is of infinite extent, and in conjunction with a multitude of other truths, 270. Truths without good are not in themselves good, because they have no life, 186. All truths, wheresoever they are, whether in the heavens or out of them, are lucid, 132. Divine Truths are laws of order, 57, 202. So far as man lives according to order, that is, so far as he is principled in good according to divine truths, he becomes a man, 202, *note*. The truth of faith is light, 186. Civil truths relate to justice and equity, moral truths to sincerity and uprightness, and spiritual truths to the good which is of love, and the truth which is of faith, 468.

TURNED TO, to be.—All conjunction in the spiritual world depends on the degree in which individuals turn towards each other, 255. The interiors and exteriors of man are either turned to the Lord or to self, 253, 552. Turning of the face and of the body in the spiritual world, 143, 144, 151, 158, 496.

TWELVE denotes all truths and goods in the complex, 73, *note*, 807.

UNDERSTANDING, the, is the *Existere* of life, proceeding from the *Esse* of life, or the will, 26, 61, 474. It is recipient of truth, 137, 221. It is it which is enlightened, 130. The understanding and the will together constitute the man, 423. The life of the understanding proceeds from the life of the will, 26, *note*. The will and understanding of man are ruled by the Lord by means of angels and spirits, 228. The understanding of truth, after death, cannot amend or change the nature of the wicked, 508. All things which are in the understanding have relation to truth, 138.

UNIVERSE.—All things in the universe, both in heaven and in the world, have relation to good and truth, 375.

USES.—Uses are the ends for the sake of which man acts, 112, *note*; they are goods in act, or goods of charity, 391. All in the other life must perform uses, even the wicked and infernal; all derive their quality from the uses which they perform, 887, 508. Uses are the goods of love and charity, 402, 403; they are various and diverse, 405. The kingdom of the Lord is a kingdom of uses, 112, 361, 367. To serve the Lord is to perform uses, 361, 387, *note*. To perform use is to desire the welfare of others, for the sake of the common good, 64. In heaven, to promote use is the delight of the life of all, 219. Use is the first and the last, and thus the all of man, 112.

VARIETY is infinite, and in no instance is one thing the same as another, 41, *note*, 20, 405. In heaven, as in the world, there is endless variety, 231. Variety arranged in a heavenly form, makes perfection, 71, 56.

VASTATION is nothing more than being let into the internals or into the proprium of the spirit, which is the spirit itself, 551. Successive vastation of the church, 1. Concerning vastations, see 513.

VEGETABLE KINGDOM, the, 104, 108, 109, 111. Influx from the spiritual world into the subjects of the vegetable kingdom, 567.

VEIL OR COVERING, a, signifies the intellectual principle, 179.

VINE, the, 111. *A. C.* 1069.

VINEYARDS signify the spiritual church, and the truths of that church, 489. Vines correspond to the affections of truth and its uses, 520.

VIRGIN, a, signifies the affection of good, and also the church, 368, *note*.

VISIONARIES.—Who they are who become visionaries, and why they become so, 249.

VISIONS.—It is dangerous to confirm truth, by visions, with those who are in falses, because they would first believe, and afterwards deny it, and thus profane the truth itself, 456.

VOICE, the, signifies divine truth in heaven, and revealed from heaven, 1, *note*.

VOWELS.—Why in the Hebrew language vowels are not written, and are also variously expressed, 241. The angels, by vowels, express their affections, 261. Vowels are signs of sounds, and affection dwells in sounds, 241. See *Consonants* and *Sounds*.

WALK, to, signifies to live, 590, *note*. To walk with the Lord denotes to receive spiritual life, and to live with Him, 590, *note*.

WALL, a, denotes truth protecting from the assaults of falses and evil, 73, *note*.

WAY, a, signifies the truth which leads to good, and also the false which leads to evil. *To sweep the way* is to prepare for the reception of truths, 479, *note*.

WEEK, a, signifies state, and also an entire period, 165. See also *A. C.* 3845.

WEST, the, signifies love and its good in obscure perception, 150. In heaven, they dwell in the west who are in an obscure perception of the good of love, 148, 149. In hell, they who are in evils which spring from self-love, dwell from the east to the west, 151.

WHITE corresponds to truth, and in the word it signifies truth, 179.

WHOLE, the, consists of the parts, and the parts constitute the whole, 64, 267.

WHOREDOMS, in the Word, signify the perversion of truth, 384, *note*.

WICKEDNESS, concerning the, of infernal spirits, 576–581.

WIFE, a, signifies the affection of good and truth, and also the church, 368, *note*.

WILL, the, of man is the very *esse* of his life, 26, 61; it is man's essential spiritual principle, 529. It is the man himself, 508. It is the recipient of good, 473, *note*, 474, 26. The will and understanding make the all of life appertaining to man, to spirit, and to angel, 468, *note*. The life of the will is the principal life of man, and the life of the understanding flows from it, 26, 61, 474. Man is man by virtue of his will, and thence of his understanding, 26, 474. The will and understanding of man are ruled by the Lord, by means of angels and spirits, 228. The will falls into gestures, with man, according to general influx, 296, *note*. After death a man remains such as his will is, 26, 474. All things which are in the will have relation to good, 188.

WILL, to, is to love to do, 16. To will and not to do when action is possible, is in reality not to will, but a mere fantasy of thought, 475.

WINDOW, a, signifies the intellectual principle which is of the internal sight, 489, *note*.

WINGED ANIMALS signify things intellectual, 110.

WINTER signifies the privation of love and wisdom. Comp. 166 with 155.

WISDOM.—The Divine Wisdom is the light of heaven, 181. Concerning the wisdom of the angels of heaven, 265–275. This wisdom is incomprehensible and ineffable, 266. Wisdom consists in receiving the good which proceeds from the Lord, 80; and also in seeing and perceiving what is good and what is evil, and in accurately distinguishing the one from the other, by intuition and interior perception, 351. Intelligence and wisdom constitute man, 80.

The nature of spurious wisdom, 352. The nature of false wisdom, 353. See *Intelligence*.

WISE IN HEAVEN, concerning the, 346–356. Concerning the wise among the ancients, 322, 323.

WOMAN, the, acts from affection, and the man from reason. In the Word, a woman signifies the affection of good and truth, and also the church, 368.

WOOD signifies good, 223; those who have placed merit in works appear to themselves in the other life to cut wood, 513.

WORD corresponds to the ideas of thought derived from affection, 236, 241, 261, 262, 269.

WORD, the, is that which unites heaven and earth, 305. The Word is written by pure correspondences, and hence all and each of the things therein signify spiritual things, 1, 114. Man has conjunction with heaven by the Word, 114, *note*. The Word was dictated by the Lord, and is accommodated both to the wisdom of angels and the intelligence of man, therefore the angels have the Word, and read it as men do on earth, 259; hence it is that the very dots, iotas, and minutest parts of the Word contain heavenly arcana and things Divine, 260. The Word in its literal sense is natural, and because the natural is the ultimate principle, in which spiritual and celestial things, which are things interior, close, and on which they subsist, as a house upon its foundation, thus the sense of the letter is the continent of the spiritual and celestial sense, 305, *note*. The conjunction of the Lord with man is effected by the Word, through the medium of the internal sense; by the whole Word, and by every part of it, there is conjunction, and therefore the Word is wonderful above all other writings, 305, *note*. The term Word in the Sacred Scriptures signifies various things, as discourse, the thought of the mind, every thing which really exists, also something; and in the supreme sense, Divine truth and the Lord, 137, *note*.

WORD, ante-Mosaic.—This Word, which existed with the Ancient Church, is lost, 327, *note*.

WORKS derive their *esse* and *existere* and their quality from the interiors of man, which are of his thought and will; therefore such as the interiors are, such are the works; works contain the interiors in regard to love and faith, and are love and faith in effect, 358, *note*, 484.

WORLD, the natural, is all that extent which lies beneath the sun, and receives thence its heat and light, and the things of the natural world are all those which thence subsist, 89. The natural world exists and subsists from the spiritual world, as an effect from its efficient cause, 89, 106; and both from the Divine, 106.

WORLD OF SPIRITS, the, is an intermediate state or place between heaven and hell, into which man enters immediately after death, 421–431. The appearance of this world, 429. The world of spirits is in equilibrium between heaven and hell, 590.

WORLD, the spiritual, is heaven, and the things of that world are all things which are in the heavens, 89. In the spiritual world, where spirits and angels dwell, the objects which are visible are so like those which appear in the natural world, that there is no apparent difference, but still they are all from a spiritual origin, 582.

WORSHIP, concerning Divine, in heaven, 221-227. Variety of worship, 56. Worship of the ancients, 111, 188. The externals of worship are of no avail, but the internal principles from which they proceed, 495.

WRITINGS IN HEAVEN, concerning, 258-

264. Numerica. writing, and writing composed of letters, 263.

YEARS, in the Word, signify states of life in general, 155, 165.

YESTERDAY, signifies from all eternity (ab æterno), 165. A. C. 8998. See To-day and To-morrow.

YOUNG MEN, in the Word, signify the understanding of truth, or those who are intelligent, 868, note.

YOUTH.—The spirits who attend on youth and manhood are in the affection of truth and good, 295.

ZION, in the Word, signifies the church, and specifically the celestial church, 216.